DANSE
MACABRE

By Laurell K. Hamilton

DANSE MACABRE

An Anita Blake, Vampire Hunter Novel

LAURELL K. HAMILTON

www.orbitbooks.co.uk

ORBIT

First published in the United States in 2006 by
The Berkley Publishing Group, Penguin Group (USA) Inc.
First published in Great Britain in 2006 by Orbit
Reprinted 2006

A CIP catalogue record for this book is
available from the British Library.

Hardback ISBN-13: 978-1-84149-474-6
Hardback ISBN-10: 1-84149-474-7
C format ISBN-13: 978-1-84149-318-3
C format ISBN-10: 1-84149-318-X

Printed and bound in Great Britain by
Clays Ltd, St Ives plc

Orbit
An imprint of
Little, Brown Book Group
Brettenham House
Lancaster Place
London WC2E 7EN

A member of the Hachette Livre Group of Companies

www.littlebrown.co.uk

To Jonathon, who comforts me while I weep; who holds me close while I scream; who understands why I rage. Because he knows how to weep, understands that pleasure can come in a scream, and has his own rage to battle. They say opposites attract, but not for me.

Acknowledgements

To Laura Gentry (1911–2005), my grandmother, who raised me.

To Darla Cook, who helped this book come to be. She makes so much go right. To Rett MacPherson, may this acknowledgment find your life peaceful and happy. Deborah Millitello, hope we see more of each other soon. Mark Sumner, stop being a tease and finish the book. Sharon Shinn, friend and wonderful writer. Tom Drennan, so many children, so little time. Marella Sands, sorry that your vision didn't find its audience. I look forward to the next world you build.

1

IT WAS THE middle of November. I was supposed to be out jogging, but instead I was sitting at my breakfast table talking about men, sex, were-wolves, vampires, and that thing that most unmarried but sexually active women fear most of all—a missed period.

Veronica (Ronnie) Sims, best friend and private detective, sat across from me at my little four-seater breakfast table. The table sat on a little raised al-cove in a bay window. I did breakfast most mornings looking at the view out onto the deck and the trees beyond. Today, the view wasn't pretty, because the inside of my head was too ugly to see it. Panic will do that to you.

"You're sure you missed October? You didn't just count wrong?" Ronnie asked.

I shook my head and stared into my coffee cup. "I'm two weeks overdue."

She reached across the table and patted my hand. "Two weeks—you had me scared. Two weeks could be anything, Anita. Stress will throw you off that much, and God knows you've had enough stress." She squeezed my hand. "That last serial killer case was only about two weeks ago." She squeezed my hand harder. "What I read in the paper and saw on the news was bad."

I'd stopped telling Ronnie all my bad stuff years ago, when my cases as a legal vampire executioner had gotten so much bloodier than her cases as a private eye. Now I was a federal marshal, along with most of the other legal vamp hunters in the United States. It meant that I had even more access to even more awful shit. Things that Ronnie, or any of my female friends, didn't want to know about. I didn't fault them. I'd rather not have had that many nightmares in my own head. No, I didn't fault Ronnie, but it meant that I couldn't share some of the most awful stuff with her. I was just glad we'd made up a long-standing grumpiness in time to have her here for this particular disaster. I was able to talk about the bad parts of my cases with some of the men in my life, but I couldn't have shared the missed period with any of them. It concerned one of them entirely too much.

She squeezed my hand hard and leaned back. Her gray eyes were all sympathy, and apology. She was still feeling guilty that she'd let her issues about commitment and men rain all over our friendship. She'd had a brief, disastrous marriage years before I met her. She'd come here today to cry on my shoulder about the fact that she was moving in with her boyfriend, Louie Fane—*Dr. Louis Fane*, thank you very much. He had his doctorate in biology and taught at Washington University. He also turned furry once a month, and was a lieutenant of the local wererat rodere—their word for pack.

"If Louie wasn't hiding what he was from his colleagues, we'd be going to the big party afterward," she said.

"He teaches people's kids, Ronnie; he can't afford to find out what they'd do if they found out he had lycanthropy."

"College isn't kids, it's definitely grown-up."

"Parents won't see it that way," I said. I looked at her, and finally said, "Are you changing the subject?"

"It's only *two weeks*, Anita, after one of the most violent cases you've ever had. I wouldn't even lose sleep over it."

"Yeah, but your period is erratic, mine's not. I've never been two weeks late before."

She pushed a strand of blond hair back behind her ear. The new haircut framed her face nicely, but it didn't stay out of her eyes, and she was always pushing it back. "Never?"

I shook my head, and sipped coffee. It was cold. I got up and went to dump it in the sink.

"What's the latest you've ever been?" she asked.

"Two days, I think five once, but I wasn't having sex with anyone, so it wasn't scary. I mean, unless there was a star in the east I was safe, just late." I poured coffee from the French press, which emptied it. I was so going to need more coffee.

Ronnie came to stand next to me while I put more hot water on the stove. She leaned her butt against the cabinets and drank her coffee, but she was watching me. "Let me run this back at you. You've never been two weeks late, ever, and you've never missed a whole month before?"

"Not since this whole mess started when I was fourteen, no."

"I always envied you the regular-as-clockwork schedule," she said.

I started dismantling the French press, taking out the lid with its filter on a stick. "Well, the clock is broken right now."

"Shit," she said, softly.

"You can say that again."

"You need a pregnancy test," she said.

"No shit." I dumped the grounds into the trash can, and shook my head. "I can't go shopping for one tonight."

"Can't you make a quick stop on the way to Jean-Claude's little tête-à-tête tonight? It's not like this is the main event."

Jean-Claude, Master Vampire of the City of St. Louis, and my sweetie, was throwing one of the biggest bashes of the year to welcome to town the first ever mostly-vampire dance company. He was one of their patrons, and when you spend that much money, you apparently get to spend more to throw a party to celebrate that the money was helping the dance troupe earn rave reviews in their cross-country tour. There was going to be national and international media there tomorrow. It was like a Big Deal, and I, as his main squeeze, had to be on his arm, smiling and dressed up. But that was tomorrow. Tonight's little get-together was sort of a prelim to the main event. Without letting the media know, a couple of the visiting Masters of the City had snuck in early. Jean-Claude had callled them friends. Master vampires did not call other master vampires friends. Allies, partners—but not friends.

"Yeah, Ronnie, I'm riding in with Micah and Nathaniel. Even if I stop, Nathaniel will insist on going in whatever store with me, or wondering why I don't let him go. I don't want any of them to know until I've got the test and it's yes or no. Maybe it's just nerves, stress, and the test will say no. Then I won't have to tell anybody."

"Where are your two handsome housemates?"

"Jogging. I was supposed to go with them, but I told them you'd called and needed me to hold your hand about moving in with Louie."

"I did," she said, and sipped her coffee. "But suddenly me being nervous about sharing space with a man for the second time in my life doesn't seem like such a big deal. Louie is nothing like the asshole I married when I was young and stupid."

"Louie sees the real you, Ronnie. He's not looking for some trophy wife. He wants a partner."

"I hope you're right."

"I don't know much today, but I'm sure Louie wants a partner, not a Barbie doll."

She gave me a weak smile, then frowned. "Thanks, but I'm supposed to be comforting you. Are you going to tell them?"

I leaned my hands against the sink, and looked at her through a curtain of my long dark hair. It had gotten too long for my tastes, but Micah had made me a deal: If I cut my hair, he'd cut his, because he preferred his hair shorter, too. So my hair was fast approaching my waist for the first time since junior high, and it was really beginning to get on my nerves. Of course, today everything was getting on my nerves.

"Until I know for sure, I don't want them to know."

"Even if it's yes, Anita, you don't have to tell them. I'll close up my agency for a few days. We'll go away on a girls' retreat, and you can come back without a problem."

I pushed my hair back so I could see her clearly. I think my face showed what I was thinking, because she said, "What?"

"Are you honestly saying that I don't tell any of them? That I just go away for a while and make sure that there's no baby to worry about?"

"It's your body," she said.

"Yeah, and I took my chances by having sex with this many men on a regular basis."

"You're on the pill," she said.

"Yeah, and if I'd wanted to be a hundred percent safe I'd have still used condoms, but I didn't. If I'm . . . pregnant, then I'll deal, but not like that."

"You can't mean you'd keep it."

I shook my head. "I'm not even sure I'm pregnant, but if I was, I couldn't not tell the father. I'm in a committed relationship with several of them. I'm not married, but we live together. We share a life. I couldn't just make this kind of choice without talking to them first."

She shook her head. "No man ever wants you to get an abortion if you're in a relationship. They always want you barefoot and pregnant."

"That's your mother's issues talking, not yours. Or at least not mine."

She looked away, wouldn't meet my eyes. "I can tell you what I'd do, and it wouldn't involve telling Louie."

I sighed and stared out the little window above the sink. A lot of things to say went through my head, none of them helpful. I finally settled for, "Well, it isn't you and Louie having this particular problem. It's me, and . . ."

"And who?" she said. "Who got you knocked up?"

"Thanks for putting it that way."

"I could ask, who's the father, but that's just creepy. If you are, then it's this little tiny, microscopic lump of cells. It's not a baby. It's not a person, not yet."

I shook my head. "We'll agree to disagree on that one."

"You're pro-choice," she said.

I nodded. "Yep, I am, but I also believe that abortion is taking a life. I agree women have the right to choose, but I also think that it's still taking a life."

"That's like saying you're pro-choice *and* pro-life. You can't be both."

"I'm pro-choice because I've never been a fourteen-year-old incest victim pregnant by her father, or a woman who's going to die if the pregnancy continues, or a rape victim, or even a teenager who made a mistake. I want women to have choices, but I also believe that it's a life, especially once it's big enough to live outside the womb."

"Once a Catholic, always a Catholic," she said.

"Maybe, but you'd think being excommunicated would've cured me." The Pope had declared that all animators—zombie raisers—were excommunicated until they repented their evil ways and stopped doing it. What His Holiness didn't seem to grasp is that raising the dead was a psychic ability, and if we didn't raise zombies for money on a regular basis, we'd eventually raise the dead by accident. I had accidentally raised a deceased pet as a child, and a suicidal teacher in college. I'd always wondered if there had been others that never found me. Maybe some of the accidental zombies that occasionally show up are the result of someone's psychic abilities gone wrong, or untrained. All I knew was that if the Pope had ever woken up as a child with his dead dog curled up in bed with him, he'd want the power controlled. Or maybe he wouldn't. Maybe he'd believe that it was evil and he'd pray it into submission. My prayers just didn't have that kind of punch to them.

"You can't mean you'd actually have this . . . thing, baby, whatever."

I sighed. "I don't know, but I do know that I could never just go away, get an abortion, and never tell my boyfriends. Never tell them that one of them might have made a child with me. I just couldn't do it."

She was shaking her head so hard that her hair fell around her face, covered the upper half of it. She ran her hands through it sharply, like she was pulling on it. "I've tried to understand that you're happy living with not one, but two men. I've tried to understand that you love that vampire son of a bitch, somehow. I've tried, but if you actually breed . . . actually have a baby, I just don't get that. I won't be able to understand that."

"Then don't, then go. If you can't deal, then go."

"I didn't mean that. I just meant that I can't understand why you would complicate your life this way."

"Complicate, yeah, I guess that's one way of putting it."

She crossed her arms tight over her chest. She was tall, slender and leggy, and blond. Everything I'd wanted to be as a child. She was small-chested enough that she could fold her arms over her breasts instead of under them, something I couldn't have done. But her legs went on forever in a skirt, and mine did not. Oh, well.

"Okay, then if you're going to tell them, tell Micah and Nathaniel and get a test and test yourself."

"I told you, I don't want anyone to know until I know for sure."

She looked up at the ceiling, closed her eyes, and sighed. "Anita, you live with two of them. You sleep over with two more of them. You are never alone. When are you going to have time to run in and get a test, let alone have the privacy to use it?"

"I can pick one up at work on Monday."

She stared at me. "Monday! It's Thursday. I'd go fucking crazy if I had to wait that long. You'll go crazy. You can't wait nearly four days."

"Maybe my period will start. Maybe by Monday I won't need it."

"Anita, you wouldn't have told me if you weren't pretty sure you needed a pregnancy test."

"When Nathaniel and Micah get back, they'll jump in the shower, we'll get dressed up, and go straight to Jean-Claude's. There won't be time tonight."

"Friday, promise me that Friday you'll get one."

"I'll try, but . . ."

"Besides, when you start asking your lovers to use condoms, won't they figure something out?"

"Jesus," I said.

"Yeah, I heard you say if you'd used condoms you'd be safe. Don't tell me that you're not going to want to use them for a while. Could you really have unprotected sex right now, and enjoy it?"

I shook my head. "No."

"Then what are you going to tell the boys about this sudden need for condoms? Hell, Micah had a vasectomy before you even met him. He's like super-safe."

I sighed again. "You're right, damn it, but you are."

"So pick up the test on the way to the thing tonight."

"No. I'm not going to rain all over Jean-Claude's meeting. He's planned this for months."

"You didn't mention it to me."

"I didn't plan it, he did. The ballet isn't really my thing." Truthfully, he hadn't mentioned it to me until they were coming to St. Louis, but I kept that part to myself. It would just give Ronnie another reason to say that Jean-Claude was keeping secrets from me. He'd finally admitted that the Masters of the City all coming here had been something he hadn't planned, at least not from the beginning. He'd just negotiated it so the vampire dancers could cross many different vamp territories without problems. Jean-Claude agreed the meet was a good idea, but he was also nervous about it. It would be the largest gathering of Masters of the City in American history.

And you don't bring that many big fish together without worrying about shark attacks.

"And how will Mr. Fang-Face feel about being a father?"

"Don't call him that."

"Sorry, how will Jean-Claude feel about being a daddy?"

"It's probably not his."

She looked at me. "You're having sex with him, a lot. Why isn't it his?"

"Because he's more than four hundred years old and when vampires get that old, they aren't very fertile. That goes for Asher and Damian, too."

"Oh, God," she said. "I'd forgotten that you had sex with Damian."

"Yeah," I said.

She covered her eyes with her hands. "I'm sorry, Anita. I'm sorry that it's weirding me out that my uptight monogamous friend is suddenly sleeping with not one, but three vampires."

"I didn't plan it that way."

"I know that." She hugged me, and I stayed stiff against her. She wasn't being comforting enough for me to relax in her arms. She hugged me tighter. "I'm sorry, I'm sorry, I'm being a jerk. But if it's not the vampires then who else but your houseboys."

I pulled away from her. "Don't call them my houseboys. They have names, and just because I like living with someone, and you don't, don't make that my problem."

"Fine, that leaves Micah and Nathaniel."

"Micah is fixed, remember? So it can't be him."

Her eyes went wide. "That leaves Nathaniel. Jesus, Anita, *Nathaniel* as the father-to-be."

A moment ago I might have agreed with her, but now it pissed me off. It wasn't her place to disparage my boyfriends. "What's wrong with Nathaniel?" I said, and my voice was not entirely happy.

She put her hands on her hips and gave me a look. "He's twenty and a stripper. Twenty-year-old strippers are the entertainment at your bachelorette party. You don't have babies with them."

I let the anger seep into my eyes. "Nathaniel told me you didn't see him as real, as a person. I told him he was wrong. I told him you were my friend, and you wouldn't disrespect him like that. I guess *I* was wrong."

She didn't back down or apologize. She was angry and staying that way. "Last time I checked, Nathaniel was supposed to be food, just food, not the love of your life."

"I didn't say he was the love of my life, and yeah, he started out as my *pomme de sang*, but that doesn't . . ."

But she interrupted me. "Your apple of blood, right, that's what *pomme de sang* means?"

I nodded.

"If you were a vampire you'd be taking blood from your little stripper, but thanks to that bloodsucking son of a bitch you have to feed off sex. *Sex*, for God's sake! First that bastard made you his blood whore, and now you're just a—" She stopped abruptly, a startled, almost-frightened look on her face, as if she knew she'd gone too far.

I gave her a flat, cold look. The look that says my anger has moved from hot to cold. It's never a good sign. "Go on, Ronnie, say it."

"I didn't mean it," she whispered.

"Yeah," I said, "you did. Now I'm just a whore." My voice sounded as cold as my eyes felt. Too angry and too hurt to be anything but cold. Hot anger can feel good, but the cold will protect you better.

She started to cry. I just stared at her, speechless. What the hell was going on? We were fighting—she wasn't allowed to cry in the middle of it. Especially not when she was the one being a cruel bastard. I could count on one hand the times I'd seen Ronnie cry and still have fingers left over.

I was still angry, but I was puzzled, too, and that took a little of the edge off. "Shouldn't I be the one in tears here?" I asked, because I couldn't think of what else to say. I was mad at her and I'd be damned if I would comfort her right now.

She spoke in that breathless, hiccuping voice that serious crying can give you. "I'm sorry, oh, God, Anita, I'm sorry. I'm just so jealous."

I raised my eyebrows at her. "What are you talking about? Jealous of what?"

"The men," she said in that shivering, uncertain voice. It was like she was someone else for a moment, or maybe this was just part of Ronnie that she didn't let people see. "All the damned men. I'm about to give up everybody. Everybody but Louie, and he's great, but damn it I've had lovers. I hit triple digits."

I wasn't sure that being able to number your lovers at over a hundred was a good thing, but it was something that Ronnie and I had agreed to disagree over a long time ago. I did not say, *Look who's the whore*, or other hurtful remarks I could have made. I let all the cheap shots I could have made go. She was the one crying.

"And now I'm giving it all up, all of it, for just one man." She leaned her hands against the cabinet as if she needed the support.

"You said sex with Louie was great. I think you've used words like *fantastic* and *mind-blowing*."

She nodded, her hair spilling around her face so that I couldn't see her eyes for a moment. "It is, he is, but he's just one man. What if I get bored, or he gets bored with me? How can just one be enough? The last time we were both cheating a month after the wedding." She looked up at that last remark, her gray eyes wide and frightened.

I made a small helpless gesture, and said, "You're asking the wrong person, Ronnie. I'd planned on monogamy. It seemed like a good idea to me."

"That's exactly what I mean." She wiped at the tears on her face in harsh, angry motions, as if the touch of them made her even more upset. "How is it that you, my girlfriend who had only three men in her entire life, ends up dating and fucking five men?"

I didn't know what to say to that, so I tried to concentrate on the hard facts. "Six men," I said.

She frowned at me, her eyes taking on that look that meant she was counting in her head. "I only count five."

"You're leaving someone out, Ronnie."

"No"—and she started counting on her fingers—"Jean-Claude, Asher, Damian, Nathaniel, and Micah. That's it."

I shook my head, again. "I had unprotected sex with one more man last month." I could have said it differently, but maybe if we got back to my personal disaster, we could stop talking about Ronnie's penis envy. She needed more therapy than I knew how to give lately.

She frowned harder, then she got it. "Oh, no, no," she said.

I nodded. Happy to see from her expression that she got the full awfulness of it.

"You just had sex with him once, right?"

I shook my head no, over and over again. "Not just once."

She was looking at me so hard that I couldn't hold her gaze. Even with the tear tracks drying on her face, she was suddenly Ronnie again. Ronnie had a good hard stare. I couldn't meet it, and was left looking at the cabinets. "How much more than 'not just once'?" she asked.

I started to blush and couldn't stop it. Damn it.

"You're blushing—that's not a good sign," she said.

I stared down at the countertop, using my long hair to hide my face.

Her voice was gentler when she said, "How many times, Anita? How many times in the month you've been back together?"

"Seven," I said, still not looking up. I hated admitting it, because the number alone said louder than any words just how much I enjoyed being in Richard's bed.

"Seven times in a month," she said. "Wow, that's . . ."

I looked up, and the look was enough.

"Sorry, sorry, just . . ." She looked as if she wasn't sure whether she was going to laugh, or be sad about it. She controlled herself, and finally sounded sad when she said, "Oh, my God, Richard."

I nodded again.

"Richard." She whispered his name, and looked suitably horrified. It was worth a little horror.

Richard Zeeman and I had been off-again, on-again, for years. Mostly off. We'd been engaged briefly until I saw him eat someone. Richard was the leader—Ulfric—of the local werewolf pack. He was also a junior high science teacher, and an all-around Boy Scout. If Boy Scouts were six foot one, muscled, amazingly handsome, and had an amazing ability to be self-destructive. He hated being a monster, and he hated me for being more comfortable with the monsters than he was. He hated a lot of things, but we'd made up just enough to have fallen into bed in the last few weeks. But as my Grandma Blake told me, once was enough.

Of all the men in my life, the worst possible choice to be the father would be Richard, because he of all of them would try for the white picket fence and a normal life. Normal wasn't possible for me, or him, but I knew that and he didn't, not really, not yet. Even if I was pregnant, even if I kept being pregnant, I wasn't going to marry anyone. I wasn't going to change my living arrangements. My life worked the way it was, and Richard's idea of domestic bliss was not mine.

Ronnie gave an abrupt laugh, then swallowed it. I was glaring at her. "Come on, Anita, I'm allowed to be impressed that you've managed to have sex with him seven times in the space of a month. I mean, you don't even live together, and you're having more sex than some of our married friends."

I kept giving her the look that makes bad guys run for cover, but Ronnie was my friend, and it's harder to impress your friends with the scary look. They know you won't really hurt them. The fight was dying under the weight of friendship, and of my problem being more immediate than her years of issues unresolved.

Ronnie touched my arm. "Oh, it wouldn't be Richard's. You're having sex with Nathaniel at least every other day."

"Sometimes twice a day," I said.

She smiled. "Well, my, my . . ." Then waved her hand as if to keep from distracting herself. "But the odds are that it's Nathaniel's, right?"

I smiled at her. "You sound happy about that now."

She shrugged. "Well, a choice of evils, ya know."

"Thanks a lot, Ronnie."

"You know what I meant," she said.

"No, I don't think I do." I think I was ready to be angry about her thinking the men in my life were a choice of evils, but I didn't get a chance to be angry, because two of the men in my life were coming through the front door.

I heard them unlocking the door before it opened, and their voices came raised and a little breathless from the run. They'd been able to run faster, and farther, without me along. I was, after all, still human, and they were not.

Standing between the island and the cabinets we couldn't see the door, but only heard them laughing as they came toward the doorway to the kitchen.

"How can you do that?" Ronnie asked, voice soft.

"What?" I asked, frowning.

"You were smiling."

I looked at her.

"You smiled just at the sound of their voices, even with everything . . ."

I stopped her with a hand on her arm. One way I knew I didn't want them to find out about the maybe-baby was by overhearing a conversation. Their hearing was a little too keen to risk it. And here they came, my two live-in sweeties.

Micah was in front, looking back over his shoulder, still laughing, talking. He was my height, short, slender, and muscular in that swimmer sort of way. He had to have his suits tailored because he needed an extra-small athletic cut. You didn't get that off the rack. He'd come to me tanned, and stayed that way from jogging outside, mostly shirtless, all summer and autumn. He'd added a T-shirt to the short-shorts today. His hair was that deep, rich brown that some people get after starting life as very blond. His dark hair was tied back in a low ponytail that couldn't hide how curly it was, almost as curly as mine. He'd taken off his sunglasses, so when I moved into his arms I could look up into his chartreuse eyes. Yellow-green leopard eyes in his delicate face. A very bad man had once forced him to stay in leopard form until, when he came back to human, he couldn't come all the way back.

We kissed and our arms just seemed to automatically glide around each other, to press our bodies as close together as we could with clothes on. He'd affected me this way almost from the moment we had seen each other. Lust at first sight. They say it doesn't last, but we were six months and counting.

I melted against his body and kissed him fiercely, deeply. Partly it was what I always wanted to do when I saw him. Partly I was scared, and touching and being touched made me feel better. Not long ago I'd have been more discreet in front of company, but my nerves just weren't good enough to pretend today.

He didn't get embarrassed, or tell me, "Not in front of Ronnie," the way Richard would have done. He kissed me back with the same drowning intensity. His hands holding me like he'd never let me go. We drew back, breathless and laughing.

"Was that for my benefit?" Ronnie asked, and her voice was not happy.

I turned around, still half in Micah's arms. I looked at her angry eyes and suddenly was ready to be angry back. "Not everything is about you, Ronnie."

"Are you telling me you kiss him like that every time he comes home?" The anger was back, and she used it. "He's been gone, what, an hour? I've seen you greet him after a day's work, and it was never like that."

"Like what?" I asked, voice sliding down. If she wanted to fight, we could fight.

"Like he was air and you couldn't breathe him in fast enough."

Micah's voice was mild, placating, trying to talk us both down. "Did we interrupt something?"

I turned to face Ronnie, squarely. "I'm allowed to kiss my boyfriend the way I want to kiss him without getting your permission, Ronnie."

"Don't try and tell me you weren't rubbing my face in it, just now, with the show."

"Go get some therapy, Ronnie, because I am fucking tired of your issues raining all over me."

"I confided in you," she said, voice strangled with some emotion I didn't understand, "and you put on a show like that in front of me. How could you?"

"Oh, that wasn't a show," Nathaniel said from just inside the doorway, "but if it's a show you want, we can do that, too." He glided into the kitchen on the balls of his feet, showing both the grace of his dance training and that otherworldly grace of the wereleopard. He pulled his tank top off in one smooth gesture and let it fall to the floor. I actually backed up a step before I caught myself. I hadn't realized until that moment that he was angry with Ronnie. What little cutting remarks had she been making to him, that I hadn't heard? When he told me she didn't see him as real, he'd been trying to tell me more than I had heard. That I'd missed something big was there in his angry eyes.

He tore the tie from his ponytail and let his ankle-length auburn hair fall around his nearly naked body. The jogging short-shorts just didn't cover that much.

I had time to say, "Nathaniel—" and he was in front of me. That otherworldly energy that all lycanthropes could give off shivered off his skin and along my body. He was five-six, just tall enough for me to have to look up to meet his eyes. His anger had turned them from lavender to the deeper color of lilacs, if flowers could burn with anger and force of personality. Nathaniel was in those eyes and with that one look he dared me, challenged me, to turn him down.

I didn't want to turn him down. I wanted to wrap his body and that skin-crawling energy around me like a coat. Lately almost any stress seemed to feed into sex. Scared? Sex would make me feel better. Angry? Sex would calm me. Sad? Sex would make me happy. Was I addicted to sex? Maybe. But Nathaniel wasn't offering actual sex. He just wanted as much attention as I'd given Micah. Seemed fair to me.

I closed the distance between us with my hands, my mouth, my body. The energy of his beast spilled around us like being plunged into a warm bath that had a mild electric charge. He'd been one of the least of my leopards until a metaphysical accident had taken him from *pomme de sang* to my animal to call. I was the first human servant to a vampire to gain the vampire ability to call an animal. All leopards were mine to call, but Nathaniel was my special pet. We'd both gained from the magical bonding, but he'd gained more.

He lifted me up, using just his hands on my thighs. Even through my jeans he made sure I knew he was happy to be pressed against my body. So happy that it forced a small sound from me.

Ronnie's voice came harsh, ugly, like she was choking on her anger. "And when the baby comes, are you going to fuck in front of it, too?"

Nathaniel froze against me. Micah's voice came from behind us. "Baby?"

2

THAT ONE WORD fell into the room like a thunderbolt, except that afterward the room was quiet. So quiet that I could hear the blood pounding in my head. Nathaniel's body was so still against mine that if I hadn't felt his pulse against my hand, it would have been like he wasn't there. I was afraid to move, afraid to breathe. It was like a moment before a gunfight, when you know it's going to happen, that anything, any movement, will set it off, and you don't want to be the one that makes that happen.

Nathaniel looked down at me, and the look was enough. It broke the unnatural silence, and sound spilled around us. Micah said, "Did Ronnie say *baby*?"

"Yeah, I said *baby*." Her voice was ugly with anger.

Nathaniel let me slide to the floor, his hands going to my shoulders. His eyes were so serious that I had to fight to keep meeting them. I did it, though my eyes flinched as if the force of his questions were a light too bright to meet.

"Are you pregnant?" he asked, voice soft.

"I'm not sure," I said, and I gave Ronnie the glare she deserved. "I was going to wait until I was sure before I told any of you guys. But I had to tell someone. I thought, hey, I'll tell my best friend, but I guess I was wrong."

"The kiss with Micah may not have been for my benefit," Ronnie said in that ugly voice that I didn't recognize as hers, "but your pet stripper and you, that was for my benefit."

I turned so that I was facing her, Nathaniel at my back. "You're jealous of the men in my life, yeah, I get that now."

She opened her mouth, closed it, and said, "I guess that's fair. I tell your secret, you tell mine."

I shook my head. "Me telling Nathaniel and Micah that you are jealous of how many men are in my bed, that isn't the same as you telling them that I may be pregnant." I had a mean idea, so I said it. "But it might be close if I told Louie that you were jealous of my boyfriends. Does he know that you can number your old lovers in triple digits?" Yeah, it was mean, but she'd earned it. Only family can fight as dirty as best friends.

She paled a little, and that was enough to answer the question. "He doesn't know," I said, and made it a statement.

"I think he deserves to know," Nathaniel said, and again there was that tone in his anger that said it was more personal than it should have been between them.

"I'd planned on telling him," she said.

"When?" he asked, and he moved around me, so that he was facing her.

I glanced at Micah, and he shook his head, as if he didn't know what was going on either. Good to know we were both confused.

"When you'd moved in together, married him, or never?"

"We're not getting married," she said in a voice that was just a little desperate, as if her fear was washing her anger away. She rallied then. "You did that little show with Anita to rub my face in the fact that I'm about to become monogamous. You're always doing shit like that."

"And how many times have you said, 'Oh, it's Anita's little stripper,' or 'pet stripper,' or 'how's tricks,' or my personal favorite, 'you're damned cute for a walking, talking, beefsteak,' or is that 'beef cake'?"

"Jesus, Nathaniel." I looked at Ronnie. "Did you say all that to him?"

The anger faded around the edges as she finally looked uncomfortable. "Maybe, but not like he makes it sound."

"Then why didn't you say it in front of me?" I asked. "If there was nothing wrong with saying it, why not in front of me?"

"Or me," Micah said, "I would have told you if she'd been saying things like that to Nathaniel."

"Why didn't you tell me, Nathaniel?" I asked.

He gave me his angry eyes. "I told you she didn't see me as real, as a person."

"But you didn't tell me what she'd said; I needed to know."

He shrugged. "She's your best friend, and you'd just made up after a big fight. I didn't want to start another one."

"I was just kidding around," Ronnie said, but the tone in her voice said she didn't believe it either.

I looked at her. "How would you feel if I said stuff like that to Louie?"

"You can't call him a stripper, or an ex-prostitute, because he's not." The moment she said it, her face showed me she knew she shouldn't have. "I didn't mean . . ." she began, but it wasn't me that put her in her place, it was Nathaniel.

"I know why you call me names," he said, and he moved in closer, not touching, but invading the hell out of her personal space. "I see the way you watch me. You want me, but not like Anita does. You just want me for a night, or a weekend, or a month, then you'd be done like you're always done with everybody. I know why you don't want to commit to Louie." I'd never seen him like this, relentless. I actually made a small move, as if I'd stop him, but Micah caught my eye, and shook his head. His face was serious, almost grim. I guess he was right. Nathaniel had earned this, and Ronnie had, too. But it wasn't going to end anywhere I wanted to be.

He said again, "I know why you don't want to commit to Louie."

She said in a small, weak voice, "Why?"

"Because it torments you to know that you will never know how I am in bed."

"Oh," she said in a voice that was almost her own, "so I'm not wanting Louie because you're such a stud?"

"Not me, Ronnie, but the next me. The next guy you get obsessed about. Not love obsessed, but I-wonder-what-he'd-be-like-in-bed obsessed. And you've always been beautiful enough, hot enough, to get anyone you've ever wanted, right?"

She stared at him as if he were something horrible. He prompted her, "Right?"

She nodded, and whispered, "Yes."

"You knew Anita wasn't fucking me, so you thought if she didn't want me maybe it would be okay, but I didn't pick up on any of it. I ignored the hints, so you started to get mean about it. Maybe you didn't even know why you were doing it." He leaned in so close that she moved back until her butt hit the cabinet, and she had nowhere else to go. "You kept belittling me in front of Anita, and worse behind her back, as if you'd convince her she didn't want to keep me. That I wasn't good enough to keep. Real enough to keep. Have you ever set your sights on anyone and not fucked them, at least once?"

She gave a little trembling shake of her head. She was biting her lower lip, and tears gleamed unshed in her eyes.

"Then suddenly, Anita is going to keep me, and you don't poach your friends' guys. That is a rule. You thought I was just food, and you could have me, at least once. Suddenly I'm a boyfriend, and it's against your rules to try for me, but you still wanted me. Just once. Just once to feel me inside you . . ."

I called it then. "Enough, Nathaniel, enough." My voice was shaky. This had gotten so ugly, so fast. How had I missed it?

Nathaniel moved back from her slowly, and said, "I used to believe in women like you, Ronnie. I used to think that anyone who wanted me that badly must love me, at least a little." He shook his head. "But people like you don't love anyone, not even themselves."

"Nathaniel," Micah said, as if he'd been shocked by that one, too.

Nathaniel ignored him. "You need to find out what you're running from, Ronnie, before it ruins the best thing you've ever found."

She spoke in a harsh whisper, "You mean Louie."

He nodded. "Yeah, I mean Louie. He loves you. He really, truly loves you, not just for a night, or a month, but for years. Part of you wants that or you wouldn't still be with him."

She swallowed hard enough that it sounded like it hurt. "I'm scared."

He nodded, again. "What if you love him? What if you give him your whole heart and then he dumps you the way you dumped so many others?"

She gave that trembling nod of hers again. "Yes."

"You need help, Ronnie, professional help. I can recommend someone."

I knew Nathaniel saw a therapist, but I'd never heard him talk about it with anyone before, not like this.

"I've been with her for a few years. She's good. She's helped me a lot." His face was gentler than it had been.

Ronnie looked at him as if he were the snake and she were the helpless little bird.

He went to the corkboard above the phone. There were business cards pinned to it; important numbers, notes. He took one of the cards down. He walked back over to Ronnie and held it out to her. "If she can't take you, she'll know someone good who can."

Ronnie took the card carefully, just by the corner as if she were afraid it would bite. She gave him wide, frightened eyes, but she put the card in her jeans pocket. She let out a deep breath, and turned to me. "I'm sorry, Anita. I'm sorry about everything." She looked at Nathaniel, then back at me. "And now I'm going to leave the mess behind and let you guys clean it up like I've always done. I am sorry." And she walked out. We all waited until we heard the door close behind her.

The three of us stood for a few seconds in silence, waiting for the shock waves to settle. But of course there were other problems than just Ronnie's issues.

Micah turned to me, and said, "Are we in a mess?"

"I'm not sure yet," I said.

"But you think you're pregnant?" he said.

I nodded. "I missed last month. I'd planned on finding out for sure before I told anyone." I sighed and crossed my arms under my breasts. "I haven't bought a pregnancy test, because I wasn't sure how to take it without one of you finding out."

Nathaniel came to stand beside me, but to one side so he wouldn't block my view of Micah. "Anita, you shouldn't have to go through this alone. At least one of us should be holding your hand while you wait for the little strip to turn colors."

I looked up at him. "You sound like you've done this before."

"Once; she wasn't sure it was mine, but I was the only friend she had to hold her hand."

"I thought I was your first girlfriend."

"She found out I'd never been with a girl, so she took care of it." His voice made it seem utterly matter-of-fact. "I wasn't very good at it, but she came up pregnant. It was probably one of her customers, but it could have been mine."

"Customers?" Micah made it a question.

"She was in the game, like I was then."

I knew "the game" meant she'd been a prostitute, but "the game" usually meant when he was on the street. He'd been off the street by sixteen. "How old were you?" I asked.

"Thirteen," he said.

The look on my face made him laugh. "Anita, I'd never been with a girl, but I'd seen a lot of men. She thought I should know what it's like to be with a girl. She was my friend, protected me sometimes, when she could."

"How old was she?" Micah asked.

"Fifteen."

"Jesus," I said.

He smiled, that gentle, almost condescending smile that always let me know what a sheltered life I'd led.

"And she got pregnant," Micah said, softly.

Nathaniel nodded. "The odds were that it wasn't mine. We had sex twice. Once so I could see if I liked it. The second time so I could get better at it." His face softened in a way I'd never seen before.

"You loved her," I said, voice as gentle as I could make it.

He nodded. "My first crush."

"What was her name?" Micah asked.

"Jeanie, her name was Jeanie."

I almost didn't ask, but it was the most he'd ever talked about that part of his life, so I asked. "What happened?"

"I held her hand while the test turned positive. Her pimp paid for an abortion. I went with her. Me, and another girl." He shrugged, and the soft light faded in his eyes. "She couldn't have kept it. I knew that. We all knew it." He looked suddenly sad, lost.

I wanted to take that lost look out of his eyes, so I hugged him, and he let me, and he hugged me back.

"What happened to Jeanie?" Micah asked.

He stiffened in my arms, and I knew then it would not be a good answer. "She died. She got into the wrong car one night, and the date killed her."

I hugged him tighter. "I am so sorry, Nathaniel."

He hugged me, one fierce, tight hug, then he moved back enough to see my face. "I was thirteen and she was fifteen. We were street hookers. We were both drug addicts. There wasn't going to be a baby." His eyes were so serious. "I'm twenty, and you're twenty-seven. We both have good jobs, money, a house. I've been clean for three, almost four years."

I pulled back from him. "What are you saying?"

"I'm saying we have choices, Anita. Choices that I didn't have the last time."

My pulse was in my throat, threatening to choke me. "Even if I am—" and it took me two tries to say—"pregnant, I'm not sure I'm keeping it. You understand that, right?" My chest was so tight I could barely breathe.

"It's your body," he said. "I respect that. I'm just saying that we have more than one way to go here, that's all. It has to be mostly your choice."

"Yes," Micah said, "you're the woman, and like it or not, the final choice has to be yours."

"Your body, your choice," Nathaniel said, "but we need a pregnancy test. We need to know."

"We're running late now," I said. "You guys need to shower and we have to go to Jean-Claude's place."

"Can you really just go to the cocktail party with this hanging over us?" Nathaniel asked.

"I have to."

He shook his head. "It's fashionable to be late, and once he knows why, Jean-Claude won't mind."

"But . . ." I said.

"He's right," Micah said, "or am I the only one that thinks I would go crazy smiling and nodding tonight, and not knowing?"

I hugged myself tighter. "But what if it's positive, what if . . ." I couldn't even finish it.

"Then we'll deal with it," Micah said.

"Whatever happens, Anita, it will be okay. I promise," Nathaniel said.

It was my turn to look into his face and realize how young he was. We were only seven years apart in age, but they could be an important seven years. He promised it would be all right, but some promises you can't keep no matter how hard you try.

That tight feeling climbed up my throat and spilled out my eyes. I started to cry, and couldn't stop it. Nathaniel wrapped his arms around me, held me against his body, and a moment later Micah moved in behind me. They both held me, while I cried my fear and confusion and anger at myself. Self-loathing didn't even begin to cover it.

When the crying slowed, and I could breathe without hiccuping, Nathaniel said, "I'll go out and get the test. Micah can shower while I'm gone. I should be back in time to clean up and we'll only be a little late."

I pushed myself away, enough to see his face. "But what if it's a yes, I mean how can I go to the party if it's a yes?"

Micah leaned over my shoulder, putting his face next to mine. "You don't want to know," he said, "because you'll find it easier to pretend tonight, if you don't know."

I nodded, my cheek sliding against his.

"I'll get the test," Nathaniel said, "and we'll use it later tonight, after the party. But we are getting one, or two, to take with us." For someone who was supposed to be a submissive his voice held no compromise. It was simple fact.

"What if someone finds it in our stuff?" I asked.

"Anita, you're going to have to tell Jean-Claude and Asher sometime," Nathaniel said.

"Only if it's positive," I said.

He gave me a look, but nodded. "Okay, only if it's positive."

Positive. It seemed like such the wrong word. If I was pregnant it was definitely a negative. A really big, scary negative.

3

AN HOUR AND a half later we were parked in the employee lot behind the Circus of the Damned. Nathaniel had helped me with my eye shadow. He could blend about a dozen different colors and make it look like I wasn't wearing anything, yet make my eyes look amazing. He did his own eyes for the stage, so he had the practice. My dress was actually a skirt outfit. Black, stiff material, so that the gun in its holster at the small of my back didn't show through the dark cloth. Nor did the knife in its spine sheath. My hair hid the hilt. I'd left my cross in the glove compartment, because the chances of no one "accidentally" using vamp powers on me tonight were between zero and nothing. Yeah, they were our "friends" but they were still Masters of the City, and I was the Executioner. Someone wouldn't be able to resist trying me out, just a little. Like someone who shakes your hand too hard. But this "handshake" could make the cross burn against my skin. I did not want another cross-shaped burn scar.

Both the men were in Italian-cut suits, tailored to their bodies. Nathaniel was in black with a lavender shirt shades paler than his eyes. His tie was rich, purple silk. He'd braided his hair, so that it gave the illusion that his hair was short, until you saw the braid waving around his ankles. His black leather shoes gleamed, the cuffed pants long enough to hide the fact that he wore no socks. Micah was in charcoal gray with a thin black pinstripe. His shirt was a green with yellow undertones, almost the same shade as his eyes. Depending on how the light hit the shirt it brought out either the green or the yellow of his eyes, so that the color of his eyes changed with almost every breath. It was a nice effect.

I was wearing jogging shoes, but there was a pair of four-inch black heels in the overnight bag. Four-inch spikes, with open heels, and laces that wrapped around my ankles. When Jean-Claude couldn't persuade me into a skimpier outfit for the night, we'd compromised with the totally impractical shoes. Though strangely, they weren't uncomfortable. They looked like they should have been, but they weren't. Either that, or I was getting better at walking in high heels. Jean-Claude's fault. I'd put the shoes on when we reached the bottom of the stairs, before we saw our guests.

I had a key to the new back door of the Circus of the Damned. No more waiting around for someone to let us inside. Yea!

I'd actually turned the key and felt the lock click over, when the door started opening inward. Security was pretty good at the Circus of late, since we'd made a deal with the local wererats. But it wasn't a wererat that opened the door; it was a werewolf.

Graham was tall enough and muscular enough to make it impossible to move through the door without brushing him. He stood for a moment looking down at me, at us, I guess, though it felt more personal than that. His perfectly straight black hair managed to fall decoratively over his brown eyes, and still be very, very short on the bottom, so the strong line of his neck was left bare and strangely tempting. His eyes tilted up at the edges, and I now knew that he had his Japanese mother's eyes and hair, but the rest of him seemed to have been copied from his ex-navy and very Nordic-looking father.

Graham was the only one of the lycanthropes I'd ever known to have his parents visit his place of work. Since his usual job was security at Guilty Pleasures, a vampire and furry strip club, that had been an interesting night.

I thought for a moment Graham would stay in the doorway and make me push past him. I think for a moment, so did he. I was almost sure he would have moved, given us room, but Micah stepped up, just a little in front of me. "Give us some room, Graham." He didn't say it mean, or even call any of that otherworldly energy. He even made it a little bit of a request, but Graham's face darkened just the same.

I watched Graham think about it. Think about not moving. He was already dressed in what all the security would be wearing tonight; black slacks, black T-shirt, though the shirt should probably have been a size larger. The one he was wearing looked like it was having trouble holding on, as if one flex too many and it would shred. Micah looked fragile beside him.

Micah let down some of his careful control. He let just a whisper of the power that lived inside him breathe through the night. My skin shivered with it. His voice came lower, deeper, an edge of growl to it. "We are Nimir-Raj and Nimir-Ra and you are not. Move."

"I am wolf and not leopard; you have no authority over me." He actually tensed, as if he were bracing for the fight.

I'd had enough. "But I have authority over you, Graham," I said.

His eyes did not move from Micah, as if I weren't a threat. There were so many reasons Graham had not made the leap from bodyguard to breakfast snack for me.

His ignoring me pissed me off, and the first thread of anger brought my own version of the beast. That warm, prickling thread of power breathed over my skin and danced around the men around me. I was not a true shapeshifter, because I couldn't shift, but I carried four different strains of lycanthropy in my bloodstream. If you catch one type of lycanthropy, it protects you from any other strain. You can't carry more than one disease at a time, but I did. A medical impossibility, but blood tests don't lie. I carried wolf, leopard, lion, and one mystery strain that the doctors couldn't identify running through my veins. That, and some metaphysical impossibilities, meant I had power to call. Power to use, up to a point.

Nathaniel rubbed his arms and said, "Easy, Anita."

He was right. Because I couldn't shift, it was possible to call the beast, but impossible to finish the call, so it was like having a seizure. Not pleasant, and I'd ruin the dress. But I was tired of Graham. Tired of him in so many ways. The energy had made him look at me, and for the first time I saw him remember that I was something besides a piece of ass he wanted, and hadn't had, yet.

"I am the lupa of your pack, Graham, until Richard picks another mate." I stepped up, and Micah moved back so I could do it. I kept moving, pushing my power into that tall, muscular body, so that it was Graham who moved out of my way. "But I will always be Bolverk of the Thronnos Rokke Clan, Graham. I will always be the doer of evil deeds for your Ulfric, your wolf king. I am the executioner of bad little werewolves who don't remember their place. I think you've forgotten that."

I'd backed him up among the boxes in the storeroom. His head actually hit the lone light that hung from the ceiling. The light swung and filled the room with shadows, and darkness.

I could feel that part of me that had begun life as Richard's beast, but now, somehow, was mine, pacing just below the surface of my mind. It was as if my body were a cage in the zoo, and my beast paced the narrow confines of its prison. Paced, and did not like it. Trapped, so trapped, and so wanting to break free.

I staggered. Micah and Nathaniel caught me before Graham could reach me. Micah growled, "Don't touch her!"

Nathaniel said, "She's called wolf; if another wolf touches her right now, it will make it harder to control."

I clung to them, my two cats. I put my face against the warmth of Micah's neck, and drew in a deep breath of his scent. But underneath the warm scent of him, the sweetness of his cologne, was the nose-wrinkling musk of leopard. It helped chase back the wolf, helped me fight free before things got out of hand.

Graham dropped to his knees, head bowed. "Forgive me, lupa, I forgot myself."

"Size doesn't make you dominant, Graham, power does. You are submissive to me in our pack. You are always submissive to Micah, because he is the leader of another people that has a treaty with the wolves. You will treat him accordingly or it will not be as lupa that I talk to you next, but as Bolverk."

He looked up, startled, as if he hadn't expected me to say that last. He'd been playing, and I'd upped the stakes so high he didn't like the game anymore. Maybe if I hadn't been so tense about the maybe-baby I wouldn't have invoked Bolverk, or maybe I was just tired of Graham.

Once Nathaniel moved from *pomme de sang* to my animal to call, then I'd needed a new *pomme de sang*. As my animal to call he was bound metaphysically too close to be just food. Jean-Claude and some of the other vamps had put their heads together and finally realized that there was a reason that an animal to call, human servant, and *pomme de sang* are three separate jobs. The first two are so closely bound to you metaphysically that though they can feed you, it's a little like eating your own arm. You can do it, but it has a price. It fills your belly, but it also takes energy from other places. It was actually Elinore, one of the vamps we invited in from England to join our vampire kiss, who figured out why I was having to feed so often from all my men. Because almost all the men I was feeding the *ardeur* from were bound to me metaphysically—Jean-Claude as my master, Richard as my Ulfric and Jean-Claude's animal to call. We were a triumvirate of power, but we needed fuel from outside that triumvirate sometimes. I'd accidentally made another triumvirate of power with Nathaniel as my animal to call, and Damian as my vampire servant (another impossibility), and again they weren't a complete meal. So no matter how much I "fed" off any of them, I just didn't stay filled up. Asher, Jean-Claude's second-in-command, and our sweetie, was a full meal. Requiem would probably have been a full meal if I'd allowed myself to have full-blown intercourse with him. Byron had been emergency food, and frankly just wasn't enough my type to be a permanent part of my bedroom. He enjoyed sex with me, but he liked boys better. I don't mind not being someone's main squeeze, but being the wrong sex, that just made my head hurt.

Jason, Jean-Claude's *pomme de sang*, was great, but he couldn't feed both me and Jean-Claude every day. I needed to find someone else to fill the spot, or maybe a couple of someones, until I got more control of the ardeur.

Graham had been one of the local men that Jean-Claude had encouraged me to "interview" as my new *pomme de sang*. Jean-Claude thought that if I'd "interview" them a little more intimately, I'd have a new *pomme* by now. He'd called me stubborn. Asher had called me foolish, to refuse to sample such bounty. Maybe it was foolish. I hadn't told Ronnie that all the men in my life had given me a short list of other men to try out. She'd have freaked even worse than she already had, because if Louie had been that generous with her, she'd have been a happy camper. But Ronnie wasn't me, and what might have made her happy just seemed to confuse me.

Of all the men who had come to my bed, to sleep and cuddle, Graham had been the most pushy. He'd made it clear he wanted more from me than I wanted to give. Of course, if I hadn't been so stubborn, he'd be in the running for would-be daddy. The thought made me cold down to my toes. Let's hear it for not fucking everyone who bunks over.

"I beg forgiveness, lupa." His face still showed the shock of hearing me invoke Bolverk, but the words were not begging words. Not really. To beg forgiveness among the wolves meant only one thing—something closer and more intimate than I wanted from Graham—but if I refused the gesture, then it would be a breach between us, one that could grow and eventually harm Richard's pack. Shit.

"Then beg, Graham." My words didn't come out uncomfortable, they came out angry. Anger was always my shield. I was trying to learn other things to hide behind, but anger was still my tried and true, and for that moment, it worked.

He stood, and standing he towered over me. So broad, so muscled, so big, but there was fear in his face. Finally, he believed that I might, if he pissed me off enough, hurt him. That I might have the right to hurt him. It was not a bad thing to see fear on his face. He was overdue for it. We'd tried being nice, Micah, Nathaniel, and me, but some people won't take nice treatment. If a person won't take nice, there are always alternatives.

He could have used the submissive gesture to take me in his arms, but he did it the way it had been shown to me. He touched my face lightly with his fingers, just enough to steady himself. If we'd been in public he would have laid a very light kiss against my lips, but we weren't in public so it got to be more interesting. He leaned over me, and the prelude was too like a kiss for my comfort.

It made me want to back up, but I was dominant to him. A dominant does not back away from a submissive, no matter how much bigger he is. It's not about size and strength. It's about who's tougher, and no matter how big he was, Graham was not the toughest person in the room. Not even close.

He bent down, and down, his mouth hovering over mine so that I could feel his breath warm against my lips. I think even at the last second he thought about stealing the kiss I'd never allowed him, but he thought better of it. He did what he was supposed to do, though frankly the kiss would have been less embarrassing. In some ways, at least.

 He was supposed to lick across my lower lip. It was a version of the gesture a submissive wolf uses toward a dominant. It's based on the food-begging behavior of wolf pups. But saying all that didn't change the fact that his fingers were gentle against my face, and his breath was warm against my mouth. The tip of his tongue touched my lip, and slid across it. Wet, gliding, sensual, wetter than the first real kiss should be. Wet, as if I'd taken a drink of wine and spilled just a little across my lower lip. Just enough so that I had to lick across my lip in an echo of what he had just done to me. As if I were drinking down the touch of his mouth.

He shivered, his breath trembling on the air. "That was nice."

"It was supposed to be you begging the forgiveness of your pack's lupa," I said, but my voice was a little shaky, and not nearly firm enough.

He gave a quick smile, the one that ruined the hip-tough-guy image, and made him look his age. Graham had yet to see twenty-five. "I do ask forgiveness, but it's still the most you've ever let me touch you."

I shook my head and pushed past him. Micah and Nathaniel followed me. Nathaniel was carrying the overnight bag that held, among other things, the pregnancy tests. I knew when he came out of the store with them why I'd put off buying them. It made the whole problem more real. Stupid, but it did.

"You've slept in the same bed with me, Graham," I called back over my shoulder as I headed for the big door that led underground.

"Sleeping's not what I want," he said.

I stopped at the door, and just turned and stared at him. The other men moved to either side to let me see him better.

Graham looked at me, his eyes peeking through the silky fringe of his overly long bangs. It always made me think of an animal peering at me through the grass. The upper layer hadn't been this long when I met him.

"I do not need your shit tonight, Graham."

"Why are you always mad at me?"

"I am not always mad at you, Graham."

"If you're not mad at me, then why don't you like me better?"

"I don't dislike you, Graham, I just don't want to fuck you. I'm allowed not to fuck you, even though you want to fuck me."

"Don't fuck me then, just feed the *ardeur* off me. Feed it the way you fed off Nathaniel for months without intercourse."

I shook my head. "I don't want to introduce the passion of the *ardeur* to someone I'm not keeping. It's cruel."

"The *ardeur* is the greatest orgasmic experience that any of the vampire lines can give to a mortal." Graham's face was full of such eagerness, his hands reaching out to the air as if he could draw the *ardeur* out of it, and hug it to him. "I just want to know what it feels like. The real deal, not the little tastes I've had by accident. Why is that wrong, Anita? Why is it wrong to want that?"

"She's afraid you'll become addicted," Micah said, voice soft.

Graham shook his head. "I've never been addicted to anything in my life."

"Lucky you," Nathaniel said.

"Please, Anita, don't go to strangers to feed the *ardeur*. Don't go to strangers when there are people right here who would do almost anything to feed your need."

I made an exasperated sound, almost a scream of frustration, and went for the door. I opened it and we headed down the stone steps that led down, down, to the actual home of the Master of the City.

The steps were too wide, too something, as if they'd been carved for something that didn't walk on two feet. The stairs were always awkward, which was why I was still in jogging shoes. Micah took my hand anyway, and I let him. If it looked to Graham like I was needing help down the stairs, fuck him, or rather don't. I needed the comfort of touch tonight. Nathaniel stayed on my other side, but didn't try to take my right hand in his. I'd need that hand for the gun or the blade. Yeah, these vamps were supposed to be Jean-Claude's friends. But they weren't *my* friends, not yet.

We were at the landing just before the stairs took a turn. It was a blind turn, but if you hugged the far wall, you didn't stay blind for long.

"Wait," Graham said, "please, wait. I should go first."

We all turned and watched him walk the few steps down to us. He gave a smile that was almost nervous. "I am the bodyguard, remember?"

I looked him up and down, and said, "Are you carrying?"

He sighed. "No. Richard says we're dangerous enough without guns."

I shook my head. "Not if everyone else has them, Graham. Silver bullets don't let you get close."

He shrugged those massive shoulders. "Richard is Ulfric; if you want to change policy, take it up with him. I'm just doing what I'm told."

I sighed. I loved Richard, really I did, but we had some serious differences of opinion.

Graham eased past us, but stopped on the step below the landing. He looked up, but not like he was happy. "I was hoping that Jean-Claude would have joined us by now."

I gave him a look. "What do you mean, joined us? Jean-Claude is waiting downstairs with our guests, right?"

He shook his head. "There was an emergency upstairs."

"Asher is managing the Circus; he should be able to take care of any emergencies."

Graham licked his lips. "I don't know the details, because I was left down here to wait for you, but Meng Die did something. Something that made Asher call for Jean-Claude to help him."

Meng Die was a petite Chinese doll, or that's what she looked like. But she, like me, didn't really match the packaging. She'd been the second-in-command in San Francisco, before Jean-Claude called in all the vamps he'd made in this country to help bolster his defenses. Her master had been happy to let her go, because she'd been nights away from a palace revolt that would have left him dead and her in charge. In fact, he wouldn't take her back, though Jean-Claude had offered.

Meng Die wanted to be Jean-Claude's second-in-command, but that was Asher's job. Then all the vamps had come from London after their master went crazy and had to be killed. Suddenly Meng Die was just another master vampire in a kiss that was lousy with master vamps. She was powerful enough to be third, or maybe even second, but temperamentally, she wasn't suited to be that close to any throne. Too dangerous. Too ambitious.

"What the hell did she do now?" I asked.

Graham shrugged. "I don't know."

"I thought you were almost her *pomme de sang*," Nathaniel said.

"I was," he said.

"You don't seem too worried about her."

He shrugged those big shoulders. "She keeps promising to make me, or Clay, her *pomme de sang*, but she never makes the decision. She was still fucking Requiem, too, until he started turning her down."

"Requiem isn't sharing Meng Die's bed anymore?" I asked.

"No."

I frowned. "Did he find a new girlfriend?"

Graham licked his lips again. "Sort of."

"I know that look, Graham, that's your I-have-more-bad-news-and-I-don't-want-to-tell-it look. Spill it, all of it."

He sighed again. "Damn it, if you're not my girlfriend you shouldn't be able to read me that easily."

It was my turn to shrug. "Just tell me."

"Requiem thinks that the reason you've turned him down as your new *pomme de sang* is because he was fucking Meng Die. He said you're not a woman who shares your men."

I didn't know whether to scream, or curse, or laugh. "Did he tell Meng Die that?" I asked.

"I don't know. He told me. He told Clay."

"Did you tell Meng Die?" I asked.

He shook his head. "I am not that stupid. She takes bad news a hell of a lot worse than you do."

"Is Clay that stupid?" I asked.

"Requiem told her," Micah said, voice soft.

We all looked at him. "You know that?" I asked.

He shook his head. "But it would be something he would do, not to cause trouble, but to be honest with her."

I thought about it, then had to agree. "Damn, he would. I wonder if he told her recently?"

"Did you turn her down?" Nathaniel asked Graham.

He gave the quick grin again. "No. She may not hold the *ardeur*, but the sex is still amazing. I've done vamps before, but never Belle Morte's blood-line. If Meng Die is an example of what they have to offer in bed, then my new goal in life is to be one of their *pommes de sang*."

"I thought you wanted to be Anita's *pomme*," Nathaniel said.

Graham looked a little startled, as if he'd said more than he'd meant to say. "If Anita would feed the *ardeur* off me, just once, I might never look at another woman, but until she does . . ." He let the sentence fade, but it summed up why Graham was not a strong contender for me. He didn't really want me, he wanted the *ardeur*. If any of the other female vamps from London had held the *ardeur*, he'd have chased them instead of me, or as well as me. Not very flattering—to him, or to me.

"Until I do, you're keeping your options open," I said.

He shrugged. "I gave all my options up for Meng Die, and she kept Clay and Requiem on her string. I shared her with Clay in a way I've never shared anyone." He looked sad for a moment, then it passed. I wasn't sure if it passed because his sorrow was that shallow, or he had pushed it away. "Anita isn't going to give up all of you guys for me. Why should I give up everyone else just for a chance to be in her bed? I mean, just for a chance, not even the certainty of it."

"I didn't ask Requiem to sacrifice his libido to me."

"You never ask anyone to give up other people for you, but if they don't, you don't sleep with them," Graham said.

And that was a little closer to the truth than I wanted to hear. I hadn't asked Requiem to give up Meng Die, but the fact that he was fucking her had been a point against him. Why? One, because I simply did not like her. Two, Graham was right, I didn't share my men. Not with other women. The fact that I then expected them to share me with about half a dozen other men, well . . . Not fair. Not fair at all.

4

THE STAIRS ENDED in a small room with a door at the other end of it. The door was heavy wood and metal like the door to a dungeon, and in front of that door stood Clay, werewolf and bodyguard. He came toward us, hurrying, which wasn't good. The look on his face wasn't good either. He looked worried.

Graham was all business, the mantle of bodyguardness sliding over him so that that was all that was left. When he actually concentrated on business instead of trying to get into my pants, he was one of the best of the wolves for bodyguard duty. "What's wrong?" he asked.

Clay shook his head. "Jean-Claude isn't with you?" His tone of voice made it half question.

"No," Graham said.

"What's wrong?" I asked, thinking maybe if we kept asking the question he'd answer it.

"Nothing." He looked at me, and smiled an apology. "Nothing except that we've got a room full of guests and no hosts. It's just me and the four other bodyguards in the room. We aren't even allowed to offer refreshments without one of the dominants being present."

"Are you this worried because you think we're being bad hosts?" Micah asked.

Clay seemed to think about it, then nodded. He did that apologetic smile again. "Yeah, I guess I am."

Clay was as tall as Graham, but his hair was blond, curly, and careless. Where Graham took time and attention with his appearance, Clay just didn't seem to care. He wasn't sloppy, just comfortable. He was wearing the same black-on-black outfit, but he'd put black jogging shoes with his slacks, not dress shoes. He looked good, but a little uncomfortable out of his jeans. I sympathized.

"Stupid," he said, "but yeah, I think the evening is starting off badly. I mean, Jean-Claude gets a message and has to run out. The two Masters of the City are all right so far, but the two women are sniping at each other. The muscle, or food, or whatever they are, just stands around looking grim, or pouty-seductive. It has the feel of something that could go south if we don't have someone to help keep it friendly."

I took that last seriously. Clay worked security at Guilty Pleasures, and he was good at spotting trouble before it got started. It made him invaluable at the club.

"Exactly what did Meng Die do to make Asher send for Jean-Claude tonight of all nights?" I asked.

He sighed. "I'm not a hundred percent sure, but it had to be bad or Asher wouldn't have called him away from the other masters."

I could have opened the vampire marks between us and found out what Jean-Claude was doing, but he'd warned me against doing that with new vamps in town. One, we were trying to hide some of my powers under the proverbial basket; two, Jean-Claude wasn't a hundred percent certain that some of the Masters of the City might not be able to listen in to such communications. His phrase: *such communications*. So, unless it was a true emergency, no mind-to-mind communication until everyone left town.

Did he need my help? No. Not against Meng Die. She was mean, and powerful, but not that powerful. I also trusted her to be smarter than to start shit bad enough that the only penalty would be death. She was like most of the old vamps, a survivor at heart.

Micah was looking at me, almost like he'd followed my line of reasoning. Out loud he said, "Jean-Claude and Asher can handle it."

"You didn't read my mind," I said.

He smiled, that smile that made him seem so gentle. "I read your face."

"Great."

He raised his eyebrows, and shrugged, as if, sorry.

Nathaniel said, "How can both of you still be wanting to be Meng Die's *pomme*? She's not dependable."

Graham laughed, a loud abrupt sound that almost startled. "Dependable. I don't want to be her *pomme* because she's *dependable*. I want to be her *pomme* because we are fucking amazing together."

Clay shrugged. "I love her, at least I thought I did."

"You don't sound very sure," Nathaniel said.

"Jean-Claude made us both bunk over with you and Anita a couple of times. Meng-Die was upset, but not that upset. I thought it was because she knew that we'd be back. That I cared about her enough not to be lured away. Then Requiem turned her down because he thought that was why Anita wouldn't take him as her next *pomme de sang*." Clay's face showed something close to pain. "She went ballistic. Jean-Claude rips us out of her bed, forces us to sleep with you, and she's cool about it. Losing Requiem bothered her, more than losing us."

I watched the look in his pale eyes. That had hurt him. He really did care for her. Damn. "Some women, especially of Belle Morte's line, seem to take rejection really badly. You guys had no choice. Jean-Claude said bunk over, and you had to do it. Requiem chose to leave her. That cuts a certain type of woman, or man, real deep."

Clay put those puzzled, pain-filled eyes on me. "You mean it hurt her pride."

I nodded. "Trust me, most master vamps have more than their share."

He shook his head. "I know you're trying to make me feel better, Anita, but what you've just said is that her hurt pride means more to her than whatever she feels for me. Thanks for trying to make me feel better."

"But I failed miserably," I said.

He actually touched me voluntarily, rare for Clay lately; he squeezed my shoulder, very guy. "Yeah, you really suck at this whole comfort thing, but thanks."

He had never been very handsy, but after he bunked over and felt the *ardeur* rise in the bed, he'd touched me only when he absolutely had to. I think he was afraid to touch me. The hints of the *ardeur* made Graham chase me harder. The same kind of hints scared Clay. One man's heaven, another man's hell.

"We should introduce ourselves to our guests," Micah said, "and you need to change shoes."

I sighed. "So we're on our own for this little cocktail party." I knelt down, careful of my hose on the stone floor, and took off the jogging shoes.

"I'm afraid so," Clay said.

"Great, just great." I stood up and let Nathaniel slip the first high heel on, then Micah balanced me while Nathaniel did the other shoe. Four-inch heels, what had I been thinking? I never did like cocktail party talk, but that wasn't the problem this time. I could fake small talk if I had to. The problem was that the two masters in the other room had brought along candidates to be my new *pomme de sang*.

It was my own damn fault. I hadn't chosen from any of the local talent. I had also expressed concern about bringing this many Masters of the City into our territory. It just didn't sound safe to me. So Elinore, one of our new British vamps, had an idea. A wonderfully, awful idea. Since Masters of the City were coming from all over the United States, why didn't we have a sort of contest? The masters could bring some candidates for my new *pomme de sang*.

I'd said no. In fact, I'd said hell no, but Jean-Claude had pointed out that I could simply turn them all down. That the chances of my finding someone I liked well enough to keep were slim. He had a point. And Elinore was right, it was a way to get all the masters to behave themselves while they were visiting us. I mean, if you're looking at what amounts to your new in-laws, you mind your manners. I couldn't argue with the reasoning, but it meant that I felt like a piece of prize beef. Or would that be cheesecake?

Why was I such a prize? Because I was Jean-Claude's human servant and he was the first American master to become his own *sourdre de sang*, fountain of blood. Bascially he'd hit the power curve where he was his own bloodline. It was rare, very rare, for any master vamp to hit that level of power, and he was our first in this country. It was a very big deal. We hadn't advertised the fact, but the Vampire High Council over in Europe knew it, and apparently they hadn't kept it entirely secret. We'd gotten a lot of overtures of friend-ship in the last few weeks. All right, we'd gotten a lot of people trying to align themselves with us. Not the same thing as friendship, actually, but bet-ter than the alternatives.

But when I agreed to all of it, I had never dreamt that I'd be doing the first introductions without Jean-Claude on my arm. Shit.

Micah took my arm in his. "It's going to be fine."

Nathaniel hugged me. "We'll help you be charming."

"I'm just not the Cinderella type," I said.

"But you're not Cinderella, Anita, you're the prince. You're Prince Charming."

I stared into Nathaniel's lavender eyes, and felt the first cold hand of fear in my stomach. Me, Prince Charming? There had to be some mistake.

Though I guess if you have to choose between being the woman who is trying to catch the prince's eye, or the prince who doesn't want to be caught, prince is better. Or at least that's what I told myself as Clay led us through the door, and the drapes that formed the walls of the living room.

I let Micah and Nathaniel each take an arm. Yeah, I couldn't get to my weapons fast, but what was waiting for me in the next room wasn't a prob-lem that guns and knives could solve. It was a problem that only diplomacy, witty banter, and sly seduction could maneuver us through. We were so screwed without Jean-Claude and Asher.

5

THE ROOM WAS all gold and white and silver from the drapes to the couch, the love seat, and the two chairs framing the empty white brick of the fireplace. It looked denuded without the picture of Jean-Claude, Asher, and their lost love, Julianna. A picture painted about five hundred years before I was born. Yeah, the wall looked bare, but the room didn't. The room seemed positively drowning in vamps and shapeshifters. I really did not want to play hostess without Jean-Claude. Really, really didn't.

Stepping into the room I gave them the smile I'd learned at work for clients. The smile that was bright and shiny, and only reached my eyes if I pushed hard. I pushed hard, but my hands were literally clutching at Micah and Nathaniel, as if they were the last pieces of wood in the ocean. I finally realized that I was scared. Scared of what? Polite banter, cocktail party talk? Surely not. I mean, no one here was going to try to kill me. Usually if no one tried to kill me, or I didn't have to kill anyone else, it was a good night. So why the major case of nerves?

Micah was introducing us, while I tried to get a handle on this sudden outbreak of rabid shyness. It wasn't like me. I didn't like small talk and parties with strangers, but I wasn't shy.

Clay and Graham took up their posts at our backs. There were more of our guards scattered around the room, but none of them could help us with the part that was scaring me.

Micah leaned in and whispered, "Anita."

I did the long blink, the one that means I'm thinking really hard, and trying not to show it. You have to know what it is to spot it, honest. "Welcome to St. Louis, and I hope our hospitality will be better from this moment on." There, that wasn't horrible. Point for me.

One of the vamps came forward smiling. He wasn't much taller than me, but broad enough through the shoulders that he looked almost misshapen. The way some short bodybuilders do in suits. "We are all Masters of the City here, Ms. Blake; we all know that some business cannot wait for niceties."

He just stood there, waiting, smiling, pleasant. It was my turn to prove that we weren't country bumpkins. To prove that we did indeed know the niceties. I got myself loose from Micah and Nathaniel. I stood on my own two feet and offered him my hand. "Welcome, Augustine, Master of the City of Chicago." Jean-Claude had described everyone to me, so at least I was pretty sure who I was talking to. That was all I was sure about.

Most master vamps tried to be scary, or mysterious, or sexy. This one smiled wide enough to flash fangs, and said, "Auggie. My friends call me Auggie." His hair was short, blond, but still had lots of small, stylized curls to it. The haircut didn't match the suit and the approach.

He took my offered hand gently in his, as if I were too delicate to touch. Some muscular men do that. Usually it bugged me, but tonight I was okay with it. He turned my hand over and began to raise my wrist to his mouth. I did not raise my own arm. You end up hitting people in the face when you do that. I'd been practicing with Jean-Claude and Asher. My hand had to sit passive in his as he raised my wrist toward his mouth. He was a Master of the City and I was just a human servant. If Jean-Claude had been here, it would have been Auggie offering up his wrist, but I was officially outranked, so I got to offer up.

He bowed over my wrist, and raised his eyes to me at the same time. His eyes were a gray so dark they were almost black. But they were just eyes, and I could meet them. Most masters aren't used to humans doing that. Auggie's eyes widened at it, and I think my smile slipped from welcoming to just a little bit arrogant. That I could meet his eyes with impunity made me feel better, more myself.

His lips curled into a close, secretive smile, not at all the wide grin he'd greeted me with. He laid his lips against my wrist, where the blood runs shallow below the skin. Even then it was just lips on skin, then he kissed my wrist, and a little jolt of power went through my body. It tightened things low and intimate in my body. Tightened them so quick and hard that it caught my breath, and made me stumble.

I felt movement at my back, but I shook my head. My voice was breathy, but I said, "No, I'm all right. It's okay." I felt rather than saw everyone pull back. I had eyes only for the vampire still hovering over my wrist. I didn't pull away from him. I looked into his eyes, until I saw that they were like the sky when it goes black, just before it falls down and destroys everything you own. But I wasn't just a human servant gaining all my power through my ties to Jean-Claude. I'd come to him with partial immunity to vampire gaze, and what I did next was my power, my magic. Necromancy.

I put a little bit of power down my hand, into his skin, like you'd push someone away who'd invaded your space. I told him, metaphysically, *Back off.*

He pulled his hand away, dropped that strange gray gaze. His breath came out in a sharp sound. "I apologize if my little push of power caused you discomfort, but I am trying to behave myself, Ms. Blake. Forcing me to show more of my power might not be wise."

He raised his face as he finished, gave me a glimpse of a face that was no longer boyishly handsome, or cute, in an ordinary sort of way. Now his face was simply beautiful. The bone structure more delicate than it had looked a moment ago. The eyes were rimmed with a lace of dark lashes. If I hadn't spent the last few years staring into Jean-Claude's lashes, I'd have said they were the prettiest eyelashes I'd ever seen on a man. Only the color of his eyes remained unchanged. That extraordinary charcoal gray with its shades of black.

I stepped back enough to look him up and down. His body was the same, and not. He was still short, for a man, but the suit fit him better. I'd gone suit shopping with enough men to know expensive when I saw it. It had been made for his body, and when a short man lifts enough weights to get an upper body that broad, it needs to be made to fit. But the suit looked good now, sleek and stylish, rather than fitting oddly.

He'd been using mind games to appear less beautiful and more ordinary. All I'd meant to do was stop him from doing what amounted to metaphysical foreplay. What I'd done instead was strip him of his camouflage.

I shook my head. "I've seen vamps waste energy to make themselves scarier, but never to appear ordinary."

"Yes," a woman's voice said, "why would you hide so much of yourself, Augustine?" I looked at the woman who went with the voice. She sat on the white love seat, tucked in very close to the only other vamp in the room who made my skin tighten when I met his eyes. The man was dark-haired, dark-eyed, and handsome in an ordinary sort of way. After looking into Augustine's face, it wasn't really fair to compare. But I knew who he had to be.

"Welcome, Samuel, Master of the City of Cape Cod. As Jean-Claude's human servant I welcome you and yours to St. Louis."

He stood, and he hadn't had to. He could have made me come to him. His hair was a dark, dark brunette, almost black, but I'd spent too many years staring at my own hair to mistake it for true black. The careless fall of short curls reminded me of Clay's hair. Cut well, but not fussed with. He was taller than Nathaniel, but not by much, maybe five-seven tops. He looked neat and trim, well-built but not obviously muscular in a simple black suit. He wore a nice green T-shirt underneath it. If Jean-Claude had dressed him, it would have been silk, and closer fitting. The T-shirt, like the suit, hinted, but hid more than it showed. A thin gold chain graced the neck of the shirt. On the end of the chain was a very old coin set in more gold. The coin was one of those ancient pieces they find in shipwrecks sometimes. Or maybe the shipwreck imagery came because I knew what his animal to call was: mermaids. No, really, mermaids. Samuel was unique among now-living vamps in his animal to call.

His wife was one. The man and woman standing behind the love seat had to be merpeople, too. I'd never actually met any of the sea people before.

I fought the urge to look away from the vampire in front of me. I mean, I'd seen vamps, but mermaids, that was new. I offered Samuel my hand. He took it more solidly than Auggie had, like he'd shake hands well. Then he raised my wrist to his mouth. Like Auggie, he rolled his eyes up to gaze at me as he did it. Samuel's eyes were hazel, pale brown with an edge of grayish green around the pupil. The green shirt brought out more of the green, so his eyes were almost an olive green, but they were definitely hazel, not true green. But then I had high standards for true-green eyes.

Samuel's eyes were just eyes, and when he laid a chaste kiss across my wrist it was just a kiss, no extras. I rewarded his restraint with a smile.

"Ah, Samuel, always the gentleman," Auggie said.

"Something you could learn from," said the woman in white, who had to be Samuel's wife, Thea.

"Thea," Samuel said, a slight warning in his tone, but it was very slight. Jean-Claude had warned us all that Samuel's only weakness was his wife. She got her way most of the time, so when dealing with the Master of Cape Cod, you had to negotiate with both of them.

"No, she's right," Auggie said, "you were always a better gentleman than I."

"Perhaps," Samuel said, "but one does not have to say such things out loud." There was an edge of heat in his voice, the first stirrings of anger.

She bowed a body that was inches taller than his, bowed and hid her face. I was betting it was because her face just didn't look sorry enough. Her dress was somewhere between cream and white, and it matched her skin and her hair. She was all whites and creams and pearls. At first glance you might think albino, but then she raised her eyes back up to us both. Her eyes were black, so black that her pupils were lost in the color of her irises. Her lashes were golden, her eyebrows gold and white.

Muscles played under her thin arms as she stood and smoothed her long dress around her body. Her coloring was odd, but not outside human norms. Her white-blond hair fell to her waist. Her only jewelry was a circlet of silver set with three pearls, the biggest in the middle and two smaller to either side, surrounded by tiny but brilliant diamonds, so that the light flashed and winked as she moved her head. Her pale neck was smooth and unadorned, with no gill slits. Jean-Claude had told me that when they wished, the maids of the sea—his phrase—could look very human.

"May I present my wife, Leucothea. Thea." He took her by the hand and drew her into a low curtsey.

Did I curtsey back? Did I tell her to get up? What should I do? What could Meng Die have done that was taking Jean-Claude this long to sort out? She was so on my shit list.

Not knowing what else to do I offered her a hand up. She took my hand, raising a softly startled face to me. Her fingers were cool against my skin.

"Are you helping me rise like a queen taking pity on a commoner, or do you acknowledge that I am your superior?"

I helped her to her feet, though she moved like a dancer and hadn't needed the help. I dropped her hand, and said what I was thinking. When in doubt I usually do. "Okay, truthfully, I'm not sure who outranks who between the two of us. If Jean-Claude had been here then you could offer up to him, but it's me, and I don't mean to be insulting, but I'm just not sure who tops who here."

Thea's pale face looked surprised, but Samuel looked pleased.

Auggie laughed an abrupt, very human-sounding laugh, turning me to look at him. "Jean-Claude said you were a breath of fresh air, Anita, but such an honest breeze, I'm not sure we're up to it."

"I like it," Samuel said.

"Only because you are hopeless at deceit," Auggie said.

Samuel gave him a look. "None of us who have risen to Master of the City is without deceit, old friend."

The humor in Auggie's face softened, and faded. I realized that of almost all the other master vamps I'd ever seen, his face was the most mobile, the most expressive. Now it went suddenly blank the way all the old ones could do. "Fair enough, old friend, but you do prefer honesty."

Samuel nodded. "Aye, that I do."

"You like honesty?" I said. "Then you are going to love me."

There were abrupt laughs from at least two different corners of the room. In one of the corners was Fredo, slumping artfully, his black T-shirt a little bulky in places from all the knives he hid on his body. There were other knives out in plain sight, two huge ones on either hip like an old-time gunslinger. His dark face was set in laughing lines, his black eyes glittering out from the fall of his dark hair.

The other laugh had come from almost the opposite corner. Claudia was nearly six foot six, the tallest woman I'd ever met, and a serious weight lifter. She made the too-thin Fredo look frail. Her black hair was tied back in its usual tight ponytail. She wore no makeup, and her face was still startling in its beauty. Claudia cared less about looking like a girl than I did. But even with the weight lifting, her body was all woman. Without the extreme height and the muscles, she would have been one of those women who couldn't go anywhere without getting hit on, or at least leered at. She still got the leers, but most men were afraid of her, and they should have been. She would probably be the only other woman carrying a gun tonight. At the moment her face was soft with the laughter that was still bubbling in her throat. She had a nice laugh, deep and throaty. I wasn't sure I'd ever heard her laugh before.

"What's so funny?" I asked them both.

"Sorry, Anita," she said, voice still full of laughter.

Fredo nodded. "Yeah, sorry, but you, 'honest'? Jesus, 'honest' doesn't cover it."

Micah had to clear his throat sharply, and even Nathaniel's face was sort of glowing with the effort not to smile at me.

I fought not to get angry, and finally managed it. Bully for me. "I can lie if I have to." And even to me it sounded pouty.

"But it's not your nature," Fredo said, which was a little too perceptive for someone who was supposed to be just muscle.

"He's right," Claudia said, and she'd finally managed to control her laughter. "I apologize for the outburst."

"She is like you, Samuel," Thea said, "an honest heart."

"That would be a good thing," he said. And the way he said it made me finally look at some of the other people in his party. My thought about in-laws was a little too accurate with Samuel and Thea: they were offering up their three sons as possible *pommes de sang* for me. Which I found a little creepy, but all the vamps had patiently explained to me that most of the really old vamps come from a time when arranged marriages between powers was the norm, not the exception.

The twins were easy to spot, because they were identical. I knew their names: Thomas and Cristos. They had their mother's white-blond color, but the short careless curls of their father. They were both taller than their father, somewhere around five-ten like Mom. But their bodies were slender, not enough muscle development. I searched their curious faces and found them young. Very young. They had to be legal, or Jean-Claude wouldn't have agreed, but they didn't look legal. Maybe merpeople aged slower than humans.

The other son I wasn't certain of, because there were two dark-haired men standing behind the love seat. One of them met my eyes bold as brass. The other man wouldn't meet my gaze; he actually blushed, embarrassed. I was betting that was the son. Maybe he thought it was all as weird as I did.

"They are lovely, my sons, are they not?" Thea asked, and that brought my attention back to her.

I wasn't sure what to say to that, but finally said, "Well, yeah, I guess, I mean, I wasn't looking at them for that." I felt the blush crawl up my face and cursed myself for it.

She smiled. "Let us decide which of us is of higher rank, so I may introduce you to them formally."

I thought about it, looked at Micah and Nathaniel. They both shook their heads; they didn't know either.

"I have a thought," Thea said, and the tone in her voice made it clear that she wasn't sure I'd like it. Her voice was melodious, almost like singing.

"I'm willing to hear it," I said.

"We are animal to call and human servant, but I am married to a Master of the City, and you are not. Would that be a way to decide who is higher rank?"

"Thea," Samuel said.

"No," I said, "it is a way to decide this. Marriage beats just dating, I'm okay with that."

Samuel frowned at me. "We were warned that you had a temper, Ms. Blake."

I shrugged. "I do, but Thea's reasoning is as good a way as any to decide which of us offers up a body part."

"You don't find it insulting to acknowledge her as greater than yourself?" he asked.

I shook my head. "No."

He looked at me, looked at me as if he were trying to see all the way through to my spine. It wasn't vampire tricks, it was just him trying to decide what I was, or wasn't. Once I would have squirmed under such a look, but not now. Now I just stood there and gave him calm eyes back.

Thea made some small movement that drew my attention back to her. She was waiting, outwardly patient, but there was a demand in her. Time to put up, or shut up.

I offered her my wrist.

She took my hand in hers, and again her hand was cool in mine. She wrapped her hand around mine, and used it to draw me in toward her body. She wasn't going to take the wrist, she was going for the neck.

I didn't fight, but I did pull back a little.

She hesitated, giving me those strange black eyes of hers. "If I outrank you, Anita, then it is my choice where to touch."

I shook my head. "No, that you're trying for the neck instead of the wrist means only one of three things: you don't trust me, you're showing how big and bad you are, or you're thinking sex. Which is it, Thea?"

"The second," she said. She kept trying to pull me in against her body, and I started to let her. The strength in her one hand let me know that if I really wanted to struggle I'd have a fight on my hands. She was strong, like shapeshifter strong.

She kept her grip on my wrist as she used her other hand to pull me in against her body, until the two of us were pressed together, not tight, but so our bodies brushed from chest to thighs.

I had to talk staring at her shoulder. She was just too tall for me. "Why do you want me to know that you're big and bad?"

"My wife is very competitive with other women, Anita," Samuel said. "Surely Jean-Claude mentioned that, as he mentioned your temper to us."

"He said something about it, but . . ." She let go of my wrist so she could slide that arm around my back, pressing me closer to her. Her other hand was sliding up my back toward my hair. But I hadn't understood what competitive meant, I thought. It took almost everything I had not to tense up as she entwined her body around me, close now, so close, lover close, sex close.

Her breasts were small and tight, and she wasn't wearing a bra. Eeek. I felt stupid with my arms limp at my sides, and I didn't really want to encourage her, but . . . I ended up sort of hugging her just to keep my balance on the damned high heels.

She leaned her mouth close to my face and whispered, "I do want you to understand that I am superior to you, Anita, but that is only half my reason."

My pulse sped up a little at that. I started to turn to look at her face, but she grabbed a handful of curls and kept my face turned away. I was left staring at the man who had blushed. He looked at me, full face, and he suddenly looked like a younger version of Samuel. How had I not seen it before? He mouthed, *I am sorry*.

I had trouble speaking around my pulse now, because I had that bad feeling that something was about to happen. Something I wasn't going to enjoy. "What's the other half of your reason?" I asked, voice breathy, holding that edge of nervousness that held a touch of fear.

"I want to know what you are, Anita," she whispered, and her breath was warmer than it had been. Her hands were warm now, as if she had caught a sudden fever. It reminded me of the way some of the shapeshifters felt close to the full moon.

"What's happening?" I asked, but my voice was only a whisper.

Her fingers entwined through my hair until she held my face immobile with her strong hands, and I could feel the heat of her fingers through my hair. She drew her face back from my neck, and stared down at me. She held my face tilted up to her as if for a kiss. "Are you truly what they say you are?"

I struggled to swallow so I could whisper, "What do they say I am?"

"Succubus," she whispered as she lowered her face toward mine. I knew in that instant that she was going to kiss me. "I am seeking another of my kind, Anita. Are you what I seek?" And with the last word she closed her mouth over mine.

6

HER MOUTH WAS warm, so warm against mine. Warm like hot chocolate. Something you wanted to open your mouth and sip from. It wasn't my idea, opening my mouth, it was hers. Somehow, it was her thought in my head. I didn't like that, not one little bit. The not liking helped me keep my mouth closed tight. She drew back enough to whisper, "Do not fight me."

I heard voices around us arguing. Help was coming, I just had to hold on. I just had to hold my shields in place and not let her do what she was trying to do. Just hold on, that was all. I'd held on when help was miles away; now it was just inches. I could do this.

She'd tried gentle persuasion, mind games, they hadn't worked. She tried force. She kissed me so hard, that either I opened my mouth to her, or she was going to cut my lip on my own teeth. If she'd been a man I would have just let her kiss me—was I really this homophobic? If she hadn't whispered through my mind that she wanted me to open my mouth, I might have done it, but she wanted it too badly. Part of me was just that stubborn, but part of me was afraid of why she wanted it so badly. I knew she was a siren, a sort of uber-mermaid. I knew that some of her magic dealt with seduction and sex. I knew that she could control the other mermaids. I knew all sorts of things from talks with Jean-Claude; what I didn't know was why she wanted me to open my mouth.

Her kiss bruised my mouth and I tasted blood, sweet, metallic candy on my tongue. The moment I tasted the blood, it hurt. She'd cut the inside of my lip on my own teeth.

She drew back. "Why fight so hard simply not to kiss me back? Are you so much a hater of women?"

I tried to shake my head, but she still held my face immobile. "Why do you want me to open my mouth? What difference does it make to you?"

"You are strong, Anita, so strong. The walls of your inner tower are high, and wide, but not impenetrable."

I was getting angry, and I wasn't sure what that would do to my inner tower and its walls. I did not want the beast to rise while we were still doing introductions. I took a deep breath and let it out slowly, but said what my anger wanted me to say; I just wasn't angry when I said it. "Either let me go, or breach those walls, but either way this ends."

"How so?"

"I've done all that vampire etiquette requires, so either let me go, or I call in my guards and they force you to let me go."

"Do you need help to break free of me?" she asked, and her voice was singsong again.

"Unless I'm willing to shoot you, yes."

Graham came close enough to say quietly, "Say the word, Anita, and we move her." He sounded eager, or angry. I guess I couldn't blame him. This whole thing had gone beyound grandstanding to just plain rude.

Samuel came to our side. "Thea, this is not the way."

She turned her head and looked at him. "Then what is the way?"

"Perhaps you could simply ask."

A look crossed her face, as if that would never have occurred to her, then she laughed, a high wild sound, and for a second I thought I heard the laughter of seagulls. "So simple, my darling Samuel, so simple." She released the grip on my hair so I could move my neck, which was a relief. She stayed entwined around me, but not so forcefully. We were still too close for comfort, but it was more friendly. "My deepest apologies, Anita; it has been so long since I met anyone who could withstand my desires that I simply kept trying to force. Forgive me."

"Let me go, and I will."

She gave that laugh again, and it wasn't my imagination. When she laughed I heard the sound that herring gulls make, and the whisper of surf. She let me go, stepped back. The moment she moved back the tension level in the room plummeted. All the guards on every side had thought the flags were about to go up. Me, too.

She bowed. "My deepest apologies. I underestimated you, and I am ashamed of my actions."

"I accept your apology."

She stood and regarded me with those black eyes in that pale white and gold face, as if some delicate porcelain doll had the eyes of a movie demon. "You know that we are offering our sons as your *pommes de sang*."

I nodded. "Jean-Claude told me, and I'm honored." Actually it creeped me out, but I understood that it was supposed to be an honor.

"But do you know why?"

That stopped me, because the answer was, "Jean-Claude said you wished for a stronger alliance between our two kisses."

"We do"—Samuel joined his wife—"but there is a reason that my wife was so adamant that we bring all three of our sons to your table."

"And that reason would be what?" I wanted to just skip this until I had more vampire backup, but I didn't think I'd get the choice.

Micah was suddenly at my side, taking my hand. I felt better. I wasn't alone. We could do this. We didn't have vamps, but we had each other. Nathaniel came in at my back, not quite taking my other hand in case I needed it for weapon grabbing, but close enough that he was a line of heat at my back. Better and better.

"I am a siren," Thea said.

I nodded. "I know."

"Do you understand what that means among my kind?"

"I know that most mermaids who exhibit siren abilities are killed by the other merpeople before they can reach their full power."

"Do you know why?"

"Because in full power you can control the merpeople magically."

"As a necromancer can control all types of undead," Thea said.

I shrugged. "Yeah, I have some control over a lot of undead, but it's not perfect control, and it doesn't work on everyone."

"Nor does mine work on every merperson, though it works on many. But do you know what the basis of that control is?"

I shook my head. "No."

"Sex, or seduction perhaps."

I crooked an eyebrow at her. "What does that mean exactly in this context?"

"It means that I hold something similar to the *ardeur* that you and Jean-Claude share. It attracts both my kind and mortals to me, as the *ardeur* attracts the dead and apparently lycanthropes and mortals to you."

I frowned at her. "Yeah, a lot of guys want a full taste of the *ardeur* once they get a small taste." I fought not to look for Graham when I said it. "But they aren't attracted to me because of it."

She gave that gull-and-surf laugh again. "You do not know what you are, Anita. The *ardeur* alone does not make you a succubus, or Jean-Claude an incubus. I have met others with the *ardeur*, but fewer with that next level of power. You have it. Your master has it. People are drawn to you because of it. The very touch of your skin can be addictive."

I gave her a look. "Like the touch of your skin is supposed to be addictive?"

"Yes."

I fought not to smile, but didn't quite succeed. I licked the cut she'd made in my lip, and said, "No insult meant, but I don't crave your touch."

"No, you fought me. You won."

"What do you want from me?"

"I believe that my sons have inherited my powers, but there is only one way for a siren to be fully born. Another siren must bring them into their power."

I saw where this was going, or was afraid I did. "Let me guess: the only way to bring them over is to have sex."

She nodded.

"You can't find another siren to do the job for you?"

"I am the last of my kind, Anita. I am the last siren. Unless you have the power to awaken my sons."

Micah squeezed my hand tighter. Nathaniel moved in so that our bodies touched from shoulder to hip. "Okay, if we're being honest, I'm a little disturbed by your pimping out your sons to me."

"What does 'pimping out' mean?" she asked.

I sighed. Great, one of those moments when you really don't want to explain the slang. Nathaniel said, "It means to sell someone else for sexual purposes."

She frowned, then said, "I cannot truly argue the definition. I wish you to have sex with my sons, and it will gain us both a stronger alliance. They will gain power from it. So, if that is selling, I cannot argue this 'pimping out.' "

"But if you are only a carrier of the *ardeur* and not a true succubus, then you cannot do what Thea wishes," Samuel said.

I looked at them both. "And how do we find out if I've got what Thea wants?" I couldn't keep the suspicion out of my voice.

Nathaniel stroked my shoulder like you'd settle a nervous horse, but I didn't push him away. I was getting tense, and fighting not to get angry.

"Let down your inner walls, and let my power taste yours." She said it like it was easy, a small thing.

I shook my head. "I don't know."

"The thought of my 'pimping out' my sons to you makes you uncomfortable, does it not?"

"Yeah, it does."

"If your power is not close enough to mine, then we will stay for the parties, and the ballet, but you will not have to look at them as *pommes de sang*. We will take our sons home and you will not have to worry over your discomfort."

It sounded too easy. "It sounds simple, but before I say yes, what are the possible side effects of your power exploring mine?"

She looked puzzled. "I am not certain I understand the question."

"She means," Micah said, "what bad things could happen if she allows this?"

She actually thought about it for almost a minute. "It should be only a touch of powers, like two leviathans moving in the deep, sliding their sides against each other, then passing away into the dark depths of the sea."

I felt calmer, as if I could feel those dark, peaceful depths.

"*Should* be," Micah said. "What else could happen?"

"It could call your *ardeur* to the surface and you would be forced to feed."

I was suddenly tense again, the peaceful dark depths gone like smoke in the wind. "No," I said.

Nathaniel whispered in my ear. "You can feed from me without intercourse, Anita. It's a way of getting rid of them."

Micah looked at me. "Only you can decide if the chance of having to feed the *ardeur* here and now is worth it, Anita."

I looked at the sons. The twins looked at me, smiling, somewhere between amused and embarrassed. But it was the kind of embarrassment that any teenager would have felt if his mom did something that made him squirm. The older one, behind the love seat, looked more like I felt, uncomfortable as hell.

"You must be Sampson," I said.

He looked startled, then nodded. "I am."

"What do you think about all this? I mean, do you want to be brought into your sirenhood?"

He looked down, then up. "Do you know that you are the first person to ask me how I feel about this?"

I let the surprise show on my face.

"It's no reflection on my parents. They love me. Us. But Father is over a thousand years old, and Mother is older still. Arranged marriages don't seem strange to them, and they both would love to have one of us be as powerful as Mother. It would cement our power base along the entire eastern seaboard of this country. I understand all that, or I wouldn't be standing here."

"But," I said.

He smiled, and it was his father's smile. "But, I don't know you. The thought of being forced to have sex with anyone is just . . . wrong."

I looked at the twins. "And you, Thomas and Cristos, right?"

They nodded.

"How do you feel about this?"

They looked at each other, then one blushed and the other didn't. The one who didn't blush said, "I'm Thomas, Tom, when Mom's not around to complain." He gave her a smile out of his father's hazel eyes. "I saw pictures of you before we came. I knew you were pretty, and"—now he blushed, bit his lip, and tried again—"I would love to have an excuse to have sex with you. There, that's the truth."

"How old are you?" I asked.

He glanced at his parents.

"Don't look at them, answer the question."

Sampson answered it, "They're seventeen."

"Seventeen," I said. "Jesus, that's not legal."

"It is legal in Missouri," Thea said. "We did check your laws before we brought them here."

I looked at her, and didn't know what my face showed, but it felt like nothing pleasant. "I don't do teenagers. Hell, I didn't do teenagers when I was one."

"Then let my wife taste your power, Anita," Samuel said. "It is likely that your power will not do what we need. Succubus is close to siren, but not the same creature. If your power does not recognize Thea's, then we will allow Sampson to go home with his morals intact. We will disappoint Thomas."

That reminded me. "Cristos, you never said how you feel about all this."

The one who had blushed raised his eyes to me. The look was enough—embarrassment, fear even, but under that was eagerness. The look just screamed virgin. I so was not going to be the one who took his virginity. So not doing that. The fact that his parents were encouraging it just made it creepier.

His voice was low, but deep enough. It was not the voice of a child, but the look was. "Cris, I'm Cris."

I wanted to say out loud, *Your first time should be with someone you care about. Your virginity should go to someone you love.* But I didn't want to embarrass him more than he already was, so instead I said, "Fine." I looked at Thea. "Thea can taste my power." I did not add that I hoped she didn't like the power, because nothing was going to make me pick any of their sons.

Sons. Children. It made me remember why we had pregnancy tests in our overnight bag. Would I be bargaining for some sort of arranged shacking-up for my own child some day? I mean, no matter who the father was, none of us was exactly human, and most of us were scarily powerful. Shit. I wished I hadn't thought of that.

Thea was in front of me, her head to one side, studying my face. "You look worried, Anita, very worried, as if you've thought of something new to fret over."

That was a little too perceptive. I was really going to have to work harder at hiding my facial expressions tonight. I tried for a little truth. "Samuel is only the second master vamp I've ever met with a grown child, or children. It's just . . . weird."

Micah leaned more of himself against the arm he was holding. Nathaniel cuddled in tighter to my back, though the gun kept him from being as comforting as I wanted him to be. They knew what I'd thought of, or maybe they'd been thinking the same thing, or something close to it.

Thea turned her head to the other side, and it didn't remind me of anything aquatic. It reminded me of a bird of prey judging the distance to my eye.

I shivered. *Please, God, don't let me be pregnant.*

She touched my face with fingers that were still fever warm. "It is not I who put that frown between the dark beauty of your eyes."

I drew my head back enough not to be touched. "Very poetic. Let's get this done, Thea. We're wasting moonlight."

She gave a smile that reminded me of the one that Tom had used just before he blushed and bit his lip, and admitted wanting to have sex with me. The twins looked very much like her except for the eyes.

"Very well, but your men will have to step away. I do not know what the effect would be if they were touching you while I do this. It might raise the *ardeur* for certain, or . . ."

"Or what?" I asked.

"Or they might bolster your defenses and keep me from testing your power at all." She gave a movement of pale shoulders that was almost a shrug, but not quite. "I will treat you as I treat Samuel. I will tell you the truth. I simply am not certain. If you were a vampire then I might know, but you are more, and less. You are not simply one thing or the other, but both, and many. I think it must change the rules of power and magic around you."

I took in a deep breath, let it out slow, and nodded. I moved forward and Micah and Nathaniel moved back. They gave me the room we asked for. I'm not sure any of us were sure it was a good idea, but if she found me wanting then there were three very unpalatable *pomme de sang* candidates off the table. Yippee.

Thea took me in her arms again, and I didn't fight it. I even wrapped my arms around her. She didn't try to control my head this time. She trusted me to let her kiss me.

I actually went up on tiptoe for her, which meant she was closer to six feet than I'd thought. I found myself putting a hand along the edge of her face as if this were a kiss that I wanted. Sometimes I touched someone's face because it was intimate. Sometimes I touched them because a hand on the face helps you control the kiss more if things get out of hand. Two guesses which reason it was this time, and first guess doesn't count.

7

SHE KISSED ME, and this time I didn't fight her. I let my body melt into hers, let her feed at my mouth. There is a moment in a kiss, especially an open-mouth kiss, where the caress of lips and tongue spills over some line, and beyond that line, you kiss back. I kissed her, kissed her as she was meant to be kissed, full and complete, tasting her.

I drew back enough to whisper, "You taste salty."

She breathed her answer in my mouth, as she drew me back into the kiss, "You taste of blood." Her breath filled my mouth, caressed the back of my throat. Her breath tasted fresh and clean like the wind off the ocean.

Her lips tasted like she had just that second taken a sip of the ocean. I licked her lip, and found that there was a whitish film on the fullness of her mouth. It wasn't illusion. It was real.

I swallowed the salty taste of her lips, staring up at her, feeling the surprise on my face. "How . . ." But I never finished the question, because I didn't just swallow the taste of salt, I swallowed her power.

I heard the ocean whispering against the shore. I could hear it like music. I looked around the room. I wanted to ask someone else if they could hear it. I meant to look for Micah, or Nathaniel, but that wasn't who caught my gaze. Thomas was staring at me with wide eager eyes. His brother had collapsed to the love seat, and was covering his ears with his hands, rocking back and forth. Cristos was fighting it, whatever it was, but Thomas wasn't. Sampson had a death grip on the love seat, but his eyes had drowned to black so that he looked blind. The other man and woman they'd brought with them turned black eyes to me. The woman was hugging herself, as if cold, or afraid. The man had a death grip on his own wrist, the typical jock pose turned into something harsh and struggling, as if, if he let go of his wrist, he would do something unfortunate. Last I found Samuel's eyes. His eyes had bled to vampire fire, the glowing brown with flecks of green flame in their depths. They all could hear it, that whispering, seductive sound. The ocean was calling, and I didn't know how to answer.

I was still staring into Samuel's eyes when I felt a hand glide down my shoulder. I turned, and found Thomas standing next to us. Thea began to pull out of my arms, giving me to Thomas's arms as she moved, so that it was as if the embrace never stopped, only the arms holding me had changed.

There was movement around us. I saw Micah's face, his lips moving, but I couldn't hear him. All I could hear was the sigh and echo of the sea. Thomas touched my face, turned me back to look at him. He spoke, and his words held the growling echo of surf over rocks. "You hear my voice though, don't you?"

I nodded, my face pressed against his hand. His hand was large enough to cup the entire side of my face. He leaned down, and I went up on tiptoe to help him finish the kiss. I wasn't thinking that he was seventeen. I wasn't thinking we had an audience that included his parents. I wasn't thinking that men I loved were watching. I saw nothing but his face, felt nothing but the strength of his hands on my face, his arm trailing down my back, his hand gliding down my body. The inside of my head was peaceful, full of a soft, rushing sound, like water as it spills along some peaceful shore. I wasn't the one who fought free of the mind games, it was Thomas who spoiled it. His hand slid down, down, and found the gun at the small of my back. It made him hesitate. Made him stumble as if his magic had legs to be tripped by a misplaced stone.

I pulled back from him, saw the uncertainty on his face. He was still handsome, and the compulsion to touch him was still there whispering through my head, but his eyes were wide, his face uncertain. He looked fresh and new and untried, like someone who had never hugged someone and found her wearing a gun.

The sound of the surf pulled away, and I could hear the murmuring in the room. People wondering what to do, whether they should interfere.

"That's a gun," he said, in a voice as uncertain as his face.

I nodded. I had gone back to being flat-footed on my heels, no more tiptoe, no more helping him seduce me with his mother's magic, or his own.

He'd actually missed the big knife down my spine, because he hadn't come to the midline of my body until low on my back. But it was a big weapon to miss. Baby, he was a baby. And I'd have said that if he'd been twenty-seven instead of seventeen. Baby not in years, but in my world. You don't miss a knife as long as a forearm, not and live, not for long. Not in my world.

I gazed up into his face. The black was beginning to drain away, showing the hazel of his human eyes. He was the son of a master vampire and a siren, but where he lived was a gentler, kinder place than my life. I would leave him to that gentleness.

I drew out of his arms, completely. "Go back and sit down, Thomas."

He hesitated and looked at his mother. She was watching me, not him. Watching me with those black eyes. There was a considering look on her face, as if she wasn't sure what she thought of the show.

"Do as Anita says, Thomas," she said, at last.

He went back to the love seat, to sit beside his brother. It left Thea and me staring at each other.

"He hesitated only for a moment," she said, "yet, it was enough."

"It's not his power," I said, "not yet. It's yours. You loaned him enough power to roll me."

She made a gesture that was almost a shrug, but her hands went out in a wide gesture. I think it meant, *Perhaps*, or, *You caught me*. I wasn't sure which, and wasn't sure I cared.

"You have greeted Thomas, but we have two other sons," she said.

Micah came up beside me. He took my hand. "In fairness to our other guests, I think we need to greet more of Auggie's people."

"They are only his henchmen, and his mistress. We have brought you our flesh and blood, the fruit of our lives."

Micah nodded, still smiling. "We appreciate that, but—"

I cut him off, and said, "Enough, Micah, thanks for trying to be all polite and hosty, but I've had enough of games for the night."

He squeezed my hand, as if saying, *Be nice*.

I squeezed back, but I was done being nice. I wouldn't be rude, but . . . "I'm going to greet Auggie and his people now, because they didn't try to roll me. Until Jean-Claude joins us, you and your sons are just going to have to wait to be greeted."

"So Augustine's whore is higher in rank than my sons?" Thea sounded genuinely angry.

There was a sound of outrage from the other side of the room—a woman's voice protesting and Auggie trying to calm her. I glanced to find him talking to a statuesque brunette in a very tiny dress. She was mad, and I didn't blame her.

I turned back to Samuel. "You talk to her, Samuel. You explain that your wife damn near abused our hospitality tonight."

"If we have truly abused your hospitality, then Jean-Claude could revoke our safe conduct," he said, voice deep, but strangely soft.

"I understand that."

"Did we frighten you that badly?" he asked.

"I agreed to Thea tasting my power, not Thomas. It wasn't what we negotiated for. I was told you were an honorable man; bait and switch isn't very honorable."

"Could you hear anything we said while Thomas touched you?" Micah asked.

I glanced at him, and shook my head. "I could hear his voice and the sound of the sea, that was it."

"I pointed out to Samuel that you hadn't bargained for Thomas."

"What did he say?"

"He said that for a siren to truly taste your power it needed to have a sexual flavor to it, and since you were not a lover of women, one of the boys would be helpful."

I shook my head. "I'm going to greet Auggie and his people now. Whether I let any of your other children touch me, or not, is up for a very serious debate." I put my gaze on Thea. "I don't like to be forced, or played, Thea. If you really want your sons to have a chance at my bed, or body, or power, you need to remember that."

"I saw into your mind when I embraced you," she said. "I saw what you think of my sons. You are disinclined toward them. Without magic to persuade you, I do not think they have any chance at your bed, your body, or your power."

My pulse was suddenly in my throat. I fought to keep a blank face, but wasn't sure I succeeded. How much had she read while she was playing inside my head? Did she know about the pregnancy scare?

Thea was watching me very narrowly. She saw the fear on me, but didn't understand why. Which meant either she'd only read things about her sons in my head, or she didn't understand why being pregnant would scare me. If the former, yea; if the latter, she was too odd for me to talk to.

I turned to Auggie and his angry girlfriend. She was the only woman on his side of the room. Standing in the spike heels she was over six feet tall. But whereas with Claudia it was all muscle, and menace, this woman was thin. There was no play of muscle to her arms and legs. She was making angry gestures with large hands, darkly painted nails, a diamond flashing on her right hand. Her dress was red with silver sequins. It fit her like a tiny, glittery second skin. The dress was so short that when she flounced around the couch, taking too long a step, she flashed enough flesh that I knew she wasn't wearing anything under the dress. Oh, my.

Auggie coaxed her back to me. Her face was perfect in a high-cheekboned, almost stark way. She wore enough makeup, artfully applied, that *stark* should not have been a word you used for her face. Her hair was long, and teased too high on the top, as if she'd never quite left the eighties, but it was brunette. It might even have been her natural color. The spaghetti straps of her dress and the thin material should not have been able to support her breasts. Breasts that large do not stay perky without more help than the dress could give. Her breasts sat under the dress in a way that real breasts just don't. She flounced toward me, holding Auggie's hand. The walk was good, bouncy, but her breasts didn't bounce with her. They were big, and even shapely, but they rode under her dress like they were way more solid than breasts are meant to be.

It took Micah tugging on my hand to let me know I'd missed something, staring at her chest. I shook my head and gave Auggie eye contact. "Sorry, what did you say?"

"This is Bunny; she is my mistress."

Bunny. I thought, was it her real name? I hoped so—who would choose to be Bunny? I nodded. "Hi, Bunny."

Auggie gave her a little pull, and a nod.

She gave an angry sullen face to me. "At least I'm only whoring for one man, not a dozen."

Micah actually pulled me away from her. I let him do it. I was so astounded at the rudeness of it that I was speechless. I wasn't even angry yet; it was too unexpected. Too rude.

Auggie ordered her to kneel, and when she didn't do it fast enough, he forced her. "Apologize, now!" His power filled the room like cold water, shivering along my skin.

"Why am I a whore, when his wife is pimping out her own sons, and this one is fucking everything and everyone that will stand still?"

"Benny," he said in a very quiet voice. I knew that tone of voice. It's the careful, controlled one you use when you're afraid of what you'll do if you yell.

The only vampire he'd brought with him moved around the couch to stand beside him. "Yeah, boss."

"Take her out of here. Get on a plane, take her back to Chicago, help her pack. Make sure she takes only what belongs to her."

Bunny's eyes went wide. "No, Auggie, no, I didn't mean it. I'm sorry."

He moved away, so she couldn't touch him. She tried to crawl after him, but Benny grabbed her arm. "Come on, Bunny, we gotta plane to catch."

She was human, and in five-inch heels, but she put up a fight. Benny was having trouble getting her to the door without hurting her. She'd proven to the entire room that she was naked under the tiny dress.

I said, "Claudia."

She came to me, all serious, the bodyguard's bodyguard. "Pick someone, or two someones, to help Benny get her out of here."

Claudia nodded, almost a bow, and said, "Fredo, Clay, help our guest out."

Fredo pushed himself from the wall, all boneless ease like some dark, well-armed cat. Clay just took Bunny's other arm, and helped Benny start carrying her toward the door. She used the spike heels effectively, probably drawing blood through Clay's pants. He never slowed, and neither did Benny, though his face was bleeding from nail marks. Fredo got both her ankles, and they carried her out.

Auggie gave me a very low bow. "I don't know what to say, Anita. I'm sorry that I brought her. I knew she was jealous, but not crazy jealous."

"Jealous?" I made it a question.

"She, like Samuel's Thea, is very competitive around other women."

I frowned at him. "So she and Thea were like trying to outbitch each other?"

He looked at me. "You really don't understand why she didn't like you from the moment you stepped into the room, do you?"

Micah drew me in against his body, hugging me one-armed. I looked back and forth from one to the other of them. "What?"

"No," Micah said, "she doesn't."

"Don't what?" I asked.

"You are a natural beauty," Auggie said. "Artifice gave Bunny her face, her figure; most of her best features were found under a surgeon's blade. In you walk, all natural equipment, wearing more clothes, and still get more attention from the men in the room than she did. When you were with Thea and Thomas, every man in the room was riveted. We wanted you. Wanted to touch you, in a way that is rare."

I felt myself blushing and tried to stop it, but, as usual, lost. "You're babbling, Auggie," I said.

"Watching you and a siren, two if you count the boy. Watching two creatures formed of desire, and it was not the pale beauty most eyes watched, Anita. It was the dark."

I frowned at him. "I don't need this much ego-boost, Auggie, just make your point. If you have a point?"

Nathaniel came up. "I'll translate."

"What do you mean, translate?" I said, turning to him.

He took my hand, and shook his head. His face had that I-love-you-but-you-amuse-me look. "You outvamped the sirens, Anita."

"How?"

"I believe," Auggie said, "because your power is over the dead, and the undead. I was told your animal to call was only leopard."

I nodded. "It is, but through Jean-Claude's marks, I also have ties to the wolves."

"Yes, but my men are neither. They are lion, and yet they felt your call."

I glanced behind him at the two men he'd brought along as both body-guards and food, and I was told as *pomme de sang* candidates, though Auggie, like Samuel, had a new twist on the whole *pomme* thing. Auggie was hoping to convince one of our new female vamps from London to come home with him and play house. He wanted another of Belle's line in his bed. Maybe that had predisposed Bunny to be pissy. He had come here to replace her, after all.

Auggie was offering to trade one of his werelions for a bedmate of Belle's line. I wondered how the men in question felt; did they want to stay in St. Louis? Did they want to leave Chicago? Had anyone asked them? I was betting not.

They were both tall, and muscular, and all they needed was a blinking sign over their heads that said "bodyguard." They both wore tailored suits that hid the guns I was almost one hundred percent sure were under there somewhere. One was brunette, the other pale; other than that they looked as if an unimaginative baker had used the same cookie cutter for both of them. Only the icing was different. The pale one had short spiky, blue hair, which had actually been dyed well, so that it wasn't a solid blue color, but pale blue, dark blue, all mixed together like real hair is, and dyed hair seldom is. Except that nobody has hair the color of Cookie Monster and a spring sky on the top of their head. His eyes were a pale blue made deeper, richer, by the hair color. He was a little more slender through the shoulders, and maybe an inch taller, than the other guard.

The brunette's hair looked like it might curl, but he'd cut it so short it didn't have the chance. His shoulders had a swell that I was familiar with; someone lifted weights as more than a casual hobby. Not a bodybuilder, but he worked at it. He was tall enough to carry the shoulders.

Cookie Monster had a slight smile on his slender face. It reached the blue of his eyes, as if we just amused the hell out of him. Brunette watched me like I might do something bad, and he would be ready. The smile didn't fool me; they were both professional muscle. They were dangerous, and they were totally unacceptable as *pomme de sang* candidates. Too dominant, too unbending. Yeah, it was a quick judgment, but I'd have bet almost anything I was right.

My eyes went to the other man who still stood behind the couch. I'd have said human, but the power that lurked just below that dark, elegant surface made me think, maybe not. I knew he was Octavius, Auggie's human servant. I'd have liked to just greet the two bodyguards, and let their power tell me I was right to think they were too dominant for what we wanted, but techni-cally since they weren't Auggie's special animal to call, Octavius outranked them.

Almost as if he read my face, Octavius said, "Greet them first, Ms. Blake, let us see what you think of your choices. I, too, think the night is wasting away." His voice matched the smooth elegance of the rest of him.

I nodded, and said, "Thank you." But I didn't like that Octavius had read me that easily. I moved around the couch, with Micah and Nathaniel at my back, and Graham and Claudia flanking all of us. I don't think any of our guards liked the two werelions any better than I did.

"You guys have names?" I asked.

Cookie Monster grinned at me, eyes sparkling. Why did I think he'd grin just like that while he gutted someone? "Haven, I'm Haven."

I nodded acknowledgment, then turned to Brunette. "And you would be?" "Pierce."

"You guys only have one name apiece? Like Madonna?"

Pierce frowned at me. Haven laughed, and it was a good laugh. Head back, full-throated; if he hadn't made the hairs at the back of my neck crawl, I'd have smiled.

Auggie glided up to the two men, putting a hand on each of them. Their eyes tightened, not a flinch, but noticeable. What had he done when he touched their backs, oh-so-lightly?

Auggie smiled, that happy, happy smile that filled his gray eyes with light. "My lions are like vampires, Anita; they can, if they choose, have only one name among us. Pierce and Haven do have first names, but I think they will keep them until they know if they're staying."

"What, you think I can't run them through a computer and a record check because you don't give me their real names?"

"If their criminal record worries you, then let me allay your fears. They both have one." He was still smiling when he said it.

It was all getting too weird. These were our friends, and I was already feeling like I'd been thrown into the deep end of the pool. *Jean-Claude, where are you?* I thought.

I got a confused glimpse of fighting. He and Asher were struggling to hold Meng Die down. It reminded me of watching the men carrying Bunny out. If they want to hurt you, and you don't want to hurt them, you are at a disadvantage. They were inside the building that housed the carnival's freak show upstairs. Though most of the "freaks" were rare supernaturals. I saw people looking in at them from the outer areas. They had an audience.

I thought, *Ask for help, get some guards in there and get her out of sight.*

I felt more than heard him think that asking for help with the other vamps maybe sensing it would make him look weak. I thought back, *Taking advantage of your resources is not weakness, it's good management.*

I felt him reach out to the wolves upstairs. I felt them moving toward him. Soon there'd be too many men for her to fight back. What they'd do with her once they subdued her, that was a different question. I had one more awful thought. I turned to Claudia. "Can you contact the wererat guards upstairs via mind?"

She pulled a small cell phone from one pocket. "How about phone?"

"Meng Die's animal to call is wolf; I'd like a few wererats to join everyone in the freak show."

Claudia didn't ask, she just made the call. So nice not to be questioned.

"And what does Jean-Claude need that much help with?" Auggie said.

"She's a female of Belle's line. You want her?"

He laughed. "Not if she's this wild, no."

"Auggie wouldn't need help to subdue one of his vamps," Pierce said.

"Jean-Claude could subdue her, or even kill her, but she's chosen a place where there's an audience. Committing murder in front of civilians is a no-no," I said.

"But once behind the scenes, will he kill her?" Haven asked.

I sighed. "Probably not."

"Weakness," Pierce said.

Auggie patted them both on the back, and again there was that tightening around their eyes. "Now, now, boys, some masters would have killed Bunny for her disrespect. Everyone runs his territory a little differently." He was still cheerful, and charming, but there was an edge to it.

"What are you thinking, Auggie?" I asked. I didn't really expect an answer, but I got one.

"That Jean-Claude is too sentimental for his own good sometimes."

I smiled, and knew it left my eyes cold. "You know, *sentimental* is not a word I would have used for him."

"Then he has changed."

"Don't we all," I said.

Auggie nodded, the smile melting around the edges. "Taste them, Anita. Taste your new toys."

I shook my head, and said, "Can you stop touching them while I do it? I'd hate to confuse your tie to them with their power."

He gave a small bow and stepped back. He even went to sit on the couch, where Octavius joined him. I stepped away from my own people. I fought not to look at one particular guard of ours. Our local lions were ruled by Joseph, and he was in the corner dressed as a bodyguard. He was ready to help if needed, but he and I both knew that he was mostly here to check out the new werelions. I was betting he liked them even less than I did.

I looked up at the two men in question. "Do you guys want this trade?"

That surprised them both, though Haven hid it sooner. He smiled. "I'm cool with it, if it works out." His eyes were cooler when he said it, as if the smile were beginning to melt down his face. If I asked the right question I might even see the real Haven behind the smiling, hip exterior.

Pierce glanced behind them at Auggie. I said what I'd said to the twins. "Don't look at your master, look at me, and give me an honest answer. Do you want to be traded to St. Louis?"

He started to look at the couch again. I touched his arm. A jolt of power ran through me, made me drop his arm. It stopped him midmotion, turned him back to me with his pulse pushing at the side of his throat. "What was that?"

I fought the urge to rub my hand along the side of my skirt. "I'm not sure. Power, some kind of power."

"You're not sure?" He sounded as suspicious as he looked.

"I honestly don't know why there was a power jump when we touched. I didn't like it either."

"I want to go home," he said. "I don't like being traded away, and I really don't like being offered up for sex like some kind of whore." He let the anger fill his voice, and the anger raised his power like heat across my skin.

Octavius said, "Be careful, cat."

"No," I said, "I want honesty. I've seen what happens if someone is forced to be in a group that they don't want to be in. The local lion pride works well; I don't want to queer their deal."

"So you won't taste Pierce now, will you?" Auggie asked from the couch.

I shook my head. "Take him back home, Auggie. I'm surprised you brought him, him not wanting to come."

"Bunny said Pierce was one of the best lovers she'd ever had. I thought you'd enjoy that."

I couldn't control my face fast enough.

"What's wrong with that?" Auggie asked.

"The idea of Bunny, just—" I made a push-away gesture. "I'm fighting off a visual."

"She could be crude, but she was very good at her job."

I looked at Auggie. "And her job would be?"

"Sex."

"She's your mistress, not your whore. Mistress means more than just sex."

"Now that is Jean-Claude talking."

"Maybe, but it's still true."

He shrugged those massive shoulders. "You've met her, Anita, do you really think I sat around and had stimulating conversations with Bunny?"

I laughed, I couldn't help it. "No, I guess not." Then another thought occurred to me. "Why would you date anyone that you couldn't talk to?"

He just stared at me, a look on his face that I couldn't read. "You mean that, don't you?" He smiled, almost sadly, shook his head, and wouldn't meet my gaze. "Oh, Anita, you make me feel jaded, and very old."

"Do I apologize for that?" I asked.

He looked up, smiling still. "No, but that you meant that question makes me wonder about my choices for your *pomme de sang*. I looked for good sex, dominants, because everyone needs more muscle. I did not look for good conversation, or someone with interests like yours. I wasn't looking for a date. I was looking for food and fucking."

"You need a woman in your organization, Auggie. Being all guys limits you."

"Are you saying I need a woman's touch?"

"Yeah, and there isn't a woman of Belle's line that will go with you just to be your whore. We promised them that they'd have choices when they came here."

"Are you saying I have to court them?"

I nodded. "Yeah, I am."

"And Jean-Claude agrees to this?" Octavius said.

I nodded. "He gave his word that no one would be forced to have sex against their will."

"Ah," Auggie said, then he laughed. "Dating. I haven't dated in decades. I wonder if I remember how."

"The Master of the City does not have to date," Octavius said, "he commands."

"You're in the wrong town for that attitude," I said.

"You are so certain of that?" he said.

"Absolutely."

"Taste Haven," Auggie said. "If you don't like him, then I'm going to have to send home for some less dominant take-out."

I looked up at the tall man in front of me. He looked down with that soft, laughing face, and I just didn't buy it. It was like the smile and sparkly eyes was his version of a cop face. A way to hide everything.

He dropped gracefully to his knees. Which made him not that much shorter than me. I added at least another inch to his height. He laughed, that joyous laugh that seemed so sincere. "You should see your face, so suspicious. I just thought that this way you have your choice of wrist or neck. With me standing, you can't reach my neck."

It made sense, so why didn't I like it? No answer other than the one I'd had since I saw him. Being close to him reacted with that primitive part of the brain that keeps you alive if you don't argue with it. Touching him was dangerous in some way, but in what way? The trouble with the primitive brain is that it doesn't reason, or explain, it just feels. I could just touch him, then turn him down. He'd be on his way back to Chicago, no harm, no foul.

I reached for his hand, and he gave it. I wondered if I'd get that jolt of energy like I had from Pierce, but his hand was simply warm. His hand was very passive in mine, but when I pushed back the sleeve of his jacket, he had on a French-cuffed shirt, with real cuff links. "Shit."

"You don't like French cuffs?"

I frowned down at him. "It'll take a while to unhook your wrists."

He gave me that smile again, but the blue eyes weren't quite as neutrally cheerful. I got to glimpse the coldness under that smile. For some reason it made me feel better. I liked truth, most of the time.

"Why are you smiling?" he asked, and his voice held just a hint of uncertainty. Good.

I shook my head. "Nothing." I smoothed my hand up the side of his face, turned him so the line of his neck stretched above the collar of his dress shirt. I bent over him, one hand on his shoulder for balance, the other cradling the side of his face. The neck was always so much more intimate than the wrist.

I meant to simply lay my lips against his neck. But when I was close enough to smell his skin, all my good intentions vanished. He smelled so warm, so incredibly warm. I wanted to put my mouth against that warmth, but not to kiss. I put my face so close to the warm, smooth line of his neck that a hard thought would have made my lips touch his skin. But I kept just above his neck, and breathed in the scent of him. Warm, a faint hint of some powdery sweet cologne, barely there, soap, and underneath just the scent of his body. Human, and deeper still, where my breath blew back hot from his skin, the musky hint of cat. Cleaner, less sharp than leopard. But definitely cat, not wolf, not dog. I breathed in the scent of lion as it rose from his skin, as if my breath called it forth.

My arms slid down his back, across his shoulders, folding my body around his. He'd behaved himself until then, hands at his sides, but now he reached for me, wrapped me in the strength of his arms, the force of his fingers, kneading at my body through my clothes.

I heard him whisper, "Oh, God."

I laid the gentlest of kisses against that hot, smooth skin, a feather's touch of a kiss, and it wasn't enough. I could smell what I wanted just below the surface. I could smell his blood like something sweet and metallic. I licked along his neck, licked over the warm, jumping life of his pulse. He shuddered in my arms.

I heard a voice. "Anita, Anita, don't do this." I didn't know who it was, and didn't understand what they were talking about. I needed to taste his pulse, feel it quiver between my teeth until it burst hot and scalding in my mouth.

A wrist appeared near my face. I smelled leopard. Micah called me back from that quivering edge. "Anita, what are you doing?"

I didn't unwind from Haven's body. I raised my face only enough to see Micah. "Tasting him," and my voice sounded hoarse and not mine.

"Let him go, Anita."

I shook my head, and felt Haven's fingers hard and firm, as if he had claws to sink into my body, and I wanted him to do it.

Graham came next, putting his wrist between me and that pulsing candy. But the musk of wolf was not what I wanted.

Nathaniel was next, putting the sweetness of his wrist between me and Haven's neck. He still smelled of vanilla, but that wasn't the scent I was after tonight. I shook my head. "No."

"Something's wrong, Anita, you need to stop."

I shook my head again, sending my hair flying over the kneeling man's face. He made a sound low in his throat from the sensation of it. The sound made me push Nathaniel away and lay my mouth over the shivering of Haven's pulse, not a kiss, no, my mouth was too wide for a kiss. My jaw tensed to bite him, and two things happened simultaneously. Someone grabbed a handful of my hair, and a wrist I didn't know well was suddenly in my face.

A voice that had already gone growling deep said, "If it is lion you want, then here I am."

I followed that scent upward, as he pulled my head backward with my hair. Joseph stood above me, his hair golden, his eyes already the deep, perfect amber of lion.

The man at my feet wrapped himself tighter around me, not kneading me with his fingers now, but clinging. "No," Haven said, "no, she's mine. Mine!"

"Not yours," Joseph growled. He drew his wrist upward and my body followed the line of his skin. It wasn't Haven I wanted, it was lion. Would anyone do? Maybe. It wasn't a person I chased, but a scent.

Haven came up off the floor in a movement too quick to follow. He was just suddenly moving, and Joseph was there, and the next moment they were across the room, crashing through the drapes into the stone wall beyond.

The drapes cascaded down around them, so that half the living room "wall" was ripped away, revealing the bare stone and the torch-lit corridor beyond.

The guards waded in, trying to separate them. I was left standing, staring, not entirely sure what had happened, or why. Joseph had saved me, from something, something . . .

Cloth ripped, loud and violent. Haven came up, out of the ripped drapes, and sailed across the room, to find the drapes at the other side. They collapsed around him, but he never tried to rise. He was just a shape under the cascading cloth.

Joseph stepped out of the fall of white and gold cloth, half his shirt ripped away. His hands were half-clawed, and his face was beginning to lose its human shape, like his body becoming soft clay. His hair was lengthening, starting to form the golden halo of his mane.

Auggie stepped to the edge of the spilled cloth around him, and his voice echoed through the room like the whisper of a giant. Intimate, soft, and thunderous all at once. "Lion, I am master here, not you."

Joseph growled at him with teeth gone long and dangerous. His voice was so low and growling that it was hard to understand. "I am the Rex of the St. Louis Pride. I was invited to see the lions you brought, and I have found them wanting."

Octavius came up beside Auggie, laid a hand on his back, and the power level rocked off the scale. It was like a metaphysical earthquake, except nothing moved, nothing you could see anyway. But it stumbled me on my high heels. Joseph staggered back a step from it. The others turned startled faces toward Auggie, but they weren't as affected as Joseph.

"Have you ever met a master vampire that could call your animal, Rex?" Auggie asked.

Joseph was breathing harder than he should have been, but he managed to growl, "No."

"Let me show you what you've been missing." He didn't gesture, or speak, but suddenly the air was hard to breathe. The air was so heavy with power that we should all be choking on it. But it wasn't meant for us.

Joseph collapsed to his knees, snarling, fighting, but he could not stand against it.

"Let me see your human eyes, Rex."

The growing mane began to shrink. The fur that had been climbing over his skin began to be reabsorbed. His face was reshaping itself. Only when he was Joseph again, fully human again, did the air ease a little.

"What do you want, vampire?" Joseph said, in a human voice that sounded breathy.

"Obedience," Auggie said, and there was nothing friendly about that one word. The good-natured man was gone, and the master vampire was revealed. "Come to me, Rex, crawl to me."

Joseph fought him. You could watch the struggle of it on his face, but finally he dropped to all fours.

"Stop it, Auggie," I said, "leave him alone."

"He is my beast, not Jean-Claude's. There is no tie between my host and the lions."

"There is tie between me and the lions. I invited Joseph here tonight."

He never looked at me, but Octavius did. He put those perfect chocolate eyes on me, and his face held nothing but arrogance. Which pissed me off. Anger is bad, but sometimes, well, it has its uses.

I moved toward them. I put myself between them, blocking his view of Joseph. It was like I'd taken a punch. Nathaniel was there to grab me, and the moment he touched me, I felt better. He was my animal to call now, not just my type of animal, but truly my animal to call, as Richard was to Jean-Claude. It was sort of like a furry human servant, and it gave some of the benefits. Power, extra power.

"Joseph and his people are our allies. My leopards and I have a treaty with them. To harm one is to harm both."

Auggie looked at me then, his eyes swimming gray like clouds with lightning caught inside them. "If Jean-Claude had made this treaty I would have to abide by it, but you are a human servant, Anita. You do not bind me, as your master would. Just as, if you visit us in Chicago, deals made by Octavius alone are not binding on your master."

"So you'll hurt Joseph because why, because he stopped me from doing some metaphysical shit with your lion? Is that it?"

"He is lion, and no lion can resist me."

"He is the Rex of St. Louis, Auggie, you have no authority over him," I said.

"Would you challenge me with Octavius at my back? Would you set yourself against me with your master busy elsewhere?"

I nodded. "Yes."

"I will punish him for his insult to me and mine, Anita. I will do it. You can either allow it, gracefully, or you can force me to control you, as I control Joseph."

"If you think you can control me, Auggie, knock yourself out."

It was suddenly harder to breathe again. Micah came in at my other side. He was my Nimir-Raj, and it helped me think, but it didn't help me fight. "Graham," I said.

He came to my reaching hand, and the moment I touched him, I could feel the wolves. Feel the tie through Richard to the pack. That neck-ruffling scent of wolf. The green peace of woods and fields, and . . .

I staggered, and only Nathaniel and Graham's hands kept me on my feet. Pierce the werelion was at Auggie's side.

I wanted to call Jean-Claude, but was afraid to. Auggie was his friend, but what I was feeling pushing against me, filling the very air, was more powerful than anything I'd ever felt from Jean-Claude. If I lost to Auggie, then I lost. But if Jean-Claude lost to him, then there was a chance he would be defeated as Master of the City. And right there, in that moment, I saw the real reason I hadn't wanted these bastards in our city. I hadn't trusted us to be strong enough.

I would not cost us the city. I would not be the ruin of us all. I would not. I was trying to fight him as if I were another master vampire, but that wasn't what I was. I was a necromancer. I was supposed to have control over all the dead. We would see.

I let go of the men who held me up. I took a step away from the hands of the living, and opened that part of me that I always had to shield. That part of me that was like some great closed fist, tight, tight, or who knows what we could do, by accident or by design.

I almost never unleashed my necromancy outside a cemetery. But there were no dead bodies for the power to find, there were only vampires. My power blew out from my body like a chill wind, and it found its mark.

"What is this?" Auggie asked. Octavius's face didn't look so arrogant over his shoulder. Pierce moved away from him as if something about my power had made it hard to keep touching him.

"If being human servant or Nimir-Ra gains me nothing, then there are other titles, Auggie. Other powers to be invoked."

He licked his lips, a nice nervous gesture. "What is this power?"

"Haven't you heard, Auggie, I'm a necromancer."

"There are no true necromancers," Octavius said, but his voice didn't sound so certain.

"Have it your way, but you will leave Joseph and his people alone while you're in my city."

"Or what?" Auggie asked, his eyes still full of gray light.

"I have another title among the vampires; do you know what it is?"

"The Executioner, they call you the Executioner."

"Yeah, they do."

"Are you threatening to kill me?" He managed to sound amused, even with my power breathing around his body.

"I am telling you the rules. You do not mess with our people. And all the vampires, all the shapeshifters, and other supernaturals to be named later, qualify as our people."

"We were attacked," Octavius said.

"Fine, you've proved your point. You forced him to swallow his beast. I say it's enough."

"I am a master vampire, a ruler of a city; you do not dictate to me."

"If you're vampire enough to make me back down, then come and get me, Auggie. I stand here alone, no animal to call, no Nimir-Raj, no vampire at my back. I stand here with nothing but my own power. Are you vampire enough to do the same?"

He smiled. "Are you saying to step away from Octavius and my lion, and meet you in the middle of the room, for what? A duel? You would die."

"A testing of wills then," I said.

"You cannot hope to win," he said.

"If that's true, then you have nothing to lose, do you?"

"Anita," Claudia said, "I'm not sure about this."

"Come to me, Augustine, come to me." I put everything I had into that command. I wanted him to come to me, now. Before Jean-Claude got here.

He pushed away from his human servant and his lion. He started walking toward me, just like I wanted. "Augustine," Octavius said, "do not do this."

"Come to me, Auggie, come to me."

He had taken two more steps, before he frowned at me. "You are bidding me to come. You are truly calling me."

"I told you what I was."

He shook his head. "I will not come to you."

"Afraid?"

"Cautious," he said.

"Fine, then I'll meet you halfway, that's fair."

"Anita," Graham said. I ignored him. I started walking toward the waiting vampire. "Meet me partway, Auggie."

He started toward me, not gliding, but stiffly, as if his body wasn't working quite right. He finally stopped before he reached me. Stopped with a look you don't get to see on a master vampire's face often. Nervous, he was nervous.

"What happens when we meet in the middle, Anita?"

"If you get past me, fine, but if you don't, then I win."

"That doesn't seem fair; you have only to stand your ground, but I must walk past you."

We both stopped about two feet away from each other. I coaxed my power, whispered to it what I wanted. I wanted him to obey me. I'd never tried this so overtly against any vampire. A Master of the City was probably not the place to start, but it was too late now.

He swayed on his expensive shoes. "I will not."

"Will not what?" I asked, but my voice held the power that was breathing around us. My voice knew what.

I expected him just to keep resisting. I should have remembered that there were other options.

"You want me, Anita, you can have me. I can do what I wanted to do all along, and Jean-Claude can't even get mad."

I hesitated, stumbling in my mind, the power flickering. "What . . ."

He moved faster than I could follow, closing the distance, taking me in his arms. I was suddenly pinned against his body, my arms trapped. My power pushed at him, but his power pushed back.

"I feel it, your power, and God, you are powerful. If you were just a necromancer you might even win, but you aren't just that, are you?" He lowered his face toward me, as if he meant to kiss me.

"Stop, I command you to stop."

He actually hesitated, swallowing hard, closing his eyes, but when he opened them, it was as if his power had taken a catastrophic leap. The gaze from his eyes stopped the breath in my throat. "Strong, but not strong enough." He flexed his power, like some invisible muscle, and that flexing shot through my body. It bowed my spine, and only his arms kept me upright. We half fell to our knees, as if my collapse caught him by surprise. He ripped my controls away from the *ardeur*. He did it better and quicker than Thea had dreamt of. He brought the *ardeur*, with my body wrapped in his. He brought the *ardeur* knowing that once it rose like this, he would be my food. Which, of course, was what he had meant. He could do what he'd wanted to all along, and Jean-Claude couldn't even get mad.

8

PASSION LIKE SOMETHING touchable, solid, spilled up through my body and over his. Lust like some thick, heavy paint flowed over us, covering us, trapping us.

I froze, afraid to breathe, afraid to speak, afraid most of all to move. I'd gone from finding Auggie handsome, arrogant, and beginning not to like him, to wanting to be naked with him. Even for the *ardeur* it was an abrupt switch.

I wanted to ask him what had he done to me, but was afraid to move that much, and even more afraid to draw his attention to me. Afraid of what he would do, no, not true: terrified of what I would do.

I stayed frozen in his arms. Perfectly still, only my pulse moving. If I could simply not move, I could hold on. I'd won the fight. Auggie was offering himself up as food; that made me the winner. Vampire rules: food loses. All I had to do was hold on until Jean-Claude came. I could do that. He was close. I could feel him coming down the stairs. Minutes, minutes away from help. But fighting the *ardeur* by not acting only works if the other person involved wants it to work. It needs two people trying to fight it. Auggie didn't want to fight it. He wanted to lose.

His eyes closed, and his head fell back, almost as if the sex had already started. His voice was hoarse as he said, "I had almost forgotten how it feels to be consumed by passion." He lowered his face so he could meet my gaze. "I try to forget the touch of it, Anita. I almost succeed in convincing myself it wasn't real, that nothing ever felt so amazing, then she sends me a dream."

I knew who *she* was, because when any of Belle's line said *her*, or *she*, of course, you knew who *she* was. Belle Morte. It was always Belle Morte. Their dark mistress, the creator of them all.

"Did you hear me, Anita? Did you hear me?" His arms moved so that he was gripping my upper arms, our bodies still pressed too close together. There was room to try to fight, to try for a weapon, but it was too late for that. If I went for a weapon, I wasn't certain I could make my hands grab a

gun, or a blade. My hands ached for the touch of his skin. I wasn't trustworthy. I wanted to scream in my mind for Jean-Claude, but with the *ardeur*
this strong, I wasn't sure if it could spread that way.

Auggie shook me. "Did you hear me, Anita?"

I felt movement, caught a glimpse of black at the sides. If anyone touched
us the *ardeur* would spread to them. Bad, very bad. "Stay back," I whispered,
"tell them."

Micah said, "Don't touch either of them. It spreads by touch."

"You touch her and I'll shoot you, Graham." This from Claudia.

"Look at me, Anita," Auggie said. "Me."

I swallowed my pulse, and moved, very slowly, to look at him. I met the
charcoal gray of his gaze, and whatever he saw there seemed to satisfy him.
"She sends such dreams, Anita. Dreams like this, where lust is something
touchable, holdable, caressable, and it's spilling over your skin, drowning
you in its need." He leaned in toward me, as if for a kiss.

I turned my head down, away, still careful, still slow. Move too fast and
the *ardeur* was like a predator, attracted by quick movements. But a small
turn of the head, that I could do.

"Don't turn away. Let me kiss you. Let me spill this waiting press of heat
over us. Let us drown together."

I kept my face turned away, my hands in fists, because all I could think of
was what his body would feel like under my hands. I wanted to trace his
shoulders, his chest, see the muscled promise of him nude before me. It was
like months, or years, of dating and wanting all packed into moments. Requiem, one of our imports from Britain, could cause instant body reaction,
hours of really good foreplay in seconds of power. Could Auggie hit the
emotional markers as fast as Requiem could hit the physical ones? Sweet
Mary, Mother of God, help me.

The moment the thought left me, I was calmer, could think more clearly.
For years I hadn't prayed during times like this, too embarrassed, but I'd finally realized if my faith was real, then it didn't desert me just because I was
outside societal norms.

"No," he said, "no, I will not come this close and be denied." He drew me
in against his body, and I fought to stay stiff and unyielding when all I
wanted to do in the whole wide world was touch him. He rested his cheek
against my hair. "I feel your master's nearness, Anita. You wait for rescue, but
remember, unless you actually feed from me, then you have not won this
fight." I felt the press of his lips against my temple, soft and hot. "Do you
really believe Jean-Claude will win against me? Feed and you win, and so
does he."

He was implying what I'd already thought of, that if Jean-Claude hit the door before I'd won, that we would lose, badly. I'd felt the power in Auggie, and I knew the power in Jean-Claude. If it was a straight-up battle, we would lose. I couldn't let that happen.

Micah's voice came from behind me. He didn't touch me, but he said, "There are other hungers, Anita. Other drives." He spoke carefully, as if he wasn't sure how well I could hear him.

Micah was right. The *ardeur* had a habit of swallowing the world, and my logic with it. There were other hungers and they were inside me, just like the *ardeur*. Once I'd thought to raise other hungers I had to open the marks between Richard, or Micah, or Nathaniel, but I knew better now. The beast wasn't something I got from them. It was something inside me. The fact that it had no way out, no way to make my body match its hunger, didn't make it less real.

I closed my eyes and reached down inside myself, like a metaphysical hand reaching into a sack. Searching for what I needed. Auggie inadvertently helped me. He jerked me off my knees with a crushing grip on my arms. It hurt, but the pain didn't blow my concentration, no, the beast liked anger. Anger and pain meant we had to fight, and we were good at fighting.

Always before the beast had been a process, but now it was like a switch in my head. One moment me, the next, something that wasn't thinking about sex, or even food. Escape, escape, escape!

I screamed into his face, wordless, rage-filled. He jerked me close to his face. He grabbed my hair, and tried for that kiss. But it was too late for kisses. Too late for so much.

I bit him. Sank my teeth into his pouting lower lip. The grip on my hair became painful, and he tried to control my face, my head, my mouth, with that bruising grip. He couldn't pull me off before I bit through his lip, and he seemed to know that, because his other hand went to my jaw, the way you'd grip an animal at the hinge of the jaw, pressing inward. If you have the strength you can force an animal not to bite down completely. If you have the strength you can pry him off.

He had the strength to keep me from biting his lip off, but that was all, unless he was willing to crush my jaw. I kept trying to bite him, and he kept me from doing it. If there'd been enough person left in me I'd have gone for my gun, or the knife, but I'd given up thoughts of knives and guns when I embraced my beast. All I could think of was teeth and claws. I raked my nails down his hands, bloodied him in ribbons to try to get free.

He was going to have to cripple me or let me go. But he had one other option, and he used it. He threw another burst of power into me. He raised the *ardeur* again, drowned my beast in desire, and things that are only partly about mating. If he'd been like some of Belle's line and only affected me physically, the beast wouldn't have left, but his flavor of Belle Morte's power was more . . . human. It was not just lust, but love. He had the ability to make you love him. Evil did not begin to cover what he did to me. Because in that moment, I loved him. Loved him completely and utterly. Part of me that was still sane prayed, *Don't let this be permanent.*

I went up on my knees, stretching toward that full mouth that a moment before I'd been trying to bite off. I gave him the kiss he'd wanted. The fresh blood didn't make it horrible, he was a vampire and . . . Roses, roses on the air like some cloying perfume. I was drowning in the scent of it, so that as I kissed him, the blood tasted of roses.

Auggie jerked back from me. "Roses, oh, God, you taste of roses." He pulled back enough to see my face, and the fear showed on his face. "Your eyes, Anita, your eyes."

I'd seen Belle Morte's eyes in my face before. Her pale brown eyes like dark honey filled with fire. I stared up at Auggie with her eyes, and she saw him, too. While her dark light filled my eyes she saw what I saw.

She whispered through my mind, "Did you truly believe that Jean-Claude being a *sourdre de sang* would keep you safe from me, Anita?"

Yeah, actually, I had. She knew, and thought it was funny as hell. "What do you want?" I asked. Fear like fine champagne was tingling through my body. The *ardeur*, the beast, all of it, was washed away under that rush of fear.

She gazed up at Auggie, kneeling above us, and I knew what she wanted. I felt regret in her. Regret that Auggie had gone from her bed and her body. "But you exiled him," I said.

"Stay out of my thoughts, Anita." She was sitting on the edge of her huge four-poster bed. A bed I'd seen once before in Jean-Claude's memories. She was curled there, a white gown centuries out of date covering the lushness of her body, so that she looked petite, like a dainty pouting child as she leaned against the carved wood. Her hair was a wealth of dark waves longer than my own. For the first time I realized that we looked at least superficially alike. Petite brunettes with ice-pale skin, and brown eyes.

"I was the greatest beauty in all of Europe; how dare you compare yourself to me?" Her power lashed through me, like the sharp blow of a whip.

"Forgive me," I said, because I'd meant no disrespect. I hadn't meant I was as beautiful as she, only that we shared some traits.

The thought mollified her, but it also freed her to concentrate on why she'd entered me in the first place. Not good. "Augustine," she said, her voice spilling in a lower alto purr than my normal voice. It wasn't her voice exactly, because she had to use my throat, but it wasn't my voice either. It was close enough to hers to widen Auggie's eyes, and make him go paler than death itself. I don't know if I'd ever seen a vampire go pale before.

"How is this possible?" he whispered.

"You called me," she said with my lips. "Your power and your blood called me."

He swallowed, rolling his lips when he did it, so that the blood seeped faster from the cut. The bite was healing as we watched, but it was still bleeding. "I did not mean . . ."

"You caused her to love you, Augustine, as you tried to force me to do. But no one forces Belle Morte, no one."

"Forgive me, I did not know what my powers could do." He whispered it, hands still on my arms, but gentle now. His hold was so loose that I could have broken away easily, but it was too late for that to matter. We had bigger problems than the *ardeur*.

"But I can enjoy you again, here and now, and it will not be I who falls in love, but her. It will cause her pain, and Jean-Claude pain. It will even cause you pain." She laughed, sitting on her bed hundreds and hundreds of miles away. "For as Requiem can raise the body's lust in his victim, he also raises it in himself. So, once you force a woman to love you, you love her back. It is the nature of our bloodline that our powers are two-edged."

Again, I felt regret in her. I knew in that moment that once Auggie had used his power to its full extent, the effect wasn't temporary.

"No, Anita," she said inside my head, talking to me from the firelit edge of her bed. "It is quite permanent, I assure you."

"Then you love . . ."

She lashed out again, with that sharp power. It stopped what I'd been about to say, and let her speak. "All love Belle Morte. All adore me. It is my nature to be loved."

But I'd been too close to her mind too often not to understand her better than that. "Lust," I said out loud, "all lust after Belle Morte."

"Lust, love, what difference the word, it means the same." But we were too deeply wedded together. She knew my thought on that, that lust and love aren't the same thing at all, and that thought was so loud that I felt her stumble in her mind. Felt her doubt; for half a moment, I felt doubt there. And it wasn't I who put that seed of doubt in her mind. It was already there, had been there since Jean-Claude and Asher left her side voluntarily centuries ago.

"They returned to me, Anita, don't forget that. They could not live without Belle Morte!" She was on her knees on the bed now, face beautiful in her anger. But I knew better than most what lay behind anger: fear.

"Enough of this!" she shouted, and that shout echoed through my mind, my body, and hit Auggie like a blow. He staggered, fighting to stay on his knees, to hold me. But her power was there, her version of the *ardeur*, the original. All that had come from Belle Morte were but pieces of her own power. We were reflections of her. The real thing roared over me, tore a scream from my mouth, and Auggie echoed me.

Her power tried to spill out from us, tried to fill the room and touch everything near us. Auggie threw up a wall around it. He used his will, his power as a Master of the City to hold it back. But it wouldn't last for long. I tried to call necromancy. I'd used it to chase her out before, but I couldn't shut down the *ardeur*. Until that was cleared, I was useless.

He found his words before I did. "Everyone out, out, all of you. We can't hold it like this for long. When we lose control it will fill this room."

"It spreads by touch," Micah said.

Auggie shook his head. "This isn't Jean-Claude's *ardeur*, this is Belle's. Proximity is enough." He shuddered, shoulders hunching as if some great weight were beginning to crush him. "Samuel, get your family out. You don't know what this could make you do."

A voice from behind us, with more French accent than I usually heard in it, said, "Augustine, what have you done to *ma petite*? The power, she presses . . ." I looked at him, and the words stopped. "Belle Morte." He said it, flat, as if he'd just swallowed all the emotion he had.

He was dressed in his signature colors, black and white. A black velvet jacket barely touched the top of his waist. The white lace of his shirt spilled out between that blackness, held at the neck by the cameo that had been one of my first presents to him. The pants were leather and looked poured on. The knee-high black boots were some of the plainest he owned. Of course with his body gliding toward us there was nothing plain about him. We both knew the potential of his body too intimately to ever believe such simple camouflage. Because it was a *we*. And because it was a *we*, she knew why Jean-Claude had his black curls pulled back in a ponytail. She knew why the clothes were elegant but some of his least expensive. Why he wore almost no jewelry. He had planned to appear as the visiting masters had last seen him. He was going to hide what he truly was, let them wonder about his power. It was a gamble that I had disagreed with. I thought it was like baiting them. *Look how powerless I am, try me.* Jean-Claude said that he had never gotten in trouble when dealing with other masters by hiding some of his abilities. It was a strategy that had saved his life in the past.

She used me to say, "I see you, Jean-Claude. All these simple games do not hide you from Belle Morte. But you were right to come humble before me, as I like my men."

I stared at him with Belle Morte's eyes, while she laughed, and laughed, and laughed on her big, empty bed. I thought, *empty*. Since when did Belle sleep alone? That thought made her stumble in her mind again. A moment of hesitation, but Jean-Claude took it. He used it to put himself at my back. To fold all the velvet and leather of his body around me, so that he and Auggie faced each other across me.

Belle roared back through me, but in some ways, her moment had passed. Jean-Claude was *sourdre de sang* and I was his human servant. Touching, she could not turn me against him. But she left us with a parting gift, an evil whisper in my mind. "You are *sourdre de sang*. You can chase me out, but you cannot cure what Augustine has begun. When I leave her mind, the *ardeur* will still be there. It will spread to the three of you, and you will do things together that you have not done in centuries."

She was in my head, so I couldn't hide that this was the first I'd heard of Auggie and Jean-Claude being more than friends. She laughed in her firelit bedroom all those miles away. She spoke through me, that alto purr trying to come out of my mouth. "Oh, Jean-Claude, you did not tell her that you and Augustine were lovers."

Jean-Claude was very still against my body, as if he were holding his breath. I realized he was waiting for me to react to what she'd said. He was waiting for me to be angry and make the disaster that was about to happen even worse. But I surprised us all.

I wasn't shocked. I don't know why, but I wasn't. I'd known he hadn't come to me a virgin. I even knew that he'd had other male lovers besides Asher. Of course, knowing something in the abstract wasn't the same as having the fact kneeling in front of you, holding you in his arms. I looked up at Auggie and expected to be upset, but maybe Auggie's powers had done something to me, or maybe I was picking up Jean-Claude's emotion, or even Belle's. Whatever the reason, I gazed up at the man in front of me and saw the line of his face from temple to jaw like the stroke of some fine painting. The charcoal-gray eyes had lost their fire; fear and willpower had shut down some of his vampiric powers. But even empty of anything but him, the eyes were utterly compelling. It wasn't just the lace of black lashes and the drowning color that for the first time convinced me that gray could be as beautiful as blue, but the look in those eyes. He stared down at me like a drowning man. Something of pain and loss so raw that it tightened my throat. My reaction was sympathy; Belle's was not. She was glad, so terribly glad that after all these centuries the sight of her eyes could still fill him with such pain. She wanted him to hurt. Wanted him to suffer. Wanted him to feel cast out, driven from paradise by the hand of a vengeful god, or, I guess in this case, goddess.

Augustine's power meant that I watched his pain as one freshly fallen in love, in that first blinding, overwhelming rush where you'll do or say almost anything to make each other happy. I wanted to make it all better, to kiss it and make it all go away.

"No," Belle said, "no, they lied to you. You should feel betrayed. Heart-broken."

"Sorry to disappoint you," I said, but she knew I didn't mean it.

"So calm, Anita. See through my eyes and your lovely calm will not survive."

I knew I still knelt, held between Jean-Claude and Augustine, but I was trapped in Belle's memories, so that we sat on a throne in a huge dark, torch-lit room. Augustine was tied to a metal framework, the naked line of his body exposed to all. He had come begging Belle to take him back. She had re-fused, but offered one more taste of the *ardeur*. These weren't thoughts; I was in her head so deeply that I shared her memories. She meant to humili-ate him. He had made her love him, and that she could not forgive.

Jean-Claude and Asher appeared before the throne. They were dressed in long cloaks that hid all but their faces. Asher's face had the flawless beauty that had once been his. So this memory was from a time before he and Jean-Claude left Belle to save Julianna, the woman they both loved, from Belle's jealousy. Jean-Claude and Asher were still her perfect pair. Her matched beauties that did all we asked.

I knew they were naked under the cloaks. I knew what she meant them to do.

Augustine's voice, next to my ear, startled me, but did not break Belle's memory. It was like a voice from on high. "You are her master, Jean-Claude. Do not let Belle show this to Anita."

It was as if his voice helped call me back, because the person talking was not the person tied there. The Jean-Claude he spoke to was not the servant who stood before this throne. This had happened long, long ago. It wasn't real anymore.

"It happened, Anita, just as I will show it to you."

"*Ma petite*," Jean-Claude said, "can you hear me?"

I blinked up at them, saw their faces looming over me, but Belle's power roared through my head. "No, Anita, you will see the reality of it." I was back in that torch-lit room. I could feel their hands on me, but all I could see was what Belle showed me.

"Touch her bare skin," Auggie said.

Asher and Jean-Claude began to glide around the bound man. It was almost a dance, the swaying of cloaks, the grace of their movements.

Hands glided over my bare arms. The moment his bare skin touched me, the memory began to grow dark. It was as if the lights were dimming, hiding what was happening.

"No!" Belle shouted, and she pulled me back into that dark hall, all those centuries ago.

The cloaks were gone, and their bodies were pale and perfect. I heard Augustine protest. "You promised me the *ardeur*."

"I keep all my promises, Augustine."

Jean-Claude glowed like some dark star, laying only his hand on the naked back of the other man. Augustine said, "Ah, now I understand." He lifted his face at an awkward angle to look back along his body at Jean-Claude. Jean-Claude knelt in front of him, so he didn't have to strain. He cupped Augustine's chin in his hand, and spoke, so low that Belle could have not heard it. "I have given you but a taste. If you find my touch repulsive, then I can stop." He put his face next to Augustine's mouth, as if he were kissing the other man's neck. He gave Augustine a chance to breathe his answer, "You have such fine control over the *ardeur*, so soon."

"*Oui.*"

"If this is but a taste, and all she will allow me, then I want it."

Jean-Claude pulled back enough to see the other man's face. He cupped Augustine's face in his hands. I realized that I was seeing Jean-Claude's face through Augustine's eyes. I watched Augustine see the uncertainty in the other man's eyes. "Would you risk her anger to save me?"

"I do not enjoy force."

Asher knelt beside Jean-Claude, and there was a look I'd never seen on his face. Arrogance, fierceness, something predatory, and something else. Something dangerous, and unpleasant.

Asher's voice fell into the memory. "Jean-Claude, do not let Anita see me like this." Until that moment I hadn't known Asher was somewhere in the room, waiting for us to win, or lose, this battle. And he was seeing what Belle was forcing me to see. How was she doing this?

"You are all blood of my blood, Anita. I can do many things to that which is mine."

Hands on me, cloth tearing, my body jerking with the force of it. The coolness of air on my back. Jean-Claude's chest and stomach pressed against my back, the lace of his white shirt only a frame for our flesh. But the moment that much of his skin touched mine, the memory turned black and Belle was back on the edge of her big bed in the flickering light of candles. Her anger filled her eyes with dark honey flame. She had never known that Jean-Claude gave Auggie a choice, all these long years ago.

Jean-Claude's bare arms wrapped around my nearly naked upper body. He wrapped his arms around me, cradled me as close to his body as the gun and knife at my back would allow.

Augustine's hands were still in mine, as if he couldn't, or wouldn't, let me go. But it was Jean-Claude's body that chased her back. That shut down the memory.

"Your body can stop me, but I leave you two parting gifts, Jean-Claude and Augustine. The first is the *ardeur* that will claim the three of you, and if I push hard enough will spread through the room to all that are left. I feel Asher and . . ." She closed her eyes, licked her lips. "Mmm, Requiem is there, as well. They will try to hold it back when it happens. Perhaps they will succeed, perhaps not." Then she looked directly at us, and it was as if she could see us, truly see us. Such concentration in those eyes. "My second is a question to you and a gift for Anita. Have you realized one of her talents, Jean-Claude, that she can borrow the abilities that are used against her? My ability to make living memories, I give to her now, just this once. I want her to have it to use, and I will not fight her magic's ability to take it. I will let her take this power to her mind, and I leave her with this question: Do you really believe that Augustine and Jean-Claude only had sex this one time, or were there more?"

Cloth tore, and more of Jean-Claude pressed against me. "I close this door to you, Belle, for she is mine, not yours."

"I'm going, I'm going, enjoy my gifts." But I was still tied close enough to her mind to know that she had no choice. She pretended she did, but Jean-Claude had chased her out. The last thing I felt from her was regret. Regret for the men she left me with, that I had them and she did not.

I came up gasping as if I'd been underwater. I was down to nothing but bra and panties, the skirt suit ripped away. My gun with its holster had vanished with the skirt. Jean-Claude's clothes were mostly gone, as well.

"Is there anything your bloodline does that doesn't involve getting naked?"

He laughed, that wonderful, touchable laugh. And I wasn't the only one who reacted to it. Auggie shivered as he gripped my hands. He was still in his expensive suit, even his tie tight in place. He'd behaved himself admirably.

I looked around the room and found it empty except for Asher on the side near the outer door and Requiem on the side near the hallway that led farther into the underground. Asher with his golden hair that hid the scars the Church had given him when they tried to burn the devil out of him with holy water. Requiem tall and pale, with hair almost as dark as mine and Jean-Claude's. His face was graced by a mustache and a small trimmed beard. Though tonight he looked like something big had hit him on the side of the face. They both held their arms up and out from their bodies. I could feel power radiating from them. I realized they'd thrown up the vampiric equivalent of a power circle to try to hold in the *ardeur*, and the memories. To stop it from spreading.

I relaxed in Jean-Claude's arms, squeezed Augustine's hands. There was a whisper in my mind, "Were there other times?" Was it my thought, or hers? I didn't know, and it didn't matter, because the question came, and the thought was enough.

I was thrown into the middle of a memory that had me clawing for air. Auggie on top, pressing Jean-Claude's body into a bed.

"*Non, ma petite, non.*" His body pressed against me, all that lovely nakedness, but it wasn't enough. This wasn't Belle's power imposed on me. She'd figured out what I'd only discovered recently myself, that I could borrow powers from vamps if they used those powers on me first. Some powers were more permanent than others, some didn't take at all, but this one was taking. This one was taking, and I couldn't stop it.

I screamed, and Auggie's arms were bare under my hands. But it didn't help. It didn't help.

"Then have all the memory, Anita," Auggie said, "see it all."

We were in a room, small but elegant. Auggie sat in a chair. Jean-Claude was down on one knee before him, hat in hand, head bowed.

This Auggie's yellow hair was down to his shoulders. He wore blue and silver gray with too much lace for my taste. "So the rumors are true—you have left her voluntarily."

Jean-Claude nodded, and looked up. "I have."

Auggie laughed. "You leave heaven voluntarily when I cry in hell for one last glimpse of it." He shook his head, sighed, the humor vanishing from his face. "But if you are strong enough to leave heaven I will get you to the coast. I know a ship and a captain that I trust."

"What is the destination of the ship?"

"The English colonies. The United States of America, they are called now. But honestly, Jean-Claude, does it matter where it goes as long as you are off the continent, and far from her?"

Jean-Claude bowed his head again as if whatever was in his eyes, he didn't wish to share. "I cannot pay you, Augustine, I have left with nothing."

"It is a gift in honor of your bravery at leaving paradise, not once, but twice. Twice, when I would give everything I have to go back."

Jean-Claude raised his face, beautiful and empty, his face when he was hiding what he was thinking. "Is it Belle you miss, or the *ardeur*?"

"Both."

"I cannot give you Belle, but the *ardeur* is mine to share."

Such eagerness on Augustine's face for an instant. A need so raw it filled his eyes with fire like lightning's glow behind gray clouds. Then his face stilled, all that hunger hiding away, but we had seen it. For in that instant, I was no longer seeing the room like some floating phantom. I was inside Jean-Claude's head as I had been inside him and Belle in the earlier memory.

Augustine's voice was as empty as his face when he said, "It is a gift, Jean-Claude. I would be your friend. Friends do not count the costs of favors."

We were surprised, and had been too long with Belle Morte to trust it. "I would have bargained my body to gain what you offer so freely, Augustine."

"And that is why I offer it freely. Yes, I long to be with her again. I will love her until the end of the world, but I did not always like her, or what she forced us to do." His face darkened with memories, but he waved them away, and smiled. "I would have stayed with her forever, doing her bidding, her willing slave, even though I knew her to be evil. I was too"—he seemed to search for a word—"immersed in her to ever wish to save myself, or save all those she wished me to enslave for her. If she had not cast me out, I would never have been strong enough to go."

"You refused direct orders from her. Some at her court still speak of it."

He nodded. "Even someone as weak as I am has things he will not do." Such sorrow on his face, such loss.

We laid our cheek against his hand where it lay on the chair arm. We rolled our eyes upward, so we could watch his face. His hand was very still under our cheek, as if he'd stopped breathing. "Let me share the one gift I have with my only friend."

He fought to keep the eagerness off his face, but only half succeeded. "You do not have to do this, Jean-Claude. I meant what I said. It is my gift to you." There was a tension in his hand where it lay, as if his body fought to be still but his hand betrayed him.

"I know your preference is for women."

"As is yours," Auggie said.

"Yes, but Belle does not share her personal men with other women."

Auggie smiled, and the smile was friendly but nothing more; it didn't match the growing tension in the hand that lay under our cheek. His voice was mild as he said, "Unless it is a woman she wished for us to seduce."

We smiled, too. "For money, or land, or politics, *oui*." We shared a smile made up of centuries in her bed, pawns in her great plans. "I am the only one of her line to have inherited the full power of the *ardeur*, Augustine, and there are none of our blood in this new America."

"So my last opportunity to taste the *ardeur* and yours to be with another master of Belle Morte's line is tonight."

We nodded, our face rubbing along his hand.

He took his hand, gently, out from under us. "You are frightened," he said, and his face was soft with wonder.

"I am."

"Then why leave her?"

"Because I could not stay, not and be hated by them both."

"Both?"

We could not hide the tears, except by turning our faces away. Augustine came down on the floor with us. He held us while we cried. "It is not Belle that has broken your heart, it is Asher."

We wept for the first time in months. Wept into his arms, and he kissed our tears away and we sought comfort in the only arms that we trusted. Our only friend.

The earlier memory returned of them in the sheets. But it wasn't shocking this time. I was ready for it, knew what to expect. And I knew that this Jean-Claude had been the one who spent over twenty years as a happy couple with Asher and Julianna. This Jean-Claude had lost Julianna, and Asher—Julianna burned as a witch, and Asher consumed by hatred at Jean-Claude for not getting there in time to save her. This Jean-Claude still blamed himself. Jean-Claude had taken the wounded Asher back to Belle Morte's court to save his life, and the bargain for that salvation was that Jean-Claude was her whipping boy for a hundred years. The Jean-Claude in Augustine's bed had lost everything and everyone he'd ever loved. He took the only comfort he could find, and I couldn't begrudge him that.

The memory faded round the edges, because it wasn't the sex that was important to me, or Jean-Claude, or even Augustine. It was the emotion of it. I came back gasping, pulse in my throat. "If that's a memory, then why does it almost hurt to come out of it?"

"I do not know, *ma petite*, but we have not much time. I could not stop the memory, but I was able to direct it. I wanted you to understand what happened between us, because I cannot stop what is about to happen. We have fought her to give me time to soften the blow."

"We?" I looked up at Augustine, and his eyes held sorrow the way Jean-Claude's could hold lust.

"We'll hold it as long as we can, Jean-Claude, but hurry, whatever you are going to do, hurry." Asher's voice, but it held sorrow to match Auggie's eyes. I looked at Asher, and found his face traced with the faintly reddish lines of vampire tears. I realized then that everyone in the room had shared the memory.

"I am sorry, Anita," Auggie said, and he looked across me at Jean-Claude. "Sorry to you both."

"Sorry about what exactly?" I asked.

"This," he said, softly, and it was as if they'd both been holding their breaths, and suddenly they let go. They dropped their shields, their wills broke together, and the *ardeur* was suddenly there, smothering us all.

I thought I heard laughter, dim and echoing, Belle's laughter somewhere deep inside my head.

9

THE *ARDEUR* CAME and the clothes went. The custom-made leather knife sheath ripped away with all the rest. We fell to the carpet naked, all hands and mouths. The heavy metal and glass coffee table got shoved to one side as if it weighed nothing.

I pressed Auggie's muscled body onto the carpet, lay on top of him naked, feeling that he was already hard and ready, but I wanted to start at the other end. We kissed, and his lips were as full and ripe as they'd looked. He kissed delicately, though I knew the *ardeur* rode him and what he wanted to do was anything but delicate. I licked and kissed along his neck, his upper chest. I came to his nipples, pale and hard in the muscled swell of his chest. I'd never been with anyone who was such a serious weight lifter. It was as if his skin fit tighter over all those muscles, so that it was harder to get a grip with my teeth, but worth the effort.

Sucking on his nipple raised his upper body off the floor, tore a yell from him. His eyes were wide, surprised, his hands reaching for something to hold on to. Someone grabbed one of those reaching hands, and I knew who it was, before Auggie drew him into my line of sight. Auggie drew Jean-Claude in to him, drew him down, as he lay back against the floor, and I worked lower on his body. I licked and bit along his stomach, as he drew Jean-Claude down for a kiss. Something I did raised Auggie up off the ground as their mouths touched, so that I had a good view of it. I had never seen two men kiss, not like that. Not with lips, and tongue. In the months that Asher had been in our bed they had moved toward each other a time or two, but stopped. I had never asked whose sensibilities they were saving, mine or theirs. Now, watching Jean-Claude cradling Auggie in his arms and kissing him so thoroughly . . . it tightened my body so hard and fast that it was like a mini-orgasm. I'd been told by a very smart friend that to keep saying that I didn't like to be in bed with two men at once was a little silly. A case of the lady protesting too much. My body reacted for me; the sight of them kissing just flat did it for me. I've been told that it's how a lot of men feel about seeing two women kiss. Why should I be any different?

I worked my way down Auggie's body, eyes rolled upward so I could watch them. I came to the long, hard, curve of Auggie's body. Not straight, but truly curved, so that the grace of that hard flesh curled in against his own body. He was hard enough that the head was naked above the silky foreskin. I rolled my mouth over that head, then shoved as much of him into my mouth as I could, as fast and hard as I could. It made me come up choking, but it also tore him away from Jean-Claude's mouth. Made Auggie stare down at me with wild eyes. I went down on him again, slower, lingering over the feel of him in my mouth, so ripe, so thick, and how the hard line of that curve felt going down my throat. I watched them both watch me as I did it. Auggie's eyes wild with sensation; Jean-Claude's face full of pleasure, yes, but also pride. His own vampire marks were open enough for me to know that he was thinking how long and how hard he had worked to get to this point. He started to close the marks as much as the *ardeur* would let him, but I rose up from Auggie's body and said, "Don't, don't close down. Let's do this. Do it all. He started this fight, not us, let's finish it."

"Do you know what you are asking, *ma petite*?"

I nodded, then shook my head, my hand still wrapped around the base of Auggie's body. "I don't know, but I won't blame you later."

"Please," Auggie said, his voice full of such pleading, "please, don't stop. God, don't stop."

Jean-Claude and I looked at each other. We had a moment where he weighed me with his eyes. Then he gave a small nod, and said, "As you like, *ma petite*. For you are correct, he overstepped the bounds of hospitality." He looked down at Auggie. "Bad Augustine, to force the *ardeur* on *ma petite*."

Auggie nodded, his hand gripping Jean-Claude's arm. "It's been so long, Jean-Claude, so long, and there is no going back to her."

"We must feed on you, Augustine, in such a way that no other visiting master will dare this."

He nodded, though I wasn't certain he really understood what Jean-Claude had meant. Jean-Claude was holding the *ardeur* back, just enough. Enough so we could think, a little. When he let it go, it would sweep us away, and there would be no second-chance decisions.

"He has to be our message to the other visitors, Jean-Claude, or we won't survive this little gathering. These are your friends, and they nearly rolled us." I looked at him, and I felt the part of me that allowed me to kill, to do what was necessary. This was, in its odd way, a business decision. A political decision, a survival decision. I knew we could roll Auggie; he was more powerful than Jean-Claude, but I could feel it. Feel that we could feed on him in such a way that it wouldn't matter. Not kill him, but take him, make him ours in a way that I couldn't even explain in words.

Jean-Claude spoke as if he'd read my mind, which he probably had. "I feel it also, *ma petite*, but . . ."

"No buts," I said, "we can take him, I can feel it."

"Perhaps Belle Morte is too much in your mind still."

It was Asher's voice, strangled with effort. It drew our eyes to him. His hands trembled in the air as if he were holding some great weight. "Hurry, Jean-Claude, hurry. We cannot hold the circle much longer."

"He began this fight," Requiem said, "let us finish it." His hands weren't shaking, but there was a thread of strain in his voice.

Jean-Claude looked down at Auggie. "Understand this, Augustine, we have never fed like this. I do not entirely know what will happen. Are you content with such a gamble, for it is you who will suffer if it goes badly?"

I slid my mouth over him, playing my tongue along the foreskin. He shivered, and simply said, "Yes."

"*Ma petite*, stop that, or he will not be able to think."

I went back on my knees, and stopped touching him. I put my hands in my lap and behaved. I guess it was cheating.

"Augustine, do you agree to this?"

He nodded, hands reaching for Jean-Claude. "Yes, yes, God, yes, the two of you both, yes, yes!" His grip on Jean-Claude's arm looked almost painful.

Jean-Claude stroked his hair, soothing him. "Then we will do as you ask." He looked at me, and it was as if a door opened in my mind. Some inner guard that he must have used almost constantly to keep the marks from being in full force was gone. It staggered me for a moment, made me reach out to Auggie's thigh to steady myself. The moment I touched him, the *ardeur* roared back, but this time I could feel Jean-Claude at the other end of his body. I could feel the two different *ardeurs* like different flavors of fire, and Auggie was our only wood. We'd burn him up, and he wanted us to do it.

I heard Jean-Claude in my mind, whispering, "I am letting go of my control, *ma petite*, are you ready?"

I nodded. He let go, and I fell screaming into the abyss. An abyss of skin and hands and mouths, and bodies. My own body was one huge throbbing need. And I didn't particularly care how that need got met.

I ended up on the floor with Augustine on top of me. All that curved hardness going in and out of my body, so that I screamed for him. Screamed my need, my pleasure, and my eagerness. He began propped on his arms so I could watch his flesh slide into mine, but then Jean-Claude joined us, and the angle had to change.

We had never put anyone in the middle of us when we both fed the *ardeur*. All these months with Asher, Micah, Nathaniel, Richard, and Jason, and I'd always been the one in the middle. Jean-Claude and I had fed from each other. He had fed from me while I fed at the man, or men, touching me, but never in all those nights had Jean-Claude been touched by someone other than me when we were all naked together. With the marks roaring open between us, I knew how much that had cost Jean-Claude. How horribly careful he had had to be in the middle of the one moment when you should be able to lose all control. So careful, so afraid of scaring me, disgusting me, making me turn away. So afraid of what the other men might say with a badly placed hand, or caress. So careful, so terribly careful, and now suddenly he didn't have to be careful. I felt the horrible tension in the center of his being relax, like a long-held breath released.

He explored Auggie first with fingers, and used the wetness of my body to lubricate other places that didn't normally lubricate themselves. The marks were wide open, so I got flashes of memory, of other men, and other times. Random images as they occurred to him, but even here he chased them away, still afraid of what I'd think. But Auggie's body was already inside mine, and I felt his eagerness at every probe, every touch. Everything that Jean-Claude did urged him on to more with me, so that all I could think was how would it feel to have Auggie thrusting inside me while Jean-Claude rode him.

Jean-Claude entered him slowly, and Auggie's body stilled above mine, as he concentrated on the sensation of it. It had been a long time for Auggie. As he'd said before, he preferred girls, which meant that even here, with both of us eager, Jean-Claude had to be careful, so careful. Nothing spoils great sex like unintentional pain.

But finally he had everything in he was getting in, and Auggie's body relaxed above me. Relaxed into the rhythm that Jean-Claude found on top of us both. They both found a rhythm, Auggie's body pushing in and out of mine, slowly, ramming home at the end, so that I made small sounds at the height of every stroke.

The two of them found a rhythm together so that the height of one stroke was the height of the other. So that Auggie and I cried out together, and Jean-Claude rode us both. I tried to move with them, but the combined weight pinned me to the floor, so that the best I could do was squeezing

Auggie as he came and went inside me. My legs were wrapped around them both, as much as I could, so that Jean-Claude's body brushed against my foot as he moved. I felt that heavy, delicious weight begin to grow between my legs. I knew that orgasm was coming and that this one couldn't afford to be a surprise. But I didn't have to tell Jean-Claude, he knew.

He stared down at me over Augustine's shoulder, his eyes all drowning blue fire, as if a midnight sky could burn. His hair had come loose, strands of it sticking to the sweat on his face. I knew that my eyes were dark brown flame, as if I were a vampire. It had happened before. We stared at each other over Augustine's shoulder, and I felt that weight growing, growing, growing.

Augustine whispered, "Your breathing's changed."

I came screaming, and it was as if that had been the moment both men had been waiting for, as if they had fought long and hard not to go, and suddenly they could.

Augustine shoved himself twice, three times as fast and hard as he could inside me. He brought me again, screaming and writhing on the floor, and only then did he go inside me. His body spasming above me, his body trying to dig deeper inside me, so that I cried out. Jean-Claude's head went back, eyes closed, his body bowed above us both, and we fed.

We didn't just feed off Augustine, we fed off all his people in our territory. I felt Haven, the werelion, spasm against the floor, where he still lay in the fallen curtains. I felt Benny, behind the wheel of a car, lose control and have to screech to the side of the highway. Pierce fell against a wall and slid to the floor, his body spasming. Octavius collapsed on the stairs, choking, clawing at the stone, breaking his nails to bloody bits to try to keep it from happening. But nothing could save them, any of them. If we'd been in Chicago we could have fed off every beast and vamp that owed allegiance to Auggie, and he would have let us. For this pleasure he would have sold what was left of his soul and the souls of everyone who worked for him.

We drank them down, all of them; we fed, and fed, and fed, and while we fed Augustine's body kept spasming, and every thrust of pleasure brought me again, which brought Jean-Claude. We fed and orgasmed until Augustine went still between us, collapsed, body twitching. Jean-Claude looked down at me over Auggie's sweating body, a fierce smile on his face. He stared down at me with his eyes gone to blue fire so bright that the skin of his face glowed with it. He glowed with the power we had drunk. So much power, so very much power. I felt like a distant echo that Richard was leaning against a wall somewhere, staggered by the power we'd taken, and shared.

A thought was enough. Micah and Nathaniel were sitting just outside, one against the wall, the other sitting on the floor. Nathaniel laughed with the power rush of it all. We'd shared the power with all our people, all of them. Good, bad, indifferent, everyone with a connection to us was power drunk and glowing tonight. If there had been a metaphysical satellite up there in the sky, our territory would have glowed from orbit.

10

I⊤ ⊤OOK ABOU⊤ an hour to get everyone separated to places where they could clean up. Claudia had sent for reinforcements, so that the wrecked living room was nearly a solid wall of black-shirted guards. Werewolves, were-rats, and werehyenas, the people we had treaties with for guard work, all stood around while Octavius had hysterics. If he'd had more guards with him, and we'd had less, it could have gotten violent, but when you're out-numbered, outmuscled, and your master is saying, *Let it go*, well, Octavius had to eat it. He didn't like it, neither did Pierce, but Haven, of the Cookie-Monster-blue hair, was voting with Auggie. They both liked us just fine.

Jean-Claude and I lay back in his huge bathtub. My clothes were ruined but I had my knife and gun on the edge of the tub. Nothing else had been salvageable. We'd scrubbed and cleaned, and now were just soaking in the hot water. Auggie had probably already finished in the showers down the hall, but Requiem and Asher were in charge of seeing that our guests didn't do anything unfortunate. They were both master vampires over four hundred years old, they could handle it. We'd handled everything I wanted to handle for one night.

Jean-Claude lay back against the edge of the tub, and I lay in his arms, the back of my body cradled against the front of his. He trailed his hand down my arm, and hugged me tighter against him. His body was quiet, pressed against my body. I think we'd both had all we could handle for one night.

His voice came lazy, with that edge that sleep can give it. "What are you thinking about, *ma petite*?"

"If you hadn't shut the marks down so tight, you might not have to ask." I snuggled my head into the hollow of his shoulder and chest. "You shut them down as soon as we were finished with Auggie. Why?"

His body tensed against me, even his arms where they were wrapped around me, not so comforting anymore. "Perhaps I was afraid of what you would find in my thoughts." His voice wasn't sleepy now, but had that bland emptiness that he used to hide behind.

"What would I have found?" I asked, but I wasn't cuddling now. Tension is contagious.

"If I had wanted you to know the answer to that question, I would not have shut the marks down."

I started to protest, but another thought stopped me. With the marks that wide open, it had only been chance that I hadn't thought of the baby question. Chance and the fact that the *ardeur* tended to wipe out anything that wasn't pertinent to the moment. Now the fear came crawling back, tightening my stomach, tensing my muscles. *Please, God, don't let me be pregnant.*

"What is wrong, *ma petite?*" he asked.

I let out a breath that shook around the edges and said, "You know, Jean-Claude, normally I'd push for honesty, but I think I've had all the revelations I can handle for one night. It's okay, whatever you thought, it's okay."

"It is okay without your ever knowing what the thought was?" he asked.

I settled back into his arms, willing the hot water and the touch of his body to take away that awful tension. "Yes," I said, "yes."

He moved me to the side, holding me in the water, so he could see my face. "Yes, just like that?" His face showed his skepticism.

I stared up into him; his hair was wet and slicked back from his face, so that nothing took away from it. Those eyes a blue as dark as blue could be and hold no touch of black. His lashes thick and black—it had taken me months in his bed to see his upper lashes by candlelight and realize that he had a double row of upper lashes. Him and Elizabeth Taylor. You only saw it if the light was just right, and his head turned just right. Until then, they were just this unbelievable lace around his eyes. I traced the lines and curves of his face, down to the grace of his lips. I let him see in my eyes what I saw, what I felt, gazing at him.

He leaned in, and laid a kiss upon my lips. Then he cuddled me back against him, as we'd been before the questions started. No more personal questions tonight, but there were other questions I wanted answered. "Why did Requiem look like someone had pounded his face into a wall?"

"Because someone had."

That made me turn enough to look at him. "Who?"

"Meng Die," he said, voice soft, face solemn.

"Was that the emergency?"

"*Oui.* Thank you for sending the extra guards, *ma petite*, it was wise of you."

I shrugged, and turned so that I was sitting across his legs, my hands against his chest, his arms around me still, but I could see his face now. "How did it get so out of hand?"

"I was called in rather late, *ma petite*. In truth, I do not know exactly how

Requiem and Meng Die allowed their spat to get so terribly out of hand, and so terribly public. Asher, as manager of the Circus, came down to stop it, or take it to a backstage area. That should have been the end of it." His face was closing down, hiding what he thought of the fight, and the aftermath.

"Why wasn't that the end of it?"

"Because Meng Die decided to fight them both."

I sat up in his lap. "Why fight Asher? She's never been his lover."

"But he is your lover."

I frowned at him. "So what?"

"I believe that if a master vampire had appeared who wasn't in your bed, had never been in your bed, the fight might have calmed instead of escalating."

"I'm totally lost here, Jean-Claude."

He looked directly at me, but his face was empty enough that it gave me nothing. "You have not asked the right question yet, *ma petite*."

"What is the right question?"

"What the fight was about."

I frowned harder, and said, "Okay, I give, what was the fight about?"

"You."

Now I was really lost. "What?"

"They were arguing about you."

"What about me?"

"Meng Die thinks you have stolen Requiem from her."

I pushed back enough in the water so I was kneeling, and not cuddled. The water was deep enough that it came to my shoulders. "Requiem isn't my lover. I've worked really hard to make sure he isn't my lover."

"But you have fed the *ardeur* from him."

"In an emergency, yes. It was to feed, or I was about to suck Damian's life away. I had to feed, but we didn't have intercourse, we didn't even take our clothes off." I thought about it, and added, "Not all of our clothes. I mean, Requiem was fully clothed." I started blushing and couldn't prevent it. I had to stop explaining before it sounded worse and worse.

"He has offered to feed you more completely."

"I know."

"Why have you refused him?"

I looked at Jean-Claude, trying to see behind that perfect mask of a face. "I think I was under the impression that I'm having sex with enough men."

His lips twitched. He was fighting not to smile.

"This isn't funny."

He let himself smile. "*Ma petite*, there have been women over the centuries who traded lands, titles, their honor, everything, for one more night in Requiem's bed. His master in London used him much as Belle Morte used Asher and me. Though because Requiem only did women, he wasn't as flexible as we."

I let that last part go. I still wasn't completely sure how I felt about Jean-Claude doing Auggie. At the time I hadn't minded—in fact, I'd liked it. I'd liked us both doing him at the same time. We'd fucked him in every way possible, physically and metaphysically, and it had felt a-fucking-mazing. That last part was probably going to bug me the most. But one disaster at a time.

"Are you saying you're surprised I turned him down?"

"No, it is typical of you to turn a man down at first."

"At first?" I said, and sounded a little outraged.

He laughed, and it was that touchable sound, as if it were the sound of pure sex, and it went through my head and all the way down my body. "Stop that," I said.

He smiled, face lit with suppressed laughter, but he stopped. "To my knowledge, the only man you have never said no to is your Nimir-Raj, Micah. But the *ardeur* was newly woken, and so I do not think we can count that one completely. It was your exception, not your rule."

"Fine, but I'm still lost. I have avoided Requiem. Graham made some remark that Requiem was refusing Meng Die's bed and somehow that was my fault."

"Apparently, Requiem told Meng Die that he would not be her lover any longer, because you do not share your men with other women. He seemed to believe that his being in her bed was what kept you from accepting his offer to be your new *pomme de sang*."

I shook my head. "He shouldn't have assumed that."

He nodded. "Because that isn't why you refused him, is it?"

I shook my head hard enough to move the water around my body. "No. And if Requiem had asked me why I was saying no, I would have told him it wasn't because he was screwing Meng Die."

"Then why?"

"What does it matter?"

"Because he has left his lover's bed in the hope that you will take him to your bed. He is third in rank among my vampires, and second, or perhaps third, in power. Meng Die is powerful enough to be my second-in-command, but her temperament is not suited to it. As she demonstrated today. You have set two of my most powerful vampires at each other's throats, *ma petite*. I need to know why."

"I did not start that fight," I said.

"No, but you were the cause of it, and if you are to convince Requiem that you will not take him as your *pomme de sang*, then you must give him a reason that does not include his being Meng Die's lover. His reasoning was sound, *ma petite*. You have refused all the *pomme de sang* candidates who have a female lover."

"Graham, Clay, and Requiem are all Meng Die's lovers," I said.

He gave that wonderful Gallic shrug that meant everything and nothing. "So. Is it that you will not take Meng Die's seconds?"

I shook my head. "No, that's not it. You know why not Graham; he might do for a meal, but he'd be a disaster as a permanent member of the household."

"Agreed," he said.

"Clay is in love with Meng Die, she's just about broken his heart, but he wants her, and I say more power to him."

"And Requiem?"

I leaned back against the side of the tub, out of reach. The bath had stopped being comforting. "Did we have to do this tonight?"

"Meng Die threw both Requiem and Asher around like dolls in front of humans. We will be lucky if your police do not come calling and asking questions. She tried to kill Requiem, *ma petite*, not wound him. She did not care that there was an audience, but Requiem and Asher did not want to kill her in front of an audience. I had the same problem when I arrived on the scene." He was angry now, the first thread of it filling his eyes with light. "She is even now locked in a cross-wrapped coffin. But it is a temporary measure. I must let her out tomorrow night, or kill her. She will see one night as a fit punishment, but beyond that it will be an insult, and she is too powerful to eat such an insult." He fixed those brilliant eyes on me. "So, I ask again, what will you tell Requiem when he tells you that he is free of Meng Die? What excuse will you give?"

"I'm dating three men, living with two more, and having occasional sex with two others. That's seven men. I'm like a pornographic Snow White. I think seven is plenty."

"But it is not, *ma petite*. Emotionally it may be too many, but metaphysically, and for the sake of our power base, seven is not enough. You must add a lover who is not metaphysically connected to you, and you must pick a new *pomme de sang* now that Nathaniel is your animal to call."

"I thought this was optional—you're making it sound like it's almost an emergency. And wait, did you say add a lover *and* a *pomme de sang*? I thought I was adding just one, if I added anybody."

"I tasted your power tonight, *ma petite*; it needs to be fed and fed well. You are like one of those dieting women that thinks she can survive on lettuce leaves and water. It may feel like food, but your body dies anyway."

"I'm not dying," I said.

"No, but your power is seeking a new *pomme de sang*. Don't you understand what is happening, *ma petite*? The *ardeur* is seeking *for* you."

"Okay, I'm confused now."

"It is not like Augustine to lose control. He is over two thousand years old, *ma petite*; one of the first vampires Belle made. You do not thrive for so long if you make such mistakes as he did this night."

"Belle messed with him, and with me."

He shook his head. "He raised your *ardeur* first, before she appeared, did he not?"

"Yeah, he said now he could do what he'd wanted to do all along, and no one could be mad at him."

Jean-Claude laughed, and it was just humor this time. He could control his laugh if he worked at it. "He doesn't know you very well yet. But when I said Augustine is my friend, I meant it. He would not have overstepped his bounds as my guest, not without something being wrong."

"And what's wrong?"

"The *ardeur* needs more food, *ma petite*, and like any predator it is seeking prey."

"It's just a metaphysical ability, Jean-Claude, not its own entity."

He gave me a look, and it was eloquent. "You know exactly what the *ardeur* is, *ma petite*. You know that it has a mind of its own, similar to the beasts you carry. But I believe that the *ardeur* can do something your beasts cannot. It is, I believe, putting out the welcome mat."

"Welcome mat?"

He sighed, and slid down in the water until his chin touched it. "You may not like Meng Die, but she is . . . proficient in bed. I find it inexplicable that Requiem would leave her body, on only the chance that he might be your lover. As I find it inexplicable that Augustine would purposefully insult me by raising the *ardeur* in you. He, in effect, attacked you, and through you, me."

"He told me to feed from him, because then I'd win the fight, and once you got into the room he said you'd lose."

Jean-Claude sat up so abruptly that he sloshed water in my face. I brushed my eyes clear, while he said, "He said that?"

I blinked at him, still trying to keep water out of my eyes. "Yes."

"Then it is as I have feared. The *ardeur* is seeking what it needs."

"Are you saying that the *ardeur* is putting out, what, pheromones?"

"I do not know this word."

"Pheromones, it's a chemical or hormone that some animals give out. The scent attracts mates. I think it was first discovered in moths."

"Yes, pheromones then, yes."

"I'm not agreeing with you, but say it is true; why does it only seem to work on certain people? I mean, it doesn't work on Clay, and I think Graham just wants to fuck. Why Requiem and Auggie?"

"What do they have in common?" he asked.

"They're both vamps of Belle's bloodline, and they're both masters. But thanks to all our imports from London, there are a couple more vampires in town who qualify. They aren't buzzing around me."

"But they do not approach the power level of Augustine and Requiem."

"Are you saying the *ardeur* is shopping for powerful food?"

"I offer it as an idea."

I thought about it, but finally looked at him. "If this is what's happening, and I'm not saying it is, then is it only vamps from Belle's line, or any master vampire of a certain power level?"

"I do not know."

"Then we need to know before tomorrow's big party," I said. "If there is even the faintest chance that the *ardeur* is going to do some funky shit with every master vampire above a certain power level, then no way can I go to the party tomorrow. We're going to be neck-deep in Masters of the City. It would be bad if they all decided they wanted to be my sweetie."

He nodded. "There is one other thing they both have in common, *ma petite*."

"And that would be?"

"They have both been with vampires who held the *ardeur*."

"You said *vampires*, plural. You don't mean just Belle, do you?"

"Requiem had a lover who meant as much to him as Julianna did to Asher and me. Her name was Ligeia."

"He told me that Belle killed her out of jealousy."

"*Oui*. Ligeia was the only woman of her line to acquire the *ardeur*. It wasn't the full *ardeur* that Belle, you, and I carry, but there is more: Requiem refused Belle's bed for her."

"And she killed her for that."

"You have been inside Belle Morte's head, *ma petite*, how can you sound surprised?"

He had a point. "It still seems pretty petty for a vampire who's over two thousand years old," I said.

He nodded. "*Oui*, but many of the old ones can be extremely petty." He held his hand out to me.

I stared at that hand for a heartbeat, then I took it. I let him draw me through the water and in against his body. Let him press me to the front of his body, wrap his arms around me. "You're afraid," I said, my cheek pressed to the firmness of his chest.

"*Oui*, I am afraid."

"Why?"

"There are others here who have tasted the *ardeur* and are masters. We need to test our theory, *ma petite*, but I fear we run the risk of having you tied permanently to someone, or they to you."

"Auggie isn't tied to me."

"He did not want to leave our side, *ma petite*. If he does not recover, then he will be as Belle made her victims, hungering for us forever, willing to do anything to be back between us."

"You sound sad."

"He was my friend; I did not mean to enslave him as Belle would. I saw her victims give up everything, betray every vow, every trust, for the sake of her body." He held me tight against him. "It is not a power I ever wished to possess."

"You hold the *ardeur*."

"*Oui*, but this is a level of the *ardeur* that only she possesses. We all believed that only Belle Morte could wield it at such a level."

"You don't want it."

"I want to be so powerful that no one dares challenge me or our people. But I am afraid of this, and what it will mean."

His heart was beating too fast against my ear. Had it been beating all along, or had it just started? "Mean, how?"

"There are those in Europe who already fear my growing power. Knowledge that I wielded the *ardeur* at the same level as Belle Morte might tip the scales in the council's voting. They might vote to kill us all rather than risk me making a power base in America, as strong as Belle once possessed in Europe. Or the other American masters might collude to kill us, for fear that we would become like the tyrants of the European council."

"How likely is all this?" I asked.

"Possible."

"How possible?" I asked, suddenly realizing that an accidental pregnancy might not be the worst disaster we could have.

"We must understand these new powers, and quickly, *ma petite*. We must experiment with a master we trust before I allow you to go to the party tomorrow. We must know what we are dealing with, if we can."

Raised voices on the other side of the door. Claudia yelling, "You can't just go in there!"

Richard's voice, angry. "Watch me."

Jean-Claude sighed, and I settled lower in the water. I did not want to fight with Richard tonight. But from the feel of him through the door, we weren't going to have a choice.

Jean-Claude called, "Let him in, Claudia."

The door opened, but Claudia came first, as if she didn't trust Richard in there with us. His power rode through the door like the heat edge of a forest fire, something that should have choked and killed anything in its path. We'd raised his power level along with ours, and we were about to find out how sorry that was going to make us.

11

CLAUDIA STOOD BETWEEN him and the tub, and because she was about five inches taller, she blocked our view of him. Of some of him. She was the more serious bodybuilder, but he had broader shoulders. His shoulders and what I could glimpse of his lower body let me know he was wearing blue jeans and a red shirt. There was a herd of black in the door, where the other guards waited to figure out what to do. Some of them were werewolves and he was their Ulfric; you don't stand in the way of your king, not and survive.

His power swirled through the room like invisible fire, as if the water should have boiled with it. Then I realized, it wasn't just Richard's power. Claudia had been my bodyguard off and on for months, maybe a year, but until this moment I hadn't really understood how much power was in that tall, muscular body. It was her power, too, burning down the room. She wasn't just physical muscle. The air was hard to breathe, as if it were too hot to pass over my lips, like coffee that you want to blow on before you drink it. I don't know what Richard had done outside, but it had made Claudia drop all her pretenses and show her power, like a preview, or a warning.

Her voice echoed in the room. "No farther, until you prove you've got your shit under control." Her legs bent, her body going into that partial crouch, legs moving in the space she had between the raised tub and him. It was a fighting stance. Jesus.

"Move!" Richard shouted it, in a voice gone bass with growling. Not good.

Jean-Claude and I exchanged looks. He gave a small shrug. I tried. "Richard." I had to raise my voice, and say his name three times, before he answered.

"Tell her to move, Anita," he growled.

"What will you do if she moves?" I asked.

I felt some of that burning power hesitate, grow weaker. His voice was still growly, but less sure of itself. "I don't know." He said it as if he hadn't thought beyond getting to us. That wasn't like Richard, to have no idea what he planned to do.

"Are you going to try to hurt us?" I asked, sitting up in the water enough to peer around Claudia's body. I caught a glimpse of his face. His hair was a foamy mass of waves, all brown and gold. In sunlight there would be more gold to his brown, and strands of coppery red. His hair was brown, but as if it could never quite decide if it might be blond, or auburn instead. It had finally grown back to brush the tops of his broad shoulders. The bright crimson T-shirt strained around his upper arms, because he was holding his hands in tight, tight fists. It looked as if the seams of the shirt weren't going to hold the muscles' strain. His summer tan was dark against the red of the shirt. He looked at me then, the full force of his eyes, and the shock of it thrilled down my spine. His eyes were wolf eyes: amber, gold, and no longer human. It was the beginning of the change. No wonder Claudia was on alert.

The dimple in his chin usually softened the sharp perfection of his cheekbones, and the utterly masculine beauty of his face. He, more than almost any other man in my life, was handsome, not pretty. Nothing would ever make you mistake Richard for a girl, not even from the back, not even with the hair. The body was too masculine to be anything else. Tonight the dimple didn't soften anything, because the anger in his face was too raw. Had the anger fed his power, or the other way around? Who knew; who cared? Dangerous either way.

"Control yourself, Ulfric," Claudia said.

He turned those golden-amber eyes to her. "If I don't, what then?" For the first time since I'd known him I realized he was spoiling for a fight. It wasn't like him. It was like me.

Jean-Claude and I both started to climb out of the tub at the same moment. He went for one of the huge fluffy white towels, wrapping it around his waist as he cleared the water. Shapeshifters aren't usually bothered by nudity, but tonight he might be, at least by Jean-Claude. Richard was a touch homophobic; what he'd felt us do tonight wouldn't help that.

I left the knife and the gun on the edge of the tub. I wouldn't kill him, and he knew it. One, there was a chance that if one of us died, the vampire marks would kill us all; two, most of the time I loved him too much to want him dead. Right at that moment was not one of those times. That moment was one of those times when I wished he had fewer hang-ups, and had had more therapy. He was in therapy, but not enough therapy for what he'd felt Jean-Claude and me do tonight. He was the last third of our triumvirate. Of all the ones we'd shared power with, Richard would have gotten more sensations, more real physical feedback of what we were doing. He was the one who would hate it the most and he got the most complete ride. Unfair, but true.

Jean-Claude stayed near the back wall with its mirror. It was the largest place to stand. He handed me a towel but I caught a glimpse of myself in the mirror. I stood there, framed by the black marble, nude, water dripping down my body, glistening in the light. My hair plastered to my face, leaving my eyes huge and dark in the paleness of my face. I could almost never resist any of my men fresh from the tub or shower. There was something about water streaming down naked skin that was just yummy. Here was hoping that Richard felt the same way.

"I won't ask you again, move!"

"She is doing her job, *mon ami*."

"Shut up," he screamed, "shut up, I don't want to hear you right now."

Oh, boy. I moved around the narrow edge between tub and wall on the closest side to the door. I stopped on the raised platform so I was totally framed by the cool black marble with its white and silver streaks. My pulse was in my throat, because even a few inches closer made their power hotter, like moving closer to that open flame when your skin is crying out, *Hot, hot, don't touch*.

"Richard." I whispered it, but he heard me.

He looked at me with that rage-filled face, and the moment he saw me, his eyes filled with such pain, as if the sight of me like that was a knife blow straight through his heart. I was sorry for the pain, but happy about the reaction. Almost any emotion is better for a shapeshifter than anger. Anger feeds their beasts quicker. We needed to slow things down.

"How could you do that? How could you do that with him?" I thought he meant Auggie, until he pointed a finger at Jean-Claude.

"I'm not sure what you mean by 'that,' Richard."

"Don't play me, Anita," and this was a yell. He covered his face with his hands, and staggered back a step. He screamed, wordless, and so full of pain. He dropped to his knees, and screamed again. His power filled the room as if we'd all been plunged into boiling water. It felt as if my skin were being cooked. I'd felt Richard's power before, but nothing like this. How much power had he gained from our feed on Auggie?

Claudia stayed in a fighting stance, and I didn't blame her. Graham was just inside the door, rubbing his bare arms, looking conflicted. He owed Richard his allegiance, but he was paid to keep us safe. He also knew that Richard would never forgive any of the wolves that allowed him to hurt me. Jean-Claude I wasn't so sure about, but me, he'd regret it later, and his regret had a way of raining all over everybody. Lisandro was in the room too, near the sinks. There was no conflict on his dark face. He was tall, dark, and handsome, with the longest hair of any of the male wererats. If Claudia said jump, he'd do it.

Clay was in the doorway, as tormented as Graham. We needed fewer wolves in here, and more wererats, or werehyenas, anything but people who would hesitate.

Richard lowered his hands, and his eyes were pure chocolate brown. He'd swallowed some of that awful, burning power. "You helped him rape the Master of Chicago." He wasn't yelling now, and I almost wished he had. It would have been easier to hear than the anguish in his voice.

But what he said made no sense to me. "It wasn't rape, Richard. You know that. You felt some of what Auggie was feeling. Hell, Richard, Auggie started the ball rolling. He raised my *ardeur* on purpose, picked a fight with me."

Richard looked at me, and I watched him want to believe me, but be afraid to. "Do you really think I'd rape someone?"

He shook his head. "No, but he would." He pointed toward Jean-Claude, who was standing very still behind me.

His voice came neutral, as empty as he could make it. "I have done many things over the centuries, Richard, but rape has never been to my taste."

I remembered Jean-Claude's memories with Auggie. Belle had wanted him to rape Auggie, and Jean-Claude had changed it to something gentler, or as gentle as he could make it with Belle watching. I opened my mouth to say something, but knew somehow that telling about the other two times that Jean-Claude and Auggie had had sex wouldn't help us.

"See, Anita, you can't defend him either."

"I do defend him. Jean-Claude has a lot of faults; rape isn't one of them."

"That wasn't what you started to say a second ago." He was still kneeling on the floor, but he was calming, swallowing that choking power. He was showing the control that had helped make him Ulfric of the Thronnos Rokke Clan.

Claudia moved to one side, so she could see him as she glanced at me. I gave her a small nod, but added, "I think Clay and Graham have something else they need to be doing."

She nodded, and ordered them out, and replaced them with two guards who wouldn't feel conflicted. She'd understood what I'd meant. If Richard understood what I'd done, he didn't show it, not even by a flicker of his eyes.

"I'm trying to decide what I can say that won't piss you off, Richard. That's all."

He took in a breath so deep it made his shoulders shake. "Fair enough." His voice sounded like his own now, not all growling deep. "Did the other master really pick a fight with you?"

I nodded. We'd leave the whole theory as to why he might have picked it until we were alone. "You felt his power, Richard—if it had come down to a fight, a true fight, vampire on vampire, would we have won?"

He looked down at his hands where they lay still and open on his thighs. "I don't think so."

"He raised the *ardeur*. If I feed off him, then he loses."

Richard nodded. "Food can't be dominant. I know." He looked past me to Jean-Claude. "Why would he raise the *ardeur*? Why would he pick the one way that he could lose?"

"I do not believe he wished to win," Jean-Claude said.

"That makes no sense," Richard said.

"He is already master of one territory. It is against our laws to rule a second that does not touch your own. There are lands in between our territories, so defeating me would win him nothing. But losing to the *ardeur* would give him . . ."

"Anita."

"A woman of Belle Morte's line who holds the *ardeur*, *oui*."

"I thought you said he was your friend," Richard said.

"I believe he is." Jean-Claude sighed and said, "We need privacy for this discussion, Claudia, if you would leave us?"

She looked at me, not at the men. I liked Claudia. "It's okay."

She sighed. "We'll be right outside the door, but if the power level rises again, we are back in here."

"No arguments," I said.

"I'll control myself," Richard said.

"Sure," she said, and went for the door. Lisandro stared back at us as the door closed, and it wasn't a bodyguard look. It was a man's look at a naked woman that he'd never seen naked before. Until that moment I hadn't even thought about any of the other men in the room. Richard had been all I thought of; the rest of them might as well have been eunuchs as far as I'd been concerned. But with that one look Lisandro broke two rules. First, shapeshifters didn't notice nudity; they did it too much. It would be like your cat thinking about not wearing pants. Second, it was against the bodyguard code to let clients see that you thought about them in any way other than as a target to keep safe. You did not let a female client see that you lusted after her, even if she paraded naked. That was her problem, not yours. You do not fuck those you guard, because you can't guard them while you're fucking. I guess there are exceptions to the above rules, but Lisandro hadn't earned those exceptions.

I gave him a look that let him know I'd seen his look. He just smiled, not a smidge of regret. Great, just great.

The door closed behind the guard, and we were alone. None of us moved, as if now that it was just us, we weren't certain what to do.

Richard spoke into the sudden heavy silence. "I need you to put on a towel, at least, Anita, please." He added the *please* like it hurt him to ask politely. I guess he was still angry. But he had swallowed all that rage the way he'd learned to swallow his beast. Part of me was beginning to wonder if there would come a day when he couldn't swallow all the rage, and what would happen when that day came. Once I'd thought Richard would never hurt me; now I knew better. He wouldn't hurt me on purpose, but purpose wasn't always what drove him.

Jean-Claude handed me a towel. His face was empty as he did it, nothing to help me, or give me a hint, but nothing on his face for Richard to take offense at either. I guess we were both being as careful of him as we could.

It was a big towel. I ended up covered from armpits to nearly my ankles. I tucked the end of the towel securely under and over, and voilà, I was dressed.

"Thank you," Richard said.

"You're welcome," I said, and sat down on the edge of the marble, smoothing the towel under me. Marble can be very cold to sit on bare.

Jean-Claude handed me another slightly smaller towel. I took it, and watched as he began to wrap an identical towel around his wet hair. He was right; if I didn't dry my hair well, it would be a mess tomorrow.

"How can the two of you do that?" he asked.

I looked at him from underneath the towel, while I wrapped it around my head. "What are we doing now?"

"Taking care of your hair like nothing's wrong."

I got the towel fixed in place and turned to meet Jean-Claude's look. He took the hint. "If we let our hair dry badly, it will not change what has happened, Richard. The practicalities of life do not cease needing to be done just because other things are going wrong."

Richard moved so he was sitting on the floor, rather than kneeling. He hugged his knees to him, and it was something that Nathaniel might have done, not my dominant Richard. Whatever he had experienced with us tonight, it had shaken him.

Jean-Claude came to sit beside me on the edge of the marble tub. He was careful not to touch me, only the faintest edge of our hips touching through the towels. I wanted him to wrap his arms around me, but he was probably right. Richard didn't always like to see us cuddle.

"You wanted privacy for this talk, so talk," he said. One of the side effects of the vampire marks was that we seemed to be sharing bits of our personalities. He seemed to have inherited some of my impatience and lack of anger management. A bad combination for a werewolf. But we didn't get to pick and choose what we got.

"*Ma petite*, if you will tell him, and me, what happened before I arrived." I told the shortest complete version I could of all that had happened before Jean-Claude showed up. Somewhere during the talk, I leaned in against Jean-Claude's body. It just seemed wrong to be this close and not touch. He put his arm along my shoulder.

Richard didn't seem to notice. "I thought this Samuel and Augustine were your friends?" he said.

"They are."

Then Richard said what I'd thought earlier. "If these are your friends, Jean-Claude, what are the other masters going to be like?"

"I'd thought of that, too," I said. "I mean, if these are your friends, your enemies are going to kill us."

"One of the reasons for tonight's little meeting was to see how *ma petite* reacted to other Masters of the City."

"Badly," Richard said.

"Not necessarily," Jean-Claude said. He leaned forward, curving me more into his arm to keep from knocking me off the edge. Jean-Claude started to tell his part in tonight's little drama, but Richard stopped him.

"I felt most of what happened after you touched Anita. I don't need a reminder."

"As you like," Jean-Claude said, "but the point is we may have rolled Augustine as thoroughly as Belle Morte could have done."

"I wouldn't brag about that," Richard said. He'd moved to lean his shoulder against the marble around the tub, so that he was close enough to have reached out and touched us, but he didn't try to close the distance. And because he didn't, we didn't.

"If Augustine is truly ours in the way that Belle made allies, than none of the other masters will try us. They will fear us, Richard. Fear even the touch of our hands."

Richard frowned at us. I wanted to touch the thick waves of his hair, but kept my hand around Jean-Claude's waist, and the other hand in my lap. "But you told us, before we agreed to this gathering of masters, that everyone would behave. Especially if they thought one of their people would be

Anita's new *pomme de sang*. Now, the first two masters who touch her are breaking all the rules."

"I believe there is a reason for that."

He gave us a skeptical look that was like a mirror of my own. "What reason?"

Jean-Claude told him about his theory that the *ardeur* was hunting powerful prey.

"But that means that any Master of the City who comes into contact with her will be, what, compelled to try to mind-roll her?"

"Not just Masters of the City," he said, and he told about Meng Die and Requiem. "It may have been only that these two are of our bloodline, and both had tasted the *ardeur* more than once."

"So has Asher, and he's not crazed."

"Asher was drawn to *ma petite* from the moment he came to us."

"He saw her as a way of duplicating what you and he and Julianna had," Richard said. He had moved almost as close as he could without actually touching us. I wondered if he was even aware of it.

"That, and the only way back into my bed was through Anita. But what if it was more than that, Richard?"

I had to add now, "Requiem isn't the only one of the new London vamps that had tasted the *ardeur*, and they're all of Belle's line. They don't seem particularly drawn to me."

"Perhaps they must get at least a small taste of the *ardeur* from you before it is triggered?"

"Or maybe you're wrong," Richard said, "maybe you just don't have any friends. How long has it been since you saw these guys?"

Jean-Claude gave that graceful shrug. "Almost a century for Augustine, and not since I entered this country for Samuel."

I looked at him. "Jean-Claude, just because someone was your friend a century ago doesn't mean he hasn't changed."

He nodded, as if I'd made a point. "Perhaps, but I felt something when we were with Augustine. It was such power. I believe that the *ardeur* is reaching some new power, evolving into something new, or at the very least new to us."

"What if Auggie isn't rolled completely?" I asked.

"Then what we did tonight will not be as large a deterrent."

"Tell Richard the other part, that if we really did roll another Master of the City, you're wondering if the council in Europe will use this as an excuse to kill us. Or maybe our American neighbors will decide to kill us before we try to take them all over."

Richard looked at us with that flat I-don't-believe-it look. "Well, this is a lose-lose situation. Why did you bring them all here, Jean-Claude?"

"Because their presence makes an important event of my evening of dance. It is unfair that just because an artist becomes a vampire he is no longer allowed on the stage. I want my kind to be able to pursue passions that have nothing to do with blood and power. I hope, as you for your wolves, that we can be more than just monsters."

I'd been thinking about what he said about the taste of the *ardeur* too much to be sidetracked into talking about ballet. "You know I fed the *ardeur* off Byron, too. He's not besotted with me."

"But he is not a master vampire, *ma petite*, nor will he ever be a master. He accepts that."

"If Anita has this effect only on your bloodline, we're safe for tomorrow, because there are no other Masters of the City from that line."

"But there are master vampires of Belle's line scattered throughout this country. Some will be there tomorrow. Some are part of the ballet troupe itself."

"So I stay home," I said.

"Cinderella must come to the ball, *ma petite*."

"Nathaniel says I'm not Cinderella, I'm Prince Charming."

He smiled, and gave me a little hug. "Of course, *ma petite*, whatever you say." Yeah, he was humoring me, but I let him. "But the point remains, you must go to the party tomorrow night."

Richard's knee touched my leg, his hands still clasped around his legs. His hands were mottled with the tightness of his own hold. "She can't go, not if she's going to get jumped by all of them." His hand started to reach for my leg, then he stopped himself, and went back to holding his own hand. He was fighting so hard not to touch me, to touch us. The vampire marks, at least for Belle's line, made you want to touch each other. It didn't have to be about sex, just about feeling more complete when you touched. I know Richard felt almost compelled to touch me, but I'd never had the courage to ask if he felt the same way around Jean-Claude. If he did, it might explain some of why he was so enraged about Augustine.

"We have in our camp other masters of similar power to Requiem, who have tasted the *ardeur*. One is even of Belle's line."

I shook my head. "If you're talking about London, forget it. He seriously creeps me."

Richard was shaking his head, too. "No."

"Frankly, Jean-Claude, I don't know why you agreed to take him. I mean, his own kiss nicknamed him 'the Dark Knight.' I think that says something."

He sighed and leaned his back against the wall. "You know that Belle Morte tried to demand all her bloodline back, when their master was executed. How could I refuse to save them from her?"

"Yeah, but I'd think Belle's court would be right up London's alley. A nice dark alley."

"He did not wish to go back to her. He spoke to me over the phone, he begged me not to let him go back to her court. You see, *ma petite*, Richard, London was traded to Belle for several years, then she exiled him. She tried to recall him, but he got his new master to intercede."

"Why?" Richard asked. "Auggie would give anything to go back. I felt how much he misses her." Richard shuddered. "It's like some sort of addiction."

"*Oui, mon ami, exactement*, that is precisely why London does not wish to go back. He is like an alcoholic that has become a teetotaler. He knows he has another drunken binge in him, but he does not know whether he has the strength to stop again. How could I leave him to her?"

"That's awfully sentimental for you, isn't it?" Richard said.

Jean-Claude gave him an unfriendly look. "I try for kindness when I can, Richard."

Richard sighed, and leaned his forehead on his knees. "God, this is a mess."

"You said we had other master vamps who had tasted the *ardeur* but who weren't of Belle's line—who are they?" Our list of non-Belle masters was pretty damn slim.

"Wicked and Truth," he said.

It was Richard who raised his face and said, "No, absolutely no." Then he seemed to think about it. "Not Wicked."

"Truth would be acceptable?" Jean-Claude asked.

Richard's shoulders hunched, and I thought he might break his own hands holding on so tight. "You're asking me to share her with another man. How can you ask me to help pick who it's going to be?"

"How many women have you lain with in the last month, Richard?"

Richard's power flared like a burst of fire through an innocent-looking wall. We were suddenly bathed in the biting heat of his power.

"You all right in there?" Claudia called through the door.

I looked at Richard. He gave the tiniest nod.

"We're fine," I said.

"You sure?" she asked.

"Yes."

Silence from the other side of the door.

Richard said, "Thank you," then got back to the fight. I didn't have to see his face to know he was angry. "We all agreed that I'd keep dating. Anita will be my lupa and my Bolverk, but she doesn't want to marry, or have kids, or any of that. I do. We all agreed to this, don't throw it up in my face now."

"You're going to hurt yourself, Richard," I said, softly, staring at his hands, and all the not-so-pretty colors they were turning.

He let go of his hands with a breath that held pain in it. He finally let himself wrap his hand around my calf. His power ran over my skin like a thousand tiny insects biting.

"Ow," I said.

He leaned his face on my towel-covered knee, and said, "Sorry, I'm sorry." The energy calmed, still warm, raising sweat along my spine, but it stopped hurting. He spoke with his face still on my knee. "Your feeding on Auggie raised my power level—oh God, it did. The power rush felt so good, so incredibly good, even after I knew what you'd done to get it. It still felt wonderful." His shoulders started to shake, and I realized he was crying.

I touched his hair, letting my fingers comb through those thick waves. "Richard, oh, Richard."

He wrapped his arms around my legs, holding on, putting his face in my lap, letting me touch him. Jean-Claude laid a tentative hand on his back, and when Richard didn't say no, he stroked his back. That useless stroking that you'll do for good friends and loved ones. Those endless, useless circles, where you try to say with your hands that it will be all right. I stroked his hair and brushed the tears from his face. We comforted him as his friends, his very good friends. Whatever else we were to each other, we were at least that.

12

WE ENDED UP on the floor with Richard cradled in my lap, while I sat against Jean-Claude's bare upper body as if he were a warm, silken chair. Richard's shirt was gone, so the warm muscled smoothness of his chest and shoulders lay across the pooled towel in my lap. My upper body was as bare as his; the towel just couldn't hold on during that much cuddling. Richard lay on his back, eyes peaceful, his hair like a brown and gold halo around his face.

My hands stroked his bare chest, not for sex, but for comfort. All the lycanthropes were like that; touch was good, touch was even necessary to stay sane. It was as if they had the normal human skin hunger except more, orders of magnitude more. His arm was raised along the line of my body, his hand playing with my hair, which had begun to dry in tight, frizzy curls. Jean-Claude's hand played along Richard's raised arm, stroking up and down the muscled length of it.

There were no words, just the comfort of the touching. Jean-Claude's other hand was stroking my shoulder and arm, almost mirroring what he was doing to Richard. I think we'd all been surprised that Richard let Jean-Claude touch so much as a fingertip to him, after the way he'd entered the room. I'd seen plenty of lycanthropes pet each other regardless of sexual orientation—a cuddle was a cuddle to most of them—but Richard had issues with Jean-Claude that he didn't have with the people I'd seen him be so casual with.

Richard's eyes shifted and I knew he was looking past me to the other man. "Your hair is almost as curly as Anita's."

The comment made me turn so I could see his face more clearly, too. Richard was right, Jean-Claude's hair was a mass of black curls. Not the relaxed, almost wavy curls that he always had, but something closer to mine. But his hair drying naturally was about where mine was with hair care products, not the black foam mine had turned into. "Have I never seen your natural hair texture?" I asked, staring at all those curls.

He smiled, and if it had been almost anyone else I'd have said he was embarrassed, but it just didn't quite fly for Jean-Claude. "I suppose not."

Richard moved his hand from my hair to Jean-Claude's. He rubbed the curls between his fingers, then went back to mine, comparing. "Your hair is still softer textured than Anita's, or mine, for that matter." He knelt, and took a handful of both of our hair, as if he were testing how much it weighed. "Normally your hair just looks silkier, but now, you have to touch it to feel how much difference in texture there is between you and Anita."

Jean-Claude had gone very still against my body. I think he stopped breathing, and the heartbeat that had been chugging along like any human's heart slowed. I knew he'd gone still because Richard was touching him voluntarily, and he didn't want to spook him. But I also think that in that moment he didn't know what to do. A man who had been a great lover for over four hundred years did not know what to do because someone was playing with his hair.

He didn't want to be too bold and raise that anger again, or frighten him with a homophobic possibility. If Richard had been a woman, he'd have taken it as foreplay. If Richard hadn't been a shapeshifter, he might still have taken it as an invitation of sorts. But shapeshifters were tactile junkies; touching didn't mean sex to them, any more than it did when a dog started licking the sweat off your skin. You tasted good, and they liked you, nothing sexual. But it is personal. If they didn't like you, they wouldn't touch you.

He sat pressed against my body, and I knew by his very stillness how much it meant to him that Richard was touching him. The stillness also told me he had no idea what to do about it. What does it say when a vampire who has been a great lover and seducer for centuries chooses, as his metaphysical sweeties, maybe the only two people in his territory who are going to puzzle him?

There was a knock at the door. Those of us with a heartbeat jumped. Richard's hands fell away from both of us as he turned to face the door, still on his knees.

Movement came back to Jean-Claude's body the way a human would take a breath. "Yes," he said, and his voice held just a touch of impatience.

Claudia's voice came, "It's the Master of Cape Cod and his oldest son."

Jean-Claude and I exchanged glances. Richard just frowned. "Why is he back?" Richard asked.

"We can but ask," Jean-Claude said, his voice back to almost its normal silky emptiness. The voice he used when he was hiding things, but trying not to seem like it. Samuel would know what a totally empty voice meant. Hiding, or fear, weakness. So Jean-Claude compromised with his voice, hiding from Richard and maybe from me, and not seeming to hide from Samuel. We were so not going to make it through this weekend without another disaster. The combination of metaphysics and politics was just too hard.

"We'll be right out," I yelled at the door. We all got up off the floor. Richard reached for his shirt and slipped it over his head. Jean-Claude and I had robes hanging on the back of the door. Jean-Claude's was one I'd seen and enjoyed before: heavy black brocade with black fur at the collar and lapel so that it framed a triangle of his pale chest. There was more fur at the wide cuffs, and I'd felt that fur rub down my body before. Just seeing him in the robe made me shiver.

He gave me a smile that said he'd noticed. Richard either didn't understand or ignored it.

My robe was black silk, no embroidery, no fur, just plain unrelieved black.

We had to walk in front of the mirror to get to the door, and Richard stopped us with a hand on either of our shoulders. He turned us toward our reflections, so that he stood between us. We were all black cloth and white skin, sharp contrasts. Then there he stood, in his bright red shirt, blue jeans, his hair all brown and gold. His tan, darker in contrast with how pale we were. "Which of these things does not belong?" he asked in a low voice. There was that shadow in his eyes again.

I slid my arm around his waist, hugged him, but even to me it looked like something carved of bone and darkness clinging to all that life.

"Jean-Claude, Anita, you coming?" Claudia asked, voice a little hesitant, which you didn't hear much from her.

"We're coming," I called.

"If I could set you free, *mon ami*, I would."

Richard hugged me so tight it almost hurt, then he relaxed against me, and looked at Jean-Claude. "If you had that kind of magic wand I'd let you use it, but you don't." He turned, keeping one arm around my shoulders, and reaching the other until he touched Jean-Claude's shoulder. He did that guy grip on the shoulder that some macho guys do instead of hugging another guy. "Some nights I hate you, Jean-Claude, but if I'd been with Anita tonight, touching her, Augustine wouldn't have been able to roll her. If I'd been where I should have been, none of the crap that I hated tonight would have happened. I know that. I felt it, while it was happening. I was miles away, and I felt the fight, but I didn't reach out and help. It was vampire politics, and that's not my problem." He shook his head hard enough to send his hair flying around his face. "No more lying to myself. I am your animal to call, and I hate it, and sometimes I hate you, and sometimes I hate Anita, and most of the time I hate myself. No more lies, and no more crippling us."

Jean-Claude's face was as careful as I'd ever seen it. "And what do these so-wise statements mean, *mon ami*?"

"It means when you meet with Samuel I'll be at your side, where I should have been earlier tonight." He hugged me tight with one arm, and squeezed Jean-Claude's shoulder again. "I wasn't even willing to offer up energy to help Anita. She had Micah and Nathaniel with her; I thought she didn't need another animal to call. But she did, you did. If you and Anita hadn't pulled a metaphysical miracle out of thin air, the Master of Chicago would have defeated you. Maybe he couldn't take your territory, but if one master defeats you, then it's like blood in the water; the sharks come and feed. If we'd proved weak, then not tonight, but some night soon, someone would come and kill us all."

"I agree with everything you're saying," I said, slowly, "but it doesn't sound like you."

"No, I guess it doesn't." He looked at Jean-Claude, and I felt that first warm trickle of his energy. "Are you playing puppet with me again?"

"I swear to you that I am not, not knowingly, but these are all things I have longed to hear you say. With you at our side, Richard, I fear no one who has come to our territory. With one third of our triumvirate absent, or unwilling . . . tonight has made me doubt my decision to invite others to our lands."

He dropped his hand from Jean-Claude's shoulder. "Then let's go have this meeting. I can't promise that I won't freak again. I can't promise to like any of this, but I promise to try harder not to run away." He started walking toward the door, still holding me. I looked back at Jean-Claude, and the look must have shown what I was thinking, because he shrugged, as if he didn't know what the hell had happened to Richard either. It wasn't that we weren't happy with a more reasonable response from him, but it just didn't seem real. It didn't feel like the quiet rush after the storm has passed; no, this felt more like that false calm you sometimes get where the world is hushed and waiting. It feels quiet, but the air is charged and waiting, waiting for the storm to come. That's what Richard's new attitude felt like, like it was brittle and waiting to break. I applauded the effort, and the sentiment, but the pit of my stomach was afraid of what would happen when the new attitude met the old issues.

13

SOMEONE HAD CLEANED up the living room. The torn drapes were gone, and the remaining ones had been moved to make long swags of cloth against the stone walls. It didn't make cloth walls now, but it was pretty, and helped give the illusion that the carpeted area was its own space, and not part of the larger rock room. The electric lights seemed odd now that you could see the torches in the hallway.

We walked up hand in hand, me in the middle of the men. Richard's hand was oh-so-slightly damp. He was nervous, but it didn't show on his face. I wished I could have asked what exactly was making him nervous. But even if there hadn't been company I wouldn't have asked. He was being brave and cooperative, and I wasn't going to poke at it. Honest.

Asher rose from the chair where he'd sat and entertained our guests. There were half a dozen black-garbed guards scattered throughout the room. Claudia and her crew followed behind us like an honor guard. I think she'd decided no more taking chances tonight. We had enough manpower to fill a room, so she was going to do it. None of us were going to argue.

Asher glided toward us, and it was almost as if his feet didn't touch the ground, as if he were floating. He was always graceful, but not like that. He was one of the best at levitating that I'd ever seen, so that he could do what the legends say: Asher could fly. Tonight it was as if he could barely force himself to walk when he knew he had wings and longed to use them. He was like some earthbound angel waiting to fling himself skyward. His clothes helped the angelic illusion. He was all in white with gold and copper thread worked through the frock coat, and along a pair of silk pants that ended at his knees, where white hose took up, and ended in white high heels with golden buckles. The shoes reminded me that the original high heel was meant for men.

His hair was the color of the gold thread in his clothes, as if the seamstress had used his own hair to decorate the cloth. He used that hair like a shield, to hide the scars on the right side of his face. He'd been so worried about what the other masters, many of whom knew him before the scarring, would think of him, that he had requested we take down all the paintings that showed him before. The side of the face that showed beside that fall of truly golden hair was the face of some medieval angel, if you liked your angels sensuous, and a little fallen. That full, kissable mouth smiled at us all. His eyes managed to be both pale blue, and a vibrant color, as if a winter sky could burn with pale, clear blue. Only one eye showed clear; the other one seemed to wink and burn when glimpsed through the hair, as if light were glancing off glass.

He offered his hand first to Jean-Claude, and said what Jean-Claude usually didn't like to hear. "Master, our friend from Cape Cod begs a word." His words were utterly polite, but his face glowed with some suppressed excitement. Something had filled our usually solemn Asher with delight, but what?

Jean-Claude arched an eyebrow, as if he wanted to ask what was up, too.

Asher's voice floated through my mind. "The new power level is amazing."

I felt Richard jerk, as if he'd been hit.

I looked at him, and saw from his wide eyes that he'd probably heard it, too. The next mind whisper held a trace of laughter to it. "My apologies. I only meant Jean-Claude to hear, but I confess to having some trouble controlling all the new abilities."

Jean-Claude squeezed my hand, and it was his voice that came next. "Calm, we must all be calm for our guests."

Richard let his breath out slow, and gave a small nod. His abilities didn't lie with the dead, so he wasn't used to vamps, other than Jean-Claude, talking mind-to-mind with him. Even I wasn't used to them doing it by accident. How much power had he gained from this one feeding, and how much had others of our vampires gained? There were one or two I wasn't sure I wanted more powerful than they already were. Meng Die, for one.

Samuel and Sampson stood in front of the love seat. Asher led us to the couch across from them. The white carpet seemed emptier than normal. Oh, the coffee table was missing. Had we broken it after the *ardeur* rose? I couldn't remember.

I had my best professional smile plastered on my face, the one that's bright and cheery as a lightbulb, and about as warm. But it was the best I could do. I'd had about all the out-of-town visitors I could deal with for one night.

"Samuel, Sampson, you have not met our Richard."

Samuel bowed toward us. "Ulfric, it is good to meet you at last."

Sampson bowed a little lower than his father, and let him do the talking. They both looked way too solemn for my tastes, as if something else had gone wrong.

"Samuel, what brings you back to us tonight?" Jean-Claude asked. If he was tired of visitors it didn't show in his voice. He sounded pleasant, welcoming, the perfect host.

"First, the apology I owe you on behalf of my wife. I worry that something about her nature affected your servant, and may have helped cause what happened tonight."

I blinked at him, felt my smile slip a notch. Was this all someone else's fault? Was I going to have someone else to blame? Goody.

Jean-Claude sat down on the white couch, not so much pulling me down with him as leading, as you do in a dance. He sat, and I followed his lead, and Richard followed mine. Jean-Claude kept my hand in his, but Richard let go, and put his arm along the back of the couch. He was touching mostly me, but his hand moved along Jean-Claude's back, and ended lost in the thick curls of his hair.

"Where is your lovely wife, and your other sons?" Jean-Claude asked.

Asher sat in the overstuffed chair closest to us. He matched the chair and pillows perfectly, all white and gold. He still looked entirely too pleased with himself, like the proverbial cat with cream.

Samuel sat down on the love seat, and Sampson followed his father's lead. "They are at a hotel along with our two guards. I did not feel it wise to bring Thea and Anita together again tonight."

"What did she think of the show?" I asked.

Jean-Claude's hand tightened on my hand, where he held it in his lap. The squeeze was enough: *Be nice*, he was saying. I'd be nice. My version of it.

Richard had gone very quiet beside me, his arm tensed against my back. But it wasn't a warning to be careful, because his body temperature went up, as if he was thinking what I was thinking: was there someone else to get angry with, someone besides ourselves? Richard and I both preferred to be angry at other people.

"Thea was much impressed," he said, and his voice was mild, empty. His tone told nothing.

"If she was so impressed," I said, "then why isn't she here?"

Sampson smiled, and had to turn away to hide it.

"What's so funny?" I asked.

His father gave him an unfriendly look. Sampson fought to control his face, but finally burst out laughing. Samuel gave him his best ancient

vampire disdain. "I'm sorry, Father," Sampson said in a voice still choked
with laughter, "but you must admit it is funny. 'Impressed' does not begin
to cover Mother's reaction to what Anita and Jean-Claude did tonight."

His father gave him a stony face, until the laughter faded round the edges.
Then Samuel said in a voice that held an edge of injured dignity, "My son
has been indiscreet, but he is accurate. You ask why Thea and my other sons
are not here; simply put, I did not trust her near the two of you."

"She liked the show," I said.

Samuel shook his head, gave his son another disapproving look. "More
than liked, Anita. She is all ablaze with speculative plans. Would it be possible for her and I to do what the two of you did? I find that unlikely, for
though Thea carries something similar to the *ardeur*, I do not. I believe what
you did to Augustine required similar gifts between the two of you."

Jean-Claude gave a small nod, face still empty. "I believe so."

"She is now convinced that Anita could bring our sons into the full
strength of their siren's powers." Something crossed his face, too faint to
read, but with such an empty face, it was strangely noticeable. "I do not
share her certainty. What I felt from you tonight, Anita, is a different ele-
ment of passion. It is like the difference between fire and water. They will
both consume you, but in very different manners."

I looked at Sampson's face, still softly amused. "What did your mother actually say?" I asked.

He glanced at his father before he answered. Samuel sighed, then nodded.
Sampson grinned at me, and said, "I don't think you really want to know
what she said, but what she meant was that if she had her way, Tom and Cris
would both be here. She'd be here, too. She'd be offering us all to you any
way you wanted us." His face sobered around the edges. "She can get carried away sometimes, our mother. She means well, but she doesn't think entirely like a human being, do you understand?"

"I hang around with vampires, so yeah."

He shook his head, his hands clasped on his knees. "No, Anita, vampires
start out human, as do shapeshifters, and necromancers"—he said that with
a smile—"but Mother was never human. She thinks like . . ." He seemed unsure what to say.

Samuel finished for him. "Thea is other, and she reasons in ways that do
not always make much sense to those of us who began life as human beings."
He didn't sound entirely happy about it, but he stated it as truth.

"That must make life interesting," Richard said.

Samuel gave him cool eyes, but Sampson nodded, smiling. "You have no
idea."

"What did you think of the show, Samuel?" Jean-Claude asked.

The other vampire thought about it, face careful, and his voice was just as careful when he answered, "I thought it was one of the most powerful things I have ever seen. I think it is the kind of power that made me flee the great courts, and it is exactly the sort of power that made me avoid Belle Morte's court. It is the kind of display that made me flee Europe for fear of becoming nothing but a vassal of some great vampiric lord."

"Do you fear us now?" Jean-Claude asked.

Samuel nodded. "I do."

"I would not harm you deliberately," Jean-Claude said.

"No, but your power is growing, and growing power is a wild and capricious thing. I do not want my people, or my sons, near you while your power finds its way. I think you will be incredibly dangerous, by accident, for years to come."

"Yet, you come before me with your son. Why? Why not leave my lands, if we are so dangerous?"

"Because Thea is right in one way. If she and I could by some chance duplicate what the two of you did, it would be"—he licked his lips—"worth the risk. I also agree that there is a chance that your Anita could bring my sons into their powers, if they have them."

"Do you believe your sons are so human?" Jean-Claude asked.

"Sampson is well over seventy in human years, so no, not so very human."

I looked at Sampson. He looked somewhere in his early twenties, maybe thirty at most. By no stretch of the imagination did he look seventy. "My," I said, "you're holding up well."

He grinned at me, and I liked the grin. He seemed to find the whole power game a little embarrassing, a little funny. "Clean living," he said, still grinning.

Richard moved beside me, a small, uncomfortable movement. I glanced at him, and his face was beginning to darken. One of Richard's biggest problems with our new lifestyle was jealousy. Of all the men trying to be in my life, he was the only one who found jealousy a real problem. Until I saw that look on his face, I'd been able to ignore that they were still talking about Sampson and me being lovers. I'd gotten better at pushing away the uncomfortable bits until I had to deal with them. Richard was still working on that.

"Thomas and Cristos seem to be aging at a more normal rate."

"They are only seventeen," Jean-Claude said, "too young to be certain, surely."

Samuel shrugged, a normal shrug, not that graceful Gallic movement.

"But for this, I think they are too young, too human, whatever Thea may wish."

"He's afraid you'd break them," Sampson said.

I couldn't help smiling. Richard's frown got deeper. "And your dad isn't worried about you?" I asked.

"He is my oldest," Samuel said, as if that meant more to him than it did to me.

"If you break me, he has two sons left," Sampson said, smiling to take the bite out of it.

Samuel touched his son's arm. "I hold all my children precious, you know that."

He smiled at his father, patted his hand where it lay on his arm. "I know that, Father, but for this kind of power you'd risk one of us, and I'm the most likely to survive without becoming her slave."

"My slave?" I made it a question. "I don't do slaves."

Sampson looked at me as if he were studying me, a shadow of his father's penetrating stare. "If Augustine is not your slave it will only be because he is powerful enough to recover. Not for lack of trying on your part, and I am not nearly as powerful as a Master of the City."

I opened my mouth, closed it, not sure what to say. I finally said, "I don't want anyone to be my slave."

"Then what did you want?" He kept his suddenly serious eyes on me.

I just blinked at him, trying to think. What had I wanted? What had I intended to do to Auggie? "Win," I said.

"What?" Sampson asked.

"Win. I wanted to win. Auggie and your father are supposed to be Jean-Claude's friends. But your mother had almost rolled me. She'd tried to raise the *ardeur* and make me fuck your brother, your little brother. Then Auggie raised the *ardeur*, and used his bloodline's special ability on me. If this is what Jean-Claude's friends do to us, then what are the other Masters of the City going to do?" I shook my head, leaning forward on the couch, still holding Jean-Claude's hand, but having to put my hand on Richard's thigh to keep touching him, too. "We had to win this fight. Had to."

"You had to win in such a way that the rest of us would not try your strength," Samuel said.

I nodded. "Yes."

He looked past us to the hallway beyond, so searching a look that it made Richard and me look behind us. Neither Jean-Claude, nor the silent Asher, bothered, as if they knew there was no one there.

"I believe you have succeeded, Anita. If Augustine follows you and Jean-

Claude about like a lovesick puppy, then the rest will fear you. Some may even take back their offers of *pomme de sang* for fear of having you feed off them the way you fed off Augustine's people."

"We fed from Augustine's people because he is their master," Jean-Claude said. "No others offer themselves to *ma petite*'s bed."

"Perhaps," Samuel said, "but I think if they did know what has happened with Augustine, they might be tempted. There is something about her that draws one. Even I feel it, and I am not of Belle's line."

"How strongly drawn?" Jean-Claude asked in that careful voice.

The two vampires looked at each other. There was suddenly something between them, not magic, but almost as if willpower could be something touchable.

"That is an odd question," Samuel said.

"Is it?" Jean-Claude asked, and his voice held a lilt at the end that sounded strangely chiding.

Samuel settled back against the love seat, as if he was going to be there for a while. Somehow they both knew they were negotiating. "It was surprisingly bad manners for Augustine to have started a fight with your human servant."

"Yes," Jean-Claude said, "it seemed out of character for him, don't you think?"

Samuel nodded. "I do."

Richard's free hand found mine where it rested on his leg. He began to run his thumb over my knuckles, as if he'd picked up the tension, too. Something was up, but what? What was Jean-Claude up to? I wasn't used to being shut out by both of the men, especially when we were touching, but whatever was happening tonight, Jean-Claude was holding us tight shut against each other. He usually only did that when he was afraid of what would happen if the marks opened. After our little show-down with Auggie I wasn't going to argue, but it made me head-blind around them, and I wasn't used to that. I hadn't realized that I'd started counting on getting hints from both their minds.

"I need advice, Samuel, advice from another Master of the City."

"What could I possibly advise you on? You are a *sourdre de sang*. I am but an ordinary Master of the City."

"I crave your wisdom, not your power."

The two of them stared at each other, and neither face showed a damn thing. *Note to self, never play poker with master vamps.* "I am always glad to share my wisdom with my friends."

"I need your trust, as well, Samuel."

"Friends must always trust each other."

I had a moment to wonder if "friends" meant for them what it had meant for Augustine and Jean-Claude. Not the time to ask.

"I trusted you tonight, Samuel, but Thea tried to force herself, and your Thomas, on my human servant. That is not the way a trusted friend behaves."

"I can only give you my deepest apologies, Jean-Claude. Thea is sometimes overly enthusiastic in her pursuit of our sons' powers."

Sampson and I both laughed at the same time. The vampires looked at us. "Sorry," I said, "but I think you're understating it."

"Mother overly enthusiastic in pursuit of her children's destiny." Sampson laughed again, shaking his head.

Samuel frowned at him. Then he sighed and turned back to Jean-Claude. "Once I helped you, not for money, but because Augustine was my friend, and he asked a favor."

"Your ship was my escape to the new world," Jean-Claude said.

I remembered Auggie, in Jean-Claude's memory, saying something about a ship and a captain he trusted. Had that been Samuel?

"I propose that we put aside mistrust, and speak plainly. I propose that we act as true friends and not adversaries."

"All master vampires are adversaries," Jean-Claude said.

Samuel smiled. "You speak what you have been told, not what you believe." He looked at Asher. "He is master enough to have his own territory, but he stays with you out of love. You do not fear each other."

"No, but you and I have never been close in the way of lovers."

Samuel waved his hand in the air as if Jean-Claude had missed his point. "I do not covet your lands. Do you covet mine?"

Jean-Claude smiled. "No."

"I do not covet your lady, do you covet mine?"

Jean-Claude shook his head. "No."

"We have different animals to call, so that cannot even be shared. We are no threat to each other, Jean-Claude, our powers are too different. Let us help each other, and leave off this game playing. Let us come in honesty and friendship."

Jean-Claude gave one brief nod. "Agreed." Then he gave a wide smile. "You first."

Samuel laughed, sudden and wide enough to flash fangs. It was an echo of Sampson's laughter, as if when human he'd been even more like his son.

The thought made me wonder: if I was pregnant, who would the baby be like? Would it be a little carbon copy of someone? Would there be a little

Jean-Claude running around? The thought of a baby was terrifying, but the thought of a little living version of Jean-Claude wasn't horrible. I shook my head, hard enough that they all looked at me.

"What is wrong, *ma petite*?"

"Sorry, thinking too hard. Maybe I've never seen master vamps talk about honesty and friendship. Takes some getting used to."

Samuel smiled at me. "I suppose for the Executioner, it would be a very alien concept."

I shook my head. "No, as Jean-Claude's human servant, that is where it gets weird. As the Executioner I just kill people, I don't talk to them."

He looked at me with those brown-green eyes, a long, considering look. He turned the look back to Jean-Claude. "I think we can help each other, Jean-Claude. I will begin." He gave a long sigh. "When Sampson said that Thea does not think like a human, he is quite right. She is the last of the sirens, and it preys upon her mind. She sees the promise of power in our boys, and she is determined that it be brought out." Samuel hesitated, and even through centuries of control he seemed uncomfortable. "Thea comes from a time and a people where close family relationships were not a hindrance to sex, or even marriage. Her people were worshipped as gods and goddesses. Are you familiar with the Greek mythos?"

"Anyone who is classically educated is familiar with the myths," Jean-Claude said.

"You're making this a long story, Father."

Samuel looked at him. "I admit that now that the time has come to be honest, I am having second thoughts."

Sampson touched his father's hand. "Let me, then."

He shook his head. "No, I am master, and father, and I will do it." He looked back at Jean-Claude. "Thea tried to bring Sampson into his powers as a siren."

Jean-Claude and I just blinked at him. Richard was lost, because we hadn't given him the whole story about how sirens come into their power. Or had we? I couldn't remember anymore. I was the one who said, "Do you mean that your wife tried to seduce your son?"

He nodded. "Sampson came to me, and I told her, in no uncertain terms, that if she ever tried to do it again I would kill her. When the twins began to exhibit faint signs of power, I gave her the talk again."

"Would you truly slay her?" Jean-Claude asked.

The polite mask dropped, and Samuel's eyes blazed for a second, before he lowered his eyes, and hid the anger. "I love my wife, but I love my sons, and they are children and cannot protect themselves against her."

"In my mother's defense," Sampson said, "when I said no, she took no for an answer. She didn't have to. I'm her son, but I'm not a siren yet; if she'd pushed her powers, then I wouldn't have had a choice. She stopped when she realized I was horrified. She didn't understand why it bothered me, but she accepted it."

Richard and I exchanged glances, and for the first time I think we were both thinking, *Gee, it could be worse.* That there was a vampire out there sexually more disturbing than Jean-Claude and Belle Morte. EEEK!

"I fear," Samuel said, "that Thea's restraint will not be perfect. The twins are seventeen, old enough to marry, old enough for much. I fear that she will be tempted to push with them, and they are not as strong of will as Sampson. It might take less to cloud their minds and lusts."

"And would you do as you threatened?" Jean-Claude asked. "Even if the sex were to make them full sirens?" His face and voice were back to being very neutral.

"They would come into their powers, but I am not certain that their sanity would survive it. Can you imagine someone with Thea's powers, or even more powerful because of my bloodline, but mad, completely broken in the mind? I do not wish to be forced to either imprison or kill my own child, Jean-Claude, and that is what we might have to do." He shook his head, and the worry on his face was like scars, so deep, as if he had carried this burden for a very long time.

"It would be a terrible choice," Jean-Claude said.

Samuel gathered himself, and his face was back to being neutral, hail-fellow-well-met, boy-next-door-handsome. "But if we can find a way to bring them into their powers without Thea being involved, then the choices are not horrible. The choices are wonderous, powerful, and I would be in your debt."

"It is by no means certain that sex with *ma petite* will do for your sons what you wish."

I opened my mouth to protest that I hadn't agreed to sex with any of them, but he squeezed my hand, as if, wait.

"Perhaps not, but I believe that I could convince Thea that if Anita could not make them full sirens, none could, not even Thea herself. If Anita tries and fails, then I believe that Thea would accept that they are not sirens."

Jean-Claude looked at me, then. "If you have questions, *ma petite*, Richard, now is the time for them."

Richard said, "Did you say seventeen?"

Samuel nodded.

Richard looked at me, and the look was eloquent.

"I've already turned them down as too young, Richard. You don't need the look, thanks." I took my hand out of his, because I hadn't deserved the look he gave me.

"But you'll fuck Sampson."

I stood up, letting go of both of them, and stared down at him. "Apologize to me, Richard. Apologize to me, now."

Embarrassment was on his face, but so was anger. "I shouldn't have said it, and I'm sorry I said it, but don't expect me to be happy that you're adding another man to your list of lovers. I'm not going to be happy about it, Anita, I'm just not."

"Do I ask how many women you've slept with this week?"

"No, but you don't have to meet them, either."

I couldn't argue that. "Fine, you're right. It would probably bug me to meet your dates." I threw my hands up in the air. "Damn it, Richard, do you have an opinion on this that isn't based on jealousy?"

He looked down, then got up from the couch, and paced away to the edge of the carpet. "All I can see when I look at Sampson is that he's not bad looking, and he's about my height, and . . . I don't want you fucking him. But then I don't want you fucking anyone but me, so—" He spread his hands wide, and shrugged.

"Have I raised a sore point?" Samuel asked.

"An ongoing disagreement," Jean-Claude said.

"If this is a problem," Sampson said, "then forget it. We were under the impression that everyone was okay with Anita adding to her list of men."

Richard crossed his arms across his chest, and said, "And if we don't do this, because I'm not happy about it, and your mother . . ." He closed his eyes, his face struggling with so many emotions. "God help me, but you and your brothers are actually in a more perverted sexual mess than we are. If I say no, and the worst happens . . ." He paced the edge of the white carpet as if the walls were still there. "I don't want to watch, but it has to be Anita's call. I won't say no. Neither of us is monogamous, so why should I bitch?" He stood there arms crossed, shoulders hunched as if something hurt.

"Anita," Samuel said.

I looked at him, still standing. I sighed. "I'd rather not add to my list of men either, truthfully, but as Jean-Claude has explained to me, I need a new *pomme de sang* sooner rather than later. I'm not promising, but I'll agree to try." I couldn't look at anyone when I said it, because it felt squeechy. To agree to try to take another lover, in front of three men I was already sleeping with.

"Good," Samuel said, and there was such relief in that one word that I looked at him. He was smiling, his eyes sparkling with happiness, and tears. Unshed tears glittered in his eyes. In that moment I realized that he had accepted that his wife would seduce one of their sons, and he would kill her, and the son would be mad, and he would have to kill him, and . . . too Oedipal for words. Samuel had accepted that someday the worst would happen, and suddenly he was saved. He looked like a man who had thought the executioner was coming, and the governor called instead.

I still wasn't sure how I felt about adding to my men, but it was nice, for a change, to be someone's salvation instead of their doom. Yeah, being the savior instead of the executioner, that sounded pretty damn good.

14

SAMUEL SMILED AT Jean-Claude, and it was like a lot about Samuel, a very human smile. I realized that he, like Auggie, could be more "normal" than most vamps I'd ever seen. Was it a vamp trick like Auggie's had been? Maybe. Was it any of my business to mess with it, and reveal his secret? Nope. No more grand revelations tonight, not that were my fault anyway. I wasn't messing with anyone or anything tonight if I could help it. My goal was simply to get through the rest of this interview without anything bad happening. Why was I so worried? I'd sat back down beside Jean-Claude, but Richard hadn't. Richard was still standing, arms folded, shoulders rounded as if with pain. I knew the look on his face, it was the look that usually meant we were going to have a really bad fight. I didn't want to fight tonight, not with anyone, but especially not with Richard.

Jean-Claude touched my hand. It made me jump, and turn startled to him. "What is wrong, *ma petite*?"

I gave him a look, and rolled my eyes back to our other third. "Ah," he said.

I gripped Jean-Claude's hand tight, and tried to head this fight off. "Richard?" I made his name a question.

He turned those smoldering brown eyes to me. "What?" That one word was so angry that even he flinched. "I'm sorry, what is it, Anita?"

"You don't have to pick a fight with me to leave." There, that was as honest and as calm as I could make it.

He frowned at me. "What does that mean?"

"It means that ever since we started talking to Samuel about his sons and their problem, your tension level has done nothing but rise."

"And if we were talking about me having sex with three new women, two of them seventeen years old, wouldn't you be angry?"

I thought about it, then nodded. "Yes."

"Then don't expect me to be happy about it."

"What am I supposed to do, Richard, apologize? I wouldn't even be sure what I was apologizing about. Anyway, I've told you that my answer was no on the seventeen-year-old."

"I think, Jean-Claude, Sampson and I will leave you all for the night." Samuel stood. "You seem to have much to discuss."

Sampson stood alongside his father. He was about two inches taller than Samuel, as if he'd gained height from his mother's genetics. I wondered what else he might have gained. I really didn't know much about mermaids, or sirens. I probably needed to remedy that before I got too up close and personal with any of them.

"Not yet, my friend, please," Jean-Claude said. He looked at Richard, giving a peaceful face to the unhappy one. "We need some riddles answered before we dare take *ma petite* among our brethren tomorrow night."

Samuel nodded, and sat back down. "You're wondering, if you take her among nearly a dozen Masters of the City, whether the night will be even more interesting than this one."

Jean-Claude nodded. "*Exactement.*"

"Are these questions that only a vampire can answer?" Sampson asked.

"It is from a master like your father that I need advice," Jean-Claude said.

"Then, I could go back to the hotel and check on Mother and the twins."

"I think they have enough watchdogs, Sampson," his father said.

Sampson gave his father a look like he was trying to say something with his eyes, and his father wasn't getting it.

"You're leaving because you think it will make me less upset," Richard said.

Sampson looked at him, with that open, honest face, and nodded.

"That's . . ." Richard's face struggled with his emotions, because a friendly gesture, honestly given, always touched him. "That's really . . . good of you."

"You obviously don't like sharing Anita, and now here I am asking you to share her again. We need her to help us. I don't want to lose my mother and one, or both, of my little brothers." Sampson shook his head, eyes staring off into space, but not seeing anything in this room. The look in his eyes was haunted as if he, like his father, had given up on avoiding the tragedy. As if he'd been picturing it all in his head for months, trying to make peace with it, and failing.

He looked up at Richard. "I won't give up this chance to save my family, but I am sorry that it's causing you pain." He came out into the middle of the room, facing Richard. "If my going will make you feel better, I can do that."

Richard hung his head, his newly long hair hiding most of his face. When he raised it again he looked like a man coming out of deep water, shaking his hair back from his face. "Insult to injury, damn it."

"Did I say something wrong?" Sampson asked.

"No, nothing wrong," Richard said. He sighed, and his arms started to unfold, stiffly, as if it hurt him to let go of the anger. "No, I just didn't want to like you."

Sampson looked puzzled. "I don't understand."

"If I can hate you, I can get angry, and storm out. If you'd acted like some kind of lustful asshole, I could have just gone. Wrapped my injured righteousness around me, and gotten the hell out of here."

I stood up and faced him; Jean-Claude kept my hand lightly in his. "I've already told you, Richard," I said, "you don't have to pick a fight to leave."

"Yes," he said, "I do. Because I know that I cripple us as a power by simply not being here when you need me. If I'd been here, Auggie wouldn't have rolled you. I have no one but myself to blame that you and Jean-Claude fucked Auggie." His voice held the edge of warmth, and the first bite of his power flickered through the room.

I took a few steps, leaving Jean-Claude's hand behind. "Why are you responsible for everything?" I asked. "I deal with more undead than you do; I should have been able to protect myself. And maybe I should have seen it coming, but I'm not beating myself up about it. It happened, and now we deal with it."

"Is it really that easy for you, Anita? It happened, now we deal with it, we move on?"

I thought about it, then nodded. "Yes, it is, because it has to be. My life wouldn't work if I wallowed in every disaster, every moral quandary. I can't afford the luxury of self-doubt, not to that degree."

"Luxury," Richard said. "This isn't luxury, Anita, it's morality. It's your conscience. That's not a luxury item, that's what separates us from the animals."

Here we go again, I thought. Out loud I said, "I have a conscience, Richard, and my own set of morals. Do I ever worry that I'm a bad guy? Yeah, sometimes I do. Do I wonder if I've traded away pieces of my soul, just to survive? Yeah." I shrugged. "It's the price of doing business in the real world, Richard."

"This isn't the real world, Anita. This isn't the normal workaday world."

"No, but it's our world." I was facing him now, almost close enough to touch. He was controlling himself, because his power was only a warm pressure in the air.

He waved his hands around the room. "This is not where I want to be, Anita. I don't want to live where my choices are sharing you with other men, or having people die. I don't want those choices."

I sighed, and let him see that I was tired, and sad, and sorry. "There was a time when I would have agreed with you, but I like parts of my life a lot, Richard. I hate the *ardeur*, but I don't hate everything it's brought into my life. I'd have liked to try that whole picket-fence thing, but I think even without the *ardeur* and the vampire marks, that it wouldn't have been my gig."

"I think it would have been," he said.

"Richard, I don't think you see me. I don't think you see who I am."

"How can you say that to me? If I don't shield I share your dreams, and your nightmares."

"But you're still trying to shove me in a box that I don't think fit me even when we met. Just like you're trying to shove yourself into a box that doesn't fit you, either."

He was shaking his head. "That's not true. That's not true."

"Which part?" I asked.

"I think we could have made it, our version of the white picket fence, without him," and he pointed at Jean-Claude.

Jean-Claude was giving his most peaceful, empty face, as if he were afraid to do or say anything.

"Don't try to blame all our problems on Jean-Claude."

"Why not, it's true. If he had left us alone, not marked us."

"You'd be dead," I said.

He frowned at me. "What?"

"Without the extra power of the marks with Jean-Claude you'd never have had the power to kill Marcus and keep the pack."

"That's not true."

I just stared at him. "Yeah, Richard, I was there, it is true. You'd be dead, and I'd still be living alone sleeping with my stuffed toys and guns. You'd be dead and I'd be dead inside, dying of loneliness, not just because you would be gone, but because my life was empty before. I was like a lot of people who do police work. I was my job. I had nothing else. My life was full of death, and horror, and trying to stay ahead of the next horror. But I was losing the battle, Richard, losing myself, long before Jean-Claude marked me."

"I asked you to give up the police work. I told you it was eating you up."

I shook my head. "You're not listening to me, Richard, or you're not hearing me."

"Maybe I don't want to hear you. Or maybe I'm right, and you're not listening."

We stood barely two feet apart, but it might as well have been a thousand miles. Some distances are made out of things bigger and harder to travel across than mere miles. We stood and stared at each other across a chasm of misunderstanding, and pain, and love.

I tried one last time. "Say you're right. Say if Jean-Claude had left us alone you could have your perfect picture. I still wouldn't have given up on the police work."

"You just said, it was destroying you."

I nodded. "Just because something's hard doesn't mean you give up on it." Somehow I thought I was talking about more than just police work.

"You said I was right."

"I said, say you're right. Let's just pretend that without Jean-Claude here, we would have found a way. But we are bound to him, Richard. We are a tri-umvirate of power. What we would change if life were totally different doesn't really matter."

"How can you say that?"

"What matters, Richard, is that we deal with the reality of our now, this minute. There are things we can't undo, and we all have to work together to make the best of what's true in our lives."

His face was cold with his anger. I hated his face like this, because it was both frightening and more beautiful, as if the anger cleaned away something that distracted the eye from realizing just how amazingly handsome he was. "And what is true in our lives?" His power began to flow through the room, hot water, hotter than you'd want in the bath. The guards around the room shifted uneasily.

"I am Jean-Claude's human servant. You are his animal to call. We are a triumvirate of power. We can't change that. Jean-Claude and I both carry the *ardeur*. We both need to feed the hunger, and that's not going to change."

"I thought you were hoping to be able to feed from a distance at the clubs, the way Jean-Claude did under Nikolaos."

"It crippled his power, which is what the ex–Master of the City wanted to do. I'm not going to cripple us magically because I'm squeamish. No more hiding, Richard. The *ardeur* is here to stay, and I need to feed it."

He shook his head. "No."

"No, what?"

He let down his shields. I don't know if it was on purpose, or his emotions got the better of him. Whatever the cause I suddenly heard his thoughts like clear bells in my head: he thought that once I got the *ardeur* under control I'd dump Micah and Nathaniel and live with him. Be with him. He still hoped, seriously, that some day we'd be a nice little monogamous pair.

It took only seconds for me to get all of it, but his shields coming down had brought mine down, too, and he felt my shock. My disbelief that he still thought, seriously, that that would ever happen.

I felt the next thought forming, and tried to stop it, tried to keep it half-formed, or to shut him out, but the emotions were too raw, and I wasn't fast enough. The thought was, *Even if I am pregnant, it would never work.*

Richard's face showed the shock now. He gaped at me, and whispered, "Pregnant."

I said the only thing that came to mind. "Fuck."

15

I SLAMMED EVERY shield I had in place, shut, tight, metal, closed. I thought *metal*, smooth and thick and impenetrable. I stared at the floor, afraid to meet anyone's eyes. Afraid of what I'd see in their faces, or what I wouldn't.

"Anita," Richard said, and his hand reached for me.

I stepped out of reach. I was shaking my head. I didn't know what I wanted out of this moment, didn't know what reaction would please me, and which one would piss me off. I'd hoped to keep it secret until I knew for sure. I did not want to open this can of emotional worms until it was a done deal.

It was Samuel who broke the silence. "Congratulations to both of you. A baby, joyous news indeed."

I turned slowly to look at him, because of anyone in the room I cared least what he thought about the news. Him, I could look at. Him, I could be angry with.

Sampson was already touching his father's shoulder. "Father, I think we should leave now."

Samuel was looking from his son, to me, to Jean-Claude, to most of the people around the room. He looked utterly confused. "But this is wonderful news, and you're all acting as if someone has died."

"Father," Sampson said, soft and warningly. He was looking at my face, and whatever he saw there made him grab his father's elbow and try to get him on his feet.

He stared at his son's hand until Sampson let it drop away. Samuel then met my gaze. His eyes didn't look friendly now. They looked older, full of some deep knowledge, and sad around the edges, and angry. "Why such anger, Anita?"

I started to count to twenty, knew it wouldn't be enough, and just said it, in a voice that was choking with anger, confusion. "Don't tell me how to feel, Samuel, you don't have that right."

He stood up, and pushed his son's hands away from him. "Think how powerful a child you and Jean-Claude could have."

"There's no guarantee it's his," I said.

"The odds are that if you are pregnant, it won't be any of the vampires," Richard said. His voice was low and careful, but there was something underneath all that that I hadn't wanted to hear—eagerness.

I turned to him, and I don't know what I would have said, or even done, because Jean-Claude was just suddenly there between us. "Do not do anything rash, *ma petite*."

"Rash, don't do anything rash!" I pulled away from him. "He's not unhappy about this and you're locked down so tight I don't know what you're feeling."

"I feel that anything I say, or do, in this moment, will upset you." It was the most diplomatic way I'd ever been told that I was a pain in the ass.

I fought the urge to scream at him. I managed a voice that was strangled low and tense with the effort not to yell. "Say something," I said.

"Are you with child?" he asked in that neutral, pleasant voice of his.

"I don't know, but I missed October."

Richard came closer and he tried for neutral, failed, but he tried. "Have you ever missed a whole month before?"

I shook my head. "No."

Emotions fought on his face, and finally he had to turn away, as if whatever expression he had, he was sure I wouldn't want to see it.

"Don't you dare be happy about this, damn it!"

He turned back, face mostly under control, but his eyes held that look. That soft I-love-you look that once was meant just for me, but which lately I hadn't seen much of. I'd seen lust, but not this.

"Would you prefer me to be angry, or sad?" he asked.

"No, yes, I don't know." There, that was the truth. "I don't know."

"I'm sorry," he said, and he looked it around the edges. "Sorry if I'm making this harder, but how could I be completely unhappy if we made a child together?"

He would pick the very worst way to say it. The way most guaranteed to panic me. "It's not a child, yet. It's a bunch of cells smaller than my thumb."

His eyes got more careful. "What are you saying, Anita?"

I hugged myself tight and wouldn't meet anyone's eyes. "I don't know what I'm saying." But I was beginning to have more sympathy with Ronnie's idea about just going away and making the choice without any of the men.

"Would you really be able to kill our baby?" he asked, and I didn't have to see his face to know he looked hurt; I could hear it in his voice.

"*Mon ami*, you put the cart before the horse. Let her find out if she is pregnant before we make plans." Jean-Claude tried to move between us again, tried to block my view of Richard, as if that would help.

Richard moved around him, so he could still see me. "Anita, could you really kill our baby?"

I wanted to scream *yes*, just to see the pain on his face, but on this I couldn't lie. I already knew the answer, I just didn't like it. "NO!" I yelled it, and the sound echoed against the stones without the hanging drapes to soften it.

Richard's face softened and he started to walk toward me, around Jean-Claude. The look on his face was almost beatific, as if all his dreams had come true. I felt as if I were suffocating in a nightmare, and he looked like that. I had to wipe that look off his face, I had to.

"What if it's not yours?" I asked, and my voice was ugly. I wanted it to hurt.

He hesitated, then got a look that was almost smug. "The odds are in my favor, Anita." He looked entirely too pleased with himself.

"Why, just because Jean-Claude and Asher, and hell, Damian are several hundred years old? That doesn't mean it's not theirs; look at Samuel. He has three sons, two separate pregnancies."

Richard started to frown. He wasn't walking closer now. Good.

Jean-Claude sighed, and stepped back as if he'd given up trying to stop the fight.

"And what about Micah and Nathaniel?" I asked. "They're not vampires and I've had more sex with them in the last two months than with you." I was happy when he flinched. Ugly, but true.

"Micah's fixed," he said, and his face darkened. "That leaves Nathaniel." There was such anger in those three words, that I wished I'd left it alone.

As if on cue, Micah and Nathaniel came out of the far hallway. They looked at all of us and Micah said, "Is this about what I think it's about?"

"You knew about the baby?" Richard asked.

"Are we sure?" Nathaniel asked.

"No," I said.

"You both knew?" Richard said, and his power started up again. I was suddenly standing too close to the metaphorical fire.

"Yes, we knew," Micah said.

"You told them before you told us?" Richard said, and he gestured at Jean-Claude.

"They live with me, Richard, it's harder to keep a secret from them. I didn't want any of you to know until I did a test. I didn't want to deal with all this crap, if I didn't have to."

"Let us calm down until we know for certain," Jean-Claude said.

"Doesn't it bother you that she told them before us?" Richard said.

"No, *mon ami*, it does not."

Richard glared at Micah and Nathaniel, but his gaze finally settled on Nathaniel. Not good. "You know that if she is pregnant, it's probably you, or me," Richard said. The words were neutral; the tone wasn't. The tone was a warning as clear as the heat rolling off his body.

Nathaniel had one of the most careful looks I'd ever seen on his face. He looked blank, pleasant, but not sorry, not submissive. Always before when dealing with Richard, Nathaniel had given off subservient vibes. Now, suddenly, there was nothing subservient about him. He might still bottom to me, but his days of doing it for Richard were over. It was there in the set of his shoulders, the eye contact he gave the bigger man. He wasn't being aggressive, but he wasn't giving off those subtle submissive signals either. His attitude said, clearly, he wasn't backing down. On one hand I was happy to see it, on the other hand it scared me. I'd seen Richard fight and I'd seen Nathaniel fight. I knew who would win.

Of course, if Richard started the fight, he would win the slugfest, but he'd lose the girl. I hoped he understood that.

16

I DON'T KNOW what would have happened. Something bad, almost certainly, but help came. "You guys are all being assholes." It was Claudia.

Everyone turned to look at her.

"How dare you make this about some macho ego shit. Can't you see she's scared?" She gestured in my direction. "Ulfric, if you think a baby will make her give up the police work and the execution work, or the zombie raising, you're wrong. Do you see a baby fitting into Anita's life? Are you going to quit work and stay home and play nanny, because Anita sure isn't."

We all looked at Richard. He was scowling at her.

"Well," she said, "are you? Are you willing to completely disrupt your life if it's yours?"

He scowled harder. "I don't know," he said, finally.

"I will." Nathaniel's voice, turning us all back to him. "I'm already the wife, why not the mother?"

"Have you ever taken care of a baby?" Claudia asked.

He shrugged. "No."

"I had four younger brothers, trust me, it's harder than it looks."

"I will," Micah said. "Whatever Anita wants, or needs."

"Stop being perfect," Richard said.

"You work days, Richard," Nathaniel said, "and you work a regular weekday. I can make more part-time at Guilty Pleasures than any teacher's salary I've ever heard of."

"So you'd be a good provider," Richard said, and his voice was full of scorn.

Nathaniel smiled, and shook his head. "Anita provides for herself just fine. She doesn't need my money. What I meant was that dropping my work hours down won't affect my job that much. It would ruin yours."

Richard didn't want to be mollified. He wanted to be angry, so he turned to Micah. "And what about you? You work as many hours as Anita does."

"I would need more help running the hotline and the coalition. We would have nearly a year to train someone to help me, or even replace me, if that's what was needed."

"It can't be your baby," Richard said.

"Genetically, no."

"What does that mean, genetically?"

"It means that just because it's not blood of my blood doesn't mean it's not mine. Ours."

"Yours and Anita's," and the words singed along my skin. So much power, so much anger, it actually hurt.

"No," Micah said, "Anita's and Nathaniel's, and Jean-Claude's, and Asher's and Damian's and yours, and mine. Leaving a little bit of sperm behind doesn't make you a father. It's what you do afterward, Richard."

"You can't bring up a baby with seven fathers."

"Call it what you like," Micah said, "but the only two men in this room able to totally disrupt their lives if there is a baby are Nathaniel and me." He looked at Jean-Claude. "Or am I wrong?"

Jean-Claude smiled at him. "No, *mon chat*, you are not. I do not believe that a baby could spend all its time in the underground of the Circus of the Damned and be"—he seemed to search for a word—"well-balanced. Visits, *oui*, many visits, but the world I have built here is not"—again he searched for a word—"conducive to the upbringing of small children."

"I'm a small child," came a small sweet voice from behind us. Apparently we'd all been so caught up that we hadn't heard the approach of the tiny girl. Of course, Valentina was a vampire, and the undead are quiet bastards.

Her dark hair curled just below her ears. She'd cut it recently, to look more modern. Her face was round, and soft, not long past being a baby. She was five, and would always be five, at least physically. She was wearing a red dress with white tights, and little white patent leather shoes. When she came to us she'd worn nothing designed after 1800. She still wouldn't wear pants or shorts, because it wasn't ladylike, but she had arrived in the twentieth century, at least in fashion. She blinked large dark eyes at us, her face perfectly innocent. At Belle's court she had tortured people for information, for punishment, and because she enjoyed it. Jean-Claude told me that all the child vampires go mad eventually. It was why it was against their laws to bring anyone over before puberty.

Valentina had been made by a pedophile who happened to be a vampire. He had been given an isolated territory, and there he had made his own special playmates for almost fifty years before someone discovered what he was doing. Valentina had been one of the lucky ones. He'd brought her over, but hadn't made her one of his brides, yet. Most of his "brides" and "grooms" had to be destroyed. Too mad, too savage, for anything else. That one of "her" vampires had done such things was one of her few things that Belle Morte seemed to feel guilty about.

"Yes," Jean-Claude said, "of course you are. You are our *petite fleur*." He moved forward as if he would herd her out of earshot of the grown-up talk. She may have looked five, but she was over three hundred years old. The body was a child's, the mind was not. But unless we were careful, most of us had a tendency to treat her like she looked, not like she thought.

She turned that tiny face to mine, with those solemn eyes. "Are you going to have a baby?"

"Maybe," I said.

She smiled, flashing fangs as delicate as needles. "I would have someone to play with."

Jean-Claude started to take her hand, then hesitated in midgesture. He had suffered at Valentina's hands more than once. He never truly forgot she was a monster. He said, "Where is Bartolome? He's supposed to be watching you today, isn't he?"

"I don't know where he is," she said, gazing up at Jean-Claude.

He laid the barest touch on her shoulder. She looked past him to me. The look in those eyes had nothing to do with childhood.

"She's over three hundred years old, Jean-Claude, don't shush her away like she's really five."

He looked at me. "Valentina prefers to be treated as a child, it is her choice." He gazed down at her. "Don't you, *ma dulce*?" He lied with his voice, but he did not touch her as if she were a child.

She nodded, but those eyes gazed at me. Those eyes that held centuries of power trapped in a body too delicate to do most of the things in her mind. There were nights when I felt sorry for her; then there were moments, like now, when I wasn't certain that she'd have been sane even if she'd come over as an adult. There was simply something in her that wasn't quite right. It was sort of a chicken/egg question on Valentina's sanity. She'd never hurt me. Never done anything to purposefully frighten me. But she was on my short list of people that I wouldn't have trusted if I'd been helpless and alone with her. It had taken me months to realize that the reason she creeped me out was only partly the whole trapped-in-a-child's-body thing. Months to admit to myself that I was more afraid of Valentina than any other vamp who called Jean-Claude master.

"I think having a baby around would be fun," she said.

"Fun, how?" I asked, not sure I wanted to hear the answer.

"I wouldn't be the smallest anymore," she said. It should have been an innocent statement, so why did I suddenly have the urge to tell her that if she tried to change my baby over into a vampire littler than herself, I would fucking kill her? Paranoid, or just cautious? So hard to tell the difference sometimes.

Richard moved closer to me, and I let him. I wasn't the only one who felt something was terribly wrong with her. He put his arm across my shoulders, and I let him do that, too. Staring into Valentina's eyes I would have let almost anyone comfort me.

"No," I said, slowly, "no, not too much time at the Circus."

Micah moved closer to us, not touching me, because Richard never seemed to like that. He'd tolerate Jean-Claude touching me with him, but almost no one else. But I wasn't the only one weirded out by the "little girl."

Jean-Claude looked back at us, still touching her shoulder. "I must find Bartolome, and chastise him for not watching her better."

Valentina pulled away from Jean-Claude, and he let her go. She started walking farther into the room. Richard drew me in tighter against his body. Micah moved so that he was standing almost in front of me, blocking her from coming closer to me. Normally, I might have told him it wasn't necessary, but I didn't like how interested she'd been in the whole idea of the baby.

Valentina walked around us. The tension in my shoulders eased. Richard's breath eased out in something like a sigh. Micah didn't relax. He stayed tense just in front of us, as if he didn't trust she wouldn't circle back. She walked toward Samuel and Sampson.

"What are you doing, little one?" Jean-Claude said.

She gave a perfect, and very low, curtsey, holding her little dress out with her hands, ankles crossing as she went down. "Greetings, Samuel, Master of Cape Cod."

"Greetings, Valentina," he said.

She offered him her hand. He took the tiny hand in his, and laid the barest touch of his mouth upon her wrist. It was all protocol, perfectly acceptable, but the gesture showed better than any words that he wasn't comfy with her either.

She turned to Sampson. She gazed up at him, her head tilted back, very childlike, but I would have bet anything I had that the searching look on her face wouldn't be childlike. I'd had her stare at me before, and knew that the face didn't match the intensity and personality in the eyes. "Is this your son?"

"Yes, his name is Sampson."

She held her tiny hand out to him, too. He took it, but seemed unsure what to do with it. "I am not a vampire," he said, "nor anyone's servant, or animal to call."

"But you are his son, his heir. I am just one more vampire. I am not even a true master." She was saying that he outranked her.

Sampson glanced at his father, who must have given him some look, because he raised the tiny hand to his mouth. He, like his father, did the minimum touch he could get away with. He, like his father, kept eye contact with her while he did it. It reminded me of how you bow on the mat in judo. You keep your eyes up as you do it, never looking away from your opponent, just in case. But there was a difference between the two men. One was a very master vampire. The other was not. He was part human and part mermaid, and maybe someday he would be more, but tonight, he wasn't.

"Pick me up," she said, in that high little-girl voice.

He picked her up and sat her in his lap. She cuddled against him. He was blinking out at the room, frowning. His face looked almost like he was in pain.

"Shit," I said softly. She had rolled him, rolled him with her eyes.

Jean-Claude said, "Valentina, he is our guest."

Samuel raised a hand up. "I run my kiss in the old way. He is my son, my eldest; if he cannot win free of a vampire who is not even a master . . ." He left the sentence unfinished.

"You make him earn his place constantly," Jean-Claude said.

Samuel nodded.

I'd never even heard of the rule he was talking about. I said so. "I don't even know this rule."

"It is a version of survival of the fittest, *ma petite*. If Sampson is not strong enough to break free, or avoid Valentina's trickery, then he is a little less worthy in his master's eyes. It is a way that some Masters of the City separate the weak from the strong. Those who fail these tests often are demoted, traded to other lands, or killed." His voice was matter-of-fact, but I knew him well enough to taste the faint disapproval. "Very few American masters run their lands with this rule."

"I am older than most of the American masters," Samuel said.

I looked at Jean-Claude and he met my look. "But she's our vampire, and we don't live by this rule."

Richard hugged me, one-armed, as if he were afraid of what I'd do, or say.

"If his father decrees that Sampson must break free of her gaze by himself, then it is so, but we will make it very clear to all our vampires that this gaze is illegal in our country. It is seen as coercion." He stared at Valentina as he said it.

She pouted her lower lip out at him, and snuggled in tighter to Sampson. He put his arms around her, as if in response to the cuddling, or maybe she'd used mind tricks. If she'd rolled him enough not to need words to boss him around, we were in deeper trouble than I'd thought. Because once vampires roll you that much, they own you. They can reclaim their victims at any time. They can stand under their windows and call them out into the night. Hell, some of them can call their victims across town like sleepwalkers. If Valentina had rolled him that badly, he'd give her blood anytime she asked. He'd have no choice.

I don't know what I would have done, but suddenly there was new energy in the room. The air smelled fresher, faintly of salt and sea. Sampson's eyes cleared, that confused, bemused look fading. His eyes changed from the hazel of his father's to the flat black of his mother's. He stared down at the vampire in his lap, and his face had a look that I'd seen before. It was a look that said his seemingly youthful face held wisdom decades beyond the outside packaging. He gazed down at Valentina with a face that showed he had lived every day of seventy years. That he was no more his twenty-something, nice-guy-next-door package than Valentina was a child.

He tried to lift her out of his lap, but she clung to him, playing the child for all she was worth. "Don't you like me, Sampson?"

He shook his head. "No," he said, "I do not like you."

She pouted at him, even managing to feign tears, as if he'd hurt her feelings. Maybe he had. Valentina was hard to figure.

He drew her away from his body, and set her firmly on the ground. "You will not be able to trick me again, for I felt your mind. You are not a child, Valentina. You do not think as a child." He shivered, rubbing his hands up and down his arms as if to cleanse them from the feel of holding her. "I saw what you wanted to do to me. What you tried to persuade me I wanted to do." He shivered again. "Your mind has begun to want things beyond your body's years. Pain is your substitute for sex."

She put her hands on her hips, and stomped her little foot. "I don't know what you are talking about. Perhaps it is you that desires such things." Then she turned to Jean-Claude. "Master, can you not find one among all the visitors who would let me hurt him? I miss it." She said it as if there were no contradiction in telling Sampson he was the pervert, and then asking to do what he'd accused her of wanting to do.

Jean-Claude sighed. "Asher, if you would take her back to Bartolome."

Asher pushed himself up from the chair where he'd gone nearly motionless during all the hoopla. But Nathaniel said, "I'll take her."

We all looked at him.

He smiled. "You need to talk vampire business with Samuel. Asher will be more useful for that than I will." He walked toward us to say good night, and

Micah moved out of the way, so he could lean in toward me. Richard's arm was still holding me close to his body. He tensed, and moved as if he'd take me out of Nathaniel's reach.

Nathaniel touched his arm, and Richard froze. His power lashed out like lightning scoring along my skin.

"Ouch, Richard, that fucking hurt."

Nathaniel shivered. "That really did hurt." But his voice didn't sound like a complaint.

"Back up," Richard said, his voice holding an edge of growl. He was controlling his power enough so it didn't actively hurt me, but it was like cuddling next to a stove that you just knew was going to get too hot to touch soon.

Nathaniel smiled and pushed in against us both, pressing his chest against Richard's arm. Richard moved away, but he tried to take me with him, and frankly, I just didn't want to be in the middle of it. So I stopped moving, but Nathaniel was so close I couldn't step forward either. Richard had choices: pick me up, or hurt me to move me, or let me go, or move away without me, or stay where he was, with Nathaniel touching him.

Richard tried to move back, while I tried not to move, and Nathaniel just watched us, from an inch away. Richard wasn't willing to move without me, or leave me alone with Nathaniel. The symbolism was too raw for words.

Nathaniel spoke low and soft, his lavender eyes raised to the taller man's face, his chest almost pinning Richard's arm between us. "You're like a dog marking your territory. Maybe you should piss on her, so we'll all know she's yours."

I froze between them, because this was going to be bad.

Richard growled low and deep, the sound of it vibrating over my skin, and into Nathaniel's body. We both shivered, but I don't think it was for the same reasons.

"Stop it, both of you," I said.

"She's not a bone, that only one of us can have," Nathaniel said.

Richard growled again and this time Richard's power rippled along my skin like little slaps of electricity. Nathaniel and I spoke at the same time. I said, "That hurts"; Nathaniel said, "Yummy."

"You are such a freak," Richard said, almost a yell.

"Maybe, but this freak is willing to do for the woman he loves and his baby what you won't do."

Richard jerked away so suddenly, it made me stumble. Nathaniel caught me. But Richard backed up. Nathaniel backed him down not with power, but with truth.

Nathaniel held me, and I let him, because if I'd pulled away now, the whole show would have been wasted. I'd hung around the lycanthropes long enough to understand what was happening. Nathaniel, my submissive Nathaniel, was stepping up to bat. He was showing the most dominant person in my bed that he was a force to be reckoned with. Why tonight? Why did Nathaniel have to draw his line in the sand tonight? The baby, of course, the baby. Something about the whole baby question had made Nathaniel feel like he had to be more dominant. Or maybe he, like me, was just tired of watching Richard say he was the dominant sweetie in my life, but acting like he was my fuck buddy. Nothing wrong with a fuck buddy, but you can't be the love of someone's life and a fuck buddy. They are mutually exclusive.

Nathaniel held me, and I wrapped my arms around him, hidng my face against his chest, because I wasn't sure what expression was on my face. Nathaniel had stood up to Richard and won. What else was going to change just because of the possibility of a baby?

"I'll take Valentina. You guys stay and talk business."

"You're part of the business," Micah said from behind us.

"But you can fill me in later, and I'm not really going to have an opinion on the vampire stuff." He grinned. "I'm also the least likely to object to anyone Anita is willing to take as a *pomme*, or a lover." He kissed me on the forehead, and whispered, "Besides, Valentina doesn't bother me."

I looked up at him. "And that bothers me a little, that you're not creeped."

The grin softened to a smile. "I know." He kissed me on the mouth, soft, gentle. He pulled away, and I let him go, still not sure what had changed in him.

Valentina came to him, and he took her hand. He began to lead her toward the far hallway. She looked back and stuck her tongue out at us.

Claudia sent Lisandro to accompany them. Aloud, she said, "Make sure Bartolome isn't doing anything he shouldn't." But I was pretty sure after Valentina's show with Sampson, she just didn't trust any of the non-vamps alone with her. Me, either.

17

"HOW CAN YOU love him?" Richard asked.

I turned to look at him. He stood, shoulders hunched, rubbing his hands up and down his arms, as if he were cold. But I knew he wasn't cold, or at least not the kind of cold that blankets and skin warmth could fix. It was a coldness of the heart, or the soul, or the mind. That cold that eats a hole through the middle of who you are, and leaves something dark and awful behind.

I looked at him, and wondered how to answer his question. How to answer without making the pain in his body worse. I sighed, and finally realized that the only thing I could give him was the truth. Whatever we were to each other, whatever else we might someday be to each other, truth, at least truth, was between us.

"I asked you a question," he said, and his power warmed the room like opening an oven to peek inside. The heat dissipated almost as soon as I'd felt it. He was trying to control himself.

"Why do I love Nathaniel?" I asked.

"That's what I asked," he said, in that angry voice.

"Because he never makes me feel like a freak."

"Because he is a freak," Richard snarled. "Anyone looks sane beside him."

I felt my face shutting down. Felt that flatness that I used when I was really pissed and trying to control it.

"Perhaps this is not the time for this conversation," Jean-Claude said in a careful voice.

We both ignored him.

"First," I said in a very tight, careful voice, "Nathaniel is not a freak. Second, he's willing to disrupt his entire life if he got me pregnant, and you're not. So I'd be careful before you throw stones at his character."

"If you're pregnant, I'll marry you."

The room was suddenly full of one of those silences so thick you should have been able to walk across it. I stared at him for a second, or two, then said, "Jesus, Mary, and Joseph, Richard, is that all you think it takes to fix this? Marry me so the baby won't be a bastard, and it's all better?"

"I don't see anyone else offering marriage," he said.

"It's because they know I'll say no. Every other man in my life understands that this isn't about marriage. It's about the fact that we may have created a little person. And we need to do whatever is best for that person. How will marrying anyone make this work better?"

He looked at me, and there was such pain in his face, such struggle, as if I'd said something incomprehensible. "If you get a woman pregnant, you marry her, Anita. It's called taking responsibility for your actions."

"And if it's not your baby? Could you really raise someone else's baby? Could you really stay married to me, and play Daddy, as you watched the baby grow to look like someone else?"

He covered his face with his hands, and he screamed, "No!" He showed me a face ravaged by rage. The room was suddenly hot again, as if his power were raising the actual temperature. "No, I'd go crazy. Is that what you wanted to hear? Is it?"

"No," I said, "but you needed to hear it."

He frowned at me. "What?"

"I appreciate the offer, Richard. Really, I do, but if I was going to marry anyone, it would have to be someone who would be okay no matter who turned out to be the father."

"So, you'll marry Nathaniel, or Micah?" The heat bit along my skin.

"I am not going to marry anyone, don't you get that?"

"You just said—"

I cut him off. "No, that isn't what I said, or what I meant. It's what you heard."

"You're pregnant, Anita."

"*Maybe* I'm pregnant," I said.

"Don't you want a father for your baby?"

I stared at him, wondering what could I say that he'd actually hear and understand.

Jean-Claude stepped close to us, not between us, but as if the three of us were a shallow triangle. "I believe what *ma petite* is saying, Richard, is that marriage is not part of her plans, and that having a baby will not change that." His voice was his pleasantly neutral one, the one that he used when he was trying to persuade, or calm, and not make things worse.

"And if it's my baby, then I'm just supposed to be okay with Nathaniel and Micah raising it?"

I hung my head. What could I say to that?

"Ulfric," Claudia said, yelling that one word, the way a drill sergeant yells at a bad recruit.

He looked at her. "What?" His power bit along my skin again.

"First, control your power, it's biting along everyone's skin. You're the wolf king, you need to set a better example."

"What I set for my people is my business, rat."

She continued as if he hadn't spoken. "Second, you're making Anita feel worse than she already does."

He made a wordless sound, almost a yell. His power went back to just being heat, but not painful. His voice came careful, each word thick with suppressed rage. He was swallowing it, but it was still there. "I don't want to make Anita feel worse, but if she's pregnant then she has to know that she can't keep living the life she's living."

"You still want to trap her," Claudia said, "trap her and put her in some kind of 1950s cage."

"Marriage is not a trap," he said. "You make it sound like I want her barefoot and pregnant."

"Don't you?" she asked, and her anger was softer now, as if she finally understood he wasn't being a jerk, he just didn't understand himself.

"No," he said, and he meant it. He turned back to me. "You said it yourself, Anita, whatever's best for this little person. Do you really think being a federal marshal, and dealing with all kinds of violent crime and monsters, is the kind of life that a baby needs?"

"Jesus, Richard," I said, "you're still trying to take away my life. To take away what makes me who I am. You love me, but not who I am. You love who you want me to be."

"Isn't that what you want from me?" he said. "Don't you want me to change who I am, too?"

I started to say no, then stopped myself. I thought about it. Was I asking him to change as much as he was asking me? "I want you to embrace the life you already have, and be happy in it, Richard. You want me to totally change my life, and try to fit in some white-picket-fence picture that doesn't match your life, or mine."

"I am so sick of you accusing me of wanting to put you behind a white picket fence."

"I may be pregnant, and suddenly you want me to marry you, and give up being a federal agent. We aren't even sure there is a baby, and you're already trying to impose your idea of what our life should be on me."

"Could you really keep working on serial killer cases, and killing monsters, after you have a baby?"

I stared at him. "What do you think having a baby will do to me, Richard? Do you think just because I have a baby I'll become this other person? This softer, gentler person? Is that what you think?"

"May I add something to this discussion?" Samuel asked.

Richard and I said no; Jean-Claude said yes. Samuel ignored us and did what Jean-Claude said.

"If my wife is any example of having children in these rather extraordinary circumstances, then softer is not what will happen. Thea was gentle with the children. There was indeed a new softness that I had never seen, but with everyone else . . ." He shook his head. "I had never seen her so ruthless as after Sampson was born. She was more determined than ever to make our base of power strong and secure. Any threat to us was destroyed immediately. Even with the help of servants she insisted on caring for him herself, and with the feedings, well"—he shrugged with hands up—"having to wake every two hours to breast-feed meant very little sleep. Lack of sleep makes anyone's temper worse, and makes the most expedient solution look good."

I was thinking, *Breast-feeding*? Oh, no, so not my gig.

Richard said, "You're saying that to make me feel what—worse, better?"

"Ask someone you trust then," Samuel said. "Ask a woman how exhausting and overwhelming a new baby can be. I have three children, two of them twins. I did what many fathers do when they have children later in life; I did more of the baby care with the twins than I did with Sampson. My power base was more secure, and there was less . . . business to occupy me. I think I had been too exposed to modern America. I had this odd idea that I should be very involved with the twins. It gave me a new respect for what Thea went through with Sampson, when I was more occupied with business. A child is a great blessing"—he patted his son's leg when he said it—"but like other great blessings, they require a great deal of time, attention, and energy."

I shook my head, waving my hands in the air as if to erase all of this. "I can't deal with this now. We've got to change topic, at least until I take the test and find out for sure. If the test's positive then we can talk, but until we know for sure, this topic is closed."

"You can't just change the topic," Richard said.

"Yes," Jean-Claude said, "she can."

"What if I don't want to change the topic?" Again I got the impression that Richard was spoiling for a fight.

Micah finally said something. "Anita is only asking to change the topic until we know for sure, Richard. That makes sense."

"You stay out of this!" Richard yelled it at him.

"Don't yell at Micah!" I yelled at him.

"I'll yell at whoever I want to yell at," he yelled.

Claudia yelled us both to silence. A huge, deep sound that made us all look at her. "Are your hurt feelings the only thing that matters here, Ulfric?" She shook her head. "Nathaniel's right, you'd piss on her if you could, if that would make her yours and yours alone."

He growled and took a step toward her.

"No," Jean-Claude said, "no, Richard."

"Are you picking a fight with him?" Micah asked. He sounded puzzled. He was right, it wasn't like Claudia to start the fight. She'd finish the fight, but not start it.

She actually looked at the floor. I think she was counting to ten. "I don't want to start a fight with anyone, but I'm tired of the attitude."

"What attitude?" I asked.

She pointed at Richard. "His attitude."

She wasn't the only one, but out loud, I said, "I don't think your starting a fight with Richard will make me feel better."

"I'm sorry for that." Then she gave Richard a completely hostile look. "But he's like so many men. He thinks that if he could just get you pregnant, just get you married, you'd be the perfect little woman."

"I do not think that," Richard said.

"You don't?" she said.

"No," he said.

"Then what's with the proposal?"

"You're supposed to propose if you've got someone pregnant."

She gave a nod. "And what's with Anita not being a federal marshal, or a vampire executioner?"

"The life she's living right now just doesn't seem like the kind of life that would be good for a baby."

"No," I said, "it doesn't."

He turned and looked at me. "You agree with me."

"Yes, of course, I agree that my life won't work with a baby. But this is the only life I have, Richard. This is who I am. I can't remake myself just because there may be a baby."

"Yes," he said, "you can. If you want to badly enough, you can change."

"Are you going to give up being a teacher?"

He looked away, and shook his head. "I love being a teacher."

"And I love being a federal marshal."

"You hate it, too."

"Yeah, sometimes I hate it, and maybe I'll burn out on all the violent cases. Maybe I'll reach a point where I can't do it anymore. But I do enjoy the police work, and I'm good at it."

"You enjoy seeing mutilated corpses?"

I shook my head. "Get out."

"What?"

"*Ma petite*, please," Jean-Claude said, and came to hold me. I didn't pull away, but I stayed stiff and unyielding in his arms. I was so angry I couldn't even think. All I knew for certain was that I needed Richard to be somewhere else, because if he stayed here saying stupid shit, I was going to say something unforgivable, or he was. We were close to the kind of fight that there is no fix for.

Samuel's pleasant and oh-so-reasonable voice came. "Perhaps we should discuss the topics that will allow all of you to survive this weekend, and keep sovereignty of your own territory in your own hands."

That got everyone's attention, even Richard's. "What are you talking about?" he said.

"If Anita's powers are as disruptive to other Masters of the City as they have been to Augustine, then what will you do? What will the other masters do when they see Augustine follow her and Jean-Claude around like a lovesick dog? She ordered Augustine around, she exhibited necromancy that controlled a Master of the City. That is legend among us, Ulfric, but not present reality. I saw Augustine strain against her compulsion. I do not know, even now, whether he used his full powers on Anita because he wished for sex with a woman of the *ardeur* once more, or to keep her from bespelling him completely. Better to be tied to her by love and lust than by blind obedience. In truth, I am not certain that Augustine himself knows why he did it, or what might have happened if he had chosen another defense." Samuel sighed. "You cannot take her to the ballet tomorrow without knowing if her attraction is universal, or whether it is mainly Belle's line that is susceptible to it."

"Were you drawn to her?" Jean-Claude asked.

"I feel some attraction, yes, but not to the degree that Augustine did. I am not fighting to keep from touching her, or doing what she says. I sense her power, and when she was using her necromancy, it was most impressive, but no, I did not feel compelled."

"Then is it just Belle's line?" Jean-Claude asked.

"Or perhaps only vampires that have experienced Belle's *ardeur* are strongly drawn."

I was finally relaxing into Jean-Claude's arms. "That would explain it." He didn't sound like he believed it was that simple.

"But, Jean-Claude, you must understand that I feel her power. I am over a thousand years old, and a Master of the City. I have as my animal to call a siren. I am not a small power, yet she does have a certain"—he seemed to search for a word—"attraction even to me. I am not burdened by it, but it is there. You said you wished my advice."

"I do."

"I advise that you find a way to test her powers before she meets the larger party."

"How?"

"I know that Maximillian of Vegas has one of Belle's line as his *pomme de sang* candidate. He would be thrilled if you asked to see one of his candidates early. He will see it as a point of favor."

"We would have to see at least one candidate from each of the masters, then, in private."

"But if it goes wrong?" I said. "Aren't we running the risk that whoever we 'experiment' on may be metaphysically bound to me forever?"

Samuel nodded. "Yes." He looked at me like *What's wrong with that?*

"It wouldn't be fair. I can't experiment on them, run the risk of binding them to me, if they don't know what the risks are."

"But they have come hoping to be your new *pomme de sang*," Samuel said. "They have come hoping to bind themselves to you."

"Jason has been Jean-Claude's *pomme de sang* for years, but if he decided to go back to college, or change jobs, or fell in love, and didn't want to keep being a *pomme de sang*, he could do that. We'd miss him, and I think he'd miss Jean-Claude, but he has choices. He isn't trapped into being Jean-Claude's *pomme* forever." I moved away from Jean-Claude and faced Samuel. "What you're suggesting takes away their options. It's like making them a slave without asking first if that's what they want."

Samuel smiled at me. "Freedom and fairness are very important to you, aren't they?"

I nodded, and frowned. "They're important to everybody."

He laughed. "Oh, no, Anita, you would be amazed at the number of people who try to give away their freedom at every opportunity. They much prefer that someone else make their decisions. As for fairness, you said it earlier, life isn't fair."

"No, life isn't fair, but I try to be."

He nodded, and stood, clapping his hands together. "She is a rare find, Jean-Claude."

"Thank you," he said, as if the compliment were all for him, and none for me.

"To make these experiments with their knowledge, Anita," Samuel said, "needs Jean-Claude to admit to the other masters that you, all of you, have no idea what the extent of your powers are. You would have to admit weakness, and confusion, when what you must have this weekend is strength, surety, and unassailable power."

"No one's power is unassailable," I said.

He gave a small bow. "Touché, but my point is still valid. To expose that much of your uncertainty to some of the masters would be nearly suicidal." He came to stand in front of me. "Think upon this, Anita: if you are with child, then it is no longer just your life you risk. Is your sense of fair play worth the risk of letting the other Masters of the City see your weaknesses? For what will they think, if you admit to this being a new power? Might they think that they should destroy you before you enslave us all?"

Jean-Claude moved to my side. Micah came to my other side. I just stared at Samuel.

"I mean you no harm, Anita, but I am not as insecure as some. The insecure ones will be your danger."

"If we can't tell the truth, what do you propose?" I asked.

"You couldn't simply lie?" he asked.

"I'm not very good at it," I said.

He smiled and looked at Jean-Claude. "How have you managed with her and the Ulfric? They are both most unwieldy."

"You have no idea," Jean-Claude said.

Samuel laughed again, then his face stilled, as if the laughter had been a trick of the eye. "Tell the masters that you wish to see how powerful their candidates are, and whether they can withstand your full powers. Tell them that if their candidates are too weak, they may be enslaved as any servant, for Jean-Claude is so powerful that that has happened with some lesser vampires of the Church of Eternal Life."

"That actually did happen with some of the church members," I said.

He smiled again, but it never reached his eyes. "So I had heard."

I glanced at Jean-Claude. "Did you tell him?"

"No."

"You have spies in your lands, Anita. You are too great a power not to have spies from all the masters that agreed to come here. None of us would have come to your lands without some intelligence of our own finding. None of us trust any of us that much."

"Great," I said.

"But it sets up the situation perfectly, Anita. You can tell the truth, that you wish to see if the candidates are strong enough to withstand your powers, for a true *pomme de sang*, as you so accurately stated, is not so closely bound to you metaphysically. To eat only from those who are already bound to you is like eating your own arm. It may fill your stomach, but it takes more energy from you then it gives to you."

"It took us a little while to figure that out," I said.

He gave another small bow. "Your new *pomme de sang* must be independent, and strong enough to play his part. It is a reasonable request."

"It is a good plan," Jean-Claude said.

"And what if they all fall under my, whatever, spell? What if I'm too much necromancer for any of them?"

"Then the ball is canceled," Samuel said. "You cannot play Cinderella if all the princes will want you."

"I'm not Cinderella," I said, "I'm the prince."

He smiled, but again it didn't reach his eyes. "Very well, Prince Charming, but the point remains the same. You cannot play Prince Charming if all the princesses want you, because as good as you may be, no one is that good." He looked at Jean-Claude then. "Not even Jean-Claude."

That look, and that comment, made me wonder if they really were "friends" the way that Jean-Claude and Augustine had been. They said that they weren't, but the look meant something.

"We will do as you suggest, Samuel. I know that I can rely on your discretion not to share any of this."

"You have my word," he said, then he looked back at me. "I would never endanger you. I want you to try to bring Sampson into his power, Anita. I would not insist it be done first, but I would prefer sooner to later."

"I know it won't be tonight," I said.

He smiled and this time it filled his eyes with soft humor. "No, not tonight. I think your plate is quite full enough without adding Sampson to it."

He bowed to Jean-Claude. Sampson followed suit. They turned on their heels and left.

Claudia's voice broke the silence. "Do you want me to go out and get a pregnancy test?"

"We have two of them in the overnight case," Micah said.

My throat was suddenly so tight I couldn't breathe.

Nathaniel and Lisandro came through the far hallway. "What did I miss?"

I looked at him, and the look on my face must have been a bad one, because he came to me, and wrapped his arms around me, and I let him.

"She's missed a month; you don't have to wait until morning to take the test," Claudia said.

I wanted to tell her to stop. Stop talking, stop helping, but she was right.

I wasn't just two weeks late like I'd told Ronnie. My period could move around by up to two weeks, later or earlier, depending on my hormone cycle, I guess. If I used the count that most women did, I was nearly four weeks late, not two. Two weeks into the month of November, but four weeks past when I should have bled. Four weeks, yeah, the test should work.

18

A PREGNANCY TEST is just this flat piece of plastic with little windows in it. So small, it fit in my hand with room left over, and my hands aren't that big. Such a small thing to have so many people so upset. But then, if I was pregnant, the baby would be smaller than the pregnancy test. Tiny bits of plastic, and even tinier bits of cells, and my whole life rested on them. Okay, I wouldn't die if it was a yes, but it sort of felt like I would.

First, there's no dignity to it. You have to pee on the little stick. Or pee in a cup, then put the stick in it. Then you put the cap on, and wait for lines to appear. One line: not pregnant. Two lines: pregnant. It seemed simple enough.

I prayed not to be pregnant. I prayed, and I bargained. I'd be more careful. I'd use condoms and not trust just to the pill. I'd, well, you get the idea. I'm sure I wasn't the first single woman to sit in a bathroom wishing, hoping, praying, bargaining with God, that if this mess passes me by, I'll be better. Shit.

I didn't want to sit in the bathroom for the entire three minutes. But I didn't want to go outside and face the men either. I compromised; I paced inside the bathroom. It was ten steps from the door to the edge of the tub's raised marble. Ten steps, back and forth. Marble is cold on bare feet, but I usually didn't spend this much time walking on it. I was either coming in and out, or sitting in hot water in the tub. I concentrated on anything, everything, but that little piece of plastic where it sat on the side of the sink. I tried not to look at it. If you peek early, it may not be conclusive. I was carrying a man's watch in my hands. Micah's watch. He'd taken it off his wrist and handed it to me, because mine was still sitting on the nightstand beside our bed.

I tried putting the watch in the pocket of the robe, but that made me nervous, as though if I couldn't see the watch I'd screw the time up. I tried sitting on the edge of the tub staring at the second hand, but that made the time go even slower. Now that I was only minutes away from knowing, I wanted to know. No more guesswork. I needed to know, one way or the other. I needed to know.

What I didn't know was that Micah had set an alarm on the watch. It beeped at me, and scared me. I gave that little *eep* scream that only girls seem to do.

Claudia knocked on the door. "Anita, you all right?"

"Sorry, alarm startled me. Sorry." I was already in the middle of the room, opposite the sink. All I had to do was turn around. I had a death grip on the watch. My heart was beating so hard I was sure that everyone outside the door could hear it. I didn't want to look. I wanted to know, and I didn't want to know. I wanted to have someone else look. Micah would do it, or Nathaniel. God, I was being so cowardly, and stupid, as if simply not looking would make it not true. But I had to look, I had to.

I took those last few steps to the sink, and looked down. Two lines, two fucking lines. The world swam, and I had to grab on to the sink edge to keep from sliding to one side. All I could hear was my own blood roaring in my ears. I was not going to faint, damn it. I was not going to faint.

I lowered myself to my knees, still clinging to the cabinet edges. I put my face against my arm, and waited for the dizziness to pass. Fuck.

When I thought I could do it without feeling worse, I raised my head up. The room didn't swim. Good. But I wasn't at all sure I trusted myself to walk to the door. I hated it, but apparently my body had decided that it just wasn't working yet. I could either sit on the floor until I felt less weak-legged, or I could yell for help.

I knew the men were almost as tense about it as I was, so waiting seemed cruel, or maybe it wasn't cruel. They had a few minutes more of believing the worst hadn't happened. I hated to treat the miracle of life like a disaster but that's how it felt.

I finally called, in a voice that almost sounded like mine, "Claudia."

She tapped the door, and said, "Do you want me in there?"

"Yes," I said.

She came through, and one look at me on the floor made her close the door behind her. She walked to me, looked down at the test, and said with real feeling, "Well, shit."

"Yeah," I said.

"Who do you want to tell first?"

I shook my head and leaned back against the cabinets. "No one."

She gave me a look.

"I can't call them in one at a time; Richard will get pissed, or someone else will. I have to go out to them."

She gazed around the room. "They'd all fit in here, barely."

I tucked my knees up tight and held on. "Jesus, Claudia. Jesus."

She knelt beside me. Her face was so sympathetic that I had to look away. My eyes were starting to burn, my throat to tighten. "Help me do this before I start to cry."

"What can I do to help?" she asked.

"Help me stand."

She took my offered hand and raised me effortlessly to my feet. She kept a hand on my elbow to steady me, as if she knew I needed it. I didn't argue. We made it to the door that way, then I took my arm back, and opened the door.

I thought I had my face under control, but I must have been wrong, because they all reacted to it. Only Jean-Claude and Asher showed nothing, but their lack of reaction was reaction enough.

Micah and Richard reached me first, at almost the same time. They looked at each other, and Micah bowed out, let the other man touch me first. It was good of him, but I'd have preferred to hug him, since I was almost certain Richard would say something to make me feel worse.

He half-hugged me, so he could hold me, and still see my face. "It's a yes?"

I nodded, because I didn't trust my voice. My throat was so tight it hurt, as if I were choking.

He hugged me, and picked me up, and spun me around. When I could move my face back enough to see his, he was beaming at me. Beaming at me. He was happy! Happy about it!

"Don't you dare be happy about this," I said.

His smile began to fade around the edges.

Jean-Claude said, "Would you prefer he was unhappy about it?"

Richard put me down, while I looked at the other man. I glanced back up at Richard, who didn't look happy now at all. What would I have done if he had been angry, or sad, about me being pregnant?

I hung my head, resting the top of my head against Richard's chest. "I'm sorry, Richard, I'm sorry. I'm glad someone is happy about it."

He touched my face, raised it so I had to look at him. "I can't be unhappy about this, Anita. I can't. If we made a baby . . ." He shrugged, and his eyes were full of happiness, worry, so many emotions.

"What do you want us to say, *ma petite*? If we are not to be happy, then what do you wish?"

I pulled away from Richard. I just couldn't be happy and his being happy bugged me. "I don't know, just be what you feel, I guess."

Micah touched my arm. "I'm sorry you're unhappy about it."

I smiled at him, and the fact that I could smile at anything was probably a good sign. "How do you feel about it?"

He smiled. "I love you. How could I not love a little piece of you running around?"

I shook my head. "Don't you feel cheated? I mean, it can't be yours."

He shrugged. "I knew I gave up children of my own when I had the vasectomy."

"Why did you have yourself fixed?" Richard asked. "You're not thirty yet, why would you do that to yourself?"

Micah wrapped his arms around me, held me close. "My old alpha, Chimera, liked pregnant shapeshifters. If one of the women came up pregnant by someone else, someone she cared for, Chimera would take her until she lost the baby. He got off on taking her from her lover, from fucking her while she was pregnant with someone else's child, and from her losing it."

I held him tight, held him and listened to his heartbeat speed. His voice never showed how awful it had been, but his pulse did. I had heard the story before, but Richard had not; his face showed revulsion, and something else, anger, I think.

I'd never heard a story about Chimera that made me unhappy that I'd killed him. No, that was one death I had absolutely no regrets about.

Nathaniel came up behind me, and wrapped himself against my back, holding me between the two of them. It felt so safe. Even now, even with Micah's story still horrible and fresh, even with the news about the baby, I still felt safe. That had to be a good sign, didn't it?

Jean-Claude came to our side. We all raised our heads from the various shoulders we were on, and looked at him.

He touched my face, ever so gently, and smiled. "Whatever happens, *ma petite*, we will not desert you."

Asher walked around to the other side so I stood in a box of the four of them.

"I'm not really included, am I?" Richard said, and his voice held more sadness than anger.

Micah said, "You could be if you wanted to be, Richard. No one excludes you, but you." He held his hand out toward Richard.

Richard stared at that hand, then looked at all the men. "I can't, Anita. I can't be part of this."

"A part of what, *mon ami*?" Jean-Claude asked.

"All of you together," Richard said.

Micah let his hand fall. "We're not asking you to have sex with everyone,

Richard. We're just comforting Anita, and ourselves. You're a shapeshifter; you understand the need for touch when you're worried or scared."

Richard shook his head. "It's always about sex with him." He pointed at Jean-Claude. "Don't let him fool you, Micah. He's enjoying touching you." It seemed he'd decided that of the other men, Micah was the one most likely to understand his unease.

Micah slid his arm around Jean-Claude's waist, pulled him in a little tighter against him and me. It forced Jean-Claude to put more of his arm across Micah's shoulders, put the line of their bodies against each other from hip to chest. Micah kept his gaze on Richard while he got cozy.

"If he were another shapeshifter, they'd enjoy the touch, too. We've all had a shock. We're all feeling insecure, Richard. We're all wondering how much our lives must change to accommodate a baby. We're scared, aren't you?"

"You're Nimir-Raj, are you saying you can't smell when someone's afraid?" There was derision in his voice.

"I thought you'd get angry if I told you that you smelled of fear."

Richard's hands made fists. His face darkening with anger, he fought for control of himself, visibly. It was almost painful to watch him fight his anger, and since his power never once warmed the room, he was controlling so much more than just his anger.

He started walking toward us, jerkily, as if his feet didn't want to move. He moved like some reluctant robot, until he came to the edge of the knot of men. Then he stopped. He just stood there beside us, as if he didn't know what to do next.

Jean-Claude moved, making a hole between himself and Nathaniel. It was an invitation to join the circle. Richard just stood there, eyes on the ground, hands limp at his sides. It was Nathaniel who moved even farther out, letting go of me, and only keeping Asher's hand. Nathaniel moved so that the circle became almost half a circle. Jean-Claude took his cue from Nathaniel, and moved farther away from me, his arm still around Micah. I stood alone with the men like a backdrop.

Richard stood there, unmoved, as if he hadn't noticed. I took a step forward, and touched fingertips to the fringe of his hair where it hid the edge of his face. He flinched, and raised his eyes to me. The pain in those brown eyes made my throat tight. Maybe I was just having an emotional night. Or maybe, if you love someone, you can never see that much pain in his eyes without wanting to fix it.

I had to go up on tiptoe to touch his face, one hand resting against his arm to steady myself. I rested my hand against the side of his face, just at the swell of his cheekbone, feeling the strength of that curve under my hand. His face was like him, strong, and outwardly perfect. Inside that nearly perfect male package there was a storm raging. It showed in his eyes, all that pain, that anger. His arm flexed under my hand. The smooth swell of muscle molding itself against the curve of my hand. I wasn't sure if he'd done it to remind me how strong he was, or if it was the only sign that he was still flinching. From the look in his eyes, I was betting on flinching.

He began to lean in toward me, as I stretched upward to meet him. Our lips met, but it was more a touch than a kiss. His lips moved against mine, the gentlest of kisses. I kissed him back, a soft caress of lips. Then his mouth pressed against mine, and there was nothing gentle about it. He broke from the kiss with a sound that was half sob and half sigh. He fell to his knees, dragging me with him, clinging to me as if I were the last solid thing in the universe.

I held him, stroked his hair, murmured his name, "Richard, Richard," over and over. He cried like his heart was breaking.

Jean-Claude knelt beside us. He put his hand on the back of Richard's head. When he didn't react to the touch, Jean-Claude put his arms around both of us. He laid his face against the side of Richard's head, and said something in French that I didn't catch. Whatever he said, it was low and comforting.

Nathaniel knelt on the other side opposite Jean-Claude. He touched my shoulder, but hesitated about touching Richard.

It was Clay who came and knelt at Richard's back. He gave me worried eyes, and pressed himself along Richard's back, his arms holding him tight. He said, "Smell the pack, and know that you are safe." It sounded like an old saying.

With Clay's body to protect Richard, Nathaniel hugged me and Clay, but we all hugged Richard. Clay had understood how much Richard needed the touch, but he'd also understood that he might not let leopards and vampires get that close. But another wolf of his own pack, that was safe. That one moment of understanding pushed Clay from bodyguard to friend in my book.

Micah came in at my back, hugging us close. Asher finally knelt, more by Nathaniel and me than Richard, but his hand touched Richard's hair. We all gave what we could.

The crying began to ease, then stop. I felt the tension in his arms, his body, ease. His breath went out in a long, heavy sigh. I felt him settle into the warmth and the touch. I felt all that care and worry drift away in the press of bodies, and caring.

Then he drew in a deep, full breath, and rose up higher on his knees. It was like a man rising from deep water, except that this water was hands and bodies. He rose to his knees, then started struggling to his feet. We all moved back to let him stand.

He smiled down at me, at all of us. "Thank you, all of you. I needed it. I didn't know how much . . ." He started to move out of the kneeling circle of us. Jean-Claude and Clay moved back so he could walk out.

He stopped at the foot of the bed, and took a breath so deep his body shuddered with it.

Jean-Claude stood, and helped me to my feet. I didn't protest the help; I felt shaky. Richard wasn't the only one who needed to be held tonight.

Everyone got to their feet, in ones and twos. We waited for Richard to say something, or for one of us to think of something worth saying.

He turned back and gave us a smile. It was his old smile, his Boy Scout smile, I used to call it. He looked more relaxed than I'd seen him in a while.

"I'll bunk in Jason's room tonight."

"You don't have to leave," I said.

The smile slipped a little, letting some sadness through. "I can't sleep here, Anita, not with all of them."

"I don't think everyone is staying," I said.

He shrugged. "I don't want to share you, Anita. Especially tonight. But I saw your face when Nathaniel and Micah held you. You never look that peaceful with me anymore."

I opened my mouth, to say something comforting, but he held up a hand and stopped me. "Don't deny it, Anita. I'm not angry, just . . ." He shook his head. "I don't know what to do, but I know I can't share you tonight. It will be dawn soon, and you won't want Jean-Claude with us. He's the only one I could stand to share you with tonight." He shrugged again. "But you'll want something warmer." His face struggled to look cheerful, and almost succeeded. "It's better if I just go. I'll say, or do, something to upset Anita tonight. I know I will." His frown turned into something bitter for a second. "I appreciate the comfort, I needed it, but part of me still wishes you were all gone." With that, he turned on his heel and went for the door.

"Clay," I said, "go with him."

Clay didn't argue, and when he followed him out, Richard didn't protest. I took it as a good sign. I hoped so, anyway.

19

Jean-Claude hugged me in against his body. "I am sorry, *ma petite*."

Asher came and kissed me on the cheek. "I am not sorry he is gone."

"Be nice," I said.

He cuddled in against me, his arm going around Jean-Claude's shoulders. "We all behaved ourselves admirably and your Ulfric still leaves in a huff."

Nathaniel came to stand in front of me. He pushed a lock of my hair back from my face. "Honestly, Anita, I'm not sorry he's staying somewhere else for the night. I want to hold you tonight, and Richard wouldn't let me in the bed."

They were both right, so why did I feel like I should defend Richard's honor?

"Enough of this," Jean-Claude said, "*Ma petite* is tired. We will leave her with Micah and Nathaniel." He kissed my upturned face, gently, his face showing nothing. There were nights when he asked not to be sent away, but tonight he didn't even try for it.

He let me go, and started for the door, Asher at his side.

"It seems wrong to keep kicking you out of your own bed," Micah said.

Jean-Claude turned back, and said, "*Ma petite* is not comfortable when I die at dawn. We will respect her sensibilities in this tonight. She has had enough shocks for one night."

Asher slipped his arm through Jean-Claude's. "We'll be in my room." I'd seen them arm in arm a hundred times. I'd sent them off to bunk in Asher's room dozens of times. But for the first time, I wondered what they would do once they got there. Would they have sex? Would they do with each other what Jean-Claude and I did with Auggie? Did the thought bother me? I wasn't sure.

Micah looked at me. "Damian doesn't die at dawn if he's with you. Shouldn't we find out if the same applies to Jean-Claude?"

"Don't push me, Micah." I felt almost frantic with the need for some kind of normality tonight. My voice didn't sound frantic, it sounded angry.

"He can sleep on the other side of me, so if he dies at dawn, you won't be touching him."

I shook my head. "Why is this so important to you? Why tonight?"

"I do think we need to find out if Jean-Claude has gained some of the same powers Damian has, but truthfully, Belle Morte had a harder time controlling you once he touched you. I'd like to keep him close to you tonight, just in case."

I blinked at him, then sighed. "Practical as always," I said.

"Eminently practical," Asher said. He let go of Jean-Claude's arm. "I will go to my lonely bed."

"Asher," I said, "please, I can't deal with any more hurt feelings tonight."

He smiled at me, and came back to me. He hugged me, gently, and gave me an almost brotherly kiss on the forehead. "I will not cause either of you more distress tonight. But I would like a chance to test this theory of vampires in the day. If it works for our Jean-Claude, then perhaps it might work for me."

"It only works for Damian if Nathaniel is in the room. I think without Richard it won't work for Jean-Claude either."

Asher stepped back, gave that Gallic shrug, and went for the door. He waved at us lightly, but I had too many centuries' worth of memories of his body language, thanks to Jean-Claude's memories. Asher was bothered. I guess I couldn't blame him. He was the only one kicked out of the room. But I didn't call him back. I didn't really want to have one corpse in the bed, let alone two.

I turned back to the corpse in question. He stood there in his elegant robe. A triangle of his chest showed, so pale, surrounded by the black of the fur lapel. His hair was a foam of curls, softer than mine.

Tiredness came over me in a wave. No, it wasn't being pregnant, it was just everything. I had had all I could handle for one night.

Micah hugged me from behind. Nathaniel came to stare down at me. He lifted my chin and looked into my eyes. He gave me the gentlest of smiles, then said, "You're beat."

I nodded, his fingers still under my chin.

He kissed me on the mouth, still gentle, no demand to it. He took my hand and started leading me toward the bed. Micah let his arm fall away but kept my other hand, so that Nathaniel led us both to the bed.

The bed was draped in red tonight. Crimson, from the curtains that graced the four posts to the mounds of pillows. The sheets underneath the bedspread either would match the rest perfectly, or would be some high-contrast color. Once upon a time Jean-Claude's decoration had been exclusively black and white. I'd complained. I still remembered the first night I'd seen the bed draped in red. I'd stopped complaining about the monochrome color scheme after that, afraid of what he might do next.

Nathaniel had to let go of my hand to wiggle the coverlet out from under the mound of pillows. The sheets were black, like a splash of darkness in all that red. Some of the smaller pillows would get piled in the room's two chairs, beside the false fireplace. Thanks to modern technology it could actually make flames, but in all the time I'd been with Jean-Claude I'd never seen anything in the fireplace but an antique fan framed behind glass.

Nathaniel and Micah went back and forth like busy ants until the seats were piled high with pillows, and there were still plenty left on the bed.

Jean-Claude had come to stand on the other side of the bed from me. We stood there staring across the expanse of red and black silk. When I say *expanse*, I mean it. The bed was larger than a king-size. Orgy-size is what I'd started calling it, but I hadn't actually shared that with Jean-Claude. I didn't mean to imply anything about what he was doing when I wasn't here. The bed was just the biggest one I'd ever seen. Then I realized, that wasn't entirely true. Belle's bed was this size. I really wished I hadn't thought of that. Suddenly I was cold.

"What is wrong, *ma petite*?" he asked.

I shook my head. I didn't want to share the observation, as if talking about it would make it more true.

Micah and Nathaniel came back to the bed. Micah stopped and looked from one to the other of us. Nathaniel started unbuttoning his shirt.

"I think you might want to wait on that," Micah said, still looking from one to the other of us.

Nathaniel kept unbuttoning. "They'll work it out." He slipped the shirt off, and went for the large armoire. It was dark rich wood that matched the bed. Nathaniel opened it, and started hanging up his shirt. The armoire was empty except for our extra clothes. Nathaniel's, Micah's, mine. Jean-Claude had a room the size of a small warehouse that was full of clothes. He'd started hanging an outfit at a time in the armoire, but he still kept his room as clean and empty as he could. He'd gotten in the habit when he used to entertain strangers on a regular basis. You don't keep things you value in a room where you're going to have one-night stands. Jean-Claude didn't do one-night feedings and fucks now, but old habits die hard. Vampires, I'd found, once they have a habit, really don't like giving it up. Old dogs, new tricks, that sort of thing.

Nathaniel came back to the bed wearing absolutely nothing. I had one of those moments of discomfort. I'd seen him nude more times than I could count. I'd seen him nude in front of Micah and Jean-Claude more times than I could count. So why was I blushing?

Nathaniel climbed into the bed, pulling the sheet up just enough to keep me from yelling at him. Left to his own devices I think Nathaniel would have been nude all the time. He lay back against the red and black pillows. His hair was still in its braid so that his face was framed by all that black and red silk. His face had started to fill out; bone structure that had only been a promise six months ago was somehow more real, more masculine. He was moving from the pretty handsomeness that some young men get, to the more handsome handsomeness that most of them grow into. He'd also grown nearly an inch taller in the six months we'd been together. At twenty he was growing into what some people hit at seventeen, or earlier. Genetics is a wonderful and confusing thing.

He smiled at me, and the smile was all male. That pleased smile that said he knew I was looking at him, and how much he liked the effect he had on me. He'd been in my bed for half a year, naked in it for about a month, and I was still staring at him as if it were the first time.

It made me blush and look away.

"Come to bed, Anita," he said, "you know you want to."

The anger was instantaneous. I wasn't blushing when I raised my eyes back to him. "I don't like being taken for granted, Nathaniel."

He sighed, and sat up, putting his muscular arms around his knees. "Don't let the whole baby thing push you back. You've made a lot of progress in your comfort zones, don't lose ground now."

"And what exactly is that supposed to mean?" I asked, hands on hips, glad to be angry. Anger was so much better than sad, or scared, or embarrassed.

His lavender eyes went all serious, not scared, or worried, but grown-up serious. "Are you really going to make us do this?"

"Do what?" I demanded.

He sighed, and said, "Why is my being nude bothering you?"

I opened my mouth, closed it, and finally said, quietly, "I don't know." That was the truth; stupid, but the truth.

Micah came to me, touched me tentatively. I went to him, wrapped my arms around him. He hugged me close, and I turned my face in against his neck, so I could smell the warmth of him. Just the smell of his skin made something hard and cold inside me loosen. I breathed in the scent of him, and underneath the smell of clean skin and aftershave, Micah had that nose-wrinkling smell, an almost sharp smell, of leopard. The smell of home.

He spoke against my skin, "Let's go to bed, Anita."

I nodded, still pressed against him.

I felt his mouth move in a smile against my skin. I knew exactly the feel of it, which meant I must make him smile with his mouth pressed to me a lot. I guess I did.

He drew away and started unfastening his collar. He had a tie bar to remove. I stood there and watched him begin to reveal his tanned upper body, but instead of enjoying the show, I felt the anxiety creep back.

I touched Micah's arm, stopped him in the middle of undoing one of his cuff links. "Stop for a minute." He turned puzzled eyes to me.

"You're nervous again," Nathaniel said. "Why?"

I shook my head, then looked across the bed. Jean-Claude was still across the bed, but he was leaning on one of the big wooden posts. His arms entwined around it as he watched us. His face was neutral, but I'd been further into his head tonight than ever, in one special area.

"Shit," I said.

"What?" Micah and Nathaniel asked together.

"I know what's wrong."

They both looked at me, but it was Jean-Claude that I looked at. "It's you," I said.

"I have seen your men nude before," he said in that pleasant neutral voice.

"We've been in bed all naked and sweaty, Anita," Nathaniel said.

"Yes, but you've never had sex with him. I had sex with him."

"Jean-Claude has fed off me, Anita," Micah said, "has had more of my blood than yours."

I looked at Micah. "Are you saying having him take blood is the same thing as having sex with him?"

He shrugged, and I watched his face shut down to the look he wore when he wasn't certain what look I wanted. "I've had sex that didn't feel as good as Jean-Claude's feedings."

"Then you were doing the sex wrong," I said.

He smiled. "I was young; I got better."

"Yes, you did," I said, and smiled back.

He kissed me, then moved back and gave me a searching look. He moved past me to put the first cufflink on the bedside table. He started on the other sleeve, his back to me. I glanced up and found that I wasn't the only one watching him.

Jean-Claude's neutral, beautiful face watched us all. We had been naked and sweaty in a bed together. Hell, some nights the pile had included Asher and Jason. It just depended on who had fed whom last. So why was I suddenly bothered by Jean-Claude watching Micah take off his shirt?

I suddenly had a smart idea. I don't have that many of them, not about my own emotional life anyway. "I know what's wrong," I said again.

They all looked at me. I touched Micah's naked back, but looked at Jean-Claude. "It was what we did tonight with Augustine."

Jean-Claude sat on the corner of the bed, one arm still wrapped around the bedpost. "What exactly are you referring to, *ma petite*? We did many things with Augustine tonight."

"I know that everyone thinks we're all snogging each other's brains out, but tonight was the first time I'd ever seen two men kiss. I've never even seen someone do . . ." I faltered. God, was I still such a baby? No, damn it, I was a grown-up. "I've never seen anal sex before, let alone between two men. Let alone between my lover and a stranger." I took in a big breath and let it out, and went to the edge of the bed, a little closer to Jean-Claude. "Am I making any sense?"

"You were disturbed by what you saw," he said.

"Wait," Nathaniel said. The *wait* turned me to him. He was propped up on the pillows, the sheet forgotten in his lap, so that he was barely covered at all, but his face showed he wasn't even thinking about it. "How did you feel when Jean-Claude kissed Auggie?"

I opened my mouth, then closed it, because I wasn't sure what the answer was. How had I felt? "I didn't mind it. It was . . . interesting." That wasn't true. I looked down at the bedspread and said, "No, I . . . it was interesting."

"Interesting bad, or interesting good?" Nathaniel said.

Without looking up, I answered, "Good."

Someone sighed, and I wasn't sure which of them had done it. I looked up, slowly, and no one was looking at me like I'd said something awful. I don't know why I thought anyone in this room would think it was wrong that I liked seeing Jean-Claude kiss another man, but I did think it. I was waiting for someone to tell me to be ashamed of myself. I'd seen someone I loved kiss another man, and not only hadn't I been horrified, but I'd liked it. Was that wrong? I had waited for it to feel wrong, but it hadn't. It had felt strangely right, as if I'd been waiting my whole life to see it. It had felt right in that way that only the things that truly speak to your heart can feel. I hadn't felt bad when it was happening. I was feeling bad now. Why? Was it guilt? No, I felt uncomfortable, and a little squeamish, but not guilty. So what was it?

Micah touched my arm. "So many thoughts flying over your face—what are you thinking?"

"That I don't feel bad, and shouldn't I feel bad about it."

He looked puzzled, frowned. "Bad about what?"

"Shouldn't it bother me that I saw Jean-Claude kiss another man, a stranger at that?"

"Did it bother you?"

I shook my head. "Not at the time, no."

He smiled, eyes still a little uncertain. "But it's bothering you now. Why?"

"Did it bother you to watch us like that?"

He gave me a look. "I've watched you have sex with other men before, Anita."

I suddenly felt thirteen again, embarrassed and confused about the whole thing.

"I believe, *ma petite*, he is asking how you felt about watching me with Augustine."

I looked at him, happy he'd helped me, but uncomfortable that he'd had to help me.

"Did it bother you?" Micah asked me.

I shook my head. "No, it was amazing. We did him. We owned him. It was . . ." My breath shivered out of me. "It was a rush, power and sex all mixed up together."

"Then it's okay," Micah said. "Don't feel bad because you don't feel bad."

Of course, that was exactly what I was doing. "It sounds stupid when you say it out loud."

He hugged me, and I wrapped myself around the warmth of his skin. "It's not stupid, Anita. It's how you feel. Feelings are never stupid, they just make us feel stupid sometimes."

I drew back enough to see his face. "You're okay with everything we did tonight. You don't think we're evil or something."

He chucked me under the chin. "That's Richard's voice in your head, not mine."

I nodded. He was right, on part of it.

He went to hang up his shirt in the armoire. Nathaniel reached a hand out to me. "Take off the robe and let me hold you all naked and warm."

I wanted to, in fact I couldn't think of anything better, but still I hesitated. I took his hand, but I didn't touch my robe, and I didn't climb on the bed.

Micah came up behind me, wrapping his body around me. His body pushed against the back of my robe. The silk was thin and parts of him were not.

I turned with a little gasp. "You're naked."

He frowned at me. "Yes, we always sleep naked."

I shook my head, and said, "But . . ." then I realized what was wrong. I'd sort of known before today that Jean-Claude had had male lovers. I mean, I knew that he and Asher and Julianna had been a true ménage à trois. I shared the memories to prove it. But that had been memories, and theory. It hadn't been fact, until tonight.

I tried to put it into words. "I knew in theory you liked men as well as women," I said, and looked at Jean-Claude while I said it. His face was as empty as I'd ever seen it, as though if I blinked, he'd vanish.

"But now you know in fact, and you think less of me," he said, in a voice as empty as his face.

"No, not less, just . . ." I tried again. "In college I had a friend, a girl-friend, a girl who was a friend. She and I went shopping together. Slept over at each other's dorm rooms. I undressed in front of her because she was a girl. Then toward the end of college she told me she was gay. We were still friends, but she went into that guy catagory for me. You don't undress in front of people who see you as a sex object. You don't sleep with them, or . . . oh, hell." I looked up at Micah. "Won't it weird you out to sleep nude be-side him now?"

Micah laughed. "Are you worried about my virtue more now than before?"

I frowned at him. "I don't . . ." I pushed him hard enough that he stum-bled. "Fuck you," I said, but I was starting to smile and that usually meant I'd lost the argument. I wasn't even sure it was an argument.

"Not to take anything away from the attractiveness of your Nimir-Raj, *ma petite*, but I believe I can restrain myself." His face held a hint of humor now.

I looked at Nathaniel, and he was trying not to grin at me. I was perilously close to being laughed at, and that was just not cool. "Stop it, all of you."

"Stop what?" Nathaniel said in a strained voice, but his eyes were shiny with suppressed laughter.

"Don't you dare laugh at me."

"Did you think that because I had tasted my first man in years that I would suddenly be some sort of rampaging beast?" Jean-Claude's neutral face was beginning to crumble around the edges, humor was filling his eyes, tweaking at the edges of his mouth.

"No," I said, and it sounded sullen even to me.

"Did you expect Nathaniel and me to be more shy around Jean-Claude because we saw him with Augustine?" Micah's mouth was twitching at the edges.

I glared at them all. "Maybe."

"Anita—" Micah said, but he had to stop and fight the smile that kept threatening to get away from him. He started over. "Anita, remember I thought I'd have to be coming across to Jean-Claude when I joined you. The entire preternatural community believed that Richard and Jean-Claude and you were a true ménage à trois. I considered this before I ever asked to be your Nimir-Raj."

I frowned at him. "So it doesn't bother you?"

"No. I'm not into men, but I don't seem to have the same hang-ups that you and Richard do."

"Don't compare me with him," I said, and was all set to be angry.

"If it was another woman sleeping naked with you, you'd have the same problems that he does," Micah said.

"I've slept with some of the female wereleopards before."

"But never nude, either you or them," Micah said.

I started to deny it, then stopped. Was he right? "I don't know, I . . . I might be able to sleep nude, if it's just sleep, with another woman. I don't think I'd like it, though. I'd rather sleep pressed between two men."

"And that's fine," he said, "but if you knew for a fact that a woman saw you as a potential sex partner, you'd treat her differently."

"Yes, she'd go in the boy box."

"According to your thinking, Nathaniel and I should put Jean-Claude into a different box now, right?"

I thought about it, then nodded.

He smiled. "Anita, seeing him with Auggie wasn't the first clue I had that Jean-Claude liked men."

I looked from one to the other of them. "Have I missed something?"

"Not what you are thinking, *ma petite*." Jean-Claude sat more solidly on the corner of the bed, his back against the foot of it, his knees drawn up for his arms to wrap around. "I have not seduced either of your cats behind your back."

I hadn't really thought he had, but . . . "Then what is Micah talking about?"

"Anita," Nathaniel said, "pay more attention the next time that Jean-Claude feeds off one of us, or Asher feeds off me. You won't have to ask."

"But I've been in the bed while you guys did that. What did I miss?"

The three of them exchanged a look. "No, no looks, just tell me."

"You said you were tired," Micah said. "I think you don't want to know this, or you wouldn't have to ask."

"Don't want to know what?"

Again they exchanged that look.

"Stop that," I said, and I had to fight the urge to stomp my foot at them.

"Let us cuddle together, *ma petite*. Let us hold you, and give you the comfort that we all need tonight. It has been a long night, a good one in many ways, but long. You are tired."

I was tired, but the rush of anger, and confusion, had chased back the tiredness. "I am tired, and all I want to do is crawl into bed and let you hold me. But damn it, you're all looking at each other like there's an elephant in the room, and I can't see it."

Claudia spoke from the edge of the room, where she and the rest of the bodyguards were so quiet. We were close to kicking them out of the room. Okay, *I* was close to kicking them out. "I think I can catch this one," she said.

I looked at her. "Go ahead," I said.

"Jean-Claude feeds from a man the same way he feeds from a woman. Most vampires differentiate when they feed. Hetrosexual vamps take more liberties with opposite-sex victims. Homosexual vamps take more liberties with same-sex vics. Jean-Claude doesn't differentiate, do you understand?"

"When have you seen him feed on other women?"

"Aha," Claudia said, "and that is exactly why he doesn't feed on women except at the clubs, in public. You'd be jealous of other women if he took them in private, but you aren't jealous of men. You don't see them as sexually competitive for Jean-Claude's attention."

My head was beginning to hurt. "You're giving me a headache, Claudia."

"Only because you don't want to think this one through."

"You're saying that Jean-Claude likes both men and women, but because I'd be jealous of women, he takes mostly men. I get it, I get it."

"Thank you, Claudia," Jean-Claude said.

"You're welcome."

"Do I apologize to anyone, everyone?" I asked.

"Just take off the robe and get in bed," Nathaniel said. "Silk is cold without another body to warm it up."

I smiled at him, shook my head, and started to undo my robe. I stopped, and said, "Everyone that's not getting in the bed, outside."

"If it's an invitation . . ." Graham started.

"Can it, Graham," Claudia said, and went for the door.

He hesitated, but he followed her. Lisandro was already going for the door. Claudia had sent most of the others out when things calmed earlier. Probably sent them to watch over our "guests." The bodyguards piled out. The door shut, and we were alone.

Micah crawled onto the bed, on the other side of Nathaniel, leaving room for me. "You're looking a little overdressed," he said.

I undid the sash and let the robe fall to the floor. I crawled up onto the silk with the help of their hands. They pulled me down between them, so their naked bodies pressed in against me. There was a moment where I had to close my eyes. The sensation of their warm, bare skin sliding against mine was almost overwhelming. It was like wrapping myself in a favorite blanket with my favorite stuffed toy in my arms, and my gun close at hand. Sandwiched between Micah and Nathaniel was the safest, best place I'd ever known.

Nathaniel kissed me. My arms slid around his shoulders automatically. He took that as an invitation to press his upper body against mine. Micah's hand slid across my hip, until his hand found the inside of my thigh. He stroked his hand back and forth, and without thinking about it, I moved my leg so he could reach other things if he wanted to.

My hands slid down Nathaniel's back, found the curve where his waist met lower things, traced the two dimples in his very lower back. The kiss had grown into something more, and his body responded to that promise, swelling where he lay trapped against my hip. The feel of him hard and firm against me made me shudder into his mouth.

He drew back enough to watch my eyes fluttering open and shut. "You are my most favoritest toy."

It was more effort than I would have admitted out loud to focus on his face. Micah's hand kept stroking my thigh, as if he was coaxing me to open my legs for him, but I'd already done that. His fingers kept trailing on that last inch before he touched intimate parts. I wanted him to touch me. Wanted his fingers to finish that teasing promise.

"I thought you were tired," Micah whispered, but his mouth was just above my neck, so hot, so close.

"I was." My voice was thick, but not with sleep.

"What do you want?" he breathed against my neck. That alone made me shiver.

"Touch me."

"I am touching you." His fingers trailed just below where I wanted him to touch, back and forth, back and forth, but not the back and forth I wanted.

"Please, Micah. No more teasing."

His fingers slid over me, and that first touch drew small sounds from me.

"So eager," he said, and he rose up enough to see my face. His own face was eager, too, but there was also a soft wonder to his face. He raised his hand from between my legs to touch, lightly, along my face. "I love that look on your face," he said.

"What look?" I whispered.

He smiled. "That look." He leaned in for his own kiss. Nathaniel's hand curved over my breast, as Micah's mouth found mine. Nathaniel's touch made me more eager at Micah's mouth, so that the kiss was more than it would have been. I fed at Micah's mouth, my hand running over his body. I tried to use both hands, but Nathaniel caught my hand, pressed it to the bed, so he could lower his mouth to my breast. He filled his hand with my breast, pressing it until it was just this side of pain. His tongue flicked over my nipple. Micah's tongue slipped inside my mouth, tasting me. Nathaniel's mouth slid over more of me, and he sucked, hard and fast. It brought me screaming off the bed, screaming my pleasure into Micah's mouth. I tried to raise my other hand off the bed, but Nathaniel held it trapped. He bit my breast, and I raked nails down Micah's back. Nathaniel let go of my other hand, and bit me harder. Not hard enough to draw blood, but hard enough to dance that line between pain and pleasure. I put a matching row of scratches down his back, and they let me go.

I lay gasping on the bed between them, trying to focus my eyes around the white, cottony edges of the world. Micah said, "That was fun."

Nathaniel said, "Mmmm." He flicked his tongue across my nipple, quick and gone.

I writhed across the bed, my hands grabbing at the silk sheets. "Oh, God!"

A hand caressed my ankle. That one quiet touch opened my eyes, made me gaze down my body to find Jean-Claude kneeling there. He was still wearing the robe, belted tight. His face was neutral, pleasant. "Micah invited me to touch you, but I've found that it is your invitation I need." Translation: sometimes in the midst of all the men, I got pissy if someone touched me without my saying yes first. Just because one of the men was touching me didn't mean that everyone got to touch me equally. A girl's got to try to draw a line somewhere.

"You can't have intercourse until you've fed again," I said.

He smiled. "So American. There are other ways to pleasure a woman."

"But you won't be able to . . ."

His hand slid up my calf, the most delicate of touches. "I will be content, *ma petite*."

"We can stop now," Micah said, "if you want. This was fun."

I gazed down his body and saw just how fun he thought it was. He was long, and thick, and ready, and long and thick for Micah was very long and thick indeed. I glanced down at Nathaniel, and found him just as ready. No, he wasn't as big as Micah, but then the only one of the men who could compare was Richard. Though Richard didn't seem as aware of it as Micah.

Nathaniel was definitely more, just not as more as Micah. Not in length anyway, but in width, well, yeah. Men are hung up on length; trust me, girls pay attention to width, too. Frankly an inch or two less length wasn't always a bad thing; depended on what you wanted to do with it.

I ran fingertips over both of them, and just that light touch made them shudder, and me writhe. "So pretty," I said, "seems a shame to waste them."

"We'll get more," Micah said.

"I agree with Anita," Nathaniel said, grinning.

Micah smiled at him, a bright flash of teeth in his tanned face.

"I will join Asher." Jean-Claude began to slide off the bed.

"Don't go," I said.

He looked at me; it was a very searching look. "I do not have the patience of your two cats, *ma petite*. They have served blood for Asher and myself more than once, then watched us have our way with you."

"We had to save them for the *ardeur* the next day, or next night," I said.

"*Oui*, but I am not the voyeur that Asher is, and if I am not to join in completely, I would as soon leave. It is not a complaint, merely truth."

"I still think you shouldn't go that far away," Micah said. "I don't trust Belle."

Jean-Claude smiled. "Wise, and correct." He spread his hands wide. "If it were just sex between the three of you I could watch and be content to join the cuddling afterward. But it is the emotional content that makes it difficult to be excluded."

I frowned. "I don't understand."

"I know that you love me, *ma petite*, but my arms do not fill you with that last drop of something. I see you with Micah and Nathaniel and that last drop of emotion, or contentment, is there." He held up a hand as if someone had started to speak. "It is the truth. I do not begrudge it, especially with the news we have had tonight. You will need that bond, but it is"— he shook his head—"discomforting to watch, and know that I am not a part of it."

I didn't know what to say to that. I mean what do you say to the man you love when he's just told you that he realizes that you love two other men more?

"Besides, *ma petite*, you have expressed doubts about me now. You say you enjoyed our time with Augustine, but your actions state otherwise. I think your cats are what you need tonight, *ma petite*, not the memory of . . ." He gave that Gallic shrug, and got off the bed. He stood there adjusting his robe with smooth, nervous gestures. When he was nervous, and not policing his movements, he smoothed his clothes. It was one of the few truly human gestures that had survived centuries of being dead. I liked that he did it, and that he didn't realize he did it, because once he noticed it, his hands went still, as still as his face.

The little bit of sex I'd had with Micah and Nathaniel had helped me clear my head. "Do you think that I think less of you for having seen you with another man?" I asked.

"You have implied it," he said in a voice that was almost neutral.

I raised myself up on my elbows. "I guess I did, but I don't mean it. I think I thought it should bother me, but it didn't. I tried to talk myself into it bothering me, but the truth is—" I sat up, folding my legs tailor fashion. "The truth is, Jean-Claude, I liked seeing you kiss Auggie. I don't know how I feel entirely about the rest, but it didn't bother me at the time, so why should it bother me now?" I shook my head. "I'm not going to talk myself into an issue I don't have."

He gave a small smile, uncertain around the edges. Was it my reaction that had made him uncertain? Or was it that I'd trained him that after a major metaphysical or sexual breakthrough, I pulled back and ran? I guess either way, it was my doing, that uncertain smile. I didn't want him uncertain. I loved him; I shouldn't be the one making him insecure, not if I loved him. Sometimes the hardest thing about having so many men in my life wasn't the sex; the sex we could handle, but the emotional stuff . . . The emotional stuff was harder. I couldn't help Richard tonight, because his issues were things I couldn't really help him with, but this issue, this I could fix, or I could try to.

I smiled at him, and tried to put into that smile everything a man wants to see in a woman's smile. I watched his eyes fill up with that dark light that has nothing to do with vampires and everything to do with a man. His smile matched his eyes, confident, sure of itself, anticipatory.

"What would you have of me, *ma petite?*" His voice curled over my bare skin like the tickling edge of fingernails. It made me shiver.

"You're overdressed," I said.

"Are you certain you wish to do this, *ma petite?* You have never taken three of us before, and the *ardeur* will not rise again tonight, it has been too well fed."

He was offering me an out, but if I said no, then he'd leave the room. I'd already watched Asher and Richard walk out; I did not want to lose another of my men tonight. I needed as many around me as I could manage. Saying it made me almost want to call Asher back, but . . . I'd never done the full deal with three of my guys at the same time. Four would have to wait.

"I said, you are overdressed," and I made it a very firm statement.

Jean-Claude's smile widened. "Easily remedied." He undid the robe, and let it fall to the floor. He stood there pale and perfect. I had seen him nude a thousand times or more, but I never got over the shock of him. It was as if he were some amazing work of art, and I had stolen him away from the museum where they kept him roped off and safe, stolen him so I could run my hands over the smooth, flawless surface of him.

"You're too far away," I whispered.

He smiled wide enough to flash just a hint of fang. "That, too, is easily remedied." He crawled up on the bed, and I watched his body, small and loose, more than his face. Until he fed, he'd be small, which meant I could indulge in something that I didn't get to do much. By the time you get most men out of their clothes they're not as small as they can get—no, definitely larger.

"I know what you are thinking of, *ma petite*." His voice was chiding.

"Did you read my mind?"

"*Non, ton visage.*"

He'd said he'd read my face. I was picking up a little French here and there in self-defense.

He hesitated at my feet, and I realized he was looking at Micah. "And you, Nimir-Raj, what do you say to this?"

Micah smiled at him. "I'm here to try to make things work better, not make them worse."

"I don't try to make things worse," I said.

"Shh," Micah said, "don't take it personally."

I opened my mouth, realized I was going to start a squabble if not a fight, and I didn't want to fight anymore tonight. "Fine, I won't take it personally."

"You're not going to argue about it?" Nathaniel asked.

I shook my head, and lay back against the pillows. "Nope."

Micah and Nathaniel exchanged looks.

"What?" I said.

They both shook their heads. "Nothing," Micah said.

"Nothing," Nathaniel said, but he was smiling.

"I don't argue about everything."

"Of course not," Micah said.

"I don't," I said.

"Not anymore," Nathaniel said.

I slapped his shoulder.

He grinned. "Hit me harder, if you want it to hurt."

I didn't hit him again. "You'd enjoy it too much."

He grinned wider.

"I am no longer the only one who is not ready," Jean-Claude said.

I glanced down at the other two men. He was right. They definitely weren't ready to go.

"We've talked too long," Nathaniel said.

I waited to be uncomfortable at the thought of three men and just me with no holds barred on the sex. I waited, but the discomfort didn't come. I lay there and waited to feel overwhelmed, or uncomfortable, but . . . I just wasn't.

"I think I can fix it," I said, and started to slide lower on the bed, turning toward Nathaniel as I did it. I started kissing my way down his body, then thought of something. I looked back at Jean-Claude where he knelt on the bed. "You didn't ask Nathaniel's opinion."

"Micah is your Nimir-Raj, Nathaniel is not."

"But he's still my sweetie."

"It's okay, Anita," Nathaniel said, petting my shoulder. "Thanks for thinking of me, but I'm okay with not being asked."

I looked up at his face with my face almost to his groin. If it seemed an odd time for a in-depth talk he didn't complain. "Why are you okay?"

"Jean-Claude is right, I'm not anyone's leader, and I'm okay with that. If we were all completely dominant our happy little domestic situation wouldn't work."

"But just because you're not dominant doesn't mean that your opinion doesn't count."

"No," he said, and gave a little laugh, "no, but it does mean that I don't have as many opinions."

"But . . ."

"You want me to be more dominant?" he asked.

"I'd like to know how you feel about this, yeah."

"Suck my dick, so we can fuck." He was smiling while he said it.

I blinked at him for a second or two, then shrugged, and said, "Okay."

20

I DID WHAT he wanted, and a lot more. I used hand and mouth to get both Micah and Nathaniel back to the smooth hardness that they had been before all the soul searching. I didn't want any more soul searching tonight. I wanted to touch and be touched. Sex was the only time I let myself go. Let all the worries, the issues, everything wash away. When I had sex I just concentrated on the sex. It was the only time I was truly in the moment with no hesitation and no other thought.

I held them both in my hands. When I'd first tried to play with them both at the same time, I'd found that I couldn't do it. I couldn't concentrate on both hands equally, and when you've got a handful of the most delicate bits on a man's body, you want to be able to concentrate. But practice makes perfect, and I could do it now. I could hold each of them in my hand and stroke and play with them. I'd finally found something I was ambidextrous at.

Jean-Claude stayed sitting at the foot of the bed. He made no move to join us. I looked at him, that careful face. He'd made his position clear. He didn't just want to watch. I'd never tried to entertain three of the men at once. Cuddling, blood sharing, but not for sex.

I went to him where he sat so still, his back touching the foot of the bed. He'd gone as far away as he could without leaving the bed. Had he thought I would make him watch and not touch him? The very blankness of his face said yes, he had. I had a memory, not a vision, just a memory. It just didn't happen to be my memory, not originally. I saw Belle in her big bed, so similar to this one. She had two other vampires with her. I was watching her from the foot of the bed where she had tied me to the posts. I could feel the pull in my shoulders where the ropes were a little too high for comfort. But she didn't want me comfortable. She wanted me punished. Tied to her bed where she had taught me, us, what true desire could be. Bound, helpless, knowing that I could not touch her, and that no one would touch me. When we'd been far away from her, we could resist wanting her, but standing there, smelling her skin and sweat, we couldn't help but want her. She was an addiction, and the only way to save yourself was to never take another drink, another hit, another taste of her. I fought free of the memory enough to think, Jean-Claude had been tied to that bed, not me. Too tall to be my body. Too male. Not me, but the memory still burned, still had the power to make his face close down to that carefulness.

I touched his face, and I let my face show how sorry I was that all those awful things had happened to him. So sorry that I hadn't been there to save him. We were shut down too tight behind our shields for him to read my mind, probably just as well, but he saw what I meant him to see. He came to me with a sigh that was almost a sob. He kissed me as if he would breathe me in through his lips, and I kissed him as if he were the last drop of water in the world and I were dying of thirst.

I tasted the sweet metal of blood in my mouth. It made him draw back from the kiss. "I am sorry, *ma petite* . . ."

I stopped his apology with a kiss, feeding at his mouth, and he fell into that kiss with his hands on my body, his nakedness pressed as tight to mine as it could be. The only reason his body did not respond was that it couldn't until he fed.

I drew back from the kiss, my breathing ragged, the taste of my own blood in my mouth. A drop of blood grew and trembled on my lower lip.

He kissed that drop away, and stared down at me, as he knelt in front of me. His face was fierce and full of some wonder, as if I'd done something amazing. I hadn't. I'd just finally decided to get out of my own way; out of everyone's way.

I moved back along the bed, with his hand in mine. I pulled him along with me, on our knees, until we reached Micah and Nathaniel's feet. One of the things I'd noticed in dealing with more than one man in bed at a time was there were only two ways to go about it. Choice one: the men took turns, completely separate lovemaking, except that they both got to watch each other have sex with me. Choice two: they both touched me at the same time, and they did foreplay, or more, with me at the same time. Choice two was harder to choreograph. Harder on the egos involved. It took more concentration on my part. It was just a higher level of skills needed all around, and a larger dose of secure masculinity, too. I realized now, after Auggie, that there was a choice three, but I didn't think any of us was up to it tonight. I knew I wasn't. I had no idea how to even raise the question to Micah and Nathaniel: would they kiss another man? I mean, when did this sound like a good conversation to have? Never, I think.

I let go of Jean-Claude's hand, leaving him kneeling, while I lay down between the other two men. I traced a hand down their bodies until I touched the smooth heads, the skin so soft but the flesh underneath so hard, so firm.

Micah made a soft sound as my hand smoothed over the top of him. I looked up at Nathaniel and found his face intent on me. His eyes bright and eager, alit with anticipation. A gentle caress wouldn't do it for him. I had to still my hand on Micah, to wrap my hand around Nathaniel, and squeeze hard. It fluttered his eyes shut and forced small noises from his mouth. I'd found that I could play with two at once if the pressure was the same for both hands, but if one man needed something different, I had to concentrate separately. Micah could rev up to a level that was close to Nathaniel's preference, but it took time to get Micah in that headspace. Nathaniel came out of the box wanting rougher handling than most men ever liked.

I went back to playing with both of them at the same time, running my hand up and down the shaft of them, sliding over the head, firm, but gentle. Too hard, and most men experienced the pressure as discomfort; too gentle and it wasn't enough stimulation. It had taken me a while to find a happy medium.

I loved the sensation of my hand running up and down and around all that velvet muscle. It made me close my eyes, arch my back with the anticipation of it. When I could focus again, I gazed up at Jean-Claude. He knelt where I'd left him, close enough to touch us, but not touching anyone.

"I want you in my mouth while I play with them."

He looked at Micah and Nathaniel. "Does everyone agree to this, for I will have to be very close to both of you, to be in the position that she requests?"

I tightened my grip on both the men, just enough to make their eyes flutter shut.

"*Non, ma petite*, that is cheating. Let them go long enough for them to answer without your so-persuasive touch."

I mumbled, "Sorry." I put my hands on my stomach, and behaved.

Micah swallowed hard enough for me to hear it, then nodded. "I'm fine with it."

Nathaniel smiled that lazy cat-with-cream smile that he got sometimes during sex. It usually meant he was going to suggest something that I'd never done, or that we'd never done together, or he was going to make some observation. "I just want to see if she can concentrate on all of us at once. I give it a difficulty rating of eight."

I frowned at him. "Are you saying I've never attempted anything that took more skill than an eight before?"

He shrugged. "Remember I did this professionally for a while. My ten on this scale is probably stuff that you don't even want to know is physically possible."

I opened my mouth to ask him, *Like what?* but decided that he was right. I probably didn't want to know.

"Let's try," I said.

Jean-Claude didn't ask again. He simply crawled over my body. He ended with his legs over my shoulders, so that he was sitting in front of my face, which put him exactly where I wanted him. I traced my hands across the other two bodies. Nathaniel turned on his side first, and Micah followed him. That gave me a better angle, since my movement was about to become limited.

I wrapped my hands around them, and raised my mouth up to slide over Jean-Claude's body. He was as small as he got, loose and delicate. It always amazed me how something so small could become so large. Nothing on my body could change so much—maybe that's why it fascinated me. I loved the texture when a man was totally soft. Until we shared blood, I could roll that soft, soft flesh around my mouth, suck on it all. Normally I would have tried to draw his testicles into my mouth, too, but with both my hands busy, I didn't dare. Too delicate a work to risk, when I wasn't sure I could concentrate on it all. I rolled my hands up and down Micah and Nathaniel's bodies while I sucked on Jean-Claude, drawing him harder and faster, over and over, glorying in the fact that I could take all of him in without a struggle. Like this, it was all about sensation. I could roll and flick and suck with my mouth and tongue, able to do things with his body that I could never have done with him erect.

Jean-Claude cried out, his hands clutching at the dark wood of the headboard. He looked down at me, and I rolled my eyes upward to catch that frantic look. That look that said the sensations were almost too much.

I found a rhythm for all of them, but it was the rhythm of the sucking: quick, fast, as fast as I could do it, over and over and over. I ran my hands over Nathaniel and Micah in that same frantic rhythm, pulling, firm, and quick, over and over and over.

Micah's hand grabbed mine. "Stop, or I'm going to go." He squeezed my hand, as if I'd made some move to keep going. "Please, Anita, please."

I looked up at Jean-Claude. His eyes were closed, his shoulders hunched, his body shuddering above me. I realized that though he was enjoying it, it was treading that line between *feels better than anything else* and *too much*. He probably wouldn't have said anything. He'd have let me do it as long as I wanted, but then he'd been trained by someone who was a much harsher mistress than I would ever be.

I drew back from his body. He half collapsed above me, his body spasming. He rolled to the side, and Micah gave him room. Jean-Claude lay on his back, spine bowing, hands clutching at the black sheets.

I was left with only Nathaniel in my hand. I looked at his face. Eager, happy. He leaned in toward me. "You win." He moved in for a kiss, but I squeezed him hard and tight. It threw his head back, closed his eyes, spasmed his body. No one else in the bed would have wanted me to squeeze that tight, but he loved it.

"What do I win?" I asked. I let him go.

He gazed down at me with eyes that didn't quite focus. "Everything." He kissed me. It started as a slow kiss, but then he was just suddenly kissing me as deep and hard as he could. I'd forgotten that Jean-Claude had bled me earlier. I knew that part of what made him so eager at my mouth was the taste of my blood. He kissed me as if he would crawl into my mouth, his tongue searching for every last drop of that precious fluid.

His body pressed on top of mine. He was so hard, so firm, the feel of him trapped between our bodies made me make small sounds into his mouth, as he kissed me.

He drew back from the kiss. "What do you want?" he asked.

"You, inside me," I said.

He gave me a fierce smile, and raised himself up off my body.

I grabbed at his waist and shoulders. "What are you doing?"

"You said inside, you didn't say where inside." He crawled over me, his body not touching me, and I knew where he was going.

"Is this more foreplay or do you want to finish here?"

"Finish," he said.

"Without the *ardeur*, I don't like to swallow."

"I know," he said, and straddled my chest, leaning forward using the headboard much as Jean-Claude had.

I stared up the line of his body, his face so eager, so sure of itself. I'd worked a long time to have him look like that during sex. He knew with me he could ask for what he wanted, that his pleasure was as important to me as my own. I cupped my hand under his balls. They were already tight and close to his body. The caress brought his breath in a long sigh.

I kept one hand on his balls, and spilled the other hand up and over the length of him. He smiled down at me. "What do you want Micah to do while I'm busy here?"

We'd only very recently begun having sex at the exact same time, Nathaniel, Micah, and me. I'd thought it had been my idea initially, but now, it seemed like Nathaniel initiated it more. I knew what he wanted me to say, and truthfully, dawn was going to come, and I had one other man in the bed. Whatever we were going to do, we needed to be doing it.

I kept playing lightly with Nathaniel, and called, "Micah."

He crawled until I could see him. He just looked at me with those chartreuse eyes. His face made no demands, but his body spoke for him, so hard, so eager. "You, inside me."

"We've never done this without the *ardeur*," he said.

"I know," I said.

He gave me a look, then he smiled, and crawled back down along the bed.

"Suck me while he does it." It was more a command than a request, but I'd worked long and hard to have Nathaniel that commanding anywhere in his life. Hard to bitch about it now. Besides, he was so temptingly close, so hard, so ready. I had to mound the pillows up, a little higher, to get the angle we needed.

Micah's hands slid over my hips.

I licked the tip of Nathaniel, slid my mouth over him, took him inch by inch into my mouth, slow, so slow, so we could both enjoy the sensation of it.

I went down about halfway, then back up. We needed him wetter, so he'd slide better. But there's something about putting that much of a man that far inside your mouth that makes you wet, both above and below.

Micah's hands spread my legs, his finger plunged inside me. It made me cry out, and shove all of Nathaniel inside my mouth at once.

He put his hand on the back of my head, held me against him, so that I was trapped, and had a moment of choking around him. It wasn't a gag reflex; it was a suffocation reflex.

He let me go, and I fell back from his body gasping for breath, choking. When I could talk, I said, "Don't do that again."

Micah said, "Are you okay?"

I nodded, wasn't sure he could see it, and said, "Yeah."

"You do it with the *ardeur*," Nathaniel said.

"We're doing it without tonight." I think the look I gave him was not entirely friendly.

"I'm sorry, but I'm used to being able to do that."

"Twice, we've done that twice. Twice is not a pattern."

"I'm sorry," he said, and that look came back to his face, that uncertain, lost look. He started to move, and I grabbed his hips to keep him from moving. He looked down at me, his face so fragile, so hurt, as if all the new bravado were only skin deep: scratch it, and it goes away. I did the only thing I could think of to chase that look from his face. I drew him back into my mouth, sucked him fast and hard, until his head went back and his eyes closed. When he looked at me again, he was smiling, but there was still a flinching around his eyes; a shadow of that hurt. There was only one thing that would take that hurt from his eyes, I had to prove I trusted him. I slipped my mouth over him again, and gave myself over to the pleasure of him filling my mouth. I let my face show just how much I enjoyed the sensation of all that velvet muscle inside my mouth. The sensation of it wet and slick from my own saliva. But I didn't stop at the comfort point, that point where it just feels good and full. I sucked past that point where my body told me too much. I sucked until my mouth met his body, and there was no inch to spare. I sucked until he was shoved as hard and deep inside my throat as I could manage. I sucked until my body stopped complaining about needing to gag and started to complain about needing to breathe. But I'd learned to be able to fight past that, too. I stayed there, pressed tight and solid against his body, until he looked down at me, stayed until my throat convulsed, spasming around the length of him. He stared down at me, his eyes wild, eager, and something more. His hands stayed in a death grip on the headboard, as if he didn't quite trust himself. I drew back from him, coughing, before I could get a good breath. I finally let myself swallow all that extra saliva and lay back, panting as if I were behind on my breaths and had to catch up.

His body shivered above me, a shiver of pleasure that went all the way up his body, to throw his head back, close his eyes, bow his spine, as if the memory alone were that intense, and for Nathaniel it might have been. He finally looked down at me, eyes slightly unfocused. He smiled, and said, "Thank you." And the look on his face held something much more precious to me than passion; it held soft gratitude, wonder, *love*, for lack of a better word. There were men who loved me who never wore a look like that. Maybe it was his youth, or his years of therapy, or his lack of hang-ups. What Nathaniel felt he felt down to his toes, no hiding, no holding back, not once he gave himself to someone. It had been one of the things that made him such a danger to himself with the wrong person. With the right person he was magnificent in his abandon. He put the rest of us to shame with our wariness, our unease, our holding back. He was the only one of us who simply gave.

I gazed up into that face and was happier than I knew how to say that he was in my life.

I felt the bed adjust, a moment before fingers slipped inside me. Two searching, slender fingers. Those fingers found that certain spot, and began to flick back and forth, back and forth, fast and faster, until the feeling threw my head back, and tore a scream from me. There were other men who could do that to me, but no one else was that quick at it. I knew who it was, before I looked past Nathaniel's body to see Jean-Claude kneeling between my thighs. His eyes had bled to solid blue light.

Nathaniel moved off me, and I had a moment to try to focus and find Micah, before Jean-Claude slipped his fingers back inside me and brought me again, screaming, tearing at the sheets, grabbing for the headboard, grabbing for anything to hold on to.

I found a hand, and grabbed it, nails digging into the wrist as I writhed. When I could see again, I found it was Micah. He stared down at me with such a look on his face. He spoke, staring down at me. "Wait, Jean-Claude, wait until I'm in place."

I blinked up at him. "In place where?" My voice sounded as thick and unfocused as I felt.

He squeezed my hand tight, and said, "I want you to scream your orgasm with me in your mouth."

I said, "Okay," then thought enough to say, "Can't deep-throat you from this angle."

He put his other hand against my cheek, and turned my face to the side, toward his body. "How about now?"

The way he asked made me smile, and staring at the front of his body so thick, so ready, stole the smile and made me whisper, "Let's try."

"That's our girl," he said. He put my hand on the headboard, wrapping my fingers around it. He did that when the body part closest to me wasn't somewhere he wanted nail marks.

Nathaniel came in from the other side; he took my free hand and put it against his hip. One telling me clearly, *Don't mark me there*; the other one saying, *Please, do it.*

Micah turned my face back to him. Nathaniel put my hand higher up his chest, so I could get a running start on his skin. He wouldn't be working at Guilty Pleasures this weekend, so I didn't have to worry about marking him.

Micah slipped inside my mouth; he pushed slowly, easing his way in, but he already tasted salty, bitter, and sweet all at once. He'd been enjoying the show. That taste meant he wouldn't last as long as he might have, not a bad thing in oral sex with someone his size. Intercourse you want to last as long as possible; orally, duration is not always an asset. Two very different skill sets.

I moved forward to meet his careful thrust, and it was as if I'd given him permission. He began to thrust into my mouth, hitting the back of my throat with every thrust, pulling out just before I would have to call uncle. I had a death grip on the headboard, and my hand was mostly just steadying myself against Nathaniel's side, not digging in. I was concentrating too hard on doing Micah to think about doing myself.

"Now," Micah said, and it took me a second to understand who he was talking to. Jean-Claude's fingers slid inside me, and he found that sweet spot, found it like he knew exactly where it was. He brought me with quick, sure flexing of his fingers, quick, quicker, quickest. I screamed around Micah's body, screamed and thrust my mouth harder and deeper onto him. I rode his body as I rode the orgasm, so that he suddenly didn't seem too big, too wide, but just right. I screamed and thrashed, and drove my nails into Nathaniel's hip, as if I were trying to dig my way through him.

I screamed, screamed, and screamed, screamed my pleasure, but it was a sound that would have been pain for most people. It wasn't pain; it was release. I gave myself over to that moment, completely and utterly. Jean-Claude's hand inside me, Micah's body in my mouth, Nathaniel's flesh under my nails. I let go of the headboard, and had just enough of me left to mark higher up on Micah's back, while my other hand just kept digging at Nathaniel's hip and ass.

I heard voices, and knew vaguely that they weren't us. I heard Jean-Claude say, "Get out," but I was too far gone to look, or care.

He shoved more of his hand inside me in one quick motion, and that brought me, too. He'd worked me until my body would give orgasms like a gift, so wet, so excited, so thick, so tight, swollen with pleasure.

Micah's body was beginning to lose its rhythm, he tasted close. The apex of his thrust climbed down my throat, and back out; my own saliva poured down my mouth, because there was no time to swallow.

Jean-Claude leaned over me, with his fingers still inside, but his mouth licked between my legs, while his fingers kept going in and out of me. He couldn't do the deep sucking that the others could—fangs got in the way—but I didn't need deep. He'd worked me to the point where quick flicks of his tongue, back and forth, back and forth, started to bring me. That warmth building up, up inside me, as if the center of my body were a cup, filling up drop by drop with pleasure, until with one last lick, the cup spilled, and I screamed around Micah's body. He thrust one last time, so deep that I choked, and I knew in that moment that he'd been careful, and now he wasn't, now he finally did make me take those last two inches. I finally touched his body for longer than a second. I started to pull away. His hand went to the back of my head, as if he'd hold me in place, but he moved, and let me draw back, and drew himself out.

I watched Micah fight for control. Jean-Claude moved inches to the side, so his mouth nestled in the very upper, very inside of my thigh. Jean-

Claude's fangs plunged into me, and I was to that point where pain was pleasure, and the feel of him piercing my skin, his mouth sucking on me, brought me up off the bed, throwing my upper body upward, screaming. My body brushed against the front of Micah's body, and it was that little bit too much. My body came back to rest on the bed, and Micah spilled himself across my breasts, hot, so hot, the liquid thick and heavy, running between my breasts, down the side of my body, pooling trickling down my stomach. The sensation of it made me cry out.

Jean-Claude raised his mouth off me. His mouth was smeared with my blood, and his body was hard and ready, full of my blood, so he could pleasure my body, and his. He usually started out slow for intercourse, but tonight he, like Micah, had done his slow. He was suddenly above me, held up on his arms like a push-up, but his lower body didn't stay up. He thrust into me as hard and fast as I'd ever felt him, and I could watch every thrust as he moved in and out of me. Three strokes, five, and he brought me. I thrust my hips up to meet his, writhing under him. He brought me twice more, before I felt him begin to lose the rhythm of it, and with one last thrust he spilled himself inside me. He stayed above me, holding himself on shaking arms, while he gazed down at me, lips open, fighting for breath. He normally collapsed on top of me afterward, but my chest was covered in Micah's juice. It was already growing thinner, beginning to trickle down my sides like icing melting in the heat.

He stayed above me, panting, and smiling, his mouth still smeared with my blood. He bent down, carefully, keeping his upper body and hair out of everything, but he kissed me. Kissed me with my blood like sweet copper in his mouth.

He pulled out, and left me blinking, dazed with it all. He had barely moved out of the way, and Nathaniel was there, above me. I couldn't remember when he'd moved from the head of the bed. I'd lost track.

I stared down the line of his body, poised above me, and I thought, *Didn't I promise to start using condoms?* But the worst had happened, I was already pregnant, it didn't matter anymore. Jean-Claude had caught me by surprise, but I let Nathaniel plunge himself inside me, naked, his flesh inside mine with nothing between us.

He found that rhythm that he did sometimes, like a shuddering wave down his body, like he was dancing inside me. And with each shuddering wave, he thrust into me, thrust into me, right over that spot. Jean-Claude had given himself over to the sex, but Nathaniel was doing his usual careful job of it, as if even after all the foreplay he was going to give me my money's worth. His emotions were raw, but his intercourse was controlled. He wouldn't come until I did, he just wouldn't. He'd made a game of making me come over and over, until I begged him to. It wasn't going to take long tonight.

It didn't. I felt that weight begin to build between my legs, slow and steady, but faster than normal because of all that had gone before. "Close," I whispered, "close." My hips began to rise up and down with his move-ments, so we danced for each other, my hips thrusting upward as his thrust down, so that we met again and again. The orgasm caught me, and there was no more dancing for me. There was just screaming, and nails along his sides, me writhing, but no rhythm, no control.

I came to myself panting, double-visioned, and found his body back in the same rhythm. He kept going in and out of me, as if he could do it all night. He damn near could. He brought me again, and this time I wound my upper body around him, pressed our chests together, dug claws into his back. He pressed his upper body against me, putting his upper chest against my mouth, while his body kept pumping away. I knew what he wanted, and I gave it to him. I bit him, bit him until I tasted blood. I held his upper body against mine, so that he wouldn't jerk away and cause me to hurt him more than I planned. My mouth filled with blood, and his rhythm faltered. Plea-sure he could fight off all night, but pain, pain would bring him faster.

But he brought me again first, and I tore my mouth away from his body, so I didn't bite him too much. I turned my face to the side, and screamed. I wrapped my legs around his body, locked my heels at the top of his ass, and pinned him to me, so he couldn't get the rhythm he wanted.

He raised himself up on hands and knees, with me clinging to the front of his body. He crawled us both to the head of the bed, and used one hand on my ass, and the other on the headboard, to lift me up, and put my back against the headboard. His voice came in a strangled whisper. "I want to move more." And he did, he moved in and out of me, over and over and over, while I clung to him with my arms and legs. He brought me again, and again, and finally one more time, and then he asked, "Please, please."

Some nights he liked to beg before I said yes, but tonight I didn't think either of us could stand much more. I whispered it against the sweet smell of his neck, "Yes, go, go, go inside me. God, go, please!"

He stopped trying for rhythm and thrust inside me as hard and fast as he could. He brought me again; I dug my nails into his shoulders and back, and he finally thrust up inside me. Thrust as far and hard as he could. He stayed there like that for a heartbeat, forever, then he slumped lower on his knees, while I still clung to him.

Our bodies were slick with sweat, and blood, and other things. He clung with his hands to the headboard, his heart beating so fast I could see it. "God, that was good," he said, voice breathless, and not quite like his voice at all, yet.

I tried to say yes, and couldn't do it. It was as if I couldn't figure out how to form words, and I still couldn't make my eyes work. The world was still a white-edged blur, like something wrapped in cotton.

"Anita," Micah said, "are you all right?"

I managed to give him a thumbs-up, because it was the best I could do. It wasn't the first time that Micah and Nathaniel had fucked me wordless.

"Damn," Micah said, "I thought with three of us we might finally fuck you unconscious." His voice was teasing.

It took me three tries to say, in a very hoarse voice, "You need more men."

Micah leaned in close, kissed my cheek. "I think we can arrange that."

I managed to whisper, "Not tonight."

He kissed my cheek again. "Not tonight." He turned to Nathaniel. "You need help?"

Nathaniel nodded, wordlessly.

Micah and Jean-Claude helped peel us apart, then they went into the bathroom to clean up. Nathaniel and I still couldn't move enough to leave the bed. We lay side by side, touching, but not in each other's arms. Our bodies weren't working well enough for that, yet.

"God, Anita, I love you," he said, voice still breathy.

"I love you, too, Nathaniel," I said. And I did.

21

I THOUGHT THAT Micah might protest when Jean-Claude got into bed as naked as everyone else, but he didn't. If it had been another girl cuddling up against my naked behind I might have protested, but Micah was a lot less trouble than I was to deal with. I guess someone had to be less trouble.

I fell asleep like I did most nights with my stomach cuddled against the back of Nathaniel's nude body, the warm curve of his ass tucked up tight against my stomach, one arm up so I could touch his hair, the other around his waist, or maybe a little lower. Micah cuddled in behind me, mirroring me almost exactly, except that his arm didn't curve in around my body but stretched across so that he was touching a little of Nathaniel. Jean-Claude cuddled in against Micah as if he'd done it before, putting his arm across Micah so that he could touch me. His hand curved around me, and I raised the arm around Nathaniel's waist, so I could touch Jean-Claude's arm. Dawn was close, and that warm, living arm wouldn't be warm or living for long. Vampires lost heat faster than a dead human. I wasn't sure why, but they did.

I enjoyed the warm curve of him while I could. Nathaniel snuggled closer to me, as if he'd pressed his ass through me into Micah, but I didn't mind. I liked it close. Besides, I knew he was missing me holding him tight. My fingers played on the small hairs on Jean-Claude's arm, back and forth, tracing his skin. The feel of him like that made me regret for an instant that it wasn't my body he was pressed up against.

I fell asleep in a nest of warm bodies and silk sheets. I'd had worse nights.

I came instantly awake in the pitch black, my heart in my throat. I didn't know what had woken me, but it was something bad. I lay there pressed between Micah and Nathaniel, looking around the room in the dim light from the half-open bathroom door. It was the light Jean-Claude left on for us when we slept over. The room looked empty, so why was my pulse in my mouth? Bad dream, maybe.

I lay there pressed between the men, straining to hear something, but there was nothing but their quiet breathing. Jean-Claude's arm was across

Micah's body, but it was no longer warm. Dawn had come and gone, and taken him from me again.

Then I saw a shadow. A shadow sitting on the foot of the bed. When I looked directly at it, it wasn't there, but out of the corner of my eye I could see it: a blackness that began to take on a shape, until there was a dark outline of a woman sitting at the foot of the bed. What the hell?

I shook Micah's arm, trying to wake him, but it didn't work. I tried Nathaniel, and the same thing happened, nothing. Their breathing never changed. What was happening?

I couldn't wake them. Was I dreaming and didn't know it? I drew breath to scream. If it was a dream, it wouldn't matter; if it wasn't a dream then Claudia and the guards would come. But the moment I drew a sharp breath, the voice floated through my mind. "Do not scream, necromancer."

The breath left me, as if someone had pushed on my stomach. I finally managed a whisper: "Who are you?"

"Good, this guise does not frighten you. I was hoping it would not."

"Who . . ." Then I smelled it: night. Night out of doors, night some place warm and soft with the scent of jasmine on the air. I knew who it was. "Marmee Noir" was the least rude of the nicknames the vampires called her. She was the Mother of All Darkness; she was the first vampire, and the ruler of their council, though she'd been in hibernation, or a coma, for more than a thousand years. The last time I'd seen her in a dream she'd been as big as the ocean, as black as the space between the stars. She'd scared the shit out of me.

The shadow smiled, or at least that's what it felt like. "Good."

I struggled to sit up, and the men slept on, not even moving in their sleep. Was this a dream, or was it real? If it was real we were in deep, deep shit. If it was a dream, then I'd had powerful vamps invade my dreams before.

I put my back against the wood of the headboard. It felt real and solid. But I didn't like sitting there naked in front of her. I wished I had a gown, and the thought was enough. I was suddenly wearing a white silk gown. Dream, because I'd been able to change it. Dream, it would be okay. It was just a dream. The knot in my gut didn't believe me, but the rest of me tried to believe.

I thought of several questions to ask that shadow, and finally settled for, "Why are you here?"

"You interest me."

It was like having the devil suddenly take a personal notice of you; not good. "I'll try to be less interesting."

"I am almost awake."

I was suddenly cold down to my toes.

"I can taste your fear, necromancer."

I swallowed hard, and couldn't keep my voice from being breathy. "Why are you here, Marmee Noir?"

"I need something to wake me after such a long sleep."

"What?"

"You, perhaps."

I frowned at her. "I don't understand."

The shadow began to grow more solid, until she was a small female figure in a black cloak. I could almost see her face, almost, and I knew I did not want to. To see the face of darkness was to die.

"Jean-Claude has still not made you his, still not crossed that last line with you. Until he does, another more powerful than he can take what is his, and finish it."

"I am bound to a vampire," I said.

"Yes, you have a vampire servant, but that does not close the other door." She was suddenly sitting at my feet. I tucked my feet up, and pushed myself against the headboard. It was a dream, just a dream, she couldn't really hurt me, but I didn't believe it.

She spread a hand wide, and the hand was carved of darkness. "I thought this guise would make me less frightening, but you cringe from me. I am wasting a great deal of energy to speak to you in dream, rather than invade your mind further, yet still you fear me." She sighed, and the sound of it flittered through the room. "Perhaps I have lost the knack of being human, even to pretend. Perhaps if I have lost the knack, I should stop trying—what do you think, necromancer? Should I show you my true form?"

"Is this a trick question?" I asked.

I felt her frown, rather than saw it, because I couldn't see her face yet.

"I mean, is there a good answer here? I don't think seeing your true form would be a good thing, but I don't really want you to keep playing human-ish for me, either."

"Then what do you want?"

I wanted Jean-Claude awake to help me answer this question. Out loud I said, "I don't know how to answer that question."

"Of course you do; humans always want something."

"You to go away."

I felt her smile. "This is not working, is it?"

"I don't know what was supposed to work," I said. I was hugging my knees now, because I did not want her touching me, not even in dream.

She stood, in the middle of the bed, then I realized that wasn't exactly it.

She stood, but then she kept growing, stretching up and up, like some black flame. The light reflected off whatever she was becoming, as off water, or sparkling rock. How could something gleam and give no light? How could something both reflect light and absorb it?

"If you are afraid of me anyway, then why pretend?" Her voice echoed through the room like a rush of wind. I could smell rain on the edge of that wind. "Let there be truth between us, necromancer."

She vanished; no, she became the dark. She became the darkness in the room. One minute she was a central point, almost a body, the next she was the darkness. She hung in the dark of the room, and that darkness had weight and knowledge. I was like every other human who had ever huddled around the fire because they could feel the darkness pressing around them. Feel the darkness waiting for them. She didn't try to talk to me now, she simply *was*, not words, not even images, but something I had no words for. She simply was. A summer night does not talk to you, but it exists. The dark of a moonless night does not think, but it is still alive with a thousand eyes, a thousand sounds. She was that night, with one addition: she could think. You don't want the dark to be able to think, because it won't think anything you want to know.

I screamed, but the darkness filled my throat, cut off my air. I was choking on the scent of night, drowning in jasmine and rain. I tried to call my necromancy, but it wouldn't come. The darkness in my throat laughed at me like the cold twinkling of stars, beautiful and deadly. I tried for my link to Jean-Claude, but she had severed it. I tried for my link to Nathaniel and Micah, but her animal to call was all cats, both great and small. My leopards could not help me now. The darkness whispered them to sleep.

I remembered the last time she'd been this close to me metaphysically, and thought of the only thing she hadn't been able to control. I thought of wolf. It had taken Richard's tie to me, and Jason's closeness, to waken my wolf in me and chase the darkness back, but we'd grown closer now, my wolf and I, and it came. A huge pale wolf with markings of darkness leapt out of the darkness, its eyes filled with brown fire. It put itself between me and the dark. It let me wrap my fingers in its fur, and the moment I touched it, I could breathe again. The scent of night was there, but it wasn't in me.

The darkness swelled around me like some great dark ocean, building up, up, to crash upon the shore. The wolf tensed against me, so real against my body. I could feel its bones, its muscle, under the fur, pressed tight against me. I could smell its fear, but knew it would not leave me alone. It would stay, and defend me, because if I died, so did it. It wasn't Richard's wolf, it was mine. Not his beast, but mine.

That black ocean reared above us, so that the bed was like some tiny raft. Then it fell toward us with a sound like a thousand screams. I knew those screams—victims, eons of victims.

The wolf sprang to meet that blackness, and I felt teeth sink into flesh. I felt us bite her. I had an instant to see the room where her real body lay, all those thousands of miles away. I saw her body jerk, saw her chest rise in a sharp breath. Her breath sighed through the room. "Necromancer."

The dream shattered, and I woke screaming.

22

JEAN-CLAUDE'S BEDROOM was bright with lights. Micah was on his knees looking down at me, petting my shoulder. "Anita, thank God, we couldn't wake you."

I had time to see Nathaniel on the other side of the bed, and Jean-Claude standing beside him. I'd been out of it long enough for Jean-Claude to die and come alive again. Hours lost to the dark. Claudia, Graham, and others were in the room. It must have been hours; the shift should have changed. I had time to see and think all that, then the wolf from my dream tried to climb out my body.

It was as though my skin were a glove, and the wolf were the hand. It filled me, impossibly long. I could feel its legs stretching out and out into my arms and legs. But its limbs and mine weren't the same shape; it didn't fit. The wolf tried to make me fit.

My fingers curved, tried to form paws, and when that didn't work, it tried for claws to come out of the human fingers. I screamed, holding my hands up, trying to get breath to explain. Then I didn't have to, because my body started to try to tear itself apart. It was as if every bone and muscle were trying to tear itself free from every other piece of me. The pain of it was indescribable. Parts of my body that were never meant to move were moving now. It was like the meat-and-bone of my body was trying to move out of the way so something else could take its place.

Micah pinned my arm and shoulder. Nathaniel had my other arm. Jean-Claude pinned one leg, and Claudia had the other. They were yelling, "She's shifting!" "She'll lose the baby!" Claudia yelled. "Help hold her, damn it."

Graham put his weight across my waist. "I don't want to hurt her."

I heard something in my shoulder pop, a wet sound that you never want to hear from your own body. I shrieked, but my body didn't care. It wanted to tear itself apart. It wanted to remake itself. The wolf was there, just under my skin. I felt it, pushing, pushing, trying to get out. Other bodies threw themselves on the pile, and gradually the sheer weight of them held me, but still the muscles and tendons kept writhing.

Another convulsion shook my body, forced some of them to shift their grips. An arm came close to my face, and I smelled wolf. That sweet musky smell quieted my body. My wolf sniffed at that pale skin and thought, not quite in words or in images, but somewhere in between: *pack, home, safe.*

The arm moved away and took that calming smell with it. The wolf tried to leap after that scent, tried to follow it, but the other smells held me down. Leopard, rat, and something not furred, not warm. Nothing that would help us.

The wolf clawed at my throat like it was an opening to be dug at, enlarged, so it could crawl out. The wolf couldn't get out, couldn't get out, trapped. Trapped! I tried to scream but a scream wasn't what broke out of my throat; a low, mournful howl spilled out instead. The sound cut through the frantic voices around me, froze the pressing hands. It echoed up and up, dying in the sudden silence. Then as the last quavering echo faded another voice rose, high and sweet. A third voice joined, deeper, so that for an instant their voices entwined in glorious harmony. Then one voice fell octaves lower, breaking the harmony, but the discord had a kind of harmony of its own.

I answered them, and for a moment our voices filled the air with quavering music. The bodies pressing against me slid away. The smell of wolf pressed close. A hand touched my face and I turned in against that hand, pressed it to my face, breathed in the scent of wolf. There were other scents on that hand, a scented map of everything he had touched that day, but under it all was wolf. I tried to raise both hands to press his skin against mine, but only one of my hands would rise. Something was broken in my left shoulder, something that wouldn't let me use that hand. Fear flared through me, and I whimpered, and that warm skin pressed closer to me. I'd never realized that you could cuddle a scent around yourself as if it were an arm. But I hugged that scent around me, smelling it so intently that it spread around me like someone taking me into their arms.

I kept his hand pressed over my nose and mouth, but rolled my eyes up along his arm until I found the black shirt and finally Clay's face. His eyes were wolf eyes, and my wolf knew that I had done that. I had called to his wolf, and it had answered.

The bed moved beside us. I pulled my face away from Clay's skin so I could sniff the air as I turned to look. I saw Graham, but his scent meant more than what my eyes told me. He smelled so warm, so good. I reached my good hand for him, because if I could touch him, I'd carry some of that good, warm smell with me.

My hand touched his chest and only when my hand touched bare skin did I realize he was nude. It was like the hierarchy of reporting from my senses was backward. Smell, touch, sight: primates didn't reason that way, but canids did. Vaguely, I remembered seeing Graham's smooth, muscled body, but he smelled safe and right. Clothes didn't matter to safe and right. But my hand on the warm, bare hardness of his chest startled me, as if I hadn't expected it. I wasn't thinking straight.

I stiffened my arm, pushing against his chest, as he tried to get closer to me. Now that I was seeing him, and not just looking at him, I could see that he wasn't unhappy to be nude in front of me. That pissed me off. I ached, my muscles burning, hurt in places that I shouldn't even be able to feel, and he was excited about getting our nude bodies up close and personal. Damn him.

I found I still had a human voice. "No." My voice was hoarse and abused, but it was still clear. "No."

Claudia appeared near the head of the bed. "I told him to get undressed, Anita. You need as much skin-to-skin contact as you can get."

I tried to shake my head, found it hurt, so just said, "No."

She knelt beside the bed, pleading at me with her eyes. It was a look I'd never seen from her. "Anita, they're all the wolves we have right now, please, don't make this harder."

I swallowed and it hurt, as if I'd damaged things in my throat that wouldn't heal for a while. "No."

Jean-Claude came to stand beside her kneeling figure. "Please, *ma petite*, do not be stubborn, not now."

I frowned at him. What was I missing? What was I not understanding? Something. Something important, by the looks on their faces, but I just didn't want Graham to put his naked, erect body up against my naked body. I did not want to have sex with him, and once we were naked and in bed the odds of that went up. Sure, I was hurt, and I'd supposedly fed the *ardeur* really well, but call me paranoid, I just didn't want to risk it. But for my last shreds of moral dignity, Graham could have been in the running for daddy-to-be. That, more than anything else, kept my arm straight, and my lips saying no.

Claudia said, "You don't understand, it's not over."

"What isn't over?" I managed to say it, in that deep, not-me voice, and then I knew. The wolf had thought it was getting out, getting help, that the pack would help it escape, free it from this prison, but I'd kept the feel of other wolves at bay. I'd refused to let them slide wolf scent and skin over my body, so the wolf went back to trying to get out and join them.

My arm didn't stay stiff, nothing on me did. I writhed on the bed like a bag of snakes, muscles and tendons moving in ways that should have ripped me apart. My skin should have split, and I almost wanted it to; I wanted the wolf to get out of me. To just stop hurting me. I'd thought the wolf was me; now I thought it was trying to kill me.

The smell of wolf was everywhere, thick and nose-wrinkling, sweet musk. My body lay still on the bed while tears leaked down my face, and I whimpered, not wolf sounds, but small, hurt, human ones. I thought I'd hurt before, but I'd been wrong. If you could force someone to feel this forever, they'd tell you anything, do anything, to make it stop.

I was lying between Graham and Clay. Their naked bodies were pressed as close as they could get, without putting any of their weight on top of me, as if they knew that that would hurt. They cradled me gently between them, their hands on my head, and on my good shoulder. They touched me as if I'd break, and it felt like they were right.

Graham's eyes had bled back to brown. The look on his face was worried. What had they seen that I hadn't? What was happening to me? Clay leaned over, pressed his lips against my cheek, and kissed me, gently. He whispered, "Change, Anita, just let it happen. It won't hurt like this, if you just let it happen."

He raised his face up, and I saw that he was crying.

I heard the soft click as the door opened. I wanted to turn and look, but it had hurt the last time I did it. It didn't seem worth it. Besides, Graham's chest was blocking my view in that direction.

"How dare you order me into your presence?" Richard's voice, already angry.

"I tried to make it a request," Jean-Claude said, "but you did not respond."

"So you order me, like I'm your dog?"

"*Ma petite* needs your aid," and Jean-Claude's voice held that first hint of anger, as if he was as tired of Richard's moods as I was.

"From what I can see," Richard said, "it looks like Anita has plenty of help."

Clay sat up enough to show a tear-stained face. "Help her, Ulfric. We are not strong enough."

"If you want tips for satisfying her in bed, ask Micah; I'm really not that into sharing."

"Are you Ulfric to her lupa, or not?" Micah came to stand at the foot of the bed, still nude, just like we'd woken up.

"That's wolf business, kitty-cat, not yours."

"Stop it," Clay yelled, "stop being an asshole, Richard, and be our leader. Anita is hurt."

Richard finally came to the edge of the bed to peer over Graham's reclining body. His hair was sleep tousled, a thick brown-gold mass around his arrogantly handsome face. The arrogance slipped, and the guilt I'd begun to dread almost as much replaced it.

"Anita . . ." He made a painful sound of my name, so much pain in that one word. He crawled onto the bed, and showed that he was still wearing shorts. He'd either taken the time to dress, or slept clothed, very unlycanthrope. The other men made room for him, but they didn't leave the bed. He started to crawl over me, but the first touch tore small pain noises from me. He went up on his hands and knees above me, keeping his weight off me, but my wolf was too close to the surface. Richard putting himself above us like that meant he thought he was superior to us and my wolf didn't think he'd earned that. Neither did I.

I felt the wolf crouch to spring. Felt it gather itself as if it could spring from my body to Richard's. I had a moment to realize that it could do just that. I'd felt Richard's beast and one of mine fight once. It had hurt. I was already hurt. I did not want to do this.

"Move, Richard." My voice was an abused whisper.

"It's all right, Anita, I'm here."

I put my good arm against his chest and pushed. "Move, now."

"You're in a dominant position over her," Graham said, "I don't think she likes it."

Richard looked at him, while his body stayed over mine. "She's not a wolf, Graham, she doesn't think like that."

A low growl trickled out of my throat. I didn't mean for it to.

Richard turned his head slowly, the way you do in horror movies when you finally look behind you. He stared down at me, his hair like a thick frame around the soft astonishment of his eyes. "Anita . . ." he said, but my name was a question this time, as if he wasn't sure.

That soft, deep roll of growl vibrated across my lips again. I whispered in a voice deeper than any I'd ever had, "Move."

"Please, Ulfric," Clay said, "please move."

Richard went back on his knees, still straddling me, but in a postion that a wolf couldn't exactly duplicate. It should have been enough, but my wolf had found another way out, a hole that it could climb through. Always before when I'd shared my beast with other lycanthropes I'd only felt fur and bone, as if some great beast were walking around inside me, but this time I saw it. I saw the wolf as I'd seen it in the dream. It wasn't truly white, but the color of cream, with dark markings like a saddle across its back and head. That dark cape was every shade of gray and black intermingled, and even the white and cream wasn't truly white or cream, but mixed like milk and buttermilk. I stroked my hand across that fur, and it was . . . real.

I jerked so hard it hurt, made me cry out, but I could still feel the memory of fur under my good hand, as if I'd touched something solid.

"She smells real," Graham said.

Richard had gone very still where he knelt over me. "Yes," he said in a faraway voice, "she does."

"Bring her wolf," Clay said, voice soft. "Make her change, so she'll stop hurting herself."

"She'll lose the baby," Richard said, but he was staring down at me with a look on his face that I couldn't read, or maybe didn't want to.

"She's going to lose the baby anyway," Claudia said.

He looked down at me, and his eyes were lost. "I can see the wolf inside you, Anita, just behind my eyes, I can see it. We can smell it. What do you want me to do? Do you want me to bring your beast?" His voice sounded empty, as if he were already in mourning. He didn't want to do it; that much was clear. But for once, we agreed.

"No," I said, "don't."

He didn't slump, but a tension went out of him. "You heard her. I won't do it against her will."

"Say that after you've seen the convulsions. I've never seen anyone fight like this, not for this long," Claudia said. "Once someone's this far along, they shouldn't be able to fight the change. Even her eyes are still human."

Richard gazed down at me, face solemn. "That's our girl," but he didn't sound happy when he said it. He let down his shields, not all the way, but as if he blinked metaphysically. I got a glimpse at his emotions, his thoughts, just a glimpse. If I shifted for real, he wouldn't want me. He valued my humanity, because he felt like he had none. If I shifted, I would cease to be Anita to him. He still didn't understand that being a werewolf didn't stop you being a human being.

But underneath those thoughts were others, though thoughts might be the wrong word. His beast was in there, his wolf, and it wanted me to change. It wanted me to be wolf, because then I would belong to it. Can't be lupa and Nimir-Ra if you're actually wolf for real.

The thought made me look across the bed, until I found Micah. I saw it in his eyes, the loss, as if he were already certain of it. No way. I would not lose him, not now. I turned to look around the room for my other leopard. Turned too fast, hurt the muscles in my left shoulder, muscles I'd torn.

Nathaniel came to the side of the bed as if he understood that I was looking for him.

There were tears drying on his face, as if he'd cried, and hadn't bothered to wipe them away. You could date outside your species, I knew that, but I remembered Richard saying once that dominants don't. If you were high enough up in the power hierarchy, you didn't date outside the pack. I was lupa; there was no higher-ranking female than me. I was Bolverk, which would have made me like an officer anyway. Either way you cut it, if the wolf I could touch came out for real, then I'd lose more than a surprise pregnancy.

I knew I had at least one more beast inside me. I held leopard, the way I held wolf. If I was finally going to go all the way furry, could I choose what kind of furry? Looking into Nathaniel's face, watching Micah look away so I wouldn't read his face, I knew I had to try.

I gazed up at Richard. I said it out loud: "You don't want me to change, that's why you won't help."

"You don't want to be one of us, not for real." His face was sliding back to that arrogant, angry mask.

"You're right."

His anger showed, almost a pleased anger, as if that one statement proved that I was no better than he was, no more comfortable in furry skin.

I looked at Micah and Nathaniel. Micah had moved so that he could hug Nathaniel. "Micah, Nathaniel, help me call leopard."

Micah looked startled. "It's not a choice, Anita. I can smell what you are."

I started to shake my head, but whatever I'd done to my left shoulder made it hurt too much. "I hold four different strains. Why can't I pick which way I go?"

Graham and Clay looked at Richard, as if wondering what he'd say. "I think you're out of choices," he said, "but if you want to try, I won't stop you." He was hurt, and his trying to hide it made it more painful to see. If I changed, he'd look elsewhere. I didn't think he'd find someone willing to share him with what amounted to a permanent mistress, furry or not, but hey, it wasn't my life. It was his life.

I could see the wolf in my head, like a waking dream, all subtle cream and white and black and gray. It looked at me with eyes that were an amber so dark they were almost brown. It was like looking into a piece of your soul and having it look back.

Richard slid off the bed. The wolf didn't panic; it stood there in me, patient, waiting. Graham started to follow, sliding off. The wolf paced closer to the surface again, agitated. I grabbed his arm. "Stay." He froze under my touch, half kneeling beside the bed.

Clay looked from me to Richard. "Stay until she says go," Richard said, in a voice that managed to be closed, empty, and angry all at the same time.

"Micah, Nathaniel, help me raise our beast." They didn't argue or hesitate; they simply crawled up on the bed. They crawled toward me in that graceful way that the lycanthropes had, as if they had muscles that we mere mortals didn't have, as if they could have balanced a cup on their backs.

Hurt as I was, watching them crawl toward me nude quickened my breathing, sped my pulse. It made the wolf start to pace in tight, agitated circles. I didn't have a hand to touch Clay. "Clay, touch me." He closed the small distance he'd made for Richard to straddle me. He pressed his body against the line of mine, but was careful not to touch my left shoulder. He was a quick study, and he seldom argued. It was sort of refreshing.

Micah touched my legs, but Nathaniel crawled around Clay, so he could be by my head. Micah asked, "What do you need us to do?"

I'd never tried to call one animal instead of another. We'd only learned about a month ago that I held three different kinds of lycanthropy. Wolf and leopard hadn't been all that unexpected, but lion, that had caught me off guard. Such a delicate injury, so little blood, but sometimes a nick is enough with blood-borne diseases.

"I don't know, yet." I knew how to call someone else's beast, if it matched mine. Richard had taught me the theory of that. I thought of leopard. I simply thought of it, and I felt it stir inside me. It was always the oddest sensation, as if there were some deep cave inside me, and the beast lived there until called. Now it uncurled itself, stretched, and began to rise. My body was like a dark liquid that the beast rose inside of; that was all pretty typical of being a lycanthrope. The problem was that my body lacked the switch to actually shift, and once the beast got to the surface of my body, there was no place to go. Or there hadn't been, up until now.

But somewhere during the rising liquid feel of fur curving against places that nothing should have touched, I realized that there were two shapes rising for the surface. I'd tried to call leopard, but I was about to get double for my money.

The wolf bristled, his ruff standing up, his body stiffening. I felt his fear. He knew he was about to be outnumbered, and inside my body there was no pack to call. The wolf stood his ground, making himself look as large and fierce as he could, then the cats hit the surface of my body, and the wolf fled. I could feel him running, running back the way he had come. Like he was heading home. It was the first time I realized that my body wasn't just a prison, but also a den, a place of safety.

The cats hit the surface together, and the force of it bowed my spine, threw my body upward, as if some great force had hit me from behind. I fell back to the bed, screaming with the pain of my abused body taking yet another hit tonight. I needed this to stop. We needed it to stop.

I saw the cats. The leopard looked small beside the lion. Small, sleek, and gleaming black. It had backed away from the larger cat. I didn't blame it. The lioness was huge, a great, tawny beast of a cat. Maybe it would have looked smaller if I hadn't been looking at wolf, and now leopard. The lion was staring at the leopard in a way that was patient, waiting for the leopard to decide what to do next. The lion had the confidence of several hundred pounds of extra muscle on its side.

I let go of Graham and used my good hand to reach for Nathaniel. He bent over my face so that when I touched him, his face was nearly above mine. I buried my face against the sweet warmth of his neck. He always smelled like vanilla to me, but underneath that was the scent of leopard. Sharper than the musk of wolf, less sweet, more exotic for lack of a better word. The leopard stopped being defensive, and looked up with eyes that were soft and gray, with just a hint of green in them. I didn't call *Here kitty-kitty*, but I called it all the same.

The leopard rose up through me, and hit the surface of my body. It filled me like a hand sliding inside a glove, so that I felt it stretch out and out, filling me. I waited for that fullness to finally split my skin and step out, but nothing happened. I could feel fur rubbing against my skin on the wrong side; I could feel it in there. I gazed down my body, and watched things roll under the skin of my stomach like the cat was rubbing against me. The sensation left me nauseous, but that was all. It wasn't as violent as the wolf had been, but I still wasn't shifting.

Graham and Clay slid off the bed so that Micah could move up beside me. "It's there, but it's not coming out—why?"

Nathaniel slid down so that the two men framed my body with their own. "I don't know," Micah said.

"Give your beast to me," Nathaniel said.

I looked up at him, and thought at the furred thing inside me. It was patient because I wasn't afraid of it. I'd embraced it, welcomed it. Now it slid inside me, waiting for release. A release that I couldn't give it.

"I've taken your beast once before," he said.

"I remember." I turned my head, just enough to see Micah's face. I looked a question at him.

"Give your leopard to him, Anita."

Nathaniel pressed his body closer to my side, so I could feel him pressed soft against my hip. He leaned over me, propping himself across my body with one arm, so he laid no weight on my upper body. He leaned in for a kiss, and I felt the leopard roll toward him like something half liquid and half solid fur. His mouth found mine, and we kissed. The last time I'd given him my beast had been almost as violent as tonight, but I'd been fighting; now I simply gave it to him, and Nathaniel didn't fight. He kissed me hard and deep, as if he were trying to taste that furred shape, and the next moment that shape spilled up through my mouth. I felt it as never before, as if truly it slipped up and out through my mouth. I had a moment of choking, and then it was in him. My leopard smashed into his body, smashed into his beast. The force of it pushed his body off the bed, like a blow, but he fought to keep on kissing me. Fought to kiss me as thick, heavy liquid ran over my body from his. So warm, hot, as if he were bleeding to death. I opened my eyes enough to see that the liquid was clear, but had to close my eyes to keep it from getting in them. His hands were on my face, trapping us in the kiss. But I wanted the kiss, I wanted this. I wanted, needed the release, and my body couldn't give it.

I wrapped my good arm across his back so I could feel his skin split, and the fur flow out like solid water, hot velvet under my hand. His mouth re-formed against mine, so that the kiss had to change, because the mouth he had now couldn't kiss like his human body. Not enough lip. I licked my tongue along teeth sharp enough to eat me for real. He drew back, and I was left to wipe the heavy liquid off my face, so I could see him. The face was leopard, and human, a strangely graceful mix. Leopardman worked better than wolfman, maybe because the cat had a shorter muzzle naturally.

I raised both my arms toward him, and realized that the left arm was working now. I hadn't shifted, but something about giving him my beast had given me some of the benefits of healing that shifting would have done. Interesting.

I hugged him, and found his fur dry, though my body was covered in the clear goo that shifters "bled" when they changed. I never understood how their fur came through dry, but it always did.

I ran my hands over the unbelievable softness of his fur, felt the muscled strength of him, and felt that his body wasn't at all unhappy to be pressed against mine. We'd made love once before when he was in this form, and at that moment it didn't sound like an entirely bad idea, but there was someone else inside me, waiting.

The lion roared where it was still standing, patient. It let me know that it—she—was still there.

"Shit," I whispered.

Nathaniel snuffled next to my face. "Lion."

Micah rolled off the bed. "We need a werelion, fast, before it decides to try to tear its way out."

"We have no lions," Jean-Claude said.

I thought about it. I thought, *I need a lion*. I thought about the golden fur, the dark, orange-amber eyes. I put the call out, not for my lion, but for *a* lion. I felt an answer, like a distant voice. I felt two answering tugs, almost as if I held two leashes. One was reluctant, the other was eager.

"They're coming, or at least he is," I whispered.

"Who's coming?" Nathaniel said in that growling voice.

"Cookie," I said, because for the life of me I couldn't think of his real name. All I could think of was what I'd nicknamed him in my head because of his Cookie Monster–blue hair.

We heard raised voices before anyone knocked at the door. Men's voices, arguing just outside the door. Lisandro went to the door after Claudia nodded. He opened the door to reveal Cookie with his blue spiked hair, and the brunette werelion. Cutting—no, Pierce. His name was Pierce. Cookie was smiling as he came through the door, wearing nothing but jeans, with a gun stuck inside the waistband. As if the reason for the pants wasn't modesty, but a place to put the gun. Pierce glowered as he came through the door. He was completely dressed, though his shirt was buttoned crookedly, and his jacket tucked badly on one side to flash the shoulder holster. The gun looked like a Beretta. Not my choice for concealed carry, but then I have small hands.

I wasn't surprised to see them. I'd called them. I was surprised to see Octavius, Augustine's human servant, at their heels. He was dressed as impeccably as he'd been earlier except that he had no tie, and his cuffs were loose in the sleeves of his elegant suit jacket. If the cuffs hadn't been loose, he wouldn't even have looked like he'd rushed.

"This is outrageous," he said. "First you insult and humiliate my master, then you try to steal his lions. Did you think that since Augustine is asleep for the day you could simply take them?" He got a good look at me on the bed. He stopped, I think, because some of the people in the room had moved so he could see me on the bed. Me and Nathaniel. I don't know what he thought we'd been doing, but I suddenly saw it through an outsider's eyes. Me, nude on the bed covered in clear, sticky liquid. Nathaniel nude and excited in leopardman form cuddled in my arms. Other men in the room already nude. What would I have thought if I'd walked in on all this? Probably the same thing Octavius was thinking.

The look on Cookie's face showed that he was thinking the same thing, but he was happy about it. He started toward the bed, but Pierce grabbed his arm, held him. Cookie growled at him, and that one trickle of sound made the lion inside me tense.

"Don't let her mind-fuck you," Pierce said.

"You heard her call, too," Cookie said. "You couldn't say no, either."

"But I don't want to go to her. I don't want her to use me." He turned the other man so he was facing away from the bed. Cookie had a tattoo of Cookie Monster, as in *Sesame Street*, on his right shoulder. A happy little Cookie Monster eating cookies. So the hair color wasn't an accident.

"I want her to use me."

"Fight it," Pierce said.

"I don't want to fight it," Cookie said.

"If our master were awake, you would not dare do this," Octavius said. He walked around them both, walked closer to the bed. Claudia and Lisandro stepped between him and the bed. But it was when he saw Jean-Claude stepping out from the wall that his face fell apart. Fear, fear and confusion, chased over his face. He was totally shocked to see Jean-Claude there. He fought, and finally mastered his face. But the first look was enough, the first look and his remark that Augustine was asleep. For the first time I figured it out. It wasn't that we'd slept the day away and Claudia and the rest were back on duty. It was that we'd barely been asleep at all, and Jean-Claude had not died at dawn. He, like Damian, did not die at dawn if he slept touching me.

Octavius gave arrogance, but shelved the anger, as if he didn't want to start the fight. He bowed. "Jean-Claude, I did not think you would be up. I did not see you standing there. I do have better manners than this; my anger made me forget myself. Please, forgive me." His words were clear, but he said them a little too fast. I think it was his version of babbling nervously.

"There is nothing to forgive, Octavius—if you do not hinder us, that is."

Octavius faced him, and nothing could keep the discomfort out of the set of his shoulders. "Hinder you in what way?"

Jean-Claude stood before the man, still nude, but as comfortable as any of the shapeshifters. He wore his body as if it were the most costly robe in the world, or as if he were not aware he was naked. "Augustine said that these two werelions are supposed to be *pomme de sang* candidates for *ma petite*."

Octavius gave a small nod. "That is true."

"We may have been too hasty with our rejection of them earlier. I believe that there were errors of etiquette on both sides, would you not say that was true?"

"Perhaps, perhaps we were all a little hasty earlier," Octavius admitted, his voice showing that he wasn't sure where this was going, and was trying to be cautious without being insulting. I think if Jean-Claude hadn't been stand-ing there, and his own master dead to the world, he'd have been less cautious and more angry. Hell, if it had just been me and the shapeshifters, I think he'd just have told us to go fuck ourselves, or some polite version of that.

"*Ma petite* would taste one of your lions now. I think in light of all that has happened it might be well to cement a stronger tie with your master. We are, after all, two of the most powerful masters in this country, and between us we are certainly the most powerful territories in the middle of this country." I followed the phrasing. It implied, but did not say, that between the two of them they could rule the middle of this country, and wouldn't it be better to be allies than enemies? Or maybe I was actually picking up a little of Jean-Claude's thoughts, just a touch. He had no intention of doing some sort of war of conquest, but to imply it gave us both the leverage of fear and greed. Fear of being our enemy, and greed to take part in the spoils if we did de-cide to conquer. Jean-Claude played him.

Octavius licked his lips, then stood a little straighter as if he'd realized he was slumping. "Perhaps. I know that Augustine's intent was to offer the lions as *pommes de sang*. Or as barter for one of your females."

"I do not barter my people. I believe *ma petite* made that clear to your master."

Octavius nodded. "Yes, very clear." Anger threaded through his voice, and he fought it off, so that his next words were empty and unoffensive. "I think it would please my master if you found his *pomme de sang* candidates worthy of attention."

Jean-Claude looked at me then. His face was empty, lovely, but it was his voice in my head, soft, the merest brush of contact, that told me what he wanted. "Call them."

I held my hand out to them, and said, "Come to me."

Cookie turned immediately, only Pierce's hand on his arm stopping him. "Don't make me fight you, Pierce."

"If he is not strong enough to resist," Octavius said, "release him to his fate."

Cookie looked at Octavius. "You don't understand; I don't want to resist her. I want her to take me."

Pierce tried to turn Cookie back to him. "Don't you see, that's wrong. She's already rolled you, man. She's already done you, and you don't even know it."

"Maybe, but if that's what's happening, I'm okay with it." The edge of smile I had seen vanished, and his voice was low and serious when he said, "Take your hands off me, Pierce. I won't ask again."

"Let him go," Octavius said. "That is an order, Pierce."

Pierce gave him an angry look, but he let the other man go. He even raised his hands in the air, as if it wasn't his fault.

There was a small part of me that wanted to see if I could force Pierce to come too, but Cookie was coming. One lion was enough, for now.

23

CLAUDIA STOPPED HIM, standing in his way, towering over him. It was probably the first time he'd met a woman tall enough and muscular enough to do that. Just seeing his reaction to it would say a lot about him.

"Call your rat off, Blake," Cookie said.

"Give up the gun and I move," she said.

"I was more armed than this when she touched me earlier."

"Then you were bodyguarding your master, now you're about to get up close and personal with one of mine." Her voice was low and matter-of-fact. I thought it was interesting that she implied I was one of her masters. News to me.

I could see one shoulder enough to know he shrugged, then he must have handed the gun over, because Claudia moved aside.

He padded toward the bed on bare feet, the first button of his jeans already undone. Had it been before, or had he caught the gun on it as he pulled? The last would be careless. Was he careless?

I was way too calm. I watched him come toward the bed with a detachment that surprised me. It was like a type of shock, almost, or . . . the lion was utterly dispassionate about the man walking toward us. In some ways animals are more reactive than we are; people mistake that for emotion, but it's not. There was no emotion from the cat in my head. She waited. Waited with a sort of cold, wary patience, as if she could have watched him forever, and felt nothing. It was his choice whether we got along, or chased him away. If he did something stupid, or weak, she wouldn't accept him. She'd kill him before she'd accept him, but there was no passion to the decision. It was colder than any thought I'd ever had, except when I'd decided to kill. Then there is a moment of cold clarity, a moment of something that is almost peaceful. My moment of peaceful sociopathy was stretched to an eternity in the head of that big cat.

Nathaniel moved, and that made me turn to him, but the lion in my head roared at me, swiped a claw across the inside of my body. She let me know that she needed my eyes and had no interest in leopard. The pain of her claws spasmed through me. I was partially healed from what I'd done with Nathaniel, but that one swipe showed me that I was still hurt. Hurt in places that there'd be no way to bandage. Part of me wanted to fight her, and turn to Nathaniel, but I knew if I did, she'd do worse. I fought my own stubbornness for a moment, eyes closed, concentrating. Trying to decide if I'd grown up enough to let this small loss go, or if I had to win at every damn thing. If I let the lion think it could boss me around, would that set a bad precedent for later? Then a thought came to me; the lion was me. I was fighting with myself. How terribly Freudian, or would it be Jungian? Either way, how strangely me.

The thought was so me, that it opened my eyes. Cookie was standing beside the bed. His hands were at his sides. The look on his face was eager, but wary, as if he'd finally figured out that something might be wrong. His blue hair was flattened on top as if he'd been asleep when I'd called him. His eyes were very blue as he stared down at me. I could see the tattoo on his left shoulder now: the faces of Bert and Ernie. I sensed a theme.

"Any more tattoos?"

He grinned. "Yeah, want to see?"

"I don't know," I said.

"You called me," he said, and his voice was softer, as if he wasn't sure what was happening, and was finally not sure he was happy to be here. Cautious, at last. It pleased the cat in my head. Pleased me, too, I guess.

Micah said, "She needs to give you her beast."

Cookie turned to him, frowning. "I don't understand." His nostrils flared, as he scented the air. "She smells like lion, but she smelled like leopard earlier. She smelled like wolf, too." He shook his head, as if clearing his mind from the scent. He looked down at me, frowning, speaking softly. "What are you?"

The truth would have been, I wasn't sure, but some of the people in this room weren't our friends. Octavius would be our enemy if he could. I was about to try for half-truth, when Jean-Claude stepped up beside the bed and spoke. "*Ma petite* seems to have the ability to acquire the animals of the vampires she comes in close contact with. I knew she gained wolf through me, as some servants do. She gained leopard through contact with another. It may be her closeness with your own master that has brought lion to her." Not a lie, but it certainly wasn't the whole truth. But hey, I had no better suggestions.

"That would make her very dangerous," Octavius said from near the door. He and Pierce were still close to the door as if for a quick getaway.

"It would make her powerful, yes," Jean-Claude said.

"Dangerous," Octavius said. "Do the other masters know that they risk seduction and the loss of their animals to you, Jean-Claude, or are we your first victims?"

Jean-Claude sighed, and the sound echoed through the room, and slid over my skin. The lioness paced, growled low and deep, and the sound slid from my lips. "Don't," I said.

"My apologies, *ma petite*," he said. He turned to Octavius. "Truth then between us, Octavius, before you think even worse of us. I know you of old; you will spread these rumors. So I give you truth, and I will know if you tell, because no one in this room will tell but you."

"I do not gossip."

"You have always gossiped." He motioned to me. "Anita holds different types of lycanthropy inside her."

"That is not possible."

"Nor is it possible for her to have a vampire servant, or an animal to call that is not mine, but those are true things."

"We had heard, but we thought the servant was rumor."

Jean-Claude shook his head. "Augustine is powerful enough to see truth. When he sees her with Damian, he would know the truth anyway. I tell you only a night early, oh, a day early." He said it as if he had just remembered that he was up at dawn. He had so not forgotten. "I swear to you that human doctors have drawn her blood and tested it. She carries more than one strain of lycanthropy, and yet has not shifted to any. She holds the animal but seems unable to turn. They have tried to tear their way out tonight, and still she cannot shift."

Micah added, "She's stuck at that point where the beast is trying to get out, and you don't know how to let it out."

"Ouch," Cookie said. He looked down at me, smiling. "You've had a hard morning."

"You have no idea," I said.

"Yes he does," Nathaniel growled from beside me.

The two shapeshifters looked at each other. It was a long look. "Yeah, I remember the first time, we all do."

"She fought, fought it to a standstill."

He looked at me, eyes narrowing. "You can't do that, no one can."

"Never underestimate how stubborn Anita can be," Richard said from across the room. "You'll regret it, if you do."

I looked at him. He'd taken one of the chairs near the fireplace, as far from the bed as he could get without leaving the room. He was mostly in shadow, so that I couldn't see his face well. But then again, maybe I didn't want to see his face right then.

"Don't mistake force of will for stubbornness," Micah said. "There is a difference."

"It looks the same to me," Richard said.

"It would," Micah said.

A low growl trickled from Richard, and it echoed through the room, much the way Jean-Claude's sigh had. The sound made me shiver but not with the promise of sex; it flared across my skin like heat, and the lion reacted to it. She spilled into my skin like the leopard had done, like the wolf had done. I was suddenly writhing on the bed, screaming again. I did not want to hurt again. But if I didn't want to be wolf, I sure as hell didn't want to be lion. I didn't even know the lion pride here well. Shit. If sheer force of will was keeping me in human skin, my will was getting worn down. Eventually, I'd lose this fight. I didn't want it to be now.

I reached out for Cookie. He grabbed my hand, almost by reflex. I dragged him down to me, and he didn't fight me. He could have, but he came to me. He laid his body on top of mine while the lion tried to come out. She stretched, stretched, impossibly huge, trying to thrust claws out through my fingers and toes. She couldn't come out, but those metaphysical claws cut through my skin. I screamed. I raised my hands up to hold him to me, and there was blood flowing down my fingers. *Sweet Jesus, help me.*

From far away I heard Cookie say, "What do I do?"

"Kiss her," someone said.

He kissed me. The moment his mouth touched mine, I let the lion go. I let it plow into him. With Nathaniel I'd tried to be a little controlled, but I was all out of control today.

It hurt for it to leave me, like someone had thrust a shovel down my throat and was digging out my internal organs in one ripping, burning line. I screamed into his mouth, and he screamed back. He kept his mouth on mine, even while his body began to writhe in pain. His hands dug into the bed on either side of me, holding on, holding on, while that line of tearing, ripping, burning power ripped him open. There was no moment of bones sliding, or reshaping. One minute he was human, the next his skin had exploded outward, raining on the room in thick wet globs. The body under my hands was dry and furred, and the cheek I touched had a fringe of thick, golden mane. I had to wipe thick goo out of my eyes to be able to see. I wiped off bits of him that were thicker than clear liquid. The power had literally blown him apart. I had a moment to wonder if his tattoos would survive; then I could see his face.

His eyes were golden, in a face that was a pale gold, with a mane around his head like a furry halo. The face was that strangely graceful mix of human and cat. His shoulders were broader than the leopards', everything more muscular. His suddenly nude body was pressed between my legs, but not happy to be there. I had a glimpse of his tail flicking behind him, then he collapsed, partially on me and partially beside me.

Where his weight hit, my body hurt. I made a small sound, and he rolled off me and lay there on the liquid-soaked sheets. He looked like some primitive golden god hunted to death. I lay where I was, covered in something I didn't even want to see. It felt too thick, too . . . just too. I tried not to look at it, or think about it. I lay there covered in bits of his body, and knew I'd hurt him, badly.

"I'm sorry," I said, and my voice was an abused whisper.

He rolled golden eyes up to look at me. "That fucking hurt."

Micah came to the edge of the bed. He took one of my hands in his, and looked at my fingers. "You were bleeding from under your nails. If he hadn't taken your beast when he did," he shrugged, "it might have been too late."

That scared me. It tightened my stomach, and even that hurt, as if I'd abused muscles that I didn't know I had.

"Thank you, Cookie, more than you'll know."

The lionman said, "Did you just call me Cookie?"

"Sorry, it's the hair, Cookie Monster blue, and the tat."

"Haven. My name's Haven." I think he smiled, but it was hard to tell on the lionish face, from the angle I had. "Though Cookie Monster works just fine."

"I said Cookie, not Monster."

"You haven't seen me at my best, yet" he said, and smiled for sure.

I did not understand the comment. Micah did. "He's implying he's big."

"Oh," I said, then had to smile up at Micah. "He shouldn't brag until he's seen the competition."

The lionman rolled his face to look at Micah. He wasn't looking at his face. Micah said, "You aren't seeing me at my best either."

Even through the lion's face I could see the arrogance as he looked up at me, not at Micah. "Trust me, I'll measure up. Auggie was shopping for size, not just talent."

I wasn't sure if I was supposed to say *Oh, really, Oh, goody,* or *Oh, boy.* Under normal circumstances his assumption that he was going to get to fuck me would have pissed me off. But one, I didn't have energy left to get pissy; two, he'd saved me. Saved us. Micah, Nathaniel, and me. I could ask for our local pride to give me some lions to follow me around, but this morning, right this moment, Haven had been the only rescue I had. I owed him. Also I'd ripped his body apart, and caused him massive amounts of pain. *Oops* didn't really cover that one.

"When you can walk," Nathaniel said, "I'll take you to the feeding area." Nathaniel's fur glistened under the lights, wetter from being so close to Haven's violent shift than from his own. He slipped off the end of the bed and padded around to join Micah, who was still holding my hand.

Micah pressed my hand to his face, and it left a wet glistening stain on his cheek. I was so going to need another bath.

"I can walk." Haven slipped off the side of the bed, and went straight to his knees. "Shit."

Nathaniel reached down to help him stand.

Haven asked, "Did you take her beast, too?"

"Yes."

"It didn't hit you this hard, did it?"

"No." Nathaniel didn't bother to explain that it hadn't been as violent, and no one else did either. I wasn't sure we were keeping Haven, but if we were then Nathaniel would need to establish some sort of dominance with the other man. That Nathaniel could take that much pain and keep on ticking would help.

Haven leaned against the bed, Nathaniel still holding his arm. Those golden lion eyes looked at me. "Don't take this personally or anything, but the fringe benefits better be fucking amazing."

"They are," Nathaniel said.

"Depends on what fringe benefits you're talking about," I said.

"Sex," he said, straightening up slowly, obviously still in pain. "You're Belle Morte's line, there is no other fringe benefit for you guys."

I couldn't argue with the last part, but I could with the first. "Don't assume you're getting sex, Haven."

He gave me a look. "All this and you don't think I've proved myself enough for sex? Damn, girl, what does a man have to do to meet your standards?"

"When you figure it out, let me know." This from Richard. He stopped near the bed, and looked at me. "You could have been my lupa for real, but you didn't want to be. You chose him, them, over me."

"If I'd been lupa for real, you wouldn't have wanted me. I saw it in your head."

He shook his head. "You could have been my lupa at the lupanar, with the pack."

"But I would have lost the baby."

He wouldn't meet my gaze.

"You can't stand the thought that this isn't your baby."

"No, I can't."

"I'm already your lupa," I said, "I'm already Bolverk. Nothing would have changed for you and me if I'd become wolf for real. My being wolf would have meant you looked harder for that human Ms. Right."

He stared down at me. "You won't even let me have the illusion of it, will you?"

I tried to sit up, and Micah had to help me. So stiff, so sore. "What illusion, Richard?"

"That we could be together as a couple, at least with the wolves."

"And what happens to my life when the moon isn't full?"

"Would it be so bad to be with me for real, without the others?"

I looked up into his face, and maybe I was tired, physically, mentally, emotionally. After everything I'd been through tonight, and this morning, all he could think of was himself, his problems, his pain. "Is everything about your pain, Richard, is that all you think about?"

"Answer me, Anita, answer me. Would it be so bad to have been with me for real? Just the two of us, would that be so bad?"

I tried one more time not to answer. "You don't want me to answer that question, Richard." I leaned in against Micah, let him hold me.

"*Mon ami*," Jean-Claude said, "let it go."

He shook his head again. "No, not this time. I had this idea that if he"— and he pointed at Jean-Claude—"hadn't interfered we'd be a couple, we'd have been happy. But I see you with him"—he pointed at Micah—"and him"—he pointed at Nathaniel—"and I have to know. Tell me the truth, Anita. Tell me the truth. I won't break the triumvirate. I won't run away. But tell me the truth, so I know where I stand. I need to know how hard I need to look for Ms. Right. Tell me the truth, and maybe I can move on. I know I can't stand watching you take another lover. That, I know I can't stand." He sat down on the messy edge of the bed. He gave me a solemn face. "If you'd become wolf for real, and had to live with me, give up Micah and Nathaniel, would that have been so bad?"

My throat hurt, but it wasn't from what the beasts had done. My throat was thick and tight; my eyes burned. Why did Richard always make me want to cry? "Don't make me do this," I whispered.

"Just say it, Anita, just say it."

I had to swallow twice, and the tears spilled over as I said, "Yes, it would have been bad."

"Why? Why would the two of us living together, raising our child be so bad? If it is mine I want a place in his life."

That was it, he'd brought the baby up, and suddenly in all the tears was the anger, never far behind for me. "You don't see me, Richard. You see this ideal of me, but it's not me. I don't think it was ever me."

"What does that mean, I don't see you? I see you, you're right there."

"What do you see, Richard, tell me?"

"I see you."

"I'm naked on a bed being held by a naked man, with two other naked men in the room who are also my lovers. You've just said you can't stand to watch me take another lover, when you know I'm supposed to be looking for a new *pomme de sang* to feed the *ardeur*."

"I thought you weren't really going to look, just pretend."

That should not have been said in front of our company. "I'm not sure I have a choice right now, Richard."

"The next time the wolf comes, just don't fight it, and you can be my lupa. We can be together, because you won't be able to be with anyone else."

That was it; I told him the truth. "I don't want to be just with you, Richard. I don't want to lose Micah and Nathaniel, or Jean-Claude."

"So, if I said, choose, I'd lose."

I thought, *you've already lost me.* Out loud, I said, "I can't be with just one person, Richard, you know that."

"Even if the *ardeur* cools, you're never going to choose just one of us, are you?"

We stared at each other, and the weight of his gaze was so heavy, so heavy. In his own way, he was just as stubborn as I was, and this was one of those moments when it was about to destroy us. "No, Richard, I don't think I am."

He took in a lot of air, and let it out slow. He nodded, as if to himself, stood, and said, without looking at me, "That's what I needed to hear. Not this weekend, we'll be busy, but next weekend I'll still want you to go to church with me, if you want to."

I wasn't sure what to say, so I said, "Okay."

"Family dinner afterward, like always," he said as he headed for the door. He hesitated at the door, turned with his hand touching it. "I will find someone who wants the life I want."

"I hope you do," I whispered.

"I love you," he said.

"I love you, too," I said, and meant it.

"I hate you, Anita," he said, with almost no change in his voice.

"I hate you, too, Richard," I said, and I meant it.

24

ANOTHER MESS, ANOTHER bath. Thanks to the violence of Haven's change I wasn't the only one with gobs of him in my hair, and other places. If a forensics team had come on the scene, God knows what they would have made of it. Jean-Claude and Micah got in the tub with me. Nathaniel had taken Haven to the feeding area, where they kept livestock, or I assumed it was livestock. Truthfully, I'd never seen the "feeding," but Nathaniel and Jason had both told me that it was legal food, and that meant animals. Though I loved several shapeshifters, I did not want to see them eat. Some visuals I did not need.

Octavius and Pierce had tried to go back to their rooms, but Claudia had stopped them. She'd asked where the guards on their door were. Pierce said, "They tried to stop Haven and me from leaving the room."

"That was their job," Claudia said.

"Then they aren't that good at their job," he said.

"Did you kill them?"

He looked down at the floor, then back up. "They were breathing when we left them."

That had prompted her to send Lisandro and Clay to check. She'd kept Graham with her, and made Octavius and Pierce wait for the news. Both of the wererats were alive, but hurt. Badly hurt.

Thanks to the problems we'd had with the masters of both Cape Cod and Chicago, we had extra guards. They had actually put guards on the coffin room, which was fortunate; Meng Die had cracked her coffin when she got the power rush that all of Jean-Claude's people got from our sex with Augustine. Meng Die, more powerful, not a good thought.

Now the extra guards came in handy. Claudia put four guards on Octavius and Pierce. She sent Lisandro to supervise them, with orders to check in with Fredo, who turned out to be in charge of the coffin room detail. Claudia stayed with us, and kept Clay with her. The two of them were outside in the bedroom now, while we cleaned up. Claudia and Clay were messy, too, but would wait to clean up.

Jean-Claude drew me through the warm water, until my body rested against his. I laid my head back against his shoulder and said, "Didn't we just do this?"

"Not precisely, *ma petite*," he whispered against my wet hair.

Micah moved through the water until he knelt beside us. His hair was plastered to his head, looking straight and black. His chartreuse eyes were startling in his tanned face without the hair to distract from them. He moved in close enough that a strand of his hair touched mine, and the illusion of blackness faded, because even wet his hair was not as dark as mine, or Jean-Claude's. Impossibly rich, dark brown, but not black.

I whispered against Micah's cheek, "No, not precisely."

Micah kissed me, then leaned back enough to see us clearly. "Now that we're clean, why couldn't we wake you and Jean-Claude?"

"I thought Jean-Claude was awake the whole time," I said.

"Not at first; at first he was as out of it as you were."

"How did you know he wasn't just dead to the world like normal?"

"He was breathing."

I felt Jean-Claude stir against me, as if that fact had startled him. "Breathing. How . . . interesting." His voice was very careful.

"Shouldn't you have been breathing?" I asked.

"No," he said.

I turned around in his arms until I could study his face. That face showed me nothing. It was as beautiful and unreadable as a painting, as if instead of a face with movement and breath, it were just a moment caught in time, a single lovely expression. He was at his most careful, hiding, when he was like that.

"Why is your breathing more surprising than your not dying at dawn?" I asked.

"I also dreamed," he said.

I frowned at him. "You were asleep. You dream when you're asleep."

"I have not dreamed in almost six hundred years."

"What did you dream?" Micah asked.

"A very practical question, *mon chat*."

I looked from one to the other of them. "Am I missing something?"

Jean-Claude looked at me. "What did you dream, *ma petite*? Who did you dream of?" His voice never changed from that friendly lilt.

"You ask like you already know," I said.

"You must say it, *ma petite*."

"The Mother of All Darkness," I said, softly, and just saying it seemed to make the room not quite bright enough.

"Marmee Noir," he said, nodding.

"Yes," I said. I tried to read past that pleasant exterior, and failed. "You dreamed of her, too?"

"*Oui*."

"You both dreamed of the head of the vampire council?"

"She is much more than that," Jean-Claude said. "She is the creator of our civilization. Our laws are her laws. Some say she was the first vampire, and that she truly is the mother of us all."

I cuddled in closer to him, and he tucked me under his arm, so I could wrap my arms around his waist. Somehow, close wasn't close enough when talking about the Mother of All Darkness.

"What did you dream, exactly?" Micah asked.

"She tried to play human for me, but, God, she was bad at it."

"I saw her bend over you, *ma petite*. I saw her begin to take you away from me. But I could not reach you, the darkness held me as her figure bent over you." He shuddered, and held me tight against his body. "I could not reach you, and her voice taunted me for my carelessness." He kissed the top of my head. "But she also told me that if I had given you the fourth mark, that she would have killed you, for if she could not control you, then she would destroy you."

Micah came to us, tucked himself against me, pressing Jean-Claude's arm between us, his own arm going across Jean-Claude's shoulders. Micah was on his knees beside me, because their heads came together over mine, and Micah wasn't tall enough for that without some help. "But you woke before Anita," Micah said. "Why?"

"I thought if I could break my dream, it would free *ma petite*. It did not, but I was able to break Marmee's hold on my mind. That, in itself, is a surprising thing."

"Surprising doesn't begin to cover it," I said. "How did you break free?"

"How did you?" he asked.

"I called the only animal I have that isn't a cat. She only does cats. I saw her in that room, where her real body is. I saw her body jerk. My wolf bit her, for real, I think."

The two men held me tighter, pressing me between them, as if something about what I'd said scared them. I guess it was scary, but . . . "Am I missing something here, guys? You're suddenly both even more afraid."

"The ability to send a spirit animal through dream and harm another is rare among us."

"Among vampires, you mean," I said.

"*Oui*."

"Us, too," Micah said, "but . . ." Then he stopped abruptly.

"But what?" I asked. When he didn't answer, I pulled away from them both, so I could see his face. Jean-Claude, if he wanted to, could hide anything behind his face, but Micah wasn't that good. If I looked hard enough, I might get a hint.

He lowered his eyes, as if he knew what I was doing.

I touched his face, turned him to look at me. "What, Micah, what is it?"

"Chimera could invade your dreams."

"Could he hurt someone that way?"

"No"—then he seemed to think about it—"not when he took over my original pard, he couldn't. He had grown in power in the years I was with him, so maybe? Ask some of the dominants he took, who survived. Ask them if he could hurt them in their dreams."

"It is very rare for a lycanthrope to be able to invade dreams like a vampire," Jean-Claude said.

"Chimera was a rare kind of guy," I said, and just thinking about him scared me. He was dead, I'd killed him, but he had been one of the scarier things I'd ever fought.

Micah looked at me, and his face held such pain, as if whatever he was thinking was something so awful.

"What?" I asked.

"We learned last month that you carry lion lycanthropy. That had to come from your fight with Chimera."

I nodded. "He was in lionman form when he cut me up, yeah."

Micah licked his lips, as if there were any possibility in the hot, misty tub that his lips were dry. "What if you gained more from him than just lion lycanthropy?"

I frowned at him. "I'm not following."

"He means, *ma petite*, what if you gained not simply lycanthropy, but the kind of lycanthropy that Chimera held? He was not a werelion, he was a panwere. He held over a half-dozen types of lycanthropy, did he not?"

Micah nodded. "Leopard, lion, wolf, hyena, anaconda, bear, and then he took the cobra's leader. I think if he'd lived until next full moon, he would have been cobra, too."

"Chimera thought that once he hit his first full moon, the animals he had were all he got."

"I don't think that was true," Micah said.

"Are you sure it wasn't true?" I asked.

He shook his head. "No, but it would explain what's happening to you."

"What do you mean, what's happening to me?"

"Anita, you almost shifted tonight. Blood came out from under your nails. It was close."

"We're not sure I'm a panwere."

"No, but if you are, then you won't lose the leopards when you shift."

I shook my head. "I'll pick leopard, if I have to pick, thanks, just in case."

"I agree," he said, "but if you are a panwere, and you're close to shifting . . ." He stopped talking, then looked down.

"You are thinking what I am thinking, *mon chat*, and you know she will not like it," Jean-Claude said.

"What?" I asked.

Jean-Claude answered, "If you are to be a panwere, and there is a chance that you will gain new animals until your first change of shape, then we have the opportunity to gain great power."

"What are you talking about?"

"If you are going to shift, then wouldn't it make sense to add more types of lycanthropy?" Micah said.

"Make sense, no," I said, "no, it wouldn't make sense."

"Why not, *ma petite*? You called the lions, and they came to your call. You call the leopards and they come. You call wolves, and I begin to wonder if it is my power that attracts them to you, or something more."

"You're saying I should deliberately infect myself with other types of lycanthropy?"

They exchanged glances. "Put that way, no," Micah said.

"It is a thought, *ma petite*, merely a thought."

"Are you always thinking about how I can help you be more powerful?"

He sighed. "We must be powerful, and stable. We must show the other masters that we do not pose a threat to the council in Europe or anyone else."

"Powerful we can do, but stable—" I shrugged. "I don't know about that one."

"We aren't a threat to the council," Micah said, "but they may not believe that."

"They may not," Jean-Claude said.

There was a knock on the door. "Who is it?" Jean-Claude called.

"Remus."

"Is there something you need, Remus?"

"Claudia ordered me to check in, physically, with you for the shift change."

Jean-Claude glanced at us. He held an arm out. "Come to me, *ma petite*, let us make certain you are hidden from sight, then allow him to enter."

"I don't see why he needs to enter," I said.

"We will ask him." Jean-Claude took me into the curve of his shoulder. Micah moved in front of me. I wrapped my arms around Micah's shoulders, drawing him in against my breasts. Yeah, the water covered me, but Remus was still one of the newer guards. I didn't know him well enough to be comfortable in the tub with him in the room.

"You may enter," Jean-Claude said.

The door opened; Remus stepped inside, but kept his hand on the doorknob, as if he were no happier about invading our bath than I was. His eyes were green-gray, nice eyes, if he'd ever look directly at you. He never did, or at least he never did at me, or Jean-Claude, or Micah, or Nathaniel. Why? Remus's face had been broken at some point, and been put back together. There was no one thing you could point to and say, "That's out of place," but the overall effect was lopsided, and looked almost uncomfortable, like a ceramic mask that had been glued back together wrong.

I couldn't make complete sense of Remus's face, because he wouldn't look at me. I wanted badly to tell him to just look at me, but I couldn't without raising a subject that was probably painful, and none of my business. So I let it go.

The rest of him was dressed in the usual bodyguard black. If there were injuries under the clothes, it didn't show when he moved. He moved like there were steel springs in the lean muscles of his body.

"Claudia ordered anyone who takes over to check with you in person, eye to eye. Her orders."

"Did she say why?" I asked, because it was a change.

He looked up then, gave that lopsided smile. I had a moment to see disbelief on his face, before he looked away. "She filled me in on what's been happening. She wants at least two guards in the room with you, at all times."

"I don't think so," I said.

"That's what I told her you'd say." He gave another glance at me, and I had a second of those green-gray eyes, angry, then down and away again. "With Micah with you, it's not a problem, but if it were only Jean-Claude—" he shrugged. "If you shift for the first time and it's wolf, then he may be able to control you, but if you shift to an animal he doesn't control, then what if you eat him?"

"He's a Master of the City; I think he can handle it."

"You don't get it," Remus said, and he came into the room a step, letting go of the doorknob. He finally looked at me, and held my gaze. Since I give absolute eye contact, it left us staring at each other. His eyes flinched, but he kept the gaze. It was a relief to be able to see his face straight on. "Jean-

Claude is powerful, but in plain unarmed combat, shifters beat vampires. Unless they can mind-fuck us, we will win a fight."

I glanced at Jean-Claude to see how he felt about that. He gave the same lovely, blank face. I turned back to Remus. "So, what, you guys get to watch?"

"Do you think this makes me happy?" he said, and his power flared through the room like a hot wind. He closed his eyes, and counted to ten, or something, because the heat vanished. He gave calmer eyes to all of us, but he knew it was mostly me he had to persuade, so he stared at me. The angry defiance, was back in his eyes. "You have no idea how dangerous you could be when you first shift. You won't just be a lycanthrope—that's bad enough, but you'll be this uber-preternatural power. You'll be a shifter with powers over the dead. If you lose control of one power, maybe you'll lose control of all of them. Do you have any idea what could happen?"

I stared up at him, scared, and not liking it. I could be scared, or I could get angry. Guess which I picked. "The beast blocks the necromancy. Once I give in to one hunger that completely, the others go away."

"Are you a hundred percent sure of that?" he asked.

I opened my mouth to say yes, then hesitated.

Micah answered for me, patting my arm as he did so, "No."

No was truthful, but . . . "So what do we do?"

"You have to have at least one shapeshifter with you at all times, someone powerful enough to handle the emergency."

"Handle how?" I asked.

"Keep you from hurting anyone too badly."

"Who's on the list of powerful enough?" I asked.

"Me, Claudia, Fredo, Lisandro, Socrates, Brontes, Bobby Lee, Mickey, Ixion. A lot of the wererats are ex-military and mercs. But some of them are better at killing than minimizing the damage." He shrugged. "Claudia and Bobby Lee will be in charge of the list, but I know that you won't be left with just Graham and Clay again. Maybe one of them, but they'll need to be paired up with someone with more real-world experience."

"Real-life experience?" I made it a question.

"Ex-military, merc, ex-cop, professional bodyguard. Raphael recruits from some very hardcore places."

"Narcissus doesn't?" I asked.

Remus shrugged again. "He does now. He lost nearly three hundred men when Chimera took them over. They slaughtered them. Narcissus had a lot of muscle and athletes, but he didn't have many real fighters. One of the reasons that the werehyenas got taken over by such a small force was that they weren't the real deal. Narcissus found out that martial arts training doesn't stand up to true warriors. War ain't an Olympic event; it's no place for amateurs."

"And you are not an amateur," Jean-Claude said in that pleasant, empty voice.

"No, sir," Remus said, "I am not."

25

I WENT TO the bathroom for a few minutes and came back out to find that Jean-Claude wasn't the only vampire in the bedroom. Elinore stood near the bed. She was dressed in a white gown with a high lacy collar and a cream robe that managed to look graceful, and not like jammies at all. Her long blond hair fell in a pale wave around her body, like a second robe, so long. She was a vision in pale delicate colors, then she looked at me. Her eyes were a pale icy blue, the wrong color of blue for that delicate face. Her face was a near-perfect oval, dainty and unreal, as if someone had carved her from some white, pure rock, and breathed life into her. Unless she worked at it, hers was a cold beauty. If her eyes had been a brighter blue, I think it would have made her look warmer. The eyes gave the lie to the rest of her. The eyes were serious, careful, watchful. Hidden under all those clothes was a round, curvy body, soft. She didn't believe in weight lifting, too unlady-like. But she had a body that was as lovely and desirable as the face, if a little soft for my tastes. She had the blond Nordic beauty that I'd craved as a child. Craved so I'd fit in with my blond, blue-eyed father and his new family.

I'd tried to hate her, just on principle. I'd failed, why? Under that lady-like exterior she was tough, fair, and harder than a box of nails. She just hid it much better than I did. We got along. Besides, all the male vamps were prettier than me, why shouldn't some of the female vamps be pret-tier, too?

"Elinore," I said, "what . . ." I checked my wristwatch. "What are you doing awake before noon?"

"That is what I was asking Jean-Claude," she said in that silky voice that matched all the lace and cream satin.

Jean-Claude looked at me from where he sat on the edge of the bed. He was in his black brocade robe with all the fur on it. They looked like oppo-site ends of a dream; one so pale, the other so dark.

"All our people have gained from what we did last night, *ma petite*." He motioned toward Elinore. "This is proof of just how much they may have gained."

I started walking around the end of the bed toward them. "Is this the earliest you've woken as a vampire?"

She nodded.

"How do you feel?" I asked.

She seemed to take the question seriously. She screwed that pretty little face up in a look of concentration. I was never sure if Elinore really had that many cute mannerisms or whether she'd spent so many centuries using them as camouflage that she couldn't get rid of them now. Whatever, she was always doing things that made me think, *little girl*, *doll-like*, *cute*. Until she decided not to be cute; then she was positively frightening. I wondered how many enemies had been lured in by that softness only to find the steel dagger inside all that silk. If I'd been willing to play to my packaging, I might have pulled it off, but it just wasn't in me to try.

"I feel fine," she said at last.

"Have you fed?" I asked.

"Can you not tell?" she asked, giving me a very direct blue gaze.

"You always look a little ethereal to me, so no. I can't tell with you."

She gave a small smile. "Quite a compliment that the Executioner cannot tell whether I've fed."

"Do you feel the thirst?" Jean-Claude asked.

She thought about that for a second, making the pretty little face. "No. I could feed, but I do not have to."

I felt a stab of triumph from Jean-Claude. Triumph, and right on its heels, fear. Then he closed the leak in his shields tight.

"Why afraid? Why triumphant? Why both?" I asked.

"Jean-Claude fed the *ardeur* well and truly last night, and it is sustaining me. That is very impressive," Elinore said.

"Yeah, I get that, but . . ." I tried to think how to form the question. "Why are you both so pleased?"

"If we wished to travel as a group in countries where we are illegal, only one of us would need to feed. It would mean Jean-Claude could take quite a large group of his own vampires into another territory without leaving much evidence behind. Certainly we could hide from the human authorities."

"But we're not going to invade anyone's territory."

"No," Jean-Claude said, "but it is always good to have options, *ma petite*."

"Where's your sweetie? Your knight?"

"He did not wake with me," and there was just a hint of sadness to that.

"So are you the only one who gained—" There was a knock on the door.

"Yes, Remus," Jean-Claude called.

Remus opened the door and closed it behind him. "Requiem is out here."

"Requiem," Elinore said, "interesting."

"Send him in, Remus," Jean-Claude said.

He held Jean-Claude's gaze for a moment, then looked down, and did his talking to the side of the face. "All right, but if anyone else shows up early like this, I will have to insist that you let two of the guards inside the room. So whatever secret shit you're discussing, discuss fast."

"You really think there's going to be that many more vamps waking up this early?" I asked.

"Yeah, I think there will be."

"We will discuss whether guards come back inside when someone else comes to my door," Jean-Claude said. "Let Requiem pass, Remus."

Remus's face struggled; he didn't like it. "I am caught between masters here. Claudia says don't leave you guys alone. You say I can't stay. We need a chain of command here."

"Too many generals," I said.

He gave me a quick, direct glance. "Yes."

"I am sorry, Remus," Jean-Claude said, "but Elinore's arrival has changed things."

"Fine, but Requiem is the last, or I'm calling Claudia and telling her I can't guard you, because you won't let me."

"As you see fit, Remus."

He gave another angry look around the room, then opened the door. A moment later Requiem glided through the door. He had his black, hooded cloak close around his body, so that the only thing that showed was the spill of his Vandyke beard framing the curve of his lips.

"How badly are you hurt, *mon ami*?" Jean-Claude asked.

Requiem shrugged back the hood without using his hands, the way you'd flip long hair behind your back. The hood slid down and the right side of his face was a mass of deep-purple bruises. One of his eyes was almost swollen shut, just a glimpse of that startling bright blue that had made Belle Morte try to buy Requiem from his original master. Belle had wanted to have a matching set of blue-eyed men. Asher's were the palest blue; Jean-Claude's the darkest; Requiem's the brightest. His master had refused, and they had fled France.

His long, straight hair, so dark it mingled with the black cloak, made his pale skin all the paler, and helped the bruises stand out like purple ink on his face.

"Wow," I said, "how much blood are you using to heal that?"

He looked at me then, and the look on his face said, clearly, I'd said something smart. "Much."

"How fares the rest?" Jean-Claude asked.

Requiem spread the cloak wide with a gesture of both arms, so that it was like a curtain spilled dramatically around his body. His upper body shone like white flame against the darkness. My eyes adjusted to all that contrast and I realized that some of the whiteness was bandages. His right arm, chest, and stomach were all thick with gauze and white tape.

"Jesus, did Meng Die really do all that?"

"Yes." He said that, and no more. Requiem rarely gave just a one-word answer to anything. He came toward us, the cloak flying out behind him, which said he was moving faster than that gliding walk appeared.

"*Ma petite*, if you could fetch scissors from the bathroom drawer, we can look at his wounds."

I did it without being asked. I'd noticed the bruises last night, but hadn't seen all the bandages under his shirt. I had had no idea how hurt he was. I hesitated in the bathroom with the scissors in my hand. I caught sight of myself in the mirror. I looked sort of startled. Had he really dumped Meng Die because of me? Dumped another woman on the off chance that I might take him as a *pomme de sang*? I stared at myself in the mirror and just didn't see a woman who could make a man dump someone on the possibility of sex. Elinore, maybe, but me . . . I just didn't think so.

I went back to the other room, and found Requiem sitting on the bed beside Jean-Claude, who was turning his face to the light, checking his bruises.

Requiem was talking as I entered. ". . . she said, if she could not have my pretty face on her pillow, then no one would have it."

Someone had brought one of the chairs by the fireplace so Elinore could sit and not be on the bed. "So she tried to ruin your face," she said, softly.

"Yes," he said, in that strangely clipped voice that wasn't at all his usual.

I held the scissors out to Jean-Claude. He took them and laid them on the bedside table. "I think perhaps we can take off the tape, if you will help me, *ma petite*?"

I had to move Requiem's cloak where he'd draped it on the end of the bed. The bed was tall enough that I had to make certain I was sitting far enough back from the edge so I wouldn't slide off. Silk coverlet, silk robe, makes for slippery. I took Requiem's hand in mine. The bandages wrapped around his hand, and up nearly to the elbow. "You didn't get this from her hitting you," I said.

"She had a blade," he said, and again, his voice was clipped and to the point.

I looked up at him, and even the uninjured half of his face showed me nothing. He was lovely and empty like Jean-Claude was sometimes. Like looking at a painting of some handsome prince come back from battle. Even as I cradled his arm in my hands, he was as distant and remote as if he'd been hanging on a museum wall.

Jean-Claude was already peeling tape from around Requiem's chest. I bent over his arm and worked on the tape there, holding his hand in mine while I started unwinding the gauze. His hand was crisscrossed with shallow and not-so-shallow slashes. I raised his hand as gently as I could, so I could keep unwrapping. The bandages fell away and I made a sound; I couldn't help it. I put my hand at his hand and elbow, and lifted, gently. His forearm was a mass of slashing wounds. Two of them needed stitches.

I looked at his face, and he met my eyes, and for an instant there was a flash of anger in those eyes; then it went back to being empty.

"These are defensive wounds. You held your arm up in front of your face, because that's what she was going for."

"Not entirely, *ma petite*." Jean-Claude's voice drew me back to him, and Requiem's now bare chest. I let out a hiss of breath, because he was right. His pale, muscular chest didn't have as many wounds as his arm, but the ones he did have were deeper.

I traced the one under the sternum. It was deep, and I could see the mark of the blade in his flesh. I looked up at him, and it must have shown on my face.

"So shocked, Anita, why?"

"She was trying for your heart. She was really trying to kill you."

"I told you that last night, *ma petite*."

"I know you said she was trying to kill him, but . . ." I traced my fingers just above another wound that went between his ribs. The stab wounds were well placed. She'd tried to hack his face, and the marks on the arm showed that she just wanted damage, but the wounds on his chest and stomach, they were kills. "She knew just where to place the blade." My respect for Meng Die went up, and so did my fear. "And she did all this where the customers could see?"

"Not all of it," Requiem said, "but much of it, yes."

I looked at Jean-Claude. "And no one called the cops?"

He had the grace to look away, not embarrassed, but . . . "What did you do?" I asked.

"Mass hypnosis is not illegal, *ma petite*, only personal hypnotism."

"You bespelled the crowd," I said.

"I, and Asher."

I laid my hand above the wound that looked like it had come closest to his heart. I had a bad thought. "You said she attacked Asher. Is he this hurt?"

"No."

"I think she knew that you and Jean-Claude would kill her if she slew Asher. I think she believed I was of less value to you." Again his voice was empty, but the very emptiness of it made me look at him.

"That sounded bitter," I said.

He looked away from me, a small smile on his face. "I meant it to sound like nothing."

"I've listened to a lot of empty vampire voices, and there's flavor even to the emptiness."

"I was a fool to tell her in a public place, but she pressed me, asked me, and I told the truth." He looked at me then, and I had to fight to meet his gaze, not because of vampire powers, but because the bruises looked painful, and I knew somehow, weirdly, they were my fault.

"Did you really tell Meng Die that you dumped her because you thought I'd turned you down because of her?"

"Not in those words, but yes."

I sighed, and shook my head. "Oh, Requiem. I mean I didn't think she'd take it this badly"—I motioned at some of his injuries—"but her pride wouldn't let her take it lying down."

"Pride." He nodded, then stopped in midmotion as if it had hurt. "She has much pride, and I seem to have none." He looked at me, and emotion filled his eyes, his face, and the emotion was too strong for me to keep looking into his face.

"Don't," I whispered.

He slid to the ground, went to his knees. He made a small involuntary sound. It must have hurt. He took my hand, and I let him, because pulling away seemed petty. "What must I do to be in your bed, Anita? Tell me, and I will do it."

I looked into his face, saw the pain there, and it wasn't the pain of bruises and cuts. I looked at Jean-Claude. "It's the *ardeur*, isn't it?"

"I fear so," he said.

I turned back to the vampire kneeling in front of me. I had no idea what to say.

"Am I ugly to you?" he asked.

"No," and I traced the line of his uninjured cheek. "You are very handsome, and you know it."

He shook his head, stopped in midmotion, again as if it hurt. "If I were handsome enough, you would have taken me to your bed and not turned to these strangers." He lowered his head, both hands gripping mine. He finally raised his face, and he was crying. "Please, Anita, please, do not cast me aside so easily. I know that you did not enjoy the attentions I gave you as much as I enjoyed the touch of your body. But I will be better, I swear it, if only you will give me another chance to show you pleasure. I was trying to be too careful of you. I did not understand. I can do better, be better." He buried his face against my legs, and wept.

"I believe we have our answer, *ma petite*."

I stroked Requiem's hair, and didn't know what he was talking about. I was too stunned to think. "Answer to what?" I asked.

"The effect you have on vampires that have tasted the *ardeur* before. I think you are addictive, as Belle was addictive." He motioned toward Requiem, who was clutching at me, still weeping into my legs. "He is powerful enough to be a Master of a City, *ma petite*, not powerful in the way of Augustine, or myself, but powerful. He lacks not power, but ambition. He does not wish to rule."

"There is no shame to that," Elinore said.

"*Non*," Jean-Claude said, "but I want *ma petite* to understand that her effect on Requiem is not a small thing."

Elinore had sat back in the chair, curling her legs under her, because her feet wouldn't have reached the ground. "I had no idea she had bespelled him like this."

"I didn't bespell him," I said.

She gave me a look and motioned at the vampire at my feet. "Pick a different word if you like, Anita, but the effect is the same. We can argue semantics, but Requiem is besotted with you in a way most unnatural."

I stroked his hair, so straight and thick, but not warm. He was cool to the touch. "He needs to feed," I said. "Healing is going to take a lot of blood and energy."

"I don't think blood will cure this," Elinore said, and her voice sounded almost accusatory.

"What do you want from me, Elinore? What do you want me to do?"

"Make him your lover," she said.

"I have four men that I'm the only sex they're getting, and two more that are in my bed some of the time. Hell, Jason makes it into my bed about once a month."

"Exactly," Elinore said, "one more will hardly make a difference."

"If it were just sex, maybe, but it's not just sex. It's the emotional stuff. I don't even know if there's enough of me to go around for five men, plus extras. Call me crazy, but I don't think Requiem is a low-needs item." I stroked his hair, felt him shake against my legs. "No, I think he definitely goes in the high-maintenance category. I don't think I have enough emotion left to do another high-needs man, okay? That's the truth. I'm sure he'd be a wonderful lover, but I couldn't meet his other needs."

"What other needs?" she asked.

"Talk, emotion, sharing, love."

Elinore shifted in her chair, turning her head to one side, her long hair spilling around her like a cornsilk dream. "You turned him down as your lover because you don't think you can love him?"

I thought about it for a heartbeat, then shrugged, and nodded. "Yeah, sort of."

Elinore looked at Jean-Claude. "She turned him down because she does not think she could love him."

Jean-Claude gave that graceful shrug. "She is very young."

"Don't talk about me like I'm not sitting here," I said.

Requiem's crying had slowed, so that he was mostly just kneeling with his head in my lap. I kept petting his hair, the way you'd soothe a dog, or a sick child.

"We all understand, Anita, that you are Jean-Claude's consort. We all understand that you and he and Asher are a threesome. We all understand that your triumvirate with the Ulfric and Jean-Claude must be maintained for reasons of power and safety. That maintenance includes sex, because he is of Belle Morte's line. I admit that I thought him a fool, and weak, to have allowed you such closeness with the wereleopards, but I was wrong. Out of that closeness came your own triumvirate, which has strengthed Jean-Claude's powers immensely. Your tie to Damian and Nathaniel is a wondrous thing. Your tie to Micah is a puzzlement, but I understand now that your powers are much like Belle's. She collected men, too."

"I am not like Belle Morte," I said.

"Your power is." She pointed at Requiem. "This is proof of that."

"I don't want to collect men," I said. I stared down at the man in my lap. "I certainly don't want them this . . . besotted. This a level of wanting that's just wrong."

"Why is it wrong?" Elinore asked.

"Because I don't think he has a choice about it. I didn't mean to collect Requiem."

He looked up then, as if my saying his name had called him. The tears had dried to faint reddish lines on his face. The red didn't help the bruises look any better.

I touched the unhurt side of his face, and he laid his cheek in my hand, as if that one touch were something wonderful. "How do I fix this?" I asked.

"You mean how do you set him free?" Elinore asked.

"Yes."

"You don't."

I stared at her. "What do you mean, I don't?"

"There is no cure, Anita. There is only going far away from you. He will still crave your touch, but he will not be able to act upon it."

"Like an alcoholic," I said.

She nodded. "Yes."

"There is a cure for it," Jean-Claude said.

I looked at him. "What?"

"Love," he said, "true love."

We both stared at him. "True love," Elinore said.

He nodded. "We loved Julianna, and she freed us of the addiction of Belle Morte. Belle Morte had Requiem in her bed before Ligeia ever touched him, but she sent Requiem on a long seduction far away from her. It was necessary to seduce both halves of a noble couple, so she sent Ligeia with him."

"I thought that Requiem's master fled France so Belle wouldn't keep him."

"His master met with an accident, and Belle was able to collect all the vampires of her line that the old master had made."

"The way you say *accident* makes it sound like you don't mean *accident* at all," I said.

"It *was* an accident," Requiem said, softly. He spoke with his face in my lap. "The carriage we were in overturned in a storm. We were on a cliff edge, and somewhere during the fall, a piece of wood went through his heart. It was such an ordinary death." His voice sounded relaxed, distant. "We tried removing the wood, but he did not revive. We learned later that the carriage maker was Wellsley."

"Who's Wellsley?" I asked.

Elinore answered, "He manufactured carriages in London for many years. He was a devout man, and hated the idea of his carriages being used for evil purposes, so he had them blessed. He would make a batch of them and have one of the local clergy bless them. When the blessing is fresh, some of them glow around us."

"The blessing wears off?" I made it a question.

"If enough 'evil' "—and she made quotation marks in the air with her fingers—"happens in the carriage."

"Like a cemetery that's been out of use for a while, or had black magic used in it too much," I said. "You have to reconsecrate the ground."

"The analogy will do," she said.

I looked down at Requiem. "And when your master was dead, Belle could call you to her?"

"Yes," he said, "and if Jean-Claude had not given me a home here, she would have done so again."

"How did you get away from her the second time?"

"Jean-Claude has the right of it. Ligeia and I were sent far away to seduce some nobles Belle wished to control. We did her bidding, and they did what Belle wished, but Ligeia and I fell in love with each other. When we returned to Belle's court, I was no longer drawn to her."

"Love," Jean-Claude said, "love is the only cure."

"You and Asher aren't besotted with me, not like this."

"Jean-Claude is your master, and he holds the *ardeur* as well. As for Asher"—she looked at Jean-Claude—"I think love protects him."

I looked at Jean-Claude, too, and he would not meet our gaze. I sort of assumed now that Jean-Claude and Asher were doing it like bunnies when I wasn't around, but I'd never asked. *Don't ask, don't tell* worked just fine for me. Last night, seeing him with Auggie, made me wonder if I needed to ask, or if it was confirmed. Too complicated for me.

I literally waved the thought away, and said, "I can't count on Requiem falling in love any time soon."

"*Non, ma petite.*"

"What do I do?"

"Take him as your lover," Elinore said.

"Easy for you to say; no one's making you share yourself with anyone but your knight."

"And one of the reasons I came to Jean-Claude was that he would let me be with the man I love, and not force me into the beds of others. I am more grateful for that than I can ever say." She turned those cold blue eyes on me. "But I do not carry the *ardeur*. I am not an addiction."

"*Ma petite*, you must meet this obligation."

I stared at him. "Obligation?"

"You have addicted him to you. Would you be as cruel as Belle Morte herself and cast him away, with this desire riding him?" He shuddered. "I have been as one addicted, and cast out for some minor infraction. I have felt my body ache for want of her, and no amount of sex with anyone else satisfied that need." He moved so he could lay his hand over mine where I stroked

Requiem's hair. "He is my third-in-command. He is a good and honorable man. You need more and more powerful food, *ma petite*. I think if you feed the *ardeur* well enough, it will quiet. But until you find food to its liking, it will seek its own."

"You want me to sleep with Requiem?"

"I want you to feed the *ardeur* from him, *oui*."

"I thought you weren't happy sharing me with so many men. I mean, you once threatened to kill Richard."

"I did not understand the nature of our power together then. Perhaps there is more than one reason that Belle collected lovers. Perhaps it was not merely her appetite, but more practical."

I stared at him, feeling the weight of his hand over mine, and Requiem gone very still under our hands. "I can't meet all his needs, Jean-Claude. I can't add another date to my card."

"It is not a date he needs, *ma petite*. He needs to be your food. Food is for eating, not for dating."

"Yeah, that's what I said about Nathaniel for months. It doesn't work like that, not for me."

"What do you propose, *ma petite*? Until we know the extent of your power over other vampires, we must be very careful of our visitors. We must surround you with powerful enough food that the *ardeur* will not keep drawing more."

"Why isn't your *ardeur* drawing in people?"

"You are his human servant," Elinore said, "you're taking some of the edge off his power."

"What does that mean?" I asked.

"If Jean-Claude didn't have you, then his *ardeur* would be doing this, and it would make it hard to run his territory. Your attracting people is less distracting to him."

I looked at him. "Are you doing this on purpose?"

"I swear that I am not."

"It's the nature of the power, Anita," Elinore said. "Human servants, animals to call, *pommes de sang*, they are all instruments to help their masters grow in power and control. The power will find a place to go and feed that allows the Master of the City to rule better."

"You make the power sound alive, like it can think for itself," I said.

She shrugged. "Perhaps it can. I know that I have seen the power work like this with other masters. Not the *ardeur*, but other powers."

I sighed. "Great, so I'm the *ardeur*'s pinup girl because Jean-Claude would get too distracted if it were him."

"Yes," she said.

"Wait, Belle had the full *ardeur*, more full than we have now."

"But she had no human servant, and no animal to call," Elinore said.

I looked at Jean-Claude. "I thought every master called in help."

"Belle does not share power," Jean-Claude said, "not with anyone."

"But you guys gain a lot of power from human servants and animals to call."

"She has intimates of her animals to call, but she has not chosen among them. She makes no one special to her," he said.

"I don't seem to be able to choose who I get as animal to call. I know you chose Richard, but I didn't exactly choose Nathaniel."

"Nor Haven," Jean-Claude said.

"Haven is not my animal to call," I said.

"But some lion will be, and soon, I fear," Jean-Claude said. "Joseph is bringing some of his lionmen around today so you will have more than our guests to choose from."

"Choose for what?" and I sounded as suspicious as I felt.

"So you may bring their beasts, and hold off the change."

That made sense. So many metaphysical problems that it was hard to keep track sometimes. But one problem at a time. I looked at the man in my lap.

"Fine, whatever. What am I going to do with you, Requiem?"

Jean-Claude and I moved our hands, and he raised his face, so he could look at me. "Make me your *pomme de sang*."

"I think the *pomme de sang* needs to be someone who can feed me night or day," I said.

His face filled with panic. "Please, Anita, do not cast me aside."

I looked at Jean-Claude. "A little help here."

"If you will not feed the *ardeur* from him then we must send him to another territory. He is powerful enough that many will want him as third, or even second."

"Which will weaken your power base, because Elinore is only staying until we find her her own territory," I said.

He gave a shrug that meant everything and nothing.

"I cannot believe that my"—and I hesitated because *boyfriend* seemed too junior high, *lover* not enough—"the man I love is encouraging me to take another lover."

He smiled at me. "We know now that any who have tasted Belle's *ardeur* are susceptible to your *ardeur*. I think any of her line will be too risky to taste as *pommes*. Agree to feed the *ardeur* from Requiem, *ma petite*, that is all. Agree, because we have two more things to know before the party tonight."

"What two things?"

"Will you draw and be drawn to all leopards, wolves, and lions? Do the *ardeur*'s effects travel outside Belle's line?"

I looked at Jean-Claude, tried to read past his face. "You're still shielding so hard, I can't tell how you really feel about this. Let me see inside your shields."

He shook his head. "I think it would be no help to you."

"Why not?"

"Because part of me is happy our powers are growing, no matter what the cost. Part of me is frightened of what the council may do about it. Do I want you to take another lover? No, but do I prefer that it is you whom the *ardeur* hunts to this degree, and not me, yes. I am sorry, *ma petite*, but that is the truth."

I thought about it, then nodded. "If you have a human servant who can't hold her shit together the other masters may forgive you. Like a bad marriage, not your fault. If you can't hold your shit together, they won't let that pass."

"Please, Anita," Requiem said, "please, feed the *ardeur* upon me, please."

"I will."

The look on his face was amazing, so joyous even through all the bruises. The look scared me. No one but your nearest and dearest should ever look at you like that.

"But not right now," I said.

Some of the joy faded. "Why not now? It is morning. You have slept."

I nodded. "Yeah, usually that does raise the *ardeur*." I looked at Jean-Claude. "That's a good question, why don't I feel all *ardeur*ish?"

"I, too, am well fed."

"You feasted last night," Requiem said, "on Augustine and his people."

I looked back at Jean-Claude. "Is he right? Was it such a powerful meal that we're safe for longer?"

"Perhaps."

"You don't sound convinced."

"The *ardeur* is not always a predictable power, *ma petite*. I would need more than one feeding of such magnitude before I agreed that that was the reason."

"Or perhaps," Elinore said, "you should be trying to figure out how powerful a meal you would need to abate the *ardeur*. You cannot feast on another

Master of the City and his people every night." She leaned forward in her chair, all lace and satin, but strangely, she didn't look cute. She looked too intent for words like *cute*. "Perhaps what is needed is permanent food of high power."

"Few masters would agree to become Anita's, or my, permanent *pomme de sang*. Not if they are powerful enough to rule a territory of their own."

"What if they have no choice in the matter?" she said, indicating Requiem.

"Are you suggesting that I purposefully trap other masters the way I accidentally trapped Requiem?" I asked.

"It would solve a great many problems," she said.

"It would be"—I groped for a word—"evil."

"I thought you were more pragmatic than this, Anita."

"Doing that would be no different than if we gave in to the requests we get weekly for you to join some other master's kiss, as his mistress. We give you room to choose, Elinore. How can you ask us to take that same choice away from someone else?"

"I would not be bespelled, Anita. I would know every night as he touched me, lay on top of me, that I hated him. Requiem adores you, and he will adore you until, and if, he falls in love, true love. Until that time he will be in the bed of someone he adores, having amazing sex, and enjoying every minute of it. It is not the same thing, Anita. Trust me on that."

"But it's sort of a metaphysical date-rape drug, used like that. Just because you're enjoying the abuse doesn't make it not abuse."

"Does it not, *ma petite*?"

I shook my head. "It's too late for Requiem, I'll accept that. I'll try feeding the *ardeur* on him."

He kissed my hand. "Thank you, mistress."

"Not mistress," I said, "Anita, just Anita."

"Thank you, Anita," he said, and kissed my hand again.

"Get up off the floor, Requiem, please."

He stood. "I would like very much to sit beside you."

I sighed, and nodded.

He sat on the other side of me from Jean-Claude, except that he sat close enough that his legs touched me. Great, just creepy, great.

I looked at his chest where the blades had come so close to taking his life. "What are we going to do about Meng Die? She's just proven herself too dangerous, and so not a team player."

"Kill her," Elinore said.

I looked at Jean-Claude.

"I would rather find another solution, but yes, it may come to that."

"You are overly sentimental, Jean-Claude, just because you feel guilty that you stole her mortal life. It is a great gift, not a curse."

"I feel as I feel, Elinore."

"Have a care that your feelings do not get us all killed." She looked at me. "Also, I think if Anita truly is going to be a panwere . . ."

"News travels fast," I said, looking at Jean-Claude.

"I wished an opinion of someone powerful enough to have an opinion."

I wanted to argue, but I couldn't. She was the most powerful vamp in his group right now. Her waking first had proven that.

"As I was saying, if Anita is truly going to be a panwere, then it may not simply be lions, wolves, and leopards that she attracts. It may be all were-animals, or many. Almost all the visiting masters have brought their animal to call, so we must test this theory before she is allowed near them. Augustine I believe will let the insult go, because he is besotted with you both, and he attacked you first. The breach of protocol was on his side, not ours. But if Anita entices others away from their masters, they may not be so forgiving."

"Agreed," Jean-Claude said, "and we still must see how master vampires outside Belle's bloodline react to Anita's *ardeur*."

"And where are we going to get master-level vamps and other were-animals to test these little theories on?" I asked.

There was a knock on the door. "It's Remus, Jean-Claude."

"Enter."

Remus entered, closing the door behind him. He was actually looking directly at us, and he was angry, which I guess explained the direct look. "I told you if there were any more that I wouldn't let them in without me and my guards coming in here."

"I remember," Jean-Claude said.

"I said any other vampire, but definitely these two are not coming in here without you having bodyguards on this side of the door."

"What two?" I asked.

"Wicked and Truth are out here," Remus said.

"Wicked and Truth," Elinore said, "how interesting. They are very powerful, and they are not of Belle's line."

I shook my head. "Truth already got a taste of the *ardeur* when I bound him to Jean-Claude. He's not following me around like this." I jerked my thumb at Requiem.

"Did you actually feed from Truth?" she asked.

"No," I said.

"Then you must try."

"No," I said.

"At least suggest it to them," she said.

"No," I said, and put more heat into the word.

"They have sworn loyalty to Jean-Claude. They are not leaving us," Elinore said.

"No," I said, "absolutely no."

"Very well, then perhaps not feed, but watch you feed," Jean-Claude said.

"What does that mean?" I asked.

"Samuel watched you feed and was not drawn to you, or me, that strongly. But Haven was drawn so that his companions had to drag him away, almost as they did Augustine. Perhaps if Wicked and Truth are simply in the room when you feed, that would tell us if the effect will go outside Belle's line, or no."

"We would need someone from Belle's line to be in the room too, someone close in power." I looked at Elinore.

She smiled, "I am in love, Anita, true love. It does not work on me."

"Some types of *ardeur* work anyway," I said.

"For a brief time, yes, but my being in love makes me unusable for the test."

There was another knock on the door. Remus opened it, murmured to someone, then turned back. He didn't look directly at us again. "London is out here, too. He's Belle Morte's line, isn't he?"

"Yes," Elinore said, "he is."

"So what, I feed the *ardeur*, and then they tell us how attracted they are to it?"

"It is a way of testing without impinging too far upon your morals," Elinore said.

"Just have sex in a room while a bunch of men watch, right?"

Jean-Claude shook his head and smiled. "Simply feed the arduer, *ma petite*. It does not have to be sex, if you do not wish it."

"It seems a shame to raise the *ardeur* on purpose when I'm not hungry," I said.

He sighed. "Yes, it does, but it is far better to raise it now, when we can control it, than later, when visitors have arrived, and we cannot."

Put that way, it made sense, but . . . "Who do I feed from?" I asked.

He gestured to Requiem. "The damage is already done to him."

"Great, now I'm damage," I said.

"And feeding from blood as powerful as yours will help him speed his healing."

That was true, but . . . "Fine, but only if you explain the parameters of the experiment to everyone. They have to agree to it, or I won't do it."

"Of course, *ma petite*, I would not have it any other way."

I looked into that beautiful, unreadable face, and was almost a hundred percent certain he was lying.

26

Everyone agreed to the test. Everyone seemed happier about it than I did. Okay, everyone but Remus and some of his guards. I think that was because he was pretty sure it was going to go horribly wrong and he and his people would have to pick up the pieces. I agreed with Remus.

Part of me hopes that someday I get over being so damned uncomfortable about group scenes like this; part of me hopes I don't. It's sort of the same part of me that mourns that I can kill without feeling bad about it, most of the time. Yeah, that same part thinks that doing metaphysical sex in front of a bunch of men, for any reason, is just another step down the slippery slope to damnation. But if the alternative is having the *ardeur* go off like a metaphysical bomb during the party tonight, well, what we were about to do was the lesser evil. Still it might be nice, once in a while, not to have to choose between evils. Just once, couldn't I choose the lesser good?

Requiem lay back against the fresh sheets, his hair spilling out around his upper body like a dark halo. His day job, or would that be night job, was stripping at Guilty Pleasures. The body showed that, but all I could see was the wounds. Meng Die had come very, very close to putting out his light forever. I traced fingertips across the sternum cut. His breath came out in a shuddering sigh. I couldn't tell if it had hurt, or felt good.

Normally I could read Requiem, but today there was nothing in his face that helped me. He gazed up at me as if I were the most wondrous thing he'd ever seen. It was a step above, or below, love. *Worship* was the only word I had for it. It hurt my heart to see that look on his face. There was no Requiem left in that look.

Requiem of the somber, pretty speeches. He'd earned his name because he was poetic but damned depressing. But there was no force of personality to him now, nothing but this overwhelming need.

"God, help me," I said.

Jean-Claude came to stand next to the bed, to me. "What is wrong, *ma petite?*"

"Please tell me he'll get better than this," I said.

"Better than what, *ma petite*?"

"Look at him," I said.

Jean-Claude moved close enough that the sleeve of his robe touched my robed arm. He gazed down at Requiem with me.

Requiem's gaze flickered to him, then settled back on me, as if the other man didn't matter. But he'd noticed him, because he said, "Will you force me to share your favors with another, Anita? Or will I be as the heavens stretched between the heat of the sun and the cold kiss of the moon? Will you do to me as you did to Augustine?"

"Well, at least he's back to being wordy and poetic," I said. "It's a start."

"Did he offer himself to both you and Anita?" Elinore asked, still curled in her chair.

"I believe so," Jean-Claude said.

"Requiem does not embrace men," London said from the far corner. He'd moved to the darkest, most shadowy corner he could find, as he always did. It wasn't just his short dark curls and penchant for black clothing that got him the nickname "the Dark Knight." "It was the one thing he fought against most strongly."

"Yes," Elinore said, "he was always most adamant that he did not do men."

"Belle punished him for his refusal to service men," Jean-Claude said. He stared down at Requiem with a solemn, lost look.

"Then he shouldn't be offering to do it for us," I said.

"No, he should not." Jean-Claude looked at me, and showed for an instant what he was feeling. I felt it like a stab through my heart. Anguish, anguish that he had brought Requiem here to keep him safe, and instead had enslaved him more thoroughly than Belle ever managed.

I felt the bed move a moment before a hand touched my back through the robe. I turned, but I knew whose hand was on me. Requiem had sat up, with all the damage to his chest and stomach, and he'd sat up so he could touch me. I searched his face for something familiar. I finally said, "Requiem, are you in there?"

He touched my face. "I am here," but he spoke the words with such emotion that they seemed to mean a great deal more than they should have.

I moved his hand away from my face, held it in mine, so maybe he would stop touching me. I looked at Jean-Claude. "This is awful. How do we fix this? Isn't there some faster way than finding his true love?"

Requiem's thumb began to make little circles on my hand, as if just being held wasn't enough.

"It's almost as if she's bespelled him," Elinore said, "as if she were the vampire and he the human."

"Fine, treat it like it's vampire mind tricks; how do I undo it?"

"A vampire's master can sometimes break such enchantments," Elinore said.

I looked at Jean-Claude. "Help him."

London stepped back to the edge of the light. "But it is not Anita's *ardeur*, but Jean-Claude's *ardeur* through her. He cannot fix his own *ardeur*, can he?"

"I do not know," Elinore said. She looked around the room and spoke toward the wall farthest from the door. "Wicked, Truth, you have been very silent through this discussion. Do you have any suggestions?"

The two brothers came forward into the stronger light near the bed. At first glance they didn't look that alike. They were both tall and broad-shouldered, but beyond that they were opposites. Wicked's hair was sleek and very blond, cut long so it framed a face that was all high, sculpted cheekbones, complete with a dimple in his chin deep enough that I could never decide if it looked adorable or painful. His eyes were a clear steady blue, and if I hadn't had Jean-Claude's and Requiem's eyes to compare him to, I'd have said his eyes were striking. He wore a modern tailored suit of tans and creams that made him look halfway between the college professor of your dreams and an executive gigolo. Then there was Truth.

Truth had obviously slept in his clothes. The clothes were made up of bits of leather, but not fashionable club wear, no, more like boiled leather worn smooth and soft with use and wear. His pants were tucked into boots so battered that Jean-Claude had offered to replace them, but Truth wouldn't give them up. He could have been dressed for any century from thirteenth to fifteenth. His straight brown hair was shoulder length, but stringy, as if it needed a good brushing. He didn't exactly have a beard, just stubble, as if he hadn't shaved for a while. But under all that disarray was the same bone structure, the same cleft chin, and the same blue eyes. Wicked's eyes always seemed to hold a cynical joy, but Truth's looked tired and wary, as if he was just waiting for us to disappoint him.

"What do you want from us?" Truth asked, and his voice was already defensive, as if he was ready for an argument.

Elinore uncurled from her chair and moved to stand on the other side of Jean-Claude, not quite to where London was standing, but so she could see the brothers more clearly. "You have been masterless for longer than any other master vampire. Surely, in all those centuries, some powerful vampire tried to capture the great warriors Wicked and Truth. Have you been bespelled as Requiem is?"

Wicked laughed. "Save the flattery, Elinore; we'll help if we can, if Anita tells us plainly what she wants from us." He turned those laughing eyes to me. Truth's somber eyes followed his brother's gaze.

I met their eyes. Wicked looked like it was all a big joke, which I'd finally realized was his blank face. Truth looked calmer, blanker, but he was ready to be disappointed in me. Certainty that I would not live up to his expectations was clear on his face.

"Isn't it Jean-Claude's order you need?" Elinore asked.

Truth shook his head. Wicked said, "No."

"No," Jean-Claude said.

"No," Wicked repeated, and he allowed himself a small, tasteful smirk of satisfaction.

"Who is your master?" Elinore asked.

"They are," and Truth motioned at both Jean-Claude and me.

"Then why is Jean-Claude's order not good enough?" she asked.

"He hasn't bespelled Requiem; she has," Truth said.

"You do not agree with London that it is Jean-Claude's *ardeur* flowing through Anita?"

They both shook their heads, and the movement was so well-timed that you could suddenly see how identical they almost were.

Wicked spoke for them. "Anita's will, her intent, is what we need." He stared at me. "What is your will, Anita?"

"To have him free of me."

"Would you undo the blood oath and cast him back to Belle Morte?" Wicked asked.

Requiem clutched at my hand. "Please, mistress, not that."

I patted his shoulder. "No, Requiem, you're not going back to Belle. We would never let that happen." He calmed almost instantly, and he shouldn't have. That much panic shouldn't have just vanished. It was just another sign of how far gone he was.

"Be careful with your words," said Truth, "for they are dangerous things."

I thought before I spoke the next time. "I want him to have choices. I don't want all his free will sucked away like this."

"Why?" Wicked asked. "Why is bespelling him so terrible to you?"

I looked into Requiem's face where he sat beside me. He gave me a look of absolute adoration. My stomach clenched tight. The thought of anyone being bound to anyone else like that was wrong; that I'd done it by accident made me vaguely nauseous.

"I like Requiem. He's a good guy, especially for a vampire. I don't want him like this, some sort of slave, it's just creepy."

"Is he better off dead?" Wicked asked.

"No," I said, quickly, "no."

"Then what would you have us do?" Truth asked.

Requiem said, "Do I not please you?"

I grabbed his good shoulder and said, "I know you're in there, Requiem. Come back to us. Hear me, Requiem, hear my voice, and break free of this."

"I don't wish to be free," he said, simply.

I pulled away from him, and he tried to hold on. I actually slapped his hands away from me. He looked so hurt.

"Please, Anita, how have I displeased you so? I will do anything. Anything that you ask, if you will only feed the *ardeur* from me."

"Anything," I said.

"Anything, you have but to speak it, and I will do it."

"Break free of this," I said.

"I do not understand," he said, and he looked as puzzled as his words.

"That's what I want, Requiem. I want you to break free of what I've done to you." The moment I said it, I knew it was true, that was what I wanted. "You're a master vampire. You could be a Master of the City, if you were a little more ambitious. You can fight this." I searched his face, to see if he understood what I was saying. "Come back to yourself, or I won't feed the *ardeur* on you."

"Anita, I . . . I don't . . ."

"You said you'd do anything I asked. This is an anything, and it's what I want you to do."

"You may be asking something he cannot do," Wicked said.

"I've felt his own version of the *ardeur*. Or whatever you call the other gifts of Belle's line that aren't exactly *ardeur*. He is powerful." I looked into his face and tried to show him how much I knew he could do this. "I want to see Requiem staring at me out of these eyes, not some besotted fool. Be the strong man I know you can be. Fight free of this, enough to talk to me. I won't touch you, ever again, unless you can give consent." He looked so stricken, so wounded, that I went up on my knees and cradled his face between my hands. "You told me once that you considered your power rape, because it affected only the body and not the mind. Do you remember saying that, Requiem?"

He frowned, but finally whispered, "Yes."

"If I take you like this, it's rape, and I won't do it."

I watched the emotions struggle across his face. "Anita . . . I do not know how to break these soft chains. Once love was strong enough to break them, but without love, let me be covered in your silken chains. Tie me down, and let me drown in your sweet flesh." He moved in for a kiss as he said the last, and I had to pull back. I slid off the bed, away from him. I wanted to run screaming with frustration. I had not meant to do this. Fuck.

"If another master had bespelled Requiem, what would you do, *ma petite?*" Jean-Claude said.

I thought about it, frowning. "I would try to break the spell. I would use my necromancy and try to break the spell."

"*Exactement.*"

"But, I did it. I can't break my own spell, can I?"

"Why can you not?"

I thought about it again. "Because . . . well."

"It is not your necromancy that has bespelled him, *ma petite*, but your power through the vampire marks, through me. Use your necromancy to free him, as you used your ties to the wolf to free you from Marmee Noir."

It made sense, but . . . "I don't know."

He spoke softly in my head. "You broke Willie McCoy free of the Traveller when he had possessed Willie's body. You used your necromancy to drive him out."

Willie was one of our least powerful vampires. He was manager at the Laughing Corpse, our comedy club. The Traveller was one of the vampire council. He had come to town in "person," except that he traveled by jumping from body to body. He could use any vampire body that wasn't strong enough to keep him out. He had possessed Willie, and tried to use him to hurt me. I had used my blood and my tie to Willie to find him in the dark where the Traveller had hidden him. Find him and bring him back to himself.

I thought carefully, because I was still not that good at the mind-to-mind thing. "I'd accidentally raised Willie from his coffin during the day once. I already had a tie to him that I don't have to Requiem."

He whispered through my mind, "Through the *ardeur* you have a bond to him that you did not have with Willie."

"How can I use necromancy to break him free of the *ardeur*, if I'm counting on the *ardeur* to be his bond to me? That doesn't make any sense."

"Perhaps the logic is a bit circular, but what do you have to lose, *ma petite?*" He spoke aloud, finally. "Look at him."

I pressed as much of me against as much of Jean-Claude as I could, then turned and looked at Requiem. He watched us like a man who was dying of thirst, and was only inches away from a cool, soothing pool, but there was a glass wall between him and it. I finally realized something. "It's not just the *ardeur* he's craving. It's the blood. He's hurt and he needs blood."

Jean-Claude ran his hands up and down my back in soothing motions. "*Oui*, but the *ardeur* overrides the other thirst."

"I thought that wasn't possible," I said.

"I have seen it with Belle. I have seen her give *ardeur* to vampires while they neglected their blood hunger, to the point where, one night, they did not rise from their coffins."

"She did it on purpose," I said.

"She wished to see if the *ardeur* alone was enough to sustain other vampires. She had hoped to travel with us across Europe, but the marks of blood taking give us away. The *ardeur* leaves no trace."

I stared at Requiem. "Nothing physical."

"*Oui*, there are signs, but nothing the authorities would have recognized. Nothing that would have given away her plan."

"But it didn't work," I said.

"She could share her *ardeur* with others, so they could feed upon it. She could sustain herself with it for long periods, as can I, but unless the *ardeur* is truly your gift to own, then it does not work."

"The Traveller . . ." He stopped me with a hand on my mouth.

He spoke in my head, again, "Quietly, *ma petite*."

I thought. "You said, no mind-to-mind, that some of the other vamp masters might overhear us."

"They are still dead to the world, but the people in this room can hear us."

"You don't trust them?"

"I would not like to have it well known that you were able to force a member of the council to do anything."

He had a point. I thought, slowly, carefully. "The Traveller was taking blood from me when I called Willie. I called him with the blood."

"Then feed our Requiem."

I wasn't sure that was a good idea. "He's fed from me once; what if drinking my blood is part of the problem? Asher thinks that any vampire who feeds from me is drawn to me."

"You are very tasty, *ma petite*."

"It's not just that. It's something more."

"We want our vampires bound to us, *ma petite*, that is why we blood-oath them. We simply do not wish them bound to this level of slavishness."

I was close enough in his head to feel that he believed that. He did not like to see Requiem this bespelled. "You're almost as creeped out by this as I am, why? This strengthens our power base, right?"

"Perhaps, but I did not invite Requiem, or anyone, into my lands so I could enslave them. I wanted to give them shelter, not chains."

"Auggie said you were too sentimental for your own good sometimes."

Out loud he said, "Perhaps, but you have taught me that sentiment is not always a bad thing."

I stared up at that impossibly beautiful face, and felt love swell up inside me like a physical force. It filled my body, swelling upward until it made my chest ache, my throat tighten, and my eyes burn. It sounded so stupid. But I loved him. Loved all of him, but loved him more because loving me had made him better. That he would say that I had taught him about being sentimental made me want to cry. Richard reminded me at every turn that I was bloodthirsty and cold. If that were true, then I couldn't have taught Jean-Claude about sentimentality. You can't learn, if you don't have it to teach.

He kissed me. He kissed me softly, with one hand lost in the hair to the side of my face. He drew back and whispered, "I never thought to see that look upon your face, not for me."

"I love you," I said, and touched his hand where it lay against my face.

"I know that, but there are different kinds of love, *ma petite*, they are equally real, but . . ." He smiled, and said, "Such soft tenderness I thought you had reserved for others."

"What others?" I asked, because I couldn't leave it alone.

He gave me a chiding look, as if I knew the answer to the question, and I guess I did. I knew Richard was almost desperately jealous of Micah and Nathaniel, but for the first time I realized Jean-Claude was jealous, too. And jealousy always hurts. I was sorry I ever made him doubt how much I loved him. He would never hold my hand in a delivery room, or vacuum a floor, but within the parameters of his life, I could ask anything of him.

"I don't mean to interrupt this little lovefest," London said, in a tone of voice that said clearly he did want to interrupt, and maybe be cruel on top of it, "but could you try to free Requiem? Or did you not mean to free him, and it was all just talk?"

"London," Elinore said, with a warning in that single word.

"I am allowed my cynicism, Elinore. I have been disappointed too many times in too many different masters."

"Haven't we all," Wicked said.

Truth just nodded.

I frowned at all of them, and suddenly even cuddling with Jean-Claude wasn't quite as comforting. "Thanks guys, no performance anxiety here."

"We do not mean to make things more difficult for you," Truth said, "but like most vampires who have not spent their entire existence with one master, we have been ridden hard, and cruelly, by those who were supposed to take care of us."

"The idea of the feudal system is that the people at the top take care of the needs of those on the bottom, but I have seldom seen it work that way," Wicked said.

"Yeah," I said, "it's like trickle-down economics; it only works if the people at the top are really good, decent people. The system is only as good as the people in power."

The brothers nodded, as if I'd said a wise thing. Maybe I had.

I laid a kiss on Jean-Claude's bare chest, caressing the slicker skin of the cross-shaped burn mark. I drew away from him and went for the bed. I prayed as I walked toward Requiem. "Let him be free, but don't let me hurt him."

27

I TOLD REQUIEM to lie down on the bed, and he did, without hesitation. Elinore was right. He was like a human hit by a vampire's gaze. I knelt beside him, the robe tucked up under my knees, tied close around my waist. I stared down at him and wondered if there was anything I could ask him to do that he would refuse. Was there really no limit to it? I'd seen humans rolled by vampires who had turned on their friends in the blink of an eye, and tried to kill people they loved. Would Requiem have killed for me? For no reason than that I asked it of him? I wanted to know, and I didn't.

I looked at Jean-Claude. "Is this just about sex, or would he do anything I asked, like a human rolled by a vamp?"

"I do not know, *ma petite*."

"If you never plan to do this on purpose, what does it matter?" London asked, and he let me hear all the distrust in those words. I didn't really blame him.

"I wouldn't do it to any of our people on purpose, but sometimes I'm on my own in a nest of vamps that I'm supposed to kill. They get testy about stuff like that. I'm just wondering if I could raise the *ardeur* as a weapon? Is there a way to make it an asset instead of a disaster?"

London frowned at me, but said, "I don't believe you, Anita."

"London," Elinore said, "never use that tone again with her."

"I've seen what the *ardeur* can do, Elinore. You haven't, not really." His face tightened in lines of anger so raw it almost hurt to see it. "I've seen my face look like Requiem's. I remember what it feels like." His hands gripped the bedpost until the skin changed color, just a bit. The mottling would be more after he fed. The wood creaked in protest, and he dropped his hands. "Part of me still wants to feel like that. It's like being on a drug all the time. Being pleasantly high, pleasantly happy. It may not be real happiness, but it's hard to tell the difference when you're in the middle of it." He hugged himself tight. "The world is a colder, darker place without it. But with it, you're a slave. A slave to someone who makes you do things . . ." He shook his head, so hard it looked dizzying.

"Maybe London should go before I start this," I said.

"No," he said, "no, if I can't bear to watch you feed the *ardeur* on someone else, then I need to find a new master, and a new city. If I can't bear this, then I need to go somewhere where no one carries the *ardeur*."

"Jean-Claude is your master, London; you will need his permission to leave," Elinore said.

"We have already discussed it," Jean-Claude said.

"When?" I asked.

"He is an addict, *ma petite*, an addict to the *ardeur*. I saved him from Belle Morte, who would have addicted him again, but London and I discussed that even your *ardeur*, and mine, might be too much for him. If it is"—he gave that graceful shrug—"I will find him some place far away from such temptations, but it will take time to find a home for someone as potentially powerful as London. Especially someone with his bloodline, and male. If he were female, there is a waiting list."

"But not for men," I said.

"*Non, ma petite*, the female masters seem convinced they would become bespelled by males of our bloodline. The male masters seem convinced they could master the women of our line."

"Well, isn't that just typical," I said. I looked back at London. "If this gets to be too much for you, promise me you'll leave."

"Why do you care?"

I raised a hand before Elinore could chastise him again. "Because I'm going to have enough trouble freeing Requiem's mind; I don't want to have to do it twice today."

He nodded. "I swear to you that I will leave, if I feel it is too much." The look on his face was very solemn, with none of that dark defiance, or anger.

I took a deep breath and turned back to the man on the bed. He gave me peaceful, eager eyes. It was as if the lamb wanted you to slit its throat.

I moved up beside him, so I could touch the unbruised side of his face. I cupped his face and he leaned into that touch, eyes closing for a moment as if that one innocent touch was almost too much to bear.

I called to him. "Requiem, Requiem, come back to me."

He laid his hand against mine, pressing me tighter against his face. "I am right here, Anita, right here."

I shook my head, because this wasn't him. It was his body, but whatever made Requiem who he was, that wasn't in his eyes. It was a stranger's face. What makes people *people* is not just bone structure and eye color, but the force of their personalities. The years of experience painted on their faces. *Them*, for lack of a better word. *Them*.

"Oh, Requiem, come back to us."

He gazed up at me, so puzzled. He didn't understand that he was lost.

I closed my own eyes, so I could concentrate and not have to see his eyes, so trusting and empty. My necromancy was unlike any other power I had. Maybe because it was mine. Whatever the reason, I didn't have to decide to use my necromancy, I just had to stop fighting it. Stop blocking the power. Blocking my necromancy was like making a fist, tight-clenched, squeezing, squeezing, so hard, so the power didn't get away from me. I spread that metaphorical fist wide, let go all that effort and the necromancy just was. Before, with Auggie, there had been so much happening, so many different powers, that it had distracted me, but now there was nothing but the necromancy. It felt so good to finally let go. So amazingly good.

I opened my eyes and stared down at Requiem. "Come to me," I said, "come to me." He rose up, off the bed, arms reaching for me. I put a finger on his chest, and said, "Requiem, stop." He stopped instantly. As if he were some sort of toy; hit one switch and he goes, another and he turns off. Sweet Mary, Mother of God, this was so wrong.

"*Ma petite, ma petite*, have a care."

I turned and glanced at Jean-Claude. "I'm a little busy here," I said, and couldn't keep the impatience out of my voice.

"I would be more specific with your calls, if I were you. You told only Requiem to stop. The others are still compelled." He motioned at the other vampires. London had a death grip on the bedpost. He looked panicked. Wicked and Truth were fighting at the edge of the bed. Truth wanted to get on, and Wicked was holding his brother back. Truth looked scared, and Wicked looked angry.

I found Elinore standing by her chair, holding on to it, as if only the chair's weight kept her from coming to me.

I felt myself go pale. "I didn't mean . . ."

"Your necromancy has gained in power, *ma petite*, as have your beasts. Be more specific on your orders; use his name."

I looked at Elinore. "If I called you, would you have to come to me?"

She swallowed hard enough for me to hear it. "I would fight, but the compulsion would be strong. I am not yet a Master of the City. As you must be of a certain level of power to rule a city, so the ruling of it, and the oaths that are taken, the magic that binds, gains a vampire more power. I do not have those ties, yet, so I . . . I am not Augustine, or Samuel. I think if you forced the issue it would be difficult."

It was my turn to swallow.

"We are all blood-oathed to Jean-Claude," London said, through gritted teeth. "I think her call is stronger for her ties to him."

Truth broke from his brother, and went to the chair by the fireplace. He strode to it, and hid his face in his hands. Wicked turned back to me. "He wanted to go to you. We are both blood-oathed to Jean-Claude. Why was my brother more drawn to your call?"

"He fed on *ma petite*, when he oathed to us," Jean-Claude said. "You took my blood."

"I told you when you brought him over that I had to be brought over in exactly the same way. You assured me that it wouldn't matter." He gestured angrily toward his brother. "This matters."

Requiem wrapped his arms around me, and laid a kiss upon my neck. He was bending his stomach to do it. Didn't it hurt?

I said the only thing I could think of. "I didn't know."

"We must always be bound the same," Wicked said, "we must always be the same. It is our strength. It is who we are. Whatever you have done to him, you must do to me, or undo to him."

I nodded. "I'll try."

"I'm beginning to understand why we used to kill necromancers on sight," London said.

"Is that a threat?" Jean-Claude said, voice mild.

"No, no, master."

But I understood what London meant. Requiem licked along my neck, and that one touch made me shiver, just a little. "Requiem, stop touching me."

He froze against me, but he was still touching me. He simply stopped kissing and licking me. I guess I'd have to be careful how I worded things. I had to find Requiem. Not just a vampire, or the dead. I needed him, his individual self. I'd done something similar once in the Church of Eternal Life, when the police and I were searching for a vampire murder suspect. I'd sought the flavor of one person, and that had been someone I hadn't known. I knew Requiem. I was holding him.

I wrapped my arms around him, moved all that thick hair to one side, so I could bury my face in the bend of his neck. I breathed in the scent of his skin. He didn't smell warm. I could smell his cologne, the soap he used, his shampoo, but underneath all of it was the faint smell of death. Not of corpses and rot, because vampires did not do that, but the scent of long-closed rooms, vaguely like the smell of snakes. Musty, not warm, nothing that you could cuddle. Yet his arms were strong, the edges of his wounds on the one arm catching in the silk of my robe. He was real, but he wasn't exactly alive.

I held him close, and pushed my necromancy into the body I held. Pushed it carefully, just into this one body, nowhere else. I searched not for this befuddled stranger but for that spark that was truly Requiem. I found him, in the dark, inside himself. He wasn't afraid, but softly confused, lost. I called to him. I felt him look up, hear me, but he could not come. I could see his prison, touch the door, gaze at him through the bars, but I did not have the key. Then I realized what we needed. Blood. No matter what type of undead you're dealing with, blood is usually the key.

I rose up from his neck, and swept my own hair to the side. "Feed, Requiem, feed from me."

He showed me a face with eyes wide with shock, as if he couldn't believe I would let him do it, but he didn't ask me to repeat the order. His hand wrapped in my hair, his other hand at my back. He pressed me tight against him, holding my neck to the side, and he brought me down to him, for he was sitting and I kneeling. He brought my neck down to his mouth, the way you would do for a kiss. He could not roll me with his eyes, and he didn't try. There would be nothing to change the pain to pleasure. I felt him tense, and I tried to relaxed, but you never relax. You tense up, just a bit, and it hurts more.

He bit me, fangs sinking in, pain sharp enough to make me push at his shoulders, as I tried to get away. I just couldn't take that much pain out of the box without pushing against it. I felt him begin to drink me down, his throat convulsing, swallowing. Something that could be so erotic, and it just fucking hurt like this.

But it was just like beheading a chicken to raise a zombie, or spreading blood on a vampire's lips to heal him. It was blood with a purpose, and I sent my magic down with that blood. I used it, to call Requiem. Used it to find him in the dark, and set him free.

He drew back from my throat, gasping, as if he'd been running. There was blood on his lower lip as he stared up at me. One moment he still looked dazed, the next he spilled into his eyes. They flared with blue fire, with that hint of turquoise in the center. His power danced over my skin like a cold, prickling breeze.

"I am here, Anita. You have cleared my mind. What would you have of me?"

I moved back from his arms, touching my neck, and came away with blood. Remus was already sending the young guard Cisco to the bathroom for gauze and tape.

"I wanted you free, and yourself. We've got that."

He shook his head, and winced, as if only now did the bruises hurt. He leaned back against the mounded pillows, favoring his stomach and chest, holding his injured arm carefully. "It was like being on drugs; nothing hurt that badly, when you touched me. I am free, but everything hurts."

"Isn't that always the way," I said, but I smiled. He was himself again.

I looked around at the other vampires. I looked at Elinore still gripping the back of her chair. I felt her. Felt her as if she were a flavor of ice cream that I could have put in a cone and licked. Mostly vanilla, but with chocolate chips. I looked at London. Not vanilla, definitely something darker, chunkier, full of hard crunchy bits. Wicked filled my mind like icing, chocolate icing to spread on skin and lick clean. I shook my head at the imagery, and looked for Truth, still huddling by the fireplace. Something fresh and clean, strawberries, maybe, strawberry ice cream to melt down the skin, and be licked away, so you could suck the cold around the nipples . . .

"Anita"—and it was Jean-Claude's voice—"Anita, you must stop this."

He never called me Anita. It made me look at him. "Why can't I taste you?" I asked.

"Because I am your master, and not a toy for your power."

The look on his face frightened me, because he was frightened. I licked dry lips, and said, "I guess this answers the question. I don't touch anyone else's vampires."

"No," he said, "no." He was at the edge of the bed. "Now shut it down."

It took me a second to realize what he meant. My necromancy, I needed to turn it off again. I closed my eyes, and drew it back in. I drew in tight and tighter, closed and squeezed that metaphysical fist tight and hard. But it was like the hand wasn't big enough to hold it all now. I could squeeze it down, but it leaked through as if the fingers were trying to hold sand. No, not true. I didn't want to stop. It felt so good to wander through the vampires, better than playing with zombies. The moment I realized I was the one letting the fist leak, I was able to shut it down. It almost hurt, but I did it. I could do it. But I wondered if there would come a day when there was so much power that I wouldn't be able to shut it down completely? I needed to talk to my magical mentor, Marianne, about that, sooner rather than later.

I opened my eyes and said, "How's that?"

"Good," he said, but his voice was not happy.

"That was frightening," Elinore said. "I felt your power, as if you were licking along my skin, my . . ." She shivered, not in a happy way.

"Sorry," I said.

"You could roll me," London said, "roll me the way I can roll a human. You could, I felt it."

"You must undo to my brother what you have done to him," Wicked said, "or bind me as you bind him."

I nodded. "We'll discuss it later, okay? I've got a full plate today."

"You promised me," Wicked said.

I sighed. "Look, I didn't know that taking blood from me instead of Jean-Claude would be that big a deal, okay? I'm doing the best I can here, Wicked. Truth was dying when I offered him blood. I saved his life, if I remember correctly, so stop being so pissy about it." I was getting angry, because I felt guilty, and that almost always led to anger for me.

"Anita can work on your problem another day," Requiem said. "Today is mine."

Something in the way he said it made me look at him. He lay like he hurt, but the look on his face wasn't about pain. It was almost anticipatory.

"What are you thinking, Requiem?" I asked.

"That you still need to feed the *ardeur* in front of all these good people." I shook my head. "I don't think that's a good idea."

"The test is to see what will happen if you feed the *ardeur* in front of our visitors. You know not to use your necromancy in front of them now, but this question has not been decided."

I nodded. "Yeah, I think it has."

"I'm with Anita on this one," London said, "no *ardeur* in front of the guests. No anything much in front of the other masters."

"That is not your call to make," Elinore said.

"Do you think I'm wrong?" he asked.

No one answered. So I did. "No, you're not wrong. My powers are too unpredictable to use in public right now. I just have to shield like a son of a bitch."

"Perhaps you can control the necromancy to that degree, but the *ardeur* is not broken to bit and bridle, yet," Requiem said.

"She just freed you," Wicked said. "How can you want her to enslave you again?"

"I don't want to be enslaved, but I do want her to feed. I want it more than I've wanted anything in a very long time."

I looked at Jean-Claude. "Is he free, or not?"

"You called me back so I could choose, Anita."

I looked at Requiem. "I don't understand."

"You said you would never feed the *ardeur* on me again, unless I broke free and could choose. You said it would be like rape, unless I could choose."

"I wasn't sure you'd remember everything I said."

"I remember," he said.

"I think it's too dangerous to feed the *ardeur* on you."

"You swore that you would feed from me, if I broke free. I have broken free."

"I broke you free."

"Are you certain of that? Are you certain that my will did not help you some little bit?"

I started to say no, then hesitated. "I don't . . . know."

"Then I choose for you to feed."

I was shaking my head.

"Feed, Anita, feed upon my flesh, drink deep of my will until it doth spill upon your body like blood."

"You're not thinking clearly." I started to get off the bed.

He grabbed my arm, in one of those too-quick-to-see movements. He winced, showed that it had cost him. "I have not made the choice you would make, if our places were reversed. I have not said what you wished me to say, but I have chosen."

"Let go of me, Requiem."

He looked at me, and smiled. "I do not wish to, and I am free not to obey. I fought to come back because you said only if I did, only then would you feed from me. Would you deny me now that I have fought the battle and won?"

"What if one feeding undoes it? What if the *ardeur* consumes you again?"

"If I am never again to be consumed by love, then what better than to be consumed by the *ardeur*?"

"You sound like a junkie who's had another taste after a long dry spell."

"My heart has died twice. Once when my mortal life ceased and the second when Ligeia was taken from me. I have felt nothing for so very long, Anita. You make me feel again." He sat up, drew me in toward him.

I put a hand on his chest, missing the knife wound by fractions. "The *ardeur* makes you feel again."

He touched my face with his wounded hand. "No, there is something about you that has awakened my heart."

I had a panicked feeling he was about to profess undying love. Maybe Jean-Claude did, too, because he moved forward and laid a hand on my arm.

Requiem kept his wounded hand against my cheek, but let go of my arm. He reached out to Jean-Claude, laid his hand against the other man's waist. I knew he couldn't feel much through the thick robe, but it was still the most intimate gesture I'd ever seen him make toward Jean-Claude.

"Always before your *ardeur* tasted of hers, Jean-Claude."

He wasn't talking about me. He meant Belle Morte, because *her* without appellation always meant Belle for them. "Last night, Jean-Claude, you did not taste of her. You tasted of no one's power but your own. I knew you were a *sourdre de sang*, but until last night you were still a planet circling the sun of Belle Morte's power. Last night you became the sun and she the moon."

"Belle was the moon," I said.

He looked at me, smiling. "No, Anita, you were the moon. 'The moon's an arrant thief, And her pale fire she snatches from the sun.' "

"You're quoting something," I said.

"Shakespeare, *ma petite*. He's quoting *Timon of Athens*."

"Haven't read that one," I said. My pulse was in my throat, and it was making blood trickle from the wounds he'd made in my neck. "I don't need to feed the *ardeur* right now, Requiem, and with everything going all weird, I think I'll wait until I have to feed."

"That is sense, Requiem," London said.

Requiem gazed at the other vampire. "Would you wait?"

"With permission," London said, "I would like to leave the room."

"Go," Jean-Claude said.

London didn't run for the door, but he didn't stroll either. Hell, if I could have run from it, I would have. But you can't run from yourself.

"Any who wish to go, go," Jean-Claude said.

"The test will not work if we are not here," Elinore said.

"The test is over. We are too dangerous, and we know it."

Elinore didn't argue, she just walked out. Wicked took his brother by the arm, and led him out. Truth seemed to be weeping.

"What do you want us to do?" Remus asked.

"Guard us, if you can."

"We can guard you," he said, sounding slightly offended that Jean-Claude doubted it.

"Can you guard us from ourselves?" Jean-Claude asked.

"I don't understand," Remus said.

Cisco had the gauze and tape. He stood by the bed, as if unsure what to do with the bandages. I touched my neck and came away with a little blood, but it had been a clean bite. It wouldn't bleed all that much, not if it had been done right, and knowing Requiem it had been.

"Do you need antiseptic?" Cisco asked.

Remus came to the bed, impatient. "You treat Anita like another shapeshifter."

"Oh," Cisco said. He started to set the first-aid supplies on the bed, then hesitated as if he didn't want to put them between Requiem and me. He was still wearing a gun, but the confident guard had vanished, replaced by an awkward eighteen-year-old.

"Give her some gauze so she can hold it against the wound," Remus said. "The bandage is mostly to keep the cleanup to a minimum, not really for the wound."

Cisco nodded like he understood, but he held the gauze out to me with his eyes nowhere near my face. In fact, he was sort of studiously trying not to look at me. I finally realized part of his problem. More of my chest was showing than when I'd started. Requiem's feeding had moved the front of the robe around, so that a lot of breast was showing. Not all, not more than a really low neckline would show, but it was distracting him. He was both trying not to stare at my chest, and staring at it, as he warred with himself.

I pressed the gauze to the bite, and closed my robe up with the other hand. I'd need two hands to retie, so all I could do was hold the robe closed. That let Cisco know I'd noticed what he'd been doing. He suddenly met my eyes, and he was embarrassed. It showed in the almost panic in his own eyes, and the dark blush that crawled up his neck. The panic turned to anger, and he looked away, as if I'd seen too far into his soul.

Remus took the first-aid stuff from him. "Go to the coffin room and tell Nazareth to send someone to take your place on this detail."

Cisco protested, "Why?"

"You're staring at her chest. She's not a piece of ass, kid. When you're on the job, you're on the fucking job. You can notice she's pretty, but you don't stare, you don't get distracted."

"I'm sorry, Remus, it won't happen again."

"No, it won't," Remus said. "Go to the coffin room."

"Please, Remus . . ."

"I gave you an order, Cisco, follow it."

Cisco lowered his head, not a bow, but dejection. The gesture itself, at something so small, said how young he was. But he didn't argue again. He went for the door.

When it closed behind him, Remus turned to me. "Are you still bleeding?"

I let go of the gauze; it stayed in place, pasted there by blood. "Hard to tell," I said.

He started to touch the gauze, then stopped, letting his hand drop to his side. I actually looked down to make sure my chest was completely covered. Nothing was showing. So why did Remus seem as reluctant as Cisco to touch me?

"Can you take the gauze away?" he asked.

I didn't argue, just pulled it off. It didn't hurt to move it, so I wasn't bleeding that badly. Good.

"Turn your head to the side so I can see." He added, "Please."

I did what he asked, which put me watching Jean-Claude. He looked way too solemn for comfort. "What's wrong now?" I asked.

"Are you so ashamed of us that you would hide our mark of favor under bandages and tape?"

I frowned at him. "What are you talking about?"

Remus touched more gauze to my neck. "Can you hold it in place while I get tape?"

I put my hand up to the gauze, automatically.

Jean-Claude motioned at my hand, at Remus, who had his back mostly to the other man.

Remus moved in to tape the gauze in place. I stopped him with a hand on his arm. He stepped back immediately, out of reach, the tape still in his fingers. I glanced up at his face, but he wouldn't give me a direct look, so I didn't know what was in his eyes. He'd stepped back like I'd hurt him. I hadn't.

I turned away from the guard, to Jean-Claude. Remus's problems were Remus's problem, not mine. I had enough problems. "You mean why am I bandaging the bite?"

He nodded.

"I always bandage the bites."

"*Pourquoi?*" he asked. *Why?*

I opened my mouth, closed it, and thought about it. "It's a wound. It usually pierces a vein or artery. You smear antiseptic on it, and slap a bandage on it to keep it from getting infected."

"Have you ever known a vampire bite to become infected?" he asked.

I frowned, and thought about it. It took me nearly a minute to say, "No."

"Why is that, *ma petite*?"

"Because vampires have a natural antiseptic in their saliva. Vampires actually have fewer types of bacteria in their saliva than the average human."

"You are quoting now," he said.

I nodded, and stopped because the bite was a little tight. It didn't exactly hurt, but it let me know it was there. "Yeah, they had an article in *The Animator*. Some doctor actually wondered why vampire bites don't get infected like an ordinary human bite, or an animal bite. They've known for a while that you guys have an anticoagulant in your saliva, but this was the first study on other properties of vampire saliva."

"So, I ask again, why are you hiding our mark of favor?"

I thought about it, then shrugged. "Habit." I took the gauze off the bite mark. It had two small round red circles on it, but it had almost stopped bleeding. They usually did unless you were cut up. A violent vamp bite was more like a dog bite; it bled. The two neat holes stopped sooner than you'd think, and rarely re-bled without the wound being reopened. I'd known vampire junkies who tried to hide their habit by having a vampire bite the same wound several times. It didn't really work if you knew enough about vamps to know what a bite should look like, but it fooled the tourists, or the boss at work on Monday. Repeated trauma to an area is still repeated trauma, and that was one of the few times outside of violent attacks when a vamp bite started to bruise and tear.

I handed the used gauze to Remus, who took it gingerly from me as if he didn't want to touch my fingers. "I don't need the bandages. Thanks anyway, Remus."

Jean-Claude came to me, smiling. He touched the bite delicately, coming away with minute drops of blood on his fingertips. He lifted them to his mouth, and I knew what he was going to do before he licked so delicately. I watched him lick my blood off his fingertips, and wasn't sure how I felt about it. I didn't enjoy it. I didn't not enjoy it. I felt neutral about what he'd done, but why had he done it? He usually went out of his way not to spook me, not to be too vampiric.

He leaned over me, put his hands delicately around my face, and tried to raise me up for a kiss. Normally, I would have met him halfway, but I didn't do it this time. I stayed sitting, forcing him to bend down for me. I kept my hand on the robe, holding it in place, and watched him bend lower. He stopped just before he would have kissed me, and drew back enough so I could see his face clearly. "You have kissed me many times with the taste of your sweet blood upon my lips, but now, I see reluctance on your face, feel it in your body. Why?" He searched my face, though I knew he could drop his shields and know exactly what I was thinking. Maybe he was afraid of what he'd find.

Why, he'd asked? Because he'd licked my blood off his fingers? I'd kissed him when he'd come directly off my vein. I'd kissed him when one mouth or the other had gotten nicked on his fangs. I'd learned to think of a little sweet copper taste as almost an aphrodisiac, because I'd begun to associate it with him, and others. Even Richard liked a little taste of blood; he hated that he liked it, but he did.

Jean-Claude drew back, letting my face slide between his hands as he stood. A look of such sadness came over his face. I grabbed his arm. "Don't."

"Don't what, *ma petite*? Don't stop hiding what I am? I cannot be human, *ma petite*, not even for you. I thought the worst of playing human for each other, you and I, was the crippling of our power, but that is not what hurts my heart."

I let go of his arm. I didn't want to ask the next question, but I knew I had to, or be branded a coward. I swallowed hard enough that it hurt, and asked, "What hurts your heart?" It was a whisper, but I asked it. Brownie points for me.

"That you turn away from me, for such a small thing. I licked your blood off my fingertips and now you will not kiss me."

"I would have kissed you."

He shook his head. "But you did not wish to."

That I couldn't argue with. Part of me wished I could have, part of me didn't. "What do you want me to say?" I asked.

"I want you and Richard to embrace yourselves, and I am out of time to await this miracle."

"What does that mean?" I asked.

"You promised to feed the *ardeur* from Requiem, if he fought free of your power. Will you go back on your word?"

I glanced at the other vampire, lying on the mounded pillows, then back to Jean-Claude. "The *ardeur* hasn't risen for either of us, yet. I think we should use the time we have before it does to plan strategy."

"Strategy for what, *ma petite*? This is not a battle of guns and knives. This is battle of a softer sort, though no less dangerous in the end."

I was shaking my head, and felt the first little trickle of blood down my throat. It wasn't the shaking that was making me bleed a little more, but the fact that my pulse was speeding up. "We are not going to feed the *ardeur* before we have to."

"Your power rises, and you are more like Belle Morte," Requiem said, and he sounded sad.

I glanced at him. "What are you talking about?"

Requiem answered, "Belle used to promise to feed the *ardeur* on us, then say she had not meant right this moment, but later, always later. Later could be very late indeed when she wished to play cruel games."

"I'm not playing," I said, "I'm scared."

"If you feed from him, and he becomes besotted again, then you cannot feed off any of the *pomme de sang* candidates. We will show them Requiem's state of mind and tell them you have grown too powerful for such games."

"And if he doesn't fall under my spell again?" I asked.

"Then you may taste some of the candidates without sex."

I was shaking my head.

"The *ardeur* is growing, *ma petite*, you must accept that. What we have seen today and last night proves that pretending will no longer work."

"I'm not pretending," I said.

"You are pretending."

"Pretending what?" I asked.

"I am sorry, *ma petite*, so sorry, but we must accept the truth."

I had crawled to the foot of the bed. Blood was trickling down my throat, like tickling fingers. I was so scared I could taste metal on my tongue. "I don't know what you're talking about."

"You are succubus to my incubus, *ma petite*. You feed as a vampire feeds, but on sex instead of blood."

"I know that," I said, and sounded angry, because I didn't want to sound scared.

"You say you know, but you know here"—and he touched his forehead—"not here"—and touched his heart. "You do not truly believe you are vampire."

"I'm not a vampire."

"Not in the traditional sense, *non*, but only because you have Damian and Nathaniel to draw upon. Without them to draw energy from, when you did not feed the *ardeur* in a timely fashion, your own body would feel the weakness."

"You went for years without feeding the *ardeur* for real. The old Master of St. Louis wouldn't let you feed the *ardeur*, not completely."

"*Oui*, Nikolaos feared what I would become if she allowed my powers full rein. The Master of the City that traded me to her feared me, as well. He sent me to Nikolaos because he knew that her child's body would not be something I would willingly seduce."

"She looked about twelve or thirteen; that's legal in some places."

He shook his head. "Not for me," he said, then he shivered. "You met her, *ma petite*; could you ever see me purposefully doing anything to draw her attention to me in that way?"

I shook my head. "No, she was creepy as hell, and not in a fun way."

He nodded. "*Oui, creepy* will do as an appellation, though there are other words." He shook his head, as if to clear his mind from such thoughts. "If you were a different woman, one of more casual lusts, then your being succubus to my incubus would not be a hardship. You would simply feed from whomever you wished. You are human, so your use of vampire trickery is not illegal."

"Not true," I said, "it is illegal to use magic or psychic ability to induce, or bespell, into sexual acts. It's looked on like a date-rape drug."

He nodded. "I had not realized the law had been broadened to include that."

I shrugged. "I keep track of the new laws, part of my job."

He nodded again. "But still, *ma petite*, there are many who would come eagerly to your body. You would not lack for food, if you were willing to feed on strangers."

I frowned at him.

He gave a small smile. "Do not frown so, *ma petite*, I know you do not do casual. In fact, you are the least casual person that I have ever met. So serious, you are, so deadly serious about everything."

"Is that a complaint?" I asked.

"No, but it is the truth."

I nodded, and put a hand to my throat to try to stop the blood from getting onto the silk robe. I looked for Remus. "Gauze, please, or this will have to be dry-cleaned."

Remus handed the gauze over without a word. I tried to stop the blood, but my pulse was pushing it out. I couldn't seem to calm myself enough to slow my pulse. So much for the meditation practice I'd been working on.

"What's your point?" I asked.

"That you need food that you know, and are comfortable with. A *pomme de sang* is never meant to be the only food for a vampire. It is more like food you always know is on hand. But it is assumed that the vampire will feed off many humans."

"Casually feed, you mean?"

"*Oui.*"

"I don't do casual, sorry."

"True, and that is why the *pomme de sang* candidates are even more important for you than for a normal vampire."

"I'm not following you," I said.

"You must pick *pommes de sang*, and other food. You must choose enough food that you are not a danger to others."

"You're babbling."

He came around the bed so he could touch me, but I moved out of reach. "If you bespell Requiem again, then you cannot seek a *pomme de sang* among our visitors. Your food will have to be chosen even more carefully, and quietly, behind the scenes, from the very few masters I trust. But it would be better to do it now, while we have so many willing princesses for our Prince Charming. Because choose you must, *ma petite*, choose you must."

"I thought the whole *pomme de sang* choosing was a trick to make everyone behave. Nobody wants to piss off their prospective in-laws, that sort of thing."

"Anita"—my name, not good—"we must know how dangerous you are, before Augustine wakes for the night. If you can feed from Requiem and not bespell him, then you can free Augustine. But if Requiem is not free, then he, and Augustine, will be like humans that we have let go, but we know that we can call them to us at any time. We take away our mind spell to please the human police, but we know which ones are so deeply ours that we can still whisper through their dreams. We can still call them." He stood at the foot of the bed, letting me see how scared he was, but under that fear was eagerness. "If we can control this, then we are powerful beyond my wildest dreams. If we cannot control this, then we are dangerous beyond my deepest fears. If Requiem falls to the *ardeur* again, then we must cancel everything. I dare not even take you to the ballet among so many vampires."

"And if Requiem is okay?"

"Then it is controllable, incredibly powerful, but controllable. It is something our enemies and allies will fear and lust after, but they will not fear us too much, or lust too greatly. It is the difference between having a weapon that one can use, and one that you dare never use."

"Like nuclear bombs," I said.

He nodded. "*Oui*."

I frowned at him. "Define 'feed the *ardeur*'."

He made a sound that was half *tsk* and half throat sound. "Feed, feed, *ma petite*. He is not ugly. Feed upon him, completely, no tasting, no holding back. Feed, and if he can withstand it, then the ballet tonight goes on, the party after."

I looked behind me to Requiem. He was trying for a neutral look, and failing. "Let me test my understanding: you want me to make love to another man, and feed the *ardeur* off him?"

"Yes," he said.

If Ronnie had been there, she'd have shot herself, or maybe shot me. I wasn't planning on keeping Requiem. This was supposed to be like a one-night stand. But I didn't believe it. I'd never had sex with anyone just once. "I can't do another permanent man in my life, Jean-Claude. I can't."

"Think of him as you think of Jason. What did he call himself, your fuck buddy?"

I raised my eyebrows at him, then turned and looked at Requiem. "Did you hear that?"

"I did."

"Do you understand what the term means?"

"It means someone who is your friend, that you sometimes have sex with, but it is not a relationship. Though I prefer the term *fib* for it."

"Fib?" I made it a question.

"Friends in bed, fib."

"Prettier," I said. "Fine, you okay with just being my friend in bed?"

"Your heart speaks to others, Anita, I know this. My heart speaks to no one else. But this is not a matter of hearts, but a matter of flesh and blood." He held his hand out to me. "Come to me, Anita, please. I have thrown off your silken chains for this chance to be with you; do not deny me."

Maybe it was the way Requiem talked, all poetry and so emotional sounding. I was a modern girl; I wasn't used to it. Jean-Claude could talk pretty when he wanted to, but he was my serious sweetie, and hearing it from someone who was supposed to be casual just didn't ring right. It was as if the words didn't match the situation. How could you talk about silken chains if you weren't serious? Fuck buddies didn't say things like that, did they? Of course, my experience with the whole concept of fuck buddies was pretty limited, so maybe I was just wrong. Wrong about so many things.

I stared at Requiem, and felt nothing. He was pretty, but pretty had never been enough for me. I was almost perfectly happy in parts of my personal life, for the first time in a long time. I did not want to screw that up, and I'd learned that every new addition had a chance of blowing it all sky-high.

Requiem let his arm fall. "You simply do not want me, do you?" He sounded sad, and more lost than when I'd rolled him.

I don't know what I would have said, because the door opening saved me. Asher glided in, as if his feet weren't quite touching the ground under the golden satin robe. His hair spread out around the robe, putting the shiny cloth to shame by contrast. He glanced at the bed and flashed a wide smile. "Oh, good, I'm in time to watch."

I gave him an unfriendly look.

He shrugged and smiled, way too pleased with himself. "Elinore has filled me in on what's been happening in here. When I woke early, I realized that if I was awake then so was Meng Die."

That stopped us all, made us all turn to him. Remus actually stepped away from the wall as if he'd go running.

Asher waved him back. "She's still in the coffin, though she does want out. She's agreed to behave herself."

"She vowed she would kill me, or scar me so badly that Anita would not want me," Requiem said.

Asher went to Jean-Claude where he still stood by the bed. He hugged the other man from behind, laying his head on Jean-Claude's shoulder, so that his scarred cheek was bare to the light. "Yes, I was there when she made that particular threat. She looked at me, and said she'd forgotten that Anita liked scars." His face tried for neutral when he said it, but failed. A flash of anger flared through the paleness of his eyes, making them flicker for a second like icy sapphires caught in light.

Jean-Claude hugged his arm where it lay across his chest. He leaned his face against the top of Asher's hair, and said, "How did you get Meng Die to see reason?"

"She said, for such power as she felt when you did Augustine she would play virgin. There's always another lover, but this kind of power is rare."

I looked at the two of them standing there, the light and the dark, entwined. I realized in that moment that I had never seen Asher enter a room and simply go to Jean-Claude and touch him like that. I had never seen them hug, let alone more. They touched, but it was seldom this deliberate.

Did they touch like this when I wasn't around? Did they do more? Did I care? Maybe. But did it bother me more that they were lovers, or that they were doing it behind my back? Doing it without me?

Jean-Claude pulled away from him. Asher held on for a moment, then let him go with a flash of annoyance on his face, but he didn't fight to stay closer. He simply let Jean-Claude move a little closer to the bed, and me.

I wanted to say, *You don't have to hide*, but I wasn't sure about it. I wasn't sure how I'd feel watching them act all lovey-dovey around each other. But the thought that they couldn't touch in front of me bothered me, too. I sighed and hung my head. God, I was confused even in my own head without any help from anyone.

I felt the bed move, and looked up to find Requiem getting off the bed. He stood carefully, showing how much he hurt, but he stood straight, his pale untouched back military straight like most of the older vampires. They came from a time when good posture was beaten into you, sometimes literally.

"Where are you going?" I asked.

He turned his whole body, rather than just his head, as if he knew that it would have hurt to do it otherwise. "I see how you watch Asher and Jean-Claude. I said that you do not want me, and you do not. It is plain in your face, in your lack of reaction to me. The irony cuts deep, Anita. So many women have wanted me over the centuries, but I did not want them. Now it is my turn to burn and be unquenched."

"*Non*," Jean-Claude said, "you are not going."

Requiem motioned with his good hand. "See her face, taste her lack of pulse. Her body does not respond to me. She does not even see me in that way."

"Anita sees you, or you'd have never gotten to feed the *ardeur* twice for her," Asher said. He walked wide around Jean-Claude, to climb onto the bed with me. There was a look in his face that I hadn't seen before. It was eager, almost angry, but not unhappy.

He touched my face, and his hand was cool to the touch. He hadn't fed. "I woke before noon today for the first time since I died." He leaned in toward me, as if for a kiss. "So much power running through my veins, even without blood. I feel wonderful." He stopped with his mouth just above mine, so close that it seemed wrong not to close the distance and kiss. So I did.

I meant it to be a good-morning kiss. Good, but not too sexual. But it takes two people to keep a kiss chaste and Asher wasn't feeling the least bit chaste.

He explored my mouth with lips and tongue. I melted into that kiss. I danced my tongue over the dainty points of his fangs, slid between them, deeper into his mouth. He pressed us together, hands urgent on my body. One hand undid the sash of my robe. The nude fronts of our bodies were suddenly touching. I didn't even know when he'd undone his own robe, only that the naked press of our bodies drove my hands under his open robe to slide along the smooth skin of his back and buttocks. When I cupped the tight smoothness of his ass, he drew back enough to see my face. Whatever he saw there painted a fierce look across his own. His voice came harsh and breathless. "Let me feed."

I just said, "Yes."

He wrapped his hand in my hair, hard enough for it to hurt, just a little. That little bit of hurting made me gasp, but it wasn't just the pain. It was the feeling that with that one harsh grasp he could expose my neck and hold me exposed while he fed. I might never have admitted it aloud, but there was something about a little bit of force that just flat did it for me. Asher dug his hand deeper into my hair, jerked, brought a cry from me. It wasn't exactly a cry of pain.

His free hand found my wrists, held them behind my back, while my robe slipped down my shoulders. He stretched my head to the side so that I could no longer see his face. I saw us reflected in the full-length mirror on the other side of the room. My robe had fallen like a dark frame around the paleness of my body. The robe covered our hands, and not much more. It looked in the mirror like my hands were bound. The sight of it made me strain to be free, and Asher tightened his grip, bruising my wrists just a little, just enough to let me know I couldn't get away. I trusted him. Trusted him enough to let him trap me.

Movement in the mirror, and I saw Jean-Claude reflected there. His own robe was tight in place, but his eyes glowed with midnight blue fire.

"The audience is a little large for *ma petite*."

"She's not objecting," Asher said.

"And do you not find that strange?" Jean-Claude asked.

Asher seemed to struggle to think, then finally said, "I do not know. I can't seem to think with her here in my arms." He looked out into the room. "Their presence seems to make it harder to think."

"The guards, or just certain guards?" Jean-Claude asked.

"Remus"—and he looked to the far corner of the room—"and the new one."

"And what of Pepito? Do you sense him as strongly?"

Asher's body began to relax against me. I didn't want that. I wanted him to feed. Needed him to feed. "Don't stop," I said, "please, don't stop."

Asher looked down at me with those glowing eyes. He seemed to be searching my face for some sign. "You wish me to take you here with the guards watching?"

Of course I did. "Yes," I said, "yes, God, yes."

He looked at Jean-Claude. "Something is wrong."

"Wrong, and right," Jean-Claude said. He came to the edge of the bed. "You have possessed her, completely. You could do what you wished with her, but when she sobered, then she would never forgive you."

Asher turned back to me. Whatever he saw there calmed him, tore the light from his eyes. "Anita, are you in there?"

The question made no sense at first, then I said, "I am here, Asher, right here." Some part of me heard me say it, and thought I'd heard that phrase before. I closed my eyes, tried to not see Asher's face. It helped, to look away. I knew where I'd heard the words now: Requiem. I was echoing Requiem when I'd rolled his mind. Asher had rolled me before, but not like this, never like this.

Remembering Requiem helped me think, but closing my eyes helped more. I was too big a fish for Asher's gaze to keep, but staring into his eyes had lost me, myself. I'd stared into Augustine's eyes and not been swept away, so how did Asher's gaze rate higher than a couple of thousand years of Master of the City? I was supposed to be immune to vampire gaze. My necromancy and Jean-Claude's marks should have kept me safe.

Asher let go of my wrists. I felt him move back from me. I opened my eyes and reached for my robe, drawing it back around me. "What's happening?" I asked.

Jean-Claude spoke from beside the bed. "Are you yourself, *ma petite*?"

"I think so." I glanced up at Asher's face, but he turned away, the spill of golden hair hiding his face. "Look at me, Asher."

"I did not mean to bespell you with my gaze. I did not even know that my gaze could capture you."

"It's never been able to before," I said. I looked at Jean-Claude. "What is happening? I was as bespelled as Requiem before I freed him."

"*Non*, you were able to fight free, once you realized what had happened."

"Yes, but why did it happen in the first place? What just happened, and why? And don't avoid the question again, Jean-Claude, I mean it."

He made a gesture that was half bow and half shrug. Managing to make it both apology and an I-don't-know gesture.

"Not good enough. You do know what's going on."

"I know what I believe has happened."

"Fine, tell us." I slipped off the bed so I could tie the robe in place better.

"All our people gained from what we did last night with Augustine. Asher has been a master vampire for a very long time, but he has never had many of the master-level powers that are taken for granted among many of us."

"His gaze has gone up a few notches, I get that," I said.

Jean-Claude shook his head. "*Non, ma petite*, it is more than that. What is Asher's greatest vampiric ability?"

I thought about it for a second or two, then said, "His bite is orgasmic."

Jean-Claude gave a small smile. "That may be his most alluring power for you, *ma petite*, but it is not his most powerful."

I thought harder. "Fascination. He makes you fascinated with him, once he's fed off you using full power. Once he's made love to you, it's like a sort of love spell, but it works the way that love spells never work."

"I believe his ability to fascinate has grown in power."

I glanced at Asher, who was still sitting on the side of the bed, but carefully not looking at me. I shook my head and walked closer to him. "Look at me, Asher, please."

"Why?" he asked, in a very still voice, carefully not looking at me.

"I have to know if your gaze can just roll me, or if it happened because I don't protect myself against you."

He almost glanced at me then, but gave me only the perfection of his profile and a wave of shimmering hair. "What do you mean, you do not protect yourself from me?"

"I trust you, so I don't shield from you. I want your power to take me. I don't want to fight it. But before it was a choice. Now I need to see if it's still a choice, or if you've just outgrown me."

"Give her the weight of your gaze, *mon ami*, let us see."

Asher turned, reluctance plain in the way he held his body. He gave me a face as blank and unreadable as any I'd ever seen on him. I'd perfected the art of looking at a vampire's face without meeting their gaze years ago. I was a little out of practice, grown arrogant with power, but old skills never truly desert you.

I studied the curve of his lips, then raised my eyes slowly to meet his. They were as beautiful as always, such a pale, pale blue. A pure, clear blue, but pale as a winter's dawn. I stared into those eyes and felt nothing.

"This won't work unless you try to capture me with your gaze."

"I do not wish to capture you," he said softly.

"Liar," I said.

He managed to look offended then.

"Don't try to kid me, Asher, you like power games entirely too much. You love the effect you have on me. You love that you can do to me what Jean-Claude can't. You love the fact that you are the only vamp who can vamp me."

His face went to cold neutrality. "I have never said such things to you."

"Your body said them for you."

He licked his lips then, an old gesture that he still made when he was nervous. "What do you want from me, Anita?"

"Truth."

He shook his head, and looked solemn. "You ask for truth a great deal, but it is seldom what you truly want."

I'd have liked to argue that, but I couldn't, not and be honest. "You're right, probably more right than I want to know, but right now, try to capture me with your gaze. Really try, so we'll know how careful I need to be around you."

"I do not want you to have to be careful around me."

I shook my head. "Please, Asher, we need to know."

"Why, so you can hide from me? So you can deny me the gaze of your own eyes?"

"Please, Asher, just do it, just try."

"I will ask as a friend," Jean-Claude said, "but the next request will be as master. Do as she asks." His voice sounded so sad. Sad enough that it made me look at him. I felt like I was missing something.

Once I would have just ignored the warning in my head, but I'd learned to ask questions. "Am I asking something bad here? I mean, you're both way too bothered by this. Am I missing something that's going to come back and bite us on the ass?"

Jean-Claude smiled, almost laughed. "Ah, *ma petite*, how delicately you phrase it."

"Yeah, yeah, just answer the question."

"We fear what your reaction will be if Asher can indeed capture you with his gaze."

I looked from one to the other of them. Jean-Claude's carefully pleasant face. Asher's arrogant blankness. I caught sight of Requiem against the far wall beyond them. His face was as blank as theirs, but it wasn't pleasant like Jean-Claude's or arrogant like Asher's; he simply tried to show nothing. His upper body was still decorated with the wounds Meng Die had given him. For the first time I wondered: if I fed the *ardeur* off him, would the wounds heal? I'd healed before with metaphysical sex. I frowned and turned back to Jean-Claude. "You had more than one reason for me to feed the *ardeur* from Requiem, didn't you?"

"You are not going to do it, so what does it matter?" There was the slightest flavor of anger to his words.

I turned to him. The pleasant mask was gone, and in its place something close to the arrogance that Asher hid behind. "I know I'm difficult, but let's pretend I'm not. Let's pretend that I'm not a huge pain in the ass. Just talk to me. Tell me your reasoning."

"My reasoning about what, *ma petite*?"

I walked toward him, talking as I moved. "All the reasons for me to feed from Requiem now. All the reasons why you're so nervous about Asher being able to capture me with his gaze." I was in front of him now, and realized that he must have moved back from the bed at some point, and I didn't remember him moving away. I'd been too caught up in Asher's eyes. "Just tell me. I promise not to panic. I promise not to run away. Just talk to me like I'm a reasonable human being."

He gave me a look, and it was an eloquent look. He let me watch thoughts chase over his face, but finally he said, "Asher is correct, *ma petite*; you ask for truth, but you often punish us for telling it."

I nodded. "I know, and I'm sorry about that. All I know is that I'll try to stop being a pain in the ass. I'll try to listen, and not overreact."

"Good intentions, *ma petite*, but you do know the old saying."

I nodded, again. "Yeah, the road to hell is paved with them, I know." I touched his arm where it lay folded across his chest. Even his body language had closed down. "Please, Jean-Claude, I feel like we don't have time to play to my insecurities. If we crash this weekend with all the other masters here, I don't want it to be because you were afraid to be honest with me. I don't want the disaster to be my fault. Okay?"

He uncrossed his arms, and touched my face. "So sincere, *ma petite*. What has come over you?"

I thought about that, then said it, out loud. "I'm scared."

"Of what?"

I put my hand on his, pressing his touch against my face. "Of failing us all, just because I didn't want something to be true."

"*Ma petite*, that is not it, not entirely."

I looked away from those suddenly knowing eyes of his. "I think it's the baby thing." I made myself meet his eyes. The gentleness in them was both easier to meet and harder. "If we really are going to do this, keep the baby, then we have to make this work. We have to make it all work. I don't have the luxury of being a pain in the ass, if it's going to get us hurt."

"You find out but hours ago, and you are suddenly more willing to compromise." He looked at me, considering, serious, tender, all mixed together. "I am told that pregnancy changes a woman, but so quick as this?"

"Maybe I just needed a wake-up call."

"Wake up to what, *ma petite*?"

"I keep telling Richard I've accepted my life, but he's right, I'm still hiding from parts of it. You"—and I looked at Asher then—"are all still tiptoeing around me afraid of what I'll do, aren't you?" I turned back to Jean-Claude. "Aren't you?"

"You have taught us caution, *ma petite*." He tried to hug me, but I stepped away.

"Don't comfort me, Jean-Claude, talk to me."

He sighed. "You do realize, *ma petite*, that these demands for complete honesty that come over you from time to time are another way of being a pain in the ass?"

I had to smile. "No, I hadn't realized that. I thought this was being reasonable."

"*Non, ma petite*, this is not being reasonable. This is another way of being very demanding."

"Well, hell, then tell me what to do, because I don't know how to be anything else."

"You are a high-maintenance item, as they say, *ma petite*. But I knew that before we became a couple."

"You're saying, you knew what you were getting into."

He nodded. "As much as any man can when he decides to love a woman. There are always mysteries and surprises in every love affair. But, yes, I had some idea what I was getting myself into. I did it willingly, eagerly."

"The difficulties were outweighed by what, the power you might gain?"

He frowned at me. "See, already you grow angry. You do not want truth, *ma petite*. You do not want lies either. You leave us all with no clue to what will take us safely through your rocky shoals."

"I've never heard you use a sea metaphor before."

"Perhaps seeing Samuel reminded me of my voyage to this fair land."

"Perhaps," I said, and even to me it sounded suspicious.

Asher made a sound low in his throat. "You seek a reason to be angry, so you can blame us, and run."

"Like Richard was trying to pick a fight earlier," I said.

Asher nodded.

I thought about that for a second or two. "It's not that Richard and I are too different, we're too much alike."

Jean-Claude gave me a look, like I'd finally come to something he'd understood long ago. "Too much alike in many ways, but you have compromised more, and your very alikeness in character makes him keep trying to force you to make the same decisions he has made. He sees the echo of himself in you, and understands even less why you do not see his rightness in all things."

"And it's maybe why he frustrates me, too. He's enough like me, so why can't he make the decisions I've made?"

"*Oui, ma petite*, I believe that is part of your immense anger toward each other."

"He's right, I'm trying to make him into something he's not, and he's trying to do the same to me. Shit."

"What, *ma petite*?"

"I hate being this slow about something that feels so obvious."

"It is only obvious once you have thought of it," he said.

"I'm not sure that makes sense, but okay, fine. I'm not saying I'll like hearing it, but tell me why you're so worried about Asher using his gaze on me."

"I'll answer this one," Asher said. He came to me, his robe still open over his body. It took more concentration than I'd have admitted out loud to give him eye contact and not look lower. "If I can capture you with my gaze, we are both afraid you will exile me from your bed. Your bed, and Jean-Claude's."

"I'm not in charge of Jean-Claude's bed. You and he sleep together in your bed whenever I sleep by day in his bed."

The two men exchanged a look I couldn't read. I touched Asher's arm, brought his attention back to me. "What is it?"

He looked down at me, using all that gold hair to cover the scarred side of his face. He didn't usually hide from me anymore. "What do you think that Jean-Claude and I do in my bed when you are asleep in this one?"

I frowned, then couldn't quite meet his entirely too-frank gaze. Vampire powers didn't make me look away, embarrassment did. "You're right, I don't want honesty, I just think I do."

"You are blushing," Asher said, and he gave a delighted laugh. "You think we are lovers, don't you?"

I was blushing so hard I was dizzy, and I felt like he was making fun of me. So I got angry. I crossed my arms over my stomach, and said, "Yeah."

Asher looked at Jean-Claude. "She believes what most believe of us."

I finally looked at Jean-Claude. His face was very empty. I had to lick my suddenly dry lips to say, "Are you saying that you're not doing it, when I'm not around?"

"All the touch I am allowed is when you are with us," Asher said, and it was his turn to sound angry. But his anger had warmth to it, to fill his voice.

I kept staring at Jean-Claude.

"You do not believe us?" Jean-Claude asked.

"It's not that, it's . . ." I tried to put it into words. Finally, I said, "How could you be so close to him and keep turning him down?"

"Thank you for that," Asher said.

"And what would you have done, *ma petite*, if you had found us in an embrace?"

"I . . . I don't know. I guess it depends on what you mean by *embrace*."

"Sex, *ma petite*, sex."

I opened my mouth, closed it, and didn't know what to say. "I don't know."

"I do. You would have stormed away. You would have abandoned my bed, damaged our power base, the triumvirate. You might have run to our so-conservative Richard, or left us both again. So shocked you would have been, so unready to conceive of such things."

"Maybe, but I didn't freak about you and Augustine."

"You were involved. We shared him. If you had come upon the two of us alone, you would have taken it differently."

"Well, yeah, he's a stranger for one thing."

"Wait," Asher said, "are you saying that you would share Jean-Claude with me?"

"We share each other now."

He shook his head. "We share you, Anita, we barely touch each other."

"Do not do this tonight, Asher. I ask this as your friend, and as your master. When our guests are gone, then we will continue this discussion."

"Your word on that," Asher said.

"My word."

I nodded. "When we're not ass-deep in alligators, and I've had a few days to digest the news."

"Is this news to you, that I want him as my lover?" Asher asked.

I shook my head. "Truthfully, I thought you guys were doing it like bunnies behind my back. You know, the whole *don't ask*, *don't tell* policy. It never occurred to me that all the touching you did was with me."

"I thought you would see it as cheating," Jean-Claude said.

"With another woman, yeah, but I don't have the same equipment. I mean if guys do it for you, I don't have those parts. But it wasn't guys I thought I was sharing you with, it was Asher. He's not just one of the guys to us."

"Are you saying that Asher is your exception to the rule?"

"I'm not sure I had a rule, but I won't share you casually with anyone, any more than I'd expect you to share me. But I assumed that you and Asher were lovers, without me." There, that was the truth.

"Why did you assume it?"

I motioned at Asher. "Look at him. Look at the way he watches you."

Asher laughed. "Are you saying I am so adorable, how could anyone turn me down?"

I nodded. "Yeah, I am."

His face softened, and he came to stand beside me. "Oh, Anita, you make my heart young again."

I took his hand in mine. "And sometimes you make me feel like such a baby."

"*Pourquoi?*"

"That I can take you both to bed, but I assumed you were doing each other behind my back, to save my sensibilities. It was a neat, clean solution, I thought. I didn't have to decide how I felt about you two being a couple, but we all got what we needed. Instead, Jean-Claude has been a very, very good boy, and you've felt neglected."

"Rejected," he said, and gave Jean-Claude a dark look.

I touched his face, turned him back to face me. "That was my fault, not his. He's right, Asher. You know me. I can ignore the elephant in the living room until I'm eyeball-deep in shit, but if you make me look at something before it's that big, sometimes I take it badly. If I'd walked in on you guys together, I'd have used it as an excuse to run for the hills. Jean-Claude's right about that."

"And now?" he asked.

"I'm not sure. That's the truth. Before I saw Jean-Claude kiss Auggie last night, before we shared him, I would have just said no. Not only no, but hell no." I looked down, not sure if I was embarrassed, unhappy, or just out of my depth. "But I want everyone that I love to be happy. I know that. I want us all to be happy, and to stop running." I touched my stomach, so nice and flat with all the exercise. "To stop pretending that we're something we're not." I looked up at him. "No one asked you how you feel about the baby thing. I mean, you have as good a chance at it as Jean-Claude. Being the father, I mean."

He smiled at me. "I am a selfish clod." He dropped to his knees, gazing up at me. "I wake power drunk, and forget you have been through so very much in the last few hours. Forgive me."

I shook my head. "No, I've been ignoring your problem for a lot longer."

"I am in the bed of two people I love, there is no problem. I am luckier, and happier, than I ever dreamed to be again."

"But . . ."

He put his fingertips against my mouth. "Hush. You ask how I feel about your pregnancy. How could I be anything but happy about the possibility of a little you, or Jean-Claude, coming into our lives? Julianna regretted that she never gave me a child." He said her name without aching sadness, for the very first time.

I kissed his fingers and moved his hand so I could say, "You're happy about the pregnancy."

"Not happy, or unhappy, but I am very happy with you right now. I am very proud to call you my lover. You truly want us all to be happy, Anita. You have no idea how rare it is for two people in a relationship to truly want the happiness of the other, but you juggle many hearts and seek happiness for all. It is a rare gift, this desire."

"How could you love someone and not want them to be happy?"

He smiled up at me, his hair falling back. He smiled broad enough to flash fangs, which he did rarely. A smile this broad stretched the scars, made him notice how tight the skin was, but it was the effect on others that made him not do it, or the perceived effect on others. I remembered this smile from centuries before I was born. It was a smile he had before Julianna died, before holy water was trailed over him to try to chase the devil out. I smiled back, because it eased something in my heart to see that smile again. I was almost certain that the feeling of ease was Jean-Claude's and not mine, but it felt real.

Asher hugged me, putting his face against my stomach. He went very still, as if he were listening. I stroked his hair, always a surprise, because it was soft and foamy, not as soft as Jean-Claude's, but as soft as mine. Hair that looked like spun gold shouldn't be that soft, should it?

He spoke low and soft, in French. I caught the word *bebe*. Baby. I waited to be irritated, but all I could think while I stared down at him whispering to my stomach was how cute it was. That didn't sound like me. I looked across the room, and found Jean-Claude's face gone soft with emotion. I knew who thought it was cute, and it wasn't me. But with that much of Jean-Claude's emotion going through me, I had to agree. I held my hand out to Jean-Claude, while the other hand stroked Asher's hair. Jean-Claude took my hand and hugged me from behind, pressing his body to Asher's arms around my waist. So happy, Jean-Claude was so happy. It filled us both, so warm, so good, like being wrapped in your favorite blanket cuddled against someone you love. I leaned into Jean-Claude's arm, and he laid a kiss against my neck. Asher raised his face, and smiled up at us both. His face somehow looked younger, the way he must have looked centuries ago when he was alive.

The happiness was real, touchable; then the thinnest slice of regret crept into Jean-Claude's mind. I caught the thought before he could hide it, that happiness like this does not last. That the last time he'd been this happy, it had all gone horribly wrong. He buried his face in the crook of my neck to hide his expression from Asher. I touched his face, gave him my eyes, and let him see that I'd "heard" his thought, and it was all right. It was all right to fear the-great-bad-thing coming to get you, because I believed in the-great-bad-thing, too.

When I was younger, I'd wanted someone to promise me that things would work out and nothing bad would ever happen again. But I understood now that that was a child's wish. No one could promise that. No one. The grown-ups could try, but they couldn't promise, not and mean it. I stood there between the two of them, and knew that I would do whatever it took to keep them safe, to keep them happy. I'd been willing to kill for the people I loved for a very long time; now I had to start living for them.

28

EVERYONE I CONSIDERED a boyfriend or a lover left. I wanted some alone time. But truly alone was too dangerous. Requiem and some bodyguards stayed. I dressed in the bathroom, which seemed stupid since everyone had seen me naked, but I needed some privacy.

While Jean-Claude and Asher were with me, I felt utterly calm about the baby, even happy. Once they were gone the panic set back in. One of them, I wasn't sure which, had used vampire wiles on me. Or maybe, I was just picking up someone's emotions. Hell, I was bound metaphysically to so many different men, it didn't even have to be Jean-Claude's emotions I was picking up. All I knew for certain was that they weren't mine.

I got dressed in the emergency clothes I'd started keeping in Jean-Claude's room. Jeans, black T-shirt, jogging shoes, good leather belt, and enough underwear to go under it all. The belt helped hold my shoulder holster. The familiar tightness of it made me feel better. More secure. The security had little to do with being able to shoot people. Most of the people making my life hard, I loved, and didn't want to shoot. No, the gun was more psychological-better than real-life-better. Guns only work against things you're willing to kill. If you're not willing to kill, then a gun is, in some ways, a false sense of security. The wrist sheaths and silver-edged knives, that was extra security. Short of a heart blow, most of the people in my life would survive a knife. I didn't expect to argue that hard with anybody, but the wrist sheaths helped me feel better. I left the bathroom dressed and armed. Much better.

I added another thing I kept at Jean-Claude's, an extra cross. I got it out of the bedside table. It was cool against my skin, hidden under the shirt.

"I am the only monster in the room that a cross will stop, do you distrust me that much?" Requiem said from the bed.

His comment made me glance at Remus and another new werehyena sitting near the fireplace. "It's nothing personal, Requiem, but I've been visited by Belle and Marmee Noir. The cross helps keep them at bay."

"They are terrible powers."

"Yeah." I rummaged in the overnight bag until I came up with my cell phone, then headed for the bathroom.

"You can talk in front of me, Anita. I will not bear tales."

"You're blood-oathed to Jean-Claude. You'll talk if he wants you to, but frankly, I just want some privacy. Again, nothing personal, Requiem." I sighed, because this kind of shit was one of the reasons I'd been able to keep turning him down as *pomme de sang*. He was messy, or at least not neat, and I didn't need more emotionally messy men in my life. "Look, this isn't going to work between us if you take everything so damned personally. Fuck buddies don't fret this much, okay."

His face had closed down to that handsome blankness. "Okay," he said, and that one empty word let me know his feelings were hurt. Shit, I did not need this.

I closed the bathroom door, and used my cell phone to call my gynecologist. I'd finally realized that a little piece of plastic wasn't quite good enough. It was ninety-nine percent accurate; for this, I wanted a hundred percent. It took me nearly five minutes to convince the receptionist that I needed to talk to a nurse, or the doctor. The doctor, of course, was with a patient, but five minutes on hold snagged me a nurse.

"What seems to be the problem?" she asked in a voice that was part cheerful and part impatient.

"How accurate are those home pregnancy tests? I mean I know what the box says, but really, how good are they?"

"Very good, very accurate." Her voice had softened a little.

I swallowed hard enough that she probably heard me. "So if one comes back positive, then . . ."

"Then congratulations," she said.

"But it's not a hundred percent, right?"

"No, but a false positive is very rare, Ms. Blake, very rare."

"Isn't there like a blood test that's a hundred percent accurate?"

"There is a blood test, yes, but normally the doctors trust the home tests, too."

"But if I wanted to schedule a blood test, to be absolutely sure, then I could?"

"Well, yes."

"Today."

"Ms. Blake, if you're that worried, take a second home pregnancy test, but I doubt that the second test will give you a different answer. False negatives, those we see, but false postives are very rare."

"How rare?" I asked.

I heard paper rustling. "When was the date of your last period?"

"First week of September."

"Do you have the exact date?"

"No, I don't." I fought not to sound angry. Who the hell kept track of the day of their period?

"Ms. Blake, Anita, I think we need to schedule you a prenatal visit."

"Prenatal, no, I mean, yes, I mean, oh, hell."

"Anita, I talk to a lot of women. Most of them are happy about the news, but not all of them. You don't sound like this was good news to you."

"It wasn't."

"Dr. North is just coming out, I'll let you talk to him." Silence, then the sounds of movement, cloth rustling, and a man's voice. "Hey, Anita, how's my favorite vampire hunter doing?"

"Not so good today," I said, and my voice sounded small, and hurt.

"I'm sorry about that. We need to schedule you an appointment."

"I don't want to be pregnant."

He was quiet for a moment. "You're not very far along, Anita; you still have options."

"Abortion, you mean?"

"Yes."

"I can't, not unless there's something majorly wrong. I mean, I'll need to be tested for Vlad's syndrome, and Mowgli syndrome."

"I figured the Vlad's syndrome test, but you only need the Mowgli test if you've had sex with a shapeshifter while he's in animal form."

I put my forehead against the cool marble tiles of the wall, and said, "I know that."

"Oh," he said in that overly cheerful way, the way people say it when what they really want to say is *OH MY GOD!* He recovered quickly; he was, after all, a doctor. "Peggy, I'm going take this in my office, transfer it, please. Hang on a minute, Anita, let's get some privacy." I listened to a mercifully short amount of Muzak, then the phone picked up, and he said, "Okay, Anita, we'll need you to come in as soon as possible." I heard paper rippling. "We had a cancellation at two o'clock this afternoon."

"I don't know if I can make it."

"If this were just a regular prenatal visit, Anita, I'd say fine, do it next week, but if we're testing for both of the syndromes, and you're telling me there's a chance, especially for Mowgli syndrome, then we need to do the blood work now."

I wanted to say I'd only had sex with one lycanthrope in animal form, just one time, but as they say, once is all it takes. "Doc, I've read up on Vlad's syndrome. I don't know as much about the other. I mean, if I really am pregnant, then it's just this little bunch of cells, right? I mean, I'd be at best two months along, right? There's no chance of the baby trying to eat its way out until it's bigger, right?" Just saying that made my stomach tight. There might be no option of keeping anything.

"Humans have a pretty long gestation period for a mammal. I am assuming mammalian shapeshifter, here?"

"Yes. Does that make a difference?"

"It can. You see, the problem with Mowgli syndrome is that sometimes the fetus grows at the rate of the animal, and not the human."

I flipped back through every biology class I'd ever had, and nowhere had I ever learned the gestation period of a leopard. It just hadn't been covered.

"Anita, talk to me, Anita."

"I'm here, doc, I just . . . I know if it's Vlad's syndrome that I have to abort. The baby won't live anyway, and will try to take me with it. But like I said, I'm not as clear on the other syndrome. It's a lot more rare."

"Very rare, in fact less than ten cases reported in this country. If the worst happens and it's Vlad's syndrome, then we have time to fix it. If it's Mowgli syndrome, depends on the animal." I heard computer keys clacking. "Do you know what type of shapeshifter he was?"

"It was only once, and yeah—" I stopped defending myself, and just said, ". . . leopard, okay, leopard." Sweet Jesus, I couldn't believe I was having this conversation.

I heard the computer keys again. "Leopard is between ninety and a hundred and six days, an average of around ninety-six days."

"So?" I said.

"A human's gestation is two hundred and eighty days."

"Still, so what?"

"So this: I'll assume you don't have severe Mowgli syndrome, or you'd know it by now. You'd be almost ready to deliver."

"You're joking," I said.

"No," he said, "but you don't have that, obviously. You could still have a less severe version of Mowgli syndrome. If you do, then the pregnancy could kick into high gear, and you could go from being barely pregnant to being ready to deliver, in a matter of days."

"You're joking."

"I'm looking at the medical literature as we speak. The Internet is a wonderful tool sometimes. Two cases in this country of women who had milder forms of Mowgli syndrome. Even with the test, Anita, all we can tell you is yes or no. Think of it like Down syndrome; we can test and know if you have it, but even an amnio wouldn't tell you the severity of it."

"Vlad's syndrome is an automatic abortion—what about Mowgli syndrome?" I asked.

He hesitated, then said, slowly, "Not automatic, no, but the birth defects can be pretty, um, severe."

"It's never good when your doctor sounds nervous, Dr. North. What am I missing that's put that tone in your voice?"

"If you have even a mild form of Mowgli syndrome, then by Monday the fetus could come up on an ultrasound as over the age limit for abortion in this state. You really do not want to be out of options on this particular birth defect, Anita."

O-kay, I thought. "Two o'clock, right?"

"Meet me at St. John's, just come straight up to the maternity ward."

My heart pounded up into my throat. "Maternity ward? Aren't you getting a little ahead of yourself there, doc?"

"At my office, we'll have to send out the blood for testing. At the hospital, we'll get all the results back much faster. Depending on the test results, if we want a closer look, the hospital is set up with the ultrasound equipment we'll want for this."

"You've got ultrasound at your office," I said.

"We do, but they've got more sensitive equipment at the hospital. We'll get more information much quicker, and speed really is of the essence here, Anita."

"Okay, I'll be there at two."

"Great."

"Your bedside manner sucks today, by the way."

He laughed. "I know you, Anita. If I didn't scare you, you'd find excuses to delay coming in."

"Did you exaggerate to scare me?" I asked.

"No, sorry, but no. I just told you more bluntly than I would normally have told a patient. But then most of my patients don't need rough treatment just to get them into the office."

"You're not wanting me in the office, doc, you're wanting to see me at the hospital. I only go to hospitals when I've gotten hurt in the line of duty."

"Are you backing out on me?" he asked.

I sighed. "No, no, I'll be there." I thought of something, and figured I should ask. "I can bring company with me to the maternity ward, right? I mean it's not like when I was a kid, and all restricted, is it?"

"You can bring a friend to hold your hand, if you want, but since we may have to do a pelvic exam, it should be a close friend."

Pelvic exam, shit. "At least one of them will be close enough to stay in the room. The rest can wait outside."

"The rest?" He made it a question.

"At least one boyfriend, maybe more, and bodyguards."

"Bodyguards? Are you in danger?"

"Almost always, but this isn't . . . it's not like bad guys trying to hurt me, or anything. Let's just say that I think this will be a pretty stressful visit for me, and for the foreseeable future I shouldn't be going anywhere stressful without muscle."

"Is that supposed to be a riddle?" he asked.

"Not on purpose," I said.

"You're usually pretty straightforward, Anita."

"Sorry, but this isn't something I can really explain on the phone."

"Okay, does it affect your health, and this situation?"

I thought about it, then said, "Maybe, yes. I guess it does." I realized if I shapeshifted for real that I'd lose the baby, and this entire medical emergency would be over before we'd even decided what to do about it. But I just couldn't think of a quick way to explain what had been happening to me. "Can I bring the extra people?"

"If I say no?"

"Then we have a problem."

"How many extra?"

"Hopefully no more than four." I did quick math in my head. Two bodyguards, and at least one of each beast I held inside me. "Five."

"Five," he said.

"At least two of them will be boyfriends."

"Potential fathers?"

"Yeah."

"If they're not disruptive, then I guess so."

"If anybody gets disruptive, it's gonna be me," I said, and I hung up on him. It was rude, but my nerves just couldn't take any more talk about it. I was scared, so scared that my skin felt cold with it. Cold? I touched my forehead and tried to decide if I really was cold. If I was, then I was endangering Damian, my poor vampire servant, who was the first of my metaphysical men I started draining energy from, if I went too long between feedings. Was I draining him to death, so he'd never wake from his coffin? I'd tamed the *ardeur* so that it wasn't as demanding; I could push it off for a few hours, but the price was high. And sometimes the price had almost been Damian's life. Theoretically, after Damian was dead then I'd start draining Nathaniel. I never wanted to find out if the theory was right.

I checked my watch: ten a.m. God, it had been a long, damn, morning. It was incredibly early for so many of Jean-Claude's vamps to be awake. So far only master vamps had woken up, and that didn't include Damian, but still . . . Was I already draining him, just because I hadn't fed the *ardeur* or eaten any breakfast? Real food helped keep the other hungers back, from the *ardeur* to the beasts. I hadn't even had a cup of coffee yet. It wasn't the time of day, but how long I'd been awake without eating that made it a mistake. Maybe we'd eaten a big enough meal from Auggie last night, but I couldn't chance that. I needed food. The only question was, which hunger to feed first? Sex, or coffee? Hmm, let me think.

29

IT TURNED OUT to be coffee first. Requiem wasn't in the bedroom, and Micah came through the door with a tray of breakfast. He didn't say that I'd waited too long to eat, and maybe endangered Damian, or risked raising my beasts again and hurting myself, or losing the baby, or that by neglecting myself I could make the *ardeur* more uncontrollable. No, he didn't say any of that. He just brought in the food and put it on the bedside table. Two cups of coffee, croissants, cheese, and fruit. All food in the Circus was catered because there was no kitchen. The old Master of the City hadn't kept many humans with her, and hadn't given a damn for anyone's comfort but her own. Jean-Claude had remodeled the bathrooms first. Priorities. Frankly, you could get good take-out food, but a decent bathroom, that they don't deliver. Still, as I looked down at the tray of food, I thought, *We need a kitchen.*

I took one of the chunks of cheddar first. We'd found that protein worked best at keeping my energy up. Some of us just aren't meant to be vegetarians.

"Are you all right, Anita? You look very . . ." Micah seemed to give up on finding a word.

I smiled at him. "Thanks for the food, and I've got a two o'clock appointment with my gynecologist."

"Today?" he asked, "Is that wise?"

I nodded, picking up the first cup of coffee. I'd been good and eaten a piece of cheese first, but that wasn't what I'd really wanted. I took that first sip of hot, strong coffee. Later in the day I'd drown it in sugar and cream, maybe, but first thing, I wanted it black, naked, the way I used to drink all my coffee. I closed my eyes as I sipped, letting the warmth flow through me. Was I addicted to coffee? Probably, but as addictions go, it could have been worse.

I opened my eyes and looked at him. "Good coffee."

He smiled. "I'm glad you're enjoying it, but by two we'll have most of the vampires awake and moving around down here. We'll have daywalking visitors, too."

I nodded, and took a smaller sip this time. "I know." I told Micah what the doctor had told me.

He blinked at me, that long slow blink that I used sometimes when I was trying to process too much information too quickly. "You have to go."

"I know," I said. I sat down on the edge of the bed, and made myself take a bite of croissant. The croissant was good, soft and buttery, but I wasn't hungry. I wanted the coffee, but the rest of it I was eating because I had to. Eating to keep everybody alive and well. I'd never been a big breakfast eater, but today I think I was just too nervous. Fine, too scared.

"I'll go with you, as boyfriend and leopard."

I nodded. "Nathaniel probably won't be back in human form by then, I know."

"You know that Richard had arranged today off from his job."

I nodded. "He arranged a substitute."

"He's going to want to go, you know he will."

I nodded. "Probably."

"He can be your wolf," Micah said.

Someone cleared his throat. Remus was closer to the bed than I remembered. "I couldn't help overhearing."

"I'll have to have at least two guards with me, so you needed to know anyway."

He nodded. "Good, but Anita, from what Claudia told me, Richard wouldn't let you bring his beast. What good is his wolf, if he won't let you bring it?"

I nodded. "Point, but he'll still want to go."

"How about if I make sure one of the guards is a wolf?" Remus said.

"Do it quietly."

"I'll make sure Richard doesn't know," Remus said. "Though maybe he'll come through."

I shook my head. "If he wouldn't change here in the underground, then he is so not going to want to change in the middle of St. John's maternity ward."

"Can't say that any of us would want to; it's a good way to get the cops called on you," Remus said.

I nodded. "I know, and I will do my damn level best to hold my shit together, but I'm scared, and it's going to be stressful."

"You need a lion. The new guy isn't going to be in human form in time for the appointment," Remus said.

"Didn't someone mention that Joseph is bringing some of his lions by today so I can pick someone?"

Micah nodded.

"We need to call him, and see how early he can be here," I said. I'd made myself finish the croissant, and one cup of coffee was gone. I took the lid off the second cup, and leaned back against the headboard. I had some food in me now, so I could allow myself to sip this cup without ruining it with food.

"I'll check." He pulled a tiny folding cell phone from somewhere on his person, and stepped away from the bed to give us some privacy. It was illusionary privacy, because he would hear anything we said, but I appreciated the effort.

Micah was wearing a man's white dress shirt unbuttoned around the tan of his upper body. The sleeves were buttoned tight, but he wore it more like a jacket than a shirt. The jeans had started life black, but were now sort of gray. When he curled up on the bed beside me, his feet were bare. "You're dressed in clothes you wouldn't mind shifting in," I said.

He nodded. He'd pulled his hair back in a ponytail, but missed a few curls, so they framed his face here and there. He looked very winsome, except for his eyes, which were way too serious for comfort.

"You think I'm going to have another"—I waffled my hand back and forth—"attack."

He smiled, but it didn't quite reach his eyes. "Let's just say, I'm prepared."

I drank my coffee a little faster, because it was cooling. "Have I eaten enough?"

"No," he said softly.

I hung my head. "My stomach feels like a hard knot today."

"Either one more croissant, or a whole piece of fruit, or all the cheese."

I finished the coffee, and reached for the bread. When you didn't want to eat, bread was less objectionable. I started nibbling at it.

"Jean-Claude needs to know about the appointment."

"I know."

"I could tell him."

I frowned at him. "You don't trust me to do it."

He sat up, raising his hands. "I will do whatever will make this easier for you, Anita, but he needs to know as soon as possible that you are going to take his human servant, his animal to call, and at least two or three blood donors with you this afternoon."

I tossed the half-eaten croissant back on the tray. "If there is another way to do this, tell me, and I'll do it."

"I didn't say that. All I said was that Jean-Claude needs to know."

"Then go tell him," I said, and the first flare of anger came.

He didn't give me hurt eyes, he gave me careful eyes. He tried to hold my hands, and I jerked away. "If you hold me, I'm going to fall apart."

He pulled back. "No one would blame you if you fell apart."

"I would."

He sighed. "You always have to be so strong."

I nodded. "Yeah, I do."

He slipped off the bed to stand beside it, gazing at me. I didn't want him standing there looking scrumptious. I wanted to be angry, and I always had trouble being angry when he looked cute. Hell, I had trouble keeping any fight going with any of the men in my life; all they had to do was strip, and they usually won. It was true, and that pissed me off, too.

"Anger is a luxury, Anita."

I screamed, full-throated, deep and loud. I screamed until it echoed off the walls. I screamed until the door opened and more guards poured in. I yelled at them, "Get out, get the fuck out!"

They turned in a black-shirted mass to Remus. He motioned them out, but he kept two of them, so I was back to four guards. I guess I couldn't blame him.

"Tell Jean-Claude, and send Requiem to me." My voice sounded deeper, thicker.

"Anita . . ."

"If you comfort me, I'm going to lose it." I looked up at him. "Please, Micah, please, just do what I ask."

"I'll talk to Jean-Claude, but are you sure about Requiem?"

"You mean am I sure I want to feed the *ardeur* on him?"

He nodded.

"No, I'm absolutely sure I don't want to feed on him, but Jean-Claude and I talked. If I feed on Requiem and he's mind-fucked again, then I'm too dangerous for the other *pomme de sang* candidates. I need to feed on Requiem before Auggie rises for the day. Because, if I truly freed Requiem's mind from the *ardeur*, then we may be able to use the same technique to free Auggie of us."

"A lot of *if*s and *maybe*s," he said.

"And maybe I can heal Requiem while I feed. I seem to heal during metaphysical sex, with or without intercourse, sometimes. Meng Die's little temper tantrum is not going to impress the visiting masters, and we can't hide it if he's as hurt as he is now."

"You could feed off someone else, someone who's already one of your sweeties."

"You mean, I don't need another shock for the day," I said, and I started to laugh, but it ended in a sob that I bit my lip to keep inside. Panic was eating at me, eating holes in all my bones and organs, so that I was getting more and more fragile, and when I needed it most, there'd be nothing there to use; there'd be nothing but the fear.

I whispered, because I didn't trust my voice any louder. I was either going to start screaming again, or crying. I didn't want to do either. "Jean-Claude thinks Requiem's power can overcome my reluctance. I have to feed the *ardeur*, and I so don't want to. If Requiem's power can make me want him, then send him, because right now, I don't want anyone. I just want to be left the fuck alone."

Anyone else would have looked hurt, but Micah didn't. He took it, with that quiet face. He said, quietly, "We all have a breaking point, Anita, all of us."

I shook my head, over and over. "We can't afford for me to break today, Micah."

He sighed. "Someday, I'd like for us to have a little time for you to be able to break down, if you wanted to." I realized his eyes were glittering with unshed tears.

"Don't cry," I said.

"Why not, one of us needs to." He turned away, with the first tear shining down his cheek.

I grabbed for his arm, and crawled over the bed, and pulled him in against me. And just like I'd known I would, I lost it. I cried, and screamed, and clung to him, and hated myself for doing it. So weak, so fucking weak.

30

SOMEWHERE IN THE middle of breaking down, I realized there were other hands holding me besides Micah's. I pushed at the hands, half-fought, and half-clung, as if I couldn't decide whether I wanted not to be touched, or never to be let go. I heard a voice, a hysterical voice, saying, "Don't want to do this . . . can't do this. I can't do this." I realized it was me, and even realizing it, I couldn't stop the babbling. "Can't do a baby, tests, don't want to do the *ardeur* anymore, no more, no more men, no more adding to my life." The talking fell into sobbing, and finally even that stopped. In the end, I just lay in the curve of their arms, and was quiet. Too tired to move, too tired to protest. Because somehow in the midst of it all, Richard had ended up holding me. His body cradling me. I didn't feel anything about him holding me. Nothing, I felt nothing, and I was glad. I'd been feeling too much lately, too much.

"Her energy feels different," he said, and his voice sounded farther away than it should have. He was tall, but I was only in his lap, not that far away.

Other hands touched my face, my hands, my arms. My eyes were closed and I kept them that way; I didn't want to see them. Didn't want to see any of them. "She is cold." Jean-Claude's voice, his hand moving away from my cheek.

Cold, yes, I was cold, so cold. Cold down to the core of my being, as if I'd never be warm again. Fur brushed my arm, and it made me open my eyes enough to see Nathaniel kneeling on the bed. His face was still a stranger's face behind the mix of animal and human. Once, just once, that face had been above me while we made love. Just the one time.

Hands touched my face, moved me to look at Jean-Claude and Richard. Their hands, one on either side of my face. Their hands were so warm against my skin. It took me a long second to realize that both of their hands felt warm. Had Jean-Claude gained so much power from feeding on Augustine, so much that he was hot to the touch?

I was having trouble focusing on their faces. I whispered, "Warm, you're both warm."

Richard spoke slowly, carefully, as if he thought I might have trouble understanding him, "Anita, you're colder to the touch than Jean-Claude."

I frowned at him, and tried to focus on his face. I could almost do it, but it was as if my attention kept wandering before I could make my eyes do what I wanted. "Wrong, something's wrong." Still a whisper, but I said it out loud.

"Yes," he said, "something is wrong." He looked at Jean-Claude. "I can't feel her. She's in my arms and I can't feel her energy."

"She is drawing away from us," Jean-Claude said.

"Drawing away, what does that mean?" Richard asked.

"I believe *ma petite* is trying to break the bonds that bind her to us."

"You mean break the triumvirate?"

"*Oui.*"

"Can she do that?" someone asked.

"Anita can do anything she wants to do," Nathaniel's growling voice said.

"I do not know if it is possible, but I know she is trying," Jean-Claude said.

"It will destroy your power base." Asher's voice, though I couldn't make my eyes search the room for him.

"So be it," Jean-Claude said. I fought to see him clearly, watch him look to Richard. "Why the tragic face, Richard? You could be free of the triumvirate, Richard, free of me."

"You know it's what I want, but what would it cost us? She's cold to the touch."

Jean-Claude's face loomed into view. "*Ma petite*, drop your shields. Drop them just enough for me to sense you. Let me share energy with you. You are unwell."

I shook my head, and the world swam in streamers of color. I had a moment of nausea, and that was the moment that I realized I was sick. Sick at heart, sick of soul, sick of it all. Somewhere deep inside me, I was trying to undo all my decisions. I was trying to do a take-back, on a game that had played too far for a do-over. The front part of my brain knew it was too late, but it wasn't the front part of my brain that was in charge. How do you argue with the subconscious? How do you argue with a part of your brain you don't even know is there most of the time? The real bitch of the situation was, I wasn't sure I wanted to argue.

I smelled the musk of leopard, and knew Nathaniel was beside me before his voice growled, "Damian."

I opened my eyes, and found myself staring into a black blur of a face. Nathaniel moved back far enough for me to have a chance to focus on him. I repeated what he'd said. "Damian."

"Damian will die," Nathaniel said.

I blinked at him. I'd heard what he said, but it didn't seem to make sense to me. It must have shown on my face because Jean-Claude said, "I do not know if what your despair attempts is truly possible, but if you succeed, Damian will die. His blood flows only with your power, Anita. Without your power, your vampire servant will rise no more from his grave. He will die, and remain dead."

I stared at him, and again, it was as if his words didn't truly reach me.

He gripped my arm, tight, and tighter, until it hurt, but even that was a distant hurt. "Anita, I will not be blamed for this. If you accomplish this miracle, and break free of all of us, then you will kill Damian. I will not have you later say you did not understand. I will not take the blame, not for this." He was angry, but his anger could not touch me, and I was glad. His anger was no longer mine. I could cut him out, cut them all out of me.

Micah's voice, from the other side of me: "Breaking the triumvirate won't change the fact that you're pregnant, Anita. You'll still need to go to the hospital at two o'clock. That doesn't change."

I turned and looked at him, though it seemed to take a long time for me to do it. "The *ardeur* will go away."

"Are you sure of that?" he asked, quietly.

Jean-Claude's voice: "In truth, I do not know if the gifts and curses you gain through the vampire marks will vanish if the triumvirate breaks. It may leave you as I found you, alone and safe in your own skin, if that is what you truly desire. Or you may retain some abilities, but lose the aid of . . ." He hesitated, finally finishing with, "all of us, in your struggle with the *ardeur*."

I turned until I found his face, still out of focus, like I wasn't working quite right. "The *ardeur* will go away," I whispered.

"I simply do not know what will happen, because what I feel you doing is impossible. Only true death should be able to break you free of my marks. Since what you attempt has never been done, I do not know what the outcome will be." His voice was utterly bland, empty, as if his words meant nothing.

I tried to think about what he'd said. Even my thoughts seemed sluggish. What was wrong with me? I was hysterical, that was what was wrong with me. The moment I thought it that clearly, I started to calm. I didn't feel any better, really, but I could think. That was an improvement. I thought about being free of the *ardeur*, and that was a good thought. I thought about being free of Jean-Claude's marks, and all the metaphysical mess that came with it.

My life being my own again, that sounded good. I thought about being just me, as Jean-Claude said, just me in my own skin. Just me, alone, again. Alone again. I had a moment of absolutely joyous nostalgia for my life before I'd acquired so many people. To come home to an empty house didn't seem awful, it seemed relaxing.

Micah touched my face, turned me to look at him. I could see him clearly, finally. His kitty-cat eyes were so serious. "Nothing that is happening is worth dying over, Anita, please."

I thought he meant Damian, then realized he didn't. I wasn't cold just because I was trying to break the triumvirate. There was only one way to be free. One of us had to die. Could I break free? Maybe. Would I die trying? Maybe. The thought should have scared me, but it didn't. And that scared me. I know it sounds stupid, but it didn't scare me to think I might die, but it did scare me not to be scared. Stupid, but true.

I had to do better than this, Jesus, Mary, and Joseph, I had to do better than this.

Richard hugged me from behind, bending all that six-feet-plus of warmth and muscle around me. "Please, Anita, don't do this." His breath was so warm, almost hot, against my hair.

I looked up at him, from inches away. His eyes were perfectly brown, warm, and full of so much emotion. "You'd be free."

He shook his head, his eyes shiny. "I don't want to be free that badly."

"Don't you?" I asked.

"No, this price is too high. Don't leave me, not like this." He held me close, his hair long enough now that it tickled along my face. I buried my face in the warm, sweet scent of his neck, but I knew it was a lie.

I cuddled against him, as tight and close as I could. I buried myself against the warmth and strength of him, and it still felt wonderful. It still felt so right, but I knew it wasn't. We were both too stubborn for it to work.

I was crying again, and wasn't sure why. Crying my regrets out against the warmth of Richard's neck. The coulda-beens, shoulda-beens, woulda-beens. I wrapped myself around him, legs, arms, all of it, and clung to him, clung to him and cried.

A hand stroked the back of my hair, and a voice said, "*Ma petite, ma petite,* drop these shields, let us inside again."

I turned my head to look at him while I clung to Richard. I stared up into that face, those midnight-blue eyes. His hand stroked along the edge of my face, and it wasn't enough. Whatever I'd done to myself, I'd walled myself up tight. Since I hadn't tried to cut myself off on purpose, I didn't know how to undo what I'd done. How do you undo an accident?

I tried to explain. "I'm head-blind. I can't feel anything metaphysically. I didn't mean to cut us up." I knew now I'd survive what I'd tried to do, but would everyone else? I reached out to Damian. Even dead in his coffin for the day, I should have been able to sense him. Nothing. Fear washed over me, and all the warmth I'd started to regain flowed away on that tide of fear.

I grabbed the edge of Jean-Claude's robe. "I can't feel Damian! I can't feel him, at all!"

"We must breach your shields, *ma petite*. We must reawaken your powers."

I nodded. "Yes."

"I am your master, Anita, my very marks can keep me out of your shields. We are running out of time for Damian. I would ask that you allow Asher and Requiem to help me breach your shields."

"I don't understand."

"I do not have time to explain, but it does not truly matter which of us breaks down these new stronger walls, only that they break. Once broken, then your own power will be set free, and it will find Damian."

I wanted to argue, but that emptiness where Damian should have been scared me. I nodded. "Do it."

"You must take off your cross first."

I didn't ask how he knew I was wearing one. Richard let me slide down his body enough so I could use my hands to unhook the chain. Jean-Claude had stepped away, not far, but far enough that he would not accidentally touch it. I spilled the chain into Richard's waiting hand.

I met his eyes, while his hand closed around my cross. "Put it in the bed-side drawer," I said.

He nodded. "So it won't glow."

I nodded. I admitted to myself in that one moment why I'd stopped wear-ing a cross most of the time. Oh, I kept one in my vampire-hunting bag, but I didn't wear it much. To bed, but, oh, hell. I kept waiting for the cross to glow when I did something. I kept waiting for the cross to glow because of some vampiric ability that I'd inherited from Jean-Claude. I kept waiting for it to glow against me. What was left of my nerves couldn't have handled it, today.

Richard moved across the bed enough to lean over and open the bedside table drawer. He set the cross in carefully, and closed the drawer. He crawled back across the bed, until he was kneeling in front of me again. "I spend so much effort keeping you out of my mind, my heart, and now it's like this void inside me. I keep trying to break up with you, stupid me. It's like trying to break up with your own hand. You can live without it, but you're not whole."

"Can you sense Damian?" Jean-Claude asked.

"I can sense vampires with a cross on, Jean-Claude; that's never made any difference to my necromancy."

"Humor me," he said.

I humored him. I shook my head. "Empty, like he's not there." I'd managed to chase the fear back, but it fluttered through my stomach, tingled the tips of my fingers. "Is it too late? Please, God, don't let it be too late." Inside my head, I added, *Don't let me have killed him.*

I watched Jean-Claude's eyes spill blue, until his pupils and the white were lost to the glowing, deep blue of his power. I sat on the bed only a few yards from him, while his power rose enough to fill his eyes with fire, and I felt nothing. At least my necromancy should have felt it, if not the vampire marks. I'd been psychically blind, head-blind, from shock or illness before, but never to this degree. It both scared me, and gave me hope. Maybe I couldn't sense Damian because I couldn't have sensed anyone right then.

Richard shivered beside me, then slid to the floor. "You don't feel that, do you?" His eyes were a little wide. The small hairs on his arms were standing at attention.

"No," I said.

He looked at Micah and Nathaniel, who were still on the bed, though they'd moved back to give us room. "I think we all need to clear a space for them to work."

Micah kissed my cheek. Nathaniel brushed his cheek against mine, scent-marking me. They slid off the far side of the bed. Jean-Claude moved up until he was beside the bed. He raised a hand above my face. I felt it, the press of his aura, but faintly, as if my skin were wrapped in cotton, and he could not touch me.

He laid his hand against my face, and that one touch spread in a shivering line across my skin. "*Ma petite.*" The words breathed along my spine, as if he'd spilled a line of water down my skin. I shivered for him again, and it felt great, but . . . I opened my eyes and looked up at him. "It's like years ago. I always felt your voice, your touch, but . . ."

"You have shut yourself away, *ma petite*, in a tower formed partially of my own vampire marks. You have used my own power against me."

"Not on purpose," I said.

Asher glided into view. His eyes were already full of pale blue light. He'd called power, and I'd felt nothing. He came to stand beside Jean-Claude. "More drastic measures, I think."

I looked up at him, in his satin robe, the deep burnished gold of it that was nothing to the shine of his own hair. "What did you have in mind?" I asked.

Jean-Claude stepped back, giving his place to the other man. Asher raised his hand, laying it against my face in an echo of what Jean-Claude had done moments before. They had always been able to echo each other like that, I thought, and on the tail of that thought, memory crashed over me. I'd shared Jean-Claude's memories before, but not like this. It wasn't one memory, or two, but hundreds. Hundreds of images flooding my mind, drowning me in the scent of Asher's skin, the spill of Belle's hair around our bodies like a second body to caress us all. A woman with hair the color of copper spilled across our pillows, and our mouths locked on her neck, her hands struggling at the scarves that bound her to the bed. A blond, whose breasts we marked together, so that she bore twin love bites. A man in a long, powdered wig, his pants down around his knees, and both of us between his thighs, not for sex, but for blood, and it was what he wanted. Women with their clothing in disarray, red hair in every shade from nearly blond to darkest auburn; blondes from white to gold; brunettes from deep brown to true black; skin like ripe grain, or dark coffee, or wood. Tall, short, thin, fat, starved; bodies flowing under our hands, against our bodies, so that it was as if I experienced a thousand nights of debauchery in heartbeats. But in every memory they moved like shadows of each other. Jean-Claude took the woman, or the man, for sex, or blood, or both, and knew that his golden shadow would be there. That Asher would match his movements, that he would be there to help, to catch the pleasure and make it more. I hadn't realized until that moment that they weren't lovers, but more than that. They had been truly the best and closest person in each other's lives.

I drowned in their memories, drowned in the scent of a thousand lovers, a thousand victims, a thousand pleasures won and lost. I drowned, and like any drowning man, I reached out to save myself.

I reached out metaphysically for someone, anyone. The memories hit Richard like a flood hitting a boulder. I felt the memories crash against him, sweep up and around him. I heard him cry out, and waited for him to push me away, to lock me out, but he didn't. He let me cling to him, let me try to make him my rock in the flood of sensations and memories. I felt his confusion, his fear, his revulsion, and his desire to push it all away, to not have these memories, of all memories. The thought came: there are worse memories.

Jean-Claude's voice. "*Non, ma petite, mon ami,* enough, enough." His voice was soft, coaxing. I was lying on the bed, with him holding my hand. He was rubbing my hand the way people do when they're trying to warm you.

"I'm here," I said, but my voice sounded echoing, tinny.

The bed moved violently. Richard had collapsed on it. His breathing was ragged, his eyes showing too much white. He grabbed my other hand. He felt frightened, shocky, and I realized that he'd taken over some of my reaction. He'd sucked it away like metaphysical poison.

I licked dry lips and said, "I'm sorry."

"You asked for help," he said, in a strained voice. "I gave it."

He usually cut himself out of the memories I got from Jean-Claude; of all the times to not shy away, he picked these memories.

"I would have preferred other memories to share, *ma petite*, but when you breached your unnatural shields, I did not dare restrict your access to me. I did not dare shut the marks down again." He stroked my hair like I was still sick, but he cast a worried look at Richard.

"I won't run," Richard said, "I knew what you were, what you both were." He glanced at Asher, who still stood near the bed.

Asher put his hand on Jean-Claude's shoulder, and it was too soon after the memories to see them touching. Except this time they weren't Jean-Claude's memories, I just had to wade through the fact that some of that flood of memories had stayed with me.

Richard flinched as if he'd been slapped, and I knew that I wasn't the only one who had kept some of it.

Micah yelled, "Nathaniel!"

I looked around the room for Nathaniel, and couldn't see him. Micah was on the floor. I fought to sit up, and Richard helped me. Jean-Claude was already around the bed, and kneeling with Micah, beside Nathaniel. He was human again, all that lovely hair spread around his body. He wasn't moving.

I screamed his name, and reached out to him not with hands but with power. I felt him breathe, but his heart hesitated, as if it was forgetting how to beat.

I screamed, "Nathaniel!"

Jean-Claude just suddenly appeared beside the bed. "Nathaniel is trying to keep Damian alive, but he does not know how. You must feed them energy, now, *ma petite*, right now."

"Or what?" I asked, and I leaned into the death grip I had on Richard's arm.

"Or they will die," Jean-Claude said.

31

I STARED AT him, because I believed him, but feeding the *ardeur* meant sex, and in that moment I'd never felt less like sex in my life.

Richard said, "Feed, Anita, you have to feed."

I looked at him. "You going to help?"

He shook his head. "Not me, my concentration isn't this good."

Jean-Claude's voice cut across the panic. "Requiem, your moment has come." He looked at me. "If you fight him, they will die. Drop your shields, and let his power take you. Let him awake the *ardeur*, and feed."

I was suddenly staring at a chest decorated with stab wounds. I looked up into Requiem's eyes, clear blue, an almost painful brightness. He'd raised his power, and I felt nothing. He'd crawled across the bed and I hadn't noticed. Shock had set in again, but for different reasons. Minutes ago I'd wanted to be alone, just me again, but I hadn't meant it. I prayed, *I didn't mean it*, as if somehow my thought was responsible for this new disaster.

Richard's body still cradled me. Requiem had to wrap his hands around my upper arms and pull me out of Richard's arms. Richard's fingers slid over my skin, and I felt the loss of his touch like a blow. I felt like some small animal torn out of its nest and thrown into the heart of the storm. That storm was made of flesh and bone, and eyes that glowed as if you could set the ocean afire.

Jean-Claude's voice whispered through me. "Let go, *ma petite*, let go, or all is lost."

I did what he asked. I let go. Let go, and fell into eyes the color of sea water where it runs deep and clear and cold, and the blue dark glows with the cold light of phosphorescence, shining off the backs of creatures that never saw the light of day.

I floated in that cold emptiness, with the dim light, and a voice whispered through me, but it wasn't Jean-Claude's. It was Nathaniel's voice in my head. He didn't ask for help, or chastise me. He whispered, "Love you." Those words echoed through the emptiness, and I followed them, up through the cold dark. Cold wasn't what we needed, it wouldn't keep him alive. We needed heat.

I hit the surface of Requiem's gaze, fell out of the power I'd let him try. I fell out of his eyes, and was left panting, struggling to breathe. I would not let Nathaniel go, even if it meant going with him. I reached out to him, felt his heart slowing. My chest ached with the need to draw a good breath.

I stared up into Requiem's glowing eyes, and whispered, "Help us."

He turned to Jean-Claude. "I cannot break her. I cannot get through!"

The last time he'd used his powers on me it had taken a while. We didn't have a while. He couldn't roll me, but I had rolled him before. Could I bring his powers on line? I prayed, prayed for help. I whispered, "Requiem." His voice echoed through the room, and he turned glowing eyes to me.

I didn't have enough air to say what I wanted out loud. I fell back toward the bed, and only his arms caught me. I knew what I wanted, what I needed. I willed it, I commanded it, and I shoved that command into him. I was losing my words, and it was a wordless longing that I filled him with. That longing flared like heat across my skin, threw me off the bed, gasping. My body was suddenly swollen with need, wetness dripping between my legs. My breasts ached with the need to be touched. The *ardeur* rose to that ache, and I welcomed it, embraced it. I threw the door of my self-control open wide, and didn't care where it landed.

It was Jean-Claude's mouth that found mine first. I knew the taste of him with my eyes closed tight. He gave himself up to the *ardeur*, and I fed through his kiss, fed in a rush that flowed through my body, in a tingling rush of energy. I'd fed the *ardeur* a hundred times, and it had never been like this.

He drew back from the kiss, eyes filled with midnight fire. "How do you feel?"

I tried to think past the pulse of my own body. I'd fed the *ardeur*, but the swollen longing in my body wasn't gone. I felt for Nathaniel's energy, and found him still there, still alive. Distant as a dream, Damian's spark like a match flame in a wind.

"More," I whispered, "I need more."

He nodded. "I gave you enough to bring you back to us." He moved back from me, and I tried to hold him against me. "*Non, ma petite*, you need food." I kept my arms locked around his neck, and he reached out, and brought Requiem into view. "When you helped him raise need in yourself, you raised it in him, as well. Would you deny him?"

I frowned at him. I couldn't think. I whispered, "No," but wasn't entirely sure what I was saying no to: no, I wouldn't deny him, or no, to other things?

Requiem's hand slid over my bare arm. That one touch threw my head back, fluttered my eyes shut. I knew where my need had come from, I could taste it on my tongue, taste his need.

Jean-Claude slid away, and Requiem was above me. So lonely, so heart-wrenchingly lonely. Lonely for so long. You feed the *ardeur* on sex, but its gifts are more than that. Sometimes you can see into people, see what they most desire, most need, and you can offer it to them. You can offer them their heart's desire, and sometimes you can even give them exactly what you promise.

I had an instant of seeing so far into Requiem that I started to cry. Weeping not my tears, but his. He wanted the *ardeur* again, yes, but more than that, he wanted a place of refuge. A place where he could stop being afraid; he'd been afraid for so very long. Afraid that Belle would drag him back, and make him suffer for all eternity for falling in love with someone else. I felt his fear, his loneliness, his loss, like blows to my heart, and in the end, I did the only thing that would keep him well and truly safe. I made him mine.

32

MOST OF THE clothes vanished in a blur of hands and bodies, but it was when he wrapped his hands around my belt, and tore it in two, jerking my body up off the bed, that I remembered. I had just enough presence of mind to make sure he didn't destroy the shoulder rig, but it fell to the floor with the pieces of the jeans and T-shirt. Requiem, with his poetry, his gentlemanly restraint, vanished under the crash of the *ardeur,* and the power of his own magic.

I fed on the touch of his hands, the brush of his lips, the sensation of his naked skin brushing along mine, the weight of him above me. Requiem and I had never been nude together, and that first time was shared with Nathaniel and Damian. They knew what I was doing, they could feel it, because I'd opened that mark between us, so that each touch, each kiss, each movement, fed energy to them. Nathaniel's heart began to beat sure and strong, but Damian's spark still flickered, hesitating between life and death. Nathaniel could make his own heart beat, but Damian couldn't. Damian needed more than these small touches of *ardeur.* I'd gotten to where I could feed the *ardeur* in small ways from less touching, but I needed orgasm for a full feeding. Okay, for a really, truly, full feeding you needed orgasms from everybody involved, but one was enough to get you through. We needed to get through.

Requiem rested above me, pressing every inch of his nakedness against the front of me, but he laid his body on top of mine, not inside it. He pressed me down into the bed, kissing me as if he would eat me from the mouth down, and only luck kept us from cutting our lips on his fangs. The feel of him, swollen and hard, made me spread my legs and try to wrap my legs around him, but he moved away. Moved above me, holding most of his weight away with his arms and legs, as if he were afraid to touch too much of me. It had all seemed to be going so well, and then he'd climbed back into himself, regained control somehow. Requiem in control went back to being a gentleman. In a situation where I would not have blamed him about taking full advantage, he still seemed painfully aware that he wasn't my first choice, or even my seventh. He tried to feed the *ardeur* without crossing that last barrier, because he knew, or thought he knew, I didn't want him.

"Requiem, please, please, finish it."

"Finish it," he said, voice showing the strain of his control. "Your words betray you, Anita. You use me only because you must, not because you want me."

Anger flared through me. "My body wants you, Requiem."

"But your heart does not."

I screamed, half from anger, half from the need in my body that he'd raised, and wasn't going to satisfy. The thought came that I could make the *ardeur* stronger, that I could overwhelm him with it. An old thought from Belle's memories, I think. But in his way, Requiem had made it clear he did not want to be food, or my fuck buddy. When push had come to shove, he wanted to be more than that. I understood that, but I couldn't give it to him. This was one thing I could not do. I could not love him.

"I need food, Requiem. If you aren't food, then get off."

I watched emotions struggle across his face. I think he was fighting his own body's need, but finally that so-refined sense of self won, and he slipped to the side, burying his face in his arms. He did not leave the bed, but he wasn't touching me.

The *ardeur* was still there, but faded under the anger and frustration of the riddle that was Requiem. I reached outward for Damian, and he was still fragile. The energy I felt in him now would never wake; it wasn't enough to bring him back to life for the night. If he tried to wake now, and failed, would he die? Would that fragile spark rise, and fall, never more to burn with life?

I yelled, "Jean-Claude!"

He came to stand by the bed on the other side of Requiem's softly weeping form. I reached out to him, but he stepped back, just out of reach. "I make all the other vampires of this city wake at dusk. We cannot risk trading one life for many."

I screamed, wordless, my hand reaching skyward, reaching for anyone. In that moment I used the *ardeur* to call food, not deliberately, because I'd never purposefully used it to call a victim to me. Jean-Claude had said that the *ardeur* was calling food of its choice; now I knew he had been right, because I could feel it. I felt the *ardeur* spread not randomly like some sort of shrapnel bomb, but like a high-tech heat-seeking missle. I felt the *ardeur* brush Asher; I knew the taste of him, but his energy signature was weak. He still hadn't fed. The *ardeur* brushed against a dozen lesser fires, but finally it found one it liked.

I knew only three things about the energy it called; it was vampire, it was no one I'd ever touched, and it was powerful.

A hand grabbed mine, and that one touch stabbed through me, a hard, tight thrust of energy that tightened my body, and tore a cry from my mouth. So much need, God!

It was London who crawled over the footboard of the bed. London whose hand in mine had already fed me more energy than all of Requiem's touches. I didn't know why, I didn't care. It was too late to care. He pressed his fully clothed body over me, settling between my legs, so that I could feel him tight and hard through his clothes. The sensation of it fluttered my eyes closed. I felt his face above mine, and opened my eyes to see him, so close it was startling.

I stared into his eyes from inches away, and realized they weren't brown at all, they were black. A black that made his pupils vanish into them, an island of darkness in the whites of his eyes.

His face lowered toward me, his breath escaping in a sound like a sob, before he pressed his mouth against mine. That sound made me remember that there was something important about London and the *ardeur*. Something I needed to remember, but he kissed me, and I stopped thinking about anything but the feel of his mouth on mine.

It wasn't just the force of his kiss, but that I fed from that kiss. As if his energy were some sweet liquor, spilling into my mouth, down my throat. There was no effort to feeding from London. He gave himself to the *ardeur* with an abandon that was exactly what I needed. I poured that energy into Damian, and felt his spark begin to grow to a small, flickering flame.

I wrapped my arms and legs around London's body, pressed my most intimate parts against the hardness still locked behind his clothes. He made that sobbing sound again, his breath hot inside my mouth. I thought he would pull away from the kiss, but he kissed me harder, pressing, exploring, and I kissed him back, sending my tongue between the sharpness of his fangs. It was as if I had more room to explore, as if his mouth were wider than Jean-Claude's. It was almost a clear thought, and I might have remembered what I'd forgotten, but London chose that moment to feed at my lips, kissing me fiercely, with tongue and lips and teeth, and with the intensity of his kiss, the *ardeur* fed harder. The sweet salt of blood filled my mouth, and I knew one of us had been cut on his fangs. If he'd given me time to think, I might even have known who, but he didn't give me time to think. He mounded my breast in one hand, jerked his mouth from mine, and pressed his mouth around my breast. He sucked, hard and fast, tongue flicking across my nipple. I cried out for him, my arms and legs falling away from him enough so he could move that fraction of an inch that let him suck me harder, faster, always the press of his fangs like a promise, or a threat, against my flesh.

He made a sound, eager, almost whimpering, then he bit me, fangs plunging into my breast. It brought me screaming, and only his weight kept my upper body from rising off the bed.

He rose up, his lips decorated with my blood. His eyes drowned in black fire, filled with his own power. He pressed his mouth back to mine, but raised his body off me. The taste of my own blood was like sweet metal in my mouth. I tried to draw his body back on top of mine, but only his mouth touched me. When he lay back on top of me, his pants were undone, and all that hard length pressed against my naked body. The feel of it made me break the kiss so I could cry out.

He raised his upper body off me, angling himself to enter me. I got only a glimpse of him, before he shoved himself inside me, and my gaze tore from his body, to his face above me. His eyes were wide, lost even to vampire glow; there was something frantic about them. He drove his body as deep inside me as he could, drove until there was no more room, then he froze above me. He froze with his body plunged inside mine, and stared down at me. His face was slack with need, and lust, but underneath it all, was fear. That one look, and I remembered. He was addicted to the *ardeur*. Shit.

I said, "London, London, I'm sorry, I'm sorry . . ."

He started to draw himself out of me. I thought he meant to stop. But he drew out only so much, then plunged back in, and he fucked me. He fucked me as hard and fast as he could. I stared down my own body, and watched him plunge in and out of me, and somewhere in the middle of it, I came. I came screaming, my hands clutching at his jacket, trying to find flesh to touch, but there were too many clothes. He brought me, and the *ardeur* fed on the waves of pleasure, on the sensation of him plunging in and out of me, on the sound of his breathing, as it changed. He picked me up, at the last minute, he picked me up, sat me in his lap, with his body still inside mine. He sat me across his body, and I wrapped arms and legs around him to help hold me in place. He sat back on the bed, still plunging in and out of me, but less sharp from this angle, less deep. I stared into his face from inches away, my hands in the short curls at the back of his neck. I watched his face grow frantic, felt his rhythm change. He buried his hand in the back of my hair, held me in place, so we had to stare into each other's eyes. With one last, hard thrust he came, and brought me with him. I screamed, and it would have bowed my neck back, but he held me in place, forced us to stare into each other's faces. As his body spasmed inside mine, I couldn't look away. I had to watch his pleasure, and his pain.

His hand eased from my hair, and he hugged me, his arms loose instead of frantic. His heart pounded against my body, his breath so fast, so terribly fast. He clung to me now, softly, and I hugged him back. He had given me his everything. He had let me feed. Damian was awake, I could feel it. London had helped me save him, but as I held him, his pulse thundering against my cheek, I had to wonder at what price. What had it cost the man in my arms?

33

WHEN LONDON'S PULSE had slowed, he sat me down, gently, on the bed, and asked Jean-Claude's permission to use the bathroom for cleaning up. Jean-Claude gave it. London had taken his pants off the rest of the way, so that he was nude from the waist down, though his dress shirt and suit jacket were long enough that they hid him from behind. He held his shirt up in front to keep it out of the mess, and his pants wadded in his other hand. He looked at no one as he went inside, and closed the door behind him.

He left behind him a silence so loud that I could hear the blood in my own head.

I knew that the vampires could be so still it was like they weren't there, but it was the first time I'd realized that the lycanthropes had their own version of stillness. Of course, there were fewer people in the room than we started with. It was almost as if people had fled before things got bad. Some bodyguards.

Though, admittedly, I didn't look around too much, to see who was left in the corners of the room. Maybe they were all there, huddled around each other, trying to keep the big bad succubus from getting them.

Jean-Claude moved first, and it was as if the pause on a television program had been turned off. He moved, and everyone else breathed, moved. Voices broke into a low murmur. Jean-Claude helped Requiem stand, from where he had apparently fallen on the floor. He must have left the bed sometime during London's and my little . . . feeding. Even in my own head, I heard, *So that's what they're calling it these days.*

Requiem gripped Jean-Claude's arm tight. He spoke low, urgently, as if he had something important to say.

"Damian's coming." Nathaniel's voice turned me to look at him. Micah was helping him climb onto the bed. Nathaniel lay down beside me, his lavender eyes blinking at the ceiling as if he was still having trouble focusing. He was right about Damian. I could feel him coming down the corridor from the coffin room where he'd spent his day asleep. It would take him a few minutes to get here, so I turned to Nathaniel. "Don't ever do that again."

"Try to save Damian?" He tried to make a joke of it, and I wouldn't let him. I touched his face. "Don't joke, Nathaniel."

He snuggled his cheek against my hand. "You saved us."

My throat was tight, and I'd be damned if I'd cry again today. "It was a near thing, and you know it."

Micah put a hand on both our shoulders. He gripped us tight, as if he were fighting an urge to shake us. His face said how scared he'd been, more clearly than any words.

Requiem gathered his cloak from the floor, wrapped it around himself, and went for the door. He never looked back. Maybe he understood finally that he wasn't food. I hoped so, because I needed less complication in my life, not more.

Remus went to Jean-Claude. He stood very straight and started a salute, then stopped himself in midmotion, like an old habit come back to haunt. The voice he used was one of those hardy, soldier voices. "Request permission to get me and my men out of here."

Jean-Claude looked at him, his head to one side, like Remus had done something more interesting than I was seeing. "And what if we need protecting, Remus?"

Remus shook his head. "We can't protect you from this, sir."

Jean-Claude looked behind him, closer to the fireplace. I was still lying down, so I couldn't see what he was looking at. "I think some of your men would disagree, Remus. I think several of them would have been more than happy to help protect *ma petite*, in these circumstances." His voice was mild as butter as he said it.

Remus's jaw tightened so hard that it looked painful. His voice came out strained, as if he were gritting his teeth. "I don't believe that that was what our Oba had in mind when he let you hire us, sir."

"Perhaps you should ask Narcissus what your rules of engagement are, Remus," Jean-Claude said.

Remus gave one curt nod. "I'll do that, sir, but with permission, can I get my men the hell out of here?"

I watched the thought travel across Jean-Claude's face, that he might say no. But that it was that clear to read meant he was doing it for Remus to see. "Go, and take the men with you who wish to leave."

Remus shook his head, hands in fists at his side. "No, sir, I am in command here, and I say we all go."

Jean-Claude looked around the room, as if memorizing faces. He finally nodded. "Go, and take your men, Remus. I will speak with Narcissus."

Remus looked uncertain then, but shook his head again. "I'm not saying that Narcissus wouldn't enjoy the show, sir, but I think if the detail included this kind of thing, he wouldn't have sent ex-military and ex-cops to you." He stared as hard as he could at Jean-Claude's shoulder. I realized that Remus was avoiding the vampire's gaze. "If Narcissus wanted our duties"—he seemed to search for words—"expanded, he has other . . . men to send."

"But not all the men in the room are hyena, Remus," Jean-Claude said. "Do you speak for Raphael's rats as well?"

"I am in command until relieved, so yes, yes, sir, I do."

Another voice came from the far wall, male, and deep, but I couldn't place it, at first. Pepito walked into view. "I'm Raphael's man, and I agree with Remus." Pepito was a large unshakable man, but he looked shaken now. Positively pale, he was. What had they felt when the *ardeur* moved through the room testing them for yumminess? Whatever they had felt, it had scared both Pepito and Remus badly. Or maybe offended them? Maybe.

"Then, by all means, go," Jean-Claude said, and he made a sweeping gesture toward the door.

Remus headed for the door, but he didn't go through it. He opened it, and held it. Pepito motioned to the men farther back in the room. I would have had to sit up to see past the headboard, and I wasn't sure I wanted to see. I started to tug at the sheets. For some reason I wanted a little covering as the guards trailed out.

Micah pulled the sheets up and covered most of me and Nathaniel. Micah stayed kneeling by us on the bed, while the bodyguards trooped out. I fought two opposing instincts. I wanted to hide under the sheet, so no one would see me, and I wouldn't have to meet anyone's eyes. But I knew if I did that I'd never be able to look any of them in the face again. I did the only thing I could do; I glared at them. A defiant front was all the hope I had to maintain any level of control or respect from any of them. Yeah, it had been an emergency and I had had to feed the *ardeur*. Technically, the guards understood that. But in reality, as Remus had said, most of them were ex-military or ex-cops. Which meant a woman was always working uphill with them anyway. They'd seen me have sex with one man, and once the story got around it would be more. The really weird thing about the rumors would be that some of the men who had actually witnessed everything would be convinced that I'd had sex with more men. I'd be lucky if some of them didn't claim they themselves had had sex with me. I'd had rumors start after crime scenes where I'd done nothing sexual. This had not been nothing.

Most of the guards seemed as eager to avoid eye contact as I was. But not everyone. I glared most of them down, but a few gave me bold eyes. The kind of look you don't want to see outside a strip club. The look that said you'd gone from a human being to just being tits and ass. I tried to remember who looked at me that way, so I could keep them away from me later.

Micah leaned over Nathaniel and me, whispering, "I see them." He was memorizing faces, too. Good, because I was still shaky, and didn't trust my own eyes to hold the right faces in the right places.

I always have trouble holding a glare when I'm more naked than the rest of the room. Nathaniel cuddled against me, under the sheet. He brought one arm free of the covers, so he could lay his bare arm across my covered waist. He rubbed his chin along the side of my breast, dragging the sheet down so that I had to hold it in place. I looked at him, ready to tell him to watch it, but the look on his face stopped the words before they could start.

He was staring at the men, too, but he wasn't glaring. His face held heat, and the promise of sex, but over it all was possessiveness. That look that a man gets when another man encroaches on his "woman." Nathaniel, who shared better than any man in my life, was marking his territory. That dark, possessive look never wavered from the parade of men. He rested the side of his chin against the mound of my breast, making it clear that he had a right to be there, like that, with me, and they did not. I didn't think Nathaniel would grasp the problem, but he had.

There was a holdup at the door, a confusion of movement, like a traffic jam. I saw the flash of blood-red hair, and expected it to be Damian on his own power, but it wasn't. Richard came through the door, his arm around Damian's waist, the vampire's arm over his shoulder. Damian leaned so heavily on him that Richard half-dragged him toward the bed.

I sat up, leaving the sheet at my waist and not caring that I was topless. Nathaniel sat up, too; we both reached toward them. I said, "Damian!" I reached for him with less-physical parts. His energy was weak, but it was more as if he hadn't woken up completely from his daytime torpor.

His legs gave out completely, and Richard carried him in his arms like a child the last few feet. He laid Damian beside me. The long, red hair hid the vampire's face. I moved the hair away so I could see his face. He blinked up at me, eyes a perfect bright green, green as summer grass. It was Damian's eyes that had raised the bar so high on green-colored eyes. No one else's eyes could compare. He tried to focus on me, but didn't seem able to do it.

I touched his face, and his skin was icy. "I fed the *ardeur*—why isn't he better than this?"

Jean-Claude came to lay his hand on Damian's forehead. Richard said, "I found him collapsed against the wall just down from the coffin room. When Remus called for reinforcements, all the guards came here. Damian was trying to crawl to you."

"What made you think to check on him?" Micah asked, still kneeling on the bed.

"I remembered how bad he got the last time his tie to Anita broke. I thought someone should check on him."

"Very good thinking, *mon ami*." Jean-Claude touched my cheek, then Nathaniel's while keeping his other hand on Damian's face. He finally stepped back from all of us, frowning. "I believe part of what is wrong is simply that Damian has woken too early. Only the very powerful masters among us wake before noon, even deep underground. Damian is no master. I believe you, *ma petite*, called him from his coffin, but even with extra energy it was too soon."

I held one icy hand in both of mine. "Will he be all right? Did I hurt him?"

"I'll be all right." Damian's voice was slow, heavy, as if he were drugged.

I smiled down at him. "Damian, I'm so sorry."

He managed a weak smile. "It would be nice," he took a labored breath, "if you'd stop almost killing me because you don't want to screw other people."

I didn't know whether to smile or be exasperated.

"I believe that Damian would feel better if Nathaniel touched him, as well," Jean-Claude said.

Nathaniel took Damian's other hand in his, and the power jumped between us. It made me gasp. It was as if a circuit had been completed. The energy hummed from my hand, through Damian's body, into Nathaniel's hand and back again.

Damian drew in a huge, gasping breath, almost like it hurt. He swore, softly.

"Does it hurt?" Nathaniel asked, looking worried.

"Wonderful," Damian whispered, "feels wonderful. You're so warm."

Strangely, I was almost certain he was talking to Nathaniel.

"Sir, excuse me, sir." It was Remus; nerves always made him default to military-speak. Of course, it worked. Jean-Claude and Richard both turned to look at him. We all looked at him, except for Damian, who had closed his eyes.

"Yes, Remus," Jean-Claude said.

He finally looked at me, sort of. He never liked direct eye contact, but he seemed unable to stare at my shoulder, like normal, because too much of my breasts were in the way. "I owe you an apology, Blake." He said it in such a way that, apology or no, it was obvious he didn't want to be saying it.

I gave him as good an eye contact as he'd let me. "What apology do you owe me, Remus?"

He blushed, and it filled some pieces of his face with bright color, but lines in between paled, so that you could see where all the pieces of his face didn't quite match up. "I thought you were just a . . ." He stopped, seemed to think about it, and finally said, "Well, you know what I was thinking."

I could have been mean, and said nope, I didn't know, and tried to force him to say it all out loud. But truthfully, I didn't want to hear him call me a slut. Thinking it had been enough.

"It's okay, Remus, I might think the same thing if I were on the outside of it looking in."

He gave a small smile. "If it really is life and death for you and your people, then you need to talk to Narcissus about guards and food." He almost laughed. "Maybe give them a different color of shirt." He shook his head, and just stopped talking. He turned on his heel and left, as if whatever he'd been about to say, he wanted to stop before he said it, and leaving was the only solution. When the door closed behind him, and we were totally guard-free, Micah spoke for most of us, I think. "He's an odd one."

I just nodded. *Odd one* about covered Remus. I'd thought my not understanding him was because I didn't know him that well, but I was beginning to think that months from now, I'd have no more clue to why he did or didn't do things. Some people are mysteries, and knowing them well doesn't make them less mysterious. Less confusing sometimes, but not less mysterious.

Asher leaned against the post of the bed, near us. He had a look on his face that I used to think meant teasing, but now I knew meant worse and darker things. "Richard," he said, so pleasantly, "did you truly leave us because you worried for Damian's safety?"

Richard gave him narrow eyes. "Yes."

"Really?" Asher managed to put in that one word a world of doubt.

Richard shifted, uncomfortably, as if he didn't know what to do with his hands. "I didn't want to see Anita feed on Requiem. Does that make you happy, to know that?" he asked of Asher.

Asher leaned his cheek against the carved wood, and nodded. "Actually, yes, it does."

"Why? Why does my discomfort please you?"

Asher wrapped his hands around the post, using it like a prop, as if the scene were staged. Most of the vampires had a certain flair for the dramatic.

Belle's vamps had more than their share sometimes. He didn't answer Richard's question, but made a statement. "You could have stayed, Richard, because she didn't feed on Requiem."

"Stop it, Asher," I said.

"Stop what?" he asked, and the glint in his eyes let me know he knew exactly *what* and that he was angry about something. Angry with Richard, maybe, or maybe angry about something else entirely. Mysterious and confusing didn't apply only to Remus.

"If you're mad about something, say so. If you're not, then stop the whole angry teasing routine."

Damian's grip on my hand tightened. Maybe he was just feeling stronger, or maybe he was trying to remind me not to get angry. One of his jobs as my vampire servant was to help me fight off those angry impulses. His own iron self-control had been forged by she-who-made-him. Any strong emotion was eventually punished, horribly punished. I'd shared enough of Damian's memories to know that his creator made Belle Morte seem the heart of kindness by comparison. Damian had learned to control all his emotions, his urges, because to do otherwise had been disaster.

He gripped my hand, not as tight as normal. He wasn't well, by any means, but I felt calm flow from him to me. That calm not of gentle meditation and the modern ideal of peace of mind, but of the older ideal, when control was carved from pain and hardship, and painted in scars across your flesh.

"Is Damian whispering peaceful things in your head, Anita?" Asher asked. His tone was still teasing and light, but underneath was a razor's edge of spite.

"You know how wanting total honesty is just another way for me to be a pain in the ass," I said.

Asher looked at me, his eyes like winter sky. "Yes."

"What you're doing now is your way of being angry without being angry. Teasing with a bite to it."

He wrapped his arms around the post, letting his hair slide forward to hide the scarred side of his face. It was an old trick, one he rarely did when it was just Jean-Claude and me. He gazed at the room with the perfection of his profile framed by his glittering froth of hair.

"Am I angry?" He made the question winsome.

"Yes," I said, and it was a statement. "Question is, what are you angry about?"

"I have not admitted to being angry." But he kept that perfect profile, that shine of hair, so that he showed himself to what he considered his best advantage. He was breathtaking, but I'd begun to value the full-face view, imperfections and all, more than this angry coyness. This show meant he was uncomfortable, or trying to persuade us to do something. Asher seldom flirted without an agenda. Sometimes it was foreplay, or just to make us smile, but other times . . . well, I did not trust his mood.

"Asher wants me to know who you fed on, and you don't want me to know." Richard had summed it up nicely.

I hung my head. Damian laid his lips against my knuckles, not quite a kiss. I only had to open my eyes to stare down into his face, where he lay on the bed. He gazed up at me, and his eyes held not sympathy, but strength, control. *You can do this*, his eyes seemed to say, *you can do this, because you must.* He was right.

I looked up at Richard. I thought about raising the sheet and hiding my breasts, but everyone left in the room had seen them before. Modesty wouldn't get me out of Richard's reaction to my newest conquest.

"Who was it?" he asked.

I turned to Asher, and said, "You told me earlier today that you were sorry, that you were putting your hurt feelings ahead of my disaster. You apologized, and tried to make amends. Is that all your apology is worth, Asher? An hour of remorse, and you go back to being a bastard?"

His eyes flashed with anger, and his power trailed over my body like a cold wind. Then he swallowed it, the power, the anger. He turned a mild, if empty, face to me. "I can only apologize once more, *ma cherie*, you are absolutely right. I am throwing a fit." He stepped away from the bed, and did a low, sweeping bow that trailed the edge of his hair on the floor. He rose up with a flourish, as if he were moving a cape with one hand.

"Why are you throwing a fit?" I asked.

"Truth?" He made it a question.

I nodded, not truly certain I wanted this particular truth.

"Because he will never be my lover. He will be your lover, but never ours together."

For a moment I wasn't sure which *he* he was talking about it. The confusion must have shown on my face, because he said, "You see, *ma cherie*, that is it, that is it, *exactement*. My statement could refer to so many of your men that you do not even know to whom I refer."

Damian's hand squeezed mine again. I wasn't certain whether it was to comfort me, or to comfort him. Damian was a touch homophobic, and Asher was not a comforting presence if that was your particuliar phobia.

"Are you saying you're pissed because I keep picking men who aren't bisexual?"

Asher seemed to think about it for a moment, then nodded. "I believe I am. I don't think I knew until you asked so point-blank, but yes, I believe that is why I am angry." He looked past me to Jean-Claude. "As he will not turn to me for fear you would leave him, so I do not turn to others for fear that he will use it as an excuse to pull even further away from me."

"We agreed that we would have this discussion at a later time," Jean-Claude said, in a voice that was as empty as any I'd ever heard from him.

Asher nodded. "I thought I could wait, but I am choking on things unsaid, Jean-Claude." He pointed to Richard. "But we must be careful in front of him, too. It would not do to frighten him away. We wouldn't want him to know that we find him beautiful, would we?"

"Asher," I started to say, but Micah finished it for me. "After the visiting masters leave town, and we know what we're doing about the baby, then we'll all sit down and talk about your . . . grievances."

"No, we will not," Asher said, "for there will be another crisis, another reason to put it off."

"I give you my word that Nathaniel, Anita, and I will sit down and talk to you about it. I can't promise for anyone else."

Asher turned that winter-blue gaze on me. "Does he speak for you?"

I nodded. "He does."

Asher turned to Jean-Claude. "And you, master?" There was a lot of sarcasm to the *master*.

"I will not be bound by Micah's word in all things, but on this, I will agree. We will discuss it in detail, if you but leave it alone for a little longer."

"Your word," Asher said.

Jean-Claude nodded. "You have it."

Some tension went out of Asher, almost like an energy release. The room felt lighter, the air easier to breathe. "I will behave myself." He looked at Micah. "I thank you, Micah."

"Don't thank me, Asher, you're part of Anita's life. If we're going to make this work, then we have to talk to each other."

"Always perfect, aren't you?" Richard said, and his own anger raised the heat in the room.

"No," I said, "no, no more fights. Until after I've seen the doctor this afternoon, I want every one of you to behave like a fucking adult, okay?"

Richard had the grace to look embarrassed. He nodded. "I'll try. Inheriting your temper makes it so hard not to be pissed all the time." He gave a small laugh. "If this is just a shadow of how angry you feel all the time, I'm amazed you don't just start killing things. God, such rage." He looked at me, his brown eyes full of so many emotions. "You told me once that your rage was like my beast, and I belittled you. I told you that your anger couldn't compare to my beast, that you didn't know what you were talking about. I was wrong. God, Anita, God, you are so full of rage."

"Everyone needs a hobby," I said.

He smiled and shook his head. "You have to learn to control the rage, Anita. If you're really going to shift, you have to get a handle on the rage first." His face sobered, and he stepped close enough that he could touch my face. The moment he did, our energy jumped to him, both offering energy, and asking for it. Richard and I jerked back at the same time, because it had almost hurt, a slap of electricity.

He rubbed his hand. "Jesus, Anita."

I used my free hand to touch my face. The skin tingled where he'd touched. "I've got the shields wide open between the three of us here."

"Could you piggyback the energy of Anita's two triumvirates?" Micah asked.

"Piggyback?" Jean-Claude made it a question.

"Double the energy," I said.

"Since no one has ever before forged two triumvirates at the same time, I have no answer. The energy did respond to Richard's touch."

I rubbed my cheek. "You could say that again."

"Are you hurt?" Richard asked.

I shook my head. "Just tingling."

He nodded. "Yeah." He rubbed his hand along the side of his jeans, as if he were trying to rub off the lingering sensation.

The bathroom door opened. London walked out, fully clothed now, adjusting his black-on-black tie. Except that his eyes were still drowning black with power, he looked like he always did. He stopped and looked at us all, because we were looking at him. His face was arrogant, his version of blank. I stared at him, and it didn't seem quite real that we'd had sex. He'd never really been on my guy radar, and now he was food. Funny damn world.

"Where is everyone?" His voice was coldly arrogant, and didn't match the words at all.

"The guards asked to leave," I said, "and truthfully, I don't remember when everyone else left."

London walked along the edge of the bed without looking at me. He was back to his cold, isolated self, as if the sex had never happened. He almost made it around the bed, but his foot tangled in the covers on the floor, and down he went. His arm caught at the bed, and he brought himself up to his knees. He peered at us over the bed, like a cat that's just fallen off something, and is trying to pretend it meant to do that.

He got to his feet, leaning on the bed. He jerked the fallen coverlet to one side, then kicked at it repeatedly, hands on the bed to steady himself. He kicked at the coverlet as if it were some kind of enemy that he had to vanquish. When the floor was clear enough for him, he smoothed his clothes again, then started walking carefully around the bed. His shoulder clipped the bedpost, and he fell into the bed again. This time he managed to sit on it, and not end up on the floor, but he didn't try to get up again either. He sat there on the bed, his black-suited back very straight. He kept looking at the far wall.

"You're drunk," I said.

He nodded without turning around. "Not precisely, but *drunk* will do as a description."

Jean-Claude walked around the bed until he was standing in front of the other man. He stared down at him, and I couldn't tell if London met his gaze, or not. "How do you feel?" he asked him at last.

Someone giggled, a high, almost hysterical sound. It was a moment before I realized it was London. He fell back on the bed with his arms wide, and his legs hanging off the edge. He lay there all black and stark against the pale sheets, giggling. The giggling turned into laughter. He gave himself to the laughter, as he'd given himself to the *ardeur*. The laughter was a good clean laugh, a good sound, but none of us joined him, because London did not laugh. This was not the Dark Knight with his love of shadows and dislike of everything else. This laughing, pleasant man on the bed was someone we'd never seen before.

Tears trailed from his eyes, faintly pink with blood like all vampire tears. He rolled his head back so he could see me. "I wanted to hide it from you, but I never could hide it."

"Hide what?" I asked, and my voice sounded almost afraid.

"How good the *ardeur* feels. Belle said once that she'd never known anyone who fed the *ardeur* as well as I did, or addicted to it as quickly." The laughter faded from his eyes, leaving them desolate. From such joy, to such loss, in a blink of his eyes.

"Are you addicted once more, *mon ami*?" Jean-Claude asked.

He turned his head to look at Jean-Claude. "I do not know for certain, but most likely, *oui*, I am." He sounded neither happy nor sad about it. He was almost matter-of-fact.

"God, London, I'm sorry," I said.

Damian tried to sit up, but Nathaniel and I had to help him, so that he was propped up between us. "I'm sorry, as well."

London curled himself on the bed so he was lying on his side, and could see us. "Don't be sorry, I feel better than I've felt in centuries." He closed his eyes, and drew a shivering breath. "I feel so warm, so . . . alive."

I remembered when the *ardeur* was searching for food, how he'd hit the radar. So powerful, but more than that. "The *ardeur* recognized you as the tasty power in the room. Is it because you were addicted to it once?"

"Requiem was addicted once," London said. "Did he seem tasty, too?"

"Not as yummy as you, no."

"Belle said that my power is to feed the *ardeur*. To use a modernism, I am a battery for it."

"If you are such a good feed, then why doesn't Damian feel better?" Nathaniel asked.

"I did not mean to, but I think I drank a great deal of the energy myself. It was like being lost in the desert for years, and suddenly seeing a river, running cool and deep. My skin soaked it up, I couldn't stop it. I kept most of the energy, and I'm sorry for that."

"No you're not," Nathaniel said, his voice soft, but certain.

London laughed, an abrupt, happy sound. "You're right, I'm not. I knew it would be enough energy to keep Damian alive, and beyond that I didn't care." He curled all that tall, strong frame into a ball, and looked at me with a face more uncertain than anything I'd ever seen from London. "I am at your mercy. I tried to hide how much it meant to me, but I cannot. I could never hide it from Belle either. She tortured me with it." He gazed up at me with those lost eyes, and said, "Will you torture me, Anita? Will you make me beg for another taste?"

My pulse was suddenly in my throat, not from passion, but from fear. The proud, scary London was curled on a bed staring up at me with a look I'd only seen in Nathaniel's eyes. I knew that look. It said, *You can do anything you want to do, just keep me. I'll do anything you want, just keep me.*

Ronnie had always been able to find men to have a nice uncomplicated fuck with. Me, I seemed to be running a home for amazingly complicated men. As for a nice uncomplicated fuck, I wouldn't have known one if it bit me on the ass.

34

By two forty-five we were in a maternity room at St. John's hospital. If I'd been further along someone might have called it a birthing room, but not in front of me, not if they wanted to live. To say that I was not happy to be there was an understatement of amazingly gigantic proportions.

Dr. North had taken one look at the crowd with me, and managed a private room for the exam. Or maybe he'd known me well enough to arrange it ahead of time. The room had pink flowered wallpaper, and all the furniture tried to be homey, or at least to pretend we were in a nice hotel. All except the bed. The bed was nicer than most, but it still had railings, and one of those trays on wheels at the foot of it. It was still a hospital bed no matter how dolled-up the surroundings might be.

I wasn't lying in the bed. I was pacing the room, because we were waiting for the blood test results. We'd find out in minutes just how bad the news was going to be.

Micah was in a chair in the corner, staying out of my way. Smart man. We had two werelions with us, one standing quietly against a wall, and the other in the room's only other chair, reading. Joseph had shown up with six werelions for me to choose from. Joseph seriously didn't like Haven, Auggie's lion, and was hoping I'd pick other, less dominant lions to play with. Okay by me. But how do you choose from relative strangers? How do you choose the ones who will at the very least let you change them, violently, into their animal forms? How do you trust that they won't fight you?

Joseph assured me and Jean-Claude, "I picked submissives, as I discussed with Jean-Claude. I think they'll be like Nathaniel was for you once, for the *ardeur*."

"What's that supposed to mean?" I'd asked.

"I think you'll be able to feed the *ardeur* from them without full sexual contact. If I understand how the *ardeur* works, it's only dominance and power that keeps you from feeding from a kiss."

"That's the theory," I said.

They all seemed soft and unfinished and too fragile for my life, but I chose two of them. Travis and Noel; blondish and brunette respectively. Travis was a business major and Noel an English major. Noel wore glasses and had a test Monday. He'd brought books to study. Travis just brought himself.

Noel was reading for his test and ignoring everything around him. Travis was watching everything with those pale brown eyes of his. He watched the way cops watch, as if he were memorizing everything. He seemed particularly interested in Richard.

My bodyguard shift had changed over, so Claudia and Lisandro were in the far corner near the door, doing that bodyguard casual that was almost a slump, but not quite. If either of them had ever been military or police, it never showed. They were just bad-asses, and that was enough. There were two more guards outside the room, by the door, which Dr. North had objected to, but Claudia had looked at him hard, and he'd okayed it. One of the guards outside the door was Graham, the other a werehyena that I didn't know. Ixion was his name, though he said it like he hated it, and hadn't had it long. Narcissus had more fun than he should have, passing out names to some of his new men. Ixion was so ex-military that he still had the haircut, and looked uncomfortable in civilian clothes.

We didn't really need four bodyguards, but it was the only way Claudia could see to get us a wolf who would shift for me at the hospital if I needed it, without letting Richard know that none of us trusted him to take my beast in an emergency. Graham was my wolf in the hole, so to speak, and Ixion got to come along because Claudia preferred all the guards to be in pairs. If we were pretending, we had to make it good pretend.

"You're going to wear yourself out, Anita," Richard said.

"Then I'll wear myself out," I snapped, and knew that I snapped, and didn't have nerves left to care.

He pushed away from the wall, and walked toward me. He reached out, as if he'd hug me, or comfort me.

"Don't," I said, and kept walking until the window made me stop and turn around.

"I just want to help, Anita," he said.

"Pacing helps," I said, not looking at him. Why couldn't he understand that I just wanted to be left the fuck alone? Micah understood it. Nathaniel had wanted to come, but shapeshifting so early had exhausted him. Once you hit animal form you usually spend between six and eight hours in it; if you shift back early it comes with a price. If he was going to be any good tonight he needed rest. I'd left him tucked in with Damian, so they could both feel better before nightfall.

Richard touched my shoulder as I went past. I jerked away from him and kept on walking. If we could have figured out a way to bring Damian with me, we would have. He helped me be calm, and I needed it. But vampires do not travel well in daylight.

"If you don't calm down," Richard said, "you may call your beast. You don't want that, not here."

I stopped and glared at him. "It would take care of the problem though, wouldn't it?"

"You don't mean that," he said.

"The hell I don't."

"Ulfric." It was Travis, from his corner of the wall.

Richard turned to him.

"Ulfric, she's burning off her nervous energy by pacing."

"I know that," Richard said in a less than friendly voice.

"If you make her stop pacing, then where will the energy go?"

Richard opened his mouth, shut it, and nodded. "You've made your point. I guess it's making me nervous to watch her pace."

"Then don't watch," Travis said, as if it were the easiest thing in the world.

Richard drew a deep breath, and said, "I'm going to get some air. I'll be right outside, I promise."

I paused in the pacing to say, "I know you will."

He nodded, and he walked out. When the door was shut behind him, Travis said, "Thank God. One of you that nervous is enough for a room this size."

I looked at him. "Is Richard that nervous?"

Micah laughed. "Yes."

I hugged my arms tight. "I guess I'm so nervous that I didn't notice."

"You're entitled to be nervous," Claudia said from near the door.

I nodded, but not like I believed it. There was a knock on the door. I jumped, and turned toward the door, my fingers digging into my own arms. I wasn't hugging myself now, I was clinging, as if my fingernails were digging into that last piece of rock ledge before you fall screaming into the abyss.

Graham opened the door enough to stick his head in, and said, "The doctor is here."

"Let him in," Claudia said, and her voice held tension. Was I making everyone crazy with nerves?

Dr. North came in, with a glance at Ixion, still by the door. "Your men are making the nurses and patients a little nervous. Could they come in the room?"

I looked at Claudia. She was the one in charge. She nodded, and sent Lisandro to open the door and invite Graham and Ixion inside. Graham just found a piece of wall to hold up. He gave me a nervous smile that I think was meant to be comforting. Ixion scowled at the entire room, and didn't seem to know where to stand. The room was getting a little crowded.

"The window, Ixion," Claudia said. "Not everything that hunts us comes through doors." We weren't really in that much danger from direct attack, but it gave the man somewhere to stand that was far away from the bed and whatever we'd be doing. Though if there was a pelvic exam coming up, then everyone who couldn't be the father was leaving.

When Ixion had settled against the window, Dr. North looked around the room. "Do you want this discussed in front of everyone?"

"You just had me bring two extra people inside, doc."

He smiled. "I mean, maybe you'd want some of them to go to the cafeteria."

I sighed, and shook my head. How could I explain that if the news was bad enough I might need one, or all, of my support staff? I couldn't, so I didn't. "Just spit it out, doc, okay? The suspense is getting to me."

He nodded, adjusted his glasses. The door opened behind him, and Richard came in. "Did I miss anything?"

I shook my head.

"Anita," Dr. North said, "you're going to bleed if you don't stop digging your nails into your arms."

I stared down at my hands as if they'd just appeared at the end of my arms. My fingers were stiff with tension when I peeled them away from my arms. Little half moons from my fingernails decorated my skin. Almost blood, almost.

Richard offered me his hand. I hesitated, then took it. The energy spiked between us; we were both too nervous to be of much help to each other. He shut down, shielded up, and his hand was just warm and real in my hand. I appreciated the effort on his part, after he'd seen what I'd done to my own arms, but I finally lost the battle not to look behind me at Micah. I was too scared to play to anyone's ego. Too scared not to want to wrap myself in as much comfort as I could find.

Micah came to my other hand. Richard stiffened, not wanting it, and not able to hide that he didn't want it, but he didn't throw a fit. I squeezed his hand, and bumped my head against his shoulder to let him know how much the effort meant to me, because it did. It really did. The extra attention earned me a smile, that smile that brightened his whole face. The smile that once I'd have given my heart to see.

I turned back to the doctor, clinging to both of them, and feeling better for it. I'd have liked to play it cool, but I clung to their hands as if they were the last pieces of wood in a drowning ocean.

"I had them run the blood work a second time, Anita."

"That can't be good," I said.

"Is this where you ask her to sit down?" Claudia asked.

Dr. North glanced at her. "She can sit down if she wants." He turned back to me, with a smile. "Do you want to sit down?"

"Do I need to sit down?"

His smile widened, and he glanced at the men on either side. "I don't think so, but if you do, I think you've got enough support." He nodded at Micah and Richard.

"Just tell me, doc," I said. My voice strained, but normalish. Points for me.

"Can I be absolutely candid in front of everyone in this room?" he asked.

I fought the urge to scream, and managed to say, "Yes, yes, just say it. God, please, just say it."

He nodded, again. "Are you aware that you have lycanthropy?"

I nodded, then frowned. "I'm aware that I'm carrying lycanthropy."

"Funny you should say it that way," he said. "Your blood work is just unique, Anita."

"I learned a few weeks ago that I'm carrying leopard, wolf, lion, and something that the doctors couldn't even identify."

He gave me a look. "You know that it's impossible to carry more than one strain of lycanthropy. They cancel each other out. You can't catch it more than once."

I nodded again, squeezing the hands that held me. "I know all that. It's a medical miracle, yadda-yadda-yadda, just get to the pregnancy part. Do I have Mowgli syndrome, or Vlad's syndrome?"

He gave me very good eye contact, way too serious, and said, "Yes, as far as the tests can tell us."

My knees went, and I might have hit the floor, but Micah and Richard caught me. Someone brought one of the chairs up, and the men lowered me into it. They kept their hands on mine, and each of them put a hand on a shoulder, as if they didn't trust me not to fall forward. I wasn't that bad, not yet. Not yet.

"What do you mean, 'as far as the tests can tell'?" Micah asked.

"The two syndromes are like lycanthropy; you can't have both. A fetus can't carry both Vlad's and Mowgli syndrome. If Anita weren't carrying four different kinds of lycanthropy, a medical impossibility, I'd say we might have twins, but because of the other blood work, and some of the other tests . . ."

His mouth kept moving, but all I could hear in my ears was the blood roaring through it. Richard and Micah helped me put my head between my knees, and kept me from falling out of the chair. The head between my knees helped after a few moments. But I was glad for their hands on me, holding me in place. I don't faint, but I'd passed out before, and this felt awfully similar. Jesus, twins. Talk about karmic payback, with interest. Twins with two of the worst birth defects known to modern science. *Sweet Mary, Mother of God, help me on this one.*

Dr. North's voice came from just in front of me. He was kneeling by me. "Anita, Anita, can you hear me? Anita!"

I managed to nod my head.

"I don't want to give you false hope here, because to my knowledge the only way to test positive for these syndromes is to be pregnant, but you tested negative for pregnancy. Twice."

I raised my head, slowly; one, because it was as fast as I could move it safely, and two, because I didn't believe I'd heard what I'd heard. "What?" I asked, in a voice that didn't sound like me at all.

He was kneeling in front of me, and he was tall enough and me short enough that we had perfect eye contact. His face was sincere, worried around the edges. He spoke slowly, carefully. "You tested negative for pregnancy."

I frowned at him. "But you said . . ."

He nodded. "I know. I don't understand the test results either. In fact, the nurses and interns are arm-wrestling right now for who gets to help me do an ultrasound."

"Arm-wrestling?"

"Do you want the truth?"

"Yeah."

"No matter what happens with the ultrasound this is a medical first, as far as any of us know. Either you aren't pregnant, and you've tested positive for two syndromes that we thought needed a pregnancy to test positive. Or you are carrying twins, from different fathers, and for some reason our tests deny that you're pregnant. Unusual enough. And don't forget, as we discussed on the phone, the Mowgli baby could be viable in weeks, but the other baby wouldn't be."

I just stared at him.

"What do you mean, doctor?" Richard asked it.

He gave an abbreviated lecture on Mowgli, and the potential for a speedy pregnancy. "Or something about Anita's blood work makes her test positive for all of it." He looked at me, still on his knees. "Are you a lycanthrope? I mean, do you shapeshift?"

I shook my head, then added, "Not so far."

"What does 'not so far' mean?" he asked.

"It means, I came close."

Micah said, "We thought she was going to shift earlier today."

"How long has she been carrying multiple strains of lycanthropy?"

Micah glanced at me. I shrugged. "About six months, we think. When she didn't shift, we just assumed she hadn't caught it."

Dr. North nodded as if that made sense. "Logical, up to a point. The literature says the first full moon and you shift, period. But you're saying she's had six full moons, and nothing."

"Don't talk about me like I'm not here," I said.

"I'm sorry, Anita. I thought I'd give you a few minutes to recover."

"I'm as recovered as I'm going to get," I said. I took in a deep breath and let it out slow. I pushed at their hands. "I can sit up, I'm okay."

"Anita"—and this time it was Micah—"let us help, please."

I tried to find the energy to get grumpy about it, but I didn't have it to spare. "Fine, just hold me, don't hold me down in the chair. It's like being trapped." Trapped, yeah, that about covered it.

Micah held his hand down, and after a heartbeat, I took it. Richard did the same on the other side, and I took his hand, too. I was being brave, but if the news kept being so interesting, I might need something to hold on to.

"The blood work results came back with the same results on all the tests twice. Since according to everything we think we know, that's impossible, I want to do an ultrasound. The ultrasound will show whether you're pregnant or not. We'll be able to see it. If we don't see it, then you aren't pregnant. The home test was a false positive, and the blood work is right."

"And if I am pregnant?"

He fought his face, trying to find some bedside manner that would fit. "Then we'll do this."

"Two babies, one that may grow so fast that it will be ready to deliver in weeks, and a second baby that may try to eat its way out of me, or eat its twin." My voice was mine again, matter-of-fact. I could have been talking about what to have for dinner.

Someone said, "Jesus." Richard's hand tightened on mine until it almost hurt, but I didn't tell him to let go. I wanted to feel him there. Micah added a second hand, holding my arm, too. At least neither of them told the big lie, that it would be all right. It wasn't going to be all right.

Dr. North blinked at me. It's never good to see your doctor do that slow oh-my-God blink. "I think that would be worst-case scenario, Anita. Let's get the ultrasound done, then we'll know what we're dealing with." He stood up, shaking out his pants legs, and not meeting anyone's eyes. I think I'd been a little too accurately pessimistic for Dr. North. Me, being too pessimistic, hell, yeah.

35

I GOT TO lie down on the bed. Doc North put the railings down so he could get the ultrasound equipment and himself close enough. The railings on the other side went down so that the crowd could gather round. He hadn't been exaggerating about the interns and nurses arm-wrestling. Well, maybe about the method of choosing, but they all wanted to be there. We were making medical oddity, if not medical history, no matter what happened. I felt like a display at the zoo.

Dr. North beat me to it, by saying, "We don't need this many people."

One of the interns said, "Let's clear some of her people out."

I looked right at him, and said, "Get out!"

He started to argue.

Dr. North said, "Get out."

The intern got out. The remaining junior doctors were way more polite. The nurses got squeezed out completely, though one of the doctors was a woman.

Claudia saved the day, a little, by saying, "Anita, he was an asshole, but for this, we can get some of us outside. I'm going to assume," and she glared at the white coats, "that some of these people are here to help out. Regardless of what the ultrasound shows, we don't have the medical expertise to offer suggestions." She motioned her people out, saying, "We'll be right outside if you need us."

She called to Travis and Noel. "The two of you, come with us."

"We're not guards," Travis said. "Joseph gave us to Anita, not to you."

"Now is not the time to be a pain in the ass, Travis," I said; my voice wasn't calm anymore. It was starting to crumble round the edges.

He didn't argue after that. He just walked out. Noel followed him, clutching his book and his backpack. Claudia gave me a look before she went out. I almost called her back in, but didn't. We weren't close friends, but I trusted her. I trusted Micah, and to a point I trusted Richard. But they weren't neutral parties, and we might need a cooler head, one not so personally involved. The door closed behind her before I could decide to say *Stay*. Decision made.

Dr. North started sending interns out, until we were down to three. That left enough room for Micah and Richard to stand near the head of the bed on the opposite side of the ultrasound stuff. I had only one hand to offer, and Micah got that. Richard ended up gripping my shoulder, but bless him, he didn't argue about it. Maybe grown-up reality had finally hit us all, and the squabbling would stop. We could hope.

I'd had to take my jacket off, which showed the gun and its shoulder holster. I was using the extra belt I'd kept at Jean-Claude's, but I was down two, so I'd have to send Nathaniel shopping for more leather belts soon. The lone female intern kept looking at the gun, with quick flashes of her eyes, as if she'd never seen one before.

I had to slide the belt off, and unhook the bottom part of the shoulder rig, so the doctor could snake my jeans down around my hips. The gun didn't stay put when I lay back on the bed, and I had to use both hands to pull it down. I suppose I could have taken it off and let Micah hold it, but I wanted the gun touching me. It was the only security blanket I had with me, except for Micah and Richard. And since both of them were a little responsible for my being in this mess, well, I was having mixed feelings about clinging to anyone who could even remotely have gotten me pregnant. For the first time, I wondered if a vasectomy on a lycanthrope was an absolutely sure thing.

"This is going to be cold," Dr. North said, before he squirted clear gel all over my stomach. It was cold, but it gave me something else to occupy my mind, and I was taking it.

"Micah had a vasectomy about three years ago. We'd discounted him as the possible father, but he is a lycanthrope, I mean . . ."

Dr. North looked at Micah. "Did he just burn the ends or did you put in silver clips?"

"Both, and I was tested about six months ago and came up clean."

"I've heard about using silver clips; are you aware that there've been two cases of silver poisoning from vasectomies like yours?"

Micah shook his head. "No, I wasn't aware."

"You might let your doctor run a blood test for silver levels, just to be safe." Dr. North looked down at me, and his face was all soft. Good bedside manner. He held up a chunky piece of plastic. "I'm going to run this over your skin. It doesn't hurt."

I nodded. "You explained how it works, doc, just do it."

He started running the chunky wand over my stomach, spreading the clear gel around as he worked. I watched the little TV screen behind him. He was glancing at it, too. It was gray, white, and black, and fuzzy. If it had been my television at home I'd have been calling the cable company and raising hell. The images seemed to make more sense to him than to me, because he'd glance and move the wand. Then he just started moving the wand without looking at it, looking only at the screen.

The tallest intern said, "Well, damn." He sounded terribly disappointed.

North didn't even glance at him. He just said, "Get out."

"But . . ."

"Now," and my kindly doctor sounded as mean and serious as I'd ever heard him. He might have good patient manners, but I was beginning to get the idea that his bedside manner ended by the bedside. Fine with me.

"What's wrong?" Richard said. He was leaning over me, trying to decipher the images.

I asked. "What are you seeing that I'm not?"

"Nothing's wrong, Mr. Zeeman," Dr. North said without looking at him. "And what am I seeing? Nothing."

"What does that mean, nothing?" Micah asked, and for the first time I heard a thread of tension in his voice. That iron control, cracking just a little.

North turned back to me with a smile. "You are not pregnant."

I blinked up at him. "But the test . . ."

He shrugged. "A rare, very rare, false positive. Anita, you're outside normal parameters on every other test we've run, why should we be surprised if a home pregnancy test gets a little confused with your internal chemistry?"

I stared up at him, not willing to believe it yet. "You're sure. I'm not pregnant."

He shook his head. He put the wand back on my stomach. He made a slow circle of a surprisingly small area. "We'd see it here. It would be tiny, but we would see it, if it were there to see. It's not."

"Then how did I come back positive for Mowgli and Vlad's syndrome?"

"I don't know for certain, but I would guess that the same enzymes the test looks for would come back positive if you yourself were a lycanthrope. It's designed to test human mothers, not mothers who are already lycanthropes."

"What about the Vlad's syndrome?" This from the female intern.

North frowned at her. "We'll discuss the case when the patient has had her questions answered, Dr. Nichols."

She looked suitably chagrined. "I'm sorry, Dr. North."

"No, she's got a point," I said, "what about the Vlad's syndrome?"

He touched my chin, moved my head so Requiem's bite marks showed. "Do you donate blood on a regular basis?"

"Yes," I said.

"We're testing for enzymes in the blood at this stage, Anita. I've never read a study on what regular blood donation does to blood test results. We know it can cause anemia, but beyond that, I don't think anyone's really studied it."

"May I ask a question, please?" It was the female intern, Nichols.

North gave her a cold look. "It depends on the question, doctor." He said the *doctor* part like it was an insult. I was seeing a whole new side of my doctor.

"It's not about the pregnancy, but about the bite."

"You can ask." He made it sound like he wouldn't if he were her, but Nichols was made of sterner stuff, and didn't back down, though she looked nervous bordering on scared.

"There's a lot of bruising around the bite. I thought it was just two neat puncture marks."

I looked at her. "You've only seen bite marks in the morgue, right?" I made it a question.

She nodded. "I took a preternatural forensics course."

"What are you doing in obstetrics?" I asked.

"Nichols is going to be one of the first doctors we'll graduate with a specialty in preternatural obstetrics."

I frowned at them both. "I'd think that would be a very limited specialty."

"Growing every year," North said.

I answered her question. "A vampire bite is like any other wound; if death results from the bite, then you don't get the same bruising. It can leave just two neat puncture wounds, because once the fangs go in, the blood flows easily from the anticoagulant in their saliva. It's drinking, not really eating. Some of the older vamps pride themselves on being able to leave no marks but the two puncture marks. Younger vamps will leave more impressions of teeth, but it's rare for them to break the skin, except with the fangs. The few times I've had vamps leave bite marks that involve more than the fangs, they were going for pain, not just feeding. They wanted it to hurt."

"We saw one body that they thought a vampire and a wereanimal had attacked, because they got impressions of fangs, but the collarbone and neck area were savaged."

I shook my head, and now that North had brought the wound to my attention, it ached a little. Requiem hadn't been a gentleman about this bite. In the heat of his need, he'd done more than just insert fangs.

"I don't know the case, but it could have been just a vampire."

She shook her head. "It was a lot of damage."

I held out my right arm with its mound of bite marks at the bend. "Vampire," I said. I pulled down the neck of my T-shirt, stretching the neck out a little, so I could show her the scars on my collarbone. "Different vampire. He broke my collarbone, and worried at the wound like a terrier with a rat."

She paled a little, but said, "I would love to contact the forensics program and suggest you come and lecture. I think just seeing your scars and talking to you in more detail might help coroners and medical examiners across the country in correctly attributing the damage on some of the victims." She started to reach out, then stopped herself.

I said, "You can touch the scars, if you want."

She glanced at North; he gave a small nod. She touched the collarbone scar, very tentatively, as if it were more intimate than it should have been. At the bend of my arm, she trailed her fingers over those scars like she was memorizing them. She trailed down to the claw marks lower on the arm. "Lycanthrope?"

"Shapeshifted witch, actually."

Her eyes got wide. "A real shapeshifted witch, with an animal skin object, not a lycanthrope?" She was excited about it, and I was impressed that she knew the difference; most people didn't.

"Yeah."

She finally touched the cross-shaped burn scar, a little crooked now because of the claw marks. "This should mean you're a vampire, but you aren't."

Nice that someone was sure. Out loud, I said, "Some vampire's flunkies amused themselves by branding me while we waited for their master to wake for the night."

She gave me wide eyes. "I would love to talk to you at greater length. Thank you so much for answering my questions at a time like this."

"I fall into lecture mode pretty easy," I said. "I'm used to being the resident expert on the preternatural."

"Thank you," she said, and sounded like she meant it.

I finally turned back to North. I searched his face. "I'm not pregnant, you promise, your fucking word of honor, that I'm not pregnant?"

He smiled at me. "I swear, my hand to God, that there is nothing inside you but you. You are not pregnant."

I'd needed Nichols's distraction to give my mind time to process. I'd needed time to let it sink in. I turned to Micah and Richard. I looked from one to the other of them.

The other intern was using a towel to wipe the goop off my tummy. I let him do it. I stared up at two of the men in my life, and said, as if they hadn't heard, "I'm not pregnant."

"We heard," Micah said, smiling.

"Well, say something," I said.

Richard said, "What do you want us to say?"

"Are you disappointed? Happy? Relieved?"

"We're waiting for you to tell us what reaction won't piss you off," Micah said.

For some reason that made me laugh, and the laughter turned to crying, though I had no idea why. I curled on my side and wept, while they tried to hold me. Dr. North and the interns left us to it. Left me to cry away the stress and fear, and underneath that, a tiny, tiny piece of regret.

36

THAT MICROSCOPIC BIT of regret gave way to a planet-sized wave of relief. By the time we all left the hospital, I wanted to skip and shout to strangers that I wasn't pregnant. I didn't do it, but I was as close to giddy as I get; giddy with relief. It was like being on a happy drunk. It was so bad that Micah suggested he drive us back to the Circus. Two miracles occurred; I let him do it, and Richard didn't argue that he should drive. In fact, Richard was positively quiet. He slid into the backseat without a word, a look on his face like he was thinking very serious thoughts. I left him to it, because I wasn't thinking anything sad.

Claudia and Lisandro shoved themselves into the seat beside him. The three of them had such wide shoulders that I always wondered if they'd all fit, but they did. Noel got in the very back. Travis rode with Graham and Ixion in the second car.

I started to use the cell phone to tell Jean-Claude, then realized I didn't need the phone, not for this. I opened the marks, just a little, until I could feel him down the cool line of power.

"What are you doing, Anita?" Richard asked.

"Telling Jean-Claude the good news."

"Use a phone, please, with me this close in the car."

I looked back at him. His skin was running with goosebumps from what little I'd just done. I thought about ignoring him, but that seemed cruel, and I didn't want to be cruel. But I didn't have a chance to decide; Jean-Claude whispered through my head, *"Ma petite . . ."*

Richard closed his eyes, as if it hurt him, but I knew that look. It wasn't that it hurt. It was the opposite, it felt good. He didn't like that it felt good.

I said out loud, "I'm here."

He whispered through my head, "You do not need to say it. I can read it off the tip of your mind, so loudly do you think it. You are not pregnant."

I fought the urge to bounce in my seat, but managed to say, "Yes, yes."

I felt him smile. "I am very happy that you are so happy about it. You feel light, as if you could fly."

It was how I felt, so I just agreed with him.

Richard's thread of warmth trailed through my mind. But he spoke out loud, to both me and Jean-Claude, "Will you please stop this while I'm trapped in the car with it?"

Jean-Claude's voice seemed to grow, so that it filled both of us. "We will talk later about these glad tidings." Then he was gone.

I turned in the seat so I could see Richard's face. "Why did that bother you?"

"I don't want him crawling in my head right now."

Noel's voice came from the back. "I can't study if power is crawling all over my skin, sorry."

I looked at Claudia. "Did you feel it, too?"

She fought it, then finally shivered. "I can usually tell when you are using the triumvirate, but it does seem more powerful today." She tried to rub her hands on her arms, but with the three of them squished in the seat there really wasn't room to finish the movement. But she made her point.

"Okay," I said, and turned to face front.

Micah offered his hand over the middle of the seat, and I took it. His hand was warm, but not too warm, in mine. He was trying not to up the power level in the car. I'd had small versions of the *ardeur* rise while I was driving—not good, not good at all.

I held his hand, and tried not to have my delirious relief bring my power up, and cause his beast to rise for me. Our beasts could flow in and out of each other, but that would be bad right now, so I tried to hold on to my shields, and not let happiness break them down. I knew that sorrow, and anger, could cause my concentration to break, but I'd never realized that happiness could do it, too.

I controlled my happiness all the way to the Circus. The long, stone stairs flew by under my feet. Jean-Claude met me in the living room, and I bounced into his arms, wrapping my arms and legs around him. I kissed him long and deep, and only when we came up for air did I realize that we had company.

Augustine sat on the love seat draped in a black silk shawl that left the tops of his bare shoulders like pale islands peeking out. His yellow curls were in disarray, as if all he'd done was run his fingers through them. He was wearing the bottoms of black silk pajamas that were too long for him. It seemed wrong to call such a muscular man winsome, but that was the word that came to mind. I looked at him, and I felt something similar to what I'd felt when I looked at Jean-Claude. It didn't have the depth and richness that my feelings for Jean-Claude, or Micah, or even Richard had, but it was that first burst of love when lust has worn away a little, and you realize that you still like someone. That it wasn't just lust, but something deeper. I stood there, staring at Auggie, and thought that it sounded like a good idea to wake up some morning beside him when he looked all sleep tousled and winsome. I was in love with him. I should have been terrified, or angry, but I wasn't. It wasn't vampire powers that made me stay calm about it. Maybe we could fix this, the way we'd fixed Requiem's attraction to me. There were options. We could work around it. I wasn't pregnant; we could work around anything else.

"*Ma petite.*"

I turned back to look at Jean-Claude. I hadn't even noticed the brush of the black satin shirt underneath my hands. The shirt was untucked over black jeans. He had very few jeans. He usually only wore them if he suspected he'd be ruining the clothes, or he was trying to portray himself as accessible in some media event. His feet were bare, the flesh only a little less white than the carpet.

"*Ma petite,*" he said again, and this time the nickname made me look back to his face. His hair was a careful fall of curls—his version of casual. "How do you feel when you look upon Augustine?"

I started to look back at the other vampire, but Jean-Claude caught my arm, turned me to look at him. "Answer before you look back, *ma petite.*"

"I think it sounds like a really good idea to have him wake up beside me all tousled and half naked."

"Is it merely lust?"

I shook my head. "No, no, it's the beginning of the real deal. It's love, not just lust."

"You do not sound upset."

I smiled at him. "I'm not pregnant, we can work around everything else. I mean, isn't this similar to what I did to Requiem with the *ardeur*? If I can free him, then shouldn't a Master of the City be able to free me?"

"Jean-Claude, how do you feel about Augustine?" This from Richard, who had come to stand just behind us.

"I see him as lovely, but strangely, I am not in love with him. He is not in love with me. I had hoped that meant the worst, or best, had not happened, but . . ." He looked beyond us to Augustine.

I looked with him. I noticed that from this distance Auggie's charcoal-gray eyes looked almost black.

"Do you need to ask how do I feel about your human servant?" he asked. Jean-Claude nodded.

"It is all I can do to stay here on this seat. I want to touch her, to hold her. If my heart could beat, it would break."

"Why should your heart break?" I asked, and was surprised at how ordinary I sounded, even felt.

"Because you belong to another, and I love you."

I took a step forward, and Jean-Claude's fingers began to let me go. Richard grabbed my other arm. "No, Anita, don't go to him."

"Why not?" I asked, looking up into those brown eyes.

He started to say several things, but finally said the only thing that was really true. "Because I don't want you to."

That stopped me more surely than any anger could have. I was left staring up at him, watching the pain on his face, and not knowing what to do about it. "Why is sharing me with Auggie different than sharing me with all the rest?"

"You don't love the rest."

I started to smile, stopped, then said, "Who don't I love?"

He let me go then, as if my skin had suddenly gotten hot. "I'll go get changed for the ballet." He actually started for the far hallway.

"It is a little early to change, *mon ami*."

Richard shook his head. "I can't watch this, I just can't."

"What do you think is going to happen, Richard?" I asked.

He answered without turning around. "You're going to have sex with him again. Maybe you and Jean-Claude." He shook his head again. "It was bad enough to feel some of it, I don't want to watch."

"I'm in love with him, Richard, that doesn't mean we're going to fuck. You, of all people, should know that just because someone has my heart doesn't mean they have my body."

That stopped him, just at the far doorway. He turned around, looked at me. "You don't feel compelled to fuck him?"

I shook my head.

"I am losing my touch," Auggie said.

It made me turn and waste a smile on him. My smile made him smile, that goofy smile that you only do when you're truly gone on someone. "You haven't lost anything, and you know it."

He made a gesture that was half bow, and half shrug. He managed to look modest, but not like he really meant it. "If I have lost nothing, and you do not fear what we feel for each other, then come to me, Anita."

"You come to me," I said.

He grinned at me, wide enough to flash fangs, which was rare for a vampire his age. He stood up, the shawl still covering most of him.

"Master, do not go to her." Octavius, his human servant, came around the side of the love seat. The werelion Pierce came with him. I think they meant to outflank him and keep him from touching me. He stood in front of Auggie, blocking our view of each other. "You are the Master of the City of Chicago, you go to no woman. They come to you."

Auggie moved Octavius to one side, gently but firmly. "I don't think this one will." He looked at me, half-smiling. "Will you come to me?"

"Why should I?"

He grinned again. "I don't know if it's my own power backfiring, but I see what you saw in her, Jean-Claude. An ambitious target for love, and I would think harmful to the ego, but worth the effort, oh, yes, worth the effort." He pushed past his men, flinging the shawl into the air, so that he was suddenly nude from the waist up. The sight of him like that pushed my pulse up into my throat. I remembered what it was like to be held down by that body, what it was like to hold all that muscled strength in my arms. I took a step forward, and I think we would have met in the middle of the room, but I suddenly smelled sun-warmed grass, felt heat, lion. I smelled lion.

I turned around to look for Noel and Travis. They were standing near the far door, as if they weren't sure what to do. I couldn't blame them for that, but it wasn't them I was sensing.

I turned the other way, toward the far hallway, where Richard was still standing. But it wasn't Richard who was making my skin creep with power. Haven stalked down the hallway, human again, nude, and beautiful. In truth he was a little thin for my tastes, but it wasn't truly the washboard abs, or the slender hips, the long graceful legs, or even the swelling of promise between those legs, but his beauty as a whole that drew me. If he'd been unattractive, would I have felt the same about him walking toward me? Would I have been able to resist walking toward him, if he hadn't looked so damn cute?

My view was suddenly blocked by Travis and Noel. Of all the men in the room that might interfere, they hadn't been on my list. Travis's soft face was utterly serious as he said, "Our Rex said that you weren't supposed to touch him again before you'd fed on one of us."

I could feel Haven behind them, moving closer. "Move, Travis," I said.

He shook his head. Noel's eyes were wide behind his glasses, but he added, "Joseph wants you to feed the *ardeur*, or give us your lion, before you touch him again."

I knew he was close before Haven loomed over the two shorter men. I guess he loomed over me, too, but he wasn't going to move me out of his way.

His blue eyes stared down at me with a look that was almost frantic. I felt it too, an almost overwhelming need to touch him. What was wrong with me? My hand started to lift up, to try to move between Noel and Travis, so

I could touch Haven's bare chest. I wanted, needed, to touch his skin. The look on his face said he felt the same. What the hell was happening now?

Noel and Travis moved closer together and stepped forward at the same time, bumping me, forcing me back a few inches. Farther away from the man at their backs.

I didn't want to be farther away, and neither did Haven. He tried to grab them by the collars, but they must have felt it coming, because they threw themselves forward, on top of me, bringing us all to the ground.

"Get off me," I said.

But I didn't have to worry; Haven reached down and grabbed Travis. Suddenly, Travis wasn't on top of me anymore. He was airborne, and hit the wall with a sharp, brittle sound, and I knew a bone had broken somewhere in his body. That fixed it, whatever the hell was wrong; I could think again.

Haven reached down for Noel, and I wrapped my arms and legs around him, tight, so if the big werelion threw him, he'd have to throw us both. It was the only thing I could think of in a split second.

He grabbed a handful of Noel's curls, jerked his neck back at a horrible angle.

I yelled, "Let him go!"

Haven snarled at me, and came to one knee beside us. "I am your lion, can't you feel it?"

I could, but that didn't give him the right to break Noel's neck, which was what was going to happen if he didn't stop pulling his head back. I couldn't draw my gun; it was trapped under Noel's body. If I let go of him, I was afraid of what Haven would do to him.

I slid one hand through Noel's hair, until I touched Haven's hand. The moment we touched, energy shot through my body as if I'd touched a live wire. So much energy that I cried out in pain. Noel echoed me, getting the backlash of it. Haven threw his head back and roared, a coughing, harsh sound out of his human throat.

He looked down at me with eyes that had gone lion gold. "Oh, God, yes, yes!"

I was shaking my head. I whispered, "No, no."

Auggie tried ordering Haven away from us, but it didn't do a damn thing. Octavius was a pain in the ass, but he'd been right about one thing: Haven didn't belong to Auggie anymore. He might not be mine completely, but he was no longer Auggie's.

Richard loomed up over us. "You want him moved?" His voice was low and careful, his face full of a dark eagerness. I knew that look; it was my look, the look when you want a fight. Want to hurt something, because it's simple, and you can stop thinking.

I said, "Yes." I said yes, with Haven's energy running through my body like a warm, hurtful blanket.

Richard said, "Thank you." I wasn't sure what he was thanking me for, but he knelt down beside us. He was on one knee, facing Haven. He wrapped his hand around the other man's wrist, where it was trying to pull Noel's head backward. The pressure eased on Noel's hair, and his head began to lower. Haven's hand shook with the effort to pull Noel's head backward, but Richard pushed his hand down. It was a struggle, and slow, but it was like an arm-wrestling match when one person is simply the stronger of the two. The match wasn't over, but one arm against one arm, Richard was the stronger man. He just was.

But Haven was one thing that Richard was not, a professional thug. He did two things simultaneously. He released Noel's hair, and he tried to hit Richard with his other hand. That fist going over us was a blink of the eye, too fast to see, more just an awareness of air moving, and the afterimage. Richard saw it, because when the fist tried to land on his face, he wasn't there to take the blow. He rolled backward, and pulled Haven with him, with one hand on the other man's wrist. Haven's own momentum made him fall forward, and Richard did a move that I'd showed him ages ago. His sport was karate, mine was judo. But if it had been me trying for the tomenage throw, I'd have failed. Because Haven was half-collapsed on Richard's legs, not high enough above the ground, unless you had the strength to plant your feet in the man's stomach and lift with your legs. I would have just ended with Haven on top of me, not an improvement in a fight, but Richard pushed him skyward and was strong enough to keep the momentum going.

Haven flew across the room and hit the fireplace. Richard had time to stand before the other man got to his knees, then charged him. The fight was on.

37

THE FIGHT ROLLED over the couch, and vanished from sight for a minute.

Noel shivered on top of me, and it wasn't pleasure. "Are you hurt?" I asked.

His voice was breathy from pain or fear. I didn't know him well enough to guess which. "Anita, you're about to pick an animal to call."

I patted the top of his curls, gently. "You're not thinking clearly, Noel." I started to try to sit up, but he wrapped himself around me. Not pinning me, but making it so sitting up would be an effort.

Richard was the one who staggered back from the couch, blood spattering his face. Haven got to his feet like he was on springs, and they squared off. Both of them went down into fighting stances that said that Haven knew some kind of martial art, too. Not good.

"Let me up, Noel."

He raised his face, so I could see how frightened his eyes were behind his glasses. "You are about to have another animal to call."

"Nathaniel is my animal to call."

"He's your animal for Damian and you, but Richard is your animal with Jean-Claude."

Richard and Haven were circling in the bare area just in front of the far hallway. They feinted with legs and hands, but they weren't fighting. They were getting the measure of each other. Once they had it, the fight would get serious. I didn't want that.

Noel gripped my arms, turned my attention back to him. "Joseph thinks that something about the vampire marks is giving you an animal to call to match each of your beasts."

"That's not possible."

"Everything you do is impossible, Anita. My Rex thinks it is possible. He hopes that if you feed from more than one lion, your power won't bond to any one person."

Travis collapsed to his knees beside us, blocking my view of the growing fight. He was cradling his arm tight against his chest. The side of his head was bleeding into his brown-gold curls. "But if you do have to bond to a lion, Joseph would prefer that the strongest preternatural power in his territory not bond itself to a lion who would try to take over his pride."

It seemed stupid having this conversation flat on my back with a nearly perfect stranger on top of me, but I couldn't figure out how to sit up without getting rough with Noel, and Haven had been rough enough. "Why did Joseph send you to me?"

Travis shrugged, and winced, his shoulders hunching around his arm. "Our first task is to keep you from bonding with blue-boy over there. Whatever it takes, to stop that from happening."

I looked at them both. "You're kids. You don't want to be bound to my life, to me, forever. You don't want that, you can't want that."

"I'm only five years younger than you," Travis said. "Hell, I'm two years older than Nathaniel."

"But Nathaniel needed me. You got drafted."

Noel pushed himself up on his arms, which meant I was able to get to my gun, not that it would help, but it was still a thought. His lower body was pressed a little closer to my lower body, but for once it wasn't erotic. It wasn't anything. "Our lion group, our pride, works, Anita, it's our home. I felt blue-boy's power, just walking down a hallway. You can feel it now, coming off him in waves." Noel licked his lips. "Joseph is powerful, but I'm not a hundred percent certain he's more powerful than what's behind us."

"Let me sit up, Noel."

Noel glanced at Travis, and the other man gave a small nod, then hunched over his arm again. Noel moved back so I could sit up, but he stayed kneeling between my knees, I think so he was close enough to grab me if I tried to go to Haven, again.

Richard and Haven were fighting now. Fighting with a capital F, if you're not planning to kill each other. It was a kind of fighting that I would never be able to do. Pounding the shit out of each other, and being able to take the damage. It was guy fighting, for the sake of a point, yes. I'd asked for help to move Haven and protect the other men. Haven's fist got past Richard's arms, and Richard staggered back two steps, but hunched his body, so that the blows Haven tried to rain on him hit only shoulders and arms. Richard, on the other hand, landed two solid body blows that doubled Haven over. Richard followed with a fist to his chin, and only Haven throwing himself backward kept the next blow from hitting. Richard didn't give him time to recover. He came at him with a flurry of blinding kicks that put the other man into a defensive crouch against the far wall. Richard was winning. I realized in that moment that I hadn't thought he would.

Noel touched my face, turned my gaze back to his scared face. "Anita, please don't touch him, not until you've at least tried one of us."

I checked Richard's progress one more time. Haven was against the wall, simply trying to keep the kicks from hitting him, not even trying to fight back now.

I looked at Travis and his wounds. Noel's eyes so scared. The lions' pride worked; they were one of the few wereanimal groups in town that let their people lead nearly ordinary lives. No power struggles, no hiring bodyguards. Joseph's people were people first, animals second. If Haven stayed in town, hooked up to the power that I had through Jean-Claude's marks, would the lions' world go up in flames?

"You don't think Joseph would win the fight?" I asked.

"He is not the fighter that your Ulfric is," Travis said. Travis said it like it was just true, and no big deal. That was the biggest difference between wolf and lion culture; all the big cat shapeshifters seemed to be less about combat, and more about what was best for the group. The wolf culture was much more about strong is right, weak is just dead. Someone had suggested that it was because the werewolf culture passed through the Vikings' culture, more than any other shapeshifter society. Maybe. Real wolves certainly weren't more vicious than lions, or leopards.

"Wait a minute," I said. "Joseph won his fight with Haven."

"Joseph got lucky," Travis said. He motioned at the fight. "He got real lucky."

Richard had the other man in a defensive ball against the wall. Haven had given up fighting back, and was just trying to keep the damage down. Richard did a very Richard thing. He backed up. The fight was over, as far as he was concerned. Since he wasn't going to kill Haven, the fight should have been over. But Haven's day job was mob enforcer; it's a different mentality.

Richard's voice sounded tired, but not strained, "Stay down."

Haven got to his knees, shaking his head. "I can't."

"You can't win," Richard said.

"Doesn't matter," Haven said, "still have to get up."

"Stay down," Richard said.

"No," Haven said, and he used the wall to push to his feet. He fell back to his knees, one hand holding him swaying against the wall.

I said, "Stay down, Haven."

"Can't," was all he said, and he gathered himself for a rush. He came up off the floor in a blur of speed, still dangerous, for all the damage he'd taken. Richard sidestepped him, let his own momentum send him crashing to the floor.

"This fight is over," Richard said, and he made the mistake. He offered Haven a hand up.

I had time to yell, "No!" I wasn't even sure who I was yelling it at.

Haven kicked out with everything he had left; he tried to dislocate Richard's knee. Richard had time to avoid some of it, but not all of it. His knee collapsed and he went down.

My gun was out and pointed. I got to my feet. If Haven had pushed the attack I'd have shot him, but he didn't. He lay back on the floor as if that last kick had taken all the fight out of him. "The fight is over," I said, just in case.

"Yeah," Haven said, and his voice held pain, "now, it is."

I stared down the barrel of the gun at him, and he didn't even seem to see the gun. He certainly didn't react to it. Most people don't like having guns pointed at them; if he didn't like it, it didn't show. "I'm thinking you need to go back to Chicago."

"Why? Because I hurt your boyfriend?"

"No, because you hurt two people who couldn't fight back. And, the fight was over; you gained nothing from that last kick."

"He's hurt, I gained that."

I shook my head. "That's not how we play here."

He lay on his back, covered in blood, and too tired, or too hurt, to sit up. He was still breathing hard. "Tell me the rules here, and I'll follow them. Ask Augustine—I follow the rules, once you make 'em clear to me."

I called out, without looking away from Haven. "Is that true, Auggie? Does he follow the rules, once he knows them?"

"It's true, but you have to make damn sure that he knows the rules, and the consequences if he breaks them."

That one statement let me know that I should pack his ass home to Chicago, but I couldn't do it. Standing there while he bled, knowing what he'd just done to Richard and the two young werelions, knowing all that, I still wanted to drop down and spill my body over his. Fuck.

I stilled my breath, and sighted the gun in the middle of that face. The eyes had bled back to blue; they looked almost artificial with the blood all around them. I swallowed hard, and let my body go very still. My voice was soft, but strangely carried through the room, as if everyone had gone quiet. "The rules are, you don't harm the weak. I've got no use for bullies. If you get into another fight like tonight, when you know you've lost, you've lost. You don't try for one last bit of damage. That's street fighting, and that's not what we do here."

"You won't shoot me," he said, and he sounded sure of that.

I felt myself smile, and knew it was the smile that creeped me out when I saw it in a mirror. It was a cruel smile, a smile that said *Not only would I kill you, but I'd enjoy it.*

His eyes went a little uncertain at that smile. Good.

"I will shoot you. I'll kill you, if I have to."

"Do you want to touch me?" he asked, his voice less breathy now.

"Yes," I said, "I want to strip off and roll on top of you like a dog scent-marking." I gave a very small nod. "I feel the call of your power, Haven."

"If you kill me that all goes away."

"Then it goes away. I don't compromise my rules, Haven, not for lust, or power, or love." I was going to have to either shoot him soon, or lower the gun. Important safety tip: if you're going to do the big threatening speech, be in a comfortable shooting stance when you do it. My hands hadn't started to waver, but they would soon. "Ask the men in my life, I don't compromise."

I watched him think about it. Think about coming off the floor and trying me. "Don't, Haven."

"Don't what?" he asked, all innocent, but innocent just didn't work on him.

"Don't try me right now. If you do, I'll pull the trigger."

"Why? I won't hurt you. I'll just try to take the gun away."

"I'll shoot you, because this is our moment of understanding. You will either live by my rules, or you will die by them."

"I don't believe you," he said.

I let all the air out of my body, and the two-handed shooting stance didn't seem hard to maintain at all. I was suddenly focused, and ready. I felt myself sinking away into that white, staticky place, where I killed. I don't know what my eyes look like when I'm like this, but whatever was on my face, Haven saw it. I watched his face change, and stop being sure of itself. Tension ran out of his body, his muscles, and he lay quiet on the floor, and very still, as if he were a little afraid to move suddenly. Good.

"It's my way, or no way," I said, and the words were squeezed out, because I'd let my air go, so I could shoot him.

He licked his lips, and spoke softly, carefully, being sure to move nothing but his mouth. "Your way."

"If I put this gun away, are you going to try to hurt me?"

"No," he said.

"Why not?" I asked, still staring at him down the barrel of the gun.

"You'll kill me."

"You sure of that?"

Some look passed through his eyes—pain, fear, something close to all of it. "I know that look, the one on your face. I know it, because I have one just like it. You will kill me, and I don't want to kill you. I can't win, so I won't play."

I stared at him a heartbeat longer. I thought about pulling the trigger. One, because I was ready to; two, because I was almost certain he was going to be trouble. But in the end I lowered the gun, and backed away until I was out of reach of him. I backed away, and made certain I didn't give him my back. I didn't offer him a hand up, and neither did anyone else.

38

I WENT TO one knee beside Richard, my gun not pointed at Haven anymore, but still out. We just weren't that far away from the fallen werelion. To say I didn't trust him was an understatement. The awful thing was, even knowing that he was bad news, knowing that he'd tried to cripple Richard just because he wanted him to hurt, knowing all that, part of me still wanted to touch him. Part of me wanted to go over and start licking the blood from his wounds. But the image in my head of me doing it wasn't of me, not human me. The image in my head was of a huge golden lioness licking his wounds. I shook my head hard to clear the image.

I glanced at Richard. He was huddled over his leg, hands over his knee, but not touching it, as if that had hurt. Not good. I put my gaze back to Haven. I didn't want him getting up without my knowing it. If I shot him, I didn't want it to be because he'd startled me, and years of training with a gun took over. No, if I shot him, I wanted it to be on purpose.

"How bad is it?" I asked.

He spoke through gritted teeth. "It's not dislocated, but it hurts."

I called, "Claudia."

She came to stand over us. "We need a doctor." I thought of Travis's arm. "Maybe more than one."

"Dr. Lillian is on her way." Doc Lillian was a wererat, and the local shapeshifters' most popular doctor for emergencies we didn't want anyone else to know about.

"Good." I fought the urge to look at her, and kept my gaze on Haven. He didn't seem to want to do anything but lie there and bleed, but I wanted to be sure of him. *Sure* meant looking at him. "Could you guys earn your pay, and actually secure him?" I didn't try to keep the irritation out of my voice.

"Yes, ma'am," she said. She motioned and Lisandro, Ixion, and Graham came up to stand around the fallen werelion. Haven didn't seem to notice. Had he passed out? Not my most immediate problem. I got to holster my gun without firing it, a rarity for me. I touched Richard's face. "The doc's on the way."

He just nodded, face pinched and pale with pain.

I looked up at Claudia. "Where the hell were you guys while Haven was abusing Travis and Noel?"

"If I say 'right over there,' will you get pissed?"

I stood up. "Yes."

She gave me empty cop face, though I knew she'd never been a cop. "This was a dominance challenge. We are not allowed to interfere in challenges of other animal groups."

"This wasn't a challgene for leadership of anything," I said.

Claudia gave me a look that said, clearly, I'd missed something. Whatever showed on my face finally let her know that I didn't know what the hell she was hinting at.

She sighed. "Sometimes I forget that you miss the obvious."

"What did I miss?" I asked.

"Your Ulfric has established himself as dominant to this guy." She smiled down at Richard. "Truthfully, I didn't think the Ulfric had it in him." There was a grudging compliment in her voice. "You needed for someone to establish dominance over him, if you planned to keep him." She jerked a thumb in Haven's direction. "Guys like this have to be forced to obey the hierarchy."

"You mean the hierarchy of the werelions?"

She shook her head. "Anita, if you add this guy to your men, then someone had to beat the shit out of him, at least once, so he'd know who was boss."

"I'm boss," I said.

She smiled at me. "I like you, Anita. I respect you. I take orders from you. But a guy like Haven is going to see you as a girl, a piece of ass. Unless you can personally beat him to a pulp, he's not going to behave for you. He'll tell you to your face what you want to hear, but you've got Nathaniel, Micah, Damian. I mean you have a lot of non-coms around you. You don't want to bring home a lion to play with your kittens unless you have a big dog to balance it out."

I frowned at her. "Are you saying that Richard is my big dog?"

"Maybe it's a bad example, but it's the best I've got."

"You don't think he would respect me—Haven, I mean?"

She shook her head. "He's got trouble written all over him, Anita."

"You think I should throw him back?"

Her dark eyes widened, surprised. "Does my opinion count?"

"I trust your judgment, and you're the only girl here."

"Why do you need a girl opinion?" she asked.

"Because I'm tired of all the damn testosterone."

She grinned at me. "I'm not sure I'll say anything that the men won't say on this one, Anita. Estrogen doesn't make me stupid, and you'd have to be stupid to want to keep Cookie Monster over there. I mean he could be a bodyguard, if we made the rules clear, but to take home as a lover, no way."

I nodded. "I agree."

"Then why ask?"

I hugged myself. "Because, knowing all of it, I still want to touch him."

She shrugged all that muscled upper body. "Then you're fucked."

Richard's voice came strained. "You can't want to keep him, not now, not after this."

I knelt beside him. He grabbed my hand, so hard and sudden it startled me. "I don't want to keep him."

I watched him try to think past the pain. "But," he said.

"But it's not always about what I want."

His hand convulsed around mine, until I had to fight not to cry out. "Shift, Richard, you can heal this if you shift."

He shook his head. "If I shift I'll have to spend at least four hours in animal form. Can't go to the ballet as a wolf."

"You're not going to enjoy the evening like this."

His grip on my hand loosened, just holding me for a moment. He stared into my face like he was trying to memorize it. "Do you want me not to go?"

I frowned at him. "Why would you ask that? Of course, I want you to go."

He almost smiled, but winced instead. "You've got a lot of men to juggle, maybe one less would make tonight easier."

I drew his hand against my breasts, and touched his face. "You didn't just assume I needed help to handle Haven. You asked me first, and waited for me to answer. I know you wanted to wade in and pull him off us. Thank you for asking, for waiting."

He grimaced, and tried to make it a smile. "I'm glad you're happy about it, but my waiting cost Travis a broken arm. Joseph's not going to want us to borrow his lions, if we keep breaking them."

That made me smile. "Good point, but the lioness in me is looking for someone strong." I looked at the wall, because I could feel that beast moving around inside me, as if it were pacing the cage of my body. I did not want another round of almost-shifting. I raised Richard's hand to my face. I sniffed it, and it didn't help. Yes, it was Richard, but he'd touched Haven, and the smell of lion was on his skin, along with wolf. The prickling warmth started to swell inside me.

I let go of his hand, and stood up.

"What's wrong?" Claudia asked.

"Her beast is trying to rise again," Richard said from the floor.

I nodded, and stepped farther away from Richard, and kept moving. I wanted distance between me and Haven. This didn't feel like the way I'd bonded to Nathaniel. This instant attraction to Haven felt like . . . I turned and found Micah standing there, closer than I'd realized. He hadn't wanted to interfere with me and Richard. I could feel my eyes widening. I reached out to him, and the wolf and lion quieted. Leopard stirred, and the movement almost doubled me over. Micah caught me, helped me stand up straight. But the leopard liked him too much, and I had to push him away from me. I stumbled, and Jean-Claude was there to catch me. I clung to him, burying my face against his chest, drawing in the scent of clean silk and him. I actually ripped his shirt open, so I could put my face directly against his skin. I drew in the sweet, clean, scent of him, as if he were air, and I'd been suffocating. His cologne was sweet, and always smelled as expensive as it was, but it was the scent of his skin underneath it, mixing with the cologne, that I needed. It helped clear my head, helped me ease the beasts back to sleep.

I rubbed my face along the smooth outline of his cross-shaped burn scar. Jean-Claude didn't see the scar as an imperfection, and neither did I. It was something extra to play with when I kissed his chest.

His arms held me tight, and he whispered, "I felt your fear flare to life, *ma petite*. What has happened?"

I spoke with my face still buried against his chest. "I'm trying not to make Haven my animal to call."

Jean-Claude stroked my hair, trying to soothe me, like a child who's woken from a bad dream, but this bad dream wasn't going to end with me waking up. It wasn't going to be all right.

"You are drawn to Haven, and he to you, *ma petite*. You have broken his link to Augustine."

I nodded my forehead against his chest. "Yeah, but he's not Auggie's animal to call, he's just one of his lions."

I felt Jean-Claude look behind him.

"That's right," and that was Auggie. He'd come to stand near us. "He's bound to me, but not as an animal to call."

I nodded again, my face still buried against Jean-Claude. I didn't want to see Auggie's naked chest. I didn't want to be distracted by yet another metaphysical problem; one at a time was plenty. "What did I do with the leopards before I got an animal to call, Jean-Claude?"

"I do not understand, *ma petite*, what . . ." Then he went very still. He was still holding me. I was still clinging to him, breathing in the scent of his skin, but his heart had stopped beating, his breathing stilled. He was doing that *be very still* that the old vampires could do, but this time I was pressed against him while he did it. I'd never been this close to him when he went this still. Until it stopped, I hadn't even been aware his heart was beating. It made me look up at him. Made me meet that beautiful, flawless face, and see it look unreal, masklike, as he stared, not at me, but behind me.

I turned and looked where he was looking. Micah stood there, staring at us. The look on his face was enough; he'd had the same awful thought I'd had.

I licked my lips and whispered, "Do the lions have a name for their queen?"

He said it out loud. "I felt it, when you saw him coming down the hallway. He won't be your animal to call. He'll be Rex to your Regina."

39

RICHARD ENDED UP back in Jason's room. Dr. Lillian pumped him full of painkillers, so he'd sleep and heal. I had to promise him guards I trusted at his door to make sure none of our "guests" visited him while he was drugged and helpless. Seemed like a reasonable request to me. In fact it was so practical that it gave me hope that he was finally beginning to realize that life wasn't a Boy Scout jamboree.

Lillian said if Richard had been human, he'd have been on his way to the emergency room, and on crutches for weeks afterward. But he wasn't human and two hours of sleep would heal a lot of the damage. Why not try to heal him with metaphysics? Because Richard had never let me heal him with magic. It was his choice, and I was okay with it. He'd done so much right in the last hour that I'd cut him slack. Acres of slack.

Haven was unconscious in the guest room he'd started the day in, with additional guards. He wouldn't be going anywhere for at least forty-eight hours, so said the doc. Fine with me; out of sight was just dandy for the Cookie Monster and me.

I'd started to get upset again, like pace-the-room upset, but Jean-Claude had touched me, and Auggie had joined him. I ended up on the couch cuddled between them and feeling strangely calm. "You've rolled my mind, haven't you?"

"You have the ability to keep me out, *ma petite*. Merely decide to push me out, and I will be forced to go. I think you need the calm."

I couldn't argue with that. I turned with my head in Jean-Claude's lap, and looked at Auggie, who had my legs across his lap. "But he's helping you."

"A very little bit," Auggie said, and did that face that was supposed to be humble, but never made it.

"You should really stop trying for the humble head dunk thing," I said, "it doesn't work for you."

He gave me wide eyes—innocent, I think he was going for. He didn't pull that off either. "Are you saying I am not humble?" He grinned, spoiling any attempt at innocence. That smile said he was thinking nefarious things—fun things, but nefarious nonetheless.

"You wouldn't know humble if it bit you on the ass."

He laughed, mouth wide, flashing fangs. If you hadn't seen the fangs you'd have said it was a very human laugh. Jean-Claude had once explained to me that vampires learn to control their faces, voices, every reaction, to hide from their masters. Because any strong emotion can be used against you. After a few centuries you could lose the knack of true laughter, of smiling just because you were happy, not because you thought it would get you something. Facial expressions for the very old vamps become more like flirting: something you do on purpose, for a purpose. Auggie just seemed to laugh.

I raised my head so I could look at Jean-Claude's face. I asked, "Is that real, that laugh, or is it part of Auggie's game plan?"

"Ask him, *ma petite*."

I looked at the other vampire. "Well?" I said.

"Well, what?" he asked.

"Is the laugh real, or a performance?"

He shrugged those massive shoulders, sending the black shawl sliding down a little lower. At the rate it was slipping, he'd be naked from the waist up again. I wasn't sure if I wanted the shawl to fall faster, or make him tuck it back over himself. Seeing him nude sounded good, and the wanting of it made me not want it at all. Crazy, I know, but true. I seldom trusted anything that I wanted too badly.

I smelled vanilla, warm vanilla. Nathaniel was coming. I heard bare feet running, and the next moment he was airborne above me. He caught himself with hands and toes on the couch, just before he would have landed on me. He'd done it before, but it always startled me, and made me make that girly *eep* sound. I hated that I even had that sound inside me somewhere. Nathaniel laughed, his face alight with it. I tried to be grumpy about him startling me, but failed. The grumpiness rolled away under the delight of being this close to him, and the soothing touch of vampire.

"Not pregnant," he said.

I shook my head, and laughed, too. Suddenly, I remembered how gloriously relieved I had been. He brought back the rush of joy that I'd had before Haven misbehaved.

Nathaniel let his body fall those few inches, so he pressed his weight against me. He kissed me, and I kissed him back. My hands slid over the muscled heat of his skin, and the silken warmth of his hair, unbound and sliding over us all. His body started to react to the closeness, and the kiss grew.

"If they actually have sex on our laps, do we get to join in?" Auggie asked.

I drew back from the kiss, and Nathaniel stopped, but he didn't move. I had to actually move some of the thick auburn hair to one side so I could see Auggie's face. "No," I said.

"Then I am at a loss as to where to put my hands."

I gazed past Nathaniel's shoulder to realize that the most natural resting place for Auggie's hands was probably Nathaniel's ass, where it peeked from between the fall of his own hair.

Auggie lifted a strand of that hair. "I have not seen hair like this for a century." He rubbed the hair along his cheek. "It brings back memories, though the body would be female." He gazed down at Nathaniel. "It's the longest hair I've ever seen on a man."

I didn't like the way he was looking at Nathaniel, not that we could really blame him. It wasn't Auggie who had jumped naked into our laps. I pushed at Nathaniel's chest. "Move, okay?"

He gave me a look that managed to be both innocent, and not, then he rolled to the floor. Yeah, he'd wanted to surprise me, but he was an exhibitionist, and loved to flirt. It didn't mean he wanted sex, just that he enjoyed the way people reacted to his body. Or at least that's what Micah and I thought. It was entirely possible that Nathaniel didn't know why he did it.

Micah came up behind the couch. "Your leopard didn't try to rise when Nathaniel touched you," he said.

"No, it didn't." I looked at him, and found that Jean-Claude's hair blocked my view. Micah moved so he was standing more between the two vampires, so I didn't have to strain.

"You touched a lot less of me, and it did rise."

"Try again," I said, and held out my hand to him.

He hesitated, as if he were a little afraid of what might happen, but he took my hand. I waited for my beast to rise, but it didn't. It was just Micah's hand in mine. I squeezed his hand, and gave him a smile. Some tension in him eased, as if he'd been holding his breath about something. He still seemed so serious, almost sad. Was he jealous? Was the man who shared me best suddenly jealous? There was no anxiety with the thought, it was just a thought. Jean-Claude's power let it just be a thought, without emotional baggage attached to it. Was this how well-adjusted people reasoned? If so, damn it was peaceful. I wanted to reassure him and take that worry from his eyes. There was no thought to it, no reasoning. I wanted to reassure Micah, so I sat up, and used our clasped hands to draw him downward. We kissed, but he pulled back from it. Those chartreuse eyes still held a shadow of worry. I wanted that shadow gone. I wanted him to know how much he meant to me.

I used both hands to drag him half over the couch back, and give him the kiss he deserved. I licked, kissed, ate, at his mouth, as if the taste of him were a drug, and I needed a fix. He fell into that kiss, and spilled over the couch, on top of me, and into everyone's laps. He rose from the kiss, laughing, the worry erased from his eyes. We ended up laughing together in a big pile. Not just Micah and me, but Nathaniel, and Auggie with his big, fang-flashing laugh. Jean-Claude's laughter spilled over us all, like something thick and sweet that you should be able to lick off your skin. The sensation of it made me catch my breath. Micah shivered above me. Nathaniel's hand grabbed my arm, and Micah's, his fingers convulsing against our skin. Auggie's hand tightened almost painfully on my leg. I couldn't see him past Micah's body, but I could feel his body reacting to that touchable laugh.

It wasn't just Auggie's body that reacted. His power flared from his hand, and the warmth of his lap, through the silk jammies, and my jeans. I felt his body like heat through the cloth. That heat found the *ardeur* curled inside my body. Auggie called it, and like a well-trained dog, it followed his power.

Micah whispered, "Oh, God." I think he would have rolled off and fled for safety, but Nathaniel's arm tightened on us both, and Auggie's other hand pressed into his back. He wasn't trapped, but with the *ardeur*, willpower is so hard to come by that small things can tip the balance.

Jean-Claude's power pulsed to life against me, but it wasn't his *ardeur* that rose. The cool power of the grave spread out from his body like cool, soothing water to quench the heat that Auggie had awakened. Jean-Claude's power spilled through me, over me, and spread. It spread to Micah, so that his eyes lost their panic. Nathaniel's hands began to relax in their desperate hold on our bodies. Auggie's breath came out in a long, shaking sigh.

"That was very bad of you, Augustine," Jean-Claude said in a voice that was thicker than normal with his French accent. Which meant he'd had to work harder at stopping the *ardeur* than that easy flow of power had led us to believe.

Micah half-collapsed on top of me, his head burying against my shoulder, so that I could suddenly see Auggie's grinning face. He was totally unrepentant. "Jean-Claude, can you truly blame me with all this bounty writhing on my lap?" He slapped Micah's ass.

Micah rolled off the couch, and took me with him, because I let him. We ended on the floor close to Nathaniel. Micah and I stood, drawing Nathaniel to his feet. We moved back from the couch, so the three of us faced the vampires, faces no longer friendly. I'd shut both vampires out of my head, because I wasn't sure how to shut Auggie out without shutting Jean-Claude off, too. I just didn't have the finer points of metaphysics down yet.

"I may not blame you, but they will," Jean-Claude said, and he sounded almost satisfied. I got just a flash of why: he was pleased that Auggie was falling into the same traps that once had been his own downfall. Then he shut the link between us, shut it tight, as if he didn't want me to know what else he was thinking. Fine with me; I had my own reasons for not wanting to share.

There had been a second, just a second, when the *ardeur* rising while all four of them were touching me hadn't seemed like a bad idea. Micah, Nathaniel, and Jean-Claude were one thing, but Auggie had rolled me. Yeah, I was in love with him, too, but it was because of vampire wiles. Auggie had trapped me into love, and that should be punished, not rewarded. Richard would probably say that I was pretty good at punishing true love, so love by deceit should carry a higher penalty, shouldn't it?

"I don't know you," Micah said, "and you don't get to touch me."

Auggie spread his hands wide, and made a how-was-I-to-know gesture. "My deepest apologies, but if people keep falling into my lap, I'm allowed to take a little advantage."

"No," I said, "you're not."

He narrowed those charcoal-gray eyes at me. "I love you, Anita. Do you love me?"

I almost said no, but knew he'd smell the lie. I shrugged. "Yeah, thanks to your power, yeah, I do." I shrugged again. "But what has that got to do with anything?"

"Most women who love me don't act this angry. Most women in love are generous to their lovers."

"In sex, I'm generous; everything else, you gotta work for it."

Auggie looked at Jean-Claude. "She tastes of the truth."

Jean-Claude nodded. "*Ma petite* is a demanding lover in every way."

"Usually when a man says a woman is a demanding lover, it's a good thing, but somehow I don't think that's what you mean," Auggie said.

Jean-Claude gave me a smile, that smile that was only for me, and sometimes for Asher. The smile said he loved me, and I had to smile back. I felt my face soften, and the anger fade. I wasn't angry at Jean-Claude. I had finally gotten better at not spreading my anger over everyone. "*Ma petite* and I have labored long together to form the love that you have gained by subterfuge." He turned and looked at Auggie. "I was your friend, but you have used your arts to make me feel for you what you have not earned. But I, like *ma petite*, know how to love and not be a prisoner to that love. You can win, or steal, our love, but you cannot steal a true relationship with us; that must be won." He turned, and curled his long legs up on the couch. He put his arm across the back of the couch, not quite touching the other man's bare shoulder. He cradled his head on his outstretched arm, letting all those black curls spill along the white of the couch. I couldn't see his face, but I knew the look. It was a charming, seductive look, his teasing look, when he really didn't expect anything to happen. He just wanted to remind you how scrumptious he was. He usually used the look only when he was mad, or I was. It was a look to either end a fight, or begin one.

Auggie looked at him, and the look was pained. He saw Jean-Claude, understood the potential in that body, and knew now that having had it once didn't mean you'd get it again. Jean-Claude played hard to get when he thought it would gain him an advantage. The look on Auggie's face said it was a really big advantage right now.

If it was real love, true love, then shouldn't it have made me feel bad to see Auggie wanting, hurting with doubt? Maybe, but it didn't. It made me happy, in that small, petty, vindictive way that always promises a really bad relationship. There are different kinds of love, I'd learned that—not less real, or more real, just different. Maybe what Auggie could cause a person to feel wasn't true love, after all. Maybe it was that kind of love that seems to come quick, and leave slow, but in the middle it's just fights, and pain, punctuated by great sex, until one of you has the courage to end it, and walk away.

Auggie turned that pained expression my way. "You would both turn me down." He sounded genuinely surprised. He glanced back at Jean-Claude. "I understand Jean-Claude, he's maneuvering for power, though my pride is hurt. I must not be as good with other men as I thought I was."

Jean-Claude answered with his head still poised on his arm. "If I feed your ego now, then I may lose the advantage I have gained."

Auggie nodded. "I understand that." He looked at me. "But her, I don't get her. I know I'm good with women. Hell, I'm an amazing lover."

I laughed, I couldn't help it.

He gave me a dirty look. "Do you disagree?"

I shook my head. "No, you're great." I didn't sound like I meant it, but I did. "Maybe I just like my men a little more modest, that's all."

He stabbed a thumb at Jean-Claude. "If he's ever been modest about his prowess in bed, it was false modesty."

"Why, thank you," Jean-Claude said.

Auggie shook his head. "That's not what I meant."

"What did you mean?" I asked.

"That he doesn't have a modest bone in his body."

I actually didn't agree with that, but Auggie didn't deserve the explanation that went with it, so I let it lie. "You're entitled to your opinion."

"Which means you don't agree with me," Auggie said.

"It means what I said."

Auggie shifted his gaze to Micah. He looked at him, looked at him the way that men usually reserve for women. Like he was wondering what Micah would look like without his clothes.

"Here I stand all naked, and you're not even looking at me," Nathaniel said. "Should I be insulted?" He moved a few steps ahead of Micah, tossing all that heavy auburn hair over his shoulders, so his body was framed by it. He stood there and gazed at the vampire. He gazed at him from those lavender eyes, with that beautiful body.

"Maybe I like a little modesty, too," Auggie said.

Nathaniel moved his muscular arms to cover himself, let the hair spill over one shoulder, so that more of him was hidden. He peeked coyly around his own body and hair, gave innocent eyes, let his face be as young as it was in years. I was never sure how he did it, but he could play the innocent down to his toes. He could hide those jaded eyes, and play the ingenue.

Auggie laughed, that bright, happy laugh. "He's good." He turned to Jean-Claude. "Where did you find so many beautiful men?"

"I didn't," he said.

He looked past Nathaniel to me. "Anita, you have a true eye for talent."

"They aren't talent to me. They're people I care about, and I don't like games."

He motioned to Nathaniel. "This one plays games, and very well, I think."

I nodded. "Nathaniel likes games better than I do, better than Micah does, but he doesn't play them with us."

Auggie gave me a look that seemed to imply I was being naïve. "Once a hustler, always a hustler, Anita."

"Was that meant to be mean?" I asked.

"I thought you liked honesty," he said.

"It was meant to be mean," Micah said.

"I know whore when I see it, because I was one. So was Jean-Claude, and Asher, and Requiem, and London. Mustn't leave out the ladies: Elinore, Cardinal, anyone who was ever Belle's line was a whore. We're created to be whores."

"Nathaniel is not a whore," I said, and reached for him. He pulled away from the touch, and gave me eyes full of loss. "I was."

"You researched us, before you came here," Micah said.

"You bet," Auggie said.

I touched Nathaniel's face, and tried to put into my eyes how much he meant to me. Whatever he saw in my face made him smile, a little. He pressed his hand over mine, pressing my hand against the curve of his jaw.

Micah stepped in front of us both. "You knew looking at me like that would be an insult. Nathaniel stepped up, took the attention, because it wouldn't bother him. Something about him protecting me bothered you. Why?"

Jean-Claude raised his head, curled his legs over each other in a way that let you know just how flexible he was, but still managed to be "ladylike," for lack of a better word. "I know why."

I put one arm across Nathaniel's back, and asked, "Why?"

Jean-Claude and Auggie exchanged a look. "If you think you can read me that well, go ahead," Auggie said.

Jean-Claude gave a small nod, then looked at us. "Augustine prefers women to men, but one would have to be very, very heterosexual indeed to ignore the beauty of both of you. In his defense, you did fall into his lap. He behaved himself admirably. There are vampires among our own kiss who would not have shown his restraint. He offered such a small insult, and you took it as a large one. Anita and I are not falling over each other to profess our love for him, and that irks him. It puzzles him. Then you, who are animal, thus lesser in the eyes of most vampires, insult him, too. But I think it is more than that." He looked at Auggie. "I think he watched Nathaniel use the only gift he had to protect Micah. Did it bring back old memories, Augustine? Bad memories?" He leaned in toward the other man.

Auggie stood up, abruptly, and wouldn't look at him. "My memories are my own." Then he realized what he'd said, and gave a bitter laugh. "For now, at least, until she dictates otherwise." He wasn't referring to me.

Jean-Claude lay back on the couch, spreading his hair over the arm of it, one arm carelessly above his head, the other across his stomach. One bare foot trailed over the carpet; the other was tucked up on the couch, his knee leaning against the back of the white couch. He looked fetching, and he knew it. But it was the way Auggie watched him that made the show. There was real anguish in his eyes. It hurt me to see his face like that.

"You give me another taste of heaven, and now I am in purgatory again. You, and she"—and he pointed at me—"can bring me into heaven at a whim, and cast me into hell if it is your will." He closed his eyes, his face etched with pain. "I remembered you as gentler than this, Jean-Claude. I remembered you as my friend."

"Friends do not use their powers against each other. You woke *ma petite's ardeur*, deliberately. You meant to have her. The fact that we both had you was an accident of power. You remembered me gentler, and less powerful. You underestimated me, and you have mistaken *ma petite*."

Auggie opened his eyes, and stared at the other vampire. "I don't understand what you mean by that."

"Ask our Nathaniel how he won her heart."

"I see his body; I know how he won her heart."

"You see nothing, know nothing," Jean-Claude said. "*Mon minet*, tell him how you won her heart."

"You call him 'my pussycat' and I'm wrong about him?" Auggie said.

Nathaniel leaned a little harder against the hand I had on his naked back. "I didn't hustle Anita," Nathaniel said.

"But you tried." Auggie made it a statement.

Nathaniel nodded. "I wanted her to want me. I didn't know any other way to do that."

"It worked," Auggie said.

Nathaniel glanced back at me, gave me a smile, then turned back to Auggie. "No, it didn't."

He motioned at us all. "Of course it worked."

"Only when I stopped trying to hustle her, and just tried to learn how to love her."

"Learn how to love her, you make it sound like a class, or a degree. You simply love people."

Nathaniel laughed. Jean-Claude made a noise like he was trying not to laugh. I looked at Micah. "Aren't you going to laugh, too?"

Micah shook his head. "I know better." Though there was the edge of a smile on his lips.

I scowled at them all. "Fine, laugh it up."

"I don't get the joke either," Auggie said.

"You will," Micah said, and it sounded like a threat.

"Is it really that hard to date me?"

This time Claudia and some of the other bodyguards laughed. I was just amusing the hell out of everyone.

40

"TELL ME THE joke, I could use the laugh." Travis's voice came from the far hallway. His face was tight and pinched with pain. Noel hovered beside him like he was waiting to catch him if he stumbled. They both still looked too young to drive. Was it just age that had made Joseph pick them for my feedings, or was there some other reason? I mean, there's submissive and then there's cannon fodder. Everyone he'd offered for my selection, even the jocks, had that new-car smell, like they hadn't been driven around the block enough. There had to be a reason he'd offered me lambs when what I needed was lions.

"Why haven't you shifted?" Micah asked. He was already moving across the living room toward them, walking past Auggie. The vampire reached out, tried to grab his arm. Micah moved so fast that I didn't really see Auggie try to grab him, and miss. I saw the vampire reach out, and Micah just wasn't where he was reaching. So fast, it was like magic. Micah went to the werelions, and started talking to them in a low voice. He ignored the vampire.

Auggie looked angry, and something else, something that was almost pain. "You've made your point, Jean-Claude."

"Micah does not like to be grabbed, that is all the point that has been made," Jean-Claude said, voice mild. He was still lounging decoratively on the couch. "Do you envy me my cats, Augustine?"

"I don't envy anyone."

Even I could taste the lie.

Micah started leading the werelions toward the love seat. He stopped well out of reach, and looked at Auggie. "I really don't want to play games, Augustine. I just want to get Travis sitting down."

"If you were in my territory, I'd have to make a lesson of it, of you, but you aren't my kitty-cat. Sit down, I won't bother you."

Micah walked wide round the vampire, but gave him his back. His eyes flicked to me, and I realized he was trusting my reaction to let him know what Auggie was doing. I nodded, like, it's okay. Micah led the two lions to the love seat.

"Petty games do not become you, Augustine. You are master of a powerful territory. You could have your own collection of lovers, to rival mine." He left the implication that we were all his lovers, and we let it slide. I was his lover, and neither of the other men was bothered by the rumors.

"I'm not just Master of the City of Chicago, Jean-Claude, I'm a mob boss. The mob allows you a family with a wife and kids, a mistress, whores, but nothing else."

Jean-Claude luxuriated against the couch arm. "You could never let any of them see you looking at me as you do right this moment."

Auggie shook his head. "If you were a whore or a hustler, I'd have to kill you if they saw me look at you this way."

"But your rivals cannot see you now. You can look at me any way you like."

"Fuck you, Jean-Claude, you're going to use this look on my face to punish me, and try to control me. It's just another kind of gun at my head."

"We are master vampires, we are all about control, but I do not intend to punish you, unless you punish us first."

"What does that mean?"

"It means, if you are cruel to us, we will be cruel in return. If you play nicely, then so will we."

"Define *play nicely*," I said.

"When you saw the look of pain on his face, did it not make your heart ache, *ma petite*?"

I wanted to lie, but . . . "Yeah."

The look of cynicism on Auggie's face flickered, as if he didn't know what look would help, or what look he dared give.

"But, so what? Thanks to his machinations, I don't want to see him hurting, so what?"

"Augustine could come and visit us. His mob connections could think he was trying to woo us for criminal activities, or just that he was solidifying his alliance with us, one master to another. Either way, he could visit us periodically without arousing suspicions. Since he is a known mob figure, it would explain why the visits would have to be out of the media's so-glaring eye."

Auggie watched the other vampire like a mouse that's had the cat tell him *I won't eat you, today*. Half hopeful, half afraid to hope. "What are you offering, Jean-Claude?"

"One, that you do not try to make things worse for *ma petite*. Do not try to raise her *ardeur*, or mine, against our will. Do not abuse my hospitality by using your powers on my people."

"I apologized for that," he said.

"You made a joke of your apology," Jean-Claude said. "I need to know if you are sincere."

Auggie nodded. "I am sorry, but . . ." He looked away, his hands in fists. "You don't understand what it's like to be on the receiving end of the *ardeur*. You gained the *ardeur* almost from the first moment. It awoke with your blood lust. You've never been its victim."

"Not true," Jean-Claude said. He sat up, suddenly, brisk and almost businesslike. "*Ma petite* can feed the *ardeur* from me, as I can feed my *ardeur* from her. We can be the victim of each other's *ardeurs*."

"I'm sorry, I know that. I know that you were as much enthralled by Belle as any. But still, you can feed the *ardeur*, and gain the rush of it. I have nothing unless I can find a partner who carries it. I had hoped that one, or both, of you would love me, truly love me, truly want me. I'd hoped to bargain love for the *ardeur*, and now I watch you both." Again, he looked away, as if he couldn't stand to look at either of us. "And you are not moved by me. You, Jean-Claude, you watch as Belle used to watch me. She"—he pointed at me—"she watches me like she hates me. So cold, so angry. I don't understand it. Did my power work on her, or only on me? I feel the draw of her body, but she doesn't seem to feel anything for me, except anger."

"*Ma petite* does not like to be in love. It always angers her, most especially in the beginning."

Auggie shook his head. "I don't understand that."

I shrugged. "Join the club." I went to the love seat. Nathaniel trailed me. "Why hasn't Travis shifted?"

Micah answered, "He's waiting for you."

"Waiting for me to do what?"

"Bring my beast," Travis said, and his face was almost gray with pain.

"What you do here on your little visits would be a secret from your so-conservative fellow criminals," Jean-Claude said.

"Just shift, Travis. Heal yourself."

He shook his head, huddling over his arm.

Auggie said, "And what would I be doing on these visits?"

"Perhaps we could even visit you in Chicago."

I was suddenly paying attention to their conversation. If we went to Chicago, oh, my God, the energy there would . . .

"No, no fucking way. You'd feed on all my people then. I felt what one feeding off me and the few people I had here did to your power level. No way."

"So you do not want to visit us again?"

Auggie forced himself to stand very straight, shoulders back, an echo of military something. "You know that I do, but I won't trade my people and all my power for it. I won't crawl for you, Jean-Claude."

"I don't want you to crawl, Augustine."

"What do you want?"

"You to stop trying to manipulate us. Accept that we hold the *ardeur* and you want it. Supply and demand, dear Augustine."

"You bastard."

Jean-Claude was suddenly standing, so fast I hadn't seen it. Magic, again. "You abused my hospitality first. You manipulated my human servant so you could feed on the *ardeur* again. You opened the way for Belle Morte to possess *ma petite*. I am not the bastard here."

"Fine, I'm the rat bastard. You're right; saying that I didn't understand I was inviting Belle in doesn't fix it. Yeah, I want to take back one of the women of Belle's line, but no one but Anita carries the *ardeur*. She and you, so yeah, I came with the idea that if I had a chance at it, I'd raise the *ardeur*."

"You came here wanting the *ardeur* one more time; what do you want now, Augustine?"

"Don't make me say it, Jean-Claude."

"*Ma petite* is not a subtle woman. Unless you say it, she will not understand it."

Auggie looked at me, but his eyes flinched, like someone who was expecting to be hit. "I won't sell my people, or my power base, I won't humilate myself, but short of that, I will do anything, anything, to have you and Jean-Claude feed on me again." The flinching gave way to fear. "Want someone killed, I'll do it. Money, drugs, designer anything, whatever you want, whatever you need, just don't tell me that I'll never be in your arms again." His face turned away, but not before I saw the shine of unshed tears.

"We do our own killing. We've got enough money. We are a drug-free zone; don't bring that shit here. If I want designer stuff, I'll buy it myself."

Auggie stood there, face averted, shoulders hunched, waiting for the blow to fall. "I have nothing to offer you then." His voice was thick when he said it.

"I am way past uncomfortable about what Jean-Claude and I did with you. It felt so fucking good to feed off you, and that terrifies me."

Auggie looked back at me. His eyes held the tears back by sheer willpower.

"But for better or worse, I look at you and my heart aches. I want to comfort you, and that pisses me off. I've had people I loved, really loved, use vampire powers on me. I cut them off at the knees for it. I've run from them for months, not seeing them, not even talking to them." I moved toward him as I spoke, a little closer with every sentence. "I just met you. You aren't my friend. You forced me to love you, but I don't know you."

He tried to give me angry eyes, but the unshed tears that hovered there ruined the effect. "I underestimated you, Anita."

"Most people do," I said.

"I thought you were just Jean-Claude's human servant. I felt your power as a necromancer. It should have been a warning, but I went ahead with my plan. I wanted the *ardeur*. I wanted it so badly." He smiled, but not like he was happy. "And I was arrogant. I am Master of the City of Chicago. I've been a mobster since the 1930s. I have been powerful, and a threat to anything in my path for centuries. The only thing that ever truly defeated me was Belle." The tears trembled, but still he held them back.

I stood there, staring at him, needing to look up only a little, because he wasn't that tall. Normally I liked that in a man, but now I was just pissed. I was going to hold on to that anger, because rage was the only thing that kept me from running my hands over his bare chest. My hands itched with the desire to touch him. It wasn't just love, it was more and less than that. It was a sort of magical compulsion. It felt like love, but it held elements of almost addiction. I realized that Auggie had rolled me, well and truly. His power had rolled me. I had fought free of some of it, and Jean-Claude had helped, but I wasn't free of what he'd done to me. But staring into his face, those angry, teary eyes, I realized he wasn't angry at me. He was angry at himself.

"You rolled yourself," I said.

He closed his eyes and turned away. He spoke with his face averted from me. "The blade cuts both ways," he whispered.

"But if we've got better armor, then more of your power hits you than us, doesn't it?"

He nodded, still turned away.

I had a flash of satisfaction. Served him right. But on the heels of that petty pleasure came regret. Regret like bitter ashes. "Jesus," I whispered.

He turned. He'd lost the battle with the tears. They ran in pale pinkish tracks down his face.

"Of all the powers from Belle's line that I've had used on me, Auggie, yours is the most awful."

"How can you say that?" he asked. "The *ardeur* can enslave. Requiem can rape with a thought."

"Yeah, Requiem's power would be the ultimate date-rape drug, but he doesn't use it that way."

"He did once," Auggie said.

I processed that information, tested if it was a lie, but I didn't think it was. I shrugged. "Whatever he was as a young vampire, he's not that now. But the *ardeur* is just lust, and so is Requiem's power. It doesn't steal the emotions; yours does."

"And you think that is a worse crime?"

I nodded. "Yeah, I do."

"You hate me." He whispered it.

I nodded again. "Yes."

He turned away, and took a step. I caught his arm. He froze under that one small touch, as if I'd turned him to stone. I knew that reaction. That was the reaction when the merest brush of someone's hand meant more to you than almost anything in the world, and it meant nothing to them. It was how I'd felt off and on with Richard. As if my entire life were in the hand that touched him, and he didn't care. It was one of the reasons that I'd fought free of him. It was too hard to love that much, and hate that much at the same time.

I used that touch to turn Auggie back to me. He let me do it, though he could have fought and won. I was stronger than a normal human now, but Auggie's bicep was thicker than my thigh. In a fair fight, I'd lose, but Auggie's own power had made certain he'd never have a fair fight with me.

I looked into his eyes, watching him try to be angry, instead of hurt. "What a terrible power you have, Augustine," I said, softly, "to offer true love and mean it. People must have been willing to trade anything, everything, for such a gift."

He nodded. "Without the *ardeur* to trap me back, I could have made you love me without risking this much of myself. I know everything about my power, Anita. I can make a person love me, really love me, and not love them back."

I dropped his arm. "Have you done that?"

"You're right, Anita, I have a terrible power. At first it was just the ability to make people like me, then love, but what I didn't realize, at first, was that it was a two-edged blade. I could only cut my prey as deep as I was willing to be cut."

"That changed," I said.

He nodded. The tear tracks were drying on his face. He made no move to wipe them away. "I learned control. I learned to trap others without trapping myself, as Jean-Claude learned with the *ardeur*. I don't know if Requiem ever learned how to cause lust in only one side of his equation."

"I did not." Requiem came in, moving slowly, carefully. He was wearing his usual black cloak, so the injuries were hidden, but he moved like things still hurt. Someone had used cover-up on the worst of the facial bruises. It was a good job. You had to look to see the discoloration; even then, if I hadn't known it was bruises, I might not have seen.

Auggie glanced at him, then back at me. "But most of us do, eventually."

"So if our power hadn't tripped you up, you'd have been willing to make me love you, really love you, and not love me back?"

"I didn't think that clearly, but I would not willingly have loved you, no."

"You really are a bastard," I said.

He nodded. "Chicago has no mob but the old-school Italian. I've kept out the Russians, the Ukrainians, the Chinese, the Koreans, the Japanese. No one, absolutely no one, takes power from me. While almost every other mob stronghold has been whittled away, I've held my territory against everyone. To do that, Anita, you have to be a bastard. A cold-blooded, murderous bastard."

"You hide it well," I said. "The laugh is great."

"I work at appearing human; it makes the other bosses be less afraid."

"The head of Vegas is an old-time mobster, too."

Auggie shook his head. "He stopped being a force in the mob when he became a vampire. It takes a while to recover from it, and by the time Maximillian was powerful enough to take back some of it, times had changed, and he didn't change with them. He's powerful, and runs Vegas, but he's not a boss anymore."

We stood there staring at each other.

Jean-Claude came up behind me. He touched my shoulder, and when I didn't pull away, he hugged me from behind. The look on Auggie's face, seeing us together, was painful, and strangely satisfying. If he'd had his way, it would be me with that stricken look, and him cool and calm. Evil bastard, but even thinking it, I couldn't own it. Damn it.

"The night wastes away. Soon we will have to change for the ballet," Jean-Claude said.

Auggie nodded. "Yeah, yeah."

"We need to decide if *ma petite* is too dangerous to go out among the other Masters of the City."

Auggie nodded again. "I'll help you figure it out, if I can. I owe you for the breach in hospitality. I owe Anita for what I tried to do to her." He looked away from both of us, staring at nothing. "It's been a long time since I've felt the full weight of my own power. I'd forgotten how much it fuckin' hurts."

"Excuse me." Noel was standing beside us.

We both turned and looked at him. I don't know what he saw on our faces, but he backed up fast until he was out of reach of both of us. "May I approach?"

"No," Auggie said.

"Yes," I said.

We looked at each other.

Noel dropped to all fours. He didn't bow, just dropped to all fours where he was standing. "I don't know what to do; I can't please you both."

"What is your problem, Auggie?" I said.

"He asked a question, I answered it," Auggie said.

"Fine, you answered it for yourself, not for me." I stepped away from Auggie, closer to Noel. Auggie grabbed my upper arm.

I tensed, but didn't try to pull away. I knew I'd lose if it was just brute strength. I looked at him, then at the hand on my arm. I looked back at him. "You did not just do that."

"And you did not just step away from me to go to anyone this submissive."

"Do you ever want to experience the *ardeur* again, Auggie?"

He looked puzzled for a moment, but I knew in a way that that was an act. He might have been truly puzzled, but he worked at human facial expressions. "You know I do."

"Move the hand, or you won't ever touch me again."

We stared at each other for a moment, then he let me go. "I heard you were dangerous, powerful, and quick to kill. What none of my spies caught, is that your force of will is the most dangerous thing about you. God, your eyes, the determination in your eyes." He shook his head. "You mean it. You would truly cut me off because of this."

"Damn straight."

"Why, because I grabbed your arm?"

"Because you're acting like you own me. Nobody owns me."

Micah got off the love seat and started toward us. It drew Auggie's gaze to him. "Your lion injured Travis and abused Noel. I think you owe them some consideration."

"Spoken like a leopard," Auggie said, "so practical, so willing to negotiate." He made those all sound like bad things.

"You really are very much your animal to call, aren't you?" Micah said. Auggie nodded.

"For those of us who are confused, could you explain a little more?" I said.

Micah said, "Lions are the most aggressive society among all the cats. To be a lion is to be always ready to defend your place in the pride. Unless you are very dominant or very strong, or make people fear you enough to be left alone. Noel and Travis are lesser, and Auggie treats them as if he were a dominant lion. A few dominant lions in most prides mate with all the females."

"Joseph's pride isn't run like that," I said, "it's closer to how the leopards run things."

Micah nodded. "Joseph's pride is the exception, Anita. Remember, I spent years trapped with a mixed group. It can take forever to do business with lions because everything is a pissing contest. Joseph thinks more like a leopard—very reasonable, especially for a lion."

"Pussy-whipped is what I heard," Auggie said. "His wife wouldn't tolerate sharing."

"You know, Auggie, almost everything coming out of your mouth is just digging the hole deeper."

"What does that mean?"

"You're on her shit list," Micah said, "and you keep digging yourself a deeper pile of shit." He actually smiled.

"What are you smiling at?" Auggie asked.

"I thought you might be a threat to our domestic arrangement, but you won't be able to behave yourself long enough to be a threat to any other man in Anita's life."

"Jean-Claude has already invited me down to sample the wares again."

"Sample the wares," I said, "what the fuck does that mean? Am I wares, things to be sampled? I don't fucking think so."

"See," Micah said, "you keep this up and you won't ever get the *ardeur* again."

Jean-Claude joined us. "You are being exceptionally careless with your words, Augustine. It isn't like you to be so impolitic."

"He's scared," Nathaniel said. He came in behind me, wrapping his arms around my waist, pressing his nakedness against my back. I didn't have to see his face to know the look. It was a look he'd only recently worn around me. *Possessive*, it said, *mine*, it said. *I'll share, but it's mine.* He usually only brought the look out when someone was behaving badly, or he didn't like them. I think we were all agreed on what we thought of Auggie. He was such bad news.

"Scared of what, pussycat?" Auggie asked, disdain thick in his voice.

"Wanting Anita as badly as you do," Nathaniel said.

The comment made me tense, but he pressed himself even closer, and I relaxed against him. He rested his face touching mine, so we probably looked like one of those posed engagement shots. Auggie was right about one thing; Nathaniel could play games when he wanted to. He played less and less as he got more comfortable with his life, and himself, but he hadn't forgotten how to play.

"You don't like wanting anyone that much. You see it as a weakness," Nathaniel said, "and you're beginning to realize just how hard to deal with Anita can be."

I turned and looked at him, forcing him to move his head enough for us to make eye contact. "Do you find me difficult?"

He grinned. "I like being dominated."

I started to say how hard I'd worked to ensure that he wasn't dominated, then realized what the grin meant. He was teasing me. I tried to glare at him, but I wasn't serious enough for it to work.

"Do not let your unease be your undoing in this, Augustine," Jean-Claude said.

"What's that mean?" he asked.

"It means that if you continue to say and do such things to *ma petite*, then I will not be able to offer you the *ardeur* from her."

Auggie had a moment where something flashed through his eyes. For just a second I would have said it was fear. "Maybe I am being stupid, but I came to her looking for a Julianna and what I found is Belle."

Jean-Claude's face went very still. "Why would you say that?"

"I only saw you love two women in nearly six centuries, Jean-Claude. You don't choose to love Belle Morte, she chooses it for you. You chose to love Julianna. I thought, if you had finally fallen in love again, that it would be someone like her. I thought that the tough talk, and the danger, were just surface. I thought if I scratched deep enough that Anita would be more like the only other human I ever saw you love." Auggie shook his head. "You've got a physical type you like, petite brunettes, but beyond that"— he shook his head again—"Jesus, Jean-Claude, sweet Jesus, don't you ever have anything in a woman's personality that you like every time?"

"Did you come here thinking that if you pushed *ma petite* hard enough she would crack open and be gentle and feminine in the way of Julianna?"

"It wasn't just you, Jean-Claude, but Asher, too. He never seemed to have a physical type, but personality; he liked gentle, laughing, comfortable women. Belle used to accuse him of being addicted to peasants, when it came to women."

"And you reasoned that if one woman had kept both of us happy, she must meet the criteria for both of us."

Auggie nodded.

"Logical," Jean-Claude said. "Wrong, but logical. I had forgotten that about you."

"Forgotten what?"

"That you tried to make of love and emotions something logical, something that could be understood."

Auggie frowned at him. "You're making fun of me."

Jean-Claude shook his head. "No, but I would remind you that Asher went on his own and found Julianna. I loved her with all my heart and soul, but she was not of my choosing. I came to love her, but I did not begin to love her."

"So I've got faulty data."

"If you like," Jean-Claude said.

Auggie looked at me, with Nathaniel still wrapped around me. "Micah's right. I think like a lion. I don't see Nathaniel as a problem, because he's submissive. I do feel the need to prove myself more dominant than the other dominants in your bed. But, damn, there are a lot of them."

I shrugged, holding Nathaniel's arms like you'd keep a shawl from spilling down your arms. "Is that why you tried to grab Micah, and why you stared at him like he was some kind of hooker?"

Auggie shrugged. "Maybe."

"I don't dig the macho shit, Auggie. Flex your dominance on your own time, not on mine."

Auggie pointed behind us, turning us all to look at Noel. He was still on all fours waiting to be noticed. "You say your local Rex doesn't run his pride the way most do."

"He doesn't," Micah said.

"His lion is reacting like he knows the rules."

"Joseph's pride know how to be lions. They just don't do that whole Serengeti-plains-dominance-fight at each kill," Micah said.

"That's what it means to be a lion," Auggie said.

"Actually," I said, "lions native to forested regions don't do that. The fluidity of dominance, and the complicated social system, seem peculiar to the African plains region."

Auggie gave me a look.

I actually felt myself beginning to blush, and fought it off. Nathaniel hugged me. "Smart girls are so sexy," he whispered.

I managed to say, "I have a degree in biology, and I did research on the various animal forms once the coalition got going."

Auggie gave an abrupt laugh. "I've been dealing with lions for thousands of years, and I've never picked up a book about them."

I just stared at him. "How could you not want to learn as much about them as you could?"

"I live with lions, I don't need to read about them."

"I live with vampires, and raise zombies damn near every night, but I still read my trade publication, and keep abreast of the articles on all the un-dead." I shook my head at the level of arrogance he was admitting to. The really scary part was that he didn't see it as arrogance.

I couldn't deal with Auggie anymore. I still felt the pull of his power, but it was just love. I could fight against love. Richard and Jean-Claude had given me lots of practice doing that.

I patted Nathaniel's arm. He kissed me on the cheek and let me go. I went to where Noel was waiting on the floor. "Get up, Noel."

He got up, eyes flicking behind me toward Auggie. It made me glance back, but the vampire actually wasn't doing anything but looking at him. I touched Noel's shoulder, turning him so he couldn't see Auggie. "What's up, Noel?"

"Travis and I need to talk to you." He tried to glance back at Auggie. I touched his arm, kept him from doing it.

"Fine, we'll talk." I started toward the couch. I herded Noel with me. Micah and Nathaniel came at our backs. I wasn't sure if they wanted to hear everything, or were covering my back in case Auggie decided to get all weird again.

Requiem was sitting beside Travis. He had a hand on the man's forehead. "He is going into shock."

I knelt in front of Travis. His face was gray-tinged. "Jesus, Travis, shift and heal this."

He gave a small, tight shake of his head. His voice was tight, but breathy. "Give me your beast, make me change."

"My beast is fine where it is, Travis."

"You need to feed the *ardeur* on one of us, or give us your beast, Anita, please."

I looked into his pain-filled face. "Do you really want to have metaphysical sex while you have a broken arm?"

He shook his head, grimacing. His upper body folded over his injured arm. He spoke, still bent over. "No, not really, but I also don't want you making that blue-haired freak our Rex."

"I won't . . ."

He stared at me from inches away. His face was beaded with sweat. He was shaky, and hurting, and should have seemed weak, but he didn't. There was a lot of force in that look. "Anita, if you make him your animal to call, or your Rex to your lioness, then he'll share in your power. No way would any dominant lion with that much power be able to leave the local pride alone. Lions aren't like the rest of the big cats. We aren't live and let live. We're very much about who's the biggest cat in the pool. Joseph chose his Regina for love, not power. She's nice, but she's his wife, not a power to be reckoned with. If you give that other guy your power, then he won't be able to leave us alone. The lion in him will be compelled to find us, and conquer us."

I looked back across the room at Auggie. "You agree with his assessment of the situation, Auggie?"

Auggie nodded. "Yes, but I'm not sure that Haven being your Rex is as certain as you and the other cats think. I've bound you with my power, Anita; what if your reaction to my lions is so strong because of that? Not just your beast, but my power helping make my lions more appealing." It was the smartest thing he'd said in a while. It left me wondering which was the real Auggie, thoughtful-guy or sexist-idiot-guy?

I nodded. "Okay, maybe, how do we test this little theory?"

"Anita reacted to your lions before you rolled her," Micah said.

"Shit," I said, "Micah's right. My initial reaction to Pierce and Haven was funky from the beginning, before we had our little power duel."

Auggie nodded. "Then perhaps what your lioness is seeking is a dominant. Either way, the way you react to Pierce, as opposed to these two, will tell you something. Either my power has made it worse, or your power seeks stronger prey. Jean-Claude believes that your *ardeur* seeks stronger prey; why not your beast?"

I glanced at Jean-Claude. "Getting chatty, are we?"

"I am seeking answers, *ma petite*. Augustine may not be trustworthy in all things, but when he gives his word, he keeps it."

"So you asked his opinion, after getting his word of honor he wouldn't tell our secrets anywhere."

Jean-Claude nodded.

I didn't like it, but I had to trust that Jean-Claude knew what he was doing. Besides, we did need help figuring some of this out. The list of Masters of the City that he trusted at all was damn small. It might be smaller after this visit, if I could vote on the list.

"Please, Anita," Travis said, "please, give me your beast. Feed on one of us. Don't give that freak power over us."

"I don't need to give my beast up, and I don't want to raise it on purpose. I don't know how to stop it, once it starts."

"Start it, and give it to me."

"Travis, just shift."

He shook his head stubbornly.

"Then feed the *ardeur* on me," Noel said.

I looked into his face, those eyes behind his wire-framed glasses. He looked so sincere and so young. "You don't know what you're asking, Noel."

"Just mark their necks," Nathaniel said.

I looked at him. Usually, Nathaniel liked to be the only one that I marked up. He shared with Micah, but he didn't like it when I marked anyone who was just food. "Usually you complain about that," I said.

"The jolt of power with Pierce could happen with anyone who was a preternatural. But what happened with Haven when you tried to touch his neck, that was different. Try to do the vampire greeting thing on their necks, and see if you get a similar reaction."

"Beauty and brains," Auggie said. "Lucky you."

I wasn't sure who he was calling lucky—me, Jean-Claude, or Nathaniel. We all ignored him. "All right, Nathaniel, all right. I'll try, but if this doesn't work at all, Travis has to shift and heal that arm." I looked at Travis as I said it.

Travis nodded. "If you try it on both of us, and nothing happens, okay."

Requiem tucked his black cloak closer around him. The movement made me look at him. "You are master here, Jean-Claude, but before she uses the *ardeur* again, should we not talk?"

That made me look back at Jean-Claude. He nodded. "Yes, but perhaps our young lions could go back to Dr. Lillian for a time."

Travis gave him a look that said, clearly, he wasn't moving. "You're kidding, right?"

"Are you refusing the direct order of the Master of the City?" Auggie asked.

I raised a hand, and said, "Don't start that shit again, Auggie. Not your city, not your call."

"I don't think Travis feels well enough to walk back to Dr. Lillian," Noel said. "What if we give our word that we won't tell anyone what you say?"

"You are young and live in a time where you do not truly understand what it means to give your word," Jean-Claude said.

"Besides," Micah said, "if Joseph ordered you to tell him, you'd have no choice."

Travis let out a long shaking breath, cradling his arm against his body. "Help me up, Noel."

"What can be so private that you're making him move?" I asked.

"We could move," Nathaniel said.

"Yeah," I said, "all the able-bodied, except for Noel, follow me."

"Are you really going to let her make us all move, so the lion won't have to?" Auggie said.

I stopped a few steps beyond the group, because only Nathaniel and Micah were following me. Claudia was looking from Jean-Claude to me, and the rest of the guards were looking to her. We were deep into the pissing contest and Claudia was trying to decide what would help and what would hurt.

I pointed a finger at Auggie. "I'm getting tired of you." I switched the finger to Jean-Claude. "Please, tell me you are not going to grandstand to save face in front of Auggie. It will cost us nothing to move down the hallway."

"He lost a fight," Auggie said, "it should hurt."

I waved a hand at him, as if waving him away. "I'm not talking to you, I'm talking to my master, thank you very much. Jean-Claude?"

It wasn't so much that I could see him think it through, because his face was perfect and unreadable. But I'd been staring at that empty face for years now. It was almost like I could feel him thinking it through.

He gave a small nod. "Very well." He went to me, and I held out my hand to reward this show of common sense.

"I see the local Rex isn't the only one pussy-whipped around here," Auggie said.

I started to get angry, but Jean-Claude pulled on my hand. He told me with a glance that he'd take care of it. He turned those dark-blue eyes on Auggie, and said, "And if you knew that she would cover you in the *ardeur*, and love your body, would you stay here, or would you go where she wished you to go?"

Auggie stared at him for a second, then started shaking his head, over and over again. He walked toward us, then kept walking. He walked into the far hallway, and kept walking until he was lost to sight.

"When he faces us again, *ma petite*, he will have his people at his back. I do not think he will risk himself alone with us again."

I squeezed Jean-Claude's hand. It made him look at me. "I don't think he's afraid of being pussy-whipped," I said.

Jean-Claude actually managed to look humble. "Perhaps not."

41

"WHAT DO YOU mean, I was about to bind Requiem to me forever?" We were having our super-secret meeting in the hallway. It was empty, and I didn't want to walk all the way back to Jean-Claude's room.

"I have tried to teach you different ways to feed, *ma petite*, and you have learned well."

I could have argued that, but I let it go. "Just explain what you said, Jean-Claude. You don't have to protect my ego, just say it."

"You have fed on Requiem, but always before you were holding back, or I was so deeply enmeshed with you when you did it, that I was in some way controlling what happened."

I nodded. "And?"

"It is possible to know the innermost desire of a person. The *ardeur* can give you a glimpse into his soul."

"I know that, it happens a lot."

He shook his head. "But that is exactly the point, *ma petite*, it should not happen a lot."

"But it does; that's how the *ardeur* works when I feed completely."

He shook his head again. "*Non, ma petite*, it is not necessary to know someone's heart's desire to feed completely."

"It makes a better feeding, more energy, if you know their deepest wish and give it to them."

He nodded. "*Oui*, but what is the rule for all the gifts of my bloodline?"

I frowned at him. "I don't . . . oh, that they're two-edged swords. All of Belle's powers cut both ways."

"*Oui.*"

I was still staring at him. "If you have a point to make, please make it, because if that was a hint, I don't get it."

"When you first met Micah, what did you need in your life?"

"Stop trying to make me reason this through, Jean-Claude, just tell me."

"You will not like it," he said.

"I'm getting that impression, but remember I'm a jerk-the-Band-Aid-off kind of girl. Just tell me."

"You needed help with the wereleopards, and with all the other shapeshifters that you were beginning to try to help. It was your willingness to help many kinds of shapeshifters that laid the groundwork for our so-lovely coalition. You yourself said that so much that was wrong with the lycanthrope community could be fixed if they would only talk to each other."

"I remember all this, so what?"

"You needed a man in your life who simply said yes, instead of arguing with you or running his own agenda. You needed someone to put your needs first." He looked at me, as if he'd been very clear. It wasn't clear to me.

"Doesn't everyone?" I said.

"I think I get it," Micah said, softly.

I turned to him. "Then tell me."

"My heart's desire was safety for my people, and a partner powerful enough, passionate enough, to help me save them. We both got what we wanted most, out of each other."

I frowned, trying to think, then said slowly, "Are you saying that I caused Micah to be everything I needed him to be?" I looked at Jean-Claude. "Are you saying that even now, he's like under my power? That that's why he never argues with me? That he's under a spell?" I looked back at Micah, to see if his face was as horrified as mine felt.

He looked the same as ever, calm, ready to do what was needed. So practical, so . . . so everything I needed in a man. Shit.

He smiled at me. "Don't look so horrified, Anita."

"Do you normally argue more than this?"

He shook his head. "I was always pretty easygoing, and years trapped in Chimera's group took care of most of my rebellion. It was too expensive to the people around me to be a smart-ass."

"Is everything we have just vampire tricks, except I'm the vampire? Is it all a lie?"

"This was the reaction I feared you would have," Jean-Claude said.

"What reaction am I supposed to have?" I asked, and it was almost a yell.

"You missed part of his point," Micah said.

"What part?"

"If the *ardeur* made me into your perfect mate, then it made you into mine. It's a double-edged sword, remember."

Was I under a spell? My own spell? It was too complicated for me. I turned back to Jean-Claude. "I don't understand this. I mean, if this is true, then how could we not have noticed?"

"But, *ma petite*, you did notice. Your Nimir-Raj is the first man you have ever had sex with on first meeting. He is the first man you have ever allowed yourself not to push away, is he not?"

I wanted to argue, and I couldn't. Damn it, but I couldn't. "Shit," I said.

I turned, and looked at Nathaniel. He gave me a gentle smile, like you'd give someone in the doctor's office who just got bad news.

"If this is true about Micah and me, then . . ."

"*Oui, ma petite*, the same would be true of Nathaniel."

"No, it was different, very different with both of them."

"But they are very different men. One heart's desire is not the same as another's."

"I resisted Nathaniel for months before we had sex."

"*Oui*, but it was not sex that Nathaniel wanted, not truly; he wanted to be loved and valued for himself, not just for his body. By denying him sex, but loving him, you gave him what he wanted most."

I felt like I was choking. I couldn't breathe. My back hit the wall. I leaned against it, trying to think, and failing.

"The only two men in my life that I haven't seen all the way through are you and Richard."

Jean-Claude nodded. "I knew how to keep you out, and Richard was strong enough, and conflicted enough, not to know his own heart's desire."

"But everyone else." I stared at him. "Asher, Damian, maybe even Jason, hell, I don't know."

Requiem spoke then. "I think that your *ardeur* holds not just lust, Anita, but love, as Belle's *ardeur* did. As my Ligeia's *ardeur* did."

"I've been inside Belle's head. She wouldn't know real love if it bit her on the ass."

He gave a small smile, as if I'd amused him. "She knows the *ardeur* as a warrior knows his weapon. She knows the art of causing love and devotion, even addiction, in others, without suffering it herself."

"Are you saying I'm doing it wrong?"

He seemed to think about it, then nodded.

"How do you know?" I asked.

"There was a moment when you looked deep into me. I felt you see all the way down into my soul, Anita. I felt you caress the deepest pain I own. Belle Morte would have coaxed that pain to life and used it to torment me. You were going to try to heal it."

"I was supposed to heal you, right?"

"Physically, *ma petite*, not emotionally." He touched my face, staring at me, as if he were trying to read something from my face. "And certainly not his deepest hurt." He let his hand drop away, but continued to study my face.

"I don't know how to do anything halfway, Jean-Claude. It's all or nothing for me, you should know that by now."

He nodded and looked unhappy. "You are quite right, *ma petite*. I am your master and this is all my fault. I should have seen it."

"Seen what, exactly?"

"You have been obsessed with learning to control the feedings, *ma petite*. It has made me obsess with you, but there are other things to learn about controlling it. Things I have neglected to teach you."

"You could not have taught her control of this, not when the *ardeur* was fresh, Jean-Claude," Requiem said. "I was with Ligeia from the moment she gained the power. The first few months are a wild thing. I thought she would go mad with it." He gripped Jean-Claude's shoulder. "My understanding is the *ardeur* rose for the first time with Micah. There was no controlling it." He looked at me, and at Micah. "It has actually worked out extremely well for all concerned."

I turned and looked at Micah, and Nathaniel. "I trapped you both. I rolled you."

They exchanged a look, then both looked back at me. "We love you," Micah said.

Nathaniel moved in, as if he'd hug me. I moved farther down the wall, out of reach. "But it's all vampire powers. It's a lie—doesn't that ruin it for you? I trapped you. I trapped you both; it's worse than what Auggie did to us. It's not fake, it's like real love. I made you both fall in love with me, that's like evil."

"If you made us fall in love with you, but didn't love us back, maybe it would be evil," Micah said, "but you do love us back."

"But it's a lie, Micah. It's all a lie."

He gave me a look, that look that said I was being silly. But I wasn't being silly, was I? "I've been in love before, Anita, remember."

"Becky, your high school sweetheart, college fiancée," I said.

He nodded. "That was real, Anita. She was the love of my life, and if she hadn't dumped me, I wouldn't have known that love could get any better than that."

Becky had dumped him when he survived the attack that made him a wereleopard. She just couldn't handle his being furry once a month. Of course, she'd had other problems with him before that. What I thought was a huge bonus, she'd thought was a huge downside.

Micah stepped toward me.

I slid along the wall, my hand out. I didn't want him to touch me, not right then. Mainly because if he did, I'd lose this fight. I'd always wondered at how my body reacted to him. No one had that effect on me, not to that degree. Now I knew it was vampire mind tricks, but I was the vampire who had done it. Fuck.

"I know what true love feels like, Anita. This is it. We are all happier than we've ever been. The only thing that will spoil what we have is if you freak about this."

"How can I not freak about this, Micah?"

I felt movement, a second before hands touched me. The hands brushed my bare arms, and I felt calmer. I leaned back against Damian's body, let his arms enfold me. The fear, anger, confusion, just washed away. The iron control of his emotions that he had learned at the hands of his creator was what he shared with me. I leaned back into that peaceful control for a handful of seconds. The panic was still there, but I could ride it. I was still horrified, but it wasn't the only thought screaming through my brain.

I leaned my head back against his chest, and looked up at him. He'd tied all that bloodred hair back from his face. I stared into a face that my magic had actually made prettier, more perfect. He'd been handsome before; now he was beautiful. I looked up into those eyes, like looking into the perfect green of an emerald, if it could look back at you. If a jewel could burn with intelligence and need. "Hey, Damian," and my voice sounded almost drugged, I was so calm.

"Hey," he said, smiling down at me.

I blinked at him. "I feel so good. I don't remember you ever making me feel this calm, so fast."

"You love Micah, don't you?"

I frowned at him. "Yes."

"You love Nathaniel, don't you?"

I frowned harder. "Yes, but it's all a lie."

His hand swept up the line of my neck, as his face bent toward me. "Does it feel like a lie?"

"No," and my voice was small.

He whispered the last few words against my lips. "You all love each other, isn't that more important than how you fell in love?"

With Damian touching me, it was utterly reasonable to say, "Yes."

He kissed me. Those lips that my own magic had made fuller, more kissable, covered mine. He drew back enough to whisper, "Love is too precious to waste, Anita."

He was right, of course. He was right, but it wasn't like me to see logic this quickly. This wasn't like me, at all.

Damian lowered his mouth over mine, his hand kneading my throat, as he pressed my back against his body. Always before when he was helping me be reasonable, kissing him was a cold thing. Today, I gave myself to his kiss, to his hands, even as part of me knew this was just more vampire mind games. Damian was my vampire servant. He gained power as I gained power. It hadn't occurred to me that he might be able to use that power against me.

42

I BROKE THE kiss, pushed him away hard enough to make him stumble. His eyes were drowning emerald fire. "Didn't it feel good?" he asked.

I shook my head, not trusting my voice. But the moment he wasn't touching me the panic was back. The fear, and it was worse now. I was surrounded by vampire tricks. Surrounded even inside myself, and that was one person I couldn't run from.

Micah tried to hug me again, but I moved around him, toward the living room. Nathaniel brushed my arm, and I moved away. I was shaking my head, and wasn't sure why.

"This does not have to be a disaster, *ma petite*."

"Yes," I said, "it does."

"Anita," Micah said, "I don't care that it was vampire magic that brought us together. We're together, that's what matters." He held his hand out to me.

I shook my head. "No, because if you touch me, I'll give up. I won't fight. I can never win a fight when you touch me. The effect you have on my body overwhelms everything else."

"And that's a bad thing?" He made it a question, his hand still held out toward me.

"I wondered why your touching me always overwhelmed me, and now we know. It's vampire powers. It's mind tricks. It's an aftereffect of the *ardeur*, Micah."

He let his hand drop slowly. "I love the way your body reacts to mine, Anita." He closed his eyes, hugged his hands into fists in front of his chest. "I abso-fucking love that you react to me like I'm intoxicating." He opened his eyes and gave me the full stare out of those yellow-green kitty-cat eyes. "Don't you love it, too?"

I opened my mouth to say no, but it would have been a lie. The vampires could sense lies, but wereanimals could smell them. I told the truth. "Yes, I loved it."

He shook his head. "Not loved, not past tense. You love it. You love it so much, you're afraid to let me touch you now."

"Please, Micah, don't do this."

"Do what? Make you happy? Make us both happier than we've ever been for longer than we've ever been happy in our entire lives? We're both almost thirty, Anita; it doesn't get better than what we have. We've all tried other people, other ways of living. This works for us. Don't throw it away because it started with the *ardeur*." He took a step toward me. "We always knew that you and I began with the *ardeur*, Anita."

"Maybe, but not all of it. Not . . ." I turned away from him. I couldn't keep being this stubborn and look at the anguish on his face. But looking away put me looking at Nathaniel. It wasn't an improvement. First, he was nude, and any of the men I loved only had to take their clothes off to win most arguments with me. I might never admit that out loud, but it was the truth. Nathaniel nude was a treat, but what made it even harder was the look on his face. So hurt, so terribly hurt.

"Anita," he said, "would you really throw us away? Could you just walk away? Just like that?"

My throat was tight, but not with panic anymore. The panic had company now. Can you choke to death on unshed tears?

He stared at me; those lilac eyes sparkled through the fall of all that hair. I stared at his eyes, so bright, like firelit amethyst, as he tried not to cry. Then the first tear glittered down his cheek, and I was undone.

I went to him. I hugged him, and he collapsed so suddenly in my arms that it pulled us both to the floor. He clung to me, weeping, and I was left drowning in the vanilla warmth of his hair. Micah stood there, looking down at us.

Was it a lie? It didn't feel like a lie. The man in my arms felt real, and his tears were real. The thought that I could turn away from him because of something so . . . petty, had broken his heart, just a little. Micah had said it; we knew that the *ardeur* had been the beginning of us. Hadn't I always known it was the beginning of Nathaniel and me, too? If I hadn't needed to feed the *ardeur*, I would never have allowed him to move in with me. I would never have slept with him, clothed and strangely chaste, feeding by a kiss, a touch, but never with release for him. I would never have done all that without the *ardeur* to feed. I would never have fallen in love with him, if the *ardeur* hadn't kept him in my way.

I hugged Nathaniel, and held one hand out to Micah. He smiled, and came to me, to us. He dropped to his knees, and put his arms around us both. Nathaniel cried harder. I held them both as hard as I could. Micah kissed me, and I kissed him back. The taste of his mouth was the taste of sex to me. Just the kiss, and my body reacted to it. Nathaniel's hands spilled over my breasts. Had I taught them that the only way to make up a fight was sex, or had the *ardeur* preordained that sex was our currency of healing? It was a chicken/egg sort of question. I let it go in the sensation of hands and mouths on my face and neck, and body.

We licked the tears off Nathaniel's face, and somewhere in all that closeness, I let go of my doubts. I could worry about it later. Right at that moment, nothing seemed more important than touching the two of them.

We both came up for air, to the smell of lion. Micah growled. It was Noel on hands and knees. He had his forehead pressed to the stone floor, one hand held out toward us. Travis collapsed to his knees behind him, cradling his broken arm. He leaned against the wall, heavily, and for the first time it occurred to me that maybe the broken arm wasn't the worst of his injuries. Wereanimals were tough bastards. I hadn't even asked if there were other things broken. I hadn't even asked exactly what the doc had said. They had just been another embarrassing problem. Another pint of blood to lay on the altar of the *ardeur*, and my beast.

I looked at Micah. "I agree with the lions. I don't want Haven."

I turned to Nathaniel. He smiled. "I agree with Micah. Though Jean-Claude, or someone, needs to help you not to bond with them completely."

"Agreed," I said.

I looked behind us, for Jean-Claude. "How do we do this?"

"I can help you not use the *ardeur* as deeply, but I do not know if I can control the lion within you."

"I can," and it was Auggie. He'd added a long black cloak. His shoulders were so wide that it made him look square, his head too small for all that body. The bottom of the cloak puddled on the floor, because any vampire here that the cloak could belong to was a foot taller. The cloak looked borrowed, and it was, but Octavius and Pierce were at his back, and they didn't look borrowed at all. They looked perfectly at home.

The two bodyguards at their backs looked right at home, too. Standing orders were that Pierce and Haven got four guards. I wondered if Haven, now unconscious, had two of his own? Probably.

"I want this to work, Auggie, if it can," I said. "I need your word that you won't spoil it."

"Tell me exactly what you want me to swear to, Anita," he said. His face was empty, pale with concentration. His eyes looked huge and even darker, like the sky before it goes black.

I thought about what he'd asked, then looked again to Jean-Claude. "Help me to word it, okay."

"I will second Augustine on this, *ma petite*. Tell me what you wish him to swear to."

"I want to really try to bond with Noel. I don't want him to interfere with that, but I don't want to bond to Noel the way I did with Micah and Nathaniel. I want to see if it's just lions I'm hunting, or if Auggie's lions are especially tasty."

"If my lions are more tasty, it may not be because they are my lions, but because your power seeks something more dominant than what's kneeling on the floor. I think in your Rex's zeal not to give power to a rival, he has sent you food that your inner lioness will never accept."

"My inner lioness," I said, though it's hard to be disdainful when you're on your knees with men still hanging on to you. But I managed it.

"Inner beast, then," he said, voice empty. His face showed nothing. He was finally acting more like all the other really old vamps that I'd ever met. Will the real Augustine please stand up?

"Are the lions more likely to want a dominant?" I asked.

"I thought you had read up on lions," he said.

I thought about it, then nodded. "If a new male takes over the pride, second thing he does is kill the cubs. It means he doesn't help the lion he drove off breed successfully, and it puts the females into estrus faster, so he gets to mate."

Auggie nodded. "It makes the females of most wereprides very tough to impress."

I shook my head. "You're not saying that werelion prides are run like real lion prides? That the new leader kills the children? That's ridiculous."

He shrugged those big shoulders under the long cloak. "It has happened."

I turned back to Noel and Travis. "You guys know about this happening for real?"

They both said, "No."

"They're too young to know what we did before we became legal." This from Pierce.

"Are you saying that some men do kill the babies of the old Rex?"

"I've seen it," Pierce said in a very clipped voice.

I almost asked, *Which end of the fight were you on?* but I didn't. There was a look in his eyes, almost a flinching. Either he'd been a victim, or he'd done things that haunted him. I had enough nightmares of my own; I'd let Pierce keep his to himself.

"I guess that would make you want the strongest lion around," I said, but my voice was a little thin. The pregnancy scare was too recent. How would it feel to go through nine months, then labor, and have some stranger kill your baby, after first killing your husband? I said it out loud. "If someone did that to me, he wouldn't survive very long."

"Prides with really strong females don't get taken over much," Pierce said, "because you gotta sleep sometimes." He almost smiled when he said it.

I nodded. "That's how I'd be thinking."

"Your local pride has very weak females," Auggie said, his voice still that empty master's voice, so it could have been almost anyone talking. "Your Rex's wife is weak, and since the females of the lions are just like the males, it's forced him to reject a lot of strong women."

"Are you saying that if someone killed Joseph, there wouldn't be enough fight in his pride to do much about it?"

"His brother would be a problem," Pierce said, "but other than that, yeah."

"You would definitely have to kill both of the brothers," Auggie said, "but after that the pride would be helpless." He looked past me at the lions.

Noel was staring at him with a sort of soft horror. It was Travis who said, "Sounds like you've thought this through."

"It's why you brought dominants," I said. "You came planning for Pierce or Haven to take over the local pride."

Auggie gave me flat eyes.

"You evil bastard."

"It's not me that's left his pride open, ripe for the picking, Anita. He did that himself."

"He loves his wife, that's not a crime," I said.

Auggie shrugged.

"Anita." Noel's small voice brought me back to look at him. He inched closer to me, his hand out, his face showing his fear. "Please, Anita, please, try me."

I wanted to say, *I won't let them hurt you and your people*, but I couldn't. Not and be truthful. We had an alliance with the lions, true, but if Joseph had truly let his pride get this fucked up, and it was truly the lion's way to take over the pride like this, then no other animal could interfere. We could help each other, but we couldn't interfere directly in the dominance hierarchy of the other groups. Not unless we wanted to start glomming us all into some kind of super-group. Wereanimals didn't do well in mixed-species groups. Too many cultural differences.

The only way I could send Haven home was to find another lion that my lioness liked. Shit. Noel stared at me, hand outstretched. The fear in his face made him look even younger and more inexperienced. No animal group could operate without dominants. You needed muscle and strength, and strength of will. If Joseph had truly done what Auggie said, then his pride was in the gravest of dangers. If it wasn't Haven or Pierce now, it would be someone else later. Of course, if one of them were my semipermanent *pomme de sang*, then other lions might hesitate to attack them.

Hell, master vamps from around the country who hadn't had the ballet troupe go anywhere near them were offering up *pomme de sang* candidates. We'd be seeing potential feeds for months even after this batch went home. We'd already had inquiries from animal groups that weren't aligned with any vampire. You know you're big fish, when all the sharks want to come play.

I did the only thing I could think of. I took Noel's hand and drew him toward me. I wasn't sure what we'd do when he got to me, but we'd think of something.

43

NOEL SMELLED OF fear. He smelled like food, but not food for the *ardeur*. He smelled like meat that just hadn't stopped squirming yet. I pushed him onto the floor, raised his shirt to his shoulders. I stared down at his bare chest and stomach. He was breathing so fast, so hard, that his stomach rose and fell with it. I lowered my mouth over that pale, soft flesh. I stopped with my face just above his skin, so close that my breath came back warm against me. With that warm breath, came his scent, stronger, richer. It made me close my eyes. But I was too far into beast mind for sight to help or hurt that much. It was all about the smell of him, the sound of his breathing, and his heartbeat. I laid my ear against his chest so I could hear that frantic beating, so clear, so wonderfully afraid. I put my hand on his stomach so I could ride the movement of it, as he breathed.

"Slow your breathing, Noel," Micah said, "or you're going to hyperventilate."

"I can't help it," Noel said, voice breathless, "she's not thinking about sex."

"If you act like food, then you're food," Travis said from behind us.

I lay there on the floor, my head over his heart, my hand on the quick rise and fall of his stomach. So soft, so . . . tender.

The thought slid my face down his body, until I rested at his sternum, the upper edge of his stomach. So close now that I could not so much see the fast rise and fall of his body as feel it under my cheek. I rolled my face over, and kissed his stomach.

He jerked, as if I'd bit him, and made a wonderful whimpering sound.

I buried my mouth in the soft, easy flesh of his belly. I took as much of his flesh into my mouth as I could hold, and not draw blood. I bit him, hard and deep, and it took all my willpower to rise up from that flesh, and leave it whole.

I pushed back from him, crab-walked until the wall stopped me. The sensation of all that warm, tender flesh filled my mouth. I could still feel it, a sensory memory that would haunt.

"Talk to me, Anita." Micah's calm voice.

I shook my head. "Food," I whispered, "just food."

"Noel is just food," Micah said.

I nodded, eyes still closed.

"Get up, Noel." Travis's voice, unhappy, angry.

"I'm sorry," Noel said.

I finally opened my eyes, to watch him drag his shirt back over his body. He wouldn't meet anyone's eyes, as if he'd failed.

"It's okay, Noel. Auggie and Pierce are right, Joseph shops for bottoms."

"He's not a bottom," Nathaniel said. "If he had been he'd have enjoyed the biting, and the danger. It might even have been enough to push you from food to sex." Nathaniel shrugged. "He's too straightlaced."

Once I would have argued.

"I would ask one favor," Travis said.

We looked at him.

"Can you come to me, instead of making me crawl to you?"

I remembered what I'd forgotten to ask, and asked it. "Is the broken arm the worst injury?"

"At least two cracked ribs, maybe a small break. Dr. Lillian said she'd need X-rays to be certain. No concussion, too hardheaded for it, I guess." He tried to smile and almost made it.

I crawled toward him. Micah moved so I could do it. Nathaniel crawled beside me. I glanced at him. "I don't think Travis will want company on this."

"I'm the only submissive you've collected. Everybody else is a dominant."

That stopped me, made me think about it. I actually sat back on my knees. "Damian isn't a master."

"No, but he's submissive because he doesn't have the power to be dominant. I'm submissive because I like it."

I frowned at him. "If you have a point, make it."

"Ask if the pride has anyone who swings more like I do."

I thought about all the men. Was Nathaniel right? Was everyone else a dominant personality, except for him? Richard, yep; Asher, yes; Jean-Claude, way yes; Micah, yes; Jason, no.

"Jason," I said.

"You rang?" and it was Jason coming into the hallway. His short blond hair was cut neat and tidy like a junior executive. The body would have qualified, if the executive worked out in the gym enough. He was about my height, short for a man, and boyishly handsome most of the time. But he glanced at Noel getting shakily to his feet, Travis with his obvious wounds,

Nathaniel and I so close together and him so very nude. Jason took it all in, and his face changed. I could never put my finger on it, but he looked suddenly older, more grown-up, and his eyes, the color of spring skies, filled up with a knowledge, a weight of intelligence. He hid it most of the time, but there was a very nice mind in that smiling, very nice body.

The look vanished, replaced by his usual smart-ass, flirting look, but I knew him too well, now, to be fooled.

"Jason subs if he wants to, but he's a top at heart," Nathaniel said, smiling up at his friend. We were never going to marry, Nathaniel and I, but if we did, I knew who he'd pick for best man.

"Tell me what position you want me in," Jason said, "and I'm your man." He wiggled his eyebrows and gave me that grin. That grin that said he was thinking cheerful nefarious thoughts. Most people made sex dark, but not Jason. He was a cheerful lecher.

I had to smile. He just had that effect on me. Hell, he had that effect on most people. "Sorry, I'm shopping for lions today, not wolves."

"Actually, *ma petite*, I think we are trying to establish how you react around all your beasts, but lions for now."

"Looks like I got here just in time," Jason said.

"You're not the only wolf in the hallway," Graham said, sounding sullen.

Jason gave him a look that wasn't entirely friendly. You didn't see that from Jason much. "I suppose not." His tone was dark, almost angry. I wondered what had been happening between the two of them to get that level of animosity from Jason. He was one of the most easygoing people I knew.

"As far as I'm concerned," I said, "Jason is the only wolf in the hallway."

"Why is he the only wolf that you fuck besides Richard?" Graham asked.

Ah, now I knew why Graham was pissed. Had he tried to bully the smaller man? Probably. Graham had this backward idea that size and strength were more important than anything else.

"I don't know, but comments like that are what help keep you off the list," I said.

"Step back," Claudia said to him.

He scowled at her, muscled arms folding over his chest.

She took a small movement toward him. "Are you challenging me?" Her voice was flat and empty as she said it; it made the threat all the more ominous.

Graham shook his head, and backed up until he was against the wall. He sulked, but he did what she asked. I hoped he got a girlfriend soon, because his little tantrums were really beginning to bug me.

As if the thought had conjured her out of the dimness, Meng Die appeared farther down the corridor. It was the first time I'd seen her since she'd sliced Requiem up. I did not want her here while I tested my beasts.

She was one of the few women who ever made me think, *delicate*. She was tinier than I was, so fragile looking. Maybe that was why she almost always wore black leather, very dominatrix. The clothes suited her though, catlike, skintight, scary, and sexy all at the same time. Yeah, scary, sexy, that summed Meng Die up perfectly.

She slinked on black, high-heel boots toward Graham. It was as if Claudia had seen this show before, because she said, "He's working, Meng Die."

Meng Die made that delicate triangular face pout, but it never reached those uptilted eyes. She changed direction without so much as a regretful glance at Graham. And that, that was why Graham wasn't devoted to her. Why she'd almost broken Clay's heart. She'd wanted Graham, but if she couldn't have him, that was fine. No man likes to know, for certain, that it doesn't matter to a woman if he's the man in her arms or not. Come to that, a woman doesn't like it when a man treats her that way either. Okay, no one likes knowing that they're utterly replaceable. We all like to be special.

Meng Die slinked toward Requiem. He backed away from her. Jean-Claude said, "You are not to touch him again, Meng Die."

She looked at Jean-Claude. "Never again?"

"Not unless he wishes it."

She turned that lovely face to Requiem. "Do you truly wish never to touch this body again?" She made her hands flow over her curves as she said it.

Some of the men in the hallway followed her hands down her body. Auggie and his men did. Requiem didn't. Jean-Claude didn't. None of the wereleopards did. Jason did, though. The view was nice if you didn't know the mind that went with it.

Meng Die walked past me, and the leopards, and the lions, like we weren't there. She went for Jason. He had looked, and he wasn't on the forbidden list.

She entwined herself around him, head on his shoulder. Even in the heels, she was shorter. "Come play with me, Jason."

He laughed, and shook his head. "I've got a report to give." I had no idea what report he was talking about.

"Afterward?" She made it a question.

He smiled, but said, "No. Thanks, but no."

She ran her hand over the front of his jeans. Apparently, she wasn't feeling the least bit subtle today.

He grabbed her wrist, and said, "No."

She jerked away from him. "Why is it no? Because she's here?" She pointed at me.

I hadn't known that Jason and Meng Die had had sex. It must have shown on my face, because she said, "You didn't know?"

I shook my head.

"We had a lot of fun, until you fucked him. Until you fed the *ardeur* off him."

I stood up, and Micah and Nathaniel moved with me. "I didn't know he was your boyfriend," I said.

"Meng Die doesn't have boyfriends," Jason said, "just people she fucks."

"And what's wrong with that?" she asked.

"Not wrong, just not my thing."

"You enjoyed it, Jason, I know you did."

"You're good at fucking," he said.

"So are you," and she made it a purr. Not a cat purr, but that alto, sultry sound that some women can make. I've never been able to do it.

Jason grinned at her. "But sometimes I prefer to make love, not just fuck. I couldn't explain the difference to you."

She frowned at him, the sultry look slipping around the edges. "Making love, it's all just pretty words for fucking."

I glanced at Jean-Claude. "You couldn't teach her the difference?"

He gave an elegant shrug. "Some lessons come too late. She was much abused by the time I found her."

"No," Meng Die said, "no, my story is not for her. I want no one's pity, least of all hers."

Jean-Claude gave that Gallic shrug again, that meant yes, no, everything, and nothing. "As you like," he said.

"You just fuck Anita, too." She'd turned back to Jason.

He smiled, but gentler this time. "Anita makes it impossible to just fuck her."

"What does that mean?" Meng Die asked.

"She was my friend, my good friend, before we ever had sex. You can't just fuck someone that's important to you. Because if you screw it up, you lose more than potential sex, you lose your friend. Her friendship was more important to me than the sex, so it had to be making love, not just fucking."

"I don't understand you," she said.

Requiem's voice then. "Because sex is almost never casual for Anita, it makes sex with Anita almost never casual."

Meng Die shook her head. "I don't understand."

"I know you do not," he said, "and for that I am sorry."

"Don't pity me!" She shouted it.

I couldn't see any weapons on her, but the leather could have hidden surprises. Slender surprises, but blades can be amazingly easy to hide.

"I want to fuck, who will fuck me?" Her words hit the air like a stone, and smashed into a suddenly heavy silence.

She looked at the men one at a time. She went to Damian, but he backed up, shaking his head. "Why shake your head? She is your master, not your wife."

Damian actually looked a little embarrassed, as he said, "We fuck when we can't find anyone else."

Again, news to me.

"So, I am who you fuck if you can't find anyone else, really?" That purring contralto went from sounding sexy to sounding ominous.

"You've turned me down enough, Meng Die. When Graham, or Clay, or Requiem was available, you didn't even look at me. It stops being flattering to be last on a woman's list."

She looked at Auggie, and he just said, "We're doing business."

She turned to Noel. He backed away, as if she'd struck at him. "You scare me," he said.

"But Anita does not scare you?"

"She scares me less than you do."

Meng Die frowned at him. "Why?"

I didn't expect Noel to answer, but he did. "Anita may hurt me by accident, but I think you'd hurt me just to see me bleed." Damn perceptive for walking food.

I felt London coming down the hallway. Felt him in a way that I shouldn't have been able to feel him. He was seeking me, using his vampire powers to find his fix again. I looked up, and found him coming toward us, all dark and pale.

Meng Die's face brightened when she saw London. She practically skipped toward him. He glanced at her, but that was all. His eyes were set on me as if I were his north star and he were lost at sea without me. Shit.

She slid her small hand through the bend of his arm, their black-on-black clothing blending together nicely. "Come on, London, let's leave them to their business."

"Not right now," he said, and didn't look at her when he said it. He looked at me.

She stiffened, gazing slowly up at him, then followed where he was looking. She came to me, and started shaking her head. "No," she said, "not London. You think he's dark and morose."

"He is dark and morose," I said.

"But you fucked him anyway," she said.

I shrugged, and gave her the "sorry" face. I mean, what was I supposed to say?

"You don't even like him," she said.

"It was sort of an accident," I said.

"How do you accidentally have sex?"

It was a good question. I did not have a good answer.

London walked away from her. He never looked at her as he glided toward me.

I watched her face pale with anger. Her hand slid to the small of her back, and I knew she had a weapon. I took a breath to say something, but Claudia and Lisandro were ahead of me. The guns under their arms just seemed to magically appear in their hands. Claudia's gun touched Meng Die's shining black hair. Lisandro's hand was hidden by Meng Die's slender back.

Claudia said one word. "Don't."

Everyone on our side of the hallway moved closer to us. Everyone behind Meng Die moved farther down the hallway. Everyone except the bodyguards, that is. The bodyguards on Pierce and Octavius started to join them, but I shook my head. They stayed at their posts. We had four guards on Meng Die, two of them with guns plastered to her. Two extra guards wouldn't make a difference on her, but it might on Auggie and his crew.

It was one of those moments when the world seems to hold its breath. Because the next breath may be someone's last.

"Do not die this way." Jean-Claude said it in a voice that shivered down the skin. But he was directing that voice at her, especially for her. I knew what it was like to be the target of that voice.

The tension left her shoulders. Her eyes were unfocused for a second. Lisandro used that second to take the knife out of her hand. Meng Die reacted to it, but too late.

She started to turn as if she meant to go for her blade, but Claudia pressed the gun barrel hard into the side of her head. Meng Die, wisely, chose to stop moving.

"Check her," Claudia said.

Lisandro holstered his gun and frisked Meng Die. He did it quickly, efficiently, and very, very thoroughly. "There are rivets and ridges throughout the leather. They could hide a few things. Do you want me to rip the leather open?" He asked it as if it were an everyday question.

"Your word of honor that you are not carrying anything else?" Claudia said.

Meng Die hesitated, then finally said, "There was just the one knife. This outfit doesn't leave much room for hiding weapons."

Claudia's eyes flicked to Jean-Claude. "It's your call, Jean-Claude, do we back up, or do we finish it?"

"Will you behave yourself, Meng Die?" he asked, and this time in as normal a voice as he could manage.

She gave him a look of such hatred that she didn't look quite sane. "I will not try to kill anyone tonight." Not exactly a rousing yes, but Jean-Claude nodded.

Claudia hesitated, then stepped back and lowered her gun. She didn't holster it, though. I couldn't say I blamed her.

London went to one knee in front of me, head bowed. It was a gesture that should have had a cloak and a plumed hat with it, so old-fashioned. "I am able to serve my lady again, if she has need."

It took me a second or two to work out what he meant. "You mean feed the *ardeur* again?"

He looked up. "Yes."

I looked down into that so-serious face. "You know if you act as food for the *ardeur* too often, it can be fatal?"

"Yes, but I can feed the *ardeur* every two hours or so in a twenty-four-hour period without ill effect."

I stared at him. "You're joking, right?"

"Why would I joke about such a thing?"

"I don't know, but . . . London, even the strongest, most powerful person I feed on can only feed twice in a row with a break of at least six hours between."

"It is my gift, Anita," he said.

"London is the perfect food for the *ardeur*. He can truly feed every few hours day after day, to no ill effect. In fact, Belle Morte said he seemed to gain power from it," Jean-Claude said.

"I'm scrambling to figure out how to feed and control this thing, and we have someone who is made to take care of it, and you didn't mention it to me sooner?"

"And if I had?" he said, simply.

I opened my mouth to protest, then closed it. If he had, what would I have done? "I'd have accused you of trying to set me up with London."

"Since he did not wish to be captured by the *ardeur* again, I thought it wisest not to mention his talent. To raise the possibility of it would be, I felt, a betrayal of his trust. For it would raise the issue of his being food for the *ardeur*. He was most adamant against it, *ma petite*."

"What's the downside to being able to feed the *ardeur* like this?" I asked, looking back at the vampire kneeling at my feet.

"Everyone is eventually addicted to the *ardeur*, but for me, the addiction is immediate."

"You're addicted again?" I said.

"Yes." His eyes were so peaceful, more peaceful than I'd ever seen them. He looked happier and more at home in his own skin than ever before. I looked up, and it was Nathaniel's gaze that I caught. He looked solemn, eyes not peaceful at all.

"You always look happy at the beginning of an addiction," Nathaniel said.

"What happens later?" I asked.

"You die."

44

I DID TRY sniffing Travis's neck, but he hit my radar as wounded antelope. Since I didn't want to rip his throat out, I had to back off. Touching Pierce's hand had been an electrifying experience. Shit. I made Noel take Travis to the hospital room in the back, so he could shift and heal the damage. I had to give my most solemn word that I would not bond with either Pierce or Haven, and bring disaster to their pride, while they were resting. I promised. I meant it. I wasn't sure how to keep the promise, but I did mean it.

We all went to sit in the living room while we tried to get through our list of metaphysical emergencies before we had to get dressed for the ballet.

"We are running out of time, Jean-Claude," Auggie said.

"*Ma petite* was able to free Requiem of an *ardeur*-related compulsion earlier today. We had thought to use the same technique to free you, Augustine. Are you saying that your freedom from the slavery of the *ardeur* can wait?"

"I need to send Octavius to fetch my clothes for this evening. He has expressed"—Auggie smiled—"reservations about my being here without him at my back. I came thinking I'd get my ashes hauled, and make a smash and grab on the local lions. Still might do the whole lion thing, but the rest didn't work out like I planned."

"You are not going to do the whole lion thing," I said. I was on the love seat sitting between Micah and Jean-Claude. Nathaniel and Damian were on the floor at our feet. Damian was touching my leg, and that one touch helped me think. He'd promised not to do anything but help me stay calm. There would be a learning curve on Damian's new power level, too. The grade on all of it seemed pretty damn steep.

Jean-Claude patted my knee, as if warning me to be calm. I was calm; Damian's touch almost guaranteed that. I was also determined that our invitation to the Master of Chicago was not going to rain bad stuff all over our local werelions.

"Most of the werelions in the Midwest owe allegiance to my pride."

"It's not your pride," I said, "even if your animal to call is the Rex of that pride. It's his pride, or hers."

"His," Auggie said.

"Fine, but that doesn't make it yours."

Auggie glanced at Jean-Claude. "She believes that. Doesn't she know the law?"

"*Ma petite* knows that in the vampire world all that my servants own is mine."

I had known it, but I hadn't made the logic jump. "It can't be your pride, because if something happened to your lion to call, then you couldn't hold the pride. If you can't hold the group without the help of someone else, then it's not yours, Auggie. Your lion dies and your hold on his pride dies with him."

"Is that a threat?" he said, softly.

Damian squeezed my calf, and Jean-Claude squeezed my knee. Micah moved closer to me, sliding his arm across my shoulders, so that he was holding me and Jean-Claude, really. It didn't seem to bother anyone but me.

"Not yet," I said.

Damian laid his head in my lap. Jean-Claude stroked my leg, his way of saying, *Be careful*. Micah was as close as he could get to me. Nathaniel just cuddled more solidly between Jean-Claude and me, wrapping his arm around my leg, but laying his head on Jean-Claude's knee. I'd never seen him do that before to the vampire. Jean-Claude petted his hair, absently, like you'd stroke a dog, as if it were very everyday. It wasn't everyday, and I realized that Nathaniel was helping us negotiate. Auggie had proved that he liked men, maybe not as much as he liked women, but still . . . He'd remarked on Nathaniel's hair, made a pass at Micah. Nathaniel wasn't flirting, he was lying with his body. Lying that he and Jean-Claude had a closer relationship than they did. Would it bother Auggie? And if it did, which way would it bother him? Would it disturb him because it's guy-on-guy sex, or would he be jealous? Hell, it might bother him both ways. A lot of men seemed conflicted about that sort of thing.

"Did you say that most of the prides in the Midwest owe you allegiance?" Micah said.

"Yes."

"Vampires aren't allowed to wage war on territories that don't touch their own," Micah said.

"I haven't done anything to any other Masters of the City. Vampire law only covers how we treat each other's animals to call. My lions haven't tried to take over any land where the Master of the City had lions as his, or her, animal to call." He looked at me, as if I'd like the "her" comment. Frankly, I was liking less and less about Auggie.

"So as long as you only take over prides that aren't owned by vamps, you're in the clear?" I said.

He nodded.

"If we hadn't invited you into our territory, how would you have taken over Joseph's pride?"

"Sent Pierce and Haven down on their own."

"Then what, kill Joseph, and take over?"

"Joseph and his brother, yes."

"But if lion is one of my animals to call, then since everything that I own belongs to Jean-Claude, you have to leave Joseph and his people alone, because they'll belong to another master vampire."

"I think you've already chosen a lion to call, Anita. Your reaction to Haven was pretty intense."

"My reaction to Pierce is intense, too. I haven't chosen between the two of them. The fact that they belong to you may be why I'm reacting to them. Or, like you said, my lioness is looking for something a little more dominant."

"Justin's coming to the ballet with us tonight," Jason said, from the chair near the love seat.

Everyone looked at him. "Joseph's brother?" I made it a question.

Jason nodded, then winced, pulling the collar of his leather jacket a little away from his neck. It wasn't that cold in here, but he was still wearing his leather jacket. Why? If Auggie and his people hadn't been there, I would have asked. Jason had said something about a report he had to make. What report?

"Take off the jacket, wolf," Pierce said. "We can smell the wound."

Jason looked at Jean-Claude. He nodded. Jason took the jacket off. He then turned so we could all see his neck. It was either the biggest hickey I'd ever seen, or something had tried to tear out half of his throat.

I tried to rise, but all the men pressed down just enough to let me know, *Don't.* Jason came to us. Something had bitten him, but the teeth marks were like nothing I'd ever seen. "What the hell did that?"

Jason looked at his master.

"Not everyone who wishes to join us wishes to be your *pomme de sang, ma petite.* Some of the masters have brought people that they simply wish to trade. Jason was investigating one of them." His voice held so little inflection that I knew it was the truth, but not all the truth.

"Hope the sex was good," I said.

He grinned at me. "It was."

Meng Die made a disgusted noise. She was leaning decoratively near the white fireplace.

"I thought you didn't pimp your people out, Jean-Claude," Auggie said.

"I didn't order Jason to sleep with anyone. I asked him to get to know them better. His decision to have sex was just that, his decision."

"What did you fuck?" Pierce asked. "I've never seen a bite like that."

Jason flashed a grin in their direction. "Wouldn't you like to know?"

Auggie reached up and laid a hand on Pierce's where it lay on the couch back. A look of near pain passed over Pierce's face. What did Auggie do when he touched his lions like that? Whatever it was, it wasn't pleasant. It reminded me of a shock collar for a dog.

The fact that Auggie didn't want Pierce to admit he didn't know something meant we were still negotiating. Negotiation was over as far as I was concerned.

"Is Justin meeting us here?" I asked.

"Yeah," Jason said. He settled back on the floor, on the other side of Jean-Claude, because Meng Die had taken his chair. London was in the chair closest to me. Only Requiem had taken a chair closer to Auggie's group. Or maybe he was farther away from me. Who knew with Requiem?

"If you liked Joseph's brother he would have already been on your radar, Anita. Don't let misplaced emotion trap you with someone not worthy of you," Auggie said.

"I decide who's worthy of me."

"He is the strongest dominant the pride has, but he is not as strong as your Ulfric is. He is not the survivor that your Nimir-Raj is. Would you truly bind yourself to someone who does not lead his group, Anita? Your power chooses only the strongest."

"It chose me," Nathaniel said, from where he cuddled on the floor.

"Yes," Auggie said, "there must be more to you than I can see."

"Perhaps it is love," Jean-Claude said.

Auggie looked at him. "What do you mean?"

"Perhaps what *ma petite* needs is not strength of arms and will alone. Perhaps there are other needs to be met."

Auggie smiled, and for a minute he was the friendly guy who had first stepped into our living room. "You are a romantic at heart, Jean-Claude. It was always your weakness."

"And my strength," Jean-Claude said.

Auggie shook his head. "I gave up such things long ago."

"How sad for you."

The two vampires stared at each other. It was a long, long look. It was Auggie who turned away, and put his gaze on me. "You come off as hard, but you're a romantic, too, Anita. I don't think you have it in you to bind yourself to someone just for power and safety. That's what we did, Jean-Claude and me. We chose our servants, and our animals, for power. There are dozens, hundreds that come up on the radar over the centuries, but you wait. You wait until you are either desperate enough for the choice to be forced, or you find just the right one to make you powerful." He motioned at all the men. "Since you don't choose, your power chooses for you. I must say, it's got high standards. Since you don't know how to force your power to choose the one you want it to choose, I don't think you have the ability to force your power to choose."

I couldn't keep my nervousness down. My pulse rate sped up, just a little, and I had to swallow. Auggie would notice it. He would know that his little talk had hit home. He was right. I'd never been able to force the *ardeur* to choose, or not to choose.

"She forced the *ardeur* to free me," Requiem said, from his chair.

"She fought her beast not to choose Haven," Micah said.

"I think *ma petite* is finding her footing with her powers, Augustine."

"Do you truly wish to waste such a powerful alliance with someone who does not rule a pride?"

"Justin is part of Joseph's male coalition," I said. "They rule the pride together."

"But he is still not the dominant to match your wolf or your leopard king, Anita. It seems a shame to settle for a prince when you've only bedded kings."

I didn't know what to say to that. Because he was right, in one way; Justin didn't do it for me, or he hadn't before this. Maybe my lioness would like him better than I would? Part of me was hoping yes, and part of me didn't want to have to choose at all. If I was a master vampire then I should be able to choose, or not to choose. If my power was more vampire than lycanthrope, then I had choices. If my power was more fuzzy than dead, then I was screwed.

45

WE GOT DRESSED in record time. I just gave myself over to the makeup and the primping. There wasn't time for me to argue. The outfit looked totally impractical, but the corset top was a dancer's corset. It meant it couldn't be laced as tight as Jean-Claude might like it, never tight enough to impede breathing, or movement. Jean-Claude told me I'd see similar corsets on the dancers tonight. The shoes had been dyed to match the shiny black of the dress, but they, too, were dancers' high heels. Made for ballroom dancing, actually, not ballet. When I'd seen the open-toed sandals I'd protested, hell no. There was no way to dance in them, I'd said, but damn me, Jean-Claude had been right. The shoes were actually comfortable.

The corset's piping was made of tiny diamonds, honest-to-God diamonds. The necklace he put around my neck was platinum and more diamonds. I'd almost asked how much money I was wearing, but decided that I really didn't want to know. It would have just made me more nervous, and that I did not need.

Jean-Claude's opera coat flowed like an elegant black cloak, but much more modern, with a short raised collar to frame his face, and the gleaming white of his shirt collar. The cravat at his neck was pierced by a platinum and diamond stickpin to match my necklace. His vest fit him like a glove because it was laced up the back; a corset vest. When he first suggested a corset top for me, I'd made the mistake of saying, "I'll wear a corset when you do." You'd think I'd know better by now. He'd just smiled and said yes. In fact he'd commissioned vests of various styles for all the men who would wear one. Impeccably tailored black slacks and gleaming black dress shoes completed his outfit. Oh, and a scattering of diamonds across the vest like stars tossed across a night sky. When I'd asked him why not make his vest have the same diamond pattern as my corset, he'd replied, "It is not a prom, *ma petite*."

All the other men were in black tuxes, some with tails, some just tailored.

The only difference was the color of the vests or jewelry accessories. It was damned subdued for one of Jean-Claude's parties.

The stretch limo had dropped us at the door, all eight of us. Which was why we needed the stretch. We'd done the gauntlet of flashing lights, cameras, microphones. They could call it a red carpet. It always felt like a gauntlet to me. Something to be endured, except instead of running as fast as you could, you had to smile and answer questions.

Jean-Claude always fielded the yelled questions and photo opportunities like a pro. I'd gotten better at clinging to his arm, and not glaring at the cameras. Occasionally you'd even catch me smiling. Everyone else was treated like entourage. You didn't yell questions at the entourage.

Normally, I enjoyed the Fox Theatre. It had been built in the 1920s as a movie theatre, but no movie theatre I knew had Chinese Foo dogs with glowing eyes at the bottom of a sweep of marble staircase. The interior was lush and gilt, full of carved Hindu gods, and animals from anywhere that qualified as exotic. Normally, I loved gazing at it all. Tonight, it was shelter from the storm.

We entered at the side entrance, the Fox club entrance. It was private, with valet parking, and a nice restaurant if you made reservations. People and corporations paid thousands of dollars a year to have a reserved box at the theatre. To my knowledge Jean-Claude didn't have a permanent box, but for tonight he had two reserved. The Fox club box seats actually ran out of room before they ran out of VIPs to seat. Jean-Claude had said that some of the visiting masters were actually on the floor with the peons, but in a special reserved front row section, along with many local celebrities.

The media frenzy might have been less if one of the Masters of the City coming hadn't been the Master of Hollywood, and his entourage. Hollywood likes Hollywood, and they had followed him out here. Someone had said that his newest girlfriend was some hot young star, in a new hit series I'd never heard of. When you work an average of sixty to a hundred hours a week, you don't watch much television. Funny, that. Apparently, the media was here as much for her as for anyone else. She must have been a very hot property indeed.

There were too many vampires in the VIP section to have dinner beforehand. It raised too many questions about what everyone would eat. Jean-Claude had avoided the problem by simply saying the restaurant was closed for that night. The management of the Fox was happy with that. Yeah, vamps were legal, but St. Louis is still part of the Bible Belt. No one was sure how people would take it if someone got pictures of vampires feasting on humans in the Fox club theatre. Just better to avoid the problem. Once we got to Danse Macabre, all bets would be off, but then people expected decadence at a vampire-run dance club. Not only expected it—were disappointed if they didn't see at least some salacious activities. I knew for a fact that some of the "naughty" impromptu scenes at Danse Macabre were very planned. The trick was to give the customers a thrill, not scare them to death, or make them run for a cop.

We finally got to our seats, Jean-Claude and I on one side of the little table in the middle, and Damian and Micah on the other side. Asher, Nathaniel, Jason, and Requiem took the box next to ours. Claudia and Lisandro, both in the bodyguards' black-on-black tuxes, stood near the boxes. Wicked and Truth were in the hallway leading into the box area. We had other bodyguards scattered throughout, because we'd refused to let the visiting masters bring more than two guards per, which meant we had to make certain they were safe. There were uniformed cops everywhere outside, as there usually were when you had a big event at the Fox. But it was more tonight; no one in St. Louis wanted some right-wing crazy to kill one of the master vamps in front of a television crew. No one wanted anyone to die period, but let's be honest, no one wanted that much bad publicity. Us, either, so there were wererats, werehyenas, werewolves, scattered throughout the building. The main difference was that the police were watching for hatemongers trying to kill the monsters, and our guards knew that the other job was to make sure none of the visiting monsters got out of hand. Jean-Claude was pretty sure they'd behave, but none of us was betting someone's life on it. Nor was he willing to risk ruining all this amazingly good publicity for vampires by some incident now at the last performance. Best behavior tonight, or else.

I was shielding as hard as I could. I did not want my abilities, not as Jean-Claude's servant, necromancer, or whatever the hell I was turning into, getting in the way. But some things are too powerful to hide from. Some things are too much a part of who you are, not to feel them. The lights dimmed, and I felt . . . vampires. Felt them through the shields. Felt them through Damian's sudden reach across the table, so that he could help me shield, help me control myself, help me not be overwhelmed. Jean-Claude had my other hand, but the tension in him wasn't helpful. He was excited.

I took my hand out of his with a smile, and clung to Damian. I needed something cold and calm, not nervous and excited. Damian wasn't excited, he was scared. I'd been nervous about all the masters coming to town, but not the ballet, itself. It was just a ballet, just a performance. The reactions of the two vampires let me know that maybe I should have worried about it more.

I glanced at Asher sitting so close in the next box. His froth of hair hid most of him, but there was a tension to him, too. What was about to happen?

I heard something, though that wasn't exactly it. It was as if I heard it with something deeper inside my head than my ears, or maybe felt it, and my mind could only translate what was happening into sound. I don't think they actually made any noise, but I heard a soft rustling, almost like birds.

I dropped the tiniest edge of my shields, like peeking over it in the midst of battle. I was holding hands with a vampire, surrounded by them, and sometimes when I was that wrapped up in vamps it was hard to sense other vampires. But not this one; this one was someone I didn't know. It was vampire, but unlike anything that had ever touched me before.

I glanced at Micah on the other side of Damian. Micah was shaking his head like a fly was buzzing him. He looked at me. "What's happening?"

I shook my head. "Vampire shit." Beyond that I truly didn't know. I looked over and found Nathaniel's face peaceful, waiting, as the lights dimmed. Jason's face lost its fight, too. I glanced at Damian, and his eyes were wide, a little panicked almost, then his face went peaceful, as well. I looked at Jean-Claude. He whispered, "He will try to make humans of us all."

I actually understood what he meant by that. The vampires at Guilty Pleasures and Danse Macabre would sometimes use group mind tricks to make performers appear in the midst of the human audience. Magic. Whatever vampire was doing this was trying not just to roll the human audience, but everyone. He was trying to cloud the minds of the other master vamps, so that his "performers" could appear like magic.

The theatre had gone eerily silent. There was no rustling, no movement below us. The humans had all had their minds rolled. Next would come the wereanimals, and then the vampires would fall. At least most of them would. I had never felt anything like this.

I drew my hand out of Damian's; he didn't seem to notice. He just kept staring straight ahead. I glanced behind at our bodyguards, and found Claudia staggering. Lisandro was just standing there, all peaceful. Shit, so much for the guards.

I looked back at Micah. His eyes were starting to unfocus. I grabbed his hand, and thought, *No*. No way. I pulsed a little power down his hand. My leopard flowed down my hand like warm water, spilling over his skin. He looked at me, eyes wide.

"Power up our cats," I whispered.

He nodded, closed his eyes, and I felt my leopard slip away, and follow his down the metaphysical lines to the other leopards. We had two leopards among the bodyguards.

"*Ma petite*, what are you doing?"

"Fighting back," I said.

My leopard began to swell upward, and I reached out to Richard. He was there in the crowd below with his date, a prof from a local college. He couldn't afford to be outed, but we couldn't afford not to have him here. He'd impressed the hell out of the prof by having tickets to tonight's gala event. I brushed his energy, and he whispered through my mind, "What's happening?"

I called my wolf, and the leopard quieted, but I could feel Micah reaching out further, finding the leopards. My wolf rose, and I saw through Richard's eyes. His human date stared at the stage, waiting, unseeing. My wolf touched his, and I thought what I wanted him to do, and I felt his energy, our wolves circle out from him, seeking. Where our energy touched, the wolves woke.

Having the vamp roll the Masters of the City was impressive, but rolling the guards was dangerous. I didn't like that at all. I looked behind, and found Claudia still struggling. She fell to her knees, struggling hard not to lose herself to the power. I had no tie to the rats, but it couldn't hurt to try. Besides, my wolf was starting to rise. I didn't need that.

I got out of my chair and knelt beside Claudia. Her eyes were terrified. She reached out. I grabbed her hand. I thought, *Power*. Her eyes cleared, and she gripped my hand so hard it almost hurt. Suddenly I felt Raphael. Not like I could feel Richard, or Micah, but I felt his power, like a scent on the air. Through Claudia's hand, his rat's hand, I offered power. Power enough to free his rats, who were most of our guards.

He took it, used it, and I felt it like a rock thrown into a pool. Out and out, leopards, wolves, rats, awake, alert. Pissed.

If there'd been a werehyena close enough, I'd have tried with them, too. Helping the rats had quieted my beasts. The power was awake, but they weren't trying to tear me apart. We were all waiting for the big, bad vampire to appear. We knew he was out there. We could feel him.

Jean-Claude's power flexed, suddenly and so strongly that it bent me over, nearly sent me to the floor. Claudia caught me. "You okay?"

I nodded.

Jean-Claude was waking up his vampires, but he needed my necromancy to do it. He'd borrowed without asking, but I was okay with that. There wasn't going to be time to ask nicely about a lot of things tonight.

I glanced at the box on the other side, away from Asher's box. It was Samuel and his family. Samuel looked at me. Thea glanced in our direction. His sons were lost to the magic, as were his two merpeople at his back. Whoever this was, was going to succeed at rolling everybody but the masters themselves and maybe one or two powerful servants. Impressive power, that. Impressive and scary.

Claudia helped me stand, and the curtains opened behind us. It wasn't Truth or Wicked, but a vamp I didn't know. He was tall, and meaty in an athletic sort of way, not fat, just physically bigger than I liked my men. Tall and broad the way Richard was, but unlike Richard, this one knew he was big and liked it. He moved in a glide that was already a kind of dance. Most of his body was nude, just enough covered by his leotard to not get him arrested. His upper body was beautiful even by my standards. Careless blond curls covered to just below his ears, framing a face that was more handsome than beautiful. He put all that beauty into his face so that the gaze of it was like a blow, or that's what he tried for. Claudia made a small, helpless sound. He'd rolled her, that quick.

I dug my fingers into her arm, and that didn't free her. I looked into his pale eyes, and felt the weight of his power. It said, *See me, I am beautiful, I am desirable, you want me.*

I shook my head, and had to flex power like unsheathing a blade not to fall into that gaze. Auggie hadn't been able to roll me, but this one could. I actually dropped my gaze, rather than fight it. The moment my eyes weren't being bored into by that pale gaze, I could think. Jesus, he was good.

I saw his hand coming. Claudia tried to stop him. I think he just looked at her, and she stopped moving. Lisandro tried, too, but again, a glance, and they seemed confused. The hesitation was enough. He had the time he needed to touch me. Touch makes it all worse, or better. He wanted me to look up, and I did.

I met his gaze, and again, his face was like a beautiful weapon. He leaned over me, his face painted with the stage makeup. He leaned in, as if he'd kiss me, and some part of me that was still sane knew that if he kissed me, it would be bad.

I smelled Jean-Claude's cologne, and the scent of Richard's neck. Jean-Claude had opened the marks wider. It made me startle, and take a step back, away from the blond.

I reached backward, and Jean-Claude took my hand. The touch of my master, and I was proof against the pale-eyed blond.

He smiled, an arrogant curl of lips. The smile said it all: *I almost had you.* He was right. He had almost had me. And still there was a breathing presence of power out there in the theatre, flowing over the crowd, and that power wasn't the blond in front of us. There was still something even more powerful waiting in the wings. Something even more powerful that we'd invited to our town. Sweet Mary, Mother of God, what had we done?

46

THE BLOND FLUNG himself over our heads, and out into the air. The air was full of vampires. They had flown up and over the audience, and in that instant the vampire let them go. He released his hold on the audience and they were left gasping, shrieking. Not at the fact that their minds had been messed about with, because they didn't know that, but at the vampires suddenly appearing above them like magic.

Jean-Claude helped me back to my seat. I needed the help; my knees were shaky. I looked around at all of us, and only the vampires hid their fear. The rest of us were wide-eyed and a little pale.

I leaned into Jean-Claude and whispered, "Did they do that every show?"

He shook his head, and spoke mind-to-mind. Yeah, maybe some of the other masters could overhear us, but we knew for dead certain they'd hear us whisper. "He bespelled the humans and some of the wereanimals, but he did not try for the vampires. He left them alone."

"Why now," I whispered, "why tonight?"

Of course, he didn't know. That didn't make me feel any better, strangely.

Claudia asked permission to check on the other guards. I gave it. I, like Claudia, wanted to see for sure that the other guards were up and running.

Lisandro was cursing very softly under his breath. "Fuck, fuck, fuck," over and over, like he said it with every breath.

He'd taken the words right out of my mouth.

The vampires danced on the air, at least a dozen of them. They defied gravity, and made it look effortless. It was beautiful, but I couldn't enjoy it. I was too scared.

The blond hovered in front of our box for a moment. He blew me a kiss. I smiled sweetly and gave him a one-fingered salute. He laughed, and flew away.

Other vampires flew low over the crowd, and they blew kisses at other women and other men. There were three or four women among them. It was sort of the reverse of most ballet companies, where there seemed to be more women than men.

The drapes at the back of our box opened, and it was Auggie. I got a glimpse of Pierce and Octavius on the other side of the curtain with Wicked and Truth. Auggie didn't look any happier than I felt.

He leaned over us, smiling, pretending he'd just come to say hi. "He did not do this in Chicago."

"Who didn't? Who's doing this?" I asked.

"Merlin," Auggie said, "troupe leader, dance master. The blond is Adonis. He used to be Belle's. Now he belongs to Merlin."

I felt that power breathing back on the air, like the smell of smoke drifting through the forest, when you don't know yet from which direction the flames will come, but you know they're on the way.

Auggie touched my bare shoulder. His power slid over my skin like a fall of silk. He offered his hand to Jean-Claude. "You rolled me; use it now."

Jean-Claude took his hand. To a casual viewer, they were shaking hands. Auggie's hand tensed on my bare shoulder, touching the edge of scars where a vamp had once worried at my collarbone like a dog with a rat. I wasn't entirely sure what Auggie meant for us to do. But Jean-Claude was sure, and you only need one driver on the metaphysical bus. Jean-Claude opened the marks between him and me, opened them wide. If it had been me, I couldn't have opened them that wide without involving at least Richard, but Jean-Claude had centuries of control under his belt. He used his free hand to touch my arm, and that was all we needed.

It was as if he pulled aside a curtain, a thick, velvet curtain. I could almost feel it sliding through my body, and then my necromancy flowed out from me like a chill wind. His power met mine, and the cold grew. But not the cold that blankets and coats would cure. This was the cold of the grave, spilled down our skins. Jean-Claude took that cold power and poured it down our hands and into Auggie. His power burst over Auggie, sudden enough that he had to close his eyes. His power was warmer than Jean-Claude's, warmer than my necromancy. He tasted not just of vampire, but of lion. More than any vampire I'd ever touched, he was also his beast. Interesting.

His cold warm power rose up, then spilled down his body to meet ours. It was a rush of power that tightened my throat, clenched my hand tight on Jean-Claude's. Only feasting on Auggie earlier let me know how small this power rush was compared to what we could do with him.

My lion tried to rise to roll his power. It was Auggie who soothed the lion, like a hand to stroke her quiet. But his power, far into me, found something else to rise. The *ardeur* started to flare, and it was Jean-Claude who rode it down, dampened those fires. He took the power, firm and hard, in his hand, the way he could suddenly take charge during lovemaking. You go from it being a team sport, to suddenly having him on top, and holding you still, so he can do exactly what he wants, in exactly the way he wants it, giving you more pleasure than you could have found on your own. He rode the power, and Auggie and I were just along for the ride.

The audience below us was oohing, aahing, giving little fake screams. It sounded like a crowd at a fireworks display, except this display was whirling, floating, diving bodies. I watched the dancers distantly. Their beauty no longer moved me. The power that Jean-Claude was building was the only thing that truly touched me.

But I heard the rustling of birds again; that got through the power haze. Merlin was about to pour power over the crowd again. He was going to hide the dancers, so they would vanish again, *poof.*

Jean-Claude used our power like a slap, a feint to let the other vampire know to back off. I heard birds flutter, as if they'd been disturbed in their sleep. I whispered, "Birds," and I couldn't tell if I said it out loud or not.

"His animal to call," Auggie whispered back, and that was a voice in my head.

I felt the power pull back, as if this Merlin had taken a deep breath. I had a moment to think he'd gotten the message, but the next moment that breath came back at us. Power poured over the audience. I felt the humans snuff out like matches, one by one. Vampires are allowed group hypnotism, because group mind tricks aren't permanent. Once the power is over, no harm, no foul. But this felt different. This felt like something that would linger, and change what it had touched.

"What's he doing?" and that was aloud.

Jean-Claude's voice breathed through my mind, "He is going to try to take us."

"What is he doing to the crowd?"

"He's trying to take us, all of us," Auggie said, "and that's too much power for the humans."

"He'll own them," I said.

"No," Jean-Claude said, "they are ours." He didn't try to fight for the minds of the crowd; he went straight for the source of our problem. He used the power of the three of us to smash into that mind.

The power staggered, as if we'd hit him, then the sound of birds filled the theatre. Twittering, crying, fluttering; the sound of hundreds of birds. The sound was so real that I searched the theatre for the flock, but there was nothing to see.

Nathaniel said, "I hear birds."

I didn't have time to wonder why he could hear them, too, because the birds were upon us. Feathers everywhere, touching, beating at me, trying to get me to move, to run. Jean-Claude's hand had a death grip on mine. Auggie's fingers dug into my shoulder, and the pain helped. It helped chase back the beating wings. I remembered the last time that a vampire's power had beat against my body like wings. Beat against me, not to frighten or make me run, but to be let inside. The power had cried in the dark, to be let inside me. Obsidian Butterfly, Master of the City of Albuquerque, had found her way inside me. She had filled my eyes with the blackness between suns, and the cold light of stars. She had also shared her power with me. That power came again, as if the touch of wings had called it.

Auggie cursed under his breath, his hand desperate on my shoulder. Jean-Claude said, "*Ma petite*, do not . . ." But whatever I wasn't to do he never said, because Obsidian Butterfly's gift dropped my shields and cut me open for Merlin's power. That metaphysical wind of wings and twittering calls poured inside me. The power poured inside me and I felt Merlin's triumph like the scream of some huge bird of prey. He thought he'd broken my shields, broken our shields, but he was wrong.

Jean-Claude and Auggie clung to me, trying to shore up what they, too, thought was a break in our power. But it wasn't a breach, it was a mouth.

It felt as if my body were a cave, a fleshy, soft cave, and the birds that I had heard and felt poured inside me, as if they'd found a home. I swear I could feel the brush of feathers, tiny bodies, fluttering, diving, filling me. Merlin's power poured into me, and tried to find Jean-Claude and Auggie. The power tried to find a way out of me and into them. Merlin poured more and more power into me, and I swallowed it.

Auggie and Jean-Claude clung to me, afraid to let go, afraid not to let go, I think. So much power, so much that it began to leak through into the other two vampires. The moment it touched them, they both understood. Merlin wasn't going to break me, we were going to eat him.

He must have figured it out at the same time, because he tried to stop the power, just cut it off. But I had the taste of him, and I didn't want it to stop.

The torrents of invisible birds slowed, but didn't stop. Obsidian Butterfly's power called to them, helped me know sweet words to use, to coax that power. The power kept coming, and I felt the flash of fear. It was sweet, and good, and I longed to taste the sweat on his skin. And I could, I licked down his skin, where he watched from the shadows.

He stared at me with dark eyes that held crimson like a pinpoint tear inside them. I'd seen eyes like that before. *Never were human, were you?* I thought.

He tried to break the contact, and he couldn't do it. Not with Auggie and Jean-Claude hooked up to me. He was big and bad and powerful, but he was not a Master of the City. He was not two Masters of the City, and he didn't know what the hell I was; in that moment neither did I.

I smelled jasmine and rain. I smelled a tropical night that hadn't existed for thousands on thousands of years. A voice rode the smell of rain. The Mother of All Darkness whispered, "I know what you are, necromancer."

I didn't want to ask, but it was as if I couldn't stop my mouth from forming the word. "What?"

"Mine."

47

I SCREAMED, AND I shut it down. I shut it all down. No more birds from Merlin. But in my panic, I shut down the tie with Auggie and Jean-Claude. For an instant, it was just me and her inside my head. I felt rain on my face, cool and warm. The moon rode full and bright, and I was too tall, and too male. I thought it was Jean-Claude's memory, but the hand I could see was too rough, too dark. Whose memory was I trapped in?

"Mine," she said again.

Oh, yeah, her. So why was I inside the head of the man she was about to eat? Why wasn't I inside her body?

Something moved in the moonlight. Something huge and pale, like some muscular ghost, sliding along the ground toward me. The head moved, and the eyes caught the moon, shining at me. I stared into the face of that great cat, and knew that nothing like it had walked the earth for thousands of years. "Cave lion," I thought, "huh, they were striped." The cat crouched to spring.

A wolf appeared between me and it. A white wolf with a dark saddle and head. Me, my wolf. This was a dream, which meant I was unconscious. Weird.

The wolf's hackles rose, and it gave that low, bass growl that all the canids use when they aren't kidding anymore. The wolf looked fragile beside that crouching figure. We were out of our weight class by a few hundred pounds.

I smelled wolf. I smelled pine, and forest loam. I smelled things that never grew here in this land, where the Mother of All Darkness had taken Merlin, or whoever he'd been once. I smelled the trees of home, the earth of pack land. I smelled the soft musk of wolf.

The cave lion tensed, and I knew this was it. The wolf braced for the spring, and the body I was wearing readied a spear that would not help.

Something touched my hand. I grabbed for it, without thinking, and the night exploded into white, hot light. Light, and pain, a great deal of pain.

Voices. "Let go, Anita, let go!"

Hands touching the pain. I tried to jerk away. It felt as if the blood in my hand had been replaced with molten metal. I knew that pain. A different voice, "Anita, let go!"

"Open your hand, Anita, just open your hand." Micah's voice.

My left hand was a lump of agony. I couldn't even feel my fingers. How could I open it, if I couldn't feel it? All I could feel was pain. It made me open my eyes. My vision was ruined, spotted, gray and black and white, as if I'd looked into a bright flash of light.

I had a moment to see the ring of faces: Micah, Nathaniel, Jason, Graham, and Richard. I saw them, but all my attention went to the agony that was my left hand. I looked at it, and on the outside it was fine. A thin gold chain trailed out of my fist. My hand looked fine, but I knew it wasn't.

There were heavy drapes behind us. We were still at the Fox. They'd just carried me out of the box, and put me somewhere where the audience couldn't see. I knew why there were no vampires kneeling with us. The Mother of All Darkness had tried to take me, again, and some fool had given me a cross to hold.

"Open your hand, Anita, please." Micah whispered it again, stroking my hair.

I found my voice, and whispered, "Can't."

Richard cradled my hand in his, and started trying to pry my fingers open. He peeled a finger up. I whimpered, then bit my lip. If I started making noises, I'd end up screaming, or weeping, loudly. They'd managed to hide me away from the crowd. If I started screaming that would all be for nothing.

"I'm sorry, Anita, I'm sorry." Richard whispered it over and over as he pried my hand open.

"Curse if you want to," Jason said.

I shook my head. Bad burns hurt too much for cursing to make anything better. I forced myself to feel past the pain. I could still feel my hand, but distant, as if the hand around the pain were almost asleep. The pain overrode everything else—as if the nerves just couldn't handle it all so they transmitted the important parts, that it fucking hurt, all else was secondary.

Richard made a sound and it made me glance at him. The look on his face made me look where he was looking—my hand.

Most of the blisters had burst, so that my palm and fingers were a mass of ruptured skin and clear fluid. But the glint of gold in my palm was buried inside the mass of torn flesh. The cross had melted into my hand.

I looked away then; I didn't want to think about what was going to be needed to clean it up.

Nathaniel leaned over me, blocking my view, which panicked me. I pushed him away, so I could see what Richard was doing by my hand. No way was that cross coming out without medical help. Painkillers, good painkillers, yeah, that was the ticket.

I reached my good hand back up to Nathaniel. He leaned over so I could whisper, "Doctor." I whispered because I was afraid if I talked any louder, I'd start yelling.

He nodded. "Dr. Lillian is on her way."

I nodded. Not caring how the doc was getting into the event. For once in my life, I just wanted the help. Most pain you can ride out, but burns just seem made to eat the world. The pain eats everything else. You can't think about anything but the pain. The grinding, biting, aching, nauseating pain. I'd had burns before, but this one was going to be the worst. Weeks of recovery, and depending on how deep the cross was embedded, maybe permanent damage to the hand. Shit, fucking shit.

Dr. Lillian came into sight. I didn't recognize her at first, and it wasn't just the pain. Makeup had softened her face, brought out what she must have looked like ten years ago. The soft blue of the dress complemented the soft gray of her hair, and the pastel shades of lipstick and eye shadow. I didn't look at her and think, *She must have been lovely a decade ago*. I looked up at her and thought, *She is lovely now*.

She shook her head. "What am I going to do with you people tonight?"

I swallowed hard. "Didn't do it on purpose."

She lifted the long skirt enough so she could kneel comfortably. "I would say not." Her face was neutral, pleasant, a good doctor's face. She started to reach for my hand, and I jerked away.

She leaned back, giving me a little smile. "If you promise to do everything I tell you to do, exactly the way I tell you to do it, I'll shoot you up with a painkiller before I touch your hand."

I nodded.

"Your word of honor that you won't argue with me, Anita. That you'll just do what I tell you to do?"

If I hadn't been out of my head with pain, I might have thought harder about her wording, but all I could think about was the pain. I nodded, and whispered, "I promise."

She smiled at me. "Good." She looked behind her. Claudia came into view, kneeling so the other woman could whisper to her. Claudia nodded, stood, and left.

Lillian turned away to get the shot ready. Normally, I made a fuss about needles. I was almost as phobic of needles as I was of flying. But tonight, I wasn't complaining. I was too busy fighting off the urge to start screaming, *Make it stop, make it stop.*

Lillian made Richard move, so she could kneel by my injured hand. Micah cupped my face so I couldn't see the needle. He knew how I felt about them. I let him do it, but I wasn't sure that I'd have cared tonight. I felt the pressure of the needle, then it was as if she shot hot water directly into my veins. I could feel it spreading liquid through my body. It was the oddest sensation. I'd never had anything that I could trace through my veins like that. My upper body flushed with heat. Then it was hard to concentrate, and I was dizzy. Even lying flat, I was dizzy. I started to ask if something was wrong, then the pain just washed away. The drugs bathed the inside of my upper body in hot water, and the pain just washed away.

Lillian leaned over me. "How do you feel, Anita?"

I managed a smile, and knew it was probably goofy. "Doesn't hurt now."

"Good," she said, smiling. She looked at Richard. "I think you need to go back to your date, Richard."

He shook his head. "I'm staying here."

"You're Clark Kent tonight, Ulfric, not Superman. You have to go back to your date and pretend you're a mild-mannered science teacher. I'll take care of Anita."

Richard glanced at us all. "Are they staying?"

"One of them will be," Lillian said, "but they aren't hiding what they are, Ulfric. The price of hiding is that you must stay hidden. Now, go back before the woman starts to look for you."

He started to argue.

"Don't make me be cruel about this, Ulfric," Lillian said.

"Go," I said, and my voice sounded strange. "Go, Richard, go."

He gave me a look that was full of such conflict, even pain. But tonight I didn't have any time for anyone's pain but mine.

"I'm sorry," he said. I wasn't sure what he was sorry about. That he had to go? That he had another date? That he was still hiding in his Clark Kent disguise? Or, maybe, that it was his cross embedded in my hand. The cross I'd given him for Christmas once. Yeah, that might need a sorry.

48

THEY SPREAD A tablecloth across me and another under my arm. Apparently, Requiem had "charmed" them out of the restaurant staff. He'd kept his eyes averted from me, as if he feared the cross would flare to life.

Lillian had Micah and Nathaniel distract me, though the drugs did a lot of the distracting for them. I was afraid it would hurt, but it was like the fear couldn't hold on to me, or I couldn't hold on to it. Jason pressed down on my arm. I started to protest. Nathaniel kissed me, hard. The kiss swallowed my small noises.

There was a sharp, abrupt tug on my hand. I cried out, and Nathaniel ate the sound as he did sometimes during sex. A scream lost in a kiss.

I could feel them doing something to my hand. Wrapping it in something. Nathaniel drew back from the kiss, his mouth smeared with my lipstick. He put a finger over my lips, and I fought to make only small whimpering sounds. It wasn't so much that it hurt, it was almost as if my body knew it was hurt, and wanted to react to it. But every time I tried to concentrate on the pain, it just slipped away. Maybe it seemed weird to try to concentrate on it. I guess I was trying to fight the drugs, stupid of me. But I couldn't just slip away. I couldn't not fight, even when it wasn't good for me.

Nathaniel smiled down at me, as if he knew what I was doing. He probably did. He moved his finger back from my mouth. I nodded at him to let him know I understood. We were trying not to attract attention. Sure.

I looked down and found that my hand was wrapped in gauze, like a pristine version of the mummy's hand. I got a flash of fresh blood on the tablecloths before they were bundled up. I tried to care about how we'd explain the fresh blood, but I couldn't finish caring, before it floated away. It should have felt good, to be so relaxed, but I knew that this was a night when Jean-Claude needed me, everyone needed me. The Mother of All Darkness was still out there. What would they do if she came back and I wasn't there? Fear tried to swell again, and it didn't last. I couldn't hold on to any one thought, or emotion. It was like trying to row a boat in the fog. You knew what direction you wanted to go. You'd get a glimpse of the shore, and row your hardest, then the fog slipped back over you, and when it cleared again, the shore was somewhere else. As much as the pain would have distracted me, I'd have been more functional with that than the drugs. But the burn had hurt so much, so very much. I'd wanted it to stop.

Someone picked me up, and it woke me. Though I wasn't sure I'd exactly been asleep, passed out maybe. Nathaniel was carrying me. The sleeves of his white shirt showed, and I was covered by a black tux jacket. His, probably. I was vaguely proud of myself for figuring it out.

I looked around for Micah and it was as if Nathaniel understood. "Micah is going to sit with Asher, so that neither box will be empty." He started down the steps with me in his arms.

Requiem appeared over his shoulder, following us. Lisandro was beside him. I looked down the stairs, and caught a glimpse of Doc Lillian, before the dizziness became too much. What the hell had she given me?

I lost some more time, because the next thing I knew we were all the way down and stepping out under the covered awning outside the Fox club's private entrance. I got a glimpse of Wicked standing beside the valet attendant. The attendant's face was blank and peaceful. Vampire mind tricks to make sure no one remembered us. One-on-one mind tricks were illegal, technically, partially because of shit like this. That a vampire could persuade a person that the bad things hadn't happened. It made witness testimony a bitch.

Fredo was holding the door to the limo as if he were a real chauffeur and not a walking weapons store. Nathaniel crawled inside with me in his arms. He laid me gently on the backseat, and lifted the tux jacket off me. Doc Lillian knelt beside me. She touched my face, and tried to get me to follow her fingers. I don't think I did really well at it.

She smiled at me. "I dosed you like you were one of us, and you're not. Whatever you are becoming, it's not lycanthrope."

I frowned at her. "What?"

"The morphine should have worked out of your system by now, and it hasn't. It won't be four to ten hours like a human, but two, at least two." She shook her head. "Sometimes we all forget that you are still mostly human."

"Morphine," I said.

She nodded. "Yes, Anita, morphine. If the master that tried to take us all renews his attack, without you, I don't think Jean-Claude can take him."

Did she think that all that happened had been Merlin's doing? Did she not know about the Mother of All Darkness? It seemed like I should explain it to her, but I couldn't hold all my thoughts in a row long enough to do it.

"We need you back with us now."

I nodded, then closed my eyes, because it made the inside of my head fuzzier for a moment. "Agreed," I whispered, "how?" I opened my eyes, and fought to focus on that lovely face, the gray eyes that looked blue tonight with the dress and the eye shadow.

"Call the munin, Anita. It will clear your mind, and heal much of this damage."

I frowned at her. I must have heard her wrong. "Call munin, now?"

She nodded. "Raina could heal this."

I closed my eyes and fought, fought hard to gather my thoughts and explain why this was such a bad idea. Munin were the ancestral spirits of the wolf pack. But they could be a lot more "lively" than just normal ancestor worship. Especially if you had psychic ability, or, most yummy, talent with the dead, the munin could be much, much more lively. Raina was the old lupa of the pack. I'd killed her because she was trying to kill me. The munin could "possess" people who had the talent for it. I'd become her favorite ride. I'd spent a long, long weekend in Tennessee with my spiritual teacher, Marianne, learning how to control the munin in general, and Raina in specific. Micah and Nathaniel had gone with me to "help" me deal with it. I'd asked Richard first, wolf business and all, but he had flatly refused. Raina was dead. He wanted nothing more to do with her. Neither did I, but I didn't have a choice.

She'd been a sexual sadist, but she could also heal with sex. It didn't have to be full-blown sex, she just liked it that way. I'd tapped into her power a few times to save lives, but the cost had been high. Her memories alone were worth avoiding. The *ardeur* wasn't normally a thing of healing, and Jean-Claude had speculated that the fact that I could heal with sex and metaphysics might be more because of Raina's munin than vampire powers. It was almost as if the more often I was used by, or borrowed magic from, someone else, the more likely it became that their magic would become part of my arsenal. Raina had played with me enough that it had somehow effected the *ardeur,* or that was the theory. Why not use the *ardeur* to heal the hand? Healing with the *ardeur* was catch-as-catch-can; sometimes it worked without your wanting it to work, and sometimes it didn't work at all. I did my best to explain it out loud. "Not sure I can control her, like this. Bad, if she's in charge."

"You are badly hurt, Anita. If you were truly vampire, then you'd need more blood. A lot more than normal. Jean-Claude thinks that the *ardeur* will rise and try to feed that need."

I frowned harder at her. "I don't . . ."

"You promised to do whatever I asked, if I gave you the morphine. You gave your word."

I swallowed, licked my lips, and thought about calling her a bitch, but since she was the only doctor we had, and I was hurt, it seemed unwise to piss her off. I could control Raina's munin now, if I hadn't been on drugs. I said, "No."

"Then you will miss the ballet, and the party, and you will not be there to help Jean-Claude against the other masters. Richard will not be there because he is hiding. If you think it is a good idea to strip the master of this city of both of his thirds on this night, then refuse."

Hell with it. I said, "Bitch."

She smiled, and patted my cheek. "Once you are healed, your beasts may rise, so I will leave you with people who can take your beast, if they must."

"I don't understand."

"But I think we should start with someone that Raina never touched. I knew her, you see; she always loved new conquests."

I shook my head, gently. "Don't understand."

Nathaniel appeared beside her. He was not new to Raina; she'd had him every way a woman could have a man, and some that stretched the imagination to the screaming point. He was nude, except for the amethyst and diamond collar. It had been a gift from Jean-Claude and me, though frankly, more Jean-Claude's idea than mine. It would simply never have occurred to me.

"You're not wearing any clothes."

He smiled. "We're going to try to go back inside afterward."

"Afterward what?"

He glanced at Lillian. "How much is she following all this?"

"I'm not certain."

A voice from behind us. "I don't do rape."

Jason's voice then. "None of us do."

Lillian leaned over me. "Anita, Anita, you must give permission for this."

"For what, exactly?" There, that was a clear question.

"Raise Raina's munin, heal yourself, and heal Requiem."

"Requiem?"

"Raina will like that he's someone new, and that he's badly injured."

I stared into Lillian's face. "You really did know her."

She nodded. "Better than I wanted to. I would not ask this, if I thought we would survive this night without you. Raphael felt one of the masters in the ballet. One of them can call rats, Anita. Do you understand what that means to our people?"

"Yes," I said, "if they take Raphael, then they own you all."

"Exactly."

"And we invited them here," I whispered.

Requiem's bare shoulder appeared around Lillian. "Merlin, their dance master, rolled the human audience to make his dancers appear and vanish, but he did not try to roll the other masters. Until tonight."

I wasn't so sure of that. I'd felt Merlin's mind. If he'd rolled them, then let them go, they might never have figured it out. I tried to explain it. "His mind, powerful enough. He could let them go. They might never know."

"You mean that he rolled them, and was so powerful that they don't remember it?"

"Yes."

I watched fear march over his face, swallowed by that perfect blankness that the old ones have. "Perhaps, but I do not believe that Marmee Noir appeared in the other cities."

"Who is Marmee Noir?" Lillian asked.

"Our dark mother, the first of us. It was her power added to Merlin's that did what was done tonight. It was her power that made Richard's cross melt into Anita's hand."

"Is she here, with the troupe?"

"No," I said, "she lies in the room with windows." That probably made no sense to any of them, but they let it go. They took my drugged assurance that the nightmare of all vampires wasn't physically in St. Louis. Drugged out of my ability to concentrate and they took my word about it. They shouldn't have done that. But more than Mommie Dearest, there was Auggie and Samuel, and hell, Samuel's wife, Thea. If these were the masters Jean-Claude trusted, then what would the other masters do to us? Jean-Claude didn't need to be alone tonight. Something bad would happen.

"Get out, doc."

"What?"

"Don't want you here when the wicked bitch comes."

"I'll get out, and the only ones in the car will be people you've fed on before, Anita." She glanced behind her. "With one exception."

"Exception?"

"Go, Lillian," Jason said. "Jean-Claude's nervous. Something else has happened. Not as bad, but something."

Lillian moved out of sight, and Jason knelt beside me. He was as nude as Nathaniel. He was wearing the cuff bracelet that Jean-Claude had had commissioned for him. Wolves running over a gold and platinum landscape. The wolves looked so real you expected them to move. I stared at the bracelet. "Pretty," I said.

He grinned. "And the bracelet's nice, too." He looked down at me, and his face was so serious. I couldn't feel what Jean-Claude was feeling; the morphine and my own earlier panic had shut the marks down. I didn't like how serious Jason looked. What was happening to my sweeties while I was arguing?

"Let's get you out of the clothes. You've got to have something to wear back inside."

A moment ago, I might have argued, but Jason was scared, and I couldn't feel Jean-Claude. I was too befuddled to risk opening the marks. Afraid I'd screw up Jean-Claude's concentration as badly as mine was, and that would be a disaster. Bad things were happening, and it was our fault. The vampires had invited bad things to the city, and now everyone was in danger. "Help me out of the corset."

"Thought you'd never ask," Jason said, and he leered at me, the way he usually did, but I could see his eyes, and his eyes weren't having any fun at all. Bad things, bad things, what was happening inside? I thought, *Hold on, Jean-Claude*. I felt him like a distant caress of wind against the door I'd used to shut us down. That breath of power smelled sweetly of his cologne. His words seemed to fill the car. "Feed before you come back to me, *ma petite*. Do not loose the *ardeur* on the crowd." Then he was gone, shut down and tight, shielding his ass off. But he'd raised a good point. It was perfectly me to raise munin, heal, and not feed the *ardeur*, if I could stave it off. That brief message let me know that he wanted me back fed, and ready to fight, not hungry and dangerous to the crowd. Jason helped me sit up, and Nathaniel started unlacing my corset back. Was it too small-town Midwestern of me to think it was weird that my main squeeze was encouraging me to have sex with a limo full of men before I came back inside to him? We had the mother of all vampires lurking around. A master vamp powerful enough to roll every master in town. And mustn't forget the blond dancer, Adonis, who had almost rolled me with his gaze. Powerful, dangerous shit going on, and the thing that made me squirm inside was the sex? It was one of those evenings when I'd really get to decide if it was a fate worse than death.

The corset loosened enough to spill my breasts into the open air. "Requiem," Jason said, "get over here."

The vampire came, and he used his hands to hide his nakedness. He seemed embarrassed. I was uncomfortable with it, too, but the morphine took the edge off the embarrassment, like it took the edge off everything.

They lifted the corset over my head, and other hands went to the top of my skirt. Nathaniel took the clothes away as they came off. They took everything but the diamond necklace. Apparently the jewelry was a theme tonight. There was plastic over the far seat, and he was putting the clothes under it. How messy was everyone expecting to be?

I caught movement in the far back of the limo. It was Noel. "No," I said, "get him out."

"Justin didn't get here, Anita," Jason said, "he's the only lion we got except for Auggie's bodyguard. If your lion rises, we need somewhere for it to go."

"He's a baby."

Jason nodded. "Raina loved virgins."

I shook my head too hard, made myself dizzy. I closed my eyes and tried to concentrate. "He waits outside the car. If my lion rises, then I'll bring his beast, but we are not feeding him to Raina." I opened my eyes, and the world had stopped wavering. Good.

Jason touched Requiem's shoulder, drew my attention back to him. "I don't think we'll have to, Anita. Look at Requiem through her eyes. Look at those wounds, Anita. He's fresh meat and he's wounded. She'll like that."

I looked at the knife wounds on his chest and side. His arms were cut up. "Silver blades," I said.

Requiem nodded. "Meng Die meant my death."

"A little power and she changes her mind."

"It is not a little power, Anita," Jason said.

I looked back at Requiem. "Do you know what Raina will do?"

Nathaniel knelt by us. "I told him what she liked to do during sex."

I fought to focus on Requiem's still face. "Is it"—I searched for the word I wanted—"all right?"

"I have been at the court of Belle Morte, Anita, this will be as nothing." He found a smile for me. "Heal me so that we may both serve our master well this night."

I nodded. "Okay." I looked behind them all, at Noel. He was pressed in the far back of the limo, as far from the action as he could get. "Out, now."

"Wait outside with Fredo," Jason said.

"I was told to stay close," Noel said. His eyes were big, his mouth a little parted. I realized I was naked in front of him. I'd known that, but the drugs or the emergency, or my collapsing morals, had made me not think about it. The look on his face wasn't lust. It was fear.

"Outside the car is close enough," Jason said.

Still, he hesitated.

"Get out of the car, Noel," Nathaniel said. He sounded angry.

Noel got out of the car. When the door closed behind him, Nathaniel said, "How could Joseph have sent him for this job?"

"Joseph didn't understand," Jason said.

"Didn't want to understand," Nathaniel said. His eyes had gone almost purple with anger.

"Protect the innocent," I said.

He gave me those angry eyes, then made a smile for me, and nodded. "You can control Raina. I know you can."

"The drugs . . ."

"Will make it harder, but you can do this. I was there when you learned how to do this, Anita. Drugs or no drugs, your will is stronger than hers."

I stared into his face, studied that anger, that surety. I got that glimpse that I had sometimes, of what he might be in ten years. He was going to be something special at thirty, and I planned on being there to see it. I planned on us all being there to see it. Which meant we had to get through tonight. Whatever it took.

Jason laid me back on the seat. Nathaniel gave me a quick kiss, then he moved away, too. Requiem sat on the end of the seat, like he was on an uncomfortable first date.

I held out my hand to him. "Help me."

He took my hand, and knelt beside the seat, still covering as much of his nakedness as he could. "How can I help you?"

"Use your power on me."

His eyes filled with rich blue fire, and my body jolted with it. It hurt my sore hand, but the mixture of pain and pleasure and confusion would appeal to her. I'd learned to control Raina, which meant she had to be coaxed inside me now. It was sort of like leaving a perfectly good house when you know a tiger is just outside, and oh, by the way, let's strap a raw steak around your neck. This was all such a bad idea. Problem was, I didn't have a better one.

49

THE FIRST THING you need to know in order to control something is how it feels to do it. I was a natural psychic, which meant that my gifts weren't something I had to strive for, they just came to me. The problem with being a natural is that sometimes things come so easily that you don't know how, or even when, you're doing psychic stuff. It sort of sneaks up on you. You must understand a thing to truly control it. I'd relied for most of my life on the fact that I was just such a brute psychically that I could bull my way through things. But some things can't be controlled by brute force alone, or even by sheer power alone. You need control. It's the difference between being able to throw a baseball ninety miles an hour, and being able to throw it ninety miles an hour over home plate. The speed and skill is great, but if you keep throwing wild, it'll never get you into the majors. In fact, you may kill some poor fan in the stands. Getting hit in the head with a ball going that fast, well, not good. Raina wasn't my only ninety-mile-an-hour ball, but she was the second one I learned to control, after the necromancy.

Requiem was flat on his back on the seat. I didn't remember changing places with him. The last thing I remembered, clearly, was me naked on my back, on the seat. Now, it was him lying naked. Him, looking up at me, a surprised look on his face. What had I done to put that look on Requiem's face? What had I done, while Raina was in control and I was fighting off the morphine?

I was sitting on his waist, which was an improvement over lower, I guess. I looked behind me to Nathaniel and Jason. The look on my face must have been enough, because Jason said, "You body-slammed him down on the seat."

"Your hand is bleeding," Nathaniel said.

I stared at my left hand as if it had just appeared at the end of my arm. There was fresh blood soaking through the gauze. The moment I saw the blood, the hand began to hurt. It wasn't as bad as before Lillian gave me the shot, but it was a persistent, grinding pain, with twinges of sharper things. The sharper pains promised worse to come.

"I believe you injured yourself throwing me down on the seat," Requiem said. His voice was mild, almost politely empty. His face matched it, handsome, and blank. The surpise was gone as if I'd dreamed it. He was in control of himself, once more.

I felt Raina inside me. She didn't want him in control of himself, or anything else. She wanted to break him. I'd seen far enough inside his head with the *ardeur* to know he'd been broken centuries before, and more than once. I knew that breaking someone already broken wouldn't appeal to her as much as being the first one to do it. Jason had been right; Raina liked virgins, of every sort. She loved to be in on someone's first experience, especially if she could turn pleasure to pain, joy to terror. That just flat did it for her. Not my kink, which made it easier not to do it.

Her voice whispered through my mind, not as clear as it once had been, more a wind-in-the-trees kind of sound. Marianne had informed me that Raina had come close to truly possessing me, as in almost demonic possession. That had been a scary thought. Now I knew how to keep Raina from getting that intimate a grip on me. The wind of her voice blew through my body, smelling of forest, and fur, and perfume. "You know what I want, Anita."

"You know what I'm willing to give you." I said that part out loud, because talking mind-to-mind with her spirit could give it a stronger hold on you. I thought about how close Requiem and I had come to intercourse earlier today. I thought about him rolling off, unsatisfied, and unsatisfying.

"The first fucking between you," she laughed, and my concentration wasn't pure enough to keep that laugh off my lips. Her laugh was a low, throaty, alto sound, a joyous promise of sex. I didn't own a laugh like that.

Nathaniel said, "Concentrate, Anita. You can do this."

Raina wanted me to look behind me at him, and I fought not to do it. Not because it was a bad thing, but because I had to start fighting somewhere, and it was a place to start. It was also something that if I lost the fight, it wouldn't hurt anyone.

"Petty, Anita," she whispered.

I ignored her, as best I could. Always hard to ignore people who are sharing your consciousness. I tried to concentrate on my breathing, but the pain in my hand kept distracting me. I tried concentrating on each heartbeat, on the pulse in my body, and that was a mistake. It was as if each beat of my heart hit my injured hand like a spike. As if the very pulse of blood made it hurt worse.

I shook my head, and that was a mistake. I was suddenly dizzy. Requiem's hands caught my arms, kept me from falling. I let myself collapse on top of him, my head resting against his shoulder. He made no sound, but his body flinched. I was lying across his wounds. Raina liked that a lot.

I kissed his shoulder. The skin was warm. Warm with the blood he'd taken from me earlier, but not as warm as it should have been. I gazed up into those brilliant blue eyes, with their hint of green around the iris. "Your body is using more energy trying to heal your wounds."

"Yes," he whispered.

"Do you need to feed more often when you're this badly hurt?"

"Yes, m'lady."

I smiled at him. "Somehow *m'lady* doesn't work with me naked on top of you."

He smiled, and it even reached his eyes. "You will always be *m'lady* to me, Anita."

I was suddenly drowning in the scent of wolf. The beast inside me stirred, as if Raina's power were a spoon and I were some kind of soup. Stirring, looking for just the right tidbit.

Her voice sounded inside me. "Your very own wolf, Anita. What have you been doing while I've been away?"

The wolf, my wolf, appeared inside me. I could see it forming. No, I thought, no. I turned my face into Requiem's neck where his pulse should have beat, but didn't. I pressed my mouth to that chilled flesh, and chased away the warm, prickling energy. I did not run from my wolf, for if you run things will chase you, but I turned to colder things. Things that the wolf neither understood nor entirely approved of. My wolf quieted, under the brush of dead flesh and the scent of flesh unmoving. The trouble with quieting my wolf was that Raina fled, too. I rose up from Requiem's body, enough to see his face.

"Your eyes, they are like brown diamonds, so much light in the darkness."

"Raina's gone," Jason said, softly.

I didn't look at him. I only had eyes for the vampire. I began to kiss down his body. A light kiss on his shoulder, and with each kiss, my body slid lower, and because we were both nude, that raised interesting things. And I knew that his body was swelling with blood that he'd taken from my veins. That without that ruby kiss, he would have been dead in so many more ways than just undead.

I raised my lower body enough so that we weren't touching below the waist. It felt wonderful, so much promise of things to come, but I wanted to concentrate on the feel of my mouth on his chest. I couldn't do that and have him brush the front of my body with the swelling richness of his. It distracted me.

I wanted to enjoy the smooth perfection of his skin. Cool, and moving, but not pulsing. Not alive, not completely, not really. It was like kissing my way down a dream, faintly unreal, as if Requiem's pale body should have evaporated into the first alarm of the day. Did Jean-Claude and Asher play human for me, more than this? Did they make their hearts beat, their blood pump, so I would not feel this amazing stillness? Requiem's arms caressed down my back, my sides. His chest moved, writhing with the pleasure of being touched, but he did not breathe. He did not play alive for me. He was a moving dead thing. It should have bothered me, but it didn't. The power that filled my eyes understood what he was, and liked it, liked it a lot.

I kissed down that smooth, cool flesh, until I came to coarseness, and a faint metallic taste. It made me open my eyes, and look at what I was kissing. It was the knife wound. It looked so smooth, but my lips told the truth. The edges of the wound were rough. The wound could look as pretty and neat as it wanted to but it had been violent. The knife had torn his skin, even around the edges, minute tears that the eye couldn't see, but the mouth could feel. I traced a fingertip across the lip of the wound. It drew small pain noises from him. Part of me liked the noises, and part of me worried that it hurt too much.

I gazed up at him. The look on his face as he stared down the length of his body at me wasn't a pained look. There was a tightening around his eyes that showed it hurt, but the look in those eyes was still eager. Which meant I hadn't crossed that thin line, yet. It still excited him more than it hurt him. Cool.

I concentrated on the sensation of the wound under the barest tip of my finger. I closed my eyes so that I could concentrate on it. It was coarse under my finger, not as instantly noticeable as my lips had found it, but the skin was torn and roughened by the violence of the blade. Touch also didn't give me that sweet, faint taste of blood. Was this Raina's thought, or mine? No, Jason was right, Raina was gone. I realized I was using my hand, both hands. It made me lean back from Requiem and stare at my burned hand. I'd had burns before, almost this bad, and for similar reasons. Admittedly, it had been because a vamp had pressed his flesh into the holy item. I guess this was the first time it had been just my body involved. Had it been because Marmee Noir had been possessing me, or had it been because I was using vampire powers? Huh? That was an interesting thought. I pushed it back, for so many reasons. I'd look at the implications later. Much later.

The skin had blistered, and hardened, and begun to slough off. Days, or weeks, of healing in minutes. I moved the hardened skin to one side. I wasn't quite brave enough to pull at it. I moved all that truly dead skin aside until I found the palm of my hand. The skin of the palm was soft, baby soft, but there was a new cross-shaped scar in the middle of my hand. That skin was shiny and not soft, not rough, more slick. Weeks of healing.

I hadn't used Raina to heal Requiem. I'd used her to heal me. But I understood why. I'd asked something of her munin that it could not do. She healed lycanthrope flesh, living flesh, and Requiem was not living flesh. No matter how alive he seemed, it was a trick, or a lie, or something I had no name for.

I stared down at Requiem. He gazed up at me with eyes that had gone back to their normal swimming blue. There was no power in him now. If it hadn't been silver blades, his body would have smoothed the damage over by now. But it was silver, and that meant healing would be almost human-slow, unless he had help.

"You are healed?" He made it a question.

I nodded. "A little trimming away of dead skin, but yeah."

"Trimming away the dead," he said, voice soft. He sighed, and said, "I can go back inside as I am. I will not be at my best, but it was your wounds that were most important."

I stared down at him, the two nearly fatal wounds in his upper body, the dozens of cuts and slashes on his arms. But I looked lower and found the rest of his body still hard and ready. "You should walk around nude more often," I said.

He actually frowned at me. "Why, m'lady?"

"Because you are beautiful."

He smiled. "I thank you for that."

"You say it like it's not true."

"If I were truly beautiful you would have found your way to my bed weeks ago."

I closed my eyes and drew a deep breath. My necromancy was still here, but it was changed somehow. It was like calling the munin or something about chasing out the Dark Mother had changed my own power. It was still necromancy, but it held an edge of . . . life. It was more alive, this energy. I didn't understand it, exactly, but I understood one thing: always before when I'd healed damage on vampires, small wounds, it had been in the daytime when they were dead. Once they rose, their own personality, or soul, or whatever, kept my power from recognizing them as a dead thing, the way it recognized zombies. They always hit the radar as dead, no matter how mobile they were.

I could feel the wound I had touched. I could feel it, and knew that it was a little like gathering up the bits of a zombie. One of the things I did most often in my job was to make the dead whole again.

It seemed important to do this thing. As though if I didn't heal Requiem now, I would forget how to do it. It was like a gift offered once, and wiped away if you don't use it. I wanted to use it; it would feel good to use. It always felt good to work with the dead.

I set my fingertips over his wound, and thought about it like clay. Like smoothing clay back into place. I closed my eyes so I could "see" the deeper tissues of the body knitting together, things I could not touch with my physical fingers.

There was a wind in the car, a wind that was chill, but held an edge of spring. I thought someone had opened a door, but when I opened my eyes, the car was closed. The wind was coming from me. I looked down at Requiem's body, and found my hands touching smooth, healed skin. There wasn't even a scar. I moved my hands to the wound on his side, at the ribs. I did it before my conscious mind could say, *Gosh, that's impossible*. I pressed my hands to his side, and I smoothed the wound away. The wind blew bits of my hair around my face. The hardened skin of blistered flesh fell away on its own from my hand, as I healed him. Dead flesh, all of it, dead flesh.

I grabbed his arms, and smoothed my hands from elbow to wrist, to hold his hands, and the skin smoothed behind my touch like a fast-forward camera trick. It wasn't possible, but I was still doing it.

The wind faltered, and I fell forward onto him. He caught me or I might have slipped to the floor of the car. Working with the dead always felt good, but it had its price, too. It was especially trying if there was no blood magic involved. It hadn't occurred to me it would be that similar to raising the dead in price.

Jason and Nathaniel were beside us. "What's wrong?" Jason asked.

Nathaniel answered, "She's exhausted."

I blinked up at him. "Are you exhausted, too?"

He shook his head. "When you shut the marks down, you shut them down. I can tell you're exhausted, but you aren't draining me. I don't think you're touching Damian either."

"I didn't want to risk the two of you again tonight."

"You shut everybody out," Jason said. "Jean-Claude is sensing more through me, right now, then you. A *pomme de sang* is not nearly the connection that you are to him."

"Too much happening," I said.

Requiem hugged me. "What can I do to make this right, m'lady? How do I repay such a miracle?"

"If we ever do this again, I need to have you take blood during it, just like a sacrifice at a zombie raising. Blood magic helps the energy."

"You need to feed," Jason said, and he had an abstracted look as if he were listening to something I couldn't hear. It was probably Jean-Claude whispering in his ear.

"Okay," I said, settling heavier onto Requiem's chest.

Jason and Nathaniel looked at each other, then back at Requiem. "Call your power, Requiem," Jason said, "call her *ardeur*. She's too weak to bind you with it, like she tried to do earlier. Feed her first, and you will be safe."

"It's like a ventriloquism act," I said, "your mouth moves but Jean-Claude's words come out."

Jason gave me the grin that was all his, and shrugged. "His words, or not, it's still true."

I rolled my head to look up at Requiem's face. "Is that why you stopped before? You were afraid I'd own you through the *ardeur*?"

"Yes," he said, "I feared I would end as London has ended, and I do not truly wish that."

"I don't think I'm up to binding anyone right now."

A look passed over his face that wasn't gentle, or hesitant. It was a very male look for a moment. "Then I can do as I wish with you."

I thought about arguing with the way he'd phrased it, but I just didn't have the energy for it. Too tired, and too drained. "Yes," I said, "you can."

He sat up, cradling me against the front of his body. He sat up, and half-carried me, until I was lying on the other end of the seat, and he was kneeling over me. His power danced over my body, and even that was energy, that was food. I watched his eyes drown in the blue depths of his own magic, until he stared down at me like one blind.

"Is this truly what m'lady wishes?"

I stared down the length of his body. So hard, so ready, almost hard enough that it must have hurt him a little. Too hard for too long is not always a good feeling. With his body practically screaming with need, he asked, asked permission one more time.

"Requiem," I said, "I promise I will always think of you as a gentleman, but I've already said yes."

"It is good to be certain," he whispered.

"Whoever taught you this caution, it wasn't me." I stroked my hand not across his chest, but just above it, playing in the energy of his aura. So much energy to play with. It made him close his eyes for a moment. "I promise, Requiem, I'll still respect you in the morning."

That made him smile, and he said, "And you will always be m'lady."

That made me laugh. Then he poured his power over my body, and the laughter changed to other sounds.

50

HE HELD ON to the door to raise himself above me, so that only the long, hard length of him touched me at first. His own magic had made my body tight and wet, and more than ready, so that each thrust was exquisite pleasure. A pleasure so great it was almost painful that his movement was slow, and shallow. He'd found that spot inside me, and he meant to work it, but I could feel his body fighting his own rhythm, wanting something harder, faster, less controlled. I was torn between wanting him to never stop, and knowing that we needed to hurry. But every time I opened my mouth to tell him to hurry, to let me feed, he thrust inside me again, or moved his hips just a little, and the thought died before I could say it.

The *ardeur* was raised, but even the *ardeur* seemed weak. I'd had it spread to most of the people in a room before; now, with Nathaniel and Jason trapped in a car with us, it hadn't spread to them. They were untouched. I needed to feed, not just to be strong enough to help Jean-Claude tonight, but to make certain I didn't start to suck Damian's life away.

I watched Requiem's body glide in and out of mine. In the dimness of the car I couldn't see that he was wearing the condom that Nathaniel had given him. I was glad someone was thinking about safety, because all I was thinking about was sex and food. Trouble was, they were the same thing right now. I curled my legs back, rose up so I could see him sliding in and out of me. The sight of him inside me for the first time, finally, bowed my spine back, closed my eyes, drew small sounds from me. That warm, delicious weight began to build inside me.

I found my words, and managed to say, "When I go, you go."

"I would soak your body in all the pleasure it could take," he said, voice full of the strain of all that control.

Jason said, "We don't have time to give Anita all the pleasure she can take, Requiem. Jean-Claude needs us."

Requiem nodded, but never changed his rhythm, that relentless gentle thrusting in and out, over and over that spot just inside my body.

"God, you're good," I whispered.

His hands convulsed on the car, so that it creaked under his strength. "If I get to go when you do, then I must let go of some of my control, or I will still be fighting my body."

"Can you keep doing this until I go?"

"Yes," he whispered.

It built, and built, and built, and then came the stroke of his body inside me that spilled me over. It brought me screaming, digging nails into the leather of the seat. It bucked my body against his, and he thrust deep inside me, as hard and fast as he could. He brought me again with that deep thrust, a different kind of orgasm, before the first had finished. I raked nails down his sides, and screamed.

The pain didn't make him come again as it did sometimes for Nathaniel, or even Micah. He took it, but he was done, and the pain didn't change that.

He drew himself out of me, and even that was a wondrous sensation that made me writhe on the seats. Someone touched my face and the *ardeur* jumped to him. I smelled wolf and knew it was Jason before I saw his face.

He swallowed hard, voice breathy. "You're feeling better."

I nodded.

"No offense, but we need you fed and all of us back inside, as soon as possible."

"Yes," I said, and my voice was hoarse.

"If we double up, you feed faster, and we're done faster."

I frowned at him, part postorgasmic haze, part the rising *ardeur*, and part just me. "What?"

Nathaniel appeared over his shoulder, and touched my hand. The *ardeur* leaped to him, but it had taken touch for it to transfer. My powers were still weak. "I want you to go down on me while the *ardeur* rides you."

I began to have a clue. "And what will Jason be doing while I'm going down on you?"

"Fucking you," Nathaniel said.

Jason tried to look embarrassed, but never quite managed it. He finally grinned at me. "You want me to be all gentlemanly about it."

I shook my head. "I want you to fuck me."

He looked startled for a moment, then his eyes filled with that knowledge, that darkness, that is all male. That look that is almost predatory, but not when you want it, when you've asked for it, then it's something to tighten your body low and hard. I cried out just from the look on his face.

"Let's fuck," he said.

"Let's," I said.

51

I ENDED UP sitting, facing Nathaniel, him inside me. I wrapped my legs around his waist with him buried as deep inside me as he could go. It reminded me of earlier with London, so intimate a lovemaking. But staring into Nathaniel's eyes from inches away, with his body inside mine, my hips riding him, it was more. London had had to hold my hair, force me to stare into his face. I wanted to stare into Nathaniel's face, wanted to watch his moods swim across his face. Wanted to watch him watch me.

Jason's hands slid down my back, cupped my buttocks. They'd decided to change places when Jason had mentioned that he'd never gone with me orally. Intercourse, yes, but not oral sex. Nathaniel had told him, "You have to feel her do this. She's amazing."

"I've had foreplay from her."

"That was when she was trying to be good, it's better when she's trying to be bad."

"Better than Raina?"

Nathaniel had nodded.

A look of almost pain had crossed Jason's face, and he'd said, "Can I change my order, please?"

So we'd changed the order.

Without a lot of foreplay I didn't normally go in this postion, but there'd been foreplay. Small G-spot orgasm always makes intercourse more fun. Big G-spot orgasm means you're done for the night, as in *Stick a fork in me, honey, I'm done*. Requiem had done just enough, and not too much, so that my body was tighter than normal, but still wet, still spasming with aftershocks. Every thrust of Nathaniel's body brought tiny spurts of pleasure, made me move my hips against his body, and drive him deeper inside me.

Jason licked a cool, wet line up my spine. It made me shiver, and lean a little back into his hands. Nathaniel kissed me, hard and completely, drowning his tongue inside my mouth, until I had to relax my mouth wide. He drove his body inside me, as if he were imitating himself at both openings.

It brought me screaming, the orgasm trying to bow my spine, tear my mouth off his, but his hand at the back of my head kept our mouths pressed together.

Jason bit my back, and it made me scream more. Nathaniel let go of my hair, and let my upper body fall back into Jason's arms. "I didn't feel her feed."

"She didn't feed."

Nathaniel's body started finding a new rhythm from the slightly different angle. My breathing started to change almost instantly. I kept my legs around Nathaniel's waist, his hands supporting most of my weight. "Move back," he told Jason. Jason did, and my body bowed backward, my hands seeking his body.

I was suddenly staring, upside down, at a very intimate part of Jason's anatomy. Nathaniel's hands were strong and firm at the small of my back. He gave me the foundation I needed to stretch off into space, and reach for the other man. I wrapped my hand around him, tight and firm. He made a small noise for me. I wanted him to make more.

Nathaniel's body just kept going inside me, over and over, deep, and smooth. I felt the beginnings of another orgasm building. I wanted Jason inside my mouth before that happened. I wanted to feed on them both. Nathaniel had put a condom on before being inside me, but Jason would slip naked between my lips. I could suck him clean, and naked, and I wanted it. In that moment the *ardeur*, my own special hunger, might not have cared whose body I was playing with. I needed to feed.

Jason wasn't quite at the angle I needed, and I said, "Please, please." He used his own hand to help guide himself between my lips. My hands wrapped around his thighs and ass. I started to make love to him with my mouth. To suck, lick, and writhe my mouth, my tongue, and ever so lightly my teeth, around the smooth muscled length of him. I moved my mouth, strained my throat to meet each thrust.

I lost myself in the sensations at my mouth, and Nathaniel reminded me, hard and fast, that I had two men to satisfy. I fought to keep both rhythms going: my hips writhing to meet Nathaniel's thrusts, and my mouth and throat to meet Jason's.

Jason's hands found my upper back, and he helped support me with one hand, while his other hand found something to hold on to. Their hands were like a safety net, holding me, supporting me, helping me fuck them.

"Are you close?" Jason asked, and his voice sounded strained.

For a moment I thought he was talking to me, but his body kept me from answering. Nathaniel said, "I can be."

"Either she has to slow down, or I'm going to go."

Nathaniel's hands tightened at the small of my back, and he sat up higher, and changed the angle of my hips at the same time. It was like he'd been waiting to do it. It forced my legs higher up his back, put my pelvis at a more than forty-degree angle. His next thrust made me scream around Jason's body.

"God, Nathaniel, stop that, or I'm . . ."

He thrust two, three times, with every word. "Just . . . a . . . little . . . more!" And he brought me, screaming, screaming with Jason's body thrusting inside me, so that I screamed around him. My nails dug into his body. Jason thrust one last time as deep and hard as he could down my throat, and I felt him go, felt it hot but too far down to be thick. I got only the heat, and the spasming of him inside my throat. Nathaniel thrust deep and hard between my legs, a heartbeat later. It made me scream as I was trying to swallow Jason down. It made me have to suck harder or choke.

Jason cried out, his body spasming, his nails digging into my back where he held me. He screamed my name, and the *ardeur* finally fed. I fed. I drank them both down, and the rush of energy tightened our bodies, made us all cry out. Nathaniel thrust inside me again, brought me again. Jason spasmed deep inside my throat again; I felt him spill inside me. A moment before I'd been fighting not to choke or throw up, and now the *ardeur* rode me, and I drank him down as if he were exactly what I wanted. I drank them both down; everywhere our skin touched I got small sips, but down my throat, and between my legs, that was food. It was exactly what I needed, exactly the way I needed it. Maybe the feeding would last longer if I fed on men who weren't tied to us metaphysically, but I didn't love anyone who wasn't tied to us. So I had to feed more often, so what?

We ended on the floor of the limo, with Jason on the bottom, me in the middle, and Nathaniel on top of me, as if the last orgasm had pulled us all to the floor.

"Wow," Jason said.

"Yeah," I said.

Nathaniel laughed, low and a little unsteady. "I love you, Anita," he said.

"I love you, too," I said. I could feel Jason's heart thudding against my back.

"I feel left out," he said, from underneath me.

Nathaniel didn't so much raise his head, as move his eyes, to look at the other man. "I love you, too, or I wouldn't enjoy sharing her with you this much."

I managed to roll my head back enough to glimpse Jason's face. "I love you, Jason, you are our very dear friend."

"I thought I was just everyone's fuck buddy."

I cuddled against the front of his body. Nathaniel crawled up until he managed to wedge himself around us both. "You're the best friend I've ever had."

Jason smiled at us both, his eyes full of more emotion than I think he knew what to do with. He managed a version of his usual grin. "And I thought the most interesting thing I'd ever do with a best friend was watch football."

Nathaniel smiled at him. "We can if you want, but you'll have to explain the rules to me."

"I am not watching football," I said.

"I hate football, let's just keep fucking," Jason said.

"Not tonight," I said.

"We need to get inside," he said.

"Whoever can move, stand up first and get dressed," I said.

He laughed, hugged me, and laid his head against Nathaniel's. "God I love my friends, but if you guys can fall to one side, I think I can stand."

"I'll have to work on that," I said.

"What?" he asked.

"You've recovered too quickly. I must have done something wrong."

The laughter faded around the edges, and there was suddenly a very serious look on his face. "You did everything right. You were wonderful."

"As good as the person who gave you the teeth mark hickey on your neck?"

He grinned, as he started trying to wriggle out of the pile. "Better actually, but if you tell her I said so, I'll deny it."

"Tell me who I'm supposed to be nice to, and I will."

He was opening a box of moist towelettes. Wiping a little of the sweat, and other things, off his body, he said, "Have you met all of the Cape Codders?"

"Samuel and his family, yeah."

Jason shook his head. "Not the family, the entourage."

"There was a man and woman with them."

"Her name is Perdita. Perdy." He stuffed the towelettes into an empty garbage bag, apparently there for the purpose. "Jean-Claude wanted to know some of what you could expect when you fuck Sampson."

"He sent you to fuck one of the mermaids so I'd be forewarned?"

Nathaniel got up slowly. Jason tossed him the box of towelettes, and dragged the plastic off our clothes. Hadn't really needed the plastic. We hadn't been that messy.

"He didn't send me to fuck her, just to find out what the transformation of a mermaid, and maybe male siren, could entail." He grinned at me. "Jean-Claude left it to me to decide how to get that information."

I'd forgotten that I'd agreed to try to bring Sampson's powers. So much had been happening; it was hard to keep track. It was always especially hard to keep track of things that made me uncomfortable. Having agreed to have sex with Sampson qualified.

"If the bite is a sample, ouch."

"It wasn't all ouch. I'll give you a full report after we've survived the ballet."

We got cleaned up as best we could. An emergency makeup kit for touch-ups had been in the limo. I'd thought maybe I'd smear my lipstick. It was a little more extensive than that, but we managed.

We were dressed, and almost as fresh as when we started the evening. Requiem had gone to report to Jean-Claude, or maybe he just hadn't wanted to watch. Nathaniel and Jason escorted me back inside. Lisandro was rear guard. Claudia and Truth met us at the Fox club entrance.

Underneath those stoic bodyguard faces I saw worry. But I didn't need their faces to tell me; I could feel it. It wasn't Marmee Noir, or Belle Morte. It was the vampires we'd invited to town. I wasn't sure what they were doing, but whatever it was, it was powerful.

Jason and Nathaniel shivered on either side of me. "What the hell are they doing up there?" Jason whispered.

"I don't know," I said, "but we're going to find out." I started up the stairs on Nathaniel's arm, with Jason's hand in mine. Normally, I'd have tried not to hold on to too many men at once in public, but the hell with it. One, we all needed the comfort. Two, my reputation couldn't get any more trashed than it already was.

52

OUTSIDE THE CURTAINS to the seats, I had to let go of Jason's hand so he could go back to Asher's box. I didn't want to let go of him. I wanted to wrap both him and Nathaniel around me like a security blanket. I put my arm around Nathaniel's waist, tucking myself in under his arm. He hugged me, and whispered against my hair. "You all right?"

I nodded. Jason would have called me a liar, but Nathaniel just accepted it. He might not believe me, but he wouldn't call me on it. Nathaniel parted the curtains. The music swelled around us and the world was suddenly golden. The air sparkled with glitter. Out of that scintillating cloud a vampire floated. It was Adonis, the vamp who had almost rolled me with his gaze earlier. His costume had changed to a ballet version of 1700s dress, which meant: fairly accurate from the waist up, and tights from the waist down. I'd seen vampires fly before, but not like this. He hung in the air as if he could have hung there forever. Other vampires appeared out of the glitter, hanging in the air as if they'd been pinned there. Adonis hovered just outside our box, so close I could see his blond curls moving in the wind. What wind? The wind of his own magic.

Jean-Claude and Damian turned from that vision to look at me. Jean-Claude let me see a moment of relief in his eyes, before his face became the blank, perfect mask that he would wear for the public tonight. Damian reached out for me. I gave him my free hand, without thinking that I was touching Nathaniel, too. It was as if his touch completed a circuit. It wasn't just a leap of energy, it was a feeling of deep contentment. It was like suddenly being wrapped in a warm electric blanket. It felt so good. I couldn't think of anything I wanted more than to wrap them both around me and sleep. I just knew that it would be healing and exactly what I needed. Not all psychic flashes are ambiguous, or hard to interpret. Some of them are crystal clear. Problem is, they always seem to come when you can't possibly act on them. Looking at the vampires spinning and diving through the falling glitter, somehow a nap didn't seem likely.

I took my seat beside Jean-Claude, and Nathaniel went to the seat on the other side of Damian, where Micah had started the evening. But to get everyone sitting down, I had to let go of Nathaniel. It was almost wrenching to let go of him, like giving up a shield when you know you're about to go into battle. No, not that, Nathaniel wasn't my shield. He was my warmth on a cold night. He was what kept me safe and sane. Well, not always safe. Safety lay elsewhere. I squeezed Damian's hand, and let go of it. There, it didn't feel so bad not to be touching Nathaniel. For some reason giving up them both was easier than giving up just one of them.

I took Jean-Claude's hand, and that was safety. That was armor in the face of battle. There was love there, too, but Jean-Claude sought power more than safety. Just touching his hand energized me. I wasn't thinking *nap* now, I was thinking *battle*. It was the difference between a soldier and a general. One sleeps when he can, the other has to be preparing for the next conflict.

The glitter had fallen down, so that the vampires were revealed in all their grace. They danced in the air. They held their places, and danced. Damian leaned in and whispered, "Do you have any idea how much strength it takes to do what they're doing?"

I shook my head.

Jean-Claude leaned in and gave the barest whisper. "To fight gravity, and your own body's desire to touch earth; it is impressive." He squeezed my hand a little tighter, as if watching the dozen vampires dance in their perfect, solid circle was exciting, or nerve-racking. I was too insecure to drop shields and check for sure. So much had already gone wrong tonight that caution seemed smarter.

Nathaniel was leaning forward in his seat. His face was rapturous. I glanced at our other box. Micah gave me a smile and I gave one back. But it was Jason who caught my eye. He was sitting on the edge of his chair like Nathaniel. They wore almost identical entranced looks. Not entranced by vampire powers, but by the beauty and strength of the dancers. I realized that I'd taken away from the performance the two people in our group who would have appreciated the dancing most. They both had dance training. They both danced for a living. Yeah, they took their clothes off while they did it, but Jean-Claude had insisted that all his dancers have some training. You couldn't just shake your booty on stage at Guilty Pleasures. Jason and Nathaniel were the two that had taken to the dancing most. They were the ones who helped the other dancers work up new acts. And I'd taken them away from the dancing. The looks on their faces made me regret that. Among all the regrets tonight, that was another.

Asher was very still, watching the show. It was a stillness that a stranger wouldn't recognize, but he wasn't a stranger to me. He was as enraptured by the show as the boys. He just had several hundred years of cool, and wouldn't let it show that much.

The music changed, and the vampires hesitated. They pretended not to know what was coming next. They were close enough to us that I could see their expressions of surprise, as they turned one by one, or two by two, to look at the stage below them.

A woman stepped on stage, dressed in one of those long white gossamer dresses. I would have said the dress floated around her as she tiptoed on stage, but compared to the vampires, it didn't quite float. But it was delicate, and she was lovely. Her hair was long and shining brown, tied back in a high ponytail. The hair moved with her like an extension of her body as she danced, slowly, tentatively across the stage. It reminded me of what Nathaniel did with his hair on stage some nights. Not the same kind of dance, but the same awareness of the hair as an extension of the dance.

She was young, as in not long dead. I whispered against Jean-Claude's hair, "Is she supposed to be human?"

"*Oui.*"

She was fresh enough that once upon a time, I might have believed the illusion, but that was long ago, and I knew vampire when I saw it.

The vampires above us began to circle downward, the way vultures will when they decide that the thing on the ground is finally dead.

One of the female vamps landed, lightly, on the stage. She had hair almost as dark as mine, but how much of all those curls were real and how much a wig, I couldn't tell. She went up on her toe shoes, as the girl did. They mirrored each other from across the stage. The girl held her hands out, beseeching, asking a question, or wanting something. The dark-haired vampire mimicked her, made fun of her. It was amazingly well done. Sometimes the ballet leaves me confused, but there was no confusion here. The human was asking for help, and the vampire wasn't going to give it.

Another female vamp touched down, brown hair this time, then a blonde. The three vamps linked arms and danced across the stage. The girl went to her knees, begging with graceful arms. She was wearing more base than the rest; it gave her a rosier skin tone, made her look alive.

Three male vampires alit upon the stage. They joined the dancing women, linked hands, boy, girl, boy, girl. The girl in white continued to beseech them. They laughed at her, and broke into couples. They danced around her. The men were able to do amazing leaps, and carry the weight of the women as if it truly were nothing. The leaps were amazing, but after seeing them fly, it just didn't impress. Once you've seen someone fly, what's a little *grand jeté*?

They began to circle around her, close and closer. She finally realized her danger, and began to try to run, but the circle had closed. They would grab her and throw her back into the middle. She fell like white and brown water, spilling all that hair like a shining cloak across the white dress. The vampires began to dance close and closer, the circle tightening in graceful, flowing movements, but tightening all the same.

There was movement above us. I had forgotten that there were vampires still hovering in the air. They had risen to the ceiling, using it like a rear stage area, but now they dropped delicately to the stage, and suddenly you realized that the vampires in the circle were nothing. The dancers who hit the stage now rolled power outward like a trembling line of cold. So cold, it almost burned. They stalked across the stage, in a rolling predatory dance that made me afraid for her. Silly. I knew they'd done this act across the country. I even knew that she was already dead, but still my body reacted to the menace in their movements.

The audience below us gasped. They'd seen the whole show, and they didn't know she was dead.

The circle of couples parted as the other vampires stalked forward. Two men, and three women, stalking across the stage. The girl stared at them with fear plain on her face. She begged with graceful arms, on her knees. When that didn't help, she got slowly to her feet, and her fear was palpable. Someone was projecting emotions onto the audience. There weren't many who could roll me that easily.

I looked up to find one last vamp hovering at the ornate ceiling. Adonis, the blond that had damn near gotten me with his gaze. He wasn't looking at me. His attention was all for the stage. I think he was waiting for his cue. It wasn't him. Oh, I was slow tonight. It was Merlin again. Merlin who I hadn't seen in the flesh, but only through memory. I didn't poke at his power. He wasn't hurting anyone. I was afraid if I poked at him, made him stop projecting emotions into the crowd, that it might raise Marmee Noir again. I was not up to another visit from the Mother of All Darkness tonight. So I left Merlin alone. We'd discuss his sins later, in private.

The vampires were chasing her around the stage. It was a beautifully choreographed game of cat and mouse. They would jump out at her, use that incredible speed to stop her from leaving the stage. She'd almost run past them, but they would be there, grabbing a hand, throwing her backward, sliding her prettily across the stage. I wondered how she kept the white tights so white doing all that.

I felt Adonis move forward. I felt his power reach outward. He flew slowly toward the stage, going down as if on wires, so slow, so incredibly slow. It wasn't a bird of prey, it was like a picture of some heaven-bound saint, except this one was coming down, not going up. He touched the stage and the dancers froze. A red-haired vampire came to his hand as if he'd commanded her. The dancers all formed couples, and began to dance around the girl. She was huddled in the middle, not begging anymore. She had given up on asking for help. She huddled like a white star in the center of the bright colors of the vampires.

They danced, and showed that they could do traditional ballet. Then the music changed. The couples gave themselves more room, and they began to do dancing that would have looked more at home on the stage at Guilty Pleasures than at the ballet. It was still beautiful, graceful, predatory, but it was also very sexual. Nothing that would get you arrested, but as they had been able to convey menace, pity, and derision, with a gesture and a look, now they conveyed sex.

The girl hid her face, as if it were too awful to watch. It was Adonis who stood above her. She raised a startled face, slowly, the way the actors look up in a horror movie when they hear that noise, and know, somehow, that the monster is right there. She gazed up at the handsome man, with that look on her face, in the posture of her body. No matter how beautiful he was, she made you see him as hideous, dangerous, frightening.

He grabbed her wrist, and they did a slow dance, with him half-dragging her, and her trying to stay farther away from him. Her reluctance for him to touch her screamed through her every movement. But he won, as you knew he would. He jerked her into his embrace, and went skyward. He flew her out over the audience, while she struggled, and pounded at him with little fists. So he dropped her. She actually screamed, before another vampire caught her. Caught her just over the audience's heads. The audience gasped and screamed with her. The vampires played catch with the girl. One would rise, then let her struggles make him drop her. She began to cling to them, and they tore her hands from their clothes and flung her to the air. Then Adonis caught her again, and he held her close. I caught the shine of tears on her face as he floated past us. He grabbed that shining fall of hair, and wadded his hand in it. He pulled her neck into a graceful, straining line, and pretended to bite her. Then he threw her to the next vampire, and that one bit her, too. They began to close in around her in a tight floating ball of arms and legs. When they parted, her neck was dotted with fake blood, and she went eagerly to them. Embracing them with graceful arms. It became a lovely feeding frenzy. From one set of arms to another, from one man, one woman, to another, until the vampire's faces were stained crimson, and the girl's dress looked like an accident victim's sheet. The fake blood made the dress cling to her body, so you could see the muscles, the small tight breasts. It was both alluring and utterly disturbing.

The audience was silent with tension, as the vampires landed on the stage again. They surrounded her, hiding her from view. It gave the illusion that all of them were feeding at once, though I knew logistically that wasn't possible. Too many mouths to fit like that.

A new vampire stalked onto the stage. He was dark-haired, and darker-skinned, pale, but I couldn't tell if it was makeup or skin tone. He chased back the other vamps. He saw the bloody almost-corpse, and he wept. His shoulders rose and fell with it.

Adonis laughed at him, one of those big stage laughs, with the head back.

The dark vampire raised a face livid with anger. They began to dance around the stage. They danced with her bloody corpse as their centerpiece. The other vampires vanished behind the stage. The two men danced. Adonis had more bulky muscles. The dark man was tall and lean, and more graceful than anyone I'd ever seen. He moved like a dream of water, and even that didn't do him justice.

Adonis's dancing came across as clunky, human in comparison. Somewhere in the middle of the dance, I realized I was looking at Merlin.

Merlin won the dancing fight. For that was what it became. They fought in the air, and on the ground, and it looked real. Real anger seemed to be involved, and I wondered if it was projecting, or if they were truly pissed at each other and the fight gave them an excuse to vent it.

Adonis was vanquished, not killed, and that left Merlin on stage alone with his dead love. He leaned over her, held her in his arms, and rocked her. My throat was tight, damn him. He wept and I fought not to weep with him. Jean-Claude did some of this with the audience at the clubs, but he wasn't this good. No one I'd ever met was this good at projecting emotions.

A mob entered from stage right. They had crossbows and torches. They shot the weeping vampire. The crossbow bolt appeared in his chest like magic. Even knowing it was stage trickery it looked real. He collapsed on top of his dead love, and the lights circled round the two dead lovers. He died curled around her, as if, even in death, he would protect her.

The mob came, and the weeping man who had shot the vampire picked up the dead girl. He cradled her in his arms, and a woman from the crowd joined him in weeping. Parents, I thought. They cradled her, much as the dead vampire had. They carried her offstage, weeping, and left the vampire dead.

The stage was empty for a moment, then the vampires returned. They crept out on the stage, cautious, afraid. They seemed bewildered by the dead vampire. It was Adonis who knelt by him, touched his face, and wept. He picked the fallen man up in his arms, cradling him. Then he rose skyward, and the vampires flew away with their fallen leader. They flew away weeping to the sounds of music that sounded like the violins were weeping with them.

The curtain went down and there was a moment of utter silence. Then the audience went wild, clapping, making noises of all kinds. The audience came to its feet and the curtain reopened. The humans came out first, the chorus, but the audience stayed on their feet through it all. When Adonis took the stage, they clapped louder. When the girl and Merlin came down to bow, well, the crowd actually screamed. You don't hear screaming much at the ballet, but you heard it now.

Roses were delivered to the girl, and to Merlin. More than one bouquet of them, in different colors. They bowed, and bowed again, and finally the audience began to quiet. Only then did the curtain close, and the dancers exited to the soft sound of applause and the excited babble of the audience, already asking themselves, "Did you see what I saw? Was it real?"

We'd survived the ballet. Now all we had to survive was the cast party afterward. The night was young. Damn it.

53

I WAS IN Jean-Claude's office at Danse Macabre. It was black-and-white elegant, with framed kimonos and fans on the walls as the only color. I sat behind his elegant black desk, with a drawer open. I had an extra gun in that drawer. I'd loaded it with silver shot while we waited. Asher sat beside me, in a chair pulled up so he could be close enough to touch me. He was the reason the drawer was open and the gun was loaded, but not sitting in plain sight on the desk, or in my hand already. He thought it might make the discussion get off on a hostile foot. Damian stood on my other side, hand on my shoulder. His touching me, sharing his calmness, was probably why Asher had won his argument about the gun. The other reason he'd won the fight about the gun was leaning up against the door: Claudia, Truth, and Lisandro, looking very bodyguardy against the wall. Where was Jean-Claude? He was out being the media darling. Elinore, as manager here, was also playing to the media. For public events like this, she made a much better hostess. Besides, I was handling other business. The kind the human media didn't get to know about.

Merlin was sitting in a chair facing us. Adonis and the dark-haired woman from the chorus were sitting on the couch against the wall. Her name was Elisabetta, and her vaguely Eastern European accent was thick enough to walk on. Merlin's and Adonis's accents seemed to flow with their moods, but were mostly absent.

Merlin was answering my questions in that elegant from-anywhere-and-everywhere voice: "I wanted the show to be magical for the entire audience, not just the humans."

"So you tried to roll everyone's mind, including the master vampires and lycanthropes, because you didn't want them to miss the show?" I didn't fight to keep the sarcasm out of my voice. I'd have lost the fight, so why try?

"Yes," he said, simply, as if, of course.

Damian's hand squeezed a little tighter on my bare shoulder, his fingers caressing the edge of the collarbone scars.

"I find that a little hard to believe," I said. There, that was calm. I hadn't called him a lying bastard.

"Why else would I have done it?" he asked. His face was very calm. I knew his eyes were dark, pure brown, but other than color I couldn't describe them much, because I wasn't making eye contact. This vampire had damn near rolled us all with no gaze. I wasn't chancing it. He was tall, dark, and handsome. He was not European. No, something darker, farther east, as in Middle East. There was something very Egyptian about him, or maybe Babylonian, because he was old. Old enough that he made my bones ache with his age. Not power, just age. I was a necromancer, and I could taste the power and age of most vampires. It was a natural ability that had gotten better as my power had grown. Now that ability made my bones thrum with the weight of ages that sat smiling in front of me.

"Using power that way on a Master of the City is a direct challenge to his or her authority. You know that."

"Not if you don't get caught at it," Adonis said from the couch.

I glanced at him, avoiding his eyes. That made him laugh. He liked that he could roll me with his gaze. All right, that we both thought he could.

Asher spoke then. "Are you implying that Merlin rolled the minds of all the masters in all the cities that you performed in, and they did not know it?" His voice was empty, pleasant, even happy. It was a lie. He wanted Adonis to chat himself into a corner.

Merlin raised a darkly pale hand. That one gesture stopped Adonis with his mouth parted. "No," Merlin said, "no. We have answered the question of Jean-Claude's servant. When she speaks it is with his voice. But why are you here, Asher? Why do you sit so close and join these talks?"

"I am Jean-Claude's *témoin*."

"How have you earned this place of trust and power, Asher? It is not through strength. There are at least four vampires here, perhaps more, who are more powerful than you. And you were never known for your skill in battle. So why do you sit at his right hand, and now at hers?"

"I can tell you why he's here tonight, sitting beside me," I said.

Merlin gave me a quizzical look. It was so hard not to look him in the eye when he moved. I'd lost the knack of not making eye contact with vampires. "Do enlighten me, Miss Blake."

I reached in the drawer and wrapped my hand around the gun. I felt better holding it. The moment the gun flashed to the room, the tension level rose. I felt rather than saw Adonis and Elisabetta begin to move forward on the couch.

Claudia said, "Don't."

Merlin said, "Do not react. That is what she wants."

It was probably their master's voice, not Claudia's warning, that kept them on the couch. Or hell, maybe she'd been speaking to me.

I put the gun on the desk with my hand sort of caressing it. Not exactly holding it, but touching it. "I wanted to have the gun naked on the desk when you came through the door. Asher talked me out of it."

"So he is here to see you do not do anything foolish."

"He is here because I trust him, and I don't trust you."

"You are not a fool. I would not expect you to trust me."

"And what would you do with your little gun?" Adonis asked.

"Shooting you and Merlin here seems like a possibility."

"On what grounds?" Merlin asked. "What laws have we broken? We are allowed mass hypnosis for theatrical purposes."

I hated to admit it, but he was right. I shrugged. "If I think on it, I'm sure I can come up with something."

"Would you, as you Americans say, frame us?"

I sighed, and let my hand fall away from the gun. "No, I guess I wouldn't."

"Then I say again, why are we here? What have we done to anger Jean-Claude?"

"You know exactly what you did," I said, "and why we're pissed at you."

"No, truly, Miss Blake, I do not."

"It's Ms. Blake, or Marshal Blake, to you."

He made a small gesture. "Ms. Blake, then."

"What would you have done if you had succeeded in rolling the minds of six Masters of the City?" Asher asked. His hair hid half his face, a golden distraction.

"I will not answer your question for you are not master here, nor powerful enough to be *témoin*."

"Fine, what he said."

Merlin looked at me. "What is that, Ms. Blake?"

"Don't make me repeat the question, Merlin, just answer it."

"I don't understand what you hope to gain by this little discussion, Ms. Blake. Truly, I do not."

"You tried to mind-fuck six Masters of the City, plus a half-dozen or more rulers of the local lycanthropes. Hell, we've got animals to call of several masters, plus human servants. You tried to bite off a great, big, bloody chunk, and you weren't master enough to swallow it."

"Merlin could have taken you all." This from Elisabetta.

I shook my head without looking at her. "No, he couldn't, or he'd have done it."

"What do you want from us, Ms. Blake?" Merlin asked.

"I want to know why you did it. Don't give me shit about wanting all your audience to enjoy the show. If you have truly been mind-fucking all the masters at all the performances, then you wanted to know if you could take them all here tonight. I want to know, why?"

"Why what, Ms. Blake?"

"Why try to roll everyone? Why run the risk of insulting all of them? Why throw this big a gauntlet down? You're a master vampire. You're so damn old you make my bones ache just sitting there. Vamps like you don't make mistakes, Merlin. Vamps like you always have a reason for everything they do."

"Perhaps I do not believe that a human who has barely seen three decades of mortal life would be able to understand my motives."

"Try me. Better yet, try Jean-Claude. You said it yourself; when you speak to me, you speak to him."

He went very still then. I knew the quality of that stillness. I'd surprised him in some way. Stillness could be as telling on a vampire as a gesture on a human.

"Touché, Ms. Blake." He made another small gesture with his hands. "You will not believe that I did it only to make our production more enjoyable to all."

"No," I said.

He did that hands-out gesture again. I was beginning to wonder if it was his version of a shrug. "Perhaps, after succeeding in city after city, I had simply grown arrogant. Perhaps I truly believed I could do you all."

"I believe you're arrogant. I might even believe that you rolled the rest of the masters individually. I'm not sure on that one, yet. I've felt your mind; I won't say you couldn't do it, just that you might not have tried."

"Then why did I try tonight?" he asked.

I smiled. It didn't feel like a happy smile, more like that curl of lips when I'm pissed. "That's what I'm trying to find out, and what you keep avoiding answering."

"Am I avoiding the question?" he asked.

I nodded, and this time my smile was almost happy. "Yeah, you are."

"Perhaps I have answered it, and you simply do not like the answer."

"Perhaps you're trying not to outright lie in case Damian, or Asher, or one of the others, smells or feels the lie. But you are definitely not answering the question completely."

"Do you truly believe that if I wished to lie in front of the people you have in this room, that I could not do it successfully?"

I thought about that for a second. I fought the urge to look at Asher. Damian played his hand along my shoulder. "I think you could, but not without using more mind power than you want to use around me."

"And why do I not wish to use mind powers around you, Ms. Blake?" His voice held disdain, almost amusement. I wasn't insulted; his voice was like everything about him, practiced, calculated.

"Because you're afraid that Mommie Dearest will hear it, and pay a second visit tonight."

He tried for arrogant disdain, and made it, but I could taste the change in him. The faintest, thinnest taste of fear. "And who is Mommie Dearest?"

I stared very hard at that graceful line of jaw. I'd have loved eye contact, but didn't want to risk it. "Do you really want me to say her name?"

"You can say anything you like," he said.

I nodded, and found my own heart beating faster, my newly scarred hand clenched into a fist. "Fine"—and my voice was a little breathy—"you're afraid the Mother of All Darkness will show up again."

Did the lights grow a shade less bright, or was it my imagination?

"She is lost to us, Ms. Blake. You know nothing of her."

"She lies in a room that is underground, but high up. There are windows around the front of that room that look out upon a cave, or underground building. There's always firelight down below, as if whoever watches is afraid of the dark."

"I am aware that Valentina has been inside the room you describe, and lived to tell the tale. Do not seek to impress me with secondhand stories."

I was beginning to think that Merlin didn't know that I'd been in his head with her. Did he not know that I'd seen his memory of her coming out of the darkness? "Let's try another secondhand tale, then. I saw her in the shape of a great cat, maybe a type of extinct lion, bigger than anything that we have today. I watched her stalk you in a night where the world smelled of rain and jasmine, or something like jasmine. I mean, I don't know how long jasmine has existed as a plant; maybe my mind just calls it 'jasmine' because it's the closest smell I know."

I thought he'd gone still before, but I had been wrong, because now he went so still that I had to concentrate on his chest to make sure he didn't just disappear. So still, more still than any snake, still in the way that live things don't get. Still, as if he were willing himself not to be there anymore.

His voice was as empty as his body when he said, "You shared her memory tonight."

"Yeah," I said.

"Then you know her secret."

"She's got a lot of them, but if you mean that she's a shapeshifter and a vampire, simultaneously, then yeah, I know that secret."

He drew a breath. A lot of them did that when they came back from that still-stillness. They drew a breath as if to remind themselves they aren't dead yet.

"But Ms. Blake, everyone knows that you cannot be both."

"The strain of vampirism that we have today is destroyed by the lycanthropy virus, but maybe once it wasn't, or maybe it's a different kind of vampirism. Whatever. I know what I've seen."

"Musette brought some of the Dark Lady's cats to visit us," Asher said, "they were both, and neither."

"Yes, Belle Morte says the sleeping cats of our mother have woken to her call," Merlin said. "What do you think of that, Ms. Blake? Do you think Belle Morte has grown so powerful that the servants of the mother have woken to her call?"

"No," I said.

"Why no?" he asked. His voice was still empty, his body not moving much. He wasn't trying to play human now.

"Because Belle Morte doesn't have that kind of power."

"You have never seen her in the flesh," Adonis said, "or you would not be so quick to judge." He didn't sound happy as he said it, which was interesting. It was the first time I felt that he'd lost control of his voice.

I glanced at him. "She's powerful, but it's not the same kind of power as Mommie Dearest. It's just not."

"If Belle Morte did not wake the servants of our good mother, then who did?" Merlin asked.

I had a moment of insight. I don't get them often. I debated on whether to act on it, or ask Asher's opinion first. Then I thought, to hell with it. I was tired. I'd fed, but the healing had taken more than the feeding had given back. I was too tired for games.

"Do you want her to wake up, Merlin? Or do you fear her waking up?"

He sank back into that stillness again. "I do not know how to answer that question."

"Yeah, you do."

"Then I will not answer it."

"Are you a flunky of the vampire council, is that it?"

"Merlin has been outside the circle of inner power for centuries," Asher said.

I nodded. "Yeah, you guys filled me in on the limo ride here. He grew so powerful that he was given a choice of giving up his territory, or being killed. He gave it all up, and vanished into the mists of time. Jean-Claude thought there might be a place for him here on American soil." In my head, I thought, *and the next time that Jean-Claude offers refuge to someone this fucking powerful, he better run it by me first.* I'd made that clear in the limo. He hadn't even argued with me.

"If you're not working for the council, then who are you working for?" I asked.

"If I said myself, would you believe me?"

"Maybe, maybe not, don't know, try me." My hand was on the gun again.

"Why touch your gun?"

"Because, I think if you don't want to answer the question that you may try vampire powers again. It just depends on what you're more afraid of."

"I am not afraid of your little gun," he said.

"Probably not, but you are afraid of Mommie Dearest, aren't you?"

He actually licked his lips. The gesture gave me hope that his façade was cracking, and it made me give his eyes a full glance. Which was what it was supposed to do. He tried to roll me in that moment of eye contact, and he might have done it, except that Asher and Damian touched my bare skin at the same time. It was enough to distract me, make me look away.

"There must be more to the two of you than I have been told," Merlin said, and his voice was back to emptiness again.

"He is her vampire servant," Adonis said, "it isn't rumor." His voice wasn't empty, more hollow with an edge of anger.

"But that is not what saved her," Merlin said. He looked to Asher, and I saw what I had rarely seen, one vampire look away from the gaze of another. Most vamps' power, like my own necromancy, protected them against vampire gaze. They couldn't roll each other—but Merlin could, or Asher feared he could. Scary bastard.

"You were the weakest of Belle Morte's master vampires. That vampire would not have helped save anyone from my gaze."

"I have never met you before," Asher said, his hand still on my arm, and his gaze averted from the other vampire.

"I have been closer to you than you know, Asher."

I did not like the direction this talk was taking. "Look, we brought you back here to get answers, not the other way around."

"And what answers do you think that I want from you?"

"You wanted to know how powerful we were. I don't know why, but you did. You wanted to test us. Why?"

"Perhaps I have sought long and hard for another master I could call my own. Someone who was powerful enough to make me feel that he was worthy to follow."

"You're Merlin, not Lancelot," I said.

"Lancelot was fiction, as is most of what you know today about me, and the ones I served."

I blinked in his direction. "Are you saying you're *the* Merlin, as in King Arthur and the Round Table?"

"Are you saying I am not?"

I started to argue with him, but decided not to. It was no skin off my back if he wanted to pretend to be the real Merlin. I wouldn't even point out that Merlin, himself, was a late addition to the legend of Arthur. It was his delusion. Obsidian Butterfly thought she was an Aztec goddess. She'd been powerful enough that I hadn't burst her bubble either.

"Another night, maybe, but tonight I want to get some straight answers out of you. You're talking rings around me, and I'm tired of it."

His power breathed through my mind. I was suddenly pointing a gun at his chest. "Don't try it."

"You would slay me simply for using my power?"

"I would shoot you in the chest for trying to roll my mind. One-on-one mind control is illegal, especially for nefarious purposes."

"I do not plan to take your blood, or feed upon you in any other way."

The gun was still nice and steady at his chest. "The law doesn't state you have to do mind control for feeding, just that you infringe on the free will of another. It's grounds for an order of execution."

"It takes time to get an order of execution, Ms. Blake. You cannot possibly have one with my name on it in your pocket." He was chiding again. *Silly girl*, his voice seemed to say.

I shook my head. I was being silly, wasn't I? Asher's hand found my leg. When I'd pointed the gun, his hand had had to move. His hand went up under my skirt, until he traced the edge of the hose, and found skin. It wasn't about sex, it was about helping keep me clearheaded. It was the first time a man touching my thigh had cleared my head.

I straightened my arm a little, and made it a double-handed grip. Damian's hand on my shoulder dug in, as if he was afraid of what I was about to do.

"You try to mind-fuck me again and I'll take my chances with the courts."

There were other guns out in the room, all of them in the hands of our guys, and girl. Claudia said, "If you leave the couch, you bleed."

Adonis and Elisabetta settled back against the cushions again. I didn't spare a glance to see if they were happy about it. Claudia and the others had them; I had my hands full with the vampire in front of me.

"I will not use my power on you again, Ms. Blake. I think you are a little too dangerous to tease."

"Good of you to notice," I said, voice quiet, fighting to keep my arms steady.

"Your word that you will not try to use your powers on any of us here tonight," Asher said, his hand very still on my thigh.

"I give you my word that I will not use my powers on any of you tonight."

"Broaden," I said.

"What?" Asher asked.

"His word that he doesn't use his powers on us while he's in town. I want his word that he'll be a good boy until he leaves our territory."

"You heard the lady," Asher said, and he didn't try to keep the humor out of his voice. I was glad I was amusing someone.

He gave his word, exactly as I asked him to. He was an ancient vampire. If you could ever get one of the bastards to give their word of honor, then you had them. They wouldn't break it. Weird, but true.

I lowered my gun, and Claudia and the others did the same. We didn't put the guns up, though. We had Merlin's word, not Adonis's, or Elisabetta's. I guess I should have thrown that in, but I hadn't thought about it at the time.

"You know that I am one of the few vampires she created personally. You have seen the memory of my death."

I nodded.

"I had heard rumors that she was stirring. More rumors that she has visited you in dream, or vision. I am forbidden to approach the council for any reason on pain of death. To have the rumors confirmed, or denied, I had no choice but to come here, to you and Jean-Claude."

"Why the power trip at the ballet?" I said.

"I wanted to see if I could find something in Jean-Claude that would interest her."

"And?" I said.

"I found you."

"What's that supposed to mean?"

"It means you are a necromancer, as of old."

"And that means, what?"

"You have powers that I have not seen in many long centuries."

"You haven't seen my powers used yet."

"You have a vampire servant. You have an animal to call. You gain powers as if you were a master vampire. You feed upon sex as Jean-Claude does, as Belle Morte does. It is not an option for you, or an added power from Jean-Claude. You must feed as if you were in truth a vampire. Not upon blood, true, but upon lust."

"Yeah, yeah, I'm a succubus." I tried not to think hard about what I'd just admitted, saying it quick.

"You make light of it, why?"

"Because it scares me," I said.

"You admit that?" This from Adonis.

I shrugged. "Why not?"

"Most people don't like admitting what they fear."

"It doesn't make you less afraid of it," I said.

"I find that it does," he said, and it was his real voice, I think, not a game.

"What do you fear?" Asher asked.

"Nothing I will share with a lesser master."

"Let's not start name-calling," I said. "We were actually talking."

"What do you wish to talk about, Ms. Blake?"

"You say you came here looking for answers about Mommie Dearest; ask your questions."

"And you will answer them, just like that?" He sounded like he didn't believe me.

"I won't know until I hear the questions, but maybe. Stop trying to mind-fuck and just pretend we're both civilized beings. Ask me."

He actually laughed, and it was just a laugh, not that touchable sound of Jean-Claude, or Asher, or Belle Morte. It was just a laugh. "Perhaps I am so old that I have forgotten how to simply talk."

"Practice on me, ask your questions."

"Is she waking from her long sleep?"

"Yes," I said.

"How do you know with such certainty?"

"I've seen her in dreams, and in . . ." I hesitated, searching for a word.

"Vision," Asher supplied.

"But that makes it seem like some beatific otherworldly shit, and it wasn't like that."

"What was it like?" Merlin asked.

"She sent a spirit cat once, an illusion. It sort of climbed up my body in the Jeep once. She smells of night, soft and tropical, jasmine, rain. She damn near suffocated me once with the taste of a rainy night. Belle Morte does it with the perfume of roses."

"Do you equate their power with each other?" he asked.

"Do you mean, are they similar in power?"

"Yes."

"No," I said.

"How is it no?"

"I've seen her rise above me in vision, or dream, or whatever the fuck it was, like a huge black ocean. I've seen her rise like living night, made into something real, and separate. As if night wasn't just the absence of light, but was something real, and alive. She is the reason that our ancestors huddled around the fire at night. She's why we fear the dark. She's a fear in the very fiber of our beings, something going back to the lizard part of us. We don't fear her because we fear the dark; we fear the dark because of her."

I shivered, suddenly cold. Asher took off his tuxedo jacket and laid it around my bare shoulders. It put Damian's hand against the back of my neck, under my hair, so he could keep contact. I didn't argue about it.

"Then it is true," Merlin said, in a voice that held a sliver of fear, "she is waking."

"Yes," I said, "she is." I took Asher's hand in mine. I needed the comfort.

"Belle Morte believes it is her power that has raised the mother's servants."

"That isn't it, and you know it," I said.

"They wake, because she is waking," he said.

"Yes," I said.

"Why is she so interested in a human servant?" Adonis asked, not rudely, but like he truly wanted to know.

"I believe it is not the human servant who interests her, but the necromancer." He looked at me, and again I fought not to meet his eyes. I didn't think it was mind tricks, just habit. You look in someone's eyes. You just do. "Did you know, Ms. Blake, that it is on her orders that the necromancers of old were slaughtered?"

"No," I said, "I didn't know that."

"It was her orders that all with your gifts be killed before they could grow to such power."

"I can sort of understand that."

"Can you?"

I nodded, and squeezed Asher's hand, and pressed Damian's hand closer to my skin. "I can roll a vampire's mind the way you guys roll us."

"Can you, truly?"

I realized that I'd said too much, overshared. "I am too tired to play games tonight, Merlin. When she mind-fucked us both tonight a well-meaning friend gave me a cross to hold."

"Oh, dear," he said.

I raised my left hand so he could see the new scar.

"How did you heal it so quickly? A holy item heals slowly for us."

I put my hand back on top of Damian's. "I'm not a vampire, Merlin, I'm a necromancer. It's just another kind of psychic gift. It doesn't make me evil."

"And are we evil, merely because we are vampires?"

The question was too hard for me with a vampire in each hand. "I'm too tired to debate philosophy with you. It took energy to heal this."

"We felt you feed," Adonis said.

I fought not to look at him again. "Yeah, I fed, but it wasn't enough. Dealing with Mommie Dearest takes a lot out of a girl."

"It takes a great deal out of everyone," Merlin said.

I wondered for the first time if the reason he hadn't done some major mind control after the mother left wasn't just to be polite, but because he was scared. Maybe he didn't have enough juice left. Maybe he, like me, was drained of energy.

"She can feed off other vampires, just by touching their powers, can't she?"

"Why do you ask?"

"She almost always comes to me after some other vampire has used major power on me. She used to follow Belle Morte's mind games. Tonight it was you that she followed. Does she feed off us when she does this?"

"Sometimes," he said.

"So she hasn't been asleep and not feeding for thousands of years. She's been like some kind of dark dream, feeding on energy, on power."

"I believe so."

"Why did she go to sleep in the first place?"

"How should I know?"

"Avoiding the question, aren't you?"

He gave a small smile. "Perhaps."

"Do you know why she went to sleep?"

"Yes."

"Will you tell me?"

"No."

"Why not?"

"Because it is not a story I wish to share."

"I can't make you tell me, can I?"

"You could try to see if you are necromancer enough to command me to tell you."

I grinned. "My ego isn't that big."

"More of the mother's servants have woken. Most of the council, like Belle Morte, believe it is their own growing powers that have broken the servants from their long sleeps."

"Which council members don't believe it?"

"Since I am forbidden to go near the council, how would I know that?"

"The same way you know what Belle Morte thinks."

He gave that smile again. I think it was his I'm-not-telling-you smile.

"You need to feed again, Ms. Blake, as do I. The good mother fed upon us both."

"She's not good, and she was never your mother."

He made that hand gesture again, the one that passed for a shrug. "She was mother to what I am now."

I couldn't argue with that, so I didn't try. "You wanted to know if she's waking; she is. You say you wanted to know whether Jean-Claude was a power strong enough for you to call him master."

"You do not believe that I seek a master?"

"I believe that the only master you've ever acknowledged is lying in a room somewhere in Europe, haunting my dreams."

He took a deep breath, sighing. Vamps didn't need to breathe, only air enough to talk, but I'd found that most of them sigh, from time to time, as if it's a habit that even a few millennia can't break.

Damian's hand tightened almost painfully on the back of my neck. I was being utterly calm; what was the deal? I started to look up at him, but I felt it. He let me feel it. I was sucking his energy. Taking back the energy I gave him to live. Shit.

There was a knock on the door.

Claudia looked at me. "See who it is," I said.

She checked before opening the door, good bodyguard. It was Nathaniel. She opened the door for him. He came through with his hair still back in its braid, but he'd lost his shirt and vest somewhere. His upper body gleamed with sweat, and the amethyst and diamond collar on his neck glittered as he glided into the room.

"How did you lose your shirt?" I asked.

"I got hot," he said, and grinned.

"I'll say."

He walked toward me still smiling, but there was worry around the edges of his eyes. A stranger wouldn't have seen it, but I'd spent months reading his face. He walked wide around the desk, so he'd be out of reach of Merlin. He'd learned to be a better person, and a worse victim, living with me. He came around, and put his hand on my arm, underneath Asher's jacket. Having them both touch me was as if someone had stuck an electric plug in my spine. It made me jump, but underneath the rush of power was the feeling that it was going just one way, into me. Shit. I was really, really going to have to get better at this energy thing.

"You are very new at being the center of this triumvirate of power," Merlin said, like he was certain of it, and like it was interesting to him.

"Yeah, there's a learning curve."

"There are ways to keep the good mother from feeding upon your energy."

"I'm all ears," I said.

He frowned at me.

"I mean, I'd love to hear it." Sometimes I forgot that slang does not travel well, not across countries, or centuries.

"A holy item hidden inside at least two layers of pillows will keep her at bay."

"That sounds risky," I said, raising my newly marked hand. The movement made Damian move, almost a stumble. I felt Nathaniel reach for him, knew when he had put an arm around the taller man's waist.

"Even vampires can sleep thus, if they believe and they do not call their own power."

I needed to feed, but I didn't want a mistake here. I bunked with too many vampires to want a holy item going off at the wrong moment. "A vampire can sleep with a holy item under his pillow?"

"Yes, or underneath the bed, though pillow is better."

"What happens if the holy item touches vampire flesh?"

"Look at your own hand for that answer," he said.

"Are you saying that the cross burned me because of my own power, not Mommie Dearest?"

"You are a succubus, Ms. Blake; that has long been a power associated with the demonic."

"I've come up against demons. Vampirism is a contagion, not a demonic anything. It's a blood-borne disease. A doctor back in the 1900s sort of figured out how to cure it. You don't cure demonic possession with a blood transfusion."

"Cured it?" Merlin said. "With a blood transfusion, truly?"

"Well, yeah, but the vampirism is what keeps the dead body up and running, so you take the vampirism out of the blood, and the body dies."

"Ah, then not a cure that most would seek."

I shook my head. "No."

Damian leaned over and whispered against my cheek, "All interesting, but may I ask that you speed this up?"

"The mother cannot break through your protection on her own, except in dream. But she can follow the attack of another vampire inside your defenses. You are correct on that. Fear of her was one of the reasons for the laws governing combat between masters. But she has been asleep for so long that we have forgotten caution."

"Why does she need to follow someone else's attack?"

"Because she is still a creature of nightmare and the lands of Morpheus."

"She's still asleep, you mean?"

"Yes, that is what I mean." He smiled.

Damian's hand dug into my shoulder. I said, "I don't mean to be rude here, but I need to feed. So, if you'll excuse us."

"Can't we watch?" Elisabetta asked.

"No," I said.

"Come, Elisabetta," Merlin said. He went out the door with her behind him. Adonis turned in the doorway, and stared at us all.

"You don't get to watch either," I said. "This meeting is over."

He started to say something, then seemed to think better of it. He finally shook his head, and left without another word. I'd learned more than he meant to tell, but less than there was to know. Somehow I knew I'd see him again. Just a feeling.

Claudia went to the door. "I'll make sure no one interrupts." She closed the door behind her.

I stood, and gently moved their hands off my shoulders. I took their hands in mine. "Nathaniel, take Damian to the workers' lounge or somewhere. Or find a table outside, I guess."

"Why can't we watch?"

I gave him a look, but he gave innocent, knowledgeable eyes. "It's been less than two hours, are you saying you'd go again?"

He smiled.

"I can't feed on you again this soon, Nathaniel, it's too dangerous. I don't know what the mother did to me, exactly, but I feel shaky. I don't know if I can guarantee that the *ardeur* won't spread through the room. Outside the door you'll be safe; inside, I don't know." I looked at Damian, who was clinging to Nathaniel's shoulders as if he'd fall down without the support. "If I fed on Damian right now, I think that would be bad."

"Who will you feed from then?" Asher asked from where he stood near the wall.

"If it's okay with you, you."

"A man likes to be asked."

I squeezed the others' hands, and said, "Nathaniel, Damian, go, please, and stay where someone can keep an eye on you, okay?"

"I promise," Nathaniel said, and they started for the door.

I turned to Asher. "Are you mad at me?"

"No one likes to be taken for granted, Anita."

"I don't take you for granted."

"You do, and so does Jean-Claude."

I didn't know what to say to that so I said that part out loud. "I don't know what to say to that."

He shook his head. "We do not have time to tend my emotional wounds. Forgive me."

The door closed behind us, Nathaniel and Damian were outside trying to find a place to wait while I fed enough to keep us all alive.

I reached for Asher's hand. He took it, but he wouldn't look at me. What little of his face he gave was that perfect profile, with the scars hidden behind the glory of his hair. I'd asked for sex and he was hiding from me. Not good.

"What is wrong?" I asked.

"Do you realize that this will be the first time we have ever had sex alone together?"

I started to argue with him but stopped myself. I could remember his body so intimately. So many nights and afternoons of his body against mine. Had there always been someone else with us? Had we never had a moment that was just us, just ours?

I touched his face, tried to get him to look at me, but he wouldn't do it. "It's not just Jean-Claude that you haven't gotten enough personal attention from, is it?"

He smiled then, but not like he was happy. "I spent centuries being desired by all that I touched, or wanted. Then I spent centuries being despised, ridiculed. Sex was a mercy or done as a torment to the ones Belle wished to punish."

I tried to hug him, and he kept me away, just holding my hand while he talked. I said the only thing I could think to say. "I'm sorry."

He finally looked at me with the perfect side of his face. He let me see the drowning beauty that had made people give up their fortunes, their honor, their virtue, for but one more night staring into this face. "You have healed some of my hurts. Being with you and Jean-Claude. I thought it would be enough."

I slid my hand underneath his hair, so I could touch the scarred side of his face. I cupped that which he hid, while I stared up into the face he let me see. "But you don't get enough attention from either of us."

"It sounds childish when you say it out loud, but it does not feel childish inside here." He touched his chest. "It feels like I am starving to death in the midst of a feast. But it is a feast that I share with too many. Neither of you watches only me. There is always someone else more beautiful, more desirable."

"There is no one more beautiful than you, Asher."

He jerked back, and exposed the scars on his face. "How can you say that to me?"

"What do you want me to say?"

"I want to be the center of someone's life again, Anita. Jean-Claude's center is you. Yours is beginning to be Nathaniel and Micah." He grabbed my arms and closed his eyes tight. "I am no one's darling, and I cannot bear it." He laughed, but when he opened his eyes there was a shine of unshed tears. "How stupid and childish. How selfish."

"It's not about being with men, or women, is it?" I said. "It's because none of the men I'm picking will ever put you at the center of their world."

"I want to be loved, Anita, as I once was."

"Julianna," I said, softly.

He nodded. "Once it was Jean-Claude, but he could never truly love another man the way he loves a woman. Belle's tastes and demands sent many of us to the arms of other men, but Jean-Claude could never be content with just men in his bed. He is a lover of women above all else."

"And you?" I asked, because he seemed to want me to ask.

"I think if it were the right man, I could be in love, and content, but I think the same of a woman. It is love I seek, Anita, not the package around it. I have always been needier of attention than Jean-Claude. I sought a woman for my human servant when I realized that Jean-Claude would never be content with just men, with just me."

I didn't know what to say to the pain in his voice. An emotional burden he'd carried for two or three hundred years, and I was supposed to fix it, or at least make it better, how? How was I going to do that?

I felt Damian reach out for me. It made me stagger against Asher. He had to catch me. "I'm draining Damian."

"Then I must stop being an enfant terrible, and let you feed."

"I do want you, Asher. I do love you. But right now, I don't have time to . . ."

"To heal my wounds," he finished for me.

"To make love to you the way I want to."

He gave me a look, like he didn't believe me.

"We have to feed and get back to the party, but you are not just emergency food to me. You are not just someone I share with Jean-Claude. You are special to me, Asher, you, just you. I don't have time to make you believe me tonight, but I'll try to do better later."

He drew me in against his body, held me close, whispered into my hair, "Later you will have to feed upon someone else, for I will have had my turn."

I drew back enough to see his face, and said, "Remember one thing, that I didn't make love to you that first time because I had to feed the *ardeur*. I made love to you because I wanted to, because Jean-Claude and I wanted to."

"You did it to protect me from Belle Morte's agents."

"Yeah, we did it so that Belle couldn't call you home, so you'd belong to us by her rules, but you're still the only new man in my life that I had sex with because I wanted to take care of you, not because you were food."

"Take care of me?"

I nodded. "It's what you do when you love someone."

He smiled then, and it was that rare smile. The smile that made him look terribly young, and not at all like himself, as if that smile was all that was left of what he might have been centuries ago. "You can't possibly love all the men in your life, Anita."

"No," I agreed, "but I love you. I love Jean-Claude."

"And Micah, and Nathaniel," he said.

I nodded.

"And London, and Requiem," he said.

I shook my head. "No, not them."

"Why not love them? They are beautiful and perfect."

I grinned. "Not perfect; handsome, but not perfect. Requiem's too damn moody by half. London, I'm a little embarrassed about him."

"Why embarrassed?"

"Not sure, maybe because I'm not sure I even like him, and I had sex with him." I felt Damian slumping at the table where he sat. Nathaniel caught his arm, kept him in the chair. Asher had to catch me or I might have fallen.

"You need to feed," he said.

I nodded.

"Then we have talked enough. Tonight I will take care of you, because that is what you do when you love someone."

Heat rose up in my face, and I wasn't sure why.

He laughed, not a magical vampire laugh, but a very masculine laugh. That laugh that lets you know you've pleased them in some very guy sort of way.

"What?" I asked, and wouldn't look at him, because I knew that would make the blush worse.

"You blushed because I said I loved you."

I nodded, and tried to sound churlish, as I said, "So?"

"So, I know you love me."

That made me look up at him. "Just because I blushed?"

He nodded.

"I blush a lot."

He drew me into the circle of his arms. "Yes, but this one was for me." He laid a kiss upon my forehead. "I would like to feed while you feed."

"Haven't you fed yet?"

"No, the blood hunger did not rise."

"Isn't that unusual?"

"Very."

"Then feed." I thought about it. "Though I'm sort of running out of spots for fresh fang marks."

He touched the side of my neck where Requiem's bite lay. He traced his hand over the mound of my breast, dipping a little lower than the corset top until he caressed London's bite. He dipped his fingers lower, so that he touched my nipple. Just that brought my breath in a gasp.

He laughed again, that pleased sound. His hand slid up my thigh, forced me to move my legs apart so he could find Jean-Claude's bite in my very inner thigh.

My voice came breathy, "How did you know it was there?"

"I smelled it," he whispered. "Are you ready for me?"

I nodded, because I didn't trust my voice.

"Then look at me, Anita, look into my eyes."

I looked up slowly, and found his eyes full of light like blue ice, glittering in winter moonlight, all shadows and shimmers. His eyes dazzled me.

He was carrying me, and I hadn't remembered him picking me up. "Where are we going?" I whispered.

"The couch," he said.

"We have to be quick."

He laid me down upon the couch, my knees bent, and him kneeling between them. "We can be quick now, because I know that there will be long later."

"All because I blushed for you," I said.

"Yes." There wasn't room for him to lie beside me, so he stood, and began to take off his clothes.

"If we take off the corset it will take forever to get it back on."

"The corset can stay." He threw his shirt and jacket on the arm of the couch. He stood there for a moment nude from the waist up. I stared up at him, stupidly, that *golly, wow* look on my face. I couldn't help it. He was so beautiful, and I knew that the rest of him was just as beautiful. I could look at him with knowledgeable anticipation. It made me shiver just staring up at him like that.

"The look on your face, Anita, *mon Dieu*, the look on your face."

I had to swallow twice to say, "What do you want me to take off?"

"Panties."

"Just panties," I said.

He nodded, and started unfastening his pants.

My pulse sped up. I had to sit up to take the panties off. It also helped me look away from him while I did it. Was it just that we had never been alone before? Was that this incredible anticipation? Or was it more than that? I wanted him. I wanted him to touch me. My body ached with the need, not just to be touched, but for Asher to touch me.

His hands slid over my bare shoulders, where I sat facing away from him. The smoothing of his hands down my skin made me hold my breath.

He leaned down and whispered, "What do you want?"

"Your hands on my body."

"What else do you want?"

"You inside me."

"What else?"

My pulse was hammering in my throat so hard I could barely speak around it. "Bite me while you fuck me, make me come both ways while you're inside me."

"Inside you both ways?" he whispered.

"Yes."

He grabbed a handful of my hair, and pulled until it hurt, just a little, just enough. "Say please."

"Please."

"I have to take blood to enter you. To bring you a second time with my bite, I will have to take blood again."

I tried to reason that out, and failed, but finally said the only thing I could think to say. "Please."

54

HE PUT US both on our knees on the couch, me facing away from him. His hand wrapped in my hair, hard enough to hurt, drawing my neck back in a clean, straining angle. He pressed his body against the back of mine, used his hips to raise the short skirt so I could feel his body against my bare ass. He plunged his hand down the front of the corset, so he could grip my breast, tight and hard. It made me cry out. He plunged his body against mine, but without blood, he was still soft.

He whispered in my ear, "Your blood will make me a man, again. It will fill my body with life, so that I may fill your body with life."

There was something about what he'd said that should have bothered me, but I couldn't make the thought form. He'd rolled my mind in a blissful rush, and I couldn't make my thoughts march to logic. All the logic I had was in his hands, in the soft push of his body, the growing tension as he held me.

Something stabbed through that lustful calm. Damian reached out to me with a silent scream. "Anita, damn it, feed!"

It made me slump in Asher's arms.

"What is wrong?"

"Let me feed with the first bite. Let me feed with your power."

"Damian is fading." He made it a statement.

"Yes." My voice was breathy, and not for any good reason.

"I will not fight your power, Anita. I will let you take me, then I will take you."

"Yes, but please hurry, please . . ."

He was too tall to stay pressed as he was, and bite me. He had to ease his body back enough to fold that six-feet-and-change frame over me. His hands tensed in my hair and on my breast. The sudden pain seemed to send me back into his gaze. My breath was short and eager, when he struck. There was a moment of pain, then it was gone, washed away in the first orgasm.

Asher's bite was pleasure. It was his gift, his power, and that power tightened my body, and exploded like a wave of warm pleasure across my skin. So much pleasure, so much, and as long as he fed, it would be wave after warm, thrilling wave. It felt so good, so good, that it spilled out my mouth in long, ragged screams. Somewhere in all of it, the *ardeur* rose, and fed. It fed through his mouth, his teeth on me. It fed through his hands on my body. I poured the spill of it into Damian, felt him sit up so hard in the chair, that he almost fell off it. Nathaniel steadied him, and got a taste of that pleasurable power.

I fought the energy, fought to send only food, and not the nearly overwhelming pleasure. To send only so much, and no more. It was like trying to meditate in the middle of sex; no wonder I wasn't better at it.

Asher drew back from my neck, breathing hard. "You took a great deal." He sounded shaky, and his bite didn't necessarily cause him pleasure, so that wasn't it.

"Sorry," I mumbled.

He let go of me, and I slumped forward onto all fours, head down. "God, Asher, God."

The couch moved as he shifted position, and the next thing I felt was his hands on my hips, pulling my skirt up. He pressed the tip of himself against me, and there was nothing soft about him now. He was hard, and ready, pushing against me.

"Do you still want me to pierce you twice?"

I should have said no. I'd missed so much of the evening. But I didn't want to say no. I wanted to say yes. I tried not to think about Asher much. One, it could cause mini-orgasms at odd moments. One of the side effects of his powers. Two, because I understood why people had been willing to trade everything away just for one more night of the pleasure that only Asher could bring. The rest of the metaphysical sex was great, but it was the affection I had for the people involved that made me want to be with most of them. Emergency food being the exception. I loved Asher, but it wasn't love that made me want to be with him. If I had been less stubborn, I might have chased after him simply for the pleasure. I stayed away from him when I could, because no one could quite do what he could, and it scared me.

Which is why I said, "Just fuck me."

"You do not wish me to bring you pleasure with my bite again?"

"Yes, but . . . we don't have time."

"As you wish." He used his hands to position my hips, and he began to push his way inside me. I was wet, but tight; my body spasmed around him, as he fought to be inside me.

His voice came strained, "So tight tonight, so tight. Forcing me to fight for every inch. I love it."

I just nodded, not trusting my voice. I should have said no to the sex. We'd fed. Jean-Claude needed us to schmooze the crowd. But I didn't want to say no. I could have lied to myself and thought that Asher needed this, this time just the two of us, but that wasn't why I said yes. I said yes because I wanted him inside me. I said yes because I was fighting myself not to beg for another bite. I did want him to pierce me twice. I did want it. I did.

He had himself inside me, as close as his body would let him. He rested a moment with our bodies wedded to each other. He laid his body across my back, letting me support our weight for a moment. His skin was warmer now, alive with the blood he'd taken from me. His hair fell around me like a shining curtain.

"Bite me," I whispered it.

"What?"

"Bite me, while you fuck me, take me, take me as only you can take me." My voice stayed a whisper as if that would make it all right. Make it less weak.

"As only I can take you?" He made a question of it.

"Yes," I said, "yes."

He wrapped his arms around me, forced me to hold all of our combined weight. He hugged me, hard and tight. "You do feel my power."

"Yes," I whispered.

"Are you afraid of it?"

"Yes."

"Afraid of how much you want me?"

"Yes!"

He whispered, "I like that." He raised himself off me, so that the only part of him touching was the part that was deep inside me, and the barest touch of thighs and hips.

He drew himself out slowly, so slowly.

"I'm still tight."

"Yes," he said, "yes, you are." He drew himself out of me, then used his knees to spread my legs wider. It made me lower my head to the couch, pressing my face to the leather. Asher entered me, shallow, just inside, inside over that sweet spot. He started slow and steady, pushing himself in and out, and always over that one spot. I kept expecting him to speed up or go deeper, but he kept that slow, shallow rhythm.

I started moving my hips to help, but he put his hands firmly on my hips, kept me from moving. It was strangely like all the ballroom dancing they'd made me learn for the party. A flexing of the man's hands, a squeeze in one direction or the other, and you knew what he wanted, or thought you did. He wanted me not to move, to let him do the work.

He spread my legs even farther, forced my body at a higher angle. "Up, Anita, I want you up on all fours."

I did what he asked, but my knees were spread so far that my hips protested the angle. It didn't exactly hurt, but it might if we did it long enough. And through it all he kept up that gliding, gentle rhythm inside my body.

The orgasm began to build inside me. To build with each caress of his body just inside mine. Building, building, on the gentle touch of him inside me. Most of the time sex was about the *ardeur*. The *ardeur* wasn't gentle. I fed and I fucked because I had to. I realized as Asher took me so carefully, so gently, that it had taught us all bad habits. I loved a good, hard fucking, more even than most women, but just because I could take it didn't mean that that was what I wanted, not always. This, this was perfect. This was what I had been missing in all the frantic sex. All the emergency feeding had made me forget that gentleness had its own pleasure.

I fought to stay where he wanted, and not to move, fought to keep my legs spread, fought to hold the pleasure. "I'm close."

"Then go."

"But . . ."

"Go," he said.

I might have argued, but he pushed his body over mine one last time and the orgasm caught me. Only his hands digging into my ass kept me from writhing my pleasure around him. He kept me in place, and he kept going, as if I weren't screaming, digging fingers into the leather. So much pleasure, so much pleasure, that my hands needed something to hold on to. I couldn't reach him, so I dug nails into what I could reach.

"Anita, I love you, I love you, I love you!" The rhythm changed. I felt him fight his body, not to lose himself yet. He grabbed my hair and jerked me to my knees with his body still inside mine. It changed the angle, and he didn't try to stay shallow. He used all the length of him, still pushing gently, still fighting his body not to pound into me. I felt the struggle in his chest and arms as he pulled my head to one side and exposed my neck again. "Now," he whispered.

"Please," I whispered.

He plunged his fangs into me, locked his mouth around me, and sucked. He stopped fighting his body, let himself plunge into me as hard and fast as he could. He brought me screaming again, brought me with his body, brought me with his bite, brought me with his power. He came inside me with one last powerful thrust. I raked nails down his arms, and screamed myself hoarse.

He fed at my neck, and as long as he fed the orgasms continued. For me, for him, for us. It was one of the things that made him so dangerous. While you were in the middle of all that pleasure, you could forget. Forget that this was my fourth blood donation tonight. Forget that he shouldn't open his mouth and let the blood pour down my body, because he was too full to take more. Forget that we were supposed to save something to go outside to meet and greet. Forget everything but the feel of him thrusting inside me, until he poured from between my legs, poured over his own body. Forget until my blood poured down my neck to soak into the dress and the diamonds. Forget until hands pulled us apart, and Asher turned snarling to the room.

I didn't snarl. I collapsed onto the couch, because I couldn't do anything else. I lay there like a broken doll, and even my thoughts circled lazily, white edged as if the world were covered in cotton.

Someone rolled me over. Remus's jigsaw face loomed out of the growing dimness. "Anita, Anita, can you hear me?"

I meant to say yes, but the world went black, and I was floating, and I couldn't say anything to anyone.

55

I WOKE UP in the hospital. Not the human hospital, but the lycanthrope hospital. The building that the local shapeshifters keep for just such emergencies. If they'd taken me to the humans, then Asher might have ended up with an order of execution against him. The downside to going to the furry hospital was that the blood they used for transfusing wasn't human blood. If you get the right blood type, humans can take in lycanthrope blood, and lycanthropes can take in human blood, but lycanthropes have trouble taking in blood that isn't their strain of lycanthropy. Since I carry three, I was something of a problem. But since I was also O-negative, there wasn't a lot of choice. It's not the most common blood type around, especially in a small hospital like this one.

Doc Lillian won't actually tell me what strain of lycanthropy she decided to add to my mix, or if she chose one that I already had. She thinks that if I know what it is, it could influence which beast wins. Since my mental process shouldn't have anything to do with it, I have no idea what she's babbling about, but she won't give in, so come next full moon we'll see if my mixed bag of furry picks a winner.

I slept off and on, and when I woke up again, Asher was sitting by my bed. I startled when I saw him, made a little gasp.

He looked away from me, letting all that long hair fall forward to hide his face completely. He wasn't flirting, showing that perfect profile. He was just hiding. "You are afraid of me now." His voice held regret like a light, persistent rain, one you know will go on all day.

I started to deny it, then stopped myself. Was I afraid of him? Yes. Yes, I was. But not for the reason he thought. I touched the bandage at my neck, and from the feel of it alone, I knew the bite wouldn't be some polite pricking. He'd gotten carried away at my neck, as he had elsewhere. It wasn't like collarbone-scar bad, or even the bend of my arm bad, but it wasn't what the old vamps usually did. It felt like a rookie mistake under the bandages.

He stood, and the movement looked tired, weary. "I understand, Anita. I don't blame you."

Movement by the door drew my attention. There were guards at the door, and there hadn't been when everyone else visited me. Remus was one of the guards. I remembered his face just as I passed out.

Asher started for the door.

"Don't go," I said, my voice hoarse.

He didn't turn and look at me; he just stopped moving. He stood, motionless, waiting.

"Stay," I said.

He risked a glance back at me, his eyes peering through the curtain of hair. The hair wasn't artfully messy, it was just tangled and spilled over his face, as if he hadn't bothered to touch it.

I stared at him, that tall figure. He usually had perfect posture, but tonight his broad shoulders were rounded, slumped in defeat. It was as if he were hunched from the cold. I knew that wasn't it; the dead don't feel the cold, much.

"I know you cannot forgive me, but I had to see you. I had to see you . . ." His words trailed off. He reached out with those graceful hands that tonight had lost all their grace to his grief.

I wanted to reach out to him, to offer my hand, but I was afraid of what would happen if he touched me. I wasn't afraid he would turn into some ravenous monster. I was afraid that I would. I'd almost died, and all I could think was, *Isn't he beautiful, isn't he sad*. I wanted to comfort him, hold him. He said I couldn't forgive him; he was wrong. I had forgiven him, but it wasn't a conscious thing. It was as if the sight of him just made it impossible to be angry with him. That wasn't right. That was vampire mind tricks.

"Why the guards?" I asked, finally, because I didn't know what to say out loud.

He blinked at me through the golden strings of his hair. "I do not trust myself alone with you. Jean-Claude agrees."

I looked past him at the guards. "Hey, Remus, Ixion."

They glanced at each other, then said hi.

"Remus was the last face I saw before I woke up here."

"He came to my call," Asher said, and his face was miserable.

"Your call, what do you mean your call? You don't have an animal to call."

"He does now," Remus said. He hesitated, then walked farther into the room. Ixion stayed by the door. "He called us while he was doing you. The call was . . . we had to answer. We had to leave our guard duties and go to him." He looked at Asher, who would not meet his eyes either. "Good thing we did, I guess, but Jean-Claude thinks that the reason it got so out of hand between the two of you was that Asher's new power came on line."

"You do not have to make excuses for me," Asher said.

"I didn't mean to." Remus gave me a look that I couldn't interpret, then went back to stand by the door.

"So you have an animal now?" I said.

"Yes." He didn't look any happier. "I know that you can't forgive me. I don't expect you to. I won't touch you again, Anita; you have my word."

It took me a moment to understand what he'd said. "Are you saying that you won't ever be with me again, as in sex?"

He nodded, face so solemn.

The thought of him never touching me again filled me with panic. My pulse sped up, and I fought not to yell at him. How could he deny me? I had to work to make my voice come out calm. "Sit down, Asher, please."

He hesitated, then finally sat. "I offer you the only safety I can. I give you my word that I will never touch you again."

I couldn't quite keep my voice steady as I said, "I don't want that."

He finally met my eyes. "What?"

"I don't want you to never touch me again."

"Anita, you've kicked me out of your bed for far less than this. I almost killed you. You can't forgive that. You don't forgive anything."

He had me there. "I'm working on that, okay?"

His mouth moved, almost like he fought off a smile.

"Do you know why I haven't reached out and taken your hand?"

"You are afraid to touch me." His voice spilled despair over my skin the way Jean-Claude could spill pleasure.

"Yes, but not in the way you mean."

He shook his head, hunching over his clasped hands. "I do not want you afraid of me, Anita, not in any way, but I cannot blame you for it."

"I'm afraid to touch you, because I'm afraid that I'll ask you to kiss me."

He nodded. "And you fear where that kiss will lead."

"Asher." I said it harder, more like myself, though with a voice that needed water. "Asher, look at me."

He just shook his head.

"Damn it, look at me."

It was actually hard to tell through the hair and the dimness of the room, but I think he was looking at me. "What would you have of me, Anita? I have already given up everything I ever wanted. What more do you want from me?"

"God, you are a gloomy person."

That made him sit up a little straighter, his arrogance kicking in. "I am sorry that my manner displeases you so." He sounded a little angry; good. It was better than despair.

"You're right, I should be furious with you. And you're right that I've kicked men out of my life for a hell of a lot less than this."

The anger leaked away, and that numbing depression rolled over him again. It was like watching the light fade from him. "Did you ask me to sit so you could grind the knife in deeper?"

"If I want to grind a knife in, you'll know it. I'm just trying to talk." I had to cough to clear my voice. "Is there water?"

Asher looked around the room. It was Remus who found a pitcher of water and a little cup. He poured it, then hesitated, and finally handed it to Asher. The two men had a moment where you could almost feel the battle of wills, then Asher finally took the cup, and came to the bed. He would not look at me as he offered the water with a little bendy straw in it.

The water tasted stale, but it was cool, and felt wonderful in my mouth and throat. I raised my untaped arm to help hold the cup. My fingers brushed Asher's hand. He jumped, as if it had hurt, but I knew it hadn't hurt. "Have I spilled water on you?"

"No, just a little on the sheets."

"You are the only woman except Belle who has ever made me feel clumsy."

Ixion was there with a handkerchief. Asher took it and dabbed at the few spots he'd gotten on the sheets.

"Is that a compliment, or an insult?" I asked. My voice sounded better, less hoarse. It made me wonder how long I'd been unconscious. I didn't ask, because if it had been a long time, then Asher would feel worse, and I'd be more scared. I let it go.

He finished trying to soak the water up, handing the handkerchief back as if he expected Ixion to simply be there to take it. He was, and he did, but the offhand quality of the gesture made me wonder again how long had I been out. "It is neither, just the truth. You have made me feel awkward from the moment I met you."

"I tend to have that effect on ladies' men."

He looked at me then. I tried to read his expression and failed. "I am a ladies' man, am I?"

"Belle Morte made certain that all of you were good with the ladies."

"And the men. Do not forget, Anita, she made certain we knew how to pleasure men, as well."

I nodded, and stopped, because the bandages pinched. "I've grasped that concept, thanks."

"But you are not happy with it."

"More puzzled by it."

He smoothed the sheets where he'd dampened them. I think he was looking for anything to fuss over, rather than what we were doing. I'd never seen him this uncomfortable.

I did what I'd wanted to do since he walked into the room. I laid my hand on his. He went very, very still under my touch. That awful, unnatural stillness, where it feels like you're not touching anything alive. He went away from my touch, but I kept my hand on his. If he thought a little weird vampire shit would make me move, he was wrong.

"Anita," and his voice tried to be as empty as his body, but failed.

"I'm not afraid because you almost killed me. I'm afraid because you almost killed me, and I still want to touch you."

He drew his hand out of mine. He sat down, but he would at least look at me now. "I have rolled your mind, completely and utterly. I have done what you feared that I would do."

"And don't you want to touch me?"

"Yes." He whispered it.

"You were the first one to realize that just biting me helps me gain control over a vamp. I don't think it's just you who's rolled me."

"Are you saying you have gained control of me?"

"I'm not sure what I'm saying. I just know that I don't want you gone. I don't want you to never touch me again. I want us to be together. Beyond that, I don't know."

"Together in what way, Anita?"

"We'll just need a spotter," I said.

"A spotter, what are you talking about?"

"A spotter, like you have in gymnastics. Sex with you is so good we need spotters."

"So dangerous, you mean," he said, and he stared at his hands where they lay loose in his lap.

"I'd do it again, Asher."

He looked up then, and it wasn't a happy look. "Do you really mean that?"

"Yes."

"That should frighten you, and me."

"It does scare me, but it doesn't really scare you, does it?"

"I'm terrified for your safety, but . . ."

"You've been a very good boy, haven't you?" I asked.

"What do you mean?"

I had one of those moments of seeing so deep into another person that it makes the rest of the world seem unsteady for a moment. It wasn't vampire powers, or necromancy, it was just a moment of insight so bright and painful that I couldn't look away. "Look me in the eye, Asher, and tell me that you've never done what you did with me before, and had the woman not survive it?"

He looked away then, those pale eyes hiding from me.

"Asher," I said.

He met my eyes with that blank perfect face, peering through the mess of his hair. "I have done what you accuse me of."

"It's not an accusation," I said, "it was more a statement."

"Do you not think me a monster for it?"

I thought about it. Did I think him a monster? "Did you do it on purpose?"

"Did I go into the lovemaking planning the death of my lover?" he asked.

"Yeah, that's what I mean?"

"No, save once."

"Once?"

"There was a lord from whom Belle desired money and land. He had been diagnosed with a cancer. He was a strong, proud man. He did not wish to die in pain and sickness. He requested I kill him. He wished to die by pleasure, instead of pain. He also felt that if I took his life, it was not suicide, so his soul was strangely safe."

He told the story in an empty voice, as if it meant nothing to him. It was the kind of voice that people use about trauma or tragedy when they haven't dealt with it yet.

"You liked him," I said.

"He was a decent man."

"I don't think you're a monster."

"Why am I not a monster for killing someone to give myself pleasure?"

"Put that way, you would be, but that's not what you did. It's a loop of pleasure, Asher. It's not your pleasure, but hers, mine. I could have said no. There was a point where I knew it was too much, that we should stop."

"I had rolled your mind. You had no free will."

"You can roll me, but I don't stay rolled if I don't want to, not anymore. I didn't want to stop, Asher. Do you think I'm a monster for saying it was one of the most amazing orgasmic experiences that I've ever had?"

"No, not a monster."

"We can have intercourse together alone sometimes, but no biting while we're alone."

"You do not trust me."

"I don't trust either of us," I said.

He almost smiled. "I nearly killed you. I nearly spilled all that precious blood. The sofa had to be destroyed, the carpet taken up. I almost killed you, Anita, not for food, but for pleasure."

"You were in the middle of a major power-up, Asher. An animal to call, at long last."

He glanced behind at the waiting guards. "Hyenas, yes."

"Jean-Claude says that the first time any power kicks in, it's always hard to control."

Asher took my hand. "I would not trade your love for a thousand powers. I would not trade a single strand of your hair for any territory." His eyes were glittery, not with power, but tears.

"I believe you."

"Your new laws say we are citizens, but we are monsters, Anita. If I had killed you with the birth of this new power, I would have followed you soon after."

"You're saying you would have killed yourself?"

He nodded. "I could not have borne it."

"I don't want you dead."

"Nor I you." He knelt and laid his head on my hand. "It was not blood that brought my power, Anita. It was you, you wanting me more than anyone else. In that moment I could feel it. You wanted me, not Jean-Claude, not Richard, not Micah, not Nathaniel, me. You wanted me, my body, my touch, more than anyone else's. I could see into your heart, and I saw only me there." He rose up, tears staining his face faintly pink. "You truly do love me, just me. Not because of memories you share with Jean-Claude. Not out of pity. You love me."

"Yes," I said, "otherwise I'd be wicked pissed about the whole almost-killing-me thing."

"I will never forgive myself for that. Jean-Claude would have been within his rights to slay me for such carelessness."

"He loves you."

He nodded. "Yes, he does. I doubted that, until I realized he was not going to kill me for almost killing you. I doubted everyone's love for me, Anita, but no longer. He loves me, or he would have killed me when he walked into that room and saw what I had done."

So that was it. I almost died. Asher had an animal to call. Jean-Claude didn't kill him for almost killing me. I didn't kill Asher for almost killing me. Jean-Claude has forbidden Asher and me to have feeding sex by ourselves. We didn't argue, because Asher and I both know the darkest secret of all between us. It felt so good, so incredibly good, that we didn't trust each other not to do it again.

I am a succubus. I am a vampire. Maybe not a bloodsucker, but I feed off sex. It isn't just Damian's life that can get drained away if I don't feed. Nathaniel will die. I will die. I think Jean-Claude can protect himself and Richard from me, but I could kill us all if I don't learn to manage my own personal triumvirate of power. London is the front-runner for my new *pomme de sang*. I wish I liked him better. I don't dislike him, but I'm afraid to bring him home. He doesn't strike me as the domestic type. Requiem is part of the food chain, but he is so not just food. He craves true love. I can't blame him, but I can't help him either. The sex is great, but he scares me. For centuries-old vampires, they all seem so easy to hurt emotionally. Weird.

I wrapped a cross in silk, put that in a velvet bag, and that inside a pillowcase. It seems to be working. No more bad dreams of Marmee Noir. No accidents for my vampire lovers, or me. I'd send Merlin a thank-you note if I had an address.

Sampson is staying in town so I can fulfill my promise to try to bring his powers over. He's letting me recover my strength, and my nerve for it. Nice of him. I made Auggie take Haven home to Chicago. My hands ached to touch him. So dangerous. The local werelions are trying to find me someone else, but I miss Haven. He's a dangerous thug, but I miss him. My lioness misses him. He would be such a bad idea to keep.

I wasn't pregnant, yea! But while I thought I was pregnant, I had unprotected sex with Nathaniel, Jean-Claude, Micah, and Augustine. No one handed London a condom when I fed the *ardeur* off him. But I've managed to dodge the bullet on those, too. Thank God. Pregnant by one of my boyfriends is one thing; pregnant by Augustine would be a disaster I could not deal with. I think I'll just start taping condoms to my body. Emergency sex comes up, you rip a condom off, and you're as safe as you're going to be. I'm safe from disease because my lovers aren't human, but pregnancy, that is one disease that I'm not safe from. My period is still AWOL. My doctor says there's nothing wrong with me. It could just be stress, or, there is literature about female shapeshifters having interrupted periods until their first full moon. Or, as my doctor pointed out, I am like a metaphysical miracle on two legs, so maybe it's something else. Maybe it's something we haven't even thought of. He recommended I take folic acid because there are birth defects that have nothing to do with werewolves and vampires. I did what he said. He also suggested a therapist, or a vacation. A vacation? Me? Where would I go, and what would I do? Hell, who would I take with me?

I try not to think too hard on the fact that my "vampire powers" gave me Nathaniel and Micah. Hell, gave me to them. Why didn't it work on Richard? Jean-Claude thinks it's because he does not know his own heart's desire. You can only get your wish when you truly know what it is you want. Maybe someday Richard will truly know what his heart needs. He's dating humans exclusively. I'm the only preternatural he's seeing. Richard has informed me he's shopping for his white picket fence.

I'm happy behind my black wrought-iron fence. The one with the pointy spikes on top. White never really was my color.